THE DISCOVERY OF HEAVEN

a novel

PENGUIN BOOKS

PENGUIN BOOKS

Published by the Penguin Group
Penguin Books Ltd, 80 Strand, London WC2R 0RL, England
Penguin Putnam Inc., 375 Hudson Street, New York, New York 10014, USA
Penguin Books Australia Ltd, 250 Camberwell Road, Camberwell, Victoria 3124, Australia
Penguin Books Canada Ltd, 10 Alcorn Avenue, Toronto, Ontario, Canada M4V 3B2
Penguin Books India (P) Ltd, 11 Community Centre, Panchsheel Park, New Delhi – 110 017, India
Penguin Books (NZ) Ltd, Cnr Rosedale and Airborne Roads, Albany, Auckland, New Zealand
Penguin Books (South Africa) (Pty) Ltd, 24 Sturdee Avenue, Rosebank 2196, South Africa

Penguin Books Ltd, Registered Offices: 80 Strand, London WC2R 0RL, England

www.penguin.com

First published in Dutch as *De ontdekking van de hemel* 1992
This translation first published in the USA by Viking Penguin,
a division of Penguin Putnam Inc. 1996
First published in Great Britain in Penguin Books 1998

19

Copyright © Harry Mulisch, 1992
Translation copyright © Paul Vincent, 1996
All rights reserved

The publisher wishes to acknowledge the contribution of the Foundation
for the Production and Translation of Dutch Literature

Printed in England by Clays Ltd, St Ives plc

ISBN-13: 978-0-140-27238-3

www.greenpenguin.co.uk

PART ONE

THE BEGINNING
OF THE
BEGINNING

Prologue

—Can I have a moment?

—*What is it?*

—Mission accomplished. The matter's settled.

—*What matter?*

—Oh, forgive me. The most important matter of all. The major problem.

—*The major problem? What are you talking about?*

—The testimony.

—*But of course! Good heavens, how terrible! One devotes oneself full-time to the essential questions, one focuses all one's energies on them, and at a certain moment one simply forgets them, or deals with them in a trice.*

—Perhaps you should start delegating a little more.

—*Perhaps you should be more aware of your place when someone confides in you. Delegate more! You still don't seem to understand what's hanging over us. Why do you think this project was set up? Tell me, how long have you been working on this file?*

—Over seventy years in human time.

—*Tell me about it.*

—Where shall I begin?

—*You're the best judge of that. First tell me briefly about the prelude.*

—I've seldom had to deal with such a complicated program. Thank God we generally let things run their own course, and in earlier assignments I had far more time to play with. However, because for some reason the mat-

3

ter had to be dealt with by the end of the millennium, I had four generations at most to come up with someone who could carry out the mission. The usual procedures were no good at all on such short notice. Normally, of course, we could have given the mission to any Spark we liked, but that would have been pointless. The problem was that if he was to be our envoy, he would have to remember the mission once he was in a body of flesh and blood—that is, he would have to be capable of hitting on the outrageous idea and, furthermore, have the strength of will and courage to execute it. I say "he" because it didn't seem a job for a "she." Of course, among the infinite human potential at our disposal there was a Spark who met those requirements, but how were we to get him to earth? So first we had to establish the unique DNA sequence in which he could manifest himself. I don't have to tell you that the coiled double DNA helix containing the information on a human individual, that Hermetic caduceus within the nucleus of each of the individual's hundred thousand billion cells, weighs no more than one hundred thousandth of a gram but, when extended, is approximately the same length as the individual himself, so that the number of possible sequences at the molecular level is vast. If written in the three-letter words of the four-letter alphabet, a human being is determined by a genetic narrative long enough to fill the equivalent of five hundred Bibles. In the meantime human beings have discovered this for themselves.

—*That's right. They have uncovered our profoundest concept—namely, that life is ultimately reading. They themselves are the Book of Books. In their year 1869 the wretched creatures discovered the DNA in the cell nucleus, and at the time we kidded ourselves that it was of no great significance, because they would never have the bright idea that the acid contained a code—and in any case would never be able to break it—but a hundred human years later they had deciphered the genetic code down to its subtlest details. We made them much too clever, using the very same code.*

—However, a hundred human years later I also achieved what I was after. First we managed to write down the secret name of our man, but that was nothing compared with what we had to do next: we had to find the great-grandparents, the grandparents, and the parents who could produce the desired combination within approximately fifty years. In his unfathomable wisdom, which may sometimes surprise even himself, the Chief arranged things so that in our Eternal Light we have a Spark for every possible combination of a sperm cell and an ovum. At each ejaculation a man emits three hundred million sperm: combined with a single female ovum, that is the same number of possible human beings, for which there are an equivalent number of Sparks—but a Spark is required for every combination of every sperm from every man in the present, past, and future with each ovum of each woman in the present, past, and future. That was necessary because even here no one could know when human beings would invent something that would extend their lives by hundreds or thousands of years. So there is a Spark for a particular sperm from a particular ejaculation of Julius Caesar's, which might have merged with a particular ovum of Marilyn Monroe's. And every sperm in the countless ejaculations of the possible son of that mismatch might subsequently have been able to join with every ovum of the countless possible daughters of John F. Kennedy and Cleopatra, or those of a random sculptor from the reign of the pharaoh Cheops with those of a toilet attendant living in ten thousand years' time— and all those possible permutations and their possible descendants might in turn have joined with all other possible permutations and their possible descendants in space and time, and so on and so on ad infinitum. For example, besides the Sparks for the combinations of all sperm—thousands of quarts of which are emitted century after century in a never-ending stream—with all ova from all ages, there are also those for the alternative generations of what might have been, diverging and branching into hyperinfinity: This is the Logos Spermatikos—the Absolute Infinite Light!

—*Can I ask if you are telling me all this to teach me something?*

—Holy, holy, thrice holy! I am speaking because I am still dumbstruck at the thought of our Light.

—*That does you honor. You are probably trying to say that there's a great deal of it.*

—Yes, you could put it like that.

—*But you succeeded.*

—Just don't ask me how. Decoding the genome, the full, secret name of a human being, is simply a matter of money for human beings themselves now, one dollar per nucleotide to be exact, making three billion dollars, and they're working on the project all over the world. Within the foreseeable future their biotechnology will enable them to produce the genetic essence of a particular ovum and a particular nucleus with a tail more quickly and simply than we can select them with our romantic, extremely old-fashioned breeding system—but it simply had to be done before the year 2000.

—*Precisely. And might there have been a connection, perhaps? Have you seen the light yet? It was only seventy-five human years ago that we discovered to our horror how rapidly technical skills were expanding down below and what human beings were going to do with them—not only in biotechnology, but in all other fields too. Before long our organization will be reduced to a skeleton staff, after which heaven will be wound up like a scroll. So tell me, how did you manage it?*

—Seventy human years ago, despite all the problems, I suddenly saw a way of getting the required Spark into flesh and blood not in four generations but in three.

—Well, well. Your creative gifts are even greater than I thought.

—The only snag was that there was no way of doing it painlessly. I was forced to use a terrible expedient.

—Which was?

—The First World War.

—Yes, that's an aspect of the same problem. Our alarm at the technological turn that human history was increasingly taking was finally confirmed by that senseless slaughter.

—So I was able to give it some meaning at least, in the following way: working back from the necessary sequence of amino acids to a possible paternal grandfather, my 301655722 staff, following my instructions, arrived at an Austrian, a certain Wolfgang Delius, born for no particular reason in 1892. The only possible paternal grandmother turned out to be a certain Eva Weiss, also born for no particular reason, but not until in 1908, in Brussels.

—"Weiss" doesn't sound very Flemish. Shouldn't it be De Witte?

—Her parents were German-speaking Jews from Frankfurt and Vienna. A family of diamond merchants.

—Practicing?

—Completely agnostic. They laughed at us.

—Hmm.

—Faith is not so simple for human beings; we can scarcely imagine that. For us there is no such thing as faith, only knowledge.

—Yes, I can see that you operate at the farthest edge of the Light. Perhaps you should be a little wary of too much understanding. Go on with the story.

—I received your instructions in April 1914, and that same June in Sarajevo a student, a certain Gabriel Princip, leaped forward and shot the archduke of Austria. That Christian name and surname are bound to make you chuckle to yourself. He was a follower of Nietzsche, the most gruesome figure of the whole lot of them.

—The name Nietzsche seems to me to have connotations of its own. Nichevo. He was that nihilist who spread the rumor that the Chief was dead. Well, he

wasn't far from the truth—but the fact that the Chief can't die is precisely the most dreadful limitation of his omnipotence. He exists by virtue of the paradox, but by the same token he must exist eternally and die eternally.

—Within a few months the slaughter was in full swing. I was able to use the spectacle not only to bring Wolfgang Delius and Eva Weiss into contact, but also for the following generation, which was to involve Dutch people.

—Dutch? Isn't this taking us a long way from home?

—It was the only solution. The German and Austrian high commands dusted off the old Schlieffen plan, which proposed violating Dutch and Belgian neutrality in order to invade France with a flanking movement. However, Dutch neutrality was as essential to my project as the infringement of Belgian neutrality, and through gentle promptings in Moltke's brain I was able to ensure that the plan was only implemented for Belgium.

—My memory for human affairs is like a sieve these days. Moltke?

—General Field Marshal von Moltke, the German supreme commander. Wolfgang Delius—or, as he was wont to say in the manner of his region, Delius, Wolfgang—who had just graduated from a Vienna business college, became a professional soldier and fought on the Italian, Russian, and French fronts. In Brussels he was billeted with the Weiss family, where his future wife was still sitting on the floor playing with a doll, already using it for practice, so to speak. Delius was a good-looking young officer in the mounted artillery, highly decorated and with silver spurs on his boots, but with an extraordinarily somber look in his eyes, which everyone put down to his wartime experiences—and which was partly due to them, but not entirely. There was a deeper, underlying somberness in him. In his knapsack he carried Stirner's *The Ego and His Own.* Weiss, very glad to be among compatriots and fellow German-speakers again, was by now driving along the Boulevard Anspach with the military governor in an open car, which did not escape the people of Brussels. The war had served its purpose, and when Germany and Austria capitulated, Weiss, in accordance with my plan, got into serious difficulties. The day after the armistice, all his possessions were confiscated, and in order to avoid arrest he had to flee overnight with his family—to Holland, that is, where I wanted them, because there was no other alternative. Meanwhile, Delius left for Germany on horseback at the head of his company.

—But they knew each other now.

—The foundations had been laid. Back in cold, hungry Vienna, Delius found employment as a teacher of commercial accounting in a private school for young ladies, but he remained in correspondence with Weiss. The latter soon began to prosper in Amsterdam. At the beginning of the 1920s he brought his young friend over and gave him a temporary job as an accountant in his diamond firm. Not long after, with Weiss's support, Delius set up in business for himself, trading with Germany and Austria. Within a year the business grew into quite a substantial company, he was naturalized, and in 1926 Wolfgang Delius married Eva Weiss, his benefactor's daughter, who was sixteen years his junior. The girl was eighteen at the time, and the very next year she had a baby boy—but because of a typing error in my department the angelic child died in its crib after two weeks. It turned out to be a dreadful marriage, I'm sorry to say. It was brought home to me yet again how privileged we are in being neither male nor female—but it was necessary for the sake of their second son, who was born in 1933 and whom I needed as the father of our man on earth.

—*Why was the marriage dreadful?*

—Had it not been for your instructions, it ought never to have happened. Everyone on earth always marries the wrong person, that's well known, but seldom were a couple less suited than these two. In some way the young woman and her much older husband must have hurt each other irreparably—not so much by doing or saying or failing to do anything specific, but just by being who they were. In the final analysis they married because we wanted them to, though they themselves had no idea of this, of course. The decisive factor for her may have been the interesting, obscure background suggested by the look in his bright blue eyes, which was eventually to turn against her; for him, precisely that sense of freedom in her that in the end he could not endure. Her spirit was ten times lighter and quicker than his. He was heavy and twisted like an anchor rope caught in a ship's propeller—like that of almost all Austrians since 1918, choking with hate and self-hatred in the *Sadosachermasochtorte* of their dismembered dual monarchy, which a few years later was to cease to exist as a result of the frenzy of another Austrian. In the evenings she wanted to go out, but he preferred to immerse himself in Max Stirner. While she enjoyed herself in town with Jewish friends of her own age and of both sexes, her Germanic husband, with his monocle in place, read about the ego as the Only True Being and the world as his property. According to Stirner, no one should allow themselves to be told what to do by anyone or anything: the unique ego was sovereign, even to the point of committing crime. When she came home in the evenings, she sometimes found him screaming in his sleep, fighting the Italians with his pillow. Perhaps she could have done something about it before the fatal moment, but she did not. Perhaps because she was too young; also perhaps because, in the final analysis, she was even more of a loner than he was. In 1939 Eva left her Wolfgang, taking her six-year-old son with her.

—*Fine. And what about the mother-to-be?*

—Fortunately I didn't have to work in such a roundabout way in this case. In fact it presented scarcely any problems, and certainly no international ones. I was dealing with the Dutch, and among those well-behaved trading folk everything is rather less intense. I won't deny that this is partly because they were able to keep out of the First World War. In fact, the Second World War was their first since the sixteenth-century one against Spain, which incidentally was ruled by a half-Austrian then, too. If the Second World War had passed them by as well, they would have become the same sort of frustrated virgins as the inhabitants of the Swiss valleys.

—*I'm not sure I'm too impressed by that view of things.*

—If you like, I'll retract what I said and argue the opposite.

—*That won't be necessary.*

—It needed only a slight adjustment to bring her to life. Once again starting from the end result that we required, in combination with the genetic material of Delius Junior, we discovered as a possible paternal grandfather a keeper at the Netherlands Museum of the History of Science in Leiden: a certain Oswald Brons, born for no particular reason in 1921. By pure coincidence, the necessary maternal grandmother, Sophia Haken, turned out to be living close by, in Delft, where she had been born in 1923, also for no particular reason. Because of his age, Brons was more or less in hiding in the museum at the end of the war; he often slept there, in the room containing the Surrealist contraption built by Kamerlingh Onnes for liquefying helium, which looks exactly like a monster on the right-hand-side panel of Hieronymus Bosch's *Garden of Earthly Delights*, the musical inferno, and also like the topmost figure in Marcel Duchamp's *Grand Verre*.

—*What in heaven's name are you talking about?*

—Pay no attention. Because of all that genetic fiddling about, I've still got a loose bobbin inside me, like a loom. At the end of 1944, in the last winter of the war, the German occupying forces were in the habit of parking trains carrying V-2 rockets immediately south of the Academic Hospital in the hope that this would deter the English from air attacks. They were fired at London from a launchpad nearby. Nevertheless, one December afternoon, just after midday, there was a heavy raid on the station; shortly afterward the false rumor circulated in Delft that the hospital was on fire. Although weakened by hunger and despite the cold, Sophia immediately cycled to Leiden to see whether anything had happened to her best friend, a fellow nurse. As she was passing the museum, a few hundred yards south of the station, the second attack came and she took cover in a doorway—but because the English, under my benevolent influence, were frightened of hitting the hospital, it suddenly started raining bombs around her. One devastated a wing of the museum containing brass telescopes from the eighteenth and nineteenth centuries. Amid the chaos of fire, noise, dust, screaming in Dutch and German, firemen, ambulances, and police, she bumped into Oswald Brons. Bewildered, with torn clothes and covered in grazes, he was wandering across the heaps of rubble carrying a huge lens in his arms like a baby, and she took pity on him.

—*Minor intervention. Positive effect. How many people dead?*

—Fifty-four.

—*A slight adjustment, you said?*

—Well, what do you want? I didn't invent all that manipulation business, I'm only carrying out your cherubic will. What's more, I prevented the hospital from being razed to the ground. It seems so easy to influence the normal course of events, but reality is just like water; it's liquid and mobile, but it can only be compressed a little by using a great deal of force. When someone falls onto it from a great height, it's as hard as the rock from which Moses struck water.

—*Oh, our Moses . . . you're touching a sensitive nerve there.*

—I'm sorry.

—*When was their daughter born?*

—In 1946, during the baby boom.

—*When did she meet the young Delius?*

—In May 1967.

—*Tell me the whole story from that moment on, preferably without a commentary. Just tell it in full and with all the details, so that I can select when it's my turn to report.*

—For a fuller understanding, it would be better if I started a little earlier.

—*When?*

—On Monday, February 13, 1967, at twelve midnight.

—*Which in fact is February 14.*

—Yes, human time is one great paradox.

—*What year is it down there now?*

—1985.

—*Begin, then. I'm listening.*

I

The Family Gathering

At the stroke of midnight I contrived a short-circuit. Anyone walking along the quiet avenue in The Hague with his collar turned up high against the freezing cold (though there was no one at that moment) would have seen all the lights in the detached mansion suddenly go off, as though a gigantic candle had been blown out inside. For those living in the neighborhood, the villa exuded a somewhat somber splendor: it was the home of a legendary prime minister, the strict Calvinist Hendrikus Quist. In the crowded downstairs rooms, where the party was going on, the sudden darkness and the fading of the music into a fathomless cave were greeted with laughter.

"Time for the young'uns!" cried a woman's voice, itself no longer very young.

"Is anyone here technically minded?"

"I'll see to it. Where are the fuses, Grandmother?"

"On top of the electric meter, in the cupboard next to the stairs down to the cellar."

"Someone must have been messing about with them. You don't get a short-circuit just like that."

"I'll go and have a look up in the attic, at the little ones."

"Ouch!"

"Someone must have been using that wretched toaster again. Coba?"

"Yes, ma'am?"

"Did you use that toaster?"

"No, ma'am."

"Look and see if there are any candles left in the sideboard."

"Yes, ma'am."

The only light in the rooms was that cast by the streetlamps. In the dark conservatory at the back of the house a large figure now rose from a wicker armchair. Glass in hand, he surveyed the scores of silhouettes.

"No, Mother!" he cried in a loud voice, emphasizing every syllable. "This has nothing to do with the toasters. It has begun!"

"What has begun?"

"It!" He shouted it with his head thrown back, ecstatically, like an enlightened mystic.

"He's off again," said a man's voice. "Sit down and stop drinking."

"It!"

"Yes, yes. It. It's all right."

"That's right! It's all right. It's also dark, and it's freezing outside. It was about time that it began, that thank heavens it's happened. So be it. Amen—so that the infidels may also understand."

"Onno, you're insufferable."

But the very opposition he provoked was an inspiration. He knew that he was making an exhibition of himself, but he was swept along by his own words.

"Does my ear hear the cacophonous voice of my eldest brother, the most bigoted of Calvinists? What is more terrible than being an eldest brother? I shall say it through clenched teeth: having an eldest brother! Father, make that wretched individual shut up!"

"I don't know if you remember," said a woman in the dark, "but we're celebrating Father's birthday. It's his seventy-fifth birthday, do you remember? It's meant to be a celebration."

"Isn't that my youngest sister? The fair Ophelia? Yes, I remember, I remember. I myself am thirty-three—does that perhaps ring a bell in this company of fanatics and zealots? I remember everything, because I never forget anything. Isn't this the second time in a week that we've celebrated Father's birthday? Father, where are you? I am looking for you, but I am looking through a glass darkly. There you were the day before yesterday at the head of the table, in De Wittenburg Castle: on your right the queen, on your left the crown princess; at the other end, a ten-minute walk away, our poor mother, wedged between the prince-consort and the prime minister; and between you the whole cabinet, eighty-six ex-ministers, a hundred and sixty-eight thousand generals, prelates, bankers, politicians, and industrialists as far as the eye could see; and all of you, too, all the pashas and grand viziers and moguls and satraps by marriage. *Hic sunt monstra.* If only my abominable eldest brother were not there, the governor of that backward province whose name still escapes me."

"Now I've had enough, I'm going to punch him in the nose!"

"Calm down, Diederic. You're a terrible nuisance, Onno. You yourself were sitting talking oh so timidly to the Honorable Miss Bob in your dinner jacket."

"Oh God, the Honorable Miss Bob, the sweetie. I told her the facts of life. It was all completely new to her."

Onno was enjoying himself hugely. It was mainly his own generation who were turning against him. The previous one did not say much; the next one, which was still in high school, was amused and admiring. That was the way to be. One must have the guts to be like that.

"I can't find any candles anywhere, ma'am."

A boy came in with a pocket flashlight, which gave less light than a candle. "There are no fuses left," he said.

He put the flashlight on the table, transforming the faces of some old ladies, who were nibbling gingersnaps and drinking their liqueurs, into those of Transylvanian witches. But people's eyes were adjusting to the dark, so it seemed to be getting gradually lighter. Onno still maintained the pose of a field marshal surveying the battlefield.

"Go next door, Coba," said his mother, "to Mrs. Van Pallandt's. Perhaps she can help us. But only if the lights are on."

"Yes, ma'am."

"It's less than two months since the birthday of the Lord Jesus," cried Onno, "and there's no longer a single candle to be found in this Calvinist bastion!"

"Can you please put a stop to that exasperating chatter?" asked his eldest sister's husband. "For goodness' sake clear off, man. Go to Amsterdam where you belong."

"Yes, heaven be praised that I live in Amsterdam and not in Holland."

"How many rum-and-Cokes have you had, Onno?"

"In Amsterdam," said Onno, raising his glass, "we don't call this liquid rum-and-Coke. In Amsterdam we call it a Cuba libre, but you'll eventually catch on in Holland. So I shall drink a toast to *el líder máximo. Patria o muerte—venceremos*!" He downed his glass in one.

"Long live Che Guevara!" shouted a boy.

"Hey, Maarten, have you taken leave of your senses?"

"The young monkey's showing his true colors."

"Beware of that monkey! That monkey will make short work of you and your horrible Holland. Soon Coba will be in control here, and then it will be the ex-governor of the ex-queen who will have to fetch candles from the people next door, who won't be called Van Pallandt but, for all I know, Gortzak, or some other honest working-class name. The bunch of you are Holland. Without Quists there would be no Holland, and what a blessing that would be for mankind."

"Onno—"

"Ignore him. Simply ignore him, then he'll shut up by himself."

"Anyway, you're a Quist too."

"Me? Me a Quist? What an unforgivable insult. I'm a bastard," he said solemnly. "A cuckoo in the next—that's what I am."

"You're cuckoo, all right," said one of his aunts at the table with the flashlight, which was becoming weaker and weaker.

"And who is the father of the cuckoo?" asked his eldest sister.

"Mother and I will never reveal that. Never! Isn't that so, Mother? We have sworn not to."

"What have we sworn?"

"Oh, now you're playing dumb. Don't you remember that handsome prince from that distant country who came to Holland on a white horse?"

"What on earth is he talking about?"

"If you ask me, the fellow's no longer completely *compos mentis*."

Onno put his hand on his heart.

"About the Seventh Commandment, woman."

"Did the prince have a black beard by any chance?" asked his other brother, a professor of criminal law in Groningen. "Was he dressed in a green uniform, with a pistol perhaps?"

Onno faltered, set his glass down, put both hands against the wall, and began shaking with laughter.

"He's enjoying it, the windbag."

"Mother!" shouted Onno with a choking voice. "They know! It's come out!"

"What has come out?"

"That you deceived Father with Fidel Castro."

"Me, deceive Father? Wherever did you get that idea? I don't even know the man."

"Joke, dear, joke."

"Funny kind of jokes they tell here. I've never deceived Father."

"You deceived me!" cried Onno, standing up and raising a trembling forefinger like a prophet. "With Father! By conceiving me!"

At that moment his youngest sister, two heads shorter than he, loomed in front of him and took his hand. He allowed himself to be led into the room like a clumsy circus bear.

"That's really enough, Onno," she said softly. "There are limits."

"Who told you that?"

"I don't mind at all, I can take a dig or two, but you're embarrassing Mother. She can't follow your strange sense of humor."

"Strange sense of humor?" he repeated. "I mean every word. Doesn't anyone understand that? Not even you? If even you don't understand me, who will? Oh, where is there someone who understands me!"

"Stop it. You're simply being provocative, and you're enjoying it."

"Of course, of course, but I also mean it. I also mean what I don't mean."

"Oh yes, tell me more."

"No, you don't want me to tell you more at all. When I'm dying I shall crawl to you on my knees, but even you don't understand a thing. No one understands me!" he cried pathetically and suddenly at full volume again.

"That's true," said his eldest sister's husband. "So hurry back to your crossword puzzles, then we here in Holland will make sure you can go on doing your puzzles in peace."

Onno cupped his hand behind his ear.

"Do I detect a shrill tone there? Is that because no one will believe that a certain seedy public prosecutor from the provinces is the brother-in-law of the great, unforgettable, world-famous Onno Quist?"

While he beat his chest with both fists, the door opened and admitted a flock of children, led by a little girl of about seven. She was wearing a white nightgown, which came down to her bare feet. She cried: "Who's that drunk man?"

Onno surveyed them with a look of horror. "Brood of vipers! Are they all going to become ministers and judges and ambassadors' wives in their turn? Oh God, take those children and smash them to pieces against the rocks! Otherwise there will never be an end to it."

"Uncle Onno! Uncle Onno!"

"I'm not anybody's uncle. How dare you? I'm only my own uncle. Misunderstood, sneered at by everyone, and kicked into a corner, I wander lonely and magnificent in the rarefied realms of the Utterly Different."

"That clown is beginning to make me feel ill," said the provincial governor. "Father, can't you put a stop to it?"

There was a silence. Onno, too, suddenly stopped talking. Far away, in the front room, near the plush curtains, sat Quist. Onno could not see him, and looked in his direction, eyes peering, as when one tries to focus on a faint star.

"Oh," said Quist, "the lad will turn out all right."

When Onno heard this, he put his glass on the windowsill and made his way to the front room between the heavy pieces of furniture and the outstretched legs—a journey in the course of which the average age of the guests gradually increased. At the other end of the suite his father was sitting in the winged armchair like a dark red boulder: a last erratic stone that had come to rest, having been driven along by the terminal moraine of his times. Beside him was the oak lectern, on which lay the massive seventeenth-century Authorized Version, as large as a suitcase, with silver trimmings and two heavy locks. Onno could not make out his face. He dropped to his knees and pressed his lips to his father's high black shoes. The leather was warmed by the feet it was covering.

Onno sat up, and suddenly said in a lighthearted tone, "Farewell, all. I'm going home."

"What time is it?" asked his mother. "Surely there are no more trains running?"

"I'm going to hitch a lift."

"What nonsense, you can sleep here."

His brother-in-law laughed. "I wouldn't dream of giving a lift to such a sinister figure in the middle of the night."

"We've got a bed too," said his eldest sister. "You can come in the car with us. We're all going home; it's twelve-thirty."

"I'm going to Amsterdam. I've got a date."

"Stop being silly. You haven't got a date."

"Let him have his way," said the public prosecutor.

Had the insults already been forgotten? Obviously, his family regarded him as a natural phenomenon: after the storm, the branches that have been blown down are cleared up, and there's an end of it. He spread his arms wide in farewell and went into the hall whistling softly.

"You can't find a thing here in this Stygian darkness," said his youngest sister, with the almost completely extinguished pocket flashlight in her hand.

As he began rummaging among the piles of coats, the key squeaked in the lock. "Heavens, you're muddling everything up," said Coba, retrieving his coat as she passed.

"Shall I drive you to the main Wassenaar road?" asked his sister, while he unbuttoned his coat again and this time rebuttoned it symmetrically. "It's over half an hour's walk."

"I'd like a bit of a walk."

"You're restless."

He gave her a kiss on the forehead and went out. As he closed the garden gate, the lights came on again all over the house.

The Hague lay silent in the darkness. There were scarcely any cars about. The houses were lighter-colored than in Amsterdam, but almost all the windows were dark. The civil servants were asleep and dreaming of putting an end once and for all to the disturbances in the capital that had been going on for years, with tanks on the street corners and dive bombers firing rockets at the university institutes, after which they would be appointed governor of the pacified city.

In his heavy full-length winter coat, Onno walked in the direction of the main road to Leiden. Although it was freezing he was not wearing gloves, but he did not put his hands in his pockets: he held them on his back, where they gradually became purple with cold, without him noticing. Here, where he had spent his whole youth, he knew every stone, but that awakened no nostalgic feelings in him. Moreover, he did not look around him; nor did he reflect on the evening that had just passed. Stooping a little, with a slightly labored gait in his clumsy, and as always unpolished, shoes, he walked through the deserted streets, with a circular clay tablet constantly in his mind—sometimes one side, sometimes the other.

He suddenly seemed like a different person. He kept his tongue on the left side of his mouth between his teeth and chewed on it gently, as he always did when he was thinking. There was a sleepy look on his face, but that was not because of tiredness or alcohol; it was the sleepiness of thought. Thought is never action, forward, up and at it, as people think who do not know what thinking is; it is not like a forest explorer cutting back creeping vines, but more like someone letting himself relax into a hot bath.

The tablet, the so-called Phaistos disc, was the size of a dessert plate. Both sides had a pattern, which resembled nothing so much as a hopscotch diagram of the kind that children draw on the street with chalk: a spiral moving inward in a clockwise direction, ending in a central point. It looked like a maze, but it was definitely not one. It was impossible to get lost in it—there was only one way, and that led to the center. The diagram was divided into compartments filled with primitive signs, such as a helmeted head, a number of human and animal figures in profile, an ax, something like a portable cage, and many other illustrations. Onno looked at the rebus, whose 242 signs and forty-five syllables in the sixty-one compartments he knew better than his own body, and which in another sense was still a maze—while ever new connections formed in his mind, disappeared, emerged again in modified form, linked with other linguistic facts and signs, Philistine, Lycian, Semitic . . .

There was a great silence around him.

2

Their Meeting

As Onno Quist was leaving his parents' house, in another, considerably less distinguished, area of The Hague a man of the same age had reached orgasm in four or five waves, accompanied by loud cries.

"Well, well!" he gasped when it had subsided, both surprised and appreciative. "Thank you."

He was lying on the floor, and with his eyes closed he stroked the woman who had collapsed on top of him like a half-empty balloon; and somehow, something was wrong. He felt a leg where in fact there could be no leg; her head was at a point where he expected a foot. He stroked a rounding that was probably the beginning of a breast but might also have been that of a buttock, raised his eyebrows in resignation, sighed deeply, and dozed off . . .

He had met her in Rotterdam a few hours earlier. Some students from the Economics University had organized a "revolutionary carnival" there, and he had read the announcement on a noticeboard in Leiden, where he worked. He lived in Amsterdam, but because he had nothing to do, he had driven to the party later that evening after work. Deafening music in decorated rooms, people dancing everywhere; even the stairs were full. At an improvised Cuban restaurant, Moncada, he ate a hunk of meat, and in a Flemish tavern, the Racing Shorts, he ordered an orange juice. In a side room an "occult market" had been set up: at trestle tables all kinds of individuals were offering their services, free, with Tarot cards, horoscopes, pendulums, crystal balls, and I Ching paraphernalia. He searched the throng for girls he might be able to chat up, but everyone was accompanied, had dressed up—there were scores of boys in Che Guevara berets—and were enjoying themselves; he soon began to tire of the relaxed, unerotic atmosphere. Human beings were not on earth for their pleasure, he believed—fucking was an imperative—and after an hour he decided he might as well go back to his car. He was tired, but he mustn't give in to that, either; there was still time to fix up something in Amsterdam.

On his way to the exit he again passed through the room with the wizards and witches, but in the meantime it had virtually emptied. As the atmosphere became more intense, interest in higher things had disappeared; most people were already busy packing up their supernatural equipment. Only by the stall of a woman in a purple sweater was there still a girl sitting with her hand, palm upward, in that of the lady, like a saint showing her stigmata.

She was an attractive girl. She was no more than nineteen or so, with her blond hair in a ponytail. With feigned interest he stopped and listened to what the palmist had to say. With a slim pen she drew lines, crosses, and circles alongside significant twists in the lines of the hand, which reminded him of markings on astronomical photographs. In general the patterns seem to present a favorable picture, but certain side branches of the lifeline did give cause for alarm: they pointed to a serious illness at the age of about forty; it was also better not to have a grille on the Mount of the Sun. The girl looked at her hand and nodded in understanding.

"I think what you're doing is quite scandalous," he said suddenly—first and foremost, of course, to make himself known to the girl, but he also meant what he said. "I hope she thinks it's all nonsense, because that's what it is; but meanwhile it's been planted in her head—your threat about that illness. For twenty years." The two women looked up at him, the girl with an amused look, the astrologer with a morose glance over her semicircular reading glasses. She was his own age, perhaps a little older; dark-brown hair lay in strange twists across her head, as though an enormous lizard had nestled there, an iguana. Something in her face immediately grabbed him. He saw her small breasts in her sweater, between them a pendant with a flat metal hand on it—and at that moment he knew that he wanted to go to bed not with her client, but with her.

"Scandalous," he said, still looking at her.

Perhaps the girl had seen the change; she got up, said goodbye politely, and left.

"I think we have a bone to pick with each other," he said severely.

When she got up to pack, she turned out to be very slightly built: her beastly crown did not even come up to his shoulders. Without a word she put on her coat and went outside. Wondering how he was to break through that silence, he followed her to the car park. When she had put the key into the door of a small car, she suddenly turned to him and gestured invitingly.

He burst out laughing. "I've got one too. I'll follow you."

A little later, in his dark-green sports car with the white cloth hood, which was raring to go faster, he dawdled behind her along the road to The Hague, with a constant semi-erection because of the situation.

"A fortune-teller!" he cried as they passed Delft, and banged his wooden steering wheel. "That's all I needed!" He felt in his element and began singing a Mahler song: *"Wenn mein Schatz Hochzeit macht, fröhliche Hochzeit macht . . ."* Tears welled up in his eyes. Melancholy, lust, music—suddenly everything overwhelmed him as he watched the red taillights.

"I'm alive!" he shouted. "I'm alive!"

She lived in a pedestrian apartment building, plonked down crudely in a street full of nineteenth-century workers' houses. Even as she walked along the back balcony she remained silent. In a small, warm apartment she lit candles and incense sticks, and handed him a bottle of wine with a label that did not inspire confidence. As he took the bottle between his knees and stuck the corkscrew into the cork, sitar music filled the room.

"Of course," he said. "Ravi Shankar."

They clinked glasses and drank, still looking at each other. He did not like the wine and put down his glass. What next? He was sitting in the small armchair; she was on the sofa. He got up, knelt down in front of her, and laid his right hand palm upward in her lap.

"Right, now let's see what you can do."

He felt the warmth of her thighs, but she moved his hand to one side like a book that she did not want to read and took hold of his left hand. The hand lay in hers like an item of lost property; her small hand was warmer than his, which aroused him still more. She had still not said a word; they did not even know each other's names. After casting a glance at his short, slightly deformed thumb, she began drawing crosses and circles again—but suddenly she faltered and looked at him in alarm. He was also alarmed. He read something in her look that he would not believe but which he did not want to hear.

He withdrew his hand and laid it on her hip, putting the other on her neck. Pushing his fingers into her thick hair, he pulled her head slightly toward him, which she willingly allowed him to do. He gave a short grunt, and then suddenly leaped forward across her, while she immediately parted her legs. At the same moment they were writhing and biting like fighting dogs, pulling each other's clothes off. Yelling, screaming, they were caught up in a whirlpool and dragged down to a depth of which no memory usually remains . . .

He woke with a start. He had slept for no longer than a minute. He turned his head to the side. Above the slowly fading glow of an incense stick, a thin white cone of ash bent further and further forward and broke off.

"I must be going," he said.

Again he studied the topology of the chiromancer. It was as though she were also a snake-woman; her posture was an impossible one, like in an Escher drawing. Her curls of hair had worked loose and lay over her shoulders and back like congealed lava, but it might also have been her breast. Without waking her, he wriggled out from beneath her and opened a door behind which he suspected the bedroom lay. He lifted her up. She was as light as a child; he laid her carefully on the bed and pulled the blankets over her. She had not woken. Because he felt agitated, as though he were in a hurry, he did not take a shower; he washed with cold water in the kitchen, dried himself with a clammy tea towel, dressed quickly, and scrutinized the flat.

In the Swedish whitewood bookcase there was a postcard of Jan van Eyck's *Arnolfini Wedding*: perhaps because of the pregnant bride's hand, which lay palm upward in that of the bridegroom. The back of the card was blank. He pulled a yellow pencil with an eraser on the end out of his inside pocket, produced a small pencil sharpener from a side pocket of his blazer, sharpened the pencil meticulously in an ashtray, and wrote: "I'll never forget this.—Max." For a moment he considered leaving his telephone number, but did not. He carefully placed the card on her small desk against a polished veined-pink stone, perhaps invested with magic powers, but perhaps simply a souvenir from a southern beach. Then he blew out the candles, left the incense burning, and gently closed the door behind him.

Sexual satisfaction had washed every part of him clean. He was reminded of a vacation in Venice, when violet-colored mountains suddenly appeared on the horizon after a storm. His tiredness had gone and with

Schubert's First Symphony on the radio—probably the Berlin Philharmonic under Böhm—he drove haphazardly down the empty winter streets. He was free! He wanted nothing more now! This was as wonderful as fucking itself, or the certainty beforehand that it was going to happen. Or was it even more wonderful? Was the reason that he wanted to sleep with a woman every day, a different one every day, ultimately to achieve this aim: not to want to for a short time? What a happy old man he would be. But of course that was not how it would be; when that time came, he would want to want what he was no longer capable of. Happiness was not freedom from chains but release from chains. Chains were an indispensable part of happiness!

He had no idea where he was, but by driving straight ahead as far as possible he was bound to reach the edge of town. The Hague was not that big. Suddenly he recognized a junction. On the deserted pavement stood a large man in a long overcoat, who raised his hand.

Surely a mugger would not operate like this, he thought, at one in the morning in the freezing cold. He signaled, pulled over with a rapid movement, and stopped. He saw the man come jogging up in the mirror; he turned off the radio, leaned over, and wound down the window on the other side.

Onno, bending low, looked into Max's narrow, fanatical face. It reminded him of an ibis, the Egyptian *Ibis religiosa,* with its thin neck and curved beak; there was something dangerous about it, like an ax. Max, for his part, surveyed Onno's full, domineering features. The transition from the forehead to the straight nose was classical, with no curve; beneath was an equally classical small mouth, with curved lips, scarcely broader than his nostrils. It struck him as vaguely familiar.

"Where are you headed?"

"Are you going toward Amsterdam?"

"In you get."

Onno took a step back and surveyed the car disapprovingly. "But under protest!"

"Please, I beg you," said Max in amusement.

Once, with some effort, he had managed to sit—or, rather, lie—down, Max put his foot down and the car leaped forward like a racehorse.

"Nice motor," said Onno with an expression that indicated he thought his benefactor was not quite right in the head.

Max burst out laughing. "Oh, this is nothing. When I grow up, I shall buy a white open-topped Rolls-Royce, and I'll sit on the back seat in a white fur coat, with a beautiful woman at the wheel."

Pulling a wry face, Onno was forced to laugh a little too, and turned his head to one side. He already had the beginnings of a double chin. "Why don't you buy a pram right away?"

Max glanced at him for a moment. They had found each other—this was the moment. Did they both realize it? With those few words a bridge had been built. Max knew he had been seen through by Onno as never before, just as Onno felt understood by Max, because his aggressive irony had not met with resistance, as it invariably did, but with a laugh that had something invulnerable about it. They had recognized each other. A little embarrassed by the situation, they were silent for a few minutes.

Once they had left the stately avenue through Wassenaar behind them and reached the dark motorway, Max accelerated to a hundred miles an hour and said: "I have the feeling I know you from somewhere. Wasn't your photo in the paper recently?"

"Of course my photo was in the paper recently," said Onno, as if he had been asked if he could read.

"For what reason?"

"Can't you remember? Have you already forgotten?"

"I confess my shortcomings."

"My photo was in the paper," pontificated Onno, "because I received an honorary doctorate in Uppsala."

"May I congratulate you belatedly? And what was it for?"

"So you can't remember that, either. Tell me, what do you know?"

"Almost nothing."

"It was because I made Etruscan comprehensible. The greatest minds in the world had failed—even Professor Massimo Pellegrini in Rome was too stupid—so I thought I might as well do it."

Max nodded. Now he remembered: the large man in tails, pretending to be astonished as he received the diploma from a lady in an academic cap, as though it were a complete surprise to him.

Onno looked sideways. "And what about you?" he asked. "What do you do for a living? I can't recall ever having seen your photo in the paper."

"What a shit you are," said Max, laughing. "I do astronomy." Motioned right with his head. "Over there. In Leiden."

Onno looked at the town on the edge of the bare fields. "Don't you need to turn off here, then?"

"I live in Amsterdam, thank God. That's why I have a car."

Onno put out his hand and said, "Onno Quist."

Max shook the hand. "Delius, Max."

3

I'll See You Home

Onno never answered curious questions about his discovery. "You can read all about it in the *Journal of Near Eastern Studies*," he was wont to say. "I don't work overtime." Now, however, in response to Max's question how he had deciphered the script, he explained patiently that it was not a matter of deciphering, seeing that it had been legible for donkey's years. It consisted largely of the Greek alphabet, but it was not Greek; it was incomprehensible. It was as if someone who knew no Greek were to learn the Greek alphabet and then try to read the *Iliad*. The Etruscans were an Italic people, he lectured, living in what was now Tuscany. The Roman conquerors called them "Tusci." Latin was full of Etruscan loanwords, such as *persona* for "mask," but apart from that there were only a few words whose meaning was known, such as those for "god," "woman," and "son."

The problem was that there was no long *bilingue* as there had been with Champollion's Rosetta stone, with the same text in Etruscan and a known language. So they were connected with the Greeks in some way, and at the same time their language was totally unconnected with Greek. They wrote their language phonetically with Greek characters, like first-year high school pupils did with their names, and like Dutch people did with Roman letters. So that in about the ninth century B.C. this people came from somewhere where there were also Greeks. However—and that was the decisive flash of inspiration—it was of course also possible that the Greeks had once borrowed their alphabet from the Etruscans in order to write their own language, Greek. Of course it was a totally crazy idea; but following that line of reasoning, supported by all kinds of archaeological considerations, he arrived at the Cretan languages, Linear B, deciphered fifteen years previously by his late colleague Michael Ventris, and Linear A from the eighteenth century—which in turn had Semitic origins . . .

"In short, my dear Watson," he said as they were passing Schiphol airport, "through combination and deduction and a lot of luck and wisdom, I found the answer. It's true that Professor Pellegrini still regards me as a fantasist and a charlatan, but that is largely an indication of his autistic nature."

"What did you study?"

"Law."

"Law?"

"It's a family disease."

"But all those languages . . ."

"A hobby. I'm an amateur, like the great Ventris, who was an architect by profession. If I have to, I can learn a language in a month. I could read by the time I was three."

"How many languages do you know then?"

"I'm bad at counting. That strikes me as more in your line. How many stars are there?"

"We haven't counted them all yet, and anyway, the number isn't constant. In one galaxy alone there are about a hundred billion. As many as a human being has brain cells."

"Speak for yourself."

"In addition there are about a hundred million known galactic systems, as many as I have brain cells, so you can work it out. A one and twenty-two naughts. How many languages are there?"

"A mere nothing. About two thousand five hundred."

"Can you read hieroglyphics too?"

"What kind of hieroglyphics?"

"Egyptian."

"Nothing to it. I can speak them too. *Paut neteroe her resch sep sen ini*

Asar sa Heroe nen ab maä kheroe sa Ast auau Asar. Which, being interpreted, is: 'The paut of the gods rejoice at the coming of Osiris's son Horus, upright in heart, whose word is absolute, son of Isis, heir of Osiris.' "

"Goodness me! What does 'paut' mean?"

"Well, that's a bit of a problem. How annoying of you to ask. Most experts believe that it refers to the primeval substance the gods are made of; but in fact it's even more complicated, because in the Book of the Dead the god creator says: 'I created myself from the primeval substance, which I made.' But I won't weary you with such archaic paradoxes."

"They seem quite modern to me," says Max. "Where do you live? I'll drop you off at your door."

Both turned out to live in the center, not far from each other. As they drove into the city, Onno told Max that he could read hieroglyphics by the time he was eleven, and that he had taught himself with an old English textbook, which he had bought in the market for twenty-five cents, so that by using a dictionary he learned English at the same time. That had been in the last winter of the war—when hunger and cold had finally broken him, he said—immediately wondering why he was telling something like this to a total stranger. At home, when he was young, he didn't talk about his language studies. He thought that anyone who made the slightest effort could do it.

It was always the same with talent: a writer could not imagine that there was anyone who could not write. Onno only realized that it was not so ordinary on one occasion after the war when they were on holiday in Finland. They were in their hotel in Hämeenlinna, somewhere among those depressing lakes and pine forests, and the evening before their departure the food was cold, or barely warm. His father called the manager, who then pretended to tell off the waiter but in fact said that he shouldn't worry about those stingy cheeseheads, because the next day they were already buggering off to their stupid tulips and windmills. Whereupon he, Onno, inquired whether he had taken leave of his senses, speaking about his guests like that, or whether perhaps he wanted his head smashed in with a Dutch clog. Everyone was speechless. He could speak Finnish! After three weeks! A Finno-Ugric language! And when he saw his father's perplexed face, he thought: I've got one over on you, Your Excellency.

"Are you a son of *that* Quist?" asked Max in surprise.

"Yes, *that* Quist."

"Wasn't he prime minister or something before the war?"

"Would you mind speaking a little less casually about my father, Delius, Max? The four years of the Quist cabinet are among the darkest in human civilization. The Dutch nation languished under the theocratic reign of terror of my honored father, against whom I will not hear a word of criticism, and certainly not from someone with such a ridiculous automobile."

"At least it got us home," said Max, stopping the car. "You can't even drive, if you ask me."

"Of course not! What do you take me for? A chauffeur? There are things one simply isn't allowed to know how to do. For example, something else that you are not allowed to be able to do is serve food with a fork and spoon in the fingers of one hand, because that means you're a waiter. Of course you can do it just as well, but a gentleman like me is not used to serving himself. A gentleman like me does that very clumsily, with two hands, and even then I drop half on the tablecloth, because that's the way to do it."

In the light of the streetlamps in the narrow street they could now see each other better. Onno thought Max was actually far too well groomed to be taken seriously; he was wearing the sort of Anglo-Saxon bourgeois outfit, with a blazer and checked shirt, that Onno also disliked on his brothers and brothers-in-law. Max, in his turn, felt that Onno would not cut a bad figure as an organ-grinder; around his ears and under his chin there were also various places he had missed while shaving. Perhaps he was short-sighted, having gone cross-eyed from poring over ideograms.

Onno proposed driving to Max's house; then he would walk back. They noted with satisfaction that there were still people in the street and that there were still lights on everywhere in the houses, whereas in The Hague all life had been totally extinguished. At the high gate into the park Max locked his car and put on his coat; Onno saw that he was also wearing brown suede shoes. He was about to say goodbye, but now it was Max who said: "Come on, I'll walk along with you for a little way."

There was the sound of police sirens from the direction of the Leidseplein: something was going on, perhaps the last throes of a demonstration against the Americans in Vietnam.

"Are you also an honorary doctor of the university of Uppsala?" inquired Onno, "like me?"

"I haven't got that far yet."

"You're not an honorary doctor of the university of Uppsala?" cried

Onno in dismay, and stopped. "Can someone like me really speak to you?" Suddenly he changed tone, still looking at Max. "Do you know that your face is all wrong? You have steely, extremely unsympathetic blue eyes, but at the same time a ridiculously soft mouth, which I wouldn't like to be seen with."

Max looked up at him. Onno was almost a head taller. "That's right," he said after a moment's hesitation.

"No, that isn't right."

"It's right that it's not right."

"And that nose of yours would be better cloaked totally in the mantle of love."

"Hunting dogs always have long snouts—they're better for sniffing with. You mustn't take it personally, but a Pekingese can't smell a thing. And anyway, I'm not a *doctor cum grano salis* like you, but a real one, with a thesis and all."

"I can hear it already. You're one of those fools who think that achievement is more praiseworthy than talent. What was your thesis on?"

"Hydrogen line spectra."

"What in heaven's name is that?"

"You won't understand. You have to be very clever for that."

Max mentioned that he was an astronomer at Leiden Observatory. He had recently had an offer of a fellowship at the Mount Palomar Observatory in California, where a Leiden colleague of his was presently in charge, the man who had discovered quasars; but he was more interested in radio astronomy, with which you could see what was invisible, even during the day. Optical astronomers were pale nightwatchmen, and if a cloud appeared they could just as well get on their bikes and cycle home into the wind; apart from that, he had better things to do at night. He went regularly to Dwingeloo, in Drenthe, to the radio telescope there. A huge synthetic radio telescope was being built near Westerbork, consisting of twelve mirrors, of which one was completed. It was going to be the biggest telescope in the world, and he had high hopes for it.

"By the way, you just said that it all began in the war with you— perhaps it was the same for me. In the middle of town the night sky had a clarity that today you find only at sea, or on Mount Palomar. At a certain moment I was in a kind of boarding school, run by priests. When they sang vespers in the chapel at night, I sometimes woke up and leaned out the window. I think that those quiet nights and those stars and that Gregorian chant and the war laid the foundation for my choice of career, for want of a better word. Maybe because those stars had nothing to do with the war." At the word *stars* he glanced upward, but the glow of the city was now reflected by a gray blanket of clouds.

"So you were brought up as a Catholic. Or are you still one?"

"I was brought up as nothing."

"How did you wind up in that institution, then?"

Max said nothing. He turned up the collar of his camel-colored coat and crossed the lapels, keeping hold of them with his gloved hand. The fathers below in the chapel sang:

> *"Kyrie eleison, kyrie eleison,*
> *Christe eleison, Christe eleison."*

In the sky the Great Bear, Cassiopeia, the pole star—around which the axis of the heavens turned. Where was his mother?

He looked at Onno. "Shall I tell you?"

Onno saw that he had touched a nerve. "If it's not intended for my ears, I don't want to hear."

Max, too, was now surprised at himself. Not that he had anything to hide, but it wasn't something to make polite conversation about. He never talked to his colleagues and friends about it, to say nothing of his girlfriends, and he himself rarely thought about it. It was rather like the talent that Onno had talked about: all human beings were of course unique, and they only discovered that when someone else fell in love with them or when no one ever fell in love with them—but even extraordinary circumstances could seem perfectly natural, simply because they were as they were; and in that case the awareness of their extraordinariness only dawned when others found them extraordinary. A king's son, too, only realized later that flags were not put out for everyone in the country when it was their birthday.

The canals were frozen over. In the murky depths people were still skating; silent figures glided past with their hands on their backs, braking with blades scraping the ice when they came to the bridges, below which the ice was unreliable. As they walked through their city, past the Rijksmuseum, across the bridges with their strange sandstone and wrought-iron decorations of sea monsters that had crawled over the dunes, Max told Onno how his parents—as a result of the First World War—had found themselves in Amsterdam, how they met, how they separated, after which he went to live with his mother in South Amsterdam, behind the Concertgebouw. His father did not want to see them anymore, and when the Second World War came along he must have been overcome by some fateful urge. He reestablished contact with his former Austrian friends from the First World War, who in the meantime, since the country's annexation by Germany, had become pan-German generals and SS-*Obersturmbannführer*. In fact he, Max, knew all this only by hearsay; he'd never gone into it in depth. Perhaps his father needed to prove his pro-German attitude. He was still married to a Jewish woman; he had committed "a racial crime," even fathering a child with her, and perhaps that had to be put right first.

Meanwhile, he played a leading role in commercial relations with the occupying powers. His office grew into a semigovernmental institution, in fact specializing in plunder, particularly of Jewish goods, and through a lawyer he informed Eva Delius, née Weiss that he wanted a divorce. But she refused: her marriage to an Aryan provided added protection against deportation, perhaps even more than the child she had had by him. In fact, that insistence on a divorce was already a disguised attempt to murder his wife. As emerged after the war, he finally enlisted the help of his former comrades.

One morning in 1942, Max told Onno—the year he was nine—the housekeeper picked him up from school; in the headmaster's room there was a gendarme with a tall cap, boots, and a white lanyard over his shoulder. He was told that his mother had suddenly left for an unknown destination and that he had to go with the gendarme and sort out his things. When he got home, a moving van was already outside the door, with the name PULS on it in huge letters; he remembered that distinctly. A couple of moving men were carrying the piano out.

Inside, men were walking around with lists, noting down everything, except of course the things that they were putting in their pockets. There were no Germans anywhere, just two policemen from the local force. Everything had been turned upside down, in his mother's bedroom, all the drawers and cupboards were open; her clothes lay in a heap on the floor. He was given five minutes to collect his belongings, and then he was taken to some Roman Catholic college. In his innocence, he said he wanted to go and see his father: he did not yet know that he was anathema to his father. His grandparents, the only other relations he still had in

Holland, were in hiding somewhere; he did not know where—as little as he knew that his father had meanwhile also betrayed their address—nor that, like his mother, they had been transported to Auschwitz via the transit camp at Westerbork, from where none of them returned.

The collaborator had turned into a war criminal. Everyone called Weiss—and God knows who else from their spectrum—had to be wiped off the face of the earth. Max told Onno that after a few weeks the priests placed him with a childless middle-aged Catholic couple, who did not even require him to cross himself before meals. Occasionally, he cycled past his former house: the front door and windows were bricked up. He only heard about his father again after the war when he was put on trial, and then only on one further occasion: a short newspaper report of his execution.

"Good God!" cried Onno. "Are you a son of *that* Delius? You deserve a lot of forgiveness, I believe."

They were back on the Kerkstraat. Small, narrow houses with wooden staircases up to the first floor, stone steps down to the door of the basement.

"My grandfather was a collaborator in the First World War," said Max, "my father in the Second World War, and to keep up the family tradition, I shall have to be one in the Third World War." As he lit a cigarette, he turned his head for a moment to inspect the calves of a passing woman.

"Am I correct in thinking," asked Onno, "that you're talking about your mother's death and first make a dubious joke and then look at a woman? What kind of a person are you?"

"I must be the kind of person who looks at a woman while he's talking about his mother's death. Anyway, I was also talking about my father's death."

Onno was about to say something, but did not. It was incomprehensible to him that someone could talk so coolly about such experiences. He thought of his own mother being gassed in an extermination camp and his father shot by a firing squad after the war, but the fantasy did not take any solid shape. In reality, his father had been imprisoned for eighteen months as a hostage in a sort of VIP section of Buchenwald concentration camp, where together with other prominent figures he made plans for the postwar Netherlands—beginning with the setting up of a "special judiciary" and the reintroduction of the death penalty for the worst of the scum. Both his brothers had also been in the resistance.

He looked at Max and felt completely at his mercy. There was of course no question of extending his hand, saying goodbye, and going in. "I'll see you back home," he said.

For minutes on end they walked side by side through the winter night without a word, surrounded by the old violence that Max had summoned up as unexpectedly as a blow with the fist. Max, too, felt completely at Onno's mercy. He had told his paradoxical story differently from the few times he had done so previously. When someone tells the same thing to different people he tells it in different ways, which are as different from each other as those people—but now it was as though he had told the story to himself for the first time. It had lightened his load to the same extent that it had burdened Onno. In order to say something, he pointed to the bread that had been scattered here and there at the foot of trees.

"There are still some good souls in the world."

Onno had been waiting for Max to break the silence, but he did not feel entitled to ask for details of his story.

"Shall I tell you something? Your father was naturalized on my father's authority. It was during the period of his cabinet, in the 1920s."

Max looked at Onno and laughed. "That creates a nice bond between us. Is he still alive?"

"Of course, my father is still alive. My father will never not be alive."

"Tell him that. The greatest blunder of his career."

Onno was about to say that because of it his own father actually deserved a bullet, too, but restrained himself; he was not sure whether it was acceptable to be so nonchalant, because how thick was the layer of ice around this man? Was there in fact something entirely different beneath it?

"If your mother was Jewish," he said "then you must be a Jew yourself." He immediately disliked hearing the word *Jew* from his own mouth. Maybe only Jews were allowed to use it after all that had happened; perhaps there was a taboo on it—but on the other hand, should he allow himself to be silenced by the fascists?

"According to the rabbis, I am. According to the Nazis, thank heavens, I was only half-Jewish, otherwise I wouldn't have survived. You ask yourself, 'What half? The top half? The bottom half? Left? Right?' "

"The Nazis were biologists. For them you were a kind of diluted Jew; the Jewish wine had been diluted with fifty percent Aryan water."

"Don't they call that 'adulterating'?" asked Max, laughing. "Do you know, by the way, why that is so—that according to the Orthodox you're only a Jew when you have a Jewish mother and not a Jew if you only have a Jewish father?"

"Tell me."

"It's also connected with biology. Because a man can never be one hundred percent sure that he is the real father of his child. A mother may perhaps not be sure who the father is, but one thing is one hundred percent certain: that she is the mother."

"That shows a deep insight into the basic mendacity of woman as such."

Max burst out laughing. "Are you married, by any chance? Do you have children?"

Onno was glad that the dark cloud had been dispelled. "Children! Me, children! Even I'm not that cruel. I live with a girlfriend on and off, if you must know. One of those good souls who puts out bread." He decided not to ask about Max's love life, because it was probably too dreadful for words. "By the way, didn't you say that you were nine in 1942? That makes us the same age. When's your birthday?"

"The twenty-seventh of November."

"Mine's the sixth of November. So from now on, I shall regard you as my younger friend. You can still learn a lot from me. No, wait a bit . . ." he said, and stopped. "I was born three weeks prematurely. That means that we were conceived on the same day!"

They looked at each other in surprise.

"At the same moment!" cried Max.

Both of them, the driver and the hitchhiker, had the feeling that they had discovered the reason for their shock of recognition, as though they had never not known each other. They shook hands solemnly.

"Only death can part us," said Max in the exalted tone that he associated with Winnetou and Old Shatterhand. At the same moment he also thought of the blood-brotherhood ceremony in the Red Indian books: each cut his finger, after which the wounds were pressed together. It was on the tip of his tongue to say: "Actually, we ought to . . ."—but he did not.

They were back at his house on the imposing Vossiusstraat and arranged to phone each other the following day. Max offered to drive him home in the car, but Onno refused. As he took out his keys, Max looked after him in case he turned around and waved, but he did not. As he looked for the door key in his bunch of keys, he saw the circles and crosses in the palm of his left hand.

4

Friendship

In the next few months, when their work did not take them abroad, not a day went by without their seeing each other. Max had never met anyone like Onno, Onno had never met anyone like Max—as a self-proclaimed pair of twins, they did not cease to delight in each other. Each felt inferior to the other; each was at once both servant and master, which created a kind of infinity, like two mirrors reflecting each other. Because of their inseparable appearance in the street, in cafés and pubs, people sometimes talked of them as "homo-intellectuals." They were surrounded by misunderstanding and suspicion, because it was threatening: two grown men, who were obviously not gay and seemed to have nothing in common, and who in some mysterious way, precisely because of that, merged almost symbiotically with each other.

If they had been gay, there would have been no problem—they would simply have been a loving couple. But as it was, they confronted everyone with a deficiency in themselves, sometimes provoking an unpleasant mixture of jealousy and aggression, which saw one as an eternal student, who simply could not give up playing student pranks, and the other as an arrogant prick. In order to neutralize this, they fully admitted it and even played it up for good measure. They would discuss the question of what was going on between them only when it was no longer there, when all the days had merged in their memories into one eternally unforgettable day. Even the

37

Greeks, Onno knew, who had laid the foundation of Western culture, had no word for *culture*. The words only appeared when the thing itself had gone.

Naturally, each of them had a circle of friends, who now also got to know each other, but at the same time Max and Onno became estranged from them, drifted away, leaving them behind in a joint shaking of heads. They generally met at the reading table in Café Américain, beneath the art nouveau lamps and surrounded by murals depicting scenes from Wagner operas. Max had often already eaten in Leiden, or had made himself a quick snack at home, while Onno was still having his dinner—that is, there was always a plate with four or five meat rissoles on it next to his newspaper, which he washed down with four or five glasses of milk. He never ate vegetables. "Salad is for rabbits," he was wont to say. He seemed to be totally out of proportion with his body, and perhaps that was why he was so impressively present; his meals were as slovenly as his unbrushed teeth and his clothes. Once, when his face was dripping with sweat, Max said, "Onno, you've got a temperature,"—at which Onno wiped his forehead, looked at his gleaming palm, and said, "Christ, you're right!"—only to forget all about it the following instant.

Max, on the other hand, sat regularly in the waiting room of his Communist GP, staring at a large photo of striking Belgian workers in berets, eye to eye with a heavily armed platoon of militia, while there was never anything wrong with him, apart from the occasional dose of clap; and however great his imagined fear of death, his tie never clashed with his socks.

Once, Max started talking about death, which immediately irritated Onno beyond measure.

"Talking about death is a waste of time. As long as you're alive you're not dead, and when you're no longer alive you're only dead for other people."

But that was not what Max meant. He said that on the one hand he was convinced that one day he would die of a heart attack in dreadful pain, but on the other hand he might be immortal. A person could determine his life expectancy by adding the ages at which his parents had died and dividing by two. But both his parents had died violent deaths; if that had not happened, they might have been immortal. And because, according to Cantor, infinity plus infinity divided by two was also infinity, the proposition was proved.

"An extremely embarrassing logical error for a natural scientist," said Onno. "In reality it follows that you have a fifty percent chance of being murdered and a fifty percent chance of being executed, which means that it's a hundred percent certain that you'll die a violent death."

When the rissoles were finished they walked into town, where the wintry cold had disappeared from the air. Sometimes they went to the movies first, to see a James Bond film, or the latest Stanley Kubrick, *2001: A Space Odyssey*, in which a computer called HAL took control of a spaceship. When they emerged into the street—in the washed-out state in which reality grates on one like a gray file—Onno asked why Max thought the computer was called HAL. Because of the association with "hell," suggested Max. Damn, Onno hadn't thought of that. But suppose Max counted one letter on from *H, A,* and *L* in the alphabet.

"*I,*" said Max, "*B,M.* IBM!" he cried. "I take my hat off to you, sir!"

Onno assumed a modest expression. "It's a gift."

While they were drinking a cup of coffee somewhere, with Little Richard wailing from the jukebox, Onno maintained that his eye for that kind of thing was a result of his Calvinist upbringing: it came from reading the Bible, "containing all the Holy Scripture." For him, truth could only reside in what was written, and could not, for example, be seen through a telescope. That higher form of reading was something that the Calvinists shared with the Jews; Catholics never read the Bible, and usually didn't have one—Catholics were illiterates. Pictures and photographs; that was what they understood.

Moreover, the Calvinists were more concerned with the Old Testament than with the New Testament, like the Catholics—who in a supreme display of primitivism actually sang the text. When the Jews were persecuted, Calvinists therefore joined the resistance much more often than Catholics, who were anyway the inventors of anti-Semitism—as often as the Communists, who also derived truth from a book, namely that of Marx, another Jew.

It was as though Max could see his friend's trains of thought sweeping through the air like a lion tamer's long whip, and they inspired him in turn.

"Have you ever noticed," he said, "that the area of Protestantism coincides with the area covered by polar ice in the Ice Age? In the Netherlands the border runs right through the middle: where there was ice is the territory of the Protestants, as far as Hammerfest, and where grass grew is Catholic, as far as Palermo. And where did Calvin live?" he suddenly thought. "In Switzerland! The only Protestant country in the Catholic area when there are still glaciers!"

"I'm shivering," said Onno. "There are shivers running down my spine. Only someone who is not Dutch could make such a shameful discovery. Get thee behind me, Satan! You don't belong here at all."

"Where do I belong, then?"

Onno waved an arm. "In space. You view the Netherlands from space, like an astronaut; but I'm in the middle of it, frozen in the Calvinist ice, like a mammoth. Don't get me started. Holland belongs to me and not a lost Central European woodcutter like you."

It was true. Max could not imagine what it felt like to be part of a people, a nation, a race, a religion—in brief, when one was not alone. He was Dutch, Austrian, Jewish, and Aryan all at once, and hence none of them. He belonged only with those who, like him, belonged with no one.

"I feel as Dutch," he said, "as Spinoza must have felt."

"Why Spinoza, of all people?"

"For a number of reasons. Partly because he was a lens grinder."

But their unending stream of theories, jokes, observations, and anecdotes was not their real conversation: that took place beneath these, without words, and it was about themselves. Sometimes it became visible in a roundabout way, like when in the past North Sea fishermen located a school of herring from its silvery reflection against the clouds.

In a pub in the newspaper district, full of journalists from the morning dailies, as well as the evening papers, where he ordered his first rum-and-Coke, Onno once told Max about the Gilgamesh epic, the oldest story in the world, deciphered in the previous century by his colleague Rawlinson, written as long before Christ as they were now living after Christ. Cheops's pyramid had already been built, said Onno, because that had always been there, so to speak; but Moses, the Trojan War, all of that had yet to happen.

The first story was the story of a friendship. The Babylonian king Gilgamesh dreamed of a frightening ax, with which he fell in love and on which he "lay as on a woman." His mother, obviously well acquainted with the theories of Freud, interpreted that ax as a man on which he would lie as on a woman. And a little later the man appeared: Enkidu, a tamed savage, with whom he ventured forth and slayed the monster Chuwawa. However, that deed eventually led to Enkidu's death. In his despair Gilgamesh went in search of the elixir of immortality, but when even that was finally stolen from him, by a serpent, he resigned himself to the inevitable like a Candide *avant la lettre* and found his life's fulfillment as the architect of the battlements of Uruk.

"Magnificent," said Max. "Why don't I know all that? Why doesn't everyone read that?"

"Because not everyone knows me."

"What a dreadful fate that must be, not knowing you."

"The very thought strikes me as unbearable."

"I too lived for a long time in that hell."

With the calculated precision of someone who has had too much to drink, a man sank into a chair at their table.

"Can I inquire what *les boys* are talking about?"

Onno looked into the journalist's cynical face with distaste.

"Of course you can't. That would confront you fatally with the abyss of your own worthlessness, day laborer that you are. Your sense of history extends no further than yesterday's evening paper, but we—we survey eons! Landlord!" he called to the bodybuilder who served as a waiter. "A big order! Another Cuba libre and a freshly squeezed orange juice!"

Max leaned confidentially toward the man opposite him. "Personally I like you well enough," he said softly, "but why does everyone else hate your guts?"

The man continued staring at him for a moment, digesting the insult. Then he leaped forward and grabbed Max by his lapel; perhaps he was going to pull him across the table, but while Max was helpless in his grasp, Onno jumped up and did the same to the journalist himself, causing Max to tumble from his chair. While he kept the man pressed down against the table with his left hand, he raised his right hand high in the air, as if to give him a deadly karate blow to the neck, looked around the pub, which had fallen silent, and said, "He attacked my friend—he must die!"

Max knew nothing about Gilgamesh and Enkidu, although astronomy had first originated at that time and in that place, but he did know something about different kinds of men, like Leopold and Loeb. While they had been debating in a pub with Red activists that day—or some other day—and were walking back through the city after midnight, across the square with the ruined synagogues, he told Onno the story of those two American law students, bosom friends, age eighteen and nineteen, sons of wealthy Chicago families. They read Nietzsche's *Thus Spake Zarathustra* and *Beyond Good and Evil*, and came to the conclusion that they were *Übermenschen*, above all human laws. In 1924, in order to put this to the test, they decided to commit a perfect crime, motiveless, apart from their own private motive. They murdered a fourteen-year-old boy, made his face unrecognizable with sulfuric acid, hid his body in a sewer, and went to dinner in a chic restaurant. However, Leopold, an expert ornithologist, had left his glasses behind, and everything came out. They were given life sentences plus ninety-nine years. Loeb, the charmer of the two, was later killed in a fight in prison; Leopold, the brains, had been released about ten years ago, and would now be sixty-two if he was still alive.

Onno said nothing. He knew at once what Max was really talking about. They had not talked about Max's father again since the evening of their meeting; it would certainly crop up, but Onno felt that it was not for him to decide the moment. Max, for his part, naturally understood what Onno understood, but he did not broach the subject, either. Instead, he said, "Who shall we murder, Onno?"

He was given no answer. Onno breathed in the night air deeply and said, "I smell a presentiment of spring."

Grating and sparking, a rail-cleaning tram approached across the deserted square. As it passed, they shouted "Bravo!" and applauded at the sight, whereupon the tram stopped and one of the workmen invited them to take a ride. In the iron interior, full of heavy, dirty tools, there turned out to be another passenger, a seedy-looking girl, full of drink or something else, standing on a box muttering incomprehensible words to herself. When Onno saw Max looking at her, he said sternly: "Keep your hands off her, you disgusting swine."

Feeling as though he were making a voluntary sacrifice, Max also decided that it would be advisable in this case.

"Gee up, coachman!" cried Onno to the driver.

Grinding the rails and making sparks, the tram set in motion. Onno stood with his feet wide apart, put his hands on his hips, raised his chin, and with a heroic, Bismarck-like look, cried: "I am the god of the city!"

This was how Max liked to see him; he would never forget such moments. For the workers of the transport company, of course, he was an oddball, one of many who hung around the city at night, but Max realized that he wasn't just yelling something at random, but really was personifying a god, with all that fire at his feet, a Pythian oracle on a box, and surrounded by three or four synagogues; and Onno knew that Max was the only one who understood.

And at four in the morning, in the Sterretje pub, surrounded by seedy taxi drivers, whores, pimps, thieves, and murderers, it suddenly emerged that Onno had never read Kafka's "Letter to my Father," and they went to Max's place to make good the omission.

When Onno had climbed those three flights of stairs for the first time and seen Max's flat, he said while still in the doorway: "Now I know for certain that you're crazy."

"All right. Let's assign roles once and for all: I'm crazy and you're stupid."

"Agreed!"

Onno had seen at first glance that nothing had been put down or wound up anywhere by accident. Not that it was aesthetically empty, or anxiously tidy; on the contrary, it was full, with books and folders on the floor, and on the baby grand too, but there was never a larger book on top of a smaller one, or a folder on a book, and nothing looked as though it could be lying in any other way—like in a painting. This harmonious composition extended naturally to everything in the apartment. There was no question, either, of a particular style; there were modern things, antique and semi-antique, but everything fitted in and the eye was never offended by something like a colored plastic object or an advertising brochure or even a ballpoint pen. The desk, too, was full of books and papers, but everything was carefully arranged, in parallel, at right angles, without creating a manic impression. What Onno called "madness" was admiration for something that he himself totally lacked in his everyday life.

Human nature is so conservative that in someone else's place one always tends to sit where one sat for the first time. So Onno sank into the olive-green chesterfield armchair, had a bottle of Bacardi and a bottle of cola set down next to him, together with a dish of ice cubes, and Max went to his "shelf of honor" on the mantelpiece. Between two bronze book ends, laurel-crowned satyrs with cloven hooves, were the ten or fifteen books that at a certain moment represented the sublime for him. Now and then there were changes, but what was always there was his father's copy of *The Ego and His Own*, signed "Wolfgang Delius—Im Felde 1917," which his foster parents had been given with a few items of clothing from Scheveningen prison in 1946; all his other possessions had been confiscated and had disappeared. Kafka's *Preparations for a Country Wedding*, containing his "Letter to My Father," which had never been sent, was on the shelf of honor.

The two of them there in the middle of the night—the three of them in fact, with their fathers! For hours, stopping only for their own commentary, Max read the letter aloud with no trace of an accent. Kafka, who was stripping his soul bare, wanted to get married, could not get married in the shadow of his sire, who at an early age had announced that he would "tear him apart like a fish." Each time some terrible passage like that came, Onno sank farther into his chair as though hit by a salvo of bullets, until he finally lay shaking euphorically on the ground. Max had finally gotten up with the book and shot the words vertically down at him from a height, while Onno cried:

"Mercy! Father! Not the worst! Yes, I will even make the *sacrificium intellectus* for you, yes, I will worship you forever, like the lowliest creature, I, worm that I am, not worthy to kiss your feet, crush me, that your just will may be done!"

Max slammed the book shut and pressed it against his stomach as he laughed. They were unique, immortal! No one would ever understand, but it was not necessary for anyone to understand. Onno hoisted himself back in his chair, refilled his glass to the brim half with rum and half with cola. Max said that the letter was the key to Kafka's whole work. *The Trial* could only be understood via this piece. Josef K.!

"You were brilliant enough to trace the origin of HAL, but I've discovered where that 'Josef' comes from. 'K.' stands for Kafka, of course, and the man who comes into his room at the very beginning of the novel to arrest him is called Franz like Kafka himself, but why is K. himself called Josef, and not Max, after his friend Brod, or Moritz?"

"Franz Joseph!" cried Onno.

"That's it. The arresting officer, the man arrested, and Kafka himself are the trinity of *Seine kaiserliche und königliche, apostolische Majestät*, His Imperial, Royal, and Apostolic Majesty.

The night advanced, the earth rotated on its axis, and they talked about the problem of why a flag in the wind, a stiff current of air, flutters and why the waves in Max's hair did not move as his hair grew but remained in the same place, just the opposite of the sea, where the waves moved horizontally but the water remained in the same place; and about the war, about Adolf Hitler, whom they called the *"A.H.-Erlebnis,"* and about the twin daughters of Max Planck, the founder of quantum mechanics: the first gave birth to a daughter and died in childbirth; the other looked after the child and married the widower, became pregnant herself two years later, and also died in childbirth. Added to that, one son died in the First World War, while his second son was shot in the Second. Planck's constant!

Later they might perhaps regret not having kept any record of those days; but if they had taken notes it would not have been like it was. Onno might not then have told him what he told him as morning approached: that his mother had hoped that he would be a girl. He was an afterthought, and until the age of four he had walked around with long curls, in pink dresses with ribbons. But he had systematically destroyed the evidence; not only were there no more delightful snapshots to be found in his parents' photo album, the albums of his brothers and sisters had also been purged on devious pretexts.

Max looked at him and nodded. "Now tell me," he said, "what you will really never tell anyone."

However much Onno had had to drink, there was always a point where he was sober. He put down his glass.

"Dreadful! As a student I was living in a rented room, where I was trying to get the philosophy of the concept of law into my head. Next to me there was an unmarried mother, a girl with a baby that cried nonstop. God knows what got into me. One winter evening I ran into her place, at the end of my tether. She was sitting at the table sewing baby clothes; the baby was screaming—for a father, of course! There was one of those old-fashioned coal stoves, boiling hot. I snatched the brat from its cradle, held it up by its ankle with my right hand, grabbed the poker with my left hand, raised the lid of the stove, and held the child above the glow with its head down. I said nothing, I just looked at her. She was frozen. She looked like a photo of herself. The baby, too, was silent for the first time. Terrible! I ought to have been arrested for that and thrown into prison."

He fixed Max's gaze.

"Well," he said. "Now you know. But you didn't just ask me this for no good reason, because you knew I was going to ask you in turn. You asked me because you want to tell me something yourself that you would never tell anyone. Get it off your chest."

Max nodded. "When my foster father was on his deathbed last year," he said rather flatly, "I got a letter from my foster mother. I only saw them rarely by then, because it seems you never forgive someone when they've been good to you. She wrote that he wanted to see me one last time before he died."

"That's enough," said Onno.

The alcohol had worn off instantly. After a while Max stood up and replaced the Kafka book. He stood there aimlessly, and in a sudden impulse lit a candle that was on the dining table. He turned around, looked at his watch, and said, "It's seven o'clock. I'm hungry. Let's have breakfast in the American Hotel—and come to that, I'm feeling in need of a romantic escapade. Perhaps there'll be an early bird there—you never know."

5

Coming Out to Play

Siamese twins derived their name from the brothers Eng and Chang, who in the previous century had lived to the age of sixty-three: in order to amuse Onno, Max had looked it up in his encyclopedia. Since they were joined at the chest, they were known in medical terminology as a *thoracopagus*; Onno's immediate reaction was to say that since they had grown together through their inner natures, they were a *mentopagus*.

As a result, they started to change each other's lives.

At the end of March, Onno was again spending a few days at his girlfriend's place; as always he had taken his dirty laundry with him. She lived above a bric-a-brac shop, which was usually shut, on a quiet side canal, in a narrow seventeenth-century house with a gable, the Unicorn. He had met her a few years before at the Art Historical Institute, where she was a librarian. He had fallen in love with her at once, because she looked just as he imagined a librarian should and as they seldom did: tall, slim, with hair up, and a severe Dutch face, like the lady governor of an orphanage in a painting by Frans Hals, only younger.

Now and then she cleared up the basement where he lived like a hamster in its hutch. From time to time he earned a little by writing articles and giving lectures, but it was not really necessary; he spent little and could survive on an allowance from his future inheritance. During a family dinner a six-year-old nephew had once asked him: "Uncle Onno, what are you going to be when you grow up?" After the laughter had died down, everyone had looked at him expectantly, and he had said, "That question is too good to spoil with an answer." If he had wanted, he could long ago have become a lecturer at some university at home or abroad; he repeatedly received offers, but had no wish to give up his way of life. He saw himself as an eighteenth-century gentleman scholar; he regarded the didactic industry as vulgar. In his view, professors were rather like swimming coaches: and who had ever seen a swimming coach in the water? No one had ever seen such a thing, because swimming coaches couldn't swim at all, they simply talked a lot at the poolside; but he was someone who plowed his way through the water with a relentless butterfly stroke.

It began one sunny Saturday afternoon, after spring had appeared from the wings and done the splits with great panache; the windows had been opened and balmy air filled the room. Onno had taken some papers to the Unicorn, but his work had not been going well for weeks. His great body lay on the sofa like a stranded ship.

"That wretched Pernier," he groaned. "I wish he had let the bloody thing smash to smithereens back in 1908. Yes, but then he would have glued the fragments together again. There's a whole people hidden in there somewhere, with helmets and axes, but it just stays put and won't budge."

Helga took off her reading glasses and looked up from her book. "Why don't you let it rest for a while? Start something else."

"Do you know what you are saying, woman? I know precisely which people are working on this, and they don't start anything else. What are you reading?"

As though she didn't know, she looked at the cover. *"Progress in Library Science."*

"That book, dear Helga, is printed, isn't it? And all the books it is talking about are also printed, aren't they? Everyone thinks that printing with separate stamps began in China a thousand years ago, but do you know who invented it?" He waved a photo of the Phaistos disc.

"The people who made this. Four thousand years ago! This has been stamped! And if they were such preliterate geniuses, then there'll be something very interesting here, won't there? And I must be the first person to read it, mustn't I? The wretched thing is that we only have this specimen, and of course you don't make stamps for only one tablet. There must be lots more, but nothing else has been found in Crete. For that matter, there's nothing Minoan about them. Look—this daft sedan chair. What sort of thing is it? What does it mean? We must look elsewhere, but where? In what family?"

"But don't you have anything to go on then?"

"I'll explain to you the position I'm in." He grabbed a newspaper off the floor and made a scribble in the margin. "Write the following number: eighty-five billion, four hundred and ninety-one million, seven hundred and sixty-one thousand and thirty-two." When she had noted this down on the sheet of paper she was using for notes, he continued: "Now imagine an aboriginal cryptographer in the Australian bush, who doesn't even know that they're figures; all he sees is eleven incomprehensible signs: 8 5 4 9 1 7 6 1 0 3 2, all different except for the two 1 signs. What can he deduce from that? Nothing at all. That's the point I'm at now. Imagine he has the brilliant idea that they are figures. How then is he supposed to discover that they are the alphabetically ordered numerals from 'one' to 'ten'? Beginning with the *e* of 'eight,' and ending with the *t* of 'two.' How is he supposed to discover that the numeral 'eight' is the name of the figure 8? He doesn't even know the decimal system, let alone English. How on earth is he supposed to discover that he is looking at Dr. Quist's unforgettable *Narration from A to Z*? What is the key? And yet he is determined to find out!" "What's that?" he suddenly shouted loudly at the photo. "Hello! Is anybody there? I can't hear you! The line is so bad!" He threw the photo away and put his hands over his face. "I'm completely blocked."

Helga closed her book, putting her forefinger between the pages.

"And why are you so blocked?" she asked in a sing-song tone.

"I don't know," he said with a feigned tearfulness. "I don't know. Perhaps you can only make a real discovery once in your life."

"Could it also be because of those sleepless nights with your new friend?"

The posturing disappeared from Onno's face. He sat up and looked at her. "You can't be serious."

"I'm perfectly serious. Do you realize how overwrought the whole thing is?"

"Helga!" he said in dismay. "What do you mean?"

"I don't know what you mean by that, all I know is that you've been completely blocked since you've known him. You've no idea how much you've changed recently."

"In what way?"

She put the book down and folded her arms. "If you ask me, you're thinking more of him than of your work. You only get home as I'm leaving for the institute. How does he manage it, by the way? Isn't he an astronomer? Doesn't he have to look at the stars at night?"

"I don't have to go to the museum in Heraklion to look at those symbols, do I? And I'm allowed to sleep in, aren't I?"

He got off the sofa and went over to the window. Of course he was thinking less about his work, but was that so bad? It stopped thinking from becoming fretting, and that was much more harmful to thought than not thinking. His exchange with Max was in a certain sense the "something else" that he had started on. She was jealous, of course. "You're not jealous by any chance?"

"I want the best for you."

He sighed deeply and turned around. "Listen. What there is between Max and me can never exist between you and me; and what there is between you and me can never exist between me and Max. That's as clear as crystal, we don't have to waste words on it. To be honest, I think we've already wasted too many words on it."

She got up, took a few steps, stopped and said, "Onno, be careful."

"What in heaven's name do I have to be careful of?" he asked in amazement.

She made a helpless gesture. "I don't know."

"Aha," he said, and went over to her. "Woman's intuition." He hugged her clumsily. "Sorry about that. Women have everything—brains, feeling, willpower—but only men have intuition. That's why there's no female creation of any importance, and that isn't because they've always been confined to the kitchen, because even the best cooks are men. One is forced reluctantly to accept the fact. But they can do one thing that men can't do, and that is give birth to men. That's more than enough." She freed herself from the hug.

"Why do you start waffling on the moment I try to talk to you?"

"You know what Napoleon said, don't you? All his wars were a bagatelle compared with the war that will break out one day between men and women. Therefore I now swear a sacred oath, that when it comes to that I will be the first traitor to my sex, although I know that I will pay dearly for it in the long run."

"All right, Onno. That's enough. You're impossible." She pushed the loose strands of hair back under the hairpins with both hands. "Shall we go to the Vondelpark?"

At that moment there was a shout from outside: "Yoohoo, Onno!"

They glanced at each other and each leaned out of a different window. With his hands in his pockets and a magazine under his arm, Max was leaning against a telephone box by the side of the canal.

"Mrs. Hartman," he called to Helga, putting on a whining boy's voice. "Can Onno come out to play?"

Onno and Helga looked at each other again, now along the front of the house. Disaster. They both realized at the same moment that this was the end—that in his innocence Max had suddenly laid bare the heart of their relationship.

A quarter of an hour later Onno finally came out.

"Did you have to do your homework first?" asked Max.

Onno did not look at him. He walked beside him in a rage. "The things you do to your friends. . . . It's over. All your fault. I left the front door key on the table."

"My fault? What have I done?"

"It's none of your business. I'm not talking to you anymore." He stopped and looked at him with disgust. "Do you know what's wrong with you?" When Max looked back at him with a puzzled expression, he repeated: "Don't you know?"

"Not that I'm aware of."

"Don't you know? Then I'll tell you: I don't like your intuition. I don't like your intuition one little bit."

Max had no idea what he was getting at; he knew almost nothing about Onno's relationship with Helga. They never talked about women, or about cars, money, or sports; at most, about woman as such, as Onno was in the habit of putting it—and never about their own girlfriends. Max did not talk about his, because he did not allow himself time to get to know them— and because Onno would have found it disgusting to listen to. And Onno did not talk about Helga, because that was not done. The few times that Max had met her, they had said scarcely a word to each other—not because he did not like her, but he saw her as belonging to a different world. She would never have caught his eye, even if he had sat opposite her in a train for an hour; and through her he realized how completely different he was from Onno. He couldn't imagine a woman that they would both be interested in.

He had never been in Helga's flat, and Onno never invited Max to his place on the Kerkstraat. He was in the habit of saying that mankind was divided into guests and hosts and that he simply belonged by nature to the first category; besides, it was cheaper. That was what he said, but that was not the reason. Taking Max to his parents' house and introducing him to his family, to his father, was just as inconceivable, although people in The Hague had long since heard, with raised eyebrows, about his strange friendship with Delius's son, and of course they would have liked an opportunity to size him up. No, the reason was that in himself too there was an area where he never admitted anyone—not only not Max, not only not Helga, but not even himself. There, in an inhospitable region, was a hermit's cave, a Carthusian monk's cell, where a leaden silence reigned—something that seemed to wait threateningly for him, that he would rather not think about and that he had never talked to Max about.

He walked along the canal, shoulders drooping, whining like a broken man. "What am I to do now? You've wrecked my life. I don't have a home. You have a home. I have just a humble shelter against the rain and the wind. Who'll do my laundry now? You've ruined me once and for all, and of course that was your intention all along. I'll wind up in the gutter, with unkempt hair and a beard and a crazed look in my eyes, begging for alms. What did you actually come for, you bastard?"

"I never come for any special reason," said Max, "but I have great news. I've just been to the dentist's and in the waiting room there was an old issue of *Time*. There's an important article about us in it."

"About us," Onno repeated. "In *Time*."

Max opened the magazine and pointed to a commemorative piece on the Reichstag fire, which had taken place on February 27 thirty-four years before.

"What about it?"

"Good God! Wasn't I born on November 27, 1933, and weren't you supposed to have been born on November 27 too? Didn't we come to the conclusion that we're nonidentical twins! Don't you understand? Nine months!

We were conceived during the Reichstag fire! While Van der Lubbe was setting fire to the curtains in Berlin, our parents were climbing on top of each other in The Hague and Amsterdam!"

Onno stopped, stretched his whole body, and spread his arms in triumph, while a broad smile passed across his face. "Death, where is thy sting?" he cried. "I can face life again!"

6

Another Meeting

Two months later—their delight in their friendship showed no signs of waning—Onno had a meeting with a colleague from Jerusalem in the Natural History Museum in Leiden. He had gotten no further with the deciphering, and the Israeli was as curious about his progress as he was about the Israeli's. When he emerged from the colossal building later that afternoon, Max was waiting for him outside in the sun, sitting in a strange little public garden next to the adjacent Science Museum, with his eyes closed and his head thrown back. They had agreed that Max would show him the observatory.

Onno expressed his contempt for blockheads who sunbathed—his own white Calvinist flesh had never seen the sun—but Max said it was part of his job: after all the sun was a star. They went into town for a cup of coffee first. Onno told him with relief that Landau, his most important rival, had obviously not made any progress either; so that threat had been removed for the moment. They reacted differently to the atmosphere of the little town with its low houses than to Amsterdam; they felt something like tenderness, such as someone from London or New York must feel in Amsterdam.

"We're walking this way now," said Max, "and while I was waiting for you, I was reminded of two other men who also walked this way."

"Everyone has walked this way. Even Einstein."

"With Lorentz, yes, and with De Sitter, but I don't mean him."

He meant Freud and Mahler. As far as he remembered from biographies, it had been in the summer of 1908. Freud was staying in a boardinghouse in Noordwijk, from where he was about to travel on to Italy, when a telegram arrived from Vienna: Mahler had problems. He was suffering from impotence and could no longer make love to his wife, Alma—who was later also to turn the heads of Franz Werfel, Walter Gropius, and Oskar Kokoschka. He needed immediate help. Mahler took the train to Leiden, where he met Freud in a hotel. They walked around the town for four hours, and Mahler was subjected to a sort of emergency analysis, which indeed seems to have had some effect.

A little girl ties a rope to a lamppost, starts turning the rope; a second girl moves her upper body forward and backward a couple of times in the same rhythm, jumps into the imaginary egg, and begins skipping. And as they walked along, Onno responded with the same suppleness to the anecdote.

"Well, well, *Herr Obermusikdirektor*, you are suffering from overpotency. In my psychoanalysis I have coined the term *astronomical satyriasis* for this. It is a disease that inspires the greatest possible disgust, even in specialists, despite their being familiar with the dark side of human nature."

"But what if I like it," whined Max. "Cure me, *Herr Professor*. I want to stop liking it. I want to be monogamous, like you, or impotent—whatever you are. I'll double your fee."

"The fact that you immediately bring up money points to an anal-erotic fixation, which conjures up scenes before my inner eye from which even Dante would shrink. Did I hear you say you like it? Surely it can't be true?"

"It is!"

"Occasionally, even experienced mountaineers are faced with precipices that force them to say, 'This is too much.' When I tell my friend Ferenczi about this, he'll say, 'You can convince me of lots of things, Sigi, but this is impossible.' "

"But I'm possible!"

"The fact that you are possible is certainly the ultimate *mysterium tremendum ac fascinans*. I have experienced a lot in the course of my practice—Little Hans, the Wolfman, all complete lunatics—but a phenomenon like you robs me of my last vestige of faith in mankind. I conclude from your revolting way of life that in your *Sexualhysterie* you would actually like to mount every woman that ever was but that your lewd priapic frenzy finds itself limited to the living. Those from the past have escaped your extraordinary appetite and those from the future will escape it. What you would prefer would be to possess every woman in space and time in one fell swoop, in the shape of the supreme woman: the primeval woman. Am I right in assuming, *mein Lieber*, that your mother's first name is Eva?"

"*Donnerwetter!*" laughed Max. "That hit home! Now I understand why my *Nervenarzt* recommended that I consult you." He had once told Onno his mother's name, but the slant Onno had put on it gave him a slight jolt.

"I can see right through you, *Herr Generalkapellmeister*."

"But if Eve is my mother, *verehrter Herr Doktor*, am I Cain or Abel?"

Now Onno seemed to be thrown, but not for long. He stopped and shouted: "The Lord will not see your sacrifice, seven times accursed one! Only mine shall be seen!"

As he said this, with the aplomb of which only he had the secret, Max's eye lighted on a cover in the window of a secondhand bookshop. They were in a narrow street behind the Pieterskerk, which rose like the Jungfrau above the low houses of the old town center.

"Look at that. Talk of the devil." He pointed to a copy of Alma Mahler's *Mein Leben*.

"Come on," he said, putting his hand on the door handle. "I'll buy it for you, as a fee for your analysis."

In a world full of war, famine, oppression, deceit, monotony, what—apart from the eternal innocence of animals—offers an image of hope? A mother with a newborn child in her arms? The child may end up as a murderer, or a murder victim, so that the hopeful image is a prefiguration of a pietà: a mother with her newly dead child on her lap. No, the image of hope is someone passing with a musical instrument in a case. It is not contributing to oppression, or to liberation either, but to something that continues below the surface: the boy on his bike, with a guitar in a faded mock-leather cover on his back; a girl with a dented violin case waiting for the tram. The hallowed halls beneath concert platforms where orchestral musicians open their cases everywhere on tables and chairs and on the floor and take out their shining and glittering instruments, after which imprints of those instruments remain: negative clarinets, flutes, bassoons with their mouthpieces and connections, hollowed out of soft reinforced velvet; and while the space gradually fills with the muted cacophony of all the instruments thronging around the A like sparrows and seagulls and starlings and thrushes around a hunk of bread, the lids of the cases of double basses, as tall as a man, are opened like the doors to another world . . .

Or the young woman, who after rehearsal lays her cello back in its case and closes the lid?

She takes the score that has fallen apart off the music stand and arranges the sheets until the title sheet is nicely on top: *Pohádka* (*Fairy Tale*). Spiky, almost Japanese, black hair in a ponytail frames her pale face in a pure square; swaying like silk, it follows every movement of her head, always coming to rest in mathematical order. Her face is severe, the lips a little pinched, like those of someone who knows what she wants. Her pianist, a thick-set man with lank ginger hair and an expressionless face, is sitting hunched forward with his arms folded on the grand piano, his chin resting on them, and looks at her deep-brown eyes below the dark, sharply outlined eyebrows.

"What are you thinking about, Ada?"

His studio, a large rectangular space in a formal school building, is filled with his collections: rows of old portable gramophones on shelving on the wall, dusty trumpets, violins, and other musical instruments, crowded bookshelves, heavy tables from the flea market with scores of old salon music, rows of 78 records in damaged paper sleeves, worn Persian carpets on the floor, and a pair of large brown leather armchairs for sitting in, picking up a book, and cutting off from the outside world.

"That the coda still isn't right. We simply can't perform like this."

She is younger than he is, only recently graduated from the conservatory, where he teaches piano; but it's obvious that she takes the lead in the duo they comprise. He is a good pianist, which interests him less than many other things, such as the archaeology of popular music.

He has set up a group for performing it, which people listen to with a hilarity quite out of keeping with the manner of the playing. For that matter he himself is incapable of laughter, or at least he never laughs; he has built his personality around the decision never to laugh. This is often laughed at, although people seldom cry about someone who never cries. He lacks the ambition to make his name as a pianist; the fact that he is performing with Ada has less to do with the music than with Ada, and she knows it, but she puts up with it. They have performed a few times, for student societies, but that has already produced a favorable review in the newspaper. She sees a great future for herself as a soloist, an international one, featuring cello concertos, famous conductors, concert platforms in Paris and Milan. Rostropovich! Pablo Casals!

"Shall we have a bite to eat in town later?"

She had been expecting some such question, and she is annoyed at him for embarrassing her yet again. Surely he must have realized by now that she's not interested in anything like that. Of course she can tell him she doesn't want to go to bed with him, but then he'll say that he didn't ask her, though of course that is what it comes down to. He'll think she's frigid, and maybe she is—despite being twenty-one she has never slept with a man— but it must be possible to work with someone without it immediately leading to this.

Or does she have to put an end to their partnership if things are like that? What she'd like as a next step is to form a trio, or a quartet; the repertory for cello and piano is too small to be able to continue for long. What she's looking for are musically motivated people, but until she has found them she needs him.

"Do you mind if I just go home, Bruno? I'd prefer to put in bit more practice."

"The two things aren't mutually exclusive, are they? You have to eat, after all."

She nods. "That's true. But you know how it is."

"How is it, then?"

She doesn't want to be having this conversation at all. Of course this is what it is like in ten-year-old marriages, when one can no longer see anything in the other person: insistence, hope, despair—with a threat of violence on the horizon.

"Just leave it." She's ready to go, one hand on the handle of the case, the other clenched in an unhappy fist, with the four fingers wrapped around her thumb so no one will see that she bites her nails, though of course that makes it all the more apparent. "See you tomorrow."

Carrying the cello case in her arms like a sarcophagus, she descends the stairs into the street. Bruno's studio is not far from her parents' house, where she still lives, and on the way she has a sudden flashback from a dream of the previous night: a lush bay, with a thin, high amber cloud above the sea in the form of an ancient, gnarled tree trunk, which slowly changes shape; she tries to hold on to it, to remember more—she catches a glimpse of a black figure, strangely elongated horizontally, with a pointed hat and a long lance—but the horn of a braking car and a finger pointing to a forehead puts an end to it . . .

She walks down the side alley to the back of the house and goes in through the kitchen door, where her mother is trussing the pale, decapitated carcass of a chicken with a white thread. She is tall and slim, slightly taller than her daughter, with a straight, disciplined back. Her own eyes meet Ada's from beneath a head of black hair, which is worn up, but with a colder look, more suspicious, without there being any special reason.

"How did it go?"

"Well."

"Cup of tea?"

"Yes, please."

She is about to go upstairs, but her mother says: "You can't go upstairs now. Daddy's painting your room."

Ada takes her foot off the bottom step in annoyance. "Why the hell is he doing that? Did I ask him to?"

"Don't be so horrid all the time. He's doing it for you. Sit and wait downstairs. He'll be finished in an hour or so."

"Why did he suddenly take it into his head to paint my room? Hasn't he got anything better to do?"

"You'll have to ask him. I don't know either. He went upstairs and said that your room was badly in need of a coat of paint."

"Crazy people are a pain," says Ada, and lugs her instrument into the back room, which doubles as a dining room and a living room.

She'll be glad when she's away from here and can live as she wants to. The good intentions are the worst thing, because they make you powerless. Her mother is a bitch, but her father is a well-meaning freethinker, with no malice in him. If only there were some malice in him, then he would at least be able to understand malice. His wife, for instance. Ada's dearest wish now is for a place of her own, where she can be completely alone. She wants to rehearse, travel, perform, have triumphs—but always to return to her apartment, with the doorbell and telephone disconnected, the radio and television switched off, or maybe completely absent; to be able to devote herself completely to music and reading poetry, or simply to doing nothing at all for hours on end and to thinking, without someone suddenly taking it into their head to paint her room. But for the time being she doesn't have the money; even her father can only just makes ends meet.

It makes her jump when her mother puts a cup of tea and a slice of cake next to her.

"What are you thinking about, Ada?"

"Nothing."

"How did it go with Bruno?"

"Fine." She notices with irritation that her mother is still looking at her. "What's wrong?"

"Why don't you go out with him? He's such a nice boy."

"Oh, Mama, please stay out of it. Do you ever go out with Dad?"

"Come on, don't get so worked up right away. It would do you a lot of good to relax occasionally."

"Just leave that to me."

Once her mother is out of the room, she opens the score and studies the music, pencil in hand. She holds the sheets upside down for a moment and even then she can see that it is marvelous. It is not just that she can "hear" what she sees, it is rather that she sees what the listener sees when he listens: a structural beauty, which exists in space as the sheet of a score but as heard music only in time. This is why she is not that keen on novels, which are read in silence, but does like poems, which have to be given a sound. Not that she thinks all this in so many words; but what is going on in her mind as she looks at the music, beating an imaginary time now and then with her left hand, is based on it—just as a child can speak its language without knowing the grammar.

She puts the score on the floor, lifts the cello from its case, and screws on the spike. While she is tightening the bow, she goes to the dividing door and pushes it open with her shoulder; the small space is oppressive. She takes the instrument between her legs, tunes it, and looking sideways at the music she begins playing, at the same time hearing what Bruno is not playing, and occasionally humming it.

Max opened the door of the shop and, without letting go of the handle, stopped in his tracks. As he listened he put up his forefinger.

"Janáček," he said after a few seconds. "That's not a record. Someone's playing."

No bell sounded. He put his finger to his lips, and they entered quietly. The sound of the cello hung in the narrow space, which was piled with books. They not only filled the roughly made shelves up to ceiling but were also stacked high on the left and right and in the center. A jungle of books, with narrow paths through it. Onno stopped, but Max pushed forward, up steps, down steps, past piles of books, boxes, magazines—architecture, girls' books, Jewish studies, travel guides—around a corner, up another couple of steps ... and saw Ada sitting in the back room: in a loose-fitting, long-sleeved white blouse and a small stand-up collar, her head turned away and the cello between her parted legs. Her left foot was placed elegantly a little in front of her; her full black skirt was pushed back, and he saw a slim knee and then the transition from her stockings to the light flesh of her thighs.

I'm going mad, he thought. I want to be fingered and stroked by that woman just like that.

She had not seen him. He went back on tiptoe and whispered: "Duty calls. I'll see you in a little while in the Gilded Turk."

Onno nodded pityingly. "Adieu, unfortunate one."

Max's heart was pounding. Each time was as new as the first. He positioned himself so that he could not be seen. While he listened and looked at her, something changed in him. His excitement did not disappear, but it was as though a space gradually opened up behind it, like when the curtain rises in the theater. Although she was so totally absorbed, it was as though the music actually consisted of audible silence, a silence with a shape like a geometrical figure, which she drew around herself.

Now and then she stopped for a moment and looked for something in the score with the tip of her bow: then there was a silence within silence. Her face framed in black; the gleaming reddish wood of the waisted sound box between her legs, her left hand at the neck; next to her the open case. A line of Mallarmé occurred to him: "*musicienne du silence* ..." Why should a line of Mallarmé occur to him? He wanted to go to bed with her, but that was nothing unusual, that was his daily bread—the unusual thing was that a line of Mallarmé should occur to him. Lines of Mallarmé did not normally occur to him. If he wanted, he could always dig up a couple, of course, such as "*Un coup de dés n'abolira pas le hasard*"—but that was really more of a title; it reminded him of what Einstein had said about dice, perhaps here in Leiden: "The Good Lord doesn't play dice."

Hidden among the books, he observed her. He could hear someone stumbling about above his head. Did he want something more besides going to bed with her a few times?

On impulse, he suddenly stepped into the room.

She started so violently when he appeared that her body trembled. She looked at him, wide-eyed. The reaction of her body, as though it were something stronger than herself, over which she had no control, bound him even more closely to her.

"I want to buy a book," he said, "but no one came. So I simply eaves-dropped on you. *Fairy Tale.*"

That was the title of the piece: he obviously knew it. But she was even more astonished at the natural way in which he spoke to her. Men were always a little frightened of her, as she herself was of her mother, but this one didn't seem worried in the least. "Eavesdropping is very rude, if you ask me."

Max burst out laughing. "And that's a *musicienne* talking! The hi-fi system as bugging equipment!"

Her mother came into the room with a meat knife in her hand: a handsome, buxom woman, with something severe about her; she had a broad lower jaw and a tight mouth. Dressed in a black nun's habit she would make a perfect abbess.

"Do I hear voices?"

Ada pointed to Max with her bow. "There's a customer."

"Hello."

He was looked at disapprovingly by dark eyes beneath black eyebrows, which were raised slightly at the sides. "Isn't the bell working?"

She apologized and called upstairs along the corridor: "Oswald! Someone in the shop!"

"Nice shop," said Max, going down the steps and looking around. "But you live here, and of course you never browse."

"My father usually knows what I want."

His eye was caught by an art book with color illustrations: the dazzling, jewel-encrusted eggs of Fabergé, which the Czar usually gave as a gift to the Czarina at Easter.

"Do you know Fabergé?" he asked without looking up.

"Is he a composer?"

The way in which she answered immediately convinced him that he was on the right track. "Something like that. A jeweler."

While he was leafing through the book, the bookseller appeared: a nondescript man of about fifty, with wavy gray-blond hair, slightly shorter than his wife; only his mouth was like his daughter's. He also apologized; the bell had not been working just now. Max said that he wanted the Fabergé book and also the one by Alma Mahler in the window. Laughing shyly, the secondhand bookseller looked at his hands; perhaps the gentleman would like to get it for himself. There was paint on his face too. As Max went toward it, he read on the shop window, back to front:

SECONDHAND BOOKSHOP
"IN PRAISE OF FOLLY"

He showed the prices on the flyleaves and said that there was no need to wrap them up. After he had paid, he looked at the back room again. The girl was still sitting in the same position with her cello. She met his glance. He went up to her and handed her the book on Fabergé.

"For you. A present for the coda."

No, really, she started blushing. She put the cello down and got up to receive it.

"How nice . . ." she said, laughing. Her two front teeth at the top were slightly wider and longer than the others.

Max turned to her father. "May I carry your daughter off for a cup of coffee?"

While he was trying not to get paint marks on the cash register, the scene had somewhat passed him by. He muttered that she must make up her own mind.

Max put out his hand. "Delius, Max."

Ada put her own hand in it. "Ada Brons."

7

The Observatory

The Gilded Turk was nearby, on the Breestraat. In the street Max had offered her his arm, ironically, like a cavalier of the old school; she had put her hand in it, and now, to her own astonishment, she was suddenly walking through town with a total stranger, chatting about Janáček. Hopefully, Bruno wouldn't see her.

Max warned her about his friend, who was waiting for them: a brute of a fellow, whom she should take with a pinch of salt.

In the large pub the afternoon rush was on; at the back a group of students in blazers were bragging noisily, beer glasses in hand.

They found Onno at the reading table, with the usual glass of milk and a half-eaten rissole next to his newspaper.

"There you are," said Max, putting the book down beside him. "*Mein Leben*. For you."

"Right." Onno looked up to thank him and saw that he had company.

"Onno Quist," said Max. "Ada Brons."

At the same moment a waiter dropped a tray of crockery somewhere, followed by applause and cheers from the students. Onno stood up and shook hands with her, after which he shot Max a look very like the one Max had given his rissole. They pulled up chairs, and for a moment it looked as though Onno was going to continue reading his newspaper out of moral indignation, but he finally decided not to. He leaned back, crossed one leg over the other, revealing the bluish-white flesh above his short socks, and in the manner of a complacent country psychiatrist asked: "Have you two known each other long?"

"We have never not known each other," said Max, and looked at Ada in expectation of a sign of agreement.

When none came, Onno took a liking to her. "I fail to understand how a sensible girl like you can stand an eternity with someone like this. But perhaps he has a secret side that he has always managed to keep hidden from me. What can I get you?"

"A mineral water, thanks."

"Water," repeated Onno, pulling a face in disgust. "Water is for brushing your teeth."

"That's right," said Max. "You should think of that more often."

Ada did not know what to say. She had to get used to the style of these two. Their tone was quite studentlike, and yet different from what she was familiar with from hearty Leiden types, for whom the tone was the only content of the conversation. Perhaps it was more boyish: the crazy exaggeration of little boys during recess at kindergarten. If it went on like this, she would find them a wearisome pair. Of course they were teasing each other because they were crazy about each other. There was a lot of violence in that Onno. Max was different, lighter: if Onno was a rock, then Max was water. The way he had whisked her off had been irresistible, but a little routine— of course he had done it hundreds of times before. He also looked a little too smart. Or did that mean he was a man of the world? Of course she herself was a tight-assed bitch.

They were talking to each other again, about their secret sides, which surpassed each other in fearsomeness; she was simply along for the ride. Of course they found her bourgeois, and they were quite right: she wasn't good enough. Soon her hand would be kissed, she would be given a flashing aphorism to contemplate, and then dismissed. . . . Suddenly her eyes began stinging. She mumbled an excuse and went to the toilet. With the door locked, she sat down on the seat. What was happening to her? She'd known him for ten minutes and she was already crying at the thought that she might not see him again. She knew nothing about him except that he was well-informed musically; she had not even yet been able to ask him if he was a musician himself. Was she in love, or perhaps just oversensitive because she was expecting her period?

Every period meant no baby yet again, but she had only just had her period. What was it, then? He wasn't good-looking. He wasn't ugly, either, but he was certainly very unusual. Perhaps it was the way he looked at her, so directly and openly. He had appeared in her life as unexpectedly as a falling star, a meteor entering the atmosphere—when it burned up you had to make a wish. Her wish was that he would not burn up and disappear! The thought of having to go home shortly, to her cello and her parents, and of everything continuing as before, was suddenly unbearable. But in that case she must get back quickly, before they disappeared!

After she had gotten up, Max leaned over to Onno with one hand on the back of her chair and said, "I'm not going to ask you what you think of her, because you know nothing about these matters."

Making a sound as if he were about to be sick, Onno looked at Max's hand on the warm chair back. "I've got my eye on you, you lecher."

Was that all it was? Or could it be something different from what Onno, or he himself, was thinking?

"Have you ever wondered," Max asked, "why it is that you find a chair on which somebody else has just been sitting warm, but never your own chair, after getting up for a moment?"

"Interesting question. And why is that?"

"There have been articles about it. The reason is that everyone produces his own individual warmth. Warmth is not simply heat, as used to be thought, not simply the Brownian motion of inanimate molecules; everyone gives off warmth, which is a function of their unmistakable personality. And it can be proved. If we get up, I look the other way, and you swap our chairs, or not, just as you like, then I'll tell you which one was your chair."

"Lunatic!" cried Onno. "Get up at once!"

Max got up and turned away. Watched with alarm by three ladies having tea, Onno began sliding their chairs about and making misleading movements with them.

"Right," he said with an inviting gesture. "Sit down. Which was my chair?"

Max pointed to Ada, who was approaching between the tables.

"We must get going, otherwise there'll be no one there. Observatories are always shut at night. Are you coming with us?" he asked her.

"Where to?"

"It's a surprise."

Walking down the Rapenburg between them, alongside the venerable academic canal, she gained some idea of the company she was in—albeit through solving little puzzles and puns on "storming heaven's gate" and enigmatists. At the university building they turned right and went into the Botanical Garden, where she had last been as a child, with her father. As though sensing this, Max took her hand in his. It was May; many trees and shrubs were already green. The conifers were already gloomily displaying their tropical origin through their exotic shapes (just as black people remain black in the North but lack the deep glow that they have in the African heat). The nameplates by each tree and plant prompted Onno to remark that they were obviously in paradise, where Adam had carried out his task of naming.

"Man was created to be a gardener!" he cried with an expansive gesture.

At the end of the garden, the observatory came into view: a two-story main building, surmounted by a dome, with low extensions on the left and right—everything in light colors, stylistically halfway between a nineteenth-century harbor office and a Renaissance-style church. At the back there were two smaller domes. But all those telescopes, Max informed them, were by now relics that were only used on weekends by amateur astronomical associations; the light and dust of the town made serious observations impossible. They themselves only processed the measurements of the radio telescope there.

When they went in, he was greeted by colleagues, who were busy disentangling punch cards in the stairwell: someone was holding one end on the second floor while others, on the banisters of the first floor and on the ground floor, tried to disentangle the long strands of brown spaghetti. They were soon to be fed into the computer at the Central Computer Institute, where someone would have to take them by bike.

"Can't you do it in your lightning racer, Max?"

"Of course."

The lecture room was also a complete mess: the previous day the ceiling of the library above had collapsed; students and technicians were busy taking the books off the pile of shelves and plaster.

"I feel exactly the same myself sometimes," said Onno.

In the corridor a lady shouted to him through an open door that Floris had phoned him from Dwingeloo; he had measured the H166 -recombination line at 1424.7 MHz.

"Thanks, Til."

Max gave them a guided tour, explained about the old instruments, and told Ada that all the matter in her body had actually been produced on stars; whereupon he took her hand and gallantly kissed it.

"As long as you don't think the same goes for my matter," said Onno, "because that was produced by my own dear mother."

In the computer room they were given an inquisitive nod by a slim, aristocratic gentleman of about seventy, with a balding skull and sharply etched features. Max seemed momentarily rather intimidated. That was the director, he told them as they went upstairs to the first floor—who had not only demonstrated that the Milky Way rotated, but also that it had a spiral structure.

In his office, with a view of the Botanical Garden, he told them about the research program that he himself was engaged in, the distribution of neutral hydrogen in the central part of the Milky Way, but Ada didn't understand a word of it. She looked at the orderly stacks of files on the shelves behind his desk and at the diagrams and formulae on the green chalkboard. It was a mystery to her that this was the same man who had just whisked her off—and she wondered whether she would ever be able to understand people. She listened to their conversation in silence.

Onno had inquired in a haughty tone whether in this building, where obviously everything went wrong, some doubt was perhaps being cast on God's creation. With an apologetic gesture, Max said that, unfortunately, they had known for the last three years that while there had been a beginning between fifteen and twenty billion years ago, it had been the result of a Big Bang: the explosion of a mathematical point with infinite density and an infinitely high temperature, from which not only all energy and matter, but also all space and time, derived. The echo of that explosion had been observed in 1964.

"So that before that sacrilegious Big Bang of yours there was nothing," said Onno.

"Exactly. No time, either."

"So nothing exploded."

"You could put it like that."

"So there was no Big Bang. There you are. The mocking laughter at that ridiculous theory will resound through astronomy for years. Don't listen to that idiot," said Onno to Ada. "Heaven and earth were created by God on Friday, April 1 in the year 4004 B.C., at a quarter past ten in the morning, and afterward he saw that it was good—or at least not bad for a beginner."

Max laughed. "You're capable of becoming a believer on purely logical grounds."

"Yes!" cried Onno ecstatically. "God is logic! Logic is God! Yes, I believe it—because it is absurd."

"Do you remember what you once told me about the 'paut' of the gods? About the god creator, who created himself from his creation?"

"I won't tell you anything anymore, because you'll always use it against me."

"Rid yourself of that fear of paradoxes. Shall I tell you what may be written on that disc of yours?"

"Now I'm really interested."

"What it says is: what is written here is illegible."

"Very good." Onno grinned. "Very good. Maybe it was written by Epimenides, who said that all Cretans are liars."

Ada's head was spinning. It was as though she were watching an intellectual fencing match: the masked fencers leaped back and forth with their glinting foils flashing between them, too quick to follow. How would she ever be able to keep up? Perhaps she didn't need to; perhaps it wasn't even required. Perhaps it had to remain their own private domain.

While Max phoned Floris in Dwingeloo about the most recent measurements, Onno went over to the window, put his hands in his pockets and said, half to himself, half to her: "This isn't a botanical garden at all, this is a *hortus conclusus*, if you know what that is."

"I'm sorry, I've only been to the conservatory."

"The 'closed garden' where a unicorn lives. That's a kind of terrible wild animal that can only be caught by a virgin, after which it rests its head in her lap. In iconology that stands for the Immaculate Conception." He turned around, smiled at her, and said, "Be careful, my girl."

Everyone, herself included, obviously took it for granted that she would go with them to Amsterdam. When Max asked whether she needed to phone home, she said, "Of course not."

"Won't your parents be expecting you for supper?"

"Perhaps."

His car was waiting in the forecourt. The seats were folded forward, and she had to squeeze in sideways behind the two seats as best she could. A strong wind had come up, and after the drums of punch cards had been delivered to the Computer Institute, they drove out of town. On the way Onno asked cautiously whether it would be a problem having to go to Westerbork eventually when the mirrors were ready.

"Is it near the old transit camp?"

"It's on the site of the camp," said Max, feeling a stiffening in his cheeks. "They're housing Moluccans there now."

"When will they be finished?"

"Probably at the end of next year."

Onno nodded.

They glanced at each other without saying anything.

After Onno had been dropped off at the Kerkstraat, Max and Ada went for a meal in an Italian restaurant, L'Arca, where one shook hands with the owner on arrival. Under a canopy of imitation bunches of grapes and empty Chianti bottles, they talked about Onno, about her parents, about her work—and as she was about to put her knife into the spaghetti, he showed her how to do it without using a spoon. Then she went home with him.

Everything proceeded with the relentless precision of a Bach variation. She realized that this was it. It was going to happen, and that was what she wanted—what she had wanted from the first moment. Of course she'd had boyfriends and had had petting sessions with them—sweaty struggles on beds, student hands trying to get inside her panties, musicians' knees trying to force their way between her thighs; but they always ended with someone trying to open his fly with trembling fingers, which led to breathless arguments, disheveled hair, and crumpled clothes, and sometimes resulted in her face being slapped. It had never actually happened. The thought of it provoked more a vague revulsion than a feeling of desire in her. The fact that men were always after it was part of their nature, their "positive" outward-oriented construction: a penis was like the finger of a glove, but a vagina was like a glove finger drawn inward, and it was a mystery to her that some women were also sexually obsessed.

Wasn't it the difference between visiting and having visitors: if you had to, you could visit everyone, but you didn't allow everyone into your home, did you! In fact, did you ever have to let anybody into your house? Without giving it much thought, she had always more or less resigned herself to the fact that she would never invite a guest in, and now suddenly she was both a guest and a hostess with someone she had known less than half a day. What was it? His smell, the soft consistency of his skin?

"Make yourself comfortable," said Max, after he had closed the curtains and sat down in the green armchair.

He was sophisticated. Most men were stupid and sat down on their sofa themselves, thereby creating the later problem of getting their lady visitors next to them on the sofa. She now had the choice between the other armchair and the sofa. If she were to sit in the other armchair, they would both be staring unnaturally at the exceptionally empty sofa; and in so doing she would have indicated not only what she basically did not want, being a respectable girl, but also what was on her mind. If she sat on the sofa, that might mean that such nonsense had never entered her head, but it would be all the easier for him to sit next to her with his photo album or his stamp collection.

Unlike his friend Onno, who probably had no antennae for such things, he of course registered everything precisely. She was curious about his arts of seduction; she hoped he wouldn't make a fool of himself. Holding her head horizontally, she strolled past his extensive, chronologically ordered record collection and looked at a Magritte reproduction on the wall: a man looking into the mirror and seeing his own back. On the grand piano she struck an A, the D above it, and then the A again.

"A poetic theme," nodded Max. "A pity there's no M or X on the keyboard. You find them only in the highest overtones of a Stradivarius."

"So that's how you see yourself," said Ada, sitting down on the sofa.

"Onno would say: 'I am in the ultimate, metaphysical realms of the completely unknowable.' "

"And what would you say yourself?"

"Nothing."

She was struck by a sudden change in his eyes, like a pair of spectacles misting over in winter when one enters a warm room. She wasn't quite clear what was happening, but she felt that something had been touched and that he probably did not fully understand it himself. She returned his gaze and a silence fell in the room. Outside, the wind was blowing; in the distance there was the faint three-note sound of an ambulance.

"Shall we get undressed," he asked, "and go to bed?"

She nodded. "All right."

It was as easy as that. Not even a preliminary kiss was necessary, though it was not cold or businesslike—a kiss might have made it colder and more businesslike: what was simple was at the same time complicated. She remembered a poem by Brecht, set to music by Eisler, on "Simple things, that are hard to do," a kind of love song addressed to Communism; Communism was not at issue here, but maybe there was a kind of love song in the air.

Max led her into the bathroom, laid a white robe over the edge of the bathtub, and closed the door behind him. There were no windows, but she could hear the strong wind through the ventilation grille in the ceiling. Here too there was a definite but not obsessive order, which had already struck her in the room; the bottles and jars were not arranged according to size but by type. All the tops were on, and the tube of toothpaste was not squashed, like a snake in a traffic accident, but had been rolled up to the right point.

She undressed and stood in front of the full-length mirror for a moment—counting herself lucky that she could not see the previous scenes that had undoubtedly been enacted in the glass. Her slim body with its small breasts and inverted black pyramid, which she had so often looked at with uncertain feelings, seemed suddenly transformed into something sacred: it was about to serve the other purpose for which it had been created. Outside, Max put on the prelude from *Tristan and Isolde*, which struck her as a rather melancholy choice. Placing her right hand on her heart and her left hand on her belly, she felt as if she were standing on a mother-of-pearl dish.

She was greeted by Wagner's oceanic swells as she entered the room. Max was lying in bed; he smiled at her with his head resting on his crossed arms.

"Or are you anti-German? Would you prefer Purcell?"

"I already know myself."

"What do you mean?"

"That I'd prefer to get to know you."

As she hesitantly loosened the belt of the robe, he put his hands over his eyes until she was lying next to him under the sheets. He raised himself on one elbow and looked at her. She saw that he wanted to say something, but although he said nothing, it seemed a moment later as though he had said it, and then he pressed his mouth to hers, took her firmly in his arms, and slid halfway across her.

She began trembling and whispered: "Be careful, don't hurt me . . ."

Max realized at once that it was her first time. He would have to deflower her, and with anyone else he would have dreamed up some pretext to put a stop to things: a headache; an early start next morning. Every time he had undertaken this task, he had paid for it afterward: for months the girls who had been transformed into women went on ringing the doorbell and phoning, even when he had forgotten them. When a man deflowered a woman, he assumed a place in her life which could only be compared with that of the doctor who had brought her into the world, or of the one who helped her when she was dying. But now, with Ada, it did not occur to him to stop.

She held him between her legs like her cello—and slowly, inch by inch, then back again, then a little further, she felt him penetrating her, while at the same time it was as though he enveloped her and she disappeared farther and farther into him. When she sensed that he had reached her hymen, she clung to him anxiously, while an image appeared to her, something like an eye, or the shutter of a camera. She wanted to call for her mother, but suddenly he was through and filled her completely.

Sobbing and laughing, she began kissing him. He stopped moving. She could feel his blood pounding deep in her belly. He was obviously trying to control his excitement, and when that threatened to fail, he came out of her, lay next to her, and put an arm around her shoulder.

"Perhaps we should leave it at that for today."

His paternal tone amazed her, but she was grateful to him. She said nothing. The record had finished, and she listened to the howling of the wind among the trees in front of the house. Suddenly there she was in an Amsterdam bed with an astronomer, who had put an end to years of fretting and had ushered in a new period in her life. She snuggled up to him and sighed deeply.

He too listened to the wind. He saw the house: light and warm inside, and outside, the damp, chilly night.

"If we went up onto the roof now," he said, "and I squeezed a drop of ink out of my fountain pen and let it blow against a sheet of paper, how great do you think the chance would be of the sentence *I don't want Ada to stay with me* appearing in my handwriting?"

"That's impossible."

"The chance isn't nil, but the universe is probably too small to contain all the ink needed before it happens."

8

An Idyll

In the weeks that followed, they saw each other every day in Leiden, where they walked through the Botanical Garden during the lunch hour, drank coffee in the observatory canteen, or had an Indonesian meal in town in the evening. On the weekends he took her with him to Amsterdam, sometimes with the cello in the back of the car. Those Saturdays and Sundays gave him a feeling of peace, which was new. He had had longer-term relationships a few times before, but they had not affected his restlessness in the slightest; even while those girlfriends were with him, he was dying to get away: out into the street, into the pub—not to drink, because he didn't do that, or to have a relaxed chat with someone, because he didn't do that either—but to look for something new.

The thought that somewhere in the town there was a woman walking, or sitting alone at a café table while he was at home wasting his time with his girlfriend, was unbearable. Sometimes such a woman appeared to him in a kind of vision: he saw exactly what she looked like and where she was sitting, in what café, at what table. On occasion he had found a pretext to get out of the house and run there; but when she turned out not to be sitting there, that was only because he was just too late. Afterward, he would stand on tiptoe outside and scan the street in both directions.

Of course, he had not suddenly changed into a monogamous lover: from Monday to Friday his time-consuming love life continued as before. But on the weekends, when Ada was there, the obsession left him. Not that he relaxed in front of the TV or read a thriller or did a household chore, because he had never understood what "relaxation" meant and he never would. The thought of playing a game, or a sport, or even going for a walk, was unthinkable. He took only study material with him on vacation, and left no church or museum unvisited; if he sunbathed, then it was not so much because he enjoyed it but because one had to get brown: it was less sunbathing than the exposure to light of his whole body according to a precise schedule, including his sides and the insides of his arms and legs. That was also work—because if he were not working or chasing women, he found himself peering into a threatening void that was more than just boredom. However, when he was chasing women he actually wanted to be working, and when he was working he actually wanted to be chasing women, with the result that he was never at peace. Whenever anyone brought this up, he usually answered: "Eternal peace will come in its own good time—I don't need an advance." Now, though, with Ada, he made love in a relaxed, almost bourgeois way, and afterward wanted nothing else, which sometimes worried him. Was he in the process of degenerating in the direction of marriage? At his insistence, Ada was now taking the pill.

His conversations with Onno were also part of his obsession, but with Ada it was different. He wasn't in love. In a certain sense he was in love with all women except Ada. When he looked at a woman, he often had the feeling that his blue eyes could see to the bottom of her soul, as if looking into a clear bay; and perhaps it was true. Perhaps women felt the same and this was the key to his romantic successes, for which he was envied and hated in the pubs. But when he looked at Ada, it seemed to increase his distance from her. He understood nothing about her; for him she had the unfathomable look of a creature from another world, and that was precisely what bound him to her. He experienced her presence in his house not like that of a dog, which has no secrets from human beings, but like that of a cat, which is itself a secret—and to that extent he felt free and unthreatened. And just as a dog belongs to a human being but a cat belongs to a house, so she merged with the order in his apartment and became a part of it. Dogs knock over tables, scoop cushions from armchairs, and carry things out of the room with their heads held high; cats do not even touch what they touch—except perhaps sometimes when they dig their claws into the carpet.

When she put a book on the table, it lay there precisely as he himself would have put it down: with the title upward, not on another book that was smaller, not at an angle, and along the golden section between the ashtray and the edge of the table, parallel to that edge. She would never forget to fold the newspaper. When he looked up from his desk and saw her sitting on the sofa, reading poems by Rilke, she was sitting exactly as she should sit. He had never known someone to have the same natural feel for relationships as himself, without having to make an effort and without it turning into petty-minded neatness. They did not talk much, and he liked that too. *Musicienne du silence.* You could chat with anyone, he believed; being silent together without it becoming embarrassing was a lot rarer. Only when Onno was around was there nonstop talk. If he had something to do at his desk, then Onno had long conversations with Ada, in a rather paternal tone, since that was the only way he could show his sympathy—or perhaps it was more the tone of a father-in-law. It always struck Ada that Max too said much more to her when Onno was there: it was as though she became a different person for him in Onno's presence. Without Onno, for example, he would never have explained so patiently to her that in modern science, what is observed can no longer be seen separately from the observer, since the observer changes what is observed by observing it. Max knew that kind of thing didn't interest her in the slightest, but he still did it, for Onno's benefit in fact—and she preferred him as he was without Onno.

She was not very talkative, either. She could sit for hours at the open window overlooking the Vondelpark, where children and dogs were being taken for walks, where hippies in Oriental dress danced past, singing and adorned with flowers, and where the same boy was always practicing juggling on the grass, learning nothing but how to bend down. On the other side, almost invisible from the park behind bushes and trees, there was a low building containing chapels of rest, to which hearses drove up several times a day and which tearful people went in and out of. For some reason she found this panorama ideally suited to Max: she felt a similar stark juxtaposition of life and death in him. In fact he was always in a good mood, but somehow that was so striking because it was set against a dark background, in the same way that a diamond is displayed on black velvet at the jeweler's.

Only when Max once asked her did she tell him anything about her parents, about their meeting during the bombing of Leiden and how they later set up a secondhand bookshop. She had never felt that she was the child of those two people who were so completely different from her, but rather that she was their foster child, a foundling, who in fact had nothing to do with them. Not that she had any romantic ideas in that direction, because she needed only to look in the mirror and she saw her mother.

"The reverse probably also happens," said Max, "where someone thinks that his parent are his parents, and they aren't."

After that first occasion he had never met her parents again. He, too, felt that he had nothing to do with them, and Ada did not ask him—although her parents had indicated a few times that they would like to meet her boyfriend. He knew that she was grateful to him for taking her out of the house for at least two days a week. And as far as his own parents were concerned, had she asked him about them, he would have told her his story: when she did not, he left things as they were.

Domestic happiness was in the air! He was in the habit of pacing through the rooms when he was thinking, but he never did so when he was not alone; Ada was the first person who did not inhibit him from doing this. The pacing was not simply walking back and forth, just as it is not with caged polar bears or lions, but was determined by a precise geometrical pattern, of which he was himself vaguely conscious and from which he did not deviate one inch. It was formed by the three invisible lines projecting from his furniture: the extensions of the diagonals and the center lines. His chairs, tables, and cupboards, combined with the angles of the corners of the room, were the focus of a complicated network, like an imaginary garden in Lenôtre style, which allowed him to step on many points in it, but not all. While he was pacing with his hands behind his back, he sometimes found himself thinking about the future.

When the Westerbork facility was finished in a few years' time, he would probably have to go to Drenthe more frequently than now. He contemplated the bleak evenings there, with nothing to do for miles around. Yokels playing billiards, odd girls, whom he could hardly understand and with whom he dare not try anything, for fear of being murdered with pitchforks and rakes. Wouldn't it be nice if Ada came along now and then? They could rent a pied-à-terre somewhere, in the local solicitor's house, and furnish it to their taste. Ada would have her work too, of course, and in a car you could be in Amsterdam in an hour, or an hour and half . . .

Since Bruno had realized that Ada had a boyfriend, he was routinely unable to attend rehearsals; because of this she was learning a new piece by Xenakis for solo cello, *Nomos Alpha*. This did not disturb Max when he was working—on the contrary: the fact that she was occupied, too, relieved him of the responsibility of having to say something to break the silence. Now and then they even made music together. During the war his mother had occasionally given him piano lessons, and later his foster parents had sent him to a music school, but his playing was not of a very high standard; he had bought the grand piano on impulse, at an auction—perhaps just to see it being carried into his house, thereby putting something right. When he did occasionally play with Ada, completely different things happened. She had been to the conservatory in The Hague. She was a professional musician; she knew that making music was not about expressing emotions but about evoking them: and that could only succeed when it was done professionally—that is, dispassionately, like a surgeon operating, regardless of theatrical grimaces conductors and soloists often pulled when they knew they were being watched. At home or in rehearsal, they never pulled those faces, nor did orchestral musicians, because those were the faces of listeners.

Max, on the other hand, was so far from being a musician that it was almost impossible for him to make music—not because it did not affect him, but because it affected him too much. He had an extensive record collection, four yards of records from Machaut and Dufay to Boulez and Riley, but he almost never put anything on for himself. As soon as he struck a note on his grand piano, and then the octave, it already affected him too deeply: it opened a fathomless shaft in him, making him dizzy. When the piano tuner was there, he pretended to look through the newspaper; in reality he was racked by emotions, almost more than when a great soloist was at work, because now it was harmony itself resonating in a pure medium without the intervention of a composer—just like at home the dough always tasted better than the cake itself, but one was not allowed to eat it, although he said a thousand times that he did not want cake. Milk, eggs, butter, flour, and sugar—it was true that in the oven the divine mixture was transformed into a work of culinary art, but at the same time it was ruined. Scores of times he repeated the first four bars of Schubert's Fantasie in F for four hands on the piano with Ada: what happened? A bed was laid down, a few simple notes sounded—and immediately an absolute beauty was attained: what was most exalted, most complex, most incomprehensible in the form of what was simplest. Even after the hundredth time it had lost none of its radiance and yielded nothing of its secret.

"What is it?" cried Max in despair. "What is it in heaven's name? Suddenly it reminds me of something. Yes, I've got it: Mendelssohn's *Fingal's Cave*." He got up, took out the record, and put it on the turntable. "Here, listen, at about bar one fifteen." He raised his forefinger. "Can you hear? It's almost the same, on just the same sort of bed!"

Ada kissed him on the cheek. "You have a merciless ear," she said.

He put his arm around her shoulders. "At least I can talk about it to you, even though you haven't a clue yourself—but no one has. Do you know what Onno once said when I started talking about music? He shook his great head with those quivering cheeks and said, 'Music is for girls.' Well, the girl in question is here. That was good intuition."

"Why is music supposed to be only for girls?"

"You mustn't take him so literally. Once when I bought an ice cream, he said, 'Ice cream is for vicars.' Music doesn't exist for him. He regards it as meaningless sound. For him only words have meaning. What he has against it is probably the flight from reality that it represents for many people, a kind of escape clause to the effect that if all else fails, there's always music. Perhaps he actually finds music a kind of cowardly consolation.

"He once told me that in the Middle Ages the Greek *mousikè technè*— the 'art of the muse'—was derived from the ancient Egyptian word *moys,* which means 'water.' This made Moses the discoverer of music, because according to the same erroneous etymology, his name was supposed to mean 'rescued from water.' You know—the rush basket in which he was found in the Nile as a baby: the same Moses who struck water from the rock and who had God create the world with a word in Genesis, after which his spirit moved over the waters. Everything always fits. So in fact you're practicing the Mosaic art."

"I'm sure I am. Show me your thumbs."

He put his hands in hers: they were well formed, like the rest of his body, not too broad and not too slim, but his thumbs were both short and spatula-shaped. "I invent it all by sucking on my thumbs," he said.

"Who do you take after?"

"No idea. Maybe my father. Maybe myself. That's why I can just span an octave but can't go any further. What's the name of that pianist who had an operation on his hands in order to be able to span larger chords and then couldn't play anymore?"

"No idea," said Ada, putting his hands in his lap. "And why is ice cream for vicars?"

"Because they have to spoil themselves, of course, seeing that no one else does."

Ada stared at him and nodded. "You love him, don't you?"

"Of course I love him."

Max's eyes suddenly moistened. Ada was amazed to see it happen. She did not know what to make of it, but suddenly she had the feeling that she was the mother of the pair of them.

"Do you two tell each other everything?"

"Everything." Fortunately she did not ask if he loved him more than her. "We even tell each other what we would never tell anyone. That's friendship."

9

The Demons

When the sun had reached its solstice and touched the Tropic of Cancer—
that is, at the beginning of summer—a political and musical happening was
staged, to round off the turbulent season and in happy expectation of even
more turbulent times. Since the riots of the year before, Amsterdam, as
Onno put it, had been occupied by invading Dutch troops: uniformed farmers' sons from Christian homes had temporary control of the city, and the
main issue was now its liberation, followed by the irrevocable overthrow of
the Netherlands by Amsterdam. One of the organizers of the festival had
evidently once heard a performance by Ada and Bruno, because they were
invited to perform. It was to be her first engagement in Amsterdam, and although it wasn't a real concert, it was still a great honor. Ada was apprehensive about playing her kind of music for the kind of audience that could be
expected there; but of course they must give it a try, and she persuaded
Bruno to pick up where they had left off.

Everyone would be there, Max assured her. Politics was the new popular
entertainment, in a way that it had not been since the war and as it would
not be for a long time to come; he estimated the interval at twenty-two years:
1945; 1967; 1989. . . . Before the concert Ada went for a meal with the other
musicians; she arranged to meet Max afterward in the greenroom and stay
over at his place.

Onno went too. Since he had reached an impasse with the Phaistos disc, he had gradually gotten more interested in politics; after all, even Chomsky was more preoccupied with politics than with linguistics these days, so he was in good company. His instinctive sympathies lay with the anarchistic provocateurs and revolutionaries, as did those of Max, but deep down he knew that their rabid views did not stand a chance.

Holland hated radicalism; in the swampy delta of the Rhine estuary this kind of theorizing had been isolated and disarmed in theology, while practical people struck bargains—Max, with his dangerously foreign disposition, need have no illusions at all on that score: Erasmus called the tune here. In Holland there was only one path, and that was the middle path. And in politics it was power that mattered, nothing else. What else was left? The Social Democrats had become as ossified as the Christian parties. What about a splinter group like the Communists or the Pacifist Socialists? But, with respect, they were a completely different breed. It was true that a new left-wing Liberal party had been set up, which a few months ago, at the interim elections, had been very successful and already had seven members in the Lower House; but although it was led by the same kind of people as himself, even from the same generation, Onno found this group too lacking in a sense of history; moreover, he suspected it of trying to implement purely formal constitutional reforms in order to prevent socioeconomic ones.

"You're not really going into politics, are you, Onno?" asked Max as they were on their way to the meeting.

Onno looked at him uncertainly. "Do you think it's my destiny?"

"Destiny? Surely you decide that for yourself?"

"Do you think so? In any case, you're completely unsuited to politics, because for that you need come from a large family. You learn the craft in the life-and-death struggle with your brothers and sisters. If you haven't been through this school of intrigue and deceit and intimidation, you'll never make it. That means that I have excellent qualifications, but you're an only child—you've never had to fight for your parents' favor."

"It was a very close thing. I had an older brother, but he died in his crib."

"Just the sort of thing that would happen to you. You can't tolerate anyone around you. But as things stand at the moment, all you're fit for is to be king. Who knows?; if things go on like this, that position may yet become vacant."

"Then I'd immediately appoint you to form my first and only cabinet, because after that I would abolish democracy and proclaim an absolute monarchy."

Onno bent his back and folded his hands in entreaty. "*Euere kaiserliche und königliche, apostolische Majestät,* don't you think—"

"That is my last word. The audience is at an end—there is the door. Or, rather, there is the window."

"Sire, do I really have to . . ."

"Jump!"

"Damn," said Onno, and sat up. "I don't know if you know, but it is the Bohemian practice of defenestration that is welling up in your sick mind. In the Hradčany in Prague, disgraced politicians were always thrown out of the window." He suddenly looked disapprovingly at Max's elegant summer suit with its pocket handkerchief. "I must say you're very badly dressed for a subversive assembly."

"Robespierre also followed the fashion of the ancien régime."

"Yes, till his head was lopped off at his lace collar."

"And you've got your sweater on inside out. You look ridiculous with that label at the back of your neck."

"You'd do something like that deliberately."

In the side streets dark-blue police buses full of armed provincials waited like patient cats next to the mousehole; there was a great mêlée around the revolving doors. The auditorium, a temporarily converted auction room, was decorated with red flags and posters of Marx, Lenin, Bakunin, Mao, Ho Chi Minh, and, of course El Che, the hero of heroes, who had given up his Cuban ministerial post and was now in the jungle, probably in Bolivia, participating in the guerrilla struggle whose object was the liberation of the South American continent.

There was the kind of cheerful bustle to which everyone had by now become addicted. Between the cast-iron pillars of the surrounding covered galleries there were stalls, where revolution was extolled in all tastes and styles: Moscow-line Communists, breakaway Communists, Trotskyites, anarchists, Maoists, the Socialist Youth, the Red Youth, the Student Trade Union Movement, the Netherlands-Vietnam Medical Committee, Provo, the Netherlands-USSR Association, Netherlands-GDR, Netherlands-Poland, Netherlands-Romania . . . Netherlands-Universe! The most chic stall at the revolutionary fair was undoubtedly that of the Committee of Solidarity with Cuba, because they had the use of Ernesto Che Guevara himself, whose portrait adorned even the shop windows of upmarket men's wear shops in the city. With a mixture of mockery and reverence, people looked at the well-known writer, the illustrious chess grandmaster, and the leading composer, sitting there on simple kitchen chairs conversing with two dark-complexioned men, admittedly without beards or cigars, but undoubtedly Cubans.

Also everywhere in evidence were furtive-looking types who carried reassuring, seditious, extreme left-wing literature under their arms, but whose hairstyle and features told a different story: detectives; Internal Security Service; spies of the reactionaries. Finally, even the aisles were full of spectators, who were half lying over each other, and gradually the metaphysical sweetness of wafting hemp fumes began spreading.

The evening was opened by a celebrated student leader, Bart Bork, a sociologist, who condemned American imperialism and urged the audience on to action. While he spoke, his lower eyelids were raised in a strange, leering way up to his pupils, which made a rather threatening impression, but everyone accepted this, since the threat was directed only at the enemies of the people. He spoke for too long, as virtually everyone always did, but he was rewarded by applause—after which an ensemble played music by Charles Ives and finally aroused the enthusiasm of the audience with militant tunes by Hanns Eisler, who, like Sleeping Beauty, had been kissed and awakened from a forty-year sleep by the spirit of the age.

Next a guest from Berlin appeared at the lectern, Rudi Dutschke himself, and a different tone was struck. He was about twenty-seven, small, frail, but like an anchor taking hold in the seabed, the fanatical look in his dark eyes immediately grabbed the whole auditorium. A thick-set middle-aged lady, who might have been his mother, stationed herself next to him at a separate microphone and looked at him sternly. With a raw-edged voice he began speaking, staccato, off the cuff, waiting impatiently after each few sentences for the translation: it was clear that checking the flow of his thoughts was more of an effort than formulating them.

With a theoretical frenzy alien to the practical Dutch, quoting Marcuse, Rosa Luxemburg, and Plekhanov, he revealed that radical change, subjectively not desired by the masses, was becoming objectively increasingly necessary. The late-capitalist working class, still exploited to the point where it had lost its identity, resigned itself unconsciously to its relative prosperity and to formally democratic structures, which served only to conceal the violent nature of imperialism. How, then, was the extraparliamentary opposition of students and intellectuals in the metropolitan centers—who after all did not participate in the production process—to break out of its isolation and create its necessary mass base? He asked this with an elegant gesture of his slender, sensitive hand; the translator imitated even that with her ring-covered fingers. This was to be found exclusively in the Third World. Only there was there a new proletariat, not perverted by false consciousness—and only out of solidarity with the liberation movements in Asia, Africa, and Latin-America, with the present genocide in Vietnam acting as a catalyst, could a praxis be created as a radical negation of world capitalism that at the same time could be the first impulse toward a new anthropology, which would allow us to avoid the perversion of the revolution by the Soviet Union and its satellites, since it was there that the dictatorship of the proletariat had degenerated first into the dictatorship of the Bolshevik party, then into that of the bureaucratic state apparatus, and finally into that of one man, Stalin, with the accompanying repression, brutality, torture, and cruelty; all this by way of a demonstration of the distinction—already made by Marx in his *Ökonomisch-philosophische Manuskripte*—between despotic and democratic Communism.

It had all been too fast for the translator, who was only able to stammer something about "perversion" and "Stalin," but Dutschke had been understood anyway. He received warm applause, which he did not acknowledge with so much as a nod of his head, descended from the platform to join his comrades in the front row—and suddenly there was an incident. It happened so fast that neither Max nor Onno were able to follow it. All at once the German ideologue was lost from sight, having been thrown to the ground by a screaming and kicking man. Other people came rushing up, and the whole auditorium rose to its feet. In the turmoil someone shouted that he knew the guy, an infamous fascist from West Amsterdam, whom he had seen the previous day at the Belgian frontier, but who, according to someone else, was a card-carrying Communist from east Groningen.

"If you can have two enemies like that," said Onno laconically, "you must be profoundly right."

Max's thoughts were with Ada, who was about to perform. He considered going backstage and suggesting that the duo change places with the orchestra which was to round off the evening, but stagehands were already pushing a grand piano onto the stage and setting down a chair and a music stand. While the attacker, still cursing at the top of his voice, was being conveyed to a side door with his arm twisted painfully behind his back, Bruno and Ada appeared. She held her cello. The sight of them had an immediate calming effect and everyone sat down, at least insofar as they were not forced to stand; the guest speaker seemed happy not to have incurred many injuries, because he remained in the auditorium.

Ada, now in jeans and a white shirt from Max's wardrobe, took the cello between her legs and arranged her score—she placed the bow on the strings, looked at Bruno, raised her head for the opening . . .

Janáček. At the very first notes it seemed to Max as though a rent had been made in all the political and transitory goings-on here, a rent through which something eternal was glimpsed, as though he were turning around in Plato's cave. Onno was right in his view of music—it was not of this world—and Max thought of what the German activist was now thinking, having just been kicked and beaten. Perhaps of Lenin's words: "I too should like to be moved by the *Appassionata*, but this is no time to be moved by the *Appassionata*, it is a time for chopping off heads." The music—perhaps not Eisler's, but that of Schubert or Janáček—was obviously the voice of the blackest reaction, archenemy of progressive humankind, public enemy number one. The audience, which a moment ago had been in violent tumult, listened like a well-trained concert audience. Many were undoubtedly hearing something of this kind for the first time in their lives: while at home on the radio such dreary music was always turned off and replaced by something catchy, they were now receiving an artistic knighthood.

Max looked proudly at Ada as she bowed and returned for another curtain call with Bruno.

"Take very good care of that girl," said Onno. "You don't deserve her at all."

There was some truth in that, thought Max. The whole evening his eyes had been wandering toward the back of a head in the third row, with unruly curly red hair; the woman to whom it belonged seemed to feel this, because now and then she looked to one side, not directly at him, but nevertheless in such a way that he must be at the edge of her field of vision, because he saw that she was not looking at what she was seeing but that she saw what she was not looking at, namely him. There was nothing for it. It was bound to happen, whether he wanted it to or not.

The grand piano and the music stand had disappeared, and the forum discussion was taking place at a long table. The forum consisted of the left-wing elite of the Cuba Committee—the writer, the chess player, and the composer—joined by a distinguished-looking old lady, who had been a nurse with the Reds in the Spanish Civil War and had still not regained her

Dutch nationality. The chairman was a generally respected journalist and publicist, himself no longer very young, a former anarchist and now an anarchist once again. Each member made a short statement, after which a discussion arose on the points that the rabid German had in fact already discussed exhaustively.

The old lady drew attention to the fact that the obvious primary interest of the pharmaceutical industry in a capitalist economy was that patients should not get better, and it was clear what consequences that had for the quality of medicines and hence of public health, whereupon the serial composer raised his hands above his head and praised Chinese medicine, which under the inspirational leadership of Chairman Mao could dispense with anesthetics even in serious operations.

At that moment Onno could suddenly no longer contain himself and shouted: "You hysterical fool! In ten years' time you'll be as right-wing as an American general!"

"I must disagree," said the composer, laughing.

Whereupon Onno stood up and declared with great dignity: "I don't want to be disagreed with, I want to be knocked down."

Things began to go with a swing. The writer, too, had to put up with an interruption. When he expressed his concern, without too much conviction, that the workers were leaving the intellectuals in the lurch, someone shouted:

"Why don't you piss off, mate! Go and cut sugarcane in Cuba."

"I *have* cut sugarcane in Cuba."

"Yeah, for a fraction of a second—for the cameras."

The writer leaned back with a superior smile and said no more.

"What a creep," said Max.

Onno nodded. "You're a bit like him."

At that moment someone in the auditorium stood up and said in a thunderous voice: "I'm a worker!"

All heads turned in his direction. It was true. There he stood. No doubt about it: a worker. Heavy industry, probably. Blast furnaces. A beret with a stalk on his head, his heavily lined face ravaged by exploitation, his hands held slightly open at hip height, ready to cope with any chore. There was applause here and there; the old lady bent over her microphone and invited him to have a seat at the table. The chairman tried to prevent this, but the worker was already on his way, chin aloft, exuding deep contempt for everyone who was not a worker.

"He's a nutcase," said Onno. "Anyone can see that. He hasn't done a day's work in his life."

Anyone with any experience could tell that the evening was now about to go off the rails. The worker did not deign to look at any of the members of the forum panel; he pulled the old lady's microphone toward himself and, with a fixed expression, began explaining that the Jesuits had constructed an underground network of tunnels under the streets and squares of Amsterdam, from where they planned one day to launch a merciless attack. He had written countless letters on the subject to the city council, the government, the queen, and the United Nations, but never—

"I thank you for your lucid statement," the chairman interrupted. "And now for a completely different subject: the recent attack by Israel on—"

"Be quiet when I'm speaking," said the worker, without so much as turning his head. While the members of the panel looked at each other in astonishment and the mood in the audience became more and more high-spirited, he went on unperturbed: "It is no accident that the general of the Jesuits is a Dutchman. He has his headquarters in Spain, which since the Revolt of the Netherlands and the Inquisition—"

Now again someone stood up in the auditorium and shouted: "For God's sake stop that nonsense, mate!" He was proof that a large amount of flesh could also contribute to intellectual superiority, because even the worker now fell silent. The excessively fat, bald man, a well-known restaurateur, turned with outstretched arms to the audience, which egged him on with acclamations. "What good is all this rubbish to us? Doesn't everybody know that Amsterdam is the New Jerusalem, blessed with the refined hyperbiogeometric ethics of Dante, Goethe, and Queen Esther with her thirty-six Essenes and thirty-six Saddikim and with the new, all-renewing, Messianic Pythagorean world mathematics, the primeval mathematics of the wisdom of the prehistoric world, as an interpretation of the Old and New Testaments, namely the new Jewish laws of harmony of prime numbers and the prime pairs of Moses, David, and Solomon—the new bio-algebra, bio-geometry, and bio-mechanics of William of Orange, Spinoza, Erasmus, Simon Stevin, Christian Huygens, Descartes, and Rembrandt, and the new plastic mathematics of Teilhard de Chardin, Mondrian, Steiner, Thomas Aquinas, Mersenne, Fermat, Aristotle, Nicolaus Cusanus, Wittgenstein, Weinreb—"

But he was not allowed to complete his list: at the back of the auditorium a door suddenly flew open, through which the earlier attacker again charged in.

"Where's that stinking German bastard?" he screamed, looking around in bewilderment. "Give him to me and I'll kick the shit out of him!"

With this he suddenly crossed a critical borderline: the auditorium capsized and submerged in thunderous laughter. The chairman crossed his arms, leaned back, and looked calmly at the pandemonium.

"It is no accident,"—the worker now resumed his revelations completely unperturbed—"that Princess Irene married a Catholic three years ago, a French creep who wants to be king of Spain."

"Augustine!" shouted the restaurateur. "Einstein! Euclid!"

"Give the bastard to me! I'll cut his head off!"

"Princess Beatrix for queen of Israel!"

"Good idea! Republic! Republic!"

And shortly afterward, those organizing the proceedings showed that they had had a brilliant brainwave because, blowing on saxophones, trumpets, clarinets, bassoons, and tubas, the musicians entered from both wings—playing a loud but slow, strangely Oriental melody, while at the same time from the back of the auditorium, along the central aisle, a man with a sheep was seen to be making his way toward the platform.

"A sheep! A sheep!"

It was not clear what was meant—maybe something to do with a symbolic sacrifice—but the shock was great. And maybe Max was the only person who suddenly found his eyes full of tears at the sight of the animal kicking in fright, the fathomless seriousness of it all, and the closeness of the bond linking it to the farmer leading it, who perhaps already knew that it would soon die of shock.

10

The Gypsies

In the crowd afterward, Max was able to make a quick date with the red-head in the third row, after which he went backstage to the greenroom. Other public figures had also managed to gain admittance. At the bar stood a tall, platinum-blond young man in a raincoat with an umbrella—the "rain maker" of the former Provo movement—who arranged for precipitation by magic whenever it could hamper the police. He was listening with a smile to a pale lad with a bandaged forehead: he had made a hole in his skull with a dentist's drill, and because of this new fontanel, as he explained in interviews, was constantly as high as a baby.

The writer sat making notes, still choking with laughter. In passing, Max heard him say to the chess player that they would later remember this time; but the grandmaster bent absent-mindedly over a pocket chess set, with which he may have been running through a variation for his forthcoming match with Smyslov in Palma de Mallorca.

Ada was sitting at a large round table with Bruno, some other musicians, the composer from the forum, the student leader Bart Bork, and Onno. Max kissed her and sat down next to her on the same chair.

"Congratulations," he said. "You two were the only ones who really knocked the audience out. Are you tired?"

"Dead tired. I don't want to stay very long."

Max raised his hand in the direction of Bruno, who nodded to him with a deadpan look. They had met each other a few times but had not struck up a conversation.

Onno was explaining to the composer why in ten years' time, like a second Richard Wagner, he would be as right-wing as an American general and that, like all Maoists, he would embrace the Holy Mother Church on his deathbed, since that was what he was actually looking for: the Holy Father.

"Comrade Rabbit is only a means to an end for you."

"Comrade Rabbit?"

"That's what Mao means in Chinese. Though there is the consolation that it's also the name of a constellation. I, on the other hand," he said, "will become the president of the People's Republic of the Netherlands after the revolution and in that capacity will make a state visit to Peking."

With his head slightly bent, Bork looked at him out of the corner of his eye. "After the revolution," he said slowly, "you'll be a beachcomber on Ameland."

Onno, startled, looked him in the eye. This was someone who meant what he said. He could feel the remark sinking into him, like a revolver thrown into a canal dropping through the murky water to the muddy bottom. Was that the way things were going? Imagine Bart Bork coming to power! And if it all came to nothing, which was the most probable outcome, knowing Holland, what would people like Bork do? How would they take it? For now they were borne along by massive good-humored benevolence—but if that were suddenly to disappear and they were suddenly alone? What would they do, then, in their despair? Would they turn into terrorists? Onno was shocked. Shouldn't he go into politics and do something about it?

"Onno, come and help."

Max, Ada, and Bruno had gotten up and were talking to one of the two Cubans. The latter switched with relief from his laborious American English into Spanish, or rather the sloppy Latin-American dialect in its Cuban variant. He was very impressed by the duo and wanted the address of the Dutch musicians' union; perhaps there would be an opportunity at some point for an invitation, but the *compañera* only wanted to give her own address. His instinct for power had obviously told him that he should talk to Ada and not Bruno. Through Onno, Ada explained that she had nothing to do with such an organization—that was not how musical life was organized in the Netherlands—and with some surprise the Cuban noted down her name and address.

"That would be nice," said Max, when he had gone.

"I know that kind of fellow," said Bruno. "You'll never hear another word. He's probably just talking big to impress the lady."

"Do you really think we'll get an invitation to go to Cuba?" asked Ada. "There are thousands of better duos."

"But they don't perform at left-wing demonstrations."

"I'll wait and see what happens. I don't want to think about it. Do you mind if we go home?"

Chairs were already being put on tables; everyone was getting ready to leave. Bruno said that he was going into town for a bit: there was a gypsy orchestra performing that he wanted to hear.

Ada looked at Max. "I can see from your face that you want to go too. Go ahead. I'm only off to bed."

"Can I come too, can I come too?" whined Onno, with his forefinger raised.

"Yes, darling," said Max. "You can come too."

"Hey!" cried Onno. "Have you gone completely nuts!"

Max gave Ada the front-door key, looked at her sternly, and said:

"Go up the front steps and count to four. On the far right you'll find a half brick, which is loose. Lift it up, slip the key in, and put the brick back in its place."

The gypsy orchestra was playing in a dimly lit bar behind the Rembrandt-plein. It turned out that Bruno knew the musicians. He greeted the *primas*, who was walking among the audience, followed by the second violinist, and waved to the cymbalist and the bass player in the corner. The second violinist raised his instrument inquiringly, whereupon Bruno took it from him and revealed himself as a stylish fiddler, who had no trouble with the *csárdás*, or even with shouting "Hop, hop!"

The moment Max heard the sounds, something melted in him. No one needed to tell him about the status of this music and its relationship to *Die Grosse Fuge*, for example: that was already clear from those shiny shirts with their wide sleeves. But at the same time there was something in it that was not found even in Beethoven, or in Bach, and that he experienced at home on his grand piano when he played the gypsy scale, the harmonic with its raised fourth note: the Central European Jewish gypsy sob, which bowled him over.

They now played a slow number. The *primas* leaned over him and Onno at their table, as the friends of his friend. He was about fifty; the upper eyelids of his large fleshy face were thick and heavy with melancholy, like shutters, so he could scarcely raise them over his pupils. From his ears his black hair grew down to his lower jaw: a style that in Max's student days had been called "screwing strips," because women could hold on to them while they were on the job. Onno, who heard less the music than the renewed threat of a beachcomber's existence, turned away in embarrassment and lit up a cigarette, but Max, not taking his eyes off the violinist, was suddenly reminded of his father.

Wolfgang too had listened to this music, on the spot, in Austro-Hungarian regions—Vienna, Prague, Budapest—at a time when he had only heard vaguely of Holland, as his son now had of Iceland, as something far away, Ultima Thule, where he would spend a few days if the opportunity presented itself. In 1914, in his tailored Bordeaux-red Habsburg uniform with the ornamental sword, a provocative girlfriend on each arm and a bottle of Tokay on the table, Wolfgang had listened to the father of this violinist in some Café Hungaria or other, his thoughts racing around in a gloomy enchanted circle, from which he was never able to free himself, while Austria declared war on Serbia—*Serbien muss sterben!*—and the mother of his son began school in Brussels . . .

When the piece was finished, Max ordered a bottle of white wine for the orchestra and asked Bruno what language the leader spoke; he wanted to say something to him. According to Bruno, he knew only a few words of German.

"Onno?"

"As long as you don't think that I know all the sixty-five thousand dialects these people speak."

He tried Hungarian, but that had no effect, and then took a different tack; suddenly the violinist's face broke into a broad smile. He put a hand on Onno's shoulder and turned and spoke the same language to his friends, who cried "Bravo!" and "Hop, hop!"

"What did you speak?" asked Max.

"No idea. A kind of Serbo-Croat, I think. Anyway, he understands it. What did you want to say to him?"

At dictation speed, Max said: "Tell him that I consider gypsies sacred, because they are the only people on earth who have never waged war."

Onno did as he was asked and the smile disappeared from the large face. "Was that all?"

"No. Tell him that because they are the only ones who are not murderers, they are denounced as thieves by everyone but that we have stolen even their death."

"What do you mean by that?"

"That they were gassed and exterminated just like Jews, but that is hushed up so that people can go on niggling at them, even in Holland."

"Are you sure I have to say that?"

"Yes."

The effect was shattering. With his instrument under his arm, the violinist looked at Max, while his eyes filled with tears. He turned and cried something with a choking voice to the others, which Onno translated as "Roma! Gather together!" The bass player now also came over, and the cymbalist with his instrument, making it necessary for the guests to get up and move tables aside; the second violinist took his instrument back from Bruno. A little while later the orchestra had grouped in a semi-circle around Max, and began playing and singing for him—in their own language, Onno suspected: some neo-Indian variant of Hindi from the sound of it, with borrowings from Iranian, Armenian, New Greek, South Slavic, and heaven knows what else.

One can surround someone sitting on a chair and destroy him with threats, blows, or electricity, but here someone was being broken down with gratitude in the form of music. Max cried, for the second time that evening. With a gesture of apology he glanced at Onno, who could see that the musicians were forcing him back mercilessly to his origins, without realizing what they were doing. What was happening was totally alien to Onno—it was a musical scandal—and he would have preferred to put an end to it immediately, but of course that was out of the question. On the other hand his affection for Max grew even greater. What kind of man was it who with a few words could transform a kitschy string band in a back street into an ensemble that was celebrating a *missa solemnis* for the dead? He looked at Bruno, and on his face saw an expression that said: He deserves Ada.

When the litany was finished, Max raised his hands in a ritual gesture of thanks. The musicians withdrew. He took a sip of his orange juice and said in a churned-up voice: "It's exactly twenty-one years ago today that my father was executed."

When Bruno heard that, he stood up and moved away. Onno was about to raise his glass to his lips, but put it down again. That was it—the gypsies had touched the core. This required very careful maneuvering, but he could not resist asking: "Have you lit a candle for him?"

"I've only just remembered."

"Can you still remember being told about it?"

"Scarcely. I was twelve. I don't think it had much effect on me. I was six when I'd last seen him."

Onno nodded. What next? Max had raised the subject; he must not be left alone with it now.

"Have you ever looked up the newspapers from those days? Have you studied his trial?"

"It's never occurred to me. I know almost nothing about him, not even exactly where he was born, or on what day. I've always had the feeling that getting interested in my father was something I couldn't inflict on my mother."

Pensively, he watched the *primas*, who was now again walking among the tables, bending over ladies with his violin and looking deep into their décolettés, while gentlemen who knew the etiquette folded banknotes lengthwise and tucked them into his wide sleeves like voting slips. Bruno had sat down next to the cymbalist. "Has it ever struck you that people often know a lot about things that don't concern them but very little about things that really matter to them? People who have been in camps know nothing about the structure of Himmler's *Reichssicherheitshauptamt*, but I know every intimate detail—I could draw you a diagram just like that. But I have no idea how they elect the Upper Chamber in the Netherlands."

"I'll explain it to you sometime."

"Of course. But with you it's genetic."

"True enough. Not with you, of course."

"You know all about languages, but what do they matter to you? I know all about stars, but what do they matter to me?"

"Just a moment. Surely you're not naive enough to think that our Upper Chamber means more to you than the *Reichssicherheitshauptamt*?"

Max was silent. The conversation was confusing him even more. Five years before, he had followed the Eichmann trial in Jerusalem day by day: the man with the asymmetrical face in his glass cage, like a mechanical doll from the *Tales of Hoffman*; he had read a dozen of the stream of books that had appeared about Nazism at the time. Of course he had thought of his father during that time, and of his trial; but even the fact that there were still newspapers from 1946 around had not occurred to him. In some way or other he assumed that everything had disappeared into the past, and been ground up by time. In fact, he knew more about the Leopold and Loeb trial. But of course everything was still available!

He looked up. "Shall I tell you something? I want to see it tomorrow. It had to happen sometime. Of course they've got all those old newspapers at the Press Institute. I'd like you to come, too."

Onno thought for a moment. "Perhaps we could be a little more thorough. I imagine his file is probably at the National Institute for War Documentation. Suppose we go there."

"Is it open to the public, do you think?"

"Of course not. But you're the dreadful son of that dreadful father, aren't you? What's more, you're the son of your murdered mother. If they get awkward, I'll involve my dreadful brother, or if necessary my father himself, and then I'd like to see them say no. However, because they know all that, it's actually a foregone conclusion."

They said goodnight to Bruno, and Max saw Onno to his front door, where they arranged that Onno would pick him up the following morning at ten o'clock. Max would take the morning off. They decided it would be better not to ring the institute in advance for an appointment, because that might be a pretext for postponing the matter indefinitely.

On the way home Max felt his pulse for a moment—too fast, but not irregular. Tomorrow he was going to sort out his past. He didn't even have any photos of his parents. Everything had been lost when they had been arrested. He could still remember his mother clearly: a young, cheerful woman, in rooms, at the piano, in the street, in the park, with a Star of David sewn onto the left breast of all her clothes, with the word *Jew* on it in mocking pseudo-Hebrew letters. He remembered her laughing as she said, with a sort of pathetic triumph, "It isn't yellow at all, it's orange!" But he had no image of his father apart from one frozen scene.

On *Heiligabend*—which was unknown in the Netherlands, but which they usually celebrated in Central European style—he had been instructed to stay in his room until the Christmas tree had been decorated and the candles lit. Neither his father nor his mother were believers. The only Christian thing about such a heathen Germanic seasonal symbol as a decorated tree with lights, he had realized later, was the crude wooden cross that kept it upright—but that was precisely hidden by red crêpe paper, on which the presents were to be laid. Perhaps there was an argument, or some impatience or irritation. In any case, he thought he had been summoned. He went into the room, and there it etched itself into his memory: his father next to the Christmas tree, standing on a chair, with the glittering star for the top in his hand, and in his flashing blue eyes, looking down at Max from an immeasurable height, a look as cold as liquid air . . .

In his front doorway he groped in his pocket for the key and then remembered that he had given it to Ada. He went up two steps and lifted the half brick. The shiny key lay in the dark niche, like Ada upstairs in his bed.

II

The Trial

Ada had half woken up a few times, once when Max crept into bed beside her. And when the sun was already shining on the curtains, she became entangled in a complicated dream:

On the backseat of a car an old, emaciated man is lying in her arms, and she can feel his white stubbly beard against her cheek. She tries to push him away, but the problem is that the top button of his crumpled raincoat is a button of a murderer's coat and at the same time a button of her own. She eventually has to go into the dungeon that extends under the Saturnusplein; those who know about it can see it in the shape of the square. In a large, dark space full of staircases, drawbridges, vaults, railings, dangling cables, and chains, she is forced into a cage made of wooden slats, but the tribunal is already waiting for her. The presiding judge in the middle displays an oblong silver medallion, or perhaps it is a box with a jewel in it, and a little later a group of religious Jews dressed for prayer begin singing a lament. This signals the beginning of religious confusion. Suddenly she has a glass of champagne in her hand, and a priest in his habit giving a blessing thinks that it is part of the service; then she has to ascend a long, steep staircase, but for some reason she cannot climb the stairs. When she turns around, she sees an old woman in a Buddha pose gliding or floating diagonally through the space and telling the secrets of the past for the umpteenth time . . .

She was awakened by Max's hand stroking her belly. He had an erection but was still half asleep. The erection did not count—he would have had that without her. He groaned.

"I'll make coffee first," she said, and looked at her watch. "Hey, it's already nearly nine-thirty. Don't you have to go to Leiden?"

"I'm taking a morning off."

She pulled open the curtains and went naked into the small kitchen. The morning sun shone in over the trees. In the park below, a jogger had put his heel on the back of a bench and was trying to break himself in two. There was a smell of coffee and toasting bread, birdsong in the trees, further away the roar of the traffic. Everything was as it should be. In the bedroom Max had turned on the radio for the news; she heard him telephoning, probably to the observatory. Soon he would take her to Leiden and for a few days she would see him only at lunchtimes. Every time he disappeared around the corner in his car, she had the feeling that he had never been there, or would never be there again—but where was the source of that feeling of absence, in him or in her?

When she came into the room with breakfast, he was sitting cross-legged on the bed, which reminded her vaguely of something she had dreamed, but she could not remember what. Her eyes glided over his body as quickly as a breath of wind, making her aware that she was as naked as he was: but even naked he seemed better dressed than she would ever be. He had an athletic build, nowhere deformed by sport or any other violent activity into proportions designed to impress women but in fact were only impressive to men; his skin was as soft and velvety as a child's.

They sat cross-legged opposite each other on the bed, with the tray between them, spread marmalade, bit into toast, drank coffee, spooned eggs, and now and again, very naturally, he placed his hand on her vagina for a moment, as though it were part of the process of having breakfast. The erection he gradually got pleased her more than the previous one, although she was amazed yet again at the dimensions that things can assume in this world. While he told her about the gypsies, she gently grasped his cool scrotum, as though weighing it.

" 'Be embraced, you millions,' " she said, quoting Schiller's "Ode to Joy."

His eyes clouded a little, but he had obviously decided not to hurry. "They all surrounded me . . ." he said in a slightly intoxicated voice. "It was as though I was the focus of a concave mirror . . ."

He faltered. Each of them now had their hands in the other's crotch, and

Ada could feel that he could feel how wet she was getting. As he continued looking at her his back arched a little, as though he were in pain; she started smiling. He put the tray on the ground and slid on top of her, groaning and with his eyes rolling, his tongue and penis sinking deep inside her.

"Slowly," he gasped, "slowly . . ."

He was talking to himself, because she wanted nothing better. Their bodies moved slowly across the bed, *andante maestoso*. It seemed to her as though they were floating on the waves, slowly sinking beneath the surface, where the same movement dominated, but increasingly shut off from the outside world, from the air, the light—noiseless, a darker and darker blue, more and more violet . . .

The doorbell rang.

The net was raised. Max's movement stopped; he leaned on his elbows and looked at his watch.

"Let it ring," whispered Ada with her eyes closed.

"It's Onno. We arranged to meet."

He quickly disengaged himself from her. Her arms slid off him, and he went to the intercom in the hall. "Onno?" she heard him call out. "I'll be right down. One minute."

He hurried into the room and opened the wardrobe. When he saw her lying there, her legs still wide apart, he said, "Bring yourself off," and disappeared into the bathroom.

Ada froze. What had he said? She couldn't believe that he had said what she had heard. Had he really said that she should bring herself off? Had he said that? That she should bring herself off? Eyes wide with astonishment, she looked at the ceiling, unable to move. Was it conceivable that he had been so crude?

"Max . . ." she started to say, when he appeared in the room dressed—then he pressed a hurried kiss on her forehead and said, "I'll see you at lunchtime, and I'll tell you all about it then. 'Bye now."

A moment later she heard the quick drumming of his feet as he ran down the stairs, then the fainter drumming on the next staircase; on the last staircase she could no longer hear him, and then through the open window came the slamming of the front door.

Silence.

She sat on the edge of the bed in a daze. It had still not sunk in completely, but she knew this was the end. He could never make this up to her: it was though she had suddenly seen the face of Mr. Hyde on that of Dr. Jekyll. Bring yourself off. She didn't know what the two them were going to do, but couldn't it have waited a quarter of an hour? Couldn't he have sent Onno to the pub for a while? The haste wasn't because of any particular urgency, but because it was Onno at the door. He couldn't keep Onno waiting; perhaps he was in a panic that Onno might turn away from him for good. Nonsense, of course, but even that was comprehensible. It wasn't that she could not bear Onno being more important to him than she was in certain respects, but the brutal way that he had trampled on her feelings was intolerable. A slap in the face would have been less awful.

The bathroom was still warm and damp from his shower. Under the stream of water it seemed for a moment that it had been washed away, but when she got back in the room it was there again. Bring yourself off. As though orgasm were what mattered. He hadn't come, either. Suddenly angry, she began to get dressed, and then she saw him again appearing from nowhere on the steps leading from the bookshop. Did she love him? She wasn't sure, so perhaps she did not. Perhaps you knew for sure when you loved someone, but then she'd never loved anyone yet, and perhaps she would have to accept that she never would. All she knew for certain was that she loved music. And yet, perhaps she would have liked a child by him.

Occasionally she had toyed with the idea of stopping the pill and seeing what happened. The thought of a little Max, or Maxima, tottering around the room made her feel as weak as a sugar lump dissolving in a cup of hot tea: she would certainly have loved a child. But it would have jeopardized her musical career, so a child was out of the question. She also knew that he slept with other girls, of course—the signs of it in his apartment, the blond hairs, the lipstick-covered cigarette ends in the wastepaper basket did not escape her—but she didn't mind that much, because she knew that he had forgotten those women before he had even seen them. Now, though, something irrevocable had happened.

She looked around. It was over. She sat at his empty, cleared desk, and opened the drawers, in which he kept his "stationery shop," as he called it: paper of all sizes and styles, scores of notebooks, from minute notebooks to huge ledgers with reinforced corners, notepads of all conceivable kinds, including some with yellow and light-blue paper from the United States, blank, lined, and squared index cards in carefully arranged pyramids, enough for a whole lifetime.

"As far as paper is concerned," he had once said, "I can face the Third World War with confidence."

She took out a simple sheet of typewriter paper and laid it on the desk. From the pen rack she took a yellow pencil with an eraser on the top and, lost in thought, stared at the exhibit-like row of instruments on the edge of his desk: the magnet, the prism, the hourglass, the pocket mirror, the ruler, the magnifying glass, the compass, the tuning fork . . .

The staff of the National Institute for War Documentation looked surprised when they suddenly found themselves confronted with a Quist and a Delius. And yet it was no stranger than the fact that their own neighbor on the canal should be the German Goethe Institute. In any case it seemed to them to be a matter for the director himself. Via oak staircases and marble corridors marred by shelves of files, Max and Onno were conducted to his quiet room at the back, with a view of the geometrically constructed seventeenth-century garden.

He was writing on a notepad and looked up. They knew his face; a few years before he had made a series of television programs on the German occupation. Now he had been commissioned to make a record of the period day by day, which would take up twenty thick volumes. They could see from his melancholy face that there was nothing he did not know about the war, which he himself had spent in London; he had embarked on this process of mourning, which was to take three times as long as the war, for the sake of his twin brother, who had not been able to escape to England and had been gassed. In a few brief sentences Max told him his own history, which was different.

"What it comes down to," he concluded, "is that my father was shot because he hounded my mother to her death."

"I know, Mr. Delius, I know."

"But he's still my father. I'd like to look at his file."

The director nodded. "And why do you want to do that now?"

Should he tell him about the gypsies? But of course that wasn't the reason. "Perhaps because the time has come."

"Well," said the director, "I can't see what objection there could be. After all, we live in a time of openness and democratization, if I understand it correctly. And you, Mr. Quist—what is your role in this? May I by the way congratulate you on your honorary doctorate? In fact, we're all in the same line, aren't we?"

For a moment Onno was at a loss for words. "So you never forget anything."

"That's why one is a historian."

"I'm here solely as a friend."

"That's enough for me," said the director, and picked up the telephone. "Adriaan? I have Mr. Delius and Mr. Quist with me. What?—yes, that's right. It's about the Wolfgang Delius case. Can you give them a little of your time and help them out? I'm sending them to you."

Max had not mentioned his father's Christian name; it shocked him to hear it coming so naturally from the director's mouth. It was explained to them where they had to go, and as they took their leave, the director said to Onno: "My regards to your father."

When the door closed, Onno said softly. "Now he'll be calling again, and giving instructions."

"What kind of instructions?"

"On what we mustn't see."

"What can be worse than what we already know?"

"Nothing, but of course other reputations are at stake. Not everyone was shot."

From the glances that met them in the corridors, it was clear that the news of their presence had already spread through the building. The official whom the director had called Adriaan was putting the phone down when they came in: a thick-set, slightly stooping man in his fifties, with a round face and a penetrating gaze, who introduced himself as Oud. Without further ceremony he asked them to sit down, and then went to the basement to fetch the documents.

They were sitting next to each other at a long table with well-ordered piles of papers. Onno surveyed the cupboards full of files, with code numbers, which went up to the plastered ceiling, and remarked that some people would be glad to put a match to them; but Max was silent. He realized that he was approaching the end of something. The papers would shortly be put on the table for the last time, but now that he was here, he did not want to know everything at all—precisely how it had happened, how it was reconstructed during the trial, what the witnesses said, and what other crimes his father might have committed; he no longer needed to read the verdict. What had happened had happened. The only thing he wanted to see was something concrete, something direct, which showed that his father had existed—perhaps just a photograph.

Oud came in with six thick files clasped to his chest, followed by a young man with an even higher pile of dusty archive files and boxes under his chin. After it had been laid out in front of them, Oud sat down behind it like a market trader, made a demonstrative gesture, and said: "How can I help you?"

There it was, like dirty scum in an empty bathtub.

SPECIAL COURT   THE HAGUE

Max read on a cover. He would have preferred to get up now and leave; he only stayed in his chair because Onno was there. The latter in turn had decided to outdo everyone and take matters in hand—but the amount of material paralyzed him; he was also a little frightened of the man sitting behind it, with his threatening, St. Christopher–like initials alpha and omega.

When he saw Max hesitating, Oud said: "I know my way around this file. I was involved in the preliminary investigation at the time. Do you want to see the documents where you yourself are mentioned?"

Max shivered. "So you knew him." He wanted to say "my father," but could not bring himself to.

"Knew . . . I don't think anyone ever knew him. But I met him a few times, yes."

"What did he say about me?"

"Himself? He never said anything—not about you or anything else. He didn't open his mouth during the whole of his detention, or during the hearings. There was no question of interrogating him."

"But then how was he . . ."

Max did not have to finish his question. Oud nodded, opened a file, undid the clip, and a little while later placed his flat hand on a typed letter: gray lines with narrow spacing, a signature that was half visible under his wrist.

"In this your father asks a certain General von Schumann of the Wehrmacht, who was later killed at Stalingrad, whether he can take steps to rid him once and for all of his young wife. The general was a personal friend of his, because he addresses him as *Du*. In fact, he expressly calls it a favor to a friend."

Max turned away. He must not even look at that. He hoped Oud would not ask him if he wanted to read the letter, so that he would have to hold it in both hands. Out of the corner of his eye he saw him leafing through.

"Here is the letter from Schumann to Rauter, the *Höhere SS-und Polizeiführer* in The Hague, also using *Du*. They were all good pals," said Oud, and went on looking. "He was also a witness at your father's trial— he himself was not executed until three years later. Yes, here we have his instructions for the *Sicherheitsdienst* in Amsterdam, complete with address and everything, and this is the list of the Amsterdam SD on that day, with a little *v* in front of your mother's name, indicating that it had been dealt with. With your grandparents, who were not protected by your existence, he took a much more direct route. Shall I look that up as well?"

Max swallowed and shook his head.

"But what's in all those other files?" asked Onno.

"Those concern other people," said Oud impassively, "and, apart from that, mainly robbery and plunder."

There was a silence. Max again saw the piano being taken out of the house, the pile of clothes in his mother's bedroom. In order to help him through the moment, Onno asked whether there was an explanation for Delius's consistent silence.

"Was it from a feeling of guilt? Because he had fatally incriminated himself in that letter? It appears that Ezra Pound has stopped speaking these days for a similar reason."

"According to the public prosecutor," said Oud, "it was only a last resort to escape the burden of proof. But one day something strange was found in his cell." He looked in one of the archive boxes and pulled out a thick yellow official envelope. "This," he said, taking out a cigarette packet and giving it to Max.

It was a Sweet Caporal packet, yellowed and empty. In astonishment Max took it and turned it over. On the back something was written in green ink.

" 'Only I exist,' " he read in German. " 'What does not exist cannot die.' "

"That's the same tune as Wittgenstein," said Onno. "Whereof one cannot speak, one must be silent. Another frustrated Austrian."

Max did not hear. He had never seen his father's handwriting. It was un-Dutch—sharper, more angular. He had held this same packet in his hand, there in his cell in Scheveningen, and he had written this on it, perhaps on his knee, sitting on the edge of his bed.

But it wasn't Wittgenstein, said Oud, it was Delius: he had certainly never heard of Wittgenstein, his contemporary, who was only now becoming fashionable. In a psychiatric report, that note was used as evidence of diminished responsibility: he was under the illusion that only he himself actually existed and that everything else was illusion, projection; from that point of view he could not be guilty of murder, because nobody else was alive, only he himself could die. Even his judges and his interrogators did not exist. Even his executioner, paradoxically, did not exist.

Such a patient should therefore be exempted from prosecution and detained at the government's pleasure. However, the prosecutor argued in turn that it was only the cunning maneuver of an intelligent criminal in order to escape his just punishment. Giltay Veth, on the other hand, the defense counsel Wolfgang had been assigned, who had not been able to get a word out of him, had gone into it further. He argued that Delius's cell contained the infamous book of Max Stirner, a German philosopher from the first half of the previous century, the advocate of an extreme, amoral egoism, whose *Ego* was a precursor of Nietzsche's *Übermensch*. After Hitler's downfall, Delius had obviously gone a step further and arrived at an authentic, metaphysical solipsism. Giltay Veth had subsequently sought the advice of two distinguished foreign philosophers: Russell from Cambridge and Heidegger from Freiburg im Breisgau.

"Heidegger?" said Onno in surprise. "Have you got it there?"

Oud had opened another file and put his finger on a postcard.

"Here Russell writes: 'Solipsism, although not my cup of tea, is a perfectly legitimate philosophical position. Not taking it seriously would imply a defamation of philosophy as such. In my opinion, therefore, your client should be executed without hesitation.' As you can imagine, Giltay Veth never submitted this; it has obviously found its way among these papers by accident. He only produced Heidegger's German letter. Here it is. 'The expression solipsism derives from *solus ipse:* "I alone." The germ of this kind of thinking, which turns its back on being, is to be found not in Classical antiquity, but may be linked to Descartes. The latter's universal skepticism, which called everything into doubt, apart from the self, led to the formula familiar to every schoolboy: *cogito ergo sum*. Solipsism arises when *cogito ergo sum* is sharpened to *ergo solus ergo sum*. However, this is a logical extension of Cartesianism. Dismissing it implies a rejection of the whole of post-Cartesian philosophy. Hence a death sentence passed against your client would basically imply a condemnation of the whole of philosophy.' "

All very well, but according to the public prosecutor, said Oud, Heidegger was himself a philosophical delinquent, a Nazi of the first order, who was indirectly only trying to exonerate himself, because he also felt under threat. In their judgment, the judges finally took the view that someone who could hound his wife and parents-in-law to their deaths was by definition not normal, that no murderer was normal, but that this could not mean that murderers could appeal to their deed as a mitigating circumstance, because that would mean the end of jurisprudence, which would herald the return to barbarity of human civilization—in brief, the kind of society that had just been prevented at the cost of fifty-five million dead.

"Quite right." Onno nodded.

Here and there in the corners of the cigarette packet there were still some blackened remnants of tobacco. Max closed it and a little later watched it disappear into the envelope.

"Have you got a photo of my father, perhaps?"

Oud raised his eyebrows. "I ought to have," he said with doubt in his voice, and began looking. "In any case, in his passport . . ."

"Do you know where your father's grave is?" asked Onno with feigned nonchalance.

"No," said Max, and looked at Oud.

The latter opened his eyes for a moment and made a brief apologetic gesture. Finally he found only a blurred newspaper photograph of the court, taken from a distance. Max saw an unrecognizable figure, flanked by a gendarme with a white lanyard. Perhaps the same one who had taken him out of school four years earlier.

Onno had an appointment with a couple of politicians, and Max went straight home. He felt tired and needed to talk to Ada. She knew nothing about any of this; she had been born in the year that his father had been shot. Of course, hearing the name Delius may have awakened a memory in her parents, since the name was rare in the Netherlands, but it was a long time ago, and there had been lots of trials in those days, most of which were more spectacular than his father's. She had to know now, partly because he had not behaved very elegantly that morning.

The moment he entered the room, he sensed that something was wrong. Her cello, which was always by the grand piano, had gone. On his desk lay her letter:

Dear Max,

> *When you get home, I shall have gone. Perhaps you won't understand immediately, but if you think a little, you'll be able to work it out. I've had a wonderful time with you, for which I'm grateful to you and which I will never forget. You meant a lot to me and perhaps I meant a little to you too. If we meet again, I hope that it will be as good friends.*

> *Yours ever,*
> *Ada*

He slowly put the sheet of paper down. The unexpected tone of farewell, the finality of the sentences, sank deep into him, but at the same time he knew that he would not do anything to change it. So that was it; the episode was over. He sat down and pulled open the bottom drawer of his desk, in order to do what he had planned to do in her presence. All he had to do was take out what he needed, without looking: the order he created around himself gave him an extra year of life, which other people wasted in looking.

He placed an old-fashioned fountain pen and a glasses case in front of him. The fountain pen was thick, and made of flame-patterned, dark-blue ebonite, which had become matt and lifeless; the copper clip and the decorations were dull and rusty. He unscrewed it carefully and looked at the gold nib, which was blackened with ancient ink. He turned on the desk lamp and studied the pen carefully with his magnifying glass, and he saw what he had hoped for: among the traces of ink there was a faint deep-green glow, like algae in a stagnant pond. He put the top back on; the thread had gone, but still he felt a very slight resistance at the end.

The glasses case was made of cheap beige papier-mâché. He opened it and took out the glasses. The frames were made of light, transparent celluloid; the greasy, dirty lenses had been ground positively. He was going to try them on for a moment, but when he opened them, everything crumbled into pulverized fragments. The lenses fell out, and suddenly there was nothing but a little heap of rubbish on Ada's letter. He winced. Grabbing the wastepaper basket with his left hand, he swept everything into it with his right forearm.

12

The Triangle

Max could have asked Oud, because it was bound to be in the trial papers, but he did not want to set foot in that haunted house again. At the Ministry of Justice he discovered with some difficulty that his paternal grandparents had been married in Prague and that his father, with calendary discipline, had been born in 1892, in Bielitz, Austria-Hungary, on the same day that he died—June 21. Obviously, no one had remembered that it was his birthday when he was put against the wall. He had attended primary school in Kattowitz, and later the high school in Krakau, before going to Vienna University at the age of nineteen.

Since his visit to the National Institute for War Documentation, Max had been pondering a suggestion of Onno's that this summer he should not spend his vacation at some stupid beach in France but in his father's native region—where he might finally be able to put it all into context. On the other hand, as far as the past was concerned, there would be as a massive silence surrounding such matters in those towns as there was in Brussels, where his mother had been born. However, when he consulted his atlas at home, he made a shocking discovery. The three place names from his father's youth, now situated in southern Poland, near the Czech border—Bielsko, Katowice, and Krakow—formed a pure isosceles triangle, which pointed due east like an arrowhead, while in the middle, precisely at the intersection, lay Oświęcim: Auschwitz.

He went by train—like his mother. She had probably taken a more southerly route, via Leipzig and Dresden; his transit visa for the GDR directed him first to West Berlin, Bahnhof Zoo, where he arrived early in the morning and deposited his suitcase at the left-luggage office. He strolled a little along the Kurfürstendamm in the morning sunshine, bought a Baedeker at a kiosk, and took a taxi to the ruined Reichstag, where they were hard at work on restoration. The building was bareheaded: the great central dome—Bismarck's helmet—had disappeared; but when he turned around, at the other end of the huge expanse he saw the new conference center, which had the exact shape of Hitler's cap. So that had been balanced out, too. He devoted a moment's thought to Van der Lubbe, who had celebrated their conception here with a bonfire, and walked through the park that skirted the Wall, silently screaming its multicolored messages. At the chaos of sausage stands, souvenir stalls, and parked buses, where once the Potsdamerplatz had been, he climbed onto a wooden platform and looked between the photographing and jostling tourists at the endless empty wastes on the other side, in which the octagonal form of the Leipziger Platz lay like the hoofprint of a huge monster. A few hundred yards further on, one could see the spot where the monster had taken his own life, as the last of many.

In the afternoon he collected his suitcase from left luggage and took the S-Bahn to East Berlin. He already felt as if he had been away from home for weeks. At Bahnhof Friedrichstrasse he was sent from one window to the next for an hour and a half by needling Vopos with forms and still more forms. Passport, visa, all his money on the table, take off those sunglasses at once! However, he realized that he was not just going from one half of the city to the other, not only from one country to another, but from one world to another. He looked at the fenced-off Brandenburg Gate and walked along Unter den Linden, where there was a refreshing calm. The difference between West and East Berlin was like that between the Amsterdam of 1967 and that of 1947. Everywhere on the unpainted housefronts there was nothing but ideological advertising slogans on red banners: ARTISTS AND CULTURAL WORKERS, INSPIRE THE WORKFORCE WITH YOUR ART TO ENSURE THE TRIUMPH OF SOCIALISM. Passers-by cast glances at his French summer suit, Italian shoes, American shirt, and English tie; now and again someone spoke to him, wanting to change marks at a rate of four to one.

The end of the avenue, opposite the recessed square where the book burning had taken place in 1933, he went into the Neue Wache: a small neoclassical building with a columned portico, where two motionless soldiers were resisting the giggling attentions of a group of curious onlookers. Inside, in a crystal cube, an eternal flame burned above the urns of the unknown soldier and the unknown resistance fighter. DEN OPFERN DES FASCHISMUS UND MILITARISMUS, it said in gold letters on the side wall, but he was given no time to meditate; the hall was gently cleared, and when he came outside, the relief guard was approaching along Unter den Linden with martial music and squeaking boots. The orders, the goose step, bodies that seemed to be joined together, the awesome Prussian precision with which fifty rifle butts slammed onto the pavement like a single butt, the whole unfathomable ceremonial elicited mainly giggling from the Berliners—and the only one who felt his eyes growing moist was himself, because though it was militaristic, it was nevertheless intended for the victims of fascism.

Guidebook in hand, he wandered on through the city and felt as if he were wading knee-deep through history. Finally, in the deserted Otto-Grotewohlstrasse, once the Wilhelmstrasse, he stared for minutes at a sunny lawn where the Reichskanzlei had stood. A swelling tumor indicated where the entrance to the bunker had been; below, deep in the ground, the monster had finally fired his first shot since the First World War: into his mouth. Max nodded in approval. Having a sweet tooth has its uses, he thought.

To his delight, the night train to Katowice was still pulled by a hissing and shuddering locomotive with an archaic whistle. They were kept waiting for hours at the Polish border. A succession of new officials in different uniforms walked down the corridor and slid open the compartment doors; the train moved backward, forward, bumped into other carriages, left the station, came back into the station, while outside one could see watchtowers, searchlights, jeeps full of soldiers, a boot sticking halfway out of a car. He felt utterly content. Finally, everything was different. In the sparse light he tried to read an article by some English colleagues on the discovery of a new kind of radio source, a "pulsar"; they had been rash enough to admit that they had even considered the possibility of an extraterrestrial civilization. But he could not concentrate on the technical details. Up to now he had been facing the engine; now he entered Poland with his back to it, so that he had the feeling of returning home. The guard kept returning with blacker and blacker exchange rates for the zloty, but he thought it advisable not to accept; the peasant woman on the seat opposite, with a scarf around a snorting piglet in a basket on her lap, seemed to hear nothing. Near Gliwice everyone began getting up and collecting their things—Max knew that this was the former Gleiwitz, on the former German-Polish border, where Hitler had staged an "incident" as a pretext for invading Poland the following day. This was where it had all begun.

He booked into a run-down family hotel in the center of Krakow. Had Lysenko been right after all? Were even experiences hereditary? It felt like coming home. When he opened his balcony doors overlooking the quiet, overgrown courtyard, he was surrounded by a strange, indescribably familiar smell of brown coal, linked to a temperature which must be exactly the same as that of his skin: it was as though his body were expanding as far as the walls of the surrounding buildings. Afterward, in the town, he tried to take in the thought that his father had also walked around here, with a stiff leather satchel on his back; but it would not come into focus. The high school looked like all high schools, with Ionic columns and a pediment over the entrance. In a café, where he was given a glass of water with his coffee, he looked in the telephone book to see if there was still a Delius living in the town, a male or female cousin perhaps; but of course all the German-speakers had left for the rump of Austria immediately after the First World War. Perhaps there were still Deliuses in Prague, Vienna, or Budapest, where he was planning to go next. He spent the rest of the day as a tourist— admired the cathedral, stood at the tombs of Polish kings, walked in woollen overshoes across the parquet floors of hundreds of pointless rooms in Wawel Castle.

The following morning at the crack of dawn, he took the local train back along the north side of the triangle to Katowice. Flat fields, bleak and deserted under an overcast sky, impoverished villages, children waving at the train from the courtyards of wooden farmhouses, gloomy woods, gradually changing into a black industrial landscape of mines and factories and then an endless railway yard full of goods trains. He wandered aimlessly through the silent streets for a couple of hours, inhaling the heavy, damp smell of coal and sulfur, and looked at the woman street sweepers.

Would his own child ever walk through Amsterdam and Leiden like this? He found himself thinking immediately of Ada. Did this mean that he should go back to her? Since she had left, he had had no further contact with her, had in fact half forgotten her. Imagine her ringing him up to announce that she was pregnant with his child. What would he do? But that was impossible; the pill took care of that. He put these thoughts aside and went back to the station. The train took him along the base of the triangle to Bielsko-Biala, thirty miles farther south. But in that town, too, where his grandmother had screamed at his father's birth, he heard no echo. The feeling of familiarity, which had originally inspired him, had receded. Perhaps Lysenko had not been entirely right. An hour later he traveled back along the southern side of the triangle to Krakow, looked at the crows in the fields, at the horses and horsecarts on the country roads, and wondered whether he ought to have listened to Onno.

On the third day he again took the train to Katowice; he had to change in Trzebinia and with his heart pounding traveled into the triangle to Oświęcim, at the intersection of the bisecting angles. Here too, under a misty white sky, there were extensive railway yards with shunting trains, train drivers leaning out of their shuddering locomotives and looking back along the endless rows of closed cattle trucks. A taxi took him to the camp entrance in less than five minutes.

Rust-brown buildings, looming between the trees. The tall, square chimney of the crematorium. ARBEIT MACHT FREI. He looked grimly at the wrought-iron slogan above the gate; was this National Socialist cynicism, as he had always supposed, or had it already been there when this was an Austro-Hungarian cavalry barracks, situated on the former border of the Habsburg empire and that of the Hohenzollerns? Maybe his father had been in the garrison stationed here.

There was a clammy, windless heat. At a stall he ate a spicy sausage on a slice of black bread, bought some brochures from another stall, and went in. He felt as if in some way he was trying to catch up with himself—as if his body were already walking over the raked gravel but he himself were still not here, as if it would take decades for him to arrive. Watchtowers. Double lines of bent concrete posts with barbed wire strung between insulators. Skulls and crossbones. *Halt! Stoj!* It was smaller than he had expected, a silent village of thirty-three brick buildings, in three rows of eleven, where tens of thousands of people had been beaten to death, shot, given fatal injections, and tortured, where there had been experiments with gas on wounded Russian prisoners of war and patients from surrounding hospitals; but it was still not the actual place.

Stones, moldy cellars, dark caves, iron rings on walls, chains, rusty operating tables. A couple of blocks had been turned into a museum. He looked at an infernal terrarium, twenty yards long and three feet deep, filled with women's hair, which had gone a uniform dull-gray color. Was his mother's hair in there? Another terrarium contained discarded children's shoes, with spectacles, toothbrushes, artificial limbs. There it was. Was the truth perhaps, he wondered, that it ultimately made no difference? Was everything possible and could anything be done, since it would one day irrevocably be cast aside? Even in heaven eternal bliss would be possible only by the grace of a criminal loss of memory. Should the blessed not be punished with hell for this? Everything had been wrecked for all eternity—not only here, but by thousands of earlier and later occasions, which no one remembered. Heaven was impossible; only hell might perhaps exist. Anyone who believed in God, he thought, looking at the huge display case full of toys, should be executed—put up against the black tarred wall of execution that he had seen next to Block II.

He could feel that he was working himself into a state. At the stall outside the camp he drank a glass of lukewarm mineral water, leafed through the brochures, peered at the figures and diagrams, and set out toward a hamlet a few miles further on, where the extermination camp Auschwitz II was situated. He could have rung for a taxi, but because countless thousands had been driven to their deaths along this road, he felt that he had to walk, like a Christian taking the Via Dolorosa. The deserted narrow road stretched away through the fields of stubble with occasional birchwoods, behind which loomed the towers of mine shafts and factory chimneys. The day was muggy; sweating and stooping slightly, he looked at the cobblestones over which he was walking, while around him not only the landscape, but gradually everything that tied him down—Amsterdam, Onno, his girlfriends, his colleagues, and also his work, the observatory, the absurd depths of the universe—sank into oblivion. All that remained was himself, walking at that moment over the cobbles between Oświęcim and Brzezinka, in the center of his diabolical triangle. Without thinking about anything in particular he became increasingly filled with the sense that he was there, that he existed, here and now, that he, here and now, was who he was. Why? Was he perhaps that question, that secret itself? Was the question the answer and the answer the question?

He saw his shoes advancing in turn, and suddenly he was aware of the rotation of the earth; he had to keep walking to remain in the same place, but after a while the rotation began gradually to increase, so that he had to walk faster to compensate for it, and a little later he had the feeling that he was about to fall forward.

He stopped dizzily and looked up. He was standing at a crossroads with a sandy country road full of cart ruts. A few hundred yards farther on there was a bridge over a railway line—and less than a mile beyond it, a low and large expanse in the misty sunshine, lay the entrance building of Auschwitz-Birkenau: *anus mundi*.

He stared at it numbly. There it was. With its small tower above the gate it was like a monstrous bird of prey, which had landed there with outspread wings. And above it the sky had glowed day and night with the burning men, women, and children; all around there must still be traces of their ash in the fields. There was no traffic; the silence was filled only with the twittering of birds and whistling locomotives in the distance. There was a smell of warm grass, mixed with an indefinable chemical smell. Motionless in its relentless symmetry, the building looked at him. As he began to walk toward it, he saw a small statue of the Virgin on the other side of the crossroads, mounted in a kind of bird box. The Madonna had a few withered branches in her hands and her eyes were turned upward with the look that he had seen so often—when he sat up in bed—on the pillow beneath him. At the same instant he was overwhelmed by rage. Without a second thought and without even looking around, he ran toward it, grabbed the wooden statue off its pedestal, took it by the head, and flung it as far as he could into the bushes.

No longer taking his eyes off the camp, he walked on over the railway bridge with heart pounding and saw the camp coming closer with every step: a black hole, from which nothing could escape. This was the altar, the real powerhouse of fascism. Was there a place on earth where as much good had been done as evil had been done here? If hell had this branch on earth, where was heaven's? There was no such place, because only hell existed, not heaven. This place was the exact opposite of paradise, even if there was no paradise. Only now did he realize that there were two entrances in the reddish brick building: one in the center, with the single-track railway running through it, and one on the left for other traffic. For hundreds of yards to left and right there were double rows of concrete posts with electrified barbed wire, twelve feet high, with watchtowers at short intervals. He was about to walk in through the center gate, shaped like the opening of a crematorium oven, but it was as if an invisible wall suddenly descended with a crash: he could no longer enter. The accursed ground, where millions had been murdered, had become sacred, and he could not set foot on it.

On the threshold he looked at the churned-up expanse of rubble and weeds. It was the mess of a hastily abandoned bedroom, with an unmade bed, all the drawers and cupboards open and clothes all over the floor. There was no one there. Inside, the rails branched once and then again; in the long spaces in between, the selections had taken place between those who were to die immediately and those not until later. To the left of the *Lagerstrasse* were rows of wooden barracks, to the right only the chimneys. In the distance, at the end of the tracks, he could see the ruins of the blown-up crematoria and gas chambers to the left and right; the back of the oblong sacrificial dish was too far away to see distinctly. He squatted down and put his right hand on the rusty rails. She had ridden in over these. It was as though the motionless silence penetrated him—he did not enter the camp, the camp entered him. The butchers and their victims had all gone—his father as well as his mother: what else was he but the personification of the camp as a whole?

He decided to walk slowly around the four and a half million-square yards. There was a dead person for every square yard of the way.

13

Clearing Up

At the same time as Max was making his five-mile procession in Poland, Ada overcame her indecision and phoned Onno to ask where his friend had gone. Of course Max had treated her shabbily, but on the other hand that silly bosom friendship could not be overlooked; perhaps there had been something really important on the agenda that morning—though he might have mentioned it. In any case he was still in her thoughts, and perhaps she had reacted a little drastically.

Onno sounded surprised, but could not help her. "Somewhere in Poland, or Czechoslovakia or Hungary. You know what he's like. Awful."

What he was like? The meaning of the remark escaped her. "When is he coming back?"

"In about three weeks, I think."

"Did he talk about me?"

"I had the impression that he was sorry things went wrong between you, and so am I for that matter. You were a positive influence on the idiot. But of course that was the purifying effect of music. How is your duo going?"

"It doesn't really exist anymore. Bruno couldn't see the point. I've just auditioned for the Concertgebouw Orchestra."

"And?"

"I'm waiting to hear."

"Why so suddenly?"

"I need to start earning money. I want to leave home. And what about you? Aren't you going on vacation?"

"Me? On vacation? Did you really think I indulge in such petit bourgeois pleasures? Shame on you! You're not on vacation either, are you?"

"Because I can't afford it."

"Where are you calling from?"

"From the Concertgebouw."

"Okay. Let's have a coffee at Keyzer's, on the corner. I'll be right there, and then I'll subject that bohemian horse thief of yours to the searing light of my analysis."

From her table at the window she watched him approach from the Museumplein and cross the road. Max would have seen her at once, probably before she saw him, but Onno looked down at the cobblestones in complete self-absorption, or at least with his thoughts somewhere totally different from where he was. His large, ungainly figure inspired a vague physical distaste in her, but at the same time she found it touching. She could scarcely imagine a greater contrast than that between Max and Onno: Max, whom nothing escaped, who was everywhere at once, and Onno, who always focused on a single point and for whom the rest of the world did not exist.

He seemed pleased to see her. For the first time she was even given a clumsy peck on the cheek.

"What were you so deep in thought about?"

"Do you really want to know?"

"If it's not a secret . . ."

"It's terribly secret, but I'll tell you anyway. About a magic square." He took a paper from the reading table, sat down opposite her and wrote in the margin:

$$
\begin{array}{ccc}
m & a & x \\
a & d & a \\
x & a & m
\end{array}
$$

"Have a good look at that crucifixion. I was wondering what those diagonals *xdx* and *mdm* mean, but I haven't worked it out yet. *Mdm* is probably an abbreviation of 'madman,' but what does *xdx* stand for? Perhaps something from differential calculus, but Max is better at that than I am. So, how are things? The last time we saw each other was that idiotic evening when you played."

"This is the first time I've been back in Amsterdam."

"What happened between you to make you split up so suddenly? It seemed so idyllic."

"Didn't he tell you?" asked Ada in amazement.

"I didn't ask him."

Obviously, thought Ada, they did not tell each other everything, as Max had maintained. "Then I'd prefer not to say."

Onno nodded and stirred his coffee. "So here we are. Max is in search of his roots, and we're sitting here like the two orphans."

"What kind of roots has he got there, then?"

Onno looked at her in disbelief. "Has he never talked about it?"

"He never talked much."

Onno debated with himself whether it was right for him to tell her. It wasn't as though Max wanted to keep his story a secret, and because he believed that Ada had the right to know, he told her the facts—from the war up to their visit to the National Institute for War Documentation.

When Ada heard about the visit, the penny suddenly dropped. Bring yourself off. At the same time she remained convinced that he wouldn't have reacted like that if anyone else had called to collect him to go to the Institute; it was because it was Onno who rang the bell—Onno, who might go away if he didn't open up immediately, and never, ever come back. But suddenly she understood that too: his parents had once left and never come back. She drank her coffee in silence. Max had suddenly become someone else—like when she opened the curtains in the morning and found that the familiar view had been covered in snow during the night: everything was the same, and everything was different.

To her own surprise, she had missed him there in her quiet back room in Leiden, not physically, because that was still not very important to her, but simply his presence. Except that the presence now turned out to be at the same time an absence; in all those weeks he had not considered her worthy to be told who he really was. Or was it unreasonable to pass judgment on someone who had experienced things she could not even imagine? Just suppose her own father had had her mother murdered and then himself been shot . . . inconceivable. There was only a thirteen-year age gap between Max and her, but for her the whole war, which her parents were always talking about—and to which she owed her existence—was an event from a dim past. What it finally came down to was that she was superfluous to Max. She had had that feeling the whole time, and now she knew where it came from.

She had made the right decision in leaving him, though it may have been for the wrong reason. He was locked up in himself, and he had not been prepared to give her the key, which Onno turned out to have in his pocket.

"Do you want to go back to him?" asked Onno.

"That's not possible now. Not because you've told me about this, but because he didn't tell me." She could see that Onno felt uncomfortable and was wondering whether he had done the wrong thing. "And what about you?" she asked, in order to help him. "How are you? Are you making headway with your deciphering?"

"Don't talk to me about it. Every morning when I wake up, my bankrupt existence stares out at me hollow-eyed."

"Aren't you exaggerating a bit?"

"A bit? Will you stop insulting me! I exaggerate terribly!"

"So in fact you're doing fine?"

A crooked smile crossed his face. "No, Ada, but I'm getting by."

It touched her that he should mention her name. Had Max ever used her name when he talked to her? Using someone's name during a conversation was like a casual caress, like stroking their hair—had she herself ever called Max by his name?

Onno told her that until he could get a handle on the Phaistos disc, he had decided to pass the time by changing the Netherlands. The time was ripe, and there wouldn't be another opportunity for a long time. That was why he had recently joined the Social Democratic party—not a bunch of heaven-and-earth-movers, admittedly, a rather embarrassing party actually, but ultimately the only one with a chance of real power with which one could just about associate oneself as a civilized human being. First of all, the party itself would have to be changed; he was part of the New Left, a small but select group of mutineers, journalists, and suchlike dubious figures, who were going to break the hegemony of the ossified Social Democratic elite, all those slavish followers of America with their hatred of Communists and their perverse love of Roman Catholics. At the same time, certain sinister student leaders must be prevented from seizing power; the old guard were no longer capable of doing that. In short, at present he spent most of his time in meetings.

"If you ask me, you're doing it to get at your brothers. What does your father make of it?"

"There you are again," laughed Onno. "Never tell a woman anything, because she'll misuse it in order to understand you. Deep down I'm sure that he thinks it's marvelous that there should be a Quist involved with the Reds, but he'd rather bite his tongue off than admit it. And the Socialists like having a Quist in their midst, too. I bear it all with the serene dignity that is so characteristic of me. In politics you must use the weapons you have, just as in love. All within the bounds of decency, of course."

"So you see less of Max than you used to."

"Yes," he said. "I see a bit less of Max than I used to." He lit up a cigarette and said, "I don't think I can explain it to you, because I don't really understand it myself, but to my dying day I shall be grateful to him for the fact that he exists."

"The same goes for him, as far as you're concerned. I know that." She looked at him for a moment. "But why are you suddenly making such a solemn declaration?"

"From saturnine melancholy."

"Has something unpleasant happened between you?"

"No, not at all. It's just something to do with time. We've known each other for six months now, and in the last few weeks I find myself being constantly reminded of a saying of Hegel's when I think of those first months: 'What a splendid sunrise it was.' Hegel wrote that as an old reactionary about the French Revolution, which had inspired him as a young man—at a time when everyone talked of nothing but the horrors of the Jacobin terror. But two months ago that saying never occurred to me, and that it should happen now, with that ominous past tense, is obviously a sign that something is changing. I see less of him because of my political activities, but it may also be partly the other way around, if you understand what I mean. Anyway, it's the same old story, nothing special, action is followed by reflection, a love affair by marriage. We shall always stay good friends—even though the bastard stole my girlfriend."

"Stole your girlfriend?" repeated Ada, more shocked than surprised. "And you said nothing unpleasant had happened. When was that, then?"

Onno laughed and said that it was always better not to take him too literally. He told her with amusement about his relationship with Helga, which Max had put an end to by pretending to be a playmate. In fact it had been high drama, of course. It was like the play in *Hamlet*, he said, the "play within the play," in which the king is confronted with his crime, the difference being that in Shakespeare it is deliberately staged by a cunning stepson, whereas Max had done it in his playful innocence.

"And who clears your room up now?"

"No one," said Onno with a comically strangled voice and screwing up his face, as though about to burst into sobs. "No one. I'm alone in the world."

"Poor boy," said Ada with a little laugh. "Shall I give your room a cleaning, then?"

"Yes, miss," said Onno, nodding in a way that used to be described in children's books as "eagerly." "Yes please, miss."

"Shall we go, then?"

He gave her a searching look. "Are you still joking?"

"Not at all. I'd like to see the kind of place you live in. I've heard so much about you . . ."

"Max has never seen how I live, or, rather, do not live."

"I'm not Max."

They looked at each other. Everything was suddenly changing—like a tree blown over by the wind, pulled out of the earth roots and all, teeming with insects. No, she wasn't Max, and he wasn't Max either—and at the same time she was Max, and so was he.

While Max completed his rectangular path of mourning around the megascaffold in Poland, Ada was amazed about what she was suddenly doing, and Onno about what he was allowing to happen. He lugged her cello across the Museumplein and said that he now finally understood why Max had broken it off. They walked to the Kerkstraat through the Rijksmuseum arch. He went down the four steps to the basement, opened the door of the former tradesman's entrance, and let her in.

"This is quite impossible," he said as he led the way over the cracked marble slabs of the dark corridor. One of the walls was almost hidden by the pile of red and green paraffin cans.

"Why? Aren't you allowed female visitors by your landlady?"

"My landlady is an unbelievable trollop herself. I always have to lock the door at night."

"You're acting as if I'd asked you to go to bed with me."

"Haven't you?"

"Perhaps," said Ada, to her own surprise.

Onno stopped and turned his eyes heavenward.

"What further witness is needed? This is the final proof of the unfathomable immorality of womankind! Even the miracle of music is obviously powerless to help."

Ada heard herself talking, lightheartedly, like a woman of the world.

She scarcely recognized herself; it was suddenly as though she were seeing herself in the mirror in coronation robes. She sensed that she was master of the situation—she, a little provincial from Leiden, here in Amsterdam with an internationally famous scholar from a distinguished family. She was in charge. With Max she had never been in charge—such an idea had not even occurred to her; he had graciously tolerated her, as one tolerates a cat on one's lap, before gently pushing her away. But now the cat had a bird in its jaws.

She hesitated on the threshold to Onno's room. It was certainly just as well that Max had never seen this. The chaos was complete. Beneath the narrow window in the front room, through which passersby on the pavement could be seen only up to knee height, stood a desk piled high with papers, open books, magazines, jumbled newspapers, folders, stencils, bank statements, envelopes, bills, everything topsy-turvy and garnished with overflowing ashtrays, an empty milk bottle, an open bag of sugar, a portable radio, a piece of butter on aluminum paper that had turned orange—and this continued over the floor and along the walls with their crooked bookshelves, a sagging sofa and an oil stove, into the back room, where it was rounded off by a mattress with sheets the color of the ancient varnish on the murals in the Sistine Chapel.

"Yes," said Ada, going in, "if anything is quite impossible, then this is it."

"Are you suggesting it's untidy?"

"What can I say? It's a bit different from your friend's place."

"But then I don't live with the feeling that I may have to take flight at any moment," said Onno. "For him anything can happen at any moment, so he has to be able find what he wants to take with him immediately. I can never find anything."

Ada picked up an antique brown folio with a damaged leather spine from the floor and read the title, which was printed in a dozen different typefaces: *Vollständiges Hebräisch-chaldäisches Rabbiner-Wörterbuch zum alten Testament, der Thargumim, Midraschim und dem Talmud, mit Erläuterungen aus dem Bereiche der historischen Kritik, Archäologie, Mythologie, Naturkunde etc. und unter besonderer Berücksichtigung der Dicta messiana, als Verbindung der Schriften des alten und neuen Bundes.*

"Good story?" she asked, looking up.

"Better than you'd think. It's the kind of book that the fairies compile for me, at night when I'm asleep."

There was a modern brochure in it as a bookmark: "Socialism & Democracy." Putting it carefully on a pile, she was suddenly reminded of her father's shop, which gave her a homey feeling. She opened the window and her eye was caught by two shiny photos pinned to the windowframe: a kind of hopscotch field spiraling inward in a clockwise direction.

"Is that it?"

"That's it."

Humming, with an air as if she were simply reading what was written, she ran her eyes over the signs. Onno looked at her frail figure against the light, eye to eye with the thing that had tormented him for so long. Why not? he thought. It was over with Max, and he hadn't been devastated; come to that, even in her time he had had all kinds of other girlfriends. Onno was not a lecher who simply chased everything in skirts; he had always let himself be seduced, and that was what happened with Helga. It wasn't frequently that someone took a fancy to him; but when it happened, he was not only defenseless, but experienced the other person's will as his own love for her—and that's what it was. He was in love with Ada—as she stood there with her black hair looking at the hieroglyphics—but he must give himself time. He had never seen her without Max, not only not in the flesh, but not even in his imagination: she was a part of him, and that must be gotten rid of first. He certainly wasn't going to leap into bed with her today, in Max's fashion—and anyway, it needed a change of sheets first.

She turned around and surveyed the room again. There was one more or less beautiful object to be seen—an overladen carved Chinese chest in dark wood, with handles and a copper lock; when she lifted the lid and looked at the discarded clothes and shoes, a strong camphor smell rose from it.

"What's the system here?" she asked in the tone of someone about to set to work. "So I know how I'm to clear things up."

"There is no system. The wild disorder of genius reigns."

But that was not completely true. She went into the back room, where between the bulging bookcase and the disgustingly filthy basin, opposite the bed, a large number of sheets of squared paper had been pinned to the wallpaper: carefully arranged in numbered horizontal columns, and vertical ones with headings like: *Masculine? Feminine? Nominative. Possible "accusatives." Orthographic variants. Consonant 2c before 24?* Spread over the columns were characters, from the look of them not only those from the Phaistos disc, some groups boxed with red or green ink, with captions—everything precise and clear. On his rumpled pillow lay Machiavelli's *Il principe;* the view from the window was of a dark, tiled courtyard.

Ada picked up some clothes and asked: "Have you got a washing machine?"

"There's one upstairs that I have the use of, but I'm frightened of the bloody thing. The whole house shakes when it's on; sometimes it even goes walkabout through the kitchen."

"Is there a vacuum cleaner and that kind of stuff? Buckets and mops and suchlike? Perhaps some soap as well?"

"Bloody hell, Ada, are you actually thinking of cleaning up in here? Are you a real Hercules?"

"Just you go into town for a few hours."

"Okay, have your way then." He gave her a kiss on the forehead. "Provided you don't interfere with anything."

14

Repayment

People returning from a journey carry the distances they have traveled with them like outspread wings—until they put the key in their front door. Then the wings fold up, and they are home again, as though in the center of an impassable steel ring on the horizon. The moment they close the door behind them, they can no longer imagine they have ever been away. Everything is as it was: the entrance hall, the staircase, the banisters. Max gathered up the newspapers and the mail and went slowly upstairs. He opened the windows, unpacked his case, put his washing in the laundry basket, and took a shower. Then he looked through the mail, sorted the newspapers into a chronological pile, with that from the day of his departure on top, and started leafing impatiently through them.

Only in Vienna had he been able to glance at Western newspapers for a few days; apart from that, it had not even occurred to him that there must be some news. However, after going through the first week he had had enough: what had happened had happened, what had not happened had not happened. One thing he did know was that he would now imagine for years that people who had died during those weeks were still alive.

He put the telephone on his lap and started dialing Onno's number, but when he got to the fourth digit he hesitated. Suddenly he had forgotten it. He put the receiver down and stared into space: there was a choice between three or four numbers. He'd dialed it hundreds of times, but there was nothing for it but to look it up, feeling guilty as he did so. Obviously he was more tired than he thought.

"Quist speaking."

"Onno, it's Max."

"Max! How long have you been back?"

"I've just gotten in from Budapest."

The pause between his saying "Max" and Onno's crying "Max," was a fraction longer than he had expected. There was a minimal hesitation: something was wrong.

"What are you going to do? Do you want to go to bed?"

"What are you talking about? I took the plane. Come on over."

When Onno sat down in the green chesterfield armchair half an hour later, there was again something hesitant in his manner; but Max did not think he should bring it up, like some anxious mother whom nothing escaped. As he reported on his journey, he felt as though he were talking about a dream. That same morning he had walked from his hotel on Lenin Körút to the imposing Parliament building, to take a last look at the Danube, with the old fortified castle hill on the other side with its palaces and churches and citadels—all that awesome *Europa*, which he had also seen in Vienna and particularly in Prague, and which was just as strange and at the same time familiar as the Austrian accent he had heard in all those countries. While he told Onno about his days in Berlin and in the Polish towns, he could scarcely imagine that he had really been there. Birkenau appeared before him, motionless in the mist. He was about to tell Onno about his walk around the camp, which had taken hours, but he fell silent.

"You're in a gloomy mood, Max."

Max nodded and looked at his nails. "Anyway, you were right that I had to go. It's just that it hasn't strengthened my links with Holland."

"Could you live over there?"

"Nonsense. I was born here, Dutch is my language, I grew up here and my friends are here—and we mustn't forget my girlfriends. Anyway, that wouldn't be the main problem, certainly not in Vienna or Budapest. As far as that's concerned, there's no shortage."

"Okay, okay," said Onno. "Spare me that."

"By the way, in Vienna I found another Delius in the phonebook."

"And you didn't telephone."

"That's right."

Onno nodded. He felt uncomfortable, and after a short silence he asked about Max's impressions of the situation behind the Iron Curtain.

"What do you mean?"

"What do you mean 'What do you mean?' "

"What do you mean what do you mean what do you mean? What do you want me to say? Big Soviet stars on the buildings, statues of Lenin, portraits of all kinds of local patriarchs, banners with slogans that a polyglot like you can read, but I can't. Everything shabby and grubby, a ghastly arrogant bureaucratic fuss everywhere, like here at the town hall or the post office or the job center."

"Dictatorship is the natural element of bureaucracy," said Onno in agreement. "In a dictatorship everyone's a bureaucrat."

"In Prague no one had heard of Kafka—but at the same time everyone is much friendlier than here. A lot of good things are being suppressed, I think, but probably a lot of bad things too."

"So things should stay as they are?"

"You mustn't ask me that kind thing. In any case fascism doesn't stand a chance there, if you ask me, and that's the main thing. The rest is a luxury."

"Stalinism too?"

"What are you getting at, Onno? The great villains were Hitler and Mussolini, and they were gotten rid of by Churchill, Roosevelt, and Stalin. That's the way I see it."

"That's what I'm frightened of."

"Okay," said Max. "I'm quite aware of what you're driving at, but let me test you out. Suppose God calls you before his throne and says, 'My son, I have decided that the world is going to be ruled for all eternity in the spirit of either Hitler or Stalin. You must decide which of the two it is to be—with the proviso that if you are unwilling to choose between those two villains, or if you refuse to take part in such immoral games, it will be Hitler.' What will you say then?"

"Then I suppose you'll say Stalin," said Onno.

"Without a moment's hesitation."

"And why won't you hesitate?"

"Because Stalin represents the inhumanity of rationalism, and Hitler that of irrationalism—and because by my very nature I'm on the side of rationalism. Hitler was an irresponsible madman, but Stalin calculated everything, so that he himself was responsible."

"Do you really think that? What a child you are. No wonder all the women go for you. What's the difference for their victims, by the way? Is it nicer dying in the service of reason?"

"No, it makes no difference for the individual. Everyone dies their own unique death."

Onno stared at him for a moment. "Shall I tell you something? You've not been in the Eastern bloc at all. You've been only in Hitler's pan-German Reich, and maybe also in Franz Joseph's dual monarchy."

Max smiled. "Let's say that I represent the continuity of history, and let's suppose that you have given no answer to God's question. Stalinism will disappear and the world will be governed forever in the spirit of Hitler. The end of civilization looms. A gulf opens between us."

"Perhaps there's a third possibility."

"God didn't say anything about that."

Onno nodded. "Perhaps it would be more sensible to stop this conversation."

There was something in his tone that made Max also think it would be better. "Okay, but I hope you'll still have a Cuba libre." He got up to pour him a drink. "Tell me, what have you been up to?"

Onno opened his legs and crossed them again. "I've been setting my indelible stamp on domestic politics. We're in the process of designing a strategy to obtain recognition of the GDR at the party conference. That will please you."

"Onno . . . I'm not sure if you understand me properly. Do you ever read anything except the newspaper these days?"

"Yes, I know how you feel about it. It's not about the GDR but about the Netherlands."

"Why don't you do something useless, as befits a gentleman."

Onno nodded. "We shall see which of us turns out to be more of a gentleman." After a short silence, he added, "I'm glad you're back, so that besides the socially relevant drivel of my comrades in the labor movement I can also enjoy your shameful views." He took hold of his glass of rum-and-Coke and began twisting uncomfortably in his chair. "But I have a dreadful confession to make." When he saw that Max was alarmed, and expected something really awful, he said, "Something very nice has happened between Ada and me."

In the days when chemistry was still an adventurous science, it sometimes happened that adding one liquid to another led to a completely incomprehensible fizzing, change of color, and rise in temperature: this was how Onno's news entered Max's mind. It was as though he saw Ada's figure appearing physically, moving diagonally from him to Onno, like a chess piece, the black queen.

"What a surprise, Onno. Since when?"

"A couple of weeks."

Max couldn't make head or tail of it. He was happy for Onno, but still couldn't imagine the two of them together, in bed, and he didn't want to imagine them, but at the same time he saw her naked body before him as he looked at Onno.

"Congratulations. You couldn't have done better."

"Of course I should have asked you for her hand, but you weren't there."

"No. You'd sent me away."

"Hold on, you don't think—"

"Of course not."

Max laughed. He wanted to ask how and where they had met, but it was no concern of his. It was no longer his business. If Onno didn't tell him of his own accord, he didn't want to know. Only now did it sink in that it was all finally over between him and Ada—whereas it had been over for a long time. Neither of them had gotten in touch, but the question whether he had let something slip through his fingers must no longer be asked; if that was the case, then it was his own fault, and in any case it was irrevocable.

Onno put his glass down, sank to his knees and folded his hands. "Do I have your blessing?"

"Isn't it a primary requirement of courtesy among civilized people that you should offer your woman to your friends?"

Onno hoisted himself back into his chair. "That's true. Thank you very much. Consider it a repayment for Helga."

Within a few weeks—the summer was coming to an end—Max had actually forgotten that the situation had ever been any different. The first time he saw Ada again was after a performance of the Concertgebouw Orchestra. She had gotten her job, and the season was opening with Bruckner's Seventh. He sat next to Onno in the full auditorium on his best behavior and surveyed the colossal organ, which looked like the Torah shrine in an Oriental synagogue. The adagio with its merciless cello passage churned him up. He never went to concerts, it affected him too deeply, and now it was even more intense than usual—not only because Ada was playing, but particularly because since his journey he had become more vulnerable, like someone after an operation.

Meanwhile Onno tried to pass the time by reading the program notes: the little Austrian had incorporated his emotion at Wagner's death in the adagio—and Onno thought: adagio, Ada-Gio, Giove, Iuppiter, Zeus, Ada, and the Supreme God. There she was on the platform, on the right, subject to the will of the conductor.

In order to get closer to music, he had studied a textbook on harmony— during meetings at the Amsterdam party headquarters, in pubs, and in back rooms in hotels in the woods; no longer did anyone have to explain to him what "C sharp minor" meant, but that had not helped. When another conspirator asked him why he was not listening, he had said without looking up from the book, "I don't read with my ears,"—whereupon the stern questioner was embarrassingly downgraded in the hierarchy by the laughter of the others, perhaps for the rest of his political career. Onno had, however, discovered that he had perfect pitch.

After the concert they went to a pub behind the Concertgebouw furnished with secondhand items, as crowded as a tram in the rush hour: there were grubby local artists, divorcées, students, concert-goers, orchestral musicians in tails and evening dresses. When Ada came in and fought her way over to them, Max and she had greeted each other cheerfully, with a sort of tense relaxation, kisses on the cheek, as though things had never been any different, and without alluding to the change, even with a glance.

"Great to see you again! Had a good trip?"

"Very unusual."

"What did you think of this evening?"

"Marvelous. Congratulations on getting the job."

"Marijke!" she called to a colleague. "Do you want a half of Pils too?"

He scarcely recognized her. She talked and laughed, buttonholed other people, introduced them, disappeared into the throng with them, appeared again, hung on Onno's arm, made dates, waved at people leaving, and seemed perfectly happy. What he did not know was that he had become a different person for her too, since Onno had told her about him.

"Are you coming with us?" asked Onno, when they had paid their bill.

"I'll stick around for a bit," he said, with a glance in the direction of Marijke. "Safe home."

★

Just as in the past Onno had never seen Ada without Max, Max never met her again without Onno—but they did not see each other that often. More and more of Onno's time was taken up with the party, particularly in the evenings; in general, politics tended to ruin marriages and relationships— although there were some people who went into politics precisely so as not to have to stay at home—but Ada too had her rehearsals and performances. Max himself now had to go to Dwingeloo every week.

Increasingly often, he woke up in the mornings with a dull sense of unease, which was new to him. In fact it began before he was properly awake, while he was still half asleep: a dark pessimism, particularly about his work. Doubts about the soundness of his research program, telling arguments that he could no longer remember when he had opened his eyes; but the gloom remained hanging there like the stench after a fire. Whereas he used to jump out of bed after a few seconds to turn on the shower, now he lay there for minutes on end, wondering what was wrong. He thought of his work, but there was nothing wrong with it—there was something wrong with him. In the course of the morning the gloom lifted, but when he had to go to the east of the country and sat in his car for an hour and a half, the depression sometimes returned.

It was not a real depression, requiring expert advice and pills, because he suspected that it had a demonstrable cause: his journey. What had been dominant in his memory for the first few weeks—baroque palaces and cathedrals on hills, statues of saints on Prague bridges, the Vienna Hofburg, gypsy music in the evenings in art nouveau Budapest hotels, or in shabby cafés with names like Fixmatros—had increasingly given way to the immobile expanse of Gehenna at the center of its satanic triangle. That fathomless, monstrous thing had penetrated further into him than he had thought— perhaps he should not have listened to Onno. Perhaps he needed a vacation to recover from his vacation. He considered ten days in the Canary Islands—it would do him good—but he knew that he wouldn't call his travel agent to fix it up.

Ada soon moved in with Onno. The first-floor neighbors had left, and he had rented their floor as well, so he suddenly had a real house, with its own kitchen and a front door. The basement remained his study, Ada was given the new front room, the back room became their bedroom, and a purpose would be found for the little side room.

"That's where our child will go!" Onno had exclaimed. "The dreadful brat that will keep me awake with its disgusting howling, so I shall unfortunately be obliged to smother it under a pillow."

However, he had no wish for a child, and neither had Ada. After she had spent a few weeks scrubbing, polishing, emulsioning, and painting, watched approvingly by Onno, she simply wanted to get the moving van over from Leiden, but that was too much for Onno. He felt that they should talk to her parents first. Not that it would make any difference, but she was after all their only child, and it wasn't right for him simply to whisk her off without a word. He had never even met them!

"Imagine being a mother and having your child suddenly take off into the blue!"

"And what about your parents, then? Shouldn't you introduce me to your parents? I'm whisking you off too, aren't I?"

"Good God, do you know what you're saying? They'll have a fit when they hear that I'm going to live with someone without getting married. I didn't introduce Helga to them, either. I always have to do everything behind their backs."

For Ada it was all unnecessary. Onno had wanted to meet her parents before—he was curious about them, particularly about her mother: according to him, you must always look at the mother of a child if you wanted to know how the child was going to turn out. It was that remark particularly which had led to her avoiding a meeting: the thought of becoming just like her mother filled Ada with revulsion. She hated her mother and was ashamed of her father, who always said the wrong things. On the other hand, she appreciated the fact that Onno wanted to do this. All told, Max had asked about her parents once; to him they were superfluous, as she was herself in the last resort. With Onno she did not have that feeling of superfluousness; on the contrary, she had the feeling that he could no longer do without her, although he was not the kind of man to say so. The question whether she felt the same was one she did not allow herself to ask.

She was able to avoid his going to Leiden and seeing her parents' petit bourgeois living quarters: the following Monday afternoon, when the bookshop was closed, they came to Amsterdam. In the Kerkstraat, Oswald and Sophia Brons shook hands with Onno with the awkwardness of people applying for a job. Brons struck him as a good sort, but he was immediately a little wary of her mother: she looked at him as though he were a thing, a chair in the wrong place. Next they surveyed the empty rooms, and Onno saw that she gave everything the same look: it was simply her look. In the basement, transformed from a wilderness into a reasonably well maintained garden, her father pointed to the tables, still hanging in their old place, and asked: "Don't you do astronomy anymore, Onno?"

"You're mixing up everything again, Dad," said Ada in annoyance. "That was Max, my last boyfriend."

"You haven't kept us very well informed, Ada," said her mother, glancing at Onno. "We had to drag every word out of you."

"Oh, young people these days." Onno nodded. "They do just what they like."

"How old are you yourself?" inquired Brons.

"What a mean question. I estimate that I am the same number of years older than her as you are than me, Mr. Brons."

"I'll work it out when I get home. But you're still being very formal with me."

"But I can't be informal with my father-in-law! That would undermine the whole social system."

Her mother looked at him from beneath Ada's sharply defined eyebrows. "Do you plan to get married?"

"Mama, please . . ."

"Why can't I ask?"

"Because I don't like it. As though marriage were the greatest thing on earth. When we decide to get married, you'll hear; for the time being we are not intending to, no."

They arranged to come back when everything was finished, and at the suggestion of Sophia Brons they went for tea at the Bijenkorf department store, where she wanted to do some shopping.

While Ada and her mother lost themselves in the perfumed, mirrored mazes of the store, Onno and Oswald Brons found a table in the cafeteria by the window. Feeling awkward and surrounded by women, they looked out over the crowded Dam. The wide steps of the national monument, an erect pylon of pre-Freudian innocence, were covered with hippies in multicolored garb sitting or lying about, guarded by strolling policemen in black uniforms and two mounted gendarmes. Brons said that all that lolling about down there was a desecration of those who had lost their lives, while Onno made a gesture that indicated there was something to be said for that view, but on the other hand. . . . On the other side of the square, beneath the facade of the royal palace—which Onno and his political allies believed should become the town hall again, as it had been at the time of the Dutch Republic—children were sitting in the street watching a performance of a puppet show.

To Onno's alarm Brons put a hand on his arm. "Onno, look at me. Promise me that you'll look after Ada."

"I promise," said Onno in an ironically solemn tone, as though taking an oath.

He wanted to pull his arm away, but that was out of the question, of course. The hand remained there, so that a little later he felt its warmth. He looked uncomfortably into the faithful eyes of the bookseller. It was clear that he was trying to say something but that it was difficult for him to begin; perhaps he'd prepared it and was now trying to remember.

"Ada is a very difficult girl," he said. "For herself especially. As a child she was very withdrawn; she never really had any girlfriends. She wanted to, but for some reason she always provoked aggression, without consciously trying to. At school there were constant plots against her by other girls. They talked about her behind her back, ridiculous stories were spread about her."

"Why was that?"

"No idea. Until she was about sixteen or seventeen she was in a kind of sleepy cocoon. She looked at you in a way that made you wonder whether she could really see you. And she wasn't just bad at school—we had the feeling that she didn't understand what study really meant. She went from one school to another, but it made no difference."

He took his hand away and waited for a moment until the tea had been put down in front of them. Where on earth did that asymmetry come from? Onno wondered. Why was the love of parents for their child axiomatic and the reverse not? Why should "Honor thy father and thy mother" be a commandment, and "Honor thy child" not?

"But it's all turned out well," he said.

"That's true," Brons went on, "but nature was just as aggressive toward her. Until she was eight or ten she had constant problems with her ears, and had to have them cleaned all the time. Fortunately that stopped, but then she developed eye trouble. At a certain moment it turned out she was short-sighted and far-sighted at the same time, if I've got it right. First she had one kind of glasses, then another. Fortunately that came right too, perhaps because short-sightedness and far-sightedness finally cancel each other out; but by that time she must have been to the eye specialist a hundred times. And besides that she was always accident-prone. Cycling crash, front teeth bro-

ken. Skating crash, someone skated over her hand—wham, tendons sev-
ered. Fortunately it was her right hand. I can't bear to think what would
have happened to her if she hadn't been able to play the cello any longer, because that's what finally helped her through it all: music. I've never really
understood it—I'm not musical at all, I can't even tell a requiem from a
Viennese waltz."

"Perhaps there isn't any difference."

"Yes, there you are. You understand—otherwise you wouldn't be
with Ada."

"What makes you think that?" said Onno. "I don't understand it either.
Words are day, music is night. Your daughter is a mystery to me, but maybe
understanding just gets in the way of love. Do you understand your wife, if I
may ask?"

"What?" asked Brons, and looked at him, with a sudden severity in his
eyes. "What do you mean?"

"Nothing really. All I mean is that probably not only does no one understand anything about anyone else's marriage, but they don't even understand
their own. For example, I've sometimes wondered what my father really
saw in my mother, but to be honest I really wouldn't know, and probably he
doesn't either. Perhaps that's precisely what love is."

Suddenly Ada and her mother appeared at their table. Ada looked inquiringly from Onno to her father. What had they been discussing? Had it
been set up like this by her mother?

Onno got up and looked into the sphinxlike face of Sophia Brons.
"We've been discussing developments in the stock market," he said. "I've
decided to speculate on a fall."

15

The Invitation

Even when the house on the Kerkstraat had been furnished and Onno finally had a "real home," Max wasn't invited. Because Ada preferred not to go to the Vossiusstraat, they mostly saw each other somewhere in town. One evening they'd arranged to meet at the bar of the Lucky Star, a dance hall filled with the social bouillabaisse that had been bubbling away in Amsterdam for the last few years: intellectuals, poets, writers, composers, activists, politicians, ex-Provos, mixed with frivolous industrialists, straight-faced fashion designers, giggling society hairdressers, and accepted underworld figures, all of them with their female or male retinue simmering away in the soup of keen young dancers from the working-class districts.

Max listened to "California Dreamin' " by the Mamas & the Papas on the jukebox and watched the girls walking toward the dance floor ahead of their boyfriends, with a strange kind of way of moving one arm: it did not move from front to back more or less fully extended, but was bent at right angles, with the upper arm remaining almost motionless, while the lower arm with the hand hanging down described a horizontal circular segment of approximately forty-five degrees. Above the dance floor was a revolving glitter ball, inlaid with hexagonal pieces of mirror glass; reflected beams from a couple of spotlights rotated in countless small misty dots over walls and people, and now he was dazzled by a brilliant flash. Perhaps there was something similar somewhere in space, he thought.

When Onno emerged from the split in the dark-red curtain at the entrance and saw him sitting there, he took a letter out of his inside pocket and waved it above his head.

"Push off," he said sternly to a deathly pale young man sitting on the stool next to Max, and to his own amazement his order was obeyed. "What do you think? Letter from Cuba."

"So they did write!" said Max in surprise.

The letter was addressed to *compañera* Ada Brons—which according to Onno did not mean "comrade," because that was *camarada,* but, "friend," or "companion."

"That's precisely the difference," he said.

The letter was written in poor English and came from the *Instituto Cubano de Amistad con los Pueblos*. In October a ten-day chamber-music festival was to be held in Havana, with a large number of ensembles from Eastern and Western Europe and Latin America taking part. The journey by Cuban Airlines and accommodation in the Hotel Nacional would be paid for by the ICAP; because of the precarious exchange situation, the result of the North American blockade, there was unfortunately no fee.

"Fantastic! The only problem is, the duo doesn't exist anymore, does it?"

"We'll bring it back to life," said Onno with determination.

"So she's going to do it?"

"Of course. At least, if she can get leave from the orchestra; if some anti-Communist fanatic has the last word on the board, it will be difficult. She was playing this evening, and after the concert she was going to try to get hold of someone. I'm seeing her shortly above the Bamboo. But there's one small problem," said Onno, and put his finger under the date. "The letter took two months to get to the Christian West. That's the ultimate problem of the Third World: communications."

"Has she already called the embassy?"

"If she's allowed to by those terrible grandees, we're going straight there tomorrow. I don't trust the telephone: they'll ring you back after the festival is over."

"You can come with me in the car tomorrow morning, if you like; I can take you to The Hague."

"Come on, let's go."

The room above the Bamboo Bar, from which the sound of a Dixieland band was blaring, was the home of the new left-wing liberal society; but the Social Democrats from the rebel club could also be found there, because everyone knew everyone else, and for the time being belonging to the same generation had a stronger pull than different political allegiances. At the top of the steep stairs stood the melancholy Hungarian doorman, who had fled from Budapest eleven years ago, after the uprising. Ada had just come in, he said with an expression that indicated it ultimately did not matter.

It was full; there was soft Dave Brubeck music. As he went past, Onno heard someone say, "When I've shaken hands with a Christian Democratic politician, I always count my fingers afterward." It was the owner of the bar, a prominent journalist and one of the founders of the left-wing liberals.

"Wish I'd said it myself," said Onno over his shoulder, whereupon the other looked up with a shrewd smile and said,

"You will, Onno, you will."

Ada was standing at the back, greeting people on all sides.

Onno went over to her. "Well?"

"Did it," she said, exchanging kisses with Max without looking at him. "As long as I don't broadcast the fact that I belong to the Concertgebouw Orchestra."

"And Bruno?"

"You know what he's like. He was very cool about it and said he might be able to find the time, but of course he was over the moon."

"Koen!" called Max to the man behind the bar. *"La Veuve!"*

Onno looked at him with eyebrows raised. "Since when have you drunk alcohol?"

"Since now. This must be celebrated. Cuba! Just think of it!"

The ice bucket with the champagne in it was brought to them and they clinked glasses.

"To the friendship of peoples!" said Onno, kissing Ada on the crown from his great height.

"Suppose," said Max, only thinking it as he said it, "we were to go too?"

But he realized at once that this was the obvious solution. Far away over there, in a subtropical region, the sun might pierce the Polish mists that had been shrouding him for weeks. Cattle trucks, selections, gassings—over there on that Red island the black pool might be . . . not filled in, because that was impossible with something infinite, but perhaps be illuminated by a glow which meant that mankind was not written off as a hopeless failure. Not that Cuba would be the branch of heaven he was looking for, but perhaps there might be an inkling of something like it.

Onno and Ada looked at each other.

"Yes, why not?" said Ada. "What's stopping you?"

Onno shook his head. "How do you think we are going to do that? It's in three weeks' time. We need visas and heaven knows what else. We could be terrorists out to murder Fidel Castro. We'll never make it at such short notice with those Bolshevik bureaucrats, and from the Third World at that. Even a letter takes two months."

"I haven't got a visa either."

"But you've got an invitation."

"Listen," said Max. "We can try at least. How about the three of us going to the embassy tomorrow. We'll put our passports on the table and say, 'Just give us a stamp, because we're friends of the Cuban revolution.' "

"Why is it," Onno wondered, "that I, after all one of the most sensible people I know—and that's being modest—have such a stupid friend? That's not how the world works, old boy!"

Suddenly Max felt completely sure of himself. He took a gulp of champagne, leaned forward, and said, "I don't know how the world works, Onno, but perhaps that's my strength. If you ask me, it doesn't work at all, any more than the contents of a dustbin work. If you ask me, the world, at least on earth, is one gigantic, improvised mess, which for inexplicable reasons still more or less functions. Mankind doesn't really belong in the universe at all, but now that it's there, everything is possible in all kinds of ways. After all, history has proved it, I would have thought, and you as a politician should know that. If you begin by saying, 'That's how the world works, and this is possible and that is impossible'—then you'd better go back to the Phaistos disc. It's all just fallible people, floundering about, that is, and that's perhaps why you should always simply do what your heart tells you and not limit your own room for maneuver in advance with considerations that other people may or may not raise."

Was it the champagne? In any case his words had struck home. Onno looked at Ada in astonishment, and said: "He seems to be giving me a good scolding. But he's right. Let's give it a try. What can happen? Perhaps it's a political discovery that's been staring us in the face all along. And anyway," he said, pulling the bottle out of the tinkling ice, "when Columbus set out to discover America, Cuba was where he first landed, and he thought it was the El Dorado that Marco Polo had written about."

✳

As they drove into The Hague the following morning, with Ada sitting sideways at the back, Max pointed out the spot where he'd stopped in February to give Onno a lift.

"Silent night," Onno began singing, "unholy night . . ."

"Oh, thanks," said Ada. "If he hadn't stopped, you would never have met me."

"True," said Onno. "Idiotically true, but I played a crucial part in it too, because if I hadn't had an appointment in Leiden that day, Max would not have met you."

"And," said Max to Ada, "we owe that to your father."

"To my father?"

"If he hadn't put *Mein Leben* by Alma Mahler in the window, we would never have gone into In Praise of Folly."

"Alma mater." Onno nodded. "But ultimately my father is behind it all, of course. If he hadn't seen fit to have his birthday on that first day, nothing at all would have happened."

"Or if I hadn't gone to celebrate carnival in Rotterdam," said Max. "Life is one string of coincidences. Although . . . what is one to make of Schönberg, the inventor of the twelve-tone system? He had an irrational fear of the number 13. In his compositions he often numbered the bars 12, 12-a, 14. And what do you know? He died on Friday the thirteenth."

"So he was a hysteric." Onno laughed. "All composers are hysterics."

"Not at all," said Ada. "He had a presentiment of what would happen. I believe everything is predetermined. It's all in the lines in your hand."

Still looking at the road, Max's eyes widened for a moment, but he thought it better to say nothing about what it reminded him of.

"Oh," sighed Onno passionately, "how marvelous that would be."

"On the contrary," said Max. "It would take all the fun out of it. Predetermination is impossible in this universe anyway, because of Planck's constant. That makes everything uncertain."

"God in his infinite wisdom also created Planck's constant," cried Onno with his finger raised. "Planck's constant is God's revelation in nature. That's why we have free will and are able to sin. Why are we on earth? We are on earth to sin and in so doing to glorify God."

Although they had no appointment and Ada was supposed to be at the consulate alone, the Cuban ambassador was prepared to receive them— which of course was not unconnected with the name Quist. To Max's disappointment, he was not a bearded desperado with a cigar clenched in his teeth and a pistol belt on his desk, but a refined gentleman in his late seventies, in a dark-gray suit with a waistcoat. He had thin white hair and the aristocratic pallor of a high functionary at the former Spanish court. Ada's visa was granted automatically by virtue of the letter of invitation, and the pianist could also come and report; he would notify the ICAP of their arrival today by telegram, and they could pick up their plane tickets here in a few days' time.

After Ada had been led away by a secretary to complete the formalities, the ambassador told Onno that he'd met his father a few times at official functions. As the longest-serving diplomat in the Netherlands, he was the doyen of the diplomatic corps, which was also the reason Havana refused to let him retire every year; in his position he could maintain contacts with all sorts of colleagues who were forbidden by their governments to say a word to a Cuban ambassador. He was quite prepared to do it for Fidel—back then in New York he had collected the money for Fidel's Granma expedition, which had led to the revolution—but increasingly he would rather enjoy his old age in Cuba. Not that he was criticizing the Netherlands in any way, of course, or at most the climate.

Onno saw his chance.

"Yes," he said. "It must be marvelous there. If it hadn't been on such short notice, we'd have liked to go ourselves."

"You'd like to visit our beautiful island in the company of your girlfriend?" he asked with feigned amazement. "Why don't you go another time?"

"What do you mean?"

"We have beautiful women in Cuba, too."

Onno looked at him with dismay. "But, Mr. Ambassador! I am unswervingly loyal to my girlfriend! I would never forgive myself if something so terrible were to happen."

The ambassador smiled faintly. "Mr. Quist, what happens ten thousand miles away has not happened at all." He left Onno to his fate and turned to Max. "And you—why would you like to visit Cuba?"

"Ah, in fact you've just given me the reason. Up to now I just wanted to go along as a friend of the family."

The ambassador nodded. "The new Cuba sets great store by friendship. Cuba needs friends in order to survive." He looked from one to the other for a moment. "Of course you just happen to have your passports with you?"

*

Ada and Bruno were going to stay in the Hotel Nacional; according to the ambassador it would be best if they arranged their own hotel at Havana airport, and after the sinister thump of the stamps, which countless times before all over the world had made the difference between life and death, time accelerated for all three of them.

The Cuban Airlines flight, for which Ada and Bruno had first to go to Prague, turned out to be fully booked. The only other airline that flew to Havana from Europe was Iberia—only fascist Spain broke the blockade against Communist Cuba. Onno believed that this was because it was the mother country of the former colony. National character was still stronger than ideology: Franco was a Spanish king; Fidel Castro, a Latin American *caudillo;* de Gaulle, the umpteenth Louis; Stalin, czar of all the Russias; Mao, the emperor of China; and Queen Juliana a Dutch stadholder. His political friends, who wanted to get rid of the grandees, would themselves end up as grandees, because one couldn't escape Holland—but Max must treat that prophecy as confidential.

"And what about you?"

"Me? I shall become the most appalling grandee of all. All men of goodwill will tremble before me!"

The duo rose from the ashes and Ada and Bruno had to devise and rehearse a program. Because it was too cumbersome for Ada to go to Leiden every day with the cello, and because Onno had no piano, Max gave them the use of his apartment, which he did not need during the day anyway. Ada was hesitant about the offer, but because a refusal did no one any good, she accepted. She was given the key, and on the first occasion she entered the rooms felt like someone visiting a house where there has been a death: everything untouched, everything still as it was when the dead person was alive. But in the company of Bruno, who immediately sat down at the grand piano, that soon disappeared.

When Max came home in the evening and found the two making music, and often Onno too, reading papers in his usual place, he was seized by a paternal feeling of contentment. A happy family! During the day in Leiden he looked forward to going home. Sometimes his arrival was scarcely noticed; but that superfluousness in his place did not worry him—on the contrary: to his own amazement it filled him with a sense of well-being. What was the source of this dislocation? Sometimes things were not even in their right place! He sat down somewhere, picked up a book on Cuba, and started reading as though he were their guest. He listened to the music, looked at Onno out of the corner of his eye, and reflected that the idyll would soon be over: the children would leave home and in the evening everything would be just as he'd left it in the morning.

Ada, with the cello between her thighs, sometimes felt him looking at her, but did not return the look. Things were as they were. She belonged with Onno now, and that's how it would remain, and she knew that he knew—but what she didn't like was that something still seemed to be smoldering in him, despite himself—or was she fooling herself? Was it perhaps smoldering in her? She looked at Onno in his green armchair: a child in a giant's body.

"Are you still with us?" asked Bruno.

16

The Conference

Although Ada and Bruno had left three days before, they would only arrive one day earlier: they had a twenty-hour wait in Prague for a connection, and besides that the Cubans still flew old Russian turbo-prop planes, via Scotland and Newfoundland. Max and Onno went via Madrid, with just one stopover in the Azores.

Everywhere in the plane they saw familiar faces, artistic and intellectual celebrities from all over Europe—writers, painters, philosophers, whom they recognized from photographs; there were also lots of North and South Americans, who as a result of the blockade had to take this roundabout route. They were told by the stewardess that there was some kind of cultural conference being held in Havana. Onno read Franco's party newspaper and Max looked out of the window at the unbroken carpet of clouds.

Thick cumuli like white mountains, with light-gray lakes in their valleys, which might have had names—the earth might have looked like that. The farther south they traveled, the cloud cover became thinner—until suddenly the sea became visible, frozen into blue immobility. Max dozed off and in the sound of the engines heard wonderful symphonies consisting mainly of triads, which he could conduct at will.

Land ahoy! Fasten your seat belts. Down below someone had planted countless matches upright in the earth, all of which cast their long, sharp shadows the same way: palm trees. They prescribed an arc across the bay and the white city, and landed at José Martí Airport. There were anti-aircraft batteries all around the perimeter of the airport; against the control tower was a gigantic portrait of Che Guevara—that apostolic face with the beret, which here, where it belonged, suddenly took on a very different character. Below it in letters three feet high was the slogan:

HASTA LA VICTORIA SIEMPRE

When the doors opened, the October heat flooded into the plane like a wave of warm water. At the top of the steps Onno stopped for a moment and looked around.

"This is it!" he cried. "El Dorado! Goodbye to the land of the cheeseheads!"

The sun was low and orange on the horizon but still had a ferocity it never had in the north. Max momentarily placed the palm of his left hand on the concrete, which was still as hot as a griddle: a fried egg would be cooked within a minute.

In the cool, air-conditioned arrivals hall an orchestra was accompanying the chaos with guarachas. An Aeroflot plane from Moscow had also landed, and everywhere people arriving and people meeting them were embracing each other, without it being quite clear where customs and passport control were. However, there were lots of soldiers in green uniforms and military caps, some of them doing nothing more than swaying in time with the music. Waiters were walking around with large trays full of brimming glasses; when they took two and were about to pay, he shook his head amiably.

A black girl in military uniform, with stiff, straightened hair, came over to them and asked what delegation they were. Onno said that they weren't a delegation at all, but two ordinary tourists from Holland who were looking for rooms, preferably in the Hotel Nacional. She asked for their passports and studied the visas, which were on separate stapled sheets, since otherwise they would not be admitted to the United States. She scanned a list with her index finger.

"I don't have your names here."

"That's right," said Onno.

"No, that's not right. Holland, did you say? Have a seat there for a moment."

She disappeared with the passports, the zipper of her seamlessly fitting trousers running directly between her luxuriant thighs. Onno took the opportunity to phone Ada. Max looked around and sighed deeply. This was exactly what he had wanted: something completely different, something with which he was totally unconnected. For him the journey was already a success. There were welcome signs hanging everywhere for the delegates to the Primera Conferencia de La Habana, as well as huge portraits of the bearded revolutionaries of the first hour, but not of Fidel Castro; he was able to translate a slogan in red letters as: "When the extraordinary becomes the everyday, a revolution is under way." He looked at the smiling musicians on the small platform and thought of the ill-tempered fussing at Eastern European borders. Did this have any connection with that?

Onno came back and passed on Ada's regards; she would wait for them in the lobby. The black girl also reemerged.

"Everything's okay. Would you come with me?"

Their passports were not returned immediately. They had to find their baggage, and without any further checks, they arrived in the untidy square in front of the terminal, where the heat received them like a scorching block weighing on the earth. Meanwhile, in a paroxysm of colors, the sky was indulging in a sunset of a kind that in Europe could only be dreamed up by a crazed lighting technician, resulting in his immediate dismissal. Beneath it the traffic situation resembled a fairground bumper-car ride: rattling American limousines, none of them newer than ten years old, decrepit buses belching clouds of black smoke, each driver with his hand on the horn.

"Jesús!" cried the girl, and waved.

A dented black Chrysler came puttering toward them; the front windshield was cracked and one mudguard was missing. She gave the small mulatto at the wheel an envelope containing documents and told him to take *los compañeros* to Hotel Habana Libre.

"But what kind of hotel is it?" asked Onno. "What does it cost?"

"Don't worry, we've called them. Everything's been fixed. You're the guests of the revolution."

Onno was about to say something, but flashing an angelic smile with her innocent white teeth, she disappeared into the airport building. They put their baggage in the trunk, and when Jesús slammed it shut, the open left front door fell into the street. He cursed, spat out the cigarette, started laughing, and together with Onno lifted the door onto the backseat. He was wearing a gray T-shirt full of holes, a shapeless pair of trousers, with sandals on his bare feet. The car moved off, rattling like an old coffee mill, while on the dashboard all the dials remained phlegmatically at zero. Max and Onno tried to find a place to sit among the feathers of the torn seat, and a little while later they were driving along the highway toward Havana. Because Cuba was obviously not keen on living in a twilight world, it had suddenly become almost completely dark. To the right and left of the road there were black and white schoolchildren, workers, and women cooling themselves with fans.

"So now," said Max with his hair waving, "we are the Dutch delegation at the cultural conference. If we want, we can even claim our travel expenses."

"Yes, and it's absolutely impossible. What are we to say if they ask us what kind of cultural ambassadors we are?"

"*Compañeros!*" intoned Max rhetorically. "Revolutionary insights on the creation and development of the universe are also in accord with the dialectical laws of Marx and Engels! God knows," he said in a different tone, "it may even be true. There was a famous Soviet biologist, Oparin, a real Marxist, with pioneering publications on the origin of life to his name—and what applies to the origin of life may apply by analogy to the origin of the universe."

"So you've got your speech ready. But what about me? What am I supposed to say?"

"That you've made the extremely socially relevant discovery that the syntax of all modern languages reflects the mechanisms of oppression of class relationships, as is apparent from terms like *subject, indirect object,* and *direct object.* The bourgeoisie is the class of the subjectors, the right-wing intellectuals are their accomplices, and the working class is the object. In the languages of primitive communistic, classless societies this distinction did not exist, and that's why under socialism all cases should be radically abolished."

"Interesting thesis! Could I perhaps also mention a Soviet scholar? What you're saying is a little like what was claimed by the linguist N. J. Marr, and J. W. Stalin personally wrote a not entirely stupid pamphlet against it. Compared with the writings of A. Hitler, at least, it's a marvel of intellectual acuteness." Onno looked anxiously outside. "We're making jokes about it now, but meanwhile we're caught in the trap, M. Delius. Perhaps we should say we're poets. No one can check up on us. Poems are untranslatable."

"What can they do to us? We haven't forced our way in anywhere, we've been pushed in, by that sweetie just now. We are simply what we are: I'm an astronomer; you're a linguist. We'll see."

Onno shook his head and sighed deeply. "It's irresponsible, extremely irresponsible . . ." Suddenly he raised one hand and cried: "Live dangerously!"

They drove into the city. Sparsely lit old streets, squares inlaid with marble, white churches in Spanish baroque style, statues from the colonial period. Decay was obscured by the heavy traffic of wrecks thundering along, the shabby but teeming street life, and the lines outside the shops, where skin colors extended across a spectrum from the blackest African black to the whitest Iberian white. Music blared out everywhere from windows and portable radios: cha-cha-cha, salsa, drumming. They passed old forts and a snow-white statue of Christ nearly a hundred feet high.

"Must be the Cuban image of Lenin," observed Max.

At the harbor, full of rusty Russian ships with hammers and sickles on their funnels, they turned onto a broad boulevard. On the left, where thousands of people were walking about, everything was lit; to the right lowered the darkness of the sea. Everywhere on the heavy stone balustrade, erected as a barrier against hurricanes, courting couples and old men playing chess were sitting above the surf below. Again there was music everywhere. Signs announced that across the water, a hundred and fifty miles beyond the horizon, in Florida, the enemy was lying in wait, *el imperialismo yanqui.* At the end of the long boulevard a modern district began, with high-rise buildings and better street lighting, even neon signs, where black faces no longer predominated in the street.

At the entrance to the drive of a tall, modern hotel Jesús had to show the papers; on the other side of the street, behind a barrier, stood a curious crowd. The papers were in order, because with the chilly wave of the hand that police all over the world are masters of, whether in the service of communism, capitalism, or fascism, they were allowed in. They got out of the car under a wide awning with the words *Habana Libre* on it. One could still see that it had once said *Habana Hilton,* but that had been erased. At the hotel entrance, too, people looked ominously to and fro from the photos in their passports to their faces, giving them the feeling that they might have smuggled in their faces.

"They take good care of cultural ambassadors here," said Max.

With Jesús ahead of them, they carried their cases through the cool, busy lobby to reception. While their papers were again being taken out of the envelope, they looked around the sumptuous space in astonishment.

Silent films were being shown on two large screens on either side, accompanied by loud, lively Cuban music tempting one to dance: one screen showed fighting in Vietnam, bombs raining from gray B-52's, helicopters spraying villagers with bullets, airplanes burning fields with napalm, an American sergeant spending minutes kicking to death a Vietcong soldier, tied up and lying face-down on the ground, and then, casually holding the submachine gun in one hand, firing a bullet into the back of the head, a bullet in the back, and finally a bullet in the backside for fun, so that each time the body jerked a few inches farther in the sand. By way of comparison, on the other screen American policemen were clubbing black demonstrators with truncheons. In the middle of the lobby, which was also decorated with slogans and huge photos, for example of monkeys drinking Coca-Cola, something resembling a huge totem pole was raised up to the ceiling, slung with machine guns, rifles, revolvers, sten guns, hand grenades, and anything that could sow death and destruction.

"A completely original view of culture prevails here," said Onno.

Max burst out laughing. "Maybe it's a conference about the birth of the revolution from the spirit of futurism."

They registered, and a girl from the organization asked whether they wanted to freshen up before going to the conference office. However, Onno wanted to get everything over with quickly and then go immediately to Ada, who would be amazed that her two friends were suddenly representing Dutch culture in Cuba. They left their luggage and followed the girl to the gallery, which used to house boutiques selling crocodile-leather bags and snakeskin shoes. Some of them were boarded up; others had changed into storage areas for carpenters and painters. The name Cartier was still vaguely legible on the window of the office. Amid shouting and jostling, the girl arranged their registration, handed them conference packs with the title "Primera Conferencia de La Habana" and badges with their names typed on them: MAX DELIUS, HOLANDA, DELEGADO; ONNO QUITS, HOLANDA, DELEGADO.

"The official opening is tomorrow morning at nine o'clock, and we'd like to know immediately what working parties you are thinking of sitting on."

As they walked back toward the hall and pinned on their badges, Onno said: "There's bound to be a working party on the New Man. I know an enormous amount about that, because I'm one myself. In a glowing speech I shall give Rousseau the honor that is his due, albeit as an insignificant dwarf in the mighty shadow of Marx and Engels. Man is basically good—he is only made bad by bad circumstances, which hence must be improved."

However, once they had found a seat on a soft sofa and opened the packs, they found that the working parties were not devoted to the cultural and philosophical aspects of this lofty aim but to its practical side: the Armed Struggle; Urban Guerrilla Warfare; the Role of the Peasants in Seizing Power; the Communist Parties.

They looked at each other open-mouthed.

"My God," said Onno.

"This isn't a cultural conference at all."

They began rummaging through the papers, and a minute later everything became clear. The conference was a highly political meeting of guerrilla organizations from Latin American and African countries and the Vietnamese Liberation Front on the one hand and on the other hand Black Power from the United States and of revolutionary student groups from the Western European countries, consistently ignoring, as emerged from the *lista oficial de participantes,* official party Communists loyal to Moscow; Maoist groups had obviously not been invited, either. It was an extremely exclusive meeting for the flower of the revolution, as this had been achieved only in Cuba. There was no Dutch delegation listed. The girl at the airport was for some reason obviously convinced that they were delegates; and because Holland was not on the list—while it was obviously a country that needed liberating—she had put it down to bureaucratic carelessness and included them.

Now they saw something that might have struck them earlier: not only were the cultural celebrities with whom they had shared the airplane nowhere to be seen in the lobby, but neither did any of those present have the weak, defenseless, clownlike features that artists and intellectuals tend to sport. The white, black, and yellow faces showed expressions of steely determination, although there was occasionally a glimpse of a certain melancholy—perhaps because their steeliness was rooted, hopefully, not in evil but in good. For that matter, some of them looked like ascetic saints in an El Greco painting. They were also senior Cuban officers, *comandantes*—majors, that is, because all higher ranks had been abolished after the revolution—heroes of the first hour—about forty—in battle dress without insignia but recognizable from their beards and from the bustle around them: they had succeeded in doing something that the others still had to achieve.

"So now," said Max, "we've been promoted to leaders of the revolution in Holland."

As soon as he'd said this, he was overcome by a fit of giggling. He dropped sideways onto the sofa and gasped for breath: their new status amid the most dangerous and most wanted men and women in the world, now assembled here in one room, films that showed the same atrocities in one unbroken loop, music ... it was as if suddenly a vein had been tapped deep inside him, from which living water suddenly burst. The tears ran down his face, but Onno fiddled nervously with the badge on his lapel.

"Don't laugh, you idiot! We've got to put this right straight away, explain everything and beat it. We're in mortal danger, man."

"Live dangerously?" said Max, sitting up with a red face.

"What do you think will happen when they find out that we don't belong here at all? Look. These are not the kind of guys you play around with. Just suppose they get the idea that we're from the CIA."

"And you were going to change Holland."

"Yes, but not like that!" said Onno, pointing to the stockade of weapons. "I'm a revisionist social fascist, concerned only to prevent revolution and keep the proletariat in eternal servitude—a worm, a hyena, a capitalist lackey, in the pay of the CIA, and I'll finish up on the rubbish heap of history. That kind of vulture is put up against the wall here without mercy."

The last sentence just slipped out. He glanced quickly at Max, but he nodded and smiled.

"And quite right, too. Perhaps you can look at it another way. You're a good Dutch Social Democrat, who wants to change Holland in the only way that's possible in Holland, namely the Dutch way. That will be very well understood here, I think—especially if it results in development help for Cuba. And just so you know, *compañero,* I'm going to sit on the fourth committee. I'll see how it goes. I'd never forgive myself if I shirked this one. Anything can happen in life—this is another example of it. Maybe the Americans will bomb the hotel tomorrow morning during the plenary session, and that will be that, because of course Moscow would prefer to be rid of these kinds of people. If you ask me it's pure Trotskyism here."

"But, Max," said Onno. "What if my father hears about this? His son in devilish Havana as a delegate at a conference of the world revolutionary elite!"

"The fact that it's an elite would appeal to him. You're crazy if you let this chance escape. You'll get to know people, and you'll have a chance to see politics from a different angle than that Dutch nursery school of yours. Apart from me, you'll soon be the only person who knows what he's talking about in this kind of matter. Perhaps in a few years a lot of these fellows will come to the Netherlands on a state visit, Onno Quist, and perhaps you'll then have to review the guard of honor with them."

"Okay, okay," said Onno in resignation, opening his information pack. "I'll let you talk me into it once again. But the results will be your responsibility. Anyway, the ambassador here is married to a second cousin of mine, one of the Van Lynden girls, so that may help if things go wrong. And as a Jacobin, I'm obviously not going to sit on a wishy-washy committee like you, but in the first one, *La lucha armada!* The Armed Struggle!"

After registering and changing currency at the cashier's, they took off their badges and walked out into the sultry evening. Obliquely opposite, in a park, there were long lines in front of a large ice-cream parlor, Coppelia, which looked like a flying saucer that had just landed. On the grass next to it a manned anti-aircraft battery had been set up; and on the roof of their own hotel they saw the long barrel of a cannon.

"What can be better," said Max, "than the threat of catastrophe?"

"Peace, you imbecile, peace."

"I didn't say catastrophe, but the threat of catastrophe. Perhaps politics can ultimately be reduced to aesthetics, just like science. Perhaps the ultimate criterion in the world isn't truth, but beauty."

As they walked along the busy Rampa, which sloped gently down toward the sea, Onno stared pensively at the paving stones, his tongue between his teeth—ideas were always more real to him than what was visible. Max, on the other hand, who had blurted out the thought, absorbed everything greedily. Everywhere families were out walking under the palms; an electronic composition blared from loudspeakers on the lampposts. It reminded him of Luigi Nono's music for Peter Weiss's *Die Ermittlung*, which he had a recording of at home, but it was virtually impossible to remember electronic music; moreover, countless portable radios were competing with it. "Me! Me!" boys shouted at passing mulatto girls, sometimes of such staggering beauty that they took away not only Max's breath but even his lust: it was too beautiful, it was art, one had no need, indeed no right, to add anything to it—the key to eroticism was precisely deviation from perfection.

Policewomen in green uniforms and white berets, no older than seventeen, tried to bring some order to the chaotic traffic at junctions. On the side of a movie theater there was a neon sign thirty feet high, advertising not a commercial product but a political one: the map of Vietnam, with colored facts flashing on and off about American airfields and naval bases, the numbers of soldiers, the campaigns, the occupied and liberated areas, and a bomber flying overhead, releasing dotted lines that ended in bursting red stars, whereupon the airplane suddenly disappeared in a red glow, followed by the latest total of aircraft shot down: 2,263.

"*Gracias, tovarich!*" a man called to Onno cheerfully, and raised his hand. Onno thanked him with a gracious bow.

"They think we're Russians."

On the other side of the street, in an open white pavilion, hung a huge painting of the head of Fidel Castro. It consisted of welded sheet iron, with a bunch of rockets between his teeth and a red rose by way of a cigar, the armored head threatened by a bloody eye, with an upturned chamber pot for a helmet, while all around black figures were being beaten to death; the whole thing was covered with sickles, hammers, numbers, buttocks, cigars, fishes, eggs, skulls, books, eyes, and snakes. When Max pointed it out to Onno and said something about "socialist surrealism," they suddenly heard ominous roaring from another world in the pandemonium of music and traffic. A wide staircase, below which orange flamingos stood on one leg in a pool, led up to the next floor of the pavilion. On the terrace stood a cage containing two lions; next to it, a cage with a lamb. Just behind hung an enormous reproduction of Michelangelo's *Creation of Adam* from the Sistine Chapel: the old gentleman waving with his outstretched arm, Adam raising himself laboriously, receiving the spark of life in his outstretched finger via multicolored arcs of light, which flashed from God to his creature like in a Leyden jar—accompanied at full volume and by a constantly repeated stirring passage from the second suite of Prokofiev's ballet *Romeo and Juliet*, the part about the Montagues and the Capulets.

"I'm dreaming!" cried Max. "I'm dreaming!"

"Ada!"

At the entrance to the Hotel Nacional, a huge building in the old style, she suddenly appeared from a stream of unknown faces, ran to meet them, and fell into Onno's arms. He kissed and cuddled her like a child, encouraged by the passersby. Max gave her a fraternal kiss on both cheeks.

"What do you think of it here!" she cried, proud and excited.

The twenty-four hours that she had been in Cuba already seemed to have made a different person of her: her face radiated an enthusiasm that neither of them had seen in it before. Arm in arm with the two of them, she told them about their reception by someone from the friendship institute, their visit to the conservatory, where they were also able to rehearse, their meetings with Cuban and foreign colleagues. Bruno had arranged to see a *habanera* orchestra in the old town tonight.

"It's one huge party here!"

This hotel was not cordoned off like theirs. In the crowded lobby they now saw not only the German writers, French philosophers, English poets, and Italian composers, but the space was also part of the street: the twittering townsfolk, whole families with small children, walked in one door and out the other.

"It's just like socialism here," said Onno.

Ada had also seen the writer who had been on the panel that evening in Amsterdam, and the chess grandmaster, who was there for the Capablanca tournament.

"Everyone's here, the whole world. All the left-wing intellectuals."

"You can drop that 'left-wing,' " said Onno, "because the alternative is a contradiction in terms."

On the large terrace at the back of the hotel Onno ordered his first authentic Cuba libre; Ada and Max had milk shakes. When Ada heard what had happened to them, she started laughing.

"Everything's possible here. It's like the fairy tale where an ugly frog is transformed into a handsome prince."

"When we come to power in Holland shortly," said Max, "we shall decree exactly the same kind of semitropical climate as they have here."

"Exactly," said Onno. "Now you're talking. Politics may be aesthetically conditioned, but it's definitely meterologically conditioned too."

"It's fantastic you're here. I've missed the pair of you."

"Not Max, I hope?" queried Onno.

"In a different way."

The night stayed warm. The terrace bordered a great, parklike garden, which led down to the sea. The crowds thinned a little, and Onno announced that he had something important to discuss with Ada, but it was strictly confidential and could only be discussed in private. He would see Max the following day at the opening session.

"Oh yes," said Max. "The New Man as an animal."

Once they had gone off to her room, he strolled into the darkened garden. The motionless sky was framed in the vaulting beneath the gigantic, twisted trees, while other trees, on the contrary, seemed ethereal, with their filigree foliage as delicate as Brussels lace—it was so exotic, and at the same

...ne so familiar to him because of his view of the Botanical Garden from his office in Leiden. The whole island was one huge botanical garden, but without nameplates. At the end, at a lower balustrade, he looked out over the sea. He was met by a cooling gust; the lights of fishing boats here and there on the water; the pandemonium of the city was virtually drowned out by the soft rush of the surf.

Here he was. This was where life had brought him, to this paradisal spot. He thought of his life's history, his parents, his journey to Poland—and then of the words of the Cuban ambassador: "What happens ten thousand miles away has never happened." Had Auschwitz never happened here? The irrepressible starry sky. He was exactly on the Topic of Cancer, the pole star was low in the sky; but the trees behind him obscured his view of the Southern sky, which he had never seen.

Suddenly he heard low voices. He glanced to the side and twenty yards farther on in the dark saw a small group of soldiers around a rapid-firing cannon, with its barrel pointing at the horizon. When he raised his hand, they returned his greeting. He sighed deeply, and an intense feeling of happiness flowed through him.

17

Hot Days

The official opening ceremony of the conference the following morning was conducted by the president of the republic—not to be confused with Fidel Castro, who was to address the final plenary meeting—followed by a reception in the Palace of the Revolution. In the coffee break Max and Onno strolled out of the hotel to gain some impression of the city in daylight.

Their eyes, adjusted to the artificial lighting in the conference room, were blinded by the chaos of sun in the street: it was as though it penetrated their skin and created a twilight even deep inside their bodies. There were vultures flying high in the sky: the black birds soared above the scorching city like printer's braces in lazy circles and loops, without once moving their wings. Behind the barriers on the other side there were again groups of curious people, focusing their eyes on them and trying to remember what heroes from what country they were—of course the papers had been full of this conference for weeks, with biographies of the delegates. Although ice cream was for vicars, Max wanted to buy an ice at Coppelia; but if he had joined the line, he would probably have missed his lunch. While they talked about the president's speech, in which he had made clear the results that the Cuban people, the revolutionary government, and the Communist party expected from the meeting, they walked into the shade of the park.

A little later, behind a tree, they saw a scene the illegality of which rose like stench from a suppurating wound. An elderly Cuban gentleman, with a panama on his head and even wearing a tie, was exchanging money with a young man who was obviously foreign, whom they could see from behind. When the gentleman noticed them, he immediately stuffed the bank notes into his pocket. Max and Onno were about to walk on, as though they had not noticed anything, when the young man turned his head to the side to see what was wrong.

Onno stopped and could not believe his eyes. Was this possible? Was providence really giving him this gift? His heart raced.

"Bork!"

The student leader was struck by his name like a stone in the head. He jerked around and stared at Onno in astonishment. Obviously, he was too surprised to walk away, and Onno strode over to him, followed at a distance by Max. He'd got him, he'd got him in his power, the hour of vengeance had come! What joy! Hands on hips, he stood straight in front of him.

"Call off your deal this instant, you creep! This instant, do you hear me?" He told the trembling Cuban in Spanish that he needn't be worried but that the deal was off, and then, turning back to Bork, said, "You contemptible swine! Playing the left-wing leader in Holland and changing money on the black market in Cuba. What's to become of you?"

Bart Bork was as astonished as he was, but when he saw the conference badge on Onno's lapel he was completely dumbstruck. The gentleman, who also looked at their badges in alarm, was given back his pesos, and when he groped for the dollars in his pocket, Onno told him he could keep them and should now beat it as fast as he could. Hereupon he raised his hat politely and disappeared. Reveling in his power, Onno turned back to Bork:

"Of course you know whose signature is on those banknotes, don't you, you wretched shit? Have a good look when you get the chance: Che. He's in the Bolivian jungle right now, with a rifle, but here you are doing dirty capitalist deals behind a tree. What would you think if that became known in Holland? We won't even talk about Cuba, because if we did, things could look bloody nasty for you. I won't say anything about it, but I'm wondering what you're doing here—and shall I tell you right away what I think? I think you came here on a charter on your own initiative and tried to force your way into the conference, but couldn't. You don't belong here. All your international pals are in the Habana Libre, but you're not, you're somewhere in a shabby youth hostel at your own expense—and that's just right for a beachcomber in Cuba."

The score had been settled. Onno looked at his watch and said to Max, "The committee sessions start in ten minutes."

They left Bork standing there without saying goodbye.

"Well," said Max, once they were out of earshot. "I've never seen you like that."

"I will look back on this day for the rest of my life with deep satisfaction."

"Aren't you afraid that he could get us into trouble with the conference organizers?"

"Him? Do you think it'll occur to him that we don't belong in that conference? He's just understood why he wasn't invited. Because we were invited. We've risen immeasurably in his estimation. He thought he was dealing with a couple of gullible scholars whom he could teach a lesson or two, but now he's realized that we're unspeakably important in the left-wing movement. He believes in world revolution, and if he puts the slightest obstacle in our path, he thinks that one day we'll settle accounts with him as he would have done with us. The first chance he gets he'll try and make up to us. Come to that, he may be in the Dutch Communist party, and that's why he's not welcome. Take it from me, they know that kind of thing here. What a day! How sweet revenge tastes! Imagine if I hadn't let you persuade me yesterday . . ."

"What a high-minded character you are," said Max as they showed their papers at the entrance. "Your moral indignation really strikes me as terribly sincere. Especially for someone who himself is staying free in a first-class hotel under false pretenses and is eating at the people's expense in a Third World country."

"Shut up, you swine! I shall pay it all back twice over in one way or another. In any case, money changers will be driven out of the temple."

At lunchtime the Dutch delegation was presented to *compañero* Salvador Guerra Guerra: a skinny man of about fifty, with thin gray hair, hollow cheeks, and wrists no thicker than broomsticks. He was entirely at their disposal, as interpreter, guide, and walking encyclopedia; he was also expected to have meals with them. The latter turned out to be especially important for Guerra. During lunch, which consisted of three courses and which was attended by all delegates, he told them that he had recently had a severe stomach operation: only in the Habana Libre could he hope to gain a little weight. Apart from that, he wasn't going to intrude; if they needed him, could ask for him at the conference office. Not once did he inquire about their political status in Holland—that wonderful country, as he put it, with its wonderful revolutionary history, which four hundred years ago had been the first to rebel against Spanish domination. In Cuba that had happened only a hundred years ago.

"Yes," said Onno to Max, "there's no answer to that. They've got a higher opinion of Holland here than they have in Holland itself."

"Nevertheless," Guerra went on, "Cuba did surpass Holland to some extent ten years ago."

In the evening, after dinner, which consisted of four courses with French wine, they went with Ada to the chamber-music festival, where that evening groups from a number of Eastern-bloc countries were performing. Guerra had said that there was a car with a driver available for their use at all times; but because they still had to get used to the idea that they could live like millionaires here, they had taken a taxi to the old town.

In the concert hall they now also met Bruno, who already knew everyone and behaved as though he had been living in Havana for years. After the concert Onno took Ada to his room in the Habana Libre. As in the Hotel Nacional, there was a fat middle-aged lady at a table next to the lift, who looked at him reproachfully as though she were his mother, but he took no notice; when he gave her a wink, she began beaming with complicity.

Max had stayed on a bit longer. His knowledge of Beethoven's Grosse Fuge in B major, Opus 133, performed by a Bulgarian quartet, had made a great impression on a Cuban girl studying medicine—a tall girl with long, slim fingers, which she placed high up on his thigh when he told her that the piece had originated from the conclusion of Opus 130.

In order to analyze this further, they went to a bar, where it was as dark as in the farthest recesses of the universe. The only light was given off by glowing cigars and cigarettes; the waiter, who took them to their seats through the heat, the guitar music, and the invisible petting and giggling, politely pointed his flashlight straight at the ground. On the sofa against a tall wooden partition they drank their Son, the Cuban counterpart of Coca-Cola, and, accompanied by the incessant moaning and creaking in the neighboring booths, they went further into the *Grande Fugue, tantôt libre, tantôt recherchée*. In order to unveil the fugue's ultimate secrets, they then adjourned to a *posada* a few streets away. At the counter they were each given a towel and a bar of soap, with which they had to wait in the corridor for ten minutes: on one bench sat the men, from white to black, opposite them the women. When they had finished and Max was finally strolling back to his hotel through the nocturnal city, where everywhere people were still sitting in the street in front of their houses, with all their doors and windows open, it dawned on him fully for the first time that he was no longer in Europe. At the entrance he was again checked, and in the lobby he said hello to Angel, the waiter who served them and who had to be summoned with a "Pst!" He was now in a blue militia uniform, and polishing his revolver.

However, after only two days Max began to wonder what he was doing here. He became increasingly fed up with sitting for hours in an artificially lit room in this marvelous weather, listening to the translation of endless papers, behind him the incessant hubbub of the interpreters in their cubicles, while he wanted to walk through the city outside. Was it going to go on like this for five days? In the mornings, in his bathrobe, he took the elevator down to the large open-air swimming pool on the first floor, where the tape, which had not been changed since the 1950s, was already playing: "Sentimental Journey," "Don't Fence Me In." He played truant, lying in the sun till lunchtime, and during the afternoon sessions he passed the time by reading Novalis's *Heinrich von Ofterdingen*, which he had put into his suitcase at the last moment—but he hadn't come to Cuba for that! The ideological and tactical wrangling didn't interest him, either. Apart from that the really interesting things, of course, did not come up in the committee meetings; they were discussed in hotel rooms, behind locked doors—or in the Central Committee building.

However, he was particularly shocked by the Palestinian delegation, which wanted to wipe the state of Israel off the map and was applauded by everyone because of it. That was new to him. Israel! The child and pendant of Auschwitz! Of course Israel wasn't a branch of heaven, either, but did that mean that it had to be changed into a second branch of hell? Could it be that the far left and the far right were of one mind when it came to fighting the Jews? He remembered from the war how the Palestinian grand mufti of Jerusalem had visited Hitler with a white blob on his head to discuss the extermination of the Jews in Palestine: General Rommel was already on his way with his Afrikakorps. Was "anti-Zionism" the latest euphemism for anti-Semitism, as "final solution" was for extermination? Had hell extended its tentacles as far as Cuba? If Israel was his mother, then surely it could not be that this fantastic island belonged to the world of his father.

He did not want to think about that dilemma, and he did not talk about

...at made him stay was Onno, who said that he was learning a lot, although—being the Erasmian parliamentary democrat that he ultimately was—he felt lukewarm about all that radicalism. Apart from that there was the comfort, of course. The chauffeur-driven car, the bus trips into the country, the theatrical performances, late suppers in a rustic square in the old town, at rows of ready-laid tables, each sixty feet long, with music and speeches, or a visit to a show in La Tropicana, a gigantic open-air nightclub, where white grand pianos emerged from the ground, played by black men in white dinner jackets, singing "Guantanamera," and where fifty girls with ostrich feathers on their heads high-kicked and at the finale sung the "Internationale," while around them in the undergrowth hundreds of soldiers kept watch, since there was always a chance of attacks from infiltrators from Miami.

When the time came for Ada's performance at the end of the week, Max was in bad shape. He'd had a high temperature all day long; he would have preferred to crawl into bed, but that was of course impossible, though no one would have taken it amiss. Onno had already left with Ada, and purely to help to build up Guerra's strength, Max had gone to the dining room, where he restricted himself to a fruit salad. Because no car was available, he took the smoking, juddering bus to the old town and was stared at by his cheerful fellow passengers.

The small auditorium was hot and full to overflowing, and people were even sitting in the aisles; a number of composers had come too. Ada was nervous. All their rehearsals, their free journey, their hotel, the meals, the free entry to concerts and ballet performances, everyone's kindness, must now all be counterbalanced by less than half an hour's music after the intermission. They played Saint-Saën's *Allegro apassionato*, followed by Janáček's *Fairy Tale*, and everything went well. The attentive silence persisted for a moment after the final notes, and then gave way to applause, which while not overwhelming was still above the level of mere politeness.

Afterward, daiquiris were served in the throng at the back of the platform.

When Onno saw Max's face, both tanned and pale, he said, "Go on, have one. You'll feel better."

Max clinked glasses with Ada and Bruno, and cautiously sucked the crushed ice with rum in it out of the low glass. He liked the taste. He emptied the glass, held it against his forehead for a moment, and took a second.

But after one mouthful he was suddenly drunk. It was as though a net had fallen over him, a net curtain, but at the same time he emerged from the daze in which he had been in all day long.

"Nazdrovye!" he shouted, and downed this glass too, feeling an urge to throw it over his shoulder, as he had seen a cube-shaped Russian general do in the Tropicana.

From that moment on, events quickly became increasingly confused for him. The two Cubans they had met in Amsterdam loomed up and disappeared again; his girlfriend of a few days ago offered her cheek for him to kiss and a moment later had gone. He slurped the ice-cold white mud and felt it slipping down coolingly through his chest, while he surveyed the throng contentedly. Suddenly people made as if to leave. No one could yet see that anything about him had changed. Onno said that Bruno had organized an excursion; he must put his glass down now, because they were going to a Santería ceremony. A Santería ceremony? Okay, let's go to a Santería ceremony. As long as there was daiquiri there.

But there wasn't any. They drove to a poor street in a suburb in rattling cars, with Max wedged in the backseat between three or four people he did not know. They got out in front of a wooden house with an open front door between peeling pillars. It was so full in the small rooms that they could scarcely get in. Max stood on tiptoe; something terribly occult was going on.

From the back room came the sound of a crescendo of drumming and singing; on an uptight wooden chair, flanked by candles, an emaciated black man in a light-blue flowered dress was shaking as though surges of current were being pumped through his body, while two black women were trying to keep him under control. In a trance he blurted out words and sounds, which Onno said were completely unrelated to Spanish but more like Nigerian, Yoruba, or whatever it might be. Obviously, an African spirit had taken possession of him, but on the other hand it couldn't be that heathen, because above his head there was a kitschy image of the Virgin on a pedestal, while above that was a portrait of Fidel Castro. But perhaps it was everything at once, ignoring the law of the odd man out, to the eternal shame of those who thought they understood anything.

Down and chicken feathers flew through the air. The drummers and women singers worked themselves up into a state of frantic ecstasy, which now also transmitted itself to some black men and women in the audience, so that people quickly had to give way to avoid flailing arms and legs. Max was forced into a corner, and with eyes too heavy with rum to focus prop-

suddenly found himself looking into the eyes of the Dutch writer who had sat on the forum panel in Amsterdam and who was standing beside him.

"So we meet again?" said Max. He tried to focus his eyes on him, but he was too close; there were two identical writers refusing to merge. Only because he had had too much to drink, did it occur to him to ask: "How the hell is it possible for someone to dream up a novel?"

"I never dream up anything," said the two mouths coolly. "I remember. I remember things that have never happened. Just like you do when you read my novel."

Very early the next morning—the conference was coming to an end—the delegates took their buses to the airport. From there they were going to Oriente, the sweltering province in the extreme southeast of the island. Here there were two days scheduled in the Sierra Maestra, the mountains where eleven years ago the rebels had begun their struggle with twelve men sitting around a table. Although there was a rumor that *el líder máximo* was to appear, Max and Onno remained in Havana. Ada's plane was leaving the following afternoon—they themselves were going three days later—and they had decided, despite Onno's protests, to spend her last day on the beach in Varadero. Guerra would ensure that the car was ready at ten o'clock, after which they were to pick her up from the Hotel Nacional.

At half-past nine Onno was sitting, as agreed, in the shady bar that divided the swimming pool from the dining room. Max was obviously still sleeping off his hangover. It had become quiet in the hotel. There had been a thunderstorm that night, and the swimming pool attendant was fishing leaves and insects out of the water with a net; the barman was checking the bottles in his racks on a list. The only other person sitting at the other end of the bar was a woman with a glass in front of her: whiskey, from the look of it. Onno thought of his conversations with the delegates, which he was mostly able to conduct in their own languages, on the mad tumult raging everywhere in the world, of which only a fraction had penetrated to him in Holland—at least he tried to think of it, because although the woman didn't look sideways at him, he felt an almost tangible link between them. It disturbed him and he wondered what was happening. What was this? Feeling as if he were already being unfaithful to Ada, he asked for the bill. He would phone up to Max's room and say he was waiting in the lobby. While he was signing—and again wondering how he was going to pay for all this—he felt the woman looking at him. He met her gaze, and with a smile he made a slight sideways movement of the head, signaling that he was sorry but there was nothing to be done—he was simply a mug.

However, as he walked to the telephone box in the lobby, he saw her coming down the stairs after him. He immediately realized what had happened. She'd interpreted his movement of the head completely differently, namely as "Come on, let's go"—done subtly to deceive the barman. After a moment's hesitation he went up to her; he was caught in a trap, there was no escaping—but he no longer really wanted to escape. She was in her thirties: a full-figured, luxuriant woman, dark blond, with deep-brown eyes and a skin the color of hazelnuts.

"Let's go," she said earnestly.

He could tell from her accent that she was Cuban. She looked well groomed, rather bourgeois; but maybe she was a *gusano,* as they were called here, a counterrevolutionary "worm," who would prefer to flee to the United States as soon as possible. But how could she get into the hermetically sealed hotel? He nodded and went outside with her. Was it all so simple? Of his own accord he would never have dared make that gesture of the head with the meaning that she had given it. That was more in Max's line.

He put out his hand and said, "Onno Quist."

"María."

As he sat next to her in the car, which was in reasonable condition, he wondered what had gotten into him. He had to go to the beach very shortly, it was Ada's last day, this was impossible, he had to go back at once. But it had become impossible. The soldier in the drive saluted as they passed.

"I have to make a phone call," he said.

"You can do that at my place. We'll be there in no time."

She glanced sideways and smiled sadly. It was Sunday, the streets were empty, and a few minutes later they were driving along a chic boulevard with grass and trees in the central divider, occasionally alternating with large signs with slogans on them like WHEREVER DEATH SURPRISES US, LET IT BE WELCOME. There were embassies here and in the past wealthy people had lived here, but now the well-appointed properties had been largely converted into student lodgings and all sorts of university institutes. Here too branches and leaves that had blown down were strewn everywhere. They got out at a small detached house with a well-maintained garden.

.oor opened directly onto the white, tiled living room, which
standards was virtually empty. The walls were also bare, except
a framed photograph above the sideboard: a man of about forty with a
wide smile, in uniform and wearing a beard, with a large broad-brimmed
hat on his head, like those that sugarcane cutters wore, with his arm around
María's shoulders, who was also smiling, cringing a little from the violent vi-
tality next to her.

When Onno saw the beard, the revolutionary sign of nobility, he had the
feeling that he should flee at once, out the front door and down the avenue
as fast as his legs could carry him: at any moment the man would come in
and gun him down, after which he would blow the smoke out of his pistol
barrel and burst out laughing. For once he had embarked on an adventure
and had landed in a situation like this. My own fault, he thought. I've got my
just deserts. He had landed himself in a fix and now he must simply take the
consequences. Wherever death surprises us, let it be welcome. *Dr. h.c. Onno
Quist, The Hague, November 6, 1933—Havana, October 8, 1967.*

He sat down on a wicker chair and phoned Hotel Nacional. While he
waited to be put through to Ada's room, María asked if he would like a
whiskey.

"I'd love one!" he said, so emphatically that she burst out laughing.

When he heard Ada's voice he felt ashamed and again felt sorry. He was
going to say that he'd walked into town, that he'd got lost and that he would
be at the hotel in a quarter of an hour, but he did not.

"Hello?" she repeated.

"Hi, it's me."

"Hello! I suppose Max's overslept, hasn't he? He had far too much to
drink yesterday. Doesn't matter, I'm sitting on the balcony in the sun."

"No, it's not that, or partly that. He hadn't arrived a moment ago."

"What's wrong, then? Aren't you in your hotel?"

"No. Do you mind if I don't go with you?"

"Oh, I thought so. You on the beach—it seemed odd somehow. What are
you going to do today? Where are you?"

"In church," said Onno solemnly, while he watched María filling their
glasses with ice.

"In church?" repeated Ada laughing. "Praying for the revolution?"

"I want to see how it's done here. There's going to be a solemn high mass
in a moment."

"Listen, shall I come? Where's the church?"

"You go on to the seaside with Max. It's your last chance. The day after tomorrow you'll be back in Holland in the gales and the rain."

"You really don't mind?"

"I'll see you both this evening. But call him right away. He doesn't know about it yet."

"I will."

"Okay. Pray for my soul."

As he put down the receiver, he raised the glass that had been put next to him and took a large gulp.

"What language were you speaking just then?" asked María, and sat down on the sofa.

"The language of the heroic Dutch people."

The irony of this reply was lost on her. "Holland has a splendid history." She nodded, lighting up a cigarette. "Was that your wife?"

Onno sighed deeply. "My girlfriend. What on earth gave it away?"

"Everything."

"You women in Cuba are just as dreadful as everywhere else." He pointed to the photograph. "Is that your husband?"

"Not anymore."

He looked at her with relief, and expected her to show in some way or other that she understood that relief, but her face remained impassive. Suddenly he was seized by a new uncertainty. Perhaps she was a secret agent; perhaps it was her task to find out the truth about those two Dutchmen at the conference whom nobody had ever heard of, who never spoke, and had now not joined the Sierra Maestra excursion.

"Why do those knights of the revolution still wear their beards from the guerrilla period?"

"Because they've sworn not to shave off their beards or take off their uniforms until the revolution has come to the whole of Latin America."

She got up and took a large photograph out of a drawer of the sideboard, which she handed to him.

"This is my husband."

Onno's face contorted with disgust. It was the same man, but now his naked body was lying on a bier, filthy and covered in blood, with black bullet holes in his chest, tangled, sticky hair and a beard, and one eye half open.

"Christ!" he said and looked at her in dismay. "Where did this happen?"

"In Bolivia."

He didn't know what to say. He got up, put the photograph back in the drawer, slid the drawer shut, and sat down again. It was all clear now. As the widow of a dead hero she had been given privileges by his friends—a nice house, a car, gasoline coupons, and whiskey from early morning onward. Perhaps she had children, too. He wanted to ask if she had children, but he did not. He looked at her in silence. She met his gaze and then twice gently patted the place next to her.

18

The Vanishing Point

Max was trying the get rid of his headache at the bar with black coffee and mineral water. He had had a strange dream about Cuba: white, completely covered in snow, it had been situated in a frozen polar sea—that was all he could remember. It was almost ten o'clock. Just when he was about to call Onno's room to ask where he'd gotten to, the telephone rang.

The barman picked up the phone, looked at him and asked: "*Compañero* Delius?"

It was Ada. Onno had gone to church and wasn't coming with them.

"Your weird fiancé prefers incense to sunshine," said Max. "What shall we do?"

"It's up to you. How do you feel after last night?"

"I've got a headache, and either it will get worse in the sun or it will disappear in the sea. Let's go. I was all geared up for it, and I can always sit in the shade. I'll be with you in ten minutes."

He grabbed his bag of swimming gear and went to the lobby, where Guerra was sitting reading the *Granma*, the party newspaper. He was wearing a white embroidered shirt, which was also a jacket.

"*Tovarich* Quits has a religious appointment," said Max. "He's sorry but he's gone to pray for the revolution. As far as I'm concerned, you can stay in Havana too. We'll find the way."

But Salvador Guerra would not hear of it. It was Sunday, it would be crowded in Varadero, and without him they wouldn't find the right place; and anyway, they would need a meal too.

"Apart from that, I'm responsible for your safety. We'll have to go through an area where terrorist commandos from Florida regularly land. May I introduce you . . . *compañera* Marilyn."

He gestured toward a young blond woman approaching them, in a green uniform, heavy high-heeled shoes, holding a small but formidable submachine gun across her breasts, and with a refined, razor-sharp smile on her face. She was Ada's age and was distinguished from her film-star namesake by an intelligent, alert look in her green eyes, which, however, were slightly clouded.

Max's headache immediately lightened. He shook her hand and knew that he must not say "Monroe," because everyone did that, of course. But he could not resist making an indirect allusion:

"You look amazing. It seems there's even a doctrine named after you."

She understood at once. The North American Monroe Doctrine, which prohibited external intervention in the Western Hemisphere, had again played a role five years earlier, during the Cuban missile crisis. She spoke fluent American English, and when he complimented her on it, she said that she was American, from New York, where she had studied art history, but that they need not go into that any further. She preferred not to lose her nationality; if her parents found out where she was and what she was up to, they wouldn't dare show their faces in the street anymore. So her surname was best left undisclosed.

"Where do your parents think you are, then?"

"Wandering around Europe visiting museums. Studying perspective in Italy, in Paolo Uccello and Piero della Francesca."

"Which is important too, of course."

"But in a different way."

Glancing approvingly at her rear, he followed her outside, where Jesús was waiting for them in the car. With the Kalashnikov on her lap, Marilyn sat next to the driver and they drove to the Hotel Nacional along the quiet *Rampa*. Ada was already waiting on the terrace. With the warmth that only women can immediately show each other, she and Marilyn said hello through the driver's window. Guerra got out politely and allowed her to sit between Max and himself in the backseat. Soon they were driving into the country along the rocky coast.

"What do you make of him," said Max to Ada, "the ex-Calvinist going to a Catholic mass in a Communist country. You just couldn't make up something like that."

"It's only possible in Cuba."

"Look. Even the earth here is red."

On their right, sugarcane stood above head height in the red clay, an ideal hiding place for the scum that landed here. Because it was Sunday, he had expected that it would be busy on the road, but of course because of gasoline rationing people took the train; there was almost no traffic. Sugarcane leaves that had blown down were strewn across the pavement, and there was a strange silence over the land and the sea.

Ada saw it too. "There's some doubt whether we'll be able to leave tomorrow. Bruno has heard that there's a hurricane off Haiti, which may come toward Cuba. *Fancy.*"

"That makes it the sixth this year."

"How do you know?"

"Because *f* is the sixth letter of the alphabet. It's not just people who learn the alphabet in these parts; disasters know it too. I must talk to Onno about that, but for the moment he's listening to the 'Kyrie eleison.' "

For the first time he smelled her scent again and felt her warmth with his thigh, but it only gave him a sense of familiarity. He was sitting behind Jesús, so he could see part of Marilyn's face. Below her ears, along the curve of her jaw, downy hairs glowed like a tiny blanket of light. Paolo Uccello. Piero della Francesca. Kalashnikov. How was he going to tell them about this in Holland when he got back? People there would be just as unable to understand what was happening here as what was going on in the GDR or in Poland.

The unreliable condition of the car meant that the journey would take almost two hours. In the cooling breeze blowing through the windows Guerra told them about his role in the revolution, in which he'd taken part not in the mountains but in Havana. The urban resistance against the corrupt Batista regime, mainly by students and intellectuals, which had cost many lives, had always been in the shadow of the *guerrilleros,* but that was partly because many people said afterward that they had been in the urban resistance when they had not. It was almost impossible to check.

"No one has ever dared claim," he said, bending forward and looking at Max, "that they fought in the Sierra Maestra when they did not, but in complicated situations there are always people who take advantage and pretend to be what they're not." He nodded and leaned back again.

Max stiffened. Did Guerra know the truth about the Dutch delegation? Was he letting him know that? Or was he imagining it? Of course they knew! They'd known for a long time! If they didn't know something like that, their state could not exist at all! But they left things as they were, because it was a mistake on their part. They had known for a long while that they were not dealing with two promising resistance fighters but with an innocent astronomer and a clueless cryptographer who dabbled in bourgeois politics. "Leave it," someone had said, between putting a cigar in his mouth and lighting it, "they're children"; and the matter was settled by disciplining the black girl at the airport. He glanced at Ada, but she did not give the impression of having registered a hidden message. He would have liked to confess to Guerra now, admit that they were attending the conference under false pretences and of course would repay all the expenses, but suppose he was wrong: what would he be letting himself in for?

Suddenly Jesús cried out: "Fidel!"

Max felt as though an electric shock had gone through him. In front of them was a column of military vehicles. They were being observed calmly but intently from the rear car by two heavily armed soldiers, one with binoculars and one with a walkie-talkie. A gesture was made indicating that they should keep their distance. The situation in the Chrysler changed instantly.

Jesús turned his head, pointed across his steering wheel, and said again, "Fidel!"

Ada leaned forward, Guerra stretched his neck, and Marilyn sat up straight. Five hearts suddenly beat faster because a certain man was close by, a man like all other men, flesh and blood, with two eyes, two ears, two arms, and two legs—and at the same time a man like no other: the liberator of his people, history personified. Max looked over Jesús's shoulder at the slowly proceeding column. He saw antennas and here and there a leg half out of a car and the barrel of an automatic rifle. He was there somewhere: power was on the move.

Guerra said that he always traveled like that, or rather that he was constantly roaming over the island in cars or helicopters. He had no kind of residence or department anywhere in Havana—that was his department, that was where all his intimates were; they knew everything and everyone, slept in barracks, with farmers, or in hammocks among the trees. That restless style was inherited from the guerrilla war; it had even driven Che out of the country. No one ever knew where Fidel was—he suddenly turned up all over the place—and of course that was also good for his safety, because there were lots of people who would like to see him dead.

But when the soldier with the walkie-talkie gestured that they could pass, Max wondered whether this wasn't a frivolous decision. In the front seat of their own car, on the side of the column that they were now overtaking, there was an American woman with a weapon at the ready: how were they to know that this was not the execution of a diabolically planned CIA assassination attempt, with the cynical sacrifice of a cellist and a promising astronomer? Perhaps the explanation was that their watchfulness was not based on fear. However, hands kept appearing, motioning them to drive on faster. Max bent deep across Ada's lap so as not to miss anything, Guerra leaned back so as not to obstruct his view, but it all happened too quickly to see much.

One military vehicle after another, including a mobile kitchen, an ambulance, a radio car, and suddenly a line of jeeps with *comandantes* and other officers. In a flash he saw him sitting in the front jeep: next to the black driver, wearing glasses with dark frames and reading papers, a submachine gun on an iron grille above his knees.

The bay lay like a grail of deep-blue blood beneath the cloudless sky. Standing next to the car, Max and Ada looked open-mouthed at the scores of great white pelicans flying high above the waves with their long beaks and suddenly plummeting straight down into the water like depth charges, disappearing, and a little later emerging dripping and with thrashing pouches below their beaks, to continue their flight. It seemed as though those incessant, vertical movements, like slim, invisible columns, transformed space into an enclosed dome. Woods stretched down to the wide sandy beach. As though the trees did not cast a shadow but the shadow carried the trees. Not a leaf stirred.

"This is out of this world," said Ada.

Farther along, the beach was crowded, but here there were only a few left-wing artists and intellectuals with international reputations sitting in the sun. Hidden among the trees were charming but rather dilapidated bungalows, which, Guerra told them, used to be inhabited for two months a year by Cuban and American brothel-keepers and cocaine dealers but now served as guest homes for various organizations. The villas along the open beach were for public use.

On the shady veranda of a bungalow, lunch was served by a Chinese Cuban in a white coat: gazpacho, grilled swordfish, with a dry white wine, which everyone drank apart from Marilyn, sweet hazelnut ice cream, and coffee. As he was about to go and put on his swimming trunks, Max asked Ada if she had also gotten the impression that he and Onno had been seen through as impostors.

"Don't be silly," she said. "It's just your guilty conscience."

"Do you think so?"

"Of course, but you two will have to set things straight one day."

"I hope you're right."

Her remark had reassured him, as had the wine. There was a diving mask on the chair, and as soon as he was undressed he ran across the red-hot, velvety sand toward the surf and dived into the sea with the mask over his arm. Used to the cold North Sea and cool Mediterranean, he was not prepared for a lukewarm dip. He resurfaced with a cry of pleasure and immediately fell back again. This couldn't be true! Life had originated in a sea like this! He waved to Ada, who was spreading her towel, but she indicated that she would be coming in a moment. He frolicked about in the water like a little child in a paddling pool, jumped up, dived, and had already forgotten that a short while ago he had had a headache. He put on the mask and in an instant the world that he had only known in his dreams unfolded, swaying silence, movement that had become vegetable, light wandering around on stilts, spectral colors transformed into fish, into which a gigantic pelican plunged like doom through the blinding roof of the sky and scooped up its prey; but his mask, which dated from before the revolution, filled with water and he had to return to the sunshine.

Marilyn had rid herself of her weapon and was sitting next to Ada in a bikini on a towel. Obviously, other people provided security here.

Guerra had stayed on the veranda, where he was talking to Jesús and the Chinese waiter, who had put his legs up on the table; a fat black woman in a white apron was sweeping the floor tiles. Max sat down on the other side of Ada, next to Marilyn. The bare, downy skin of her arms and legs and belly, without a submachine gun, was different than if he had never seen her with one. Then she would have simply been a young woman in a bikini, like Ada; but because of its absence, the submachine gun was somehow even more present than when it had been there. Was that what attracted soldiers to a certain kind of woman: the fact that they finally had to disarm themselves for her? Was it perhaps also a kind of justification for the women who had slept with German soldiers during the war? Were they really resistance fighters unjustly shorn of their hair after the liberation? While the enemy was on top of them, he couldn't shoot!

He did not like thinking about the war. He lay on his back, folded his hands under his head, and asked in English: "What would Fidel do now?"

"Certainly not sunbathe," said Ada. "He's never done that."

"I've seen him. My life is fulfilled. From now on things can only go downhill."

Marilyn turned her head over her shoulder and gave him a searching look. "What kind of joke is that?"

"Why do you think it's a joke? Perhaps it's not a joke. Perhaps it's a joke that's not a joke."

"You sound like Onno," said Ada.

He looked up into Marilyn's eyes and saw that he must be a little careful. He had found repeatedly that in Cuba the revolution was not devoid of good-humored features, but he had noticed little of that among the foreigners at the conference, just as he had not when he had been in Eastern Europe—and here was an American. At the same time, it titillated him and he felt like teasing her.

"Perhaps we should see everything in perspective."

"What perspective?"

"Eternity."

This time she seemed to understand him even better than he had intended. She turned onto her stomach and said didactically:

"Eternity and perspective are incompatible. Shall I tell you something,

Dutch Max? Perspective was discovered in the fifteenth century. Up till then God had always fitted very naturally into the space of the painting, a Madonna and child for example, but that space itself was unnatural. He simply sat on a throne in the blue sky, above the Madonna, with some circles and stars around him; or on the left you had St. Dionysius wearing an elegant mitre in a dungeon and on the right later after his head had been chopped off, and in the center Christ, naked on the cross hundreds of years earlier, surrounded by the twelve apostles in bishop's robes: all of that quite naturally in one impossible space at one impossible moment. But with the discovery of central perspective, natural space and natural time were defined. Someone on a chair in the sky would fall down, and things that followed each other could not happen simultaneously. So that was the beginning of the end of eternity."

He listened to her exposition in amazement. It was as though she were giving a summary of her M.A. thesis.

"Do you perhaps mean that since then nothing can worm its way from the heavenly side through the vanishing point in perspective to this world?"

"You won't hear me talking that kind of nonsense."

"Pity."

"There is no heavenly side of the vanishing point."

"How do you know? Perhaps it can no longer be made visible with artistic decency, but perhaps it's still all there just the same." He said it to tease her, but she turned out to be impervious.

"In my opinion that's all drivel. Only temporality and space are eternal."

"And probably not even them." He turned over onto his stomach too. "I believe that in astronomy it is sometimes called into question. For that matter, when I think of Michelangelo's *Creation of Adam*, which is hanging on the *Rampa* . . . that's from after the discovery of perspective, isn't it?"

"And in that, God *floats* there of necessity, in natural space, on this side of the vanishing point, which has no other side. He isn't a credible God any longer, but the brilliant fantasy of a man who overcame the laws of nature."

"Instead of having made them." Max nodded. "But wait a moment . . . nowadays—"

"Yes, I know what you mean."

"You do? What, then?"

"That modern art has abandoned perspective again."

"Exactly. Take Picasso. With him you don't see any nonsimultaneous happenings, like in medieval paintings, but you do see spacial impossibilities, like the front and side of a face at the same time, and in the theory of relativity you find all those temporal and spatial oddities in scientific form, so I've heard."

"But God hasn't reappeared. If there is another side to the vanishing point, then he's suffocated there by now, and it's only his corpse that is lying stinking in heaven."

"Do you think so? If you ask me, nothing has changed, because nothing can change in eternity. Eternity is exactly the same thing as the moment. The vanishing point is the gate of heaven, where St. Peter stands with his keys. We probably can't take them from him, but if you ask me you can easily find a way through that point with your submachine gun. I'll slip in right behind you."

"Well, I think what you're saying is all well and good, but you aren't going to tell me that you are a believer?"

"Of course not."

"You aren't going to tell me, or you aren't one?"

"Perhaps Einstein is God; he's a bit like him. *Ein Stein der Weisen*—the Philosophers' Stone." Max sighed deeply. He pushed his fingers into the hot sand to where it was a little cooler. "I can still remember very well when he died in 1955; I was twenty-two and I felt as though I had lost my father. Listen, Marilyn. I make the occasional joke. I know that's not right according to orthodox thinkers like you, but that's just how I am. What's more, I'm in Cuba too now. Just like you, I believe that it must be possible to found a just society on earth. It's true that I'm still that much of a believer—just like you. And if Fidel succeeds, if only a little, I'm quite prepared in a manner of speaking to grant him a reflection of something like the divine. Or perhaps it already applies to his intention, even if he doesn't succeed. There's definitely something apostolic about him. I've got a good nose for that."

He wanted to say to Ada in Dutch that here was finally someone who took art history seriously, and reached for a gun, but because it would be impolite suddenly to speak a secret language, he put his head on his arms and closed his eyes. He was sorry that Onno wasn't there; he would definitely have had something more to say.

Perhaps he would have praised her for not having brought in the psychology of religion, or Marx. Max listened to the surf while the sun baked his back. That sound at any rate was almost eternal. Perhaps only the sound of an erupting volcano was older. The oldest signal was of course the cosmic background radiation of 3°K, the afterglow of the Big Bang, in which Marilyn's "natural space and time" had originated; the exploding singularity, then, was Marilyn's perspective vanishing point, through which nothing could pass. The question what was behind it, or in front of it, was absurd. It was so neat: art not only as a guide for political action but also for the scientific understanding of the world!

"You're burning," said Ada. "So am I, come to that. I'll go and see if there's any sun oil."

When she went to the bungalow he leaned on one elbow, looked deep into Marilyn's eyes, and said, "If that's all true, why don't we get married?"

She returned his glance for a moment, and then, convulsed with laughter, rolled off her towel into the sand, where she lay on her back, her arms and legs spread wide apart. He was about to laugh too, but when he suddenly saw her mons veneris rising, with the thin material of her swimsuit wrapped over the curve of her labia, like a great coffee bean, his mouth hung open a little. When she realized what was suddenly happening, her laugh froze too. She sat up, put her arms around her knees, and looked at him for a while, nodding.

"What are you thinking about?" she asked.

"Terrible things."

"Put those out of your head. You've got the wrong person."

"I'm afraid I have."

"Christ, this really bugs me. Here we are having an interesting conversation, but your wife or your girlfriend has no sooner gone off than the fooling around begins."

"She's not my girlfriend. She's my friend's girlfriend." He saw that the information threw her for a moment. "You see, now you're supposed to cry: 'Darling, that changes everything!' and throw your arms around me."

It was obviously an effort for her to maintain an air of indignation—if she were to laugh now, she probably thought, things would soon get out of hand. Of course she was involved with some *comandante,* or, rather, with an earnest professor of aesthetics, or with a jovial surrealist in a messy studio—anything was possible: a man never knew who a woman was involved with. Perhaps the revolution was her only love. He decided to leave things as they were for now. The day wasn't over yet. He turned back onto his stomach, rested his chin on his hands, and looked at Ada, who was coming out of the bungalow with the oil.

19

In the Sea

In the evening Jesús again preferred to eat in the kitchen. Languidly, with red faces, they sat at the table on the veranda during the intemperate sunset; the heat scarcely abated, and, after showering, they had all put on just a shirt; Guerra was still wearing his long trousers with the embroidered jacket. As darkness quickly fell and the forest no longer stood out because of its shadow, it was filled with the chirping of legions of crickets. Melancholy at the thought of her impending departure, helped by the full-bodied red wine that was served with the roast lamb, Ada looked at the deepening violet glow above the sea.

"I'm inconsolable. This is the last time that I shall have seen the sunset here."

"Stay, then," said Guerra. "Marilyn stayed."

"If only it were as simple as that . . ."

"Suppose," said Max, dipping a piece of bread in his wine, "she were to say that she was staying. What would be in store for her—perfect happiness or the question: what next?"

"In other words," concluded Marilyn, "happiness is impossible."

He looked at her, convinced that she also knew that the two of them were simultaneously engaged in a second, unspoken conversation. He took the bottle and said, "How severe you are. Why don't you have a glass of wine? According to our friend who is otherwise engaged, water is for brushing your teeth."

"No thanks," she said. "I may have to shoot."

Laughing, he topped up the three other glasses. "That's right. It's extremely dangerous on the road—the whole coast is swarming with infiltrators. Why don't we stay the night here? I'm sure that's possible."

"Of course," said Guerra, "if you want . . ."

"Don't be silly, Max," said Ada with a girlish gesture of her elbow. "I wouldn't dream of it, my plane leaves tomorrow—and it doesn't seem a very nice way to behave toward Onno. Come to that, shouldn't we be making a move?"

Max nodded with his eyes closed, indicating that the impulse had already gone, and put down his knife and fork.

"Shall I tell you something, Marilyn? Believe it or not, I'm happy now. Because I know that one day I shall look back at this evening in the knowledge that I was happy then. Maybe you can only be happy via that mirror. One day I'll lie on my deathbed in the knowledge that I'll never get up again—and then the thought of this evening may perhaps ease my death." He took a sip, but did not swallow. He swished his tongue about in the wine, the smell of which now penetrated his nose from inside, and it seemed to him as though those few cubic inches in the darkness of his mind in some way contained the whole world, just as a drop of dew on a stalk of grass mirrors the landscape. He swallowed and said, "I've suddenly had a vision."

"Tell us," said Ada.

"I see a German soldier on the Russian steppe, twenty-five years ago. You should know that there was a war going on between us in Europe at that time, but that would take me too long to go into now. He's about twenty years old, it's forty degrees below zero and among burnt-out tanks and frozen horse carcasses he lies back in the howling snowstorm while a glowing red grenade fragment lies hissing in his guts—and in his final moments he suddenly has a vision. He sees a table on the veranda by a fairy-tale bay, it's evening, the table is covered with food and wine, and it's so warm that two beautiful women are wearing nothing but flimsy shirts . . ."

It was still for a moment. Ada gave Marilyn a look that showed a problem had now arisen.

"And why," asked Guerra, bending aside to allow the black housekeeper to take his plate away, "are we the vision of a fascist soldier and not a Soviet one?"

Max groaned. "You're right, but I can't force my visions, can I? It's *his* vision after all, isn't it?"

Guerra smiled. "You wouldn't cut a bad figure as a dialectician at the cadre school."

"If you assure me that visions are not forced there, either, I hereby apply for the post."

"We don't force anything. The new Cuba is itself a vision."

"You see," said Max to Ada, "now *I'm* staying here."

All three of them looked at him—and suddenly he felt uncomfortable. Was he talking too much? It was as though there were a sudden distance between himself and the others; suddenly he felt abandoned. Because his headache started to return, he cupped his hands and asked Ada to pour some ice water from the carafe into them, after which he parted his knees and dipped his face into it.

"Don't you feel well?"

"A little relapse," he said, his face dripping. "It'll soon pass." He got up and only knew what he was trying to say when he said it. "Shall I give Onno a call? To say we'll be home in a couple of hours?"

"Shall I do it?"

"Let me."

Without drying himself he went inside, where the black housekeeper pointed out the telephone in the hall. Marilyn's submachine gun was hanging over the arm of a chair. Her real identity was hanging there. He had been wrong about her. He must stop—otherwise he might bite off more than he could chew. But meanwhile his internal secretions had prepared themselves for it: he felt it like a hardening in his insides, something like the spongy stem sometimes put in a vase for sticking flowers into, erect from his abdomen to his heart.

As Onno was probably still at dinner, he had him paged on the terrace of the restaurant, but he was not there; there was no answer from his room either. Just as he was about to hang up, he heard Onno's soft, hoarse voice:

"*Sí?*"

"What's all this? It's Max. Were you asleep?"

"Yes. You woke me up. What's wrong? I don't want to talk to anyone. Not even you."

"What's happened?"

"None of your business."

"Onno! What's wrong?"

There was a moment's silence. He was certain that Onno had half raised himself and was leaning on one elbow to see what time it was.

"I can't look myself in the face any longer. I'm not fit for a high-minded person like you to talk to. I won't say any more, but even that must remain a secret. Can Ada hear you?"

"No, she's sitting on the terrace. We're in a wonderful *dacha* by the sea, with Guerra and Jesús, with crowds of servants around us—well, as you know, only in a Communist country can people like you and me live like capitalists. What's more, the revolution has assigned me, as future leader of the Dutch People's Republic, a breathtakingly beautiful woman with a sub-machine gun."

"Yes, I can hear, your deepest masochistic instincts are once again being satisfied. I should never have listened to you. We should never have come here, because they're serious here, and that seriousness has made a necro-philiac of me. I'm a moral wreck. Only sleep can bring me oblivion."

"Did all that happen in church? Did you spit in the holy-water font?"

"Yes! I spat in the holy-water font!"

"Onno, you're not going to tell me that you've been to bed with another woman?"

"I'm not going to tell you anything at all, you shit. When an exceptionally refined spirit reproaches itself, all you can think of is *that*. My real problem is of a completely different spiritual kind. I've allowed myself to be devoured—as a victim of my own goodness. My noble spirit will be my downfall one day. And now I'm going to hang my . . . I mean, now I'm go-ing to hang up, because I'm exhausted. Tell Ada that I'll come straight to her tomorrow to throw myself at her feet. No, don't say that last bit. You're coming back this evening, aren't you?"

"We'll be home at about twelve."

"See you tomorrow."

" 'Good night, sweet prince.' "

Max hung up and stood there lost in thought. What did it mean? Had Onno really been unfaithful to Ada, in broad daylight? Surely that was in-conceivable, but even if he had, then what he said was incomprehensible, even making allowances for all the exaggeration. What did he mean by "necrophiliac"? Had he been seduced into taking the host, perhaps? *Hoc est enim corpus meum?* Had he slunk toward the altar, with head bowed and hands folded, and stuck his tongue out? Perhaps to please someone? The priest? Perhaps because he was the only person in the church? In any case Max knew that Onno always exaggerated in the direction of truth, never in the opposite direction, and that something was really tormenting him, and that he would do better not to return to the subject if Onno did not raise it himself.

He went to the veranda, where the housekeeper, the cook, and Jesús had now joined them and sat talking softly in the dark. Ada had disappeared. Marilyn said that she had gone into the sea for a last time "to say goodbye."

"What's stopping you?" said Guerra, gesturing toward the crashing of the surf in the darkness.

Yes, why not? He had never swum in the Gulf of Mexico at night, and in a few days' time he would be shaking his English umbrella with its bamboo handle in and out in the doorway, as though fighting a gigantic bat. In the bungalow he put on his clammy swimming trunks again and went down the steps to the beach.

When he emerged from under the trees, his bare feet sinking into the sand, still warm from the sun, the moonless starry sky spread out with a gesture that he thought he could almost *hear:* like a marvelous chord played by the whole orchestra. Compared to this, the sight of the heavens from his hotel room on the twenty-fifth floor, pale because of the city lights and the exhaust fumes, was a record on an old portable gramophone. He stood still. Feeling as though his head were the dome of an observatory, he let his eyes wander.

Mars shone red and unwavering among the twinkling stars, and in the Cross of Orion, Messier 42 glimmered like a dried sperm stain on the fly of a pair of evening trousers. For him the stars to the south below Betelgeuse and Rigel, sometimes invisible even in summer at higher latitudes, did not merge into the geometrical mythical "pictures" of ancient astronomy; but even with those of the Northern Hemisphere he got no further than the few configurations that he had learned as a boy, in the war—just as doctors no longer knew the Hippocratic theory of temperaments. The capricious, faintly glowing band of the Milky Way wound across the heavens like a torn bridal veil, and for the first time in years he again realized why he had devoted his life to that magnificent dome.

The sea, which seemed even warmer than in the afternoon, received him like someone coming home. The tide was in. As he swayed and let the waves break against his chest, he tried to find Ada, but it was impossible in all that dark movement. He cupped his hands round his mouth and shouted:

"Ada!"

She hesitated. She saw his silhouette outlined against the lighter beach. Each wave lifted her up a little and set her back on her toes. But she was absorbed by the fairy-tale fact that she was here now because she could play the cello: music had carried her *auf Flügeln des Gesanges* to this spot in the sea—if only her mother could see her!

"Max!" She waved. "Over here!"

He waved back and dived.

She would have preferred to remain alone, but then of course he would have worried that she had been engulfed by the sea. Only when she was alone did she have the sense that she really existed; other people might be frightened precisely because of that sense, but she was frightened of other people because they stole it from her.

Max surfaced near her.

"What do we owe this to?" she cried.

"Our lucky stars!"

He put his hands around her waist and together they bobbed up and down in the almost black water. It had been a long time since she had seen him so close; his dripping face was lit only by the stars. She put her hands on his shoulders and laughed.

"It's as though we're dancing."

He put his right arm around her waist, took her right hand in his left, and pulled her to him. *"La valse . . ."*

She saw a mischievous twinkle in his eyes and could feel him getting an erection, but because it was under water, invisible down in the depths, it was as though she had nothing to do with it: there were so many secrets in the sea that had not yet been unveiled. He put his cheek against hers, and while he hummed the macabre theme of Ravel's orchestral piece through the roar of the surf, she saw a bright light shooting across the sky.

"Look, a falling star! We can make a wish."

He turned his head, but he did not entirely trust the grainy, slowly fading dust trail: it must be a block of one or two kilos, and meteorites were rarely that big.

"And if it doesn't come true," he said, "it was a fragment of a satellite; the sky's full of them at this latitude. What did you wish?"

"You must never say that." She looked at him in confusion.

A child is what she had instantly thought, without hesitation, as though the wish had plunged into her mind like that thing into the atmosphere— *I want a child.* She felt as disconcerted as a good husband and father who, on seeing a meteor, suddenly desires a beautiful nymph of seventeen. As far as she was aware, she did not want a child at all, nor did Onno. So was she suppressing her deepest wish every time she swallowed that little white pill?

Suddenly there was a syncopation in the rhythm of the waves: a faster, higher one arrived, which lifted them up and tumbled them over. Coughing, spewing saltwater, they surfaced again and grabbed each other again. Max gave her a kiss on the cheek and immediately afterward sought her mouth. Had he seen what she was thinking? She let herself be kissed and felt his hand disappearing down the back of her bikini bottom.

"What are you doing?"

"We need to finish something . . ." he panted.

Bring yourself off. His excitement of course also derived from the state he had gotten himself into with Marilyn; he had been given the cold shoulder and now Ada was the erotic substitute—but at the same time he harked back to that morning over three months ago, and that rendered her helpless. He had not forgotten, either; he too knew that it was wrong. At the moment that a wave lifted them up, he pulled down her bikini bottom and already had it around his arm. Almost weightlessly, she wrapped her legs around his hips and said, "Max . . . this is impossible . . . if Onno . . ."

But he could no longer hear. I made sure that a completely different force flowed through him, which cared nothing about him. She felt him penetrate her—and over his shoulder she saw that a blood-red, monstrous crescent moon had risen; in its first quarter, it lay back almost horizontally on the horizon . . .

THE MISSION

At that moment I said:

—*Spark! Yes, you! Drift toward me in slowly turning parallellepipeda through this whiter than white Light, which shines and resonates from all sides, by which we are surrounded and permeated, are ourselves a part of, light in Light, harmony in Harmony. Who would want to leave this pneumatic field, where each element coincides with the whole, where the whole is in every part, and where first here and then there figures take shape and disappear, triangles, circles, ellipses, hyperbolas, spheres, cones, cubes, octahedrons, dodecahedrons, where tumbling spheroids glow and merge in the endless harmony of the Endless Light, in which you are a single point, no, a harmoniously resonating string of Light. Can you leave? Look, there, near that convex polygon sector, there's one, whoosh, gone, something quivers for a moment, a faint echo, a tiny silence, then Light closes over itself and it is as though nothing has happened. But something has happened. Look around you—you can see it happening everywhere, continuously. Where are they going? Look hard—you can see Sparks coming back into the Light too: there, and there, and there. So is there nothing else but this eternal domain? Look into yourself, into that unbroken light that you are, without a flaw—is there perhaps a flaw in it after all? Isn't that flaw a certain vague longing, which is always with you and which you are hence not aware of, just as you are not aware of the glowing harmony that you are by being a part of it? A kind of homesickness, although you have never been anywhere else but here? Isn't it as though even perfection is not perfect? The Light is not completely luminous and Harmony is not completely harmonious? Yes, you must know now: this world is*

not the only one. There is another world. I cannot prove it, you have to believe it,
you have to take the step and only then will you really experience it. There is an
earth. The earth exists—as the innermost dungeon of the Kingdom of the Ar-
chontes. There is no point in telling you much about it, or even a little, because
you would not understand. You would not even understand what you do not
understand, because you do not yet know what "not" is. So, for example, it is not
always light on earth—but that is already beyond your understanding. I might as
well say nothing, but I am going to say it all the same: perhaps from envy, because
I will never be able to live there. In a way that is as explicable as it is mysterious,
it is sometimes light, sometimes dark; but even the earthly light of the sun is Dark-
ness compared with our Light. It is as if it were the shadow of ours, and the
shadow of that shadow is the poison of earthly darkness. I realize that I am not
making it attractive for you to depart for that impure, confused world, but I do
not wish to hold out false hopes to anyone, even though they do not understand
me—and precisely because you do not understand me, I will now reveal the deep-
est secret. Just as the germ of Darkness is hidden within our Light, so Darkness
tends toward our Light and loves it. By going there, you will bring Light, and the
only way of bringing Light is by going there. This cosmic mismatch ultimately
contains the meaning of our world. That is, only by setting out for that region of
black light, lies, deceit, violence, murder, sickness, and death do you make yourself
meaningful. By far the greater number of the infinite number of Sparks—if I can
put it like that—will never have that opportunity, because they are reserved for
contingencies that will never arise. For them eternity will never give way to tran-
sience and the finite. But you are one of the small, select band who are given the
chance. Much has already been invested in making your departure possible—
more than you will ever know, for your peace of mind. And that investment has
been made because you are being given a mission, which only you will be able to
remember. But you will not remember it as a memory; you will think that it's
your own idea, a fantastic brainwave. Because just as here you know nothing of
the earth, on earth you will know nothing of this world. You will forget all about
it. When we are mentioned, you will shrug the shoulders you will then have. Be-
cause while you are sinking through the three hundred and sixty-five eons, worlds,
and generations on your way to the earth at a point in time, you will grow heavier
and heavier; more and more litter from the cosmic spheres will attach itself to you,
shrouds, clothes, excrescences, snails, dead weight, covering your awareness of the
original Light, until you at last fall into the dark dungeon of spirit and flesh and
are finally born as a human being. That is, as a being that remembers nothing, not
even what it is, namely Light—like someone sleeping. That applies to you too.

But at the same time you are different from the others. All the others are sleepers, who have yet to awake, through faith and knowledge. Only then is there a way back for them. But the heavy accretions have mostly reconciled them with life on earth; they have forgotten that they are aliens there and that they are what they think they are: that is the greatest threat to their return. Things will be easier for you. For technical reasons, we have decided on the VIP procedure. And now your moment has come; everything is ready for your reception. Farewell! Go! Now! Retrieve the testimony for us! Adieu!

PART TWO

THE END
OF THE
BEGINNING

First Intermezzo

—Dear me, that was a close thing.

—You're telling me. The trouble with human beings is that we can lead them to the water, but we can't make them drink. For example, it's no trouble for us to make someone stand up and pace about his room, or to make him slip so that he breaks his neck; but to get someone to do something that runs counter to his feelings is less simple. People aren't puppets—they have a will of their own; before you know it, they've slipped through your fingers. Take the meeting of Max and Onno.

—Did you fix that?

—Who else?

—It might have been coincidence.

—Of course, but it wasn't.

—Quite a feat. If Delius had driven past thirty seconds later, Onno might have gotten a lift from someone else.

—Then everything would have fallen through. Thank you for the compliment, but that kind of thing is routine for my department; for us that is almost as easy as some mechanical operation or other—for example making a tree blow over, or a meteorite strike, say—although in those areas too we often face uncertainties. Of course it was part of an extensive plan of action, because we had first to ensure that Max went to Rotterdam on the day of Onno's father's birthday, and so on and so forth, but as far as that was concerned there was no resistance to be expected.

—But why would have everything have fallen through in that case? What

was the point of the meeting? After all, it's only made matters more complicated.
You could have left Onno completely out of it and simply have had Max meet Ada
and have a child.

—In the first place, he would probably not have given her a child in that
case; and in the second place, it will become clear that Onno's presence was
essential for us to achieve our ultimate objective. When you're involved in a
project like that, you work not only on the moment that is immediately present, but are constantly keeping in mind everything that has already happened, what must happen in the future, everything that can go wrong, and
how that has to be coped with and what will in that case have to be prepared,
if you are to avoid it slipping through your fingers. You can compare it with
a war: in retrospect in the history books it's a nice, rounded story, the result
of which is known; but while it was going on, you as a field marshal may
have had your plan of campaign, but it was still largely a chaotic succession
of events, stupidities, and unforeseen surprises, which demanded new decisions every moment. And in the third place. . . . Oh, I've forgotten. Excuse
me, you have touched on an essential point that we should perhaps be clear
about from the outset. You asked me to tell the story at length and in detail
and I've started. But to be honest, I don't feel like telling the story and at the
same time saying why it is like it is and where I've intervened and where I
haven't and why.

—*Have I touched on a sensitive spot?*

—To start with I have no sensitive spots, because in our pneumatic domain we exist entirely of intelligence, and moreover . . .

—*And moreover?*

—Let's leave it. I don't mind justifying myself now and then, or explaining something more fully, but I don't intend to keep biting my own tail.

—*You do have a tail, then?*

—The story may have one.

—*I don't know if you know but the Ouroboros, a serpent biting its own tail, is*
a symbol of eternity on that same earth.

—That's as may be, but if I can't tell the story in the way that is implicit
in the events themselves, then you will simply have to make do with the announcement that the matter is settled. You can ask me a hundred questions,
or a thousand or a hundred thousand; you can ask me . . . for example, why
Cuba had to be dragged in, and so on and so forth—that will all become
clear. Take it from me that nothing has happened that wasn't absolutely

necessary, at least as far as my interventions were concerned. It's no coincidence that I haven't once said "I" yet.

—*Except for those three times, that is. And let me tell you this. The fact that you are also in the top rank of the Celestial Hierarchy doesn't give you the right to strike such a damn impertinent tone with an official who is just a little superior to you. Anyway, that's how things are here these days. It's starting to depress me, but that may also be partly due to your story. You know, none of us has a view of the whole Pleroma, but if you operate at the edge of the Light, as we do, with a view of the demonic world of Darkness, things are harder for you than for those higher entities who are scarcely aware of it; and you even more than I are standing with your back to the Light and facing Darkness. If my memory serves me well, once or twice in the past you even appeared in that Archontic area, which cannot even claim to have been created by the Chief, as most of those windbags there believe, because that anthropic explosion of light, which was to lead to them, was the work of our center. Compared with me you are already almost one of them, although for them you are infinitely far removed—at least if they even have an inkling of your existence. Most of them know beings like us only in the shape of infantile fantasies like Superman or Batman. Would you like to know why that is? It's because by now they have almost all our powers themselves, in the shape of their technology. And that's our own stupid fault. For centuries we have been complacently been asleep here, and in the meantime Satan-El has been doing his work.*

—Satan-El? What's that you're saying? In what form?

—*All those characters are scum anyway: Belial-Satan, Beelzebub-Satan, Asmodee-Satan, Azazel-Satan, Samael-Satan, Mephistopheles-Satan, and so on and so on, they're all the same. But of course it was Lucifer-Satan again.*

—What was the swine doing then?

—*We only found out recently. Five hundred years ago, without our realizing it, he entered into a pact with mankind, a sort of diabolical counterpart of the Chief's testimony.*

—You must be joking! I only know the story that Mephistopheles is supposed to have entered into a pact with a certain Dr. Faust, that Faust is supposed to have sold his soul to him, but that seemed to me to belong more to literature.

—*That is true, but there now turns out to be a very dangerous aspect to it. Can I refresh your memory a moment? The historical Johannes Faust was a trav-*

eling German magician from Württemberg, with an infamous reputation, like many others in the first half of the human sixteenth century. In 1587, when he had been dead for about forty or fifty years, his legend began with the appearance of a chronicle. Historia von D. Johann Fausten dem weitbeschreiten Zauberer und Schwarzkünstler, *in which that story of the pact with the devil occurs. That Faust legend, we believe, goes back to a similar traveling character, fifteen hundred years earlier, who is mentioned in the Acts of the Apostles, Simon Magus. He fell out with Peter, because he wanted to buy the Holy Ghost. That character, a Samaritan, had gotten it into his head that he himself was the Chief.*

—Go on. Was Satan-El behind that, too?

—*We assume so now. He was going with a Phoenician whore, whom he maintained was an incarnation of Helen of Troy.*

—How can you claim such a thing?

—*On earth you can claim all sorts of things, and there are always people who will believe you. But be careful, don't underestimate him. He said that the Feminine Principle was the first Idea in Thought—that is, in the Chief's thought; that is, his own. That Principle next created us, whereupon we in our turn created the world. But according to him we do not want to be regarded as creatures, only as creators, and so we dragged our creator from Light to the Darkness of our creation and forced it into the physical shape of a centuries-old series of women, including Helen, and finally into a whore in the brothel in Tyre from where the Father, having descended to earth and become flesh, finally rescued the imprisoned Mother.*

—What a story! Of course that bit about the abduction and all those women is a scandalous lie—but how did that magician find out the truth about creation? Did Lucifer tell him about all that?

—*Can you think of another explanation?*

—And what did he have up his sleeve in doing that?

—*It was a red herring to disguise his real intention. Without anyone realizing it Simon Magus returned toward the end of the sixteenth century in the legend of Faust, the restless seeker after knowledge, who entered into a pact with the devil. The first literary adaptation was Christopher Marlowe's,* The Tragicall History of Doctor Faustus, *which was performed in London in about 1590. That was the beginning of a continuous succession of adaptations of the theme, down to the present earthly day, the high point of which was, naturally, Goethe's version, in which Helen again appears. In one of the most recent versions,* Doktor Faustus *by Thomas Mann, a syphilitic whore again crops up as the companion of the hero, and that was, significantly enough, inspired by a fatal whore in the life of Nietzsche, whom we were talking about just now. She was the cause of his fatal madness.*

—I know all about that. At the time I even dispatched that creature to get him. People shouldn't pronounce the Chief dead. But where was Lucifer's red herring? What was he trying to distract attention from?

—*The intention was to impress upon mankind that a pact with the devil was a literary matter: the noncommittal story of an imaginary individual thirsting after knowledge, who sells his soul. That was how it was possible for a dreadful, far from literary but very real event to go unnoticed until today—namely, that in that same last decade of the sixteenth century, also in London, Lucifer entered into a pact with* mankind, *a collective contract in which the whole of* mankind *sold its soul to him.*

—Good God! How should I imagine that? Did someone sign that contract on behalf of mankind?

—*Yes.*

—Who was that?

—*Francis Bacon.*

—Francis Bacon?

—*Francis Bacon. He has always been regarded as a man who prophetically foresaw the modern scientific and technological world. In a number of epochmaking works he sketched the outlines of a world in which science and technology would no longer be in the hands of a few individual amateurs, as was the case in his own days around 1600, but would have changed into an internationally organized, collective endeavor, subsidized by governments, with conferences and systematic publications. Only in that way could a full mastery of nature be obtained; and the scientific method would have to be that of induction, in which one progressed from the particular to the general, from empirical phenomena to natural laws, although you and I of course know that the only true method is the reverse one, that of deduction. At the end of his life he wrote* Nova Atlantis, *"The New Atlantis," which remained as a fragment and was published after his death. In it he sketches a central institute of a Utopian island called Bensalem, which he dubs "Solomon's House," but it is not something like the blessed temple of Solomon in Jerusalem, which is so dear to our hearts, not even something like a Christian church, but more like a modern research center, in which new biological species are manufactured.*

—From a human point of view, that all seems obvious.

—So obvious that in the twentieth century he is scarcely mentioned on earth any longer. That's the danger of being absolutely right: virtually no one realizes that things were ever any different. Just imagine, in his day even scientific experiments were virtually unknown. That is why it has always astonished us that this rational founder of modern science and technology of all people should be surrounded by mystery. He is supposed to be the founder of freemasonry, he has been called a clandestine Rosicrucian and an initiate in numerous other secret societies. There has long been a Baconian sect, which with a lot of numerological hocuspocus tries to prove that he wrote the plays and sonnets of Shakespeare. All nonsense, of course, but why is it that all this has become attached precisely to that cool, realistic combater of delusions? Not only has he been called the true author of Burton's Anatomy of Melancholy, but all kinds of acrostics have been dragged in to prove that the work of Edmund Spenser were actually by him—and of course, inevitably, that of Marlowe too. Bacon as the author of the first Faust play! It is claimed that at his funeral an empty coffin was consigned to the earth, because he is claimed to have lived for a further twenty-one years in Germany under another name.

—In Württemberg, of course!

—In the capital no less, Stuttgart. The so-called discovery finally woke us up, and we can now reconstruct the course of events. Baconians sometimes claim that he was the illegitimate son of Queen Elizabeth and the earl of Leicester, but in reality he was born in 1561 as the son of Elizabeth's Keeper of the Great Seal. Because he was the youngest son, he was left penniless on his father's death; as a twenty-three-year-old lawyer he obtained a seat in Parliament. He was determined to become as rich and powerful as his father, but his career did not progress well. His bosom friend the earl of Essex, the queen's lover, did what he could for him, but Elizabeth did not trust Bacon. When all his attempts to secure his friend a high office had failed, the loyal Essex gave him one of his own estates as a consolation. That was in 1595. However, four years later Essex himself fell out of favor, a charge of high treason was prepared against him, and now Elizabeth suddenly intervened. She asked Bacon if he would be so kind as to draw up the indictment. And now the hour of the devil had struck—because, what do you think? He did it, although he knew that it would lead to the execution of his benefactor. The serpent promised him that he would rise even higher than his father, but for that he must first put his signature to the indictment and then publish a number of books, which would be dictated to him.

—Why did Lucifer choose Bacon, of all people? Had he already written anything?

—In 1597 he had published a collection of intelligent Essayes, *which are still read, but are not anything that would have attracted the attention even of the devil. But much earlier, at the age of twenty-one, in 1583, he had published a pamphlet entitled* Temporis Partus Maximus, *"The Great Birth of Time." The fact that not a single copy of it has survived aroused our suspicions; and we now assume that it struck a tone that had made the devil prick up his ears. For some reason he later suppressed all copies of it. Be that as it may, after the prophet of the new age had signed the diabolical pact with mankind by putting his signature to the effective death sentence against his best friend, the stagnation of his career was suddenly over. In 1600 Essex was beheaded in the Tower, in 1607 Bacon became Attorney General, in 1613 Procurator General, and in 1617 he equaled his father's achievement by being appointed Keeper of the Great Seal. Two years later he confirmed his subservience to the devil by having an innocent prisoner tortured, because King James required a confession and a sentence; shortly afterward he became Lord Chancellor, the highest position in the land, thus surpassing his father. He was raised to the nobility as Lord Verulam, and later further elevated to become Viscount Saint Albans. Meanwhile he wrote the books that the devil dictated to him, and which were not prophetic but clever self-fulfilling prophecies intended to destroy mankind.*

—That means that the opportunistic traitor not only did not write the works of Shakespeare or Marlowe, but not even his own.

—That's right. But Lucifer would not be Lucifer if he had left it at that. Even those who submit themselves to him and serve him must finally be destroyed. Because after Sir Francis had finally achieved more than he had ever dreamed of, the devil appeared to him one day in the shape of an official, from whom he accepted a bribe, which led to a trial for corruption, imprisonment in the Tower, and his complete social downfall. Five years later, at the age of sixty-five, he finally went to hell.

—Long live friendship!

—Your story too is yet another demonstration of what is missing—and it saddens me that that's how it must be. That's what I have always missed most against my better judgment, here in the Light. No shortage of love, bliss, goodness, wisdom, truth, peace, beauty, all in our service, but no friendship.

—You're not my friend?

—Or even your girlfriend. In organizations there are no friendships, and certainly not in ours, and even more certainly not between superiors and subordinates. Friendship exists only in the abyss. Do you know those famous, magnificent, elevated passages on friendship that Bacon wrote shortly before his death: No re-

ceipt openeth the heart but a true friend? *Indeed, and the jugular vein! The man who had his best friend beheaded! Can you hear it? The laughter of the heartless devil, with his own temperature at absolute zero, resounds through all the halls of all eternities.*

—Now I finally understand why I made such efforts for all those years.

—*Go on. I'm listening.*

20

The Hooblei

One of the first things they did, back in autumnal Holland—Che Guevara turned out to have been murdered in Bolivia on the very night of the excursion to Varadero—was to repay the expenses incurred in Cuba. Max was not very keen in retrospect; his alarm at Guerra's words had subsided with distance, and according to him everything had disappeared into the caverns of bureaucratic oblivion. But in Onno's view it was a question of morality, of Kantian *practical reason,* about which there could be no haggling. Max inquired about the cost per day with full board at the Amsterdam Hilton, which turned out to be a lot of money; they estimated the capitalist profiteering of Conrad Hilton and his henchmen on the Wall Street stock exchange at 50 percent, then divided the amount in revolutionary fashion by two and decided to regard the excursions and car trips as Cuban investments in their future propaganda on behalf of the island. They considered sending the money to the ICAP in the form of an anonymous dollar check; but Ada told them that the conservatory in Havana urgently needed a new stencil machine, which was unobtainable in Cuba, whereupon Max selected a splendid machine and had it shipped out with the message: *Hasta la victoria siempre.—Dos amigos.*

When he later reported what he had written, Onno nodded in agreement, but Ada shot him a short glance, which hit him like a blow to the head. He looked down and thought the same as she did. *Dos amigos?* Did a friend go to bed, or rather into the sea, with his friend's girlfriend, even though she had once been his own girlfriend? In his own words friendship was that condition in which one told the other person even what one would never tell anyone. Would he ever tell Onno what he had gotten up to in the Gulf of Mexico? Whether he told him or not, wasn't it in either case the end of true *amistad*? If he told him, it need not be replaced by enmity, it could be replaced by all kinds of things, but whatever happened, something else would replace it. But since he was not going to tell him, it had created an even more false situation: for Onno everything went on as before, but Max and Ada now had something to hide—they had both deceived him. It didn't change the actual situation at all, but Onno was now like someone who had invested his fortune in a Rembrandt drawing; the thief had replaced it one night by a faultless reproduction, and for the rest of his life he would have no idea that there was a worthless fake on the wall.

What Max and Ada on their side did not know was that Onno had had an adventure of his own. But he had been seduced—he had betrayed only his girlfriend, not his friend. Max salved his conscience with the thought that it had not actually happened in October but in June, as the belated payment of a debt for something that one had once bought and no longer possessed but that nevertheless had to be paid for, and a week later it had merged harmoniously with his other incredible experiences on the island, which were summarized by the aphorism that he had seen at Havana airport: "When the impossible becomes the everyday, a revolution is under way." He felt refreshed by the intercontinental excursion, and in the observatory's lecture room he gave an enthusiastic talk on the revolution in Cuba; it even attracted people from other faculties who were interested in hearing the report of an eyewitness. Because there were a few foreigners among them he spoke in English; an American colleague from the Goldstone radio telescope, who was working on the sun, got excited about the policy of strangulation being followed by his government. He was ashamed to be American!

Onno did his duty with his political friends. He also omitted to mention that he had been a delegate at a conference of radical revolutionaries; no one would believe the true story. However, he did explain that the main problem of the Third World was communication—not only the flow of goods, but also information: it was all totally inadequate, that's why the craziest things were possible there, and he could give astonishing examples of this, but that would take him too far at this point. And then there was the ideology! In Cuba you could learn the meaning of the word *radicalism*. In the United States the left wing of the Democratic party was still farther right than a right-wing party in the Netherlands, and there was no party taken seriously here as right-wing as the Republican party, let alone its right wing; but in Cuba the government was considerably farther to the left than even the Communist party in the Netherlands. American rage at the existence of that Red bastion off its coast was therefore understandable. For them it was quite simply the Red devil; this was the home of the new redskins who had to be gunned down from the hip; and for Dutch Social Democrats it still meant that the prevailing situation there should be closely observed with the necessary attention, albeit with judicious reserve.

"I'm going into town for a bit," said Ada.

She had put her head around the door of Onno's study; she had her coat on. He had a colleague with a mustache visiting him, smoking a large bent pipe; with his back to her Onno gave a wave of his hand, without turning around.

She was still struck by the amount of grayness in Amsterdam after all those dazzling tropical colors, but it was not really unpleasant. She was at home here. People looked surly and dissatisfied, it was chilly, the trees were becoming bare, and it was getting dark early again, but it was just this variation of the seasons that were unknown in the tropics: no autumn, no winter, no spring, in fact only summer. Were Chopin or Stravinsky conceivable in a climate like that? In any case they hadn't appeared there, and nor had anything else of importance been thought of or invented there, as far as she knew. Because she had the feeling that she would be better off to leave such considerations to Onno and Max, she put these thoughts out of her mind.

She didn't feel like taking the busy streets with trams running along them, and wandered aimlessly down the Spiegelstraat toward the center of town. She felt restless; suddenly she had become too impatient to practice, like when she wanted to do something and was expecting visitors any moment. Now and then she stopped at the window of an antiques shop and looked at a serene, gleaming gold Buddha with hands outstretched as though warding something off, at a lonely, grubby green Japanese bowl on dun-colored velvet, which no one would pick up if they saw it lying in the gutter, at antique glass and silver and at glowing seventeenth-century paintings. There was no end to the beauty of the world, nor to its cruelty. She had a painful feeling in her breasts—naturally, because she had let her posture at the cello become lazy; that had been her fault from her first lessons onward, when she was six. Tomorrow evening she was playing in The Hague with the orchestra, and a tour of the United States was scheduled for March. The artistic director had impressed on her not to say a word about her performance in Havana, preferably not to the other musicians either, because that might endanger the whole tour. Anyone who had been to Cuba had the plague, "the Red Death," in Poe's words.

She walked along the Keizersgracht toward the narrow cross streets with the barbaric names that she could never remember, Berenstraat, Wolvenstraat, where small shops sold things: colorful jewelry, semi-antique knickknacks, ivory cigarette holders, rusty thimbles, dolls with yellow lace collars. Her thoughts went back to her own favorite doll, Liesje: a little bald waif with a furtive look, which was precisely what gave her a character of her own.

At the same moment she remembered the sand-colored coconut mat on which she played and the legs of the table and the country-style chairs with the frayed underside of their wicker seats. Liesje was a doll and at the same time not a doll. When she pulled its arm out, the white elastic band in its shoulder became visible; when she let go, it snapped back against the body with a click and remained in an unpredictable position: "Hello!" or "Look, over there!" She could also twist the arms and legs backward into agonizing positions, but as soon as everything had been brought back within the bounds of possibility, Liesje once again became more than a doll. Then she was also a girl, just like Ada herself, a girl who understood her, and for whom she was what her mother was to her, so that she herself was at the same time Liesje. And both Liesjes were threatened by that appalling monster, which sometimes hid in the shadows of the curtains but also wandered around somewhere near the ceiling without ever showing itself, the Hooblei.

She remembered this with a start as she was walking across the stamp market, with the shabby philatelists at their stalls, the albums covered with plastic against the drizzle. She hadn't thought of it for ten or fifteen years. The dark threat of the Hooblei had hung over her childhood like a storm that refused to break. The Hooblei wanted to stuff her in a box. There was no one she could talk to about it, only Liesje, who willingly allowed herself to be stuffed into cardboard boxes in the bookshop in order to find out what it was like. And one day the Hooblei struck and Liesje was indeed gone for good, put out for the dustman by her father, with box and all, on the edge of the sidewalk. She still managed to run after it with her father, but was only in time to see how two streets farther on, the loading compartment of the dustcart moved into a vertical position with a screech while Liesje was ground up with all the dirt and rubbish of the world . . .

Wading through pigeons she crossed the Dam and, caught up in the current of warm air behind the revolving doors, she entered the Bijenkorf department store. She strolled aimlessly for a while between women smelling the backs of their hands or having thick red stripes put on them; she stepped onto the elevator and allowed space to sink slowly downward. It made her feel a bit sick; perhaps she should eat something. At a high table in the cafeteria she ate a mackerel roll standing up, and then walked to the toy department, where she subjected herself to the gaze of dozens of dolls, each one with a more stupid expression than the last. None of them was even remotely like Liesje.

On a shelf there was a contingent of Russian *mamushkas* in all sizes; brightly painted peasant women that could be opened by twisting the top, whereupon the next one appeared. Her eye lighted on a box full of little peasant women in the same style, also hand-painted, no more than two inches high, with only a pencil sharpener hidden under their skirts. A smile crossed her face. She decided to give one to Max for his birthday in November: a woman with such alarming genitalia—that would teach him. *1 guilder, 5 cents* said the small label. She stood with it in her hands undecidedly. For some reason she had the feeling that it was already hers and that she would devalue that possession by paying for it, just as a man using prostitutes knows that the woman does not belong to him. She looked around, closed her hand over the doll, walked on, and a little later slipped it into the pocket of her raincoat.

Her deed filled her with amused satisfaction. She was reminded of Onno's argument that winning the 100,000-guilder prize in the lottery gave one deeper satisfaction than earning the same amount, and that was exactly why gambling should be prohibited. Even as a child she had never stolen anything from a shop, and she was surprised how easy it was. Touching the doll now and then, she went to the grocery department, where she immediately did the shopping for that evening. Since she had lived with Onno, she had understood her mother better; having to think every day of what to have to eat was worse than playing scales—and then she was lucky to have Onno, because at least he ate the same thing every evening. She paid for the macaroni and the ham and went to the exit. Dusk was already falling outside.

But when she had gone through the revolving door, a man suddenly barred her way.

"Would you mind showing me what you've got in your coat pocket?"

She looked in alarm at the identity card he held up in front of her, which showed his face, but differently from what she now saw: kinder, looking up in a relaxed way at something pleasant. Now she met a stony look. She handed him the pencil sharpener in embarrassment.

"Didn't they wrap it up for you? Could I see the receipt?"

"I haven't got one."

"Come with me."

People turned to look at her, trams and cars passed by, on the other side she read the sign DE ROODE LEEUW, and suddenly the matter-of-fact world of freedom disappeared over the horizon, because now she had to go back into the building.

"I'll pay for it," she said.

"You can't sort it out with me. After you."

Passing through an unobtrusive door behind the glittering cosmetics counters, they arrived in a concrete, neon-lit corridor, where in an instant the sweetness of existence had ended. Through a steel door she was admitted to a small, windowless room, which contained only a long table and a couple of chairs. She expected the man to follow her, but the door closed behind her and a key was turned in the lock.

She looked around her in alarm. She had been locked up! She suppressed a surge of despair. What could happen to her for one guilder and five cents? Of course this was the usual procedure—it was done to drum it into her; soon another official would appear, she would be given a telling off, would have to pay, and would be allowed to leave. But until the door had opened, it was still closed. She put her bag of shopping on the table and sat down. In a film she would now shout that she wanted to see her lawyer. Hordes of men, women, and children had preceded her here. The top of the table was made of grubby plastic; it had deep holes in various places. In the corridor she heard occasional voices, and the rattle of trucks bringing new goods for sale. She looked at her watch and thought of Onno, who was now conferring in his room and had no idea that she was shut up in the dungeon of a department store. She took a guilder and a five-cent coin out of her purse and put one on top of the other.

When after a quarter of an hour, twenty minutes, still no one had appeared, a wave of terror suddenly went through her. It was past five-thirty—it would soon be closing time. Suppose they had forgotten her! Imagine having to wait here till tomorrow morning! She got up in a sweat and began walking back and forth, biting her nails. Should she pound on the door? Start screaming? But perhaps that was precisely what they were waiting for; perhaps she was being observed from somewhere. She scanned the cement walls to see whether she could find anything. But just when she had decided to wait precisely five minutes longer, the key was turned.

On the threshold stood the security man who had apprehended her, with a policeman.

"What is your name?"

With eyes wide, Ada looked at the man in the black uniform, with the black boots, and with the black truncheon at his side.

"Ada Brons," she stammered, not being able to believe that she had been reported to the police.

"Do you admit that you stole this?" he asked, pointing to the doll, which the security man was holding up.

Ada took the coins and offered them in her open hand. "Here's the money. I'm sorry."

The policeman shook his head. "I must ask you to come to the station with me."

"To the station?" she repeated, perplexed. "Why?"

"So you can be charged."

He put his hand under his uniform jacket, and to her dismay, Ada saw that he was getting out handcuffs. The sight of that gleaming polished steel tore her apart. Her resistance broke and, sobbing, she threw the money at the two men.

"You're crazy! Crazy!"

"Calm down, miss. Nothing will happen to you. These are just the rules."

When the handcuffs clicked shut around her wrists, her first thought was how she could ever play the cello again. The space between her hands was not even sufficient for a ukulele. While they walked down the corridors to a back entrance, the policeman carried her shopping bag.

It was already dark outside; in a courtyard stood a small police van with barred windows. Shortly afterward they drove to the Warmoesstraat police station, which was around the corner, on the edge of the red-light district.

She was delivered to the duty officer's counter, where her handcuffs were taken off. A fat drunk woman with disheveled hair was screaming at a policeman, so young that he looked as if he had dressed up, and tried to involve Ada in her dispute; but she fell silent when two detectives brought in a semiconscious man, the front of whose shirt was red with blood. Ada was shown to Room 21, where she had to wait on a wooden bench in front of an ocher-painted door. When her handcuffs were taken off, her dismay and rage also disappeared. She felt as if she had fallen in the water but was now on shore.

Inside, she was received by a graying sergeant seated at a high black typewriter, which resembled the steps of a mausoleum. He looked at her paternally and asked her whether she had been guilty of this crime before. She was unable to explain to him why she had committed it now with such a trifling little thing. With a sigh, he put a black sheet of carbon paper between two forms straightened out on the table and put them in his machine.

When she observed that it was strange that there should be all this fuss over a guilder and five cents, he said: "It's not a matter of a guilder-five—it's about shoplifting. If a thousand people steal something worth one guilder-five and we do nothing about it, why should we prosecute someone who steals fifteen hundred guilders' worth? Or someone who's stolen fifteen hundred guilders?"

"That's true," said Ada. She had a feeling that the calculation wasn't quite right, but it seemed more sensible not to point this out.

"If we do nothing about it, then in ten years' time nothing will be done about someone who's stolen a bike or a car radio, and in fifty years' time nothing will be done about murder. You wouldn't want that to happen, would you?"

She thought of the orchestra. "Will I have to appear in court?"

"That could well happen."

"And what will I get?"

"A fine, I think, and possibly a suspended sentence as well. What's your job?"

When he heard that she was a cellist, he leaned back for a moment, took off his reading glasses, and looked at the ceiling with a thoughtful smile; it reminded him of something, but he said nothing. He took down all the facts, constantly pulling back one arm that stuck from the paper, checked on the spelling of the word *mamushka,* and pulled the sheets out of the typewriter carriage with a screeching jerk. Before he asked her to sign, he read the statement to her, in which she, the accused, Ada Brons, born July 24, 1946, in Leiden, a cellist by profession, stated that on October 27, 1967, in Amsterdam, she had removed from the premises of the Bijenkorf department store, with the purpose of unlawfully appropriating it, a *mamushka*-model pencil sharpener belonging to the Bijenkorf department store or some other person.

"You put the carbon paper in the wrong way," said Ada.

The sergeant looked at the second form: it was empty. The text was on the back of the first sheet in mirror image. He shook his head.

"Imagining that happening to me in my old age. It's time I retired. Do you know what?" he said, tearing everything in half with two large hands. "Let's say it never happened. I wish you well."

21

The News

"Can't you sleep?" whispered Onno.

"No."

It was a week and a half later. He had gone on working until after midnight and had gotten into bed beside her without putting the light on; he must have dropped off to sleep, but he had suddenly awakened again in the certain knowledge that her eyes were still open. He couldn't see her.

"Of course you're consumed by remorse because your life has taken a fatally criminal turn."

"That may be it."

He turned over onto his back, crossed his arms under his head, and stared into the darkness.

"Why is it that criminals should be beset by insomnia? Sleep is the sister of death, says the poet, but in that case murderers of all people should sleep very well. Conscience is obviously the opposite of death. Anyway, do you know why it is that human beings have to sleep?" he asked, "that we waste a third of our precious time on it? If you think about it, it's completely ridiculous and demeaning, lying there stupidly with your eyes shut—a typical prewar phenomenon. Just like unemployment in the 1930s."

"Well?"

"The stupid habit originated when our forefathers crawled out of the sea onto the land. At that time the sea had a temperature of 98.4 degrees

Fahrenheit, exactly the same temperature as our blood is at present. During the day that was no problem, because then the sun shone on the primeval Quists and the primeval Bronses, but at night it cooled down and then they became lethargic, just like bats and such creatures still do during hibernation. We ourselves are now homoiothermal, but sleep is a legacy of our poikilothermal stage, if you see what I mean."

"How do you know all that?"

"It's a result of my wretched inability to forget what I've once read. My memory's my curse—but take heart, now and again I make up things and add them. For example, I could now invent the idea that the nature of dreams is a reminiscence of our earlier existence in the sea. Things are just as idiotic in them. Take that half-floating sensation in your dreams—you know what I mean? The only other place it happens is in water. Instead of Sigmund Freud, perhaps we should turn to Jacques-Yves Cousteau."

Ada said nothing. It was as if he were alluding to things he couldn't possibly know about. A number of coarse animal cries rang out in the street, emanating from the Germanic spirit of beer. Onno listened to the faint tick of the alarm clock and, having expounded his theory, felt himself drifting off again; an animal figure appeared before him and then slowly changed into something resembling a portable cage.

"Onno?"

He woke with a start. "Yes?"

"What time is it?"

"About two o'clock."

"Do you know what day it is today?"

"Monday. Why?"

"The sixth of November. It's your birthday."

He opened his eyes wide. "Bloody hell!" he said. "Thirty-four—I've made it!"

"Made what?"

"I've survived the age Christ died at."

They kissed, and while he still had her in his arms, Ada said after some hesitation: "I've got a present for you."

"It's not stolen, I hope?"

A slight shudder went through Ada's body. It was an effort for her to keep her voice under control: "As long as you like it . . ."

"I won't look a gift horse in the mouth."

"I've missed my period."

*

Although he was a man of language, he had scarcely ever heard a sentence that heralded the possibility of a fundamental change in his circumstances. Sentences like "You're under arrest" or "You're seriously ill" or "I'm leaving you" had been spared him up to now, seeing that he did not misbehave, was healthy, and had never really become attached to a woman; he had never yet heard the news that people who were really close to him were dead. Occasionally he had heard sentences like "After the revolution you'll be a beach-comber on Ameland," and there was even one sentence that he could not decipher, but all in all his life—despite the war—still had a virginal quality. "I've missed my period . . ."—the sentence seemed to have a *shape:* dark and elongated, like a torpedo launched from the tube and disappearing into the waves. He wanted to turn on the light, but he lay there and stared in the darkness at the spot where the old school poster with the picture alphabet on it must be hanging.

"When were you due?"

"Over a week ago."

"Are you often late?"

"Never. Always bang on time."

"And you haven't forgotten to take the pill at all? Not even in Cuba?"

"I'm quite sure of it. Do you want to see the strip? All twenty-one have gone."

"No, please. And you don't have to convince me you haven't flushed them down the toilet. It's unbelievable! It's as big a mess in the pharmaceutical industry as everywhere else. If you really have a baby, we'll put it in a shoe box and send it to the complaints department at the factory. That'll teach them." He sensed that she gave a start; he put an arm around her and said in a different voice, "If you have a baby, Ada, we shall bring it up lovingly, but with an iron hand, the sole aim being that it shall honor its father."

"What do you really think, Onno?"

"To tell you the truth, I've no idea. It's obviously been on your mind for days, but how am I supposed to know what I think all at once?" He really did not know. It was a moment like when the hour of the great god Pan strikes in the classical landscape: the onset of the motionless, scorching mid-day heat. "For the whole evening I've immersed myself in the breathtaking problem of how social benefits should be linked to civil servants' salaries— and then you suddenly tell me you're pregnant. Good grief!" he cried. "Now

I hear myself say it, it's suddenly dawned on me. You can't be serious! Is it true?"

"If you were to leave the room," said Ada, "I'd be sure that I wasn't alone."

He now remembered that on a number of times in the last few days he had noticed something strange in her eyes: as though she were looking not outward but inward, as though he were seeing her from behind a two-way mirror, like they had in shops and brothels. When she looked at him, it was as though she were not seeing him but only herself.

"That's incontrovertible proof. So I won't leave the room. The three of us will stay here forever, because the family is the cornerstone of society. It's just as well that they don't know in the party how right-wing and crypto–Christian Democrat I am deep down." To his own amazement the idea that he might become a father suddenly became attractive, like when a desk-bound scholar unexpectedly has the offer of an around-the-world trip. It would turn his life upside down, but why should that always remain as it was?

She gave him a kiss on the cheek. "I was frightened you'd say that we'd have to get rid of it."

"Have to get rid of it?" he repeated, with horror in his voice. "Me *get rid of my child*? I might want to get rid of you, but certainly not my child! Get rid of a Quist—whoever heard of anything so scandalous? And of course we're getting married, because a Brons is no good to me."

They were still lying in the dark, as though they didn't dare face each other in their new situation.

"I don't care what it's called. As long as it's a normal, healthy baby."

"Healthy, yes, normal, no. For that matter the chance doesn't seem to me very great genetically. Abnormally gifted, with a wide range of interests, dazzlingly beautiful—that's what she'll be."

"She? Do you want a girl?"

"I don't want anything, but it's bound to be a girl. Real men have daughters." Suddenly he started groaning.

"What's wrong?"

"I'm thinking of the scandal in my family. A Quist marrying a pregnant woman is unheard of; my parents will never get over it. Perhaps it's time I introduced you." He felt like smoking a cigarette, but he didn't want to see the light of the match. "Do you know who else it will be a nice surprise for?"

"Max," said Ada rather flatly.

Of course, for the last few days the thought of Max had occurred to her repeatedly, like a fish breaking the surface of a pond, but she had kept suppressing it; for now she wanted to think only of her child and not of the father. Onno groped for her hand, and for a while they lay next to each other in silence.

"What if I'd said we would have to get rid of it?" he asked. "Would you have done it?"

"Not in a million years."

He turned onto his side and put his other hand on her belly. "How big do you think it is now? A sixteenth of an inch? An eighth of an inch?"

"About the size of a globule of frogspawn, I think. The same as you at that age."

"Would you mind moderating your language? Me a globule of frogspawn . . . you must be out of your mind. I emerged spontaneously from my mother's fontanel, in full regalia, with shield and spear; my father fainted at the sight, the planets left their orbits, and all over God's creation strange portents were seen." He leaned on one elbow and asked in the direction of her face, "Listen, are you sure it's all true? What will you do if you have your period tomorrow?" As he was saying this he realized that it would be a disappointment to him, too.

"I'm not going to have my period tomorrow."

"Have you been to a gynecologist?"

"Not yet."

"You're going to the gynecologist tomorrow. And if you're not pregnant, you're going to stop the pill." He could tell from the pillow that she was nodding. "When's it due? The lunar calender won't present any problems to you as a pregnant woman."

"The eighth of July."

"So it happened . . ."

"On our last night in Havana."

Onno stared into the darkness.

Again he saw her shadow appearing in the doorway of his hotel room with the light of the corridor behind her—submerged far away below the horizon in Cuba. The greatest miracle of all was surely memory. How could Max's Big Bang lead to memory? To everything that existed, okay, but how could it lead to the memory of everything that had existed up to and including the Big Bang itself? María, who had twice patted the place next to her, whereupon he had obeyed her orders like a lap dog—rendered defenseless by misunderstandings, the lying telephone conversation with Ada, and the gruesome photograph of the body on the bier.

She had taken him into her bed, where the spirit of the man with the beard and the big hat was still present, had raped him, and then—past saluting soldiers—delivered him back to the hotel, where he had lain in the bath for hours and spent the rest of the day sighing and groaning and reading the letters of Walther Rathenau to his mother, in a Spanish translation, a crumpled old edition, which the previous guest—some anarcho-syndicalist radicalinski, of course—had left on his bedside table. Disgusted with himself and consumed by guilt, he had gone to bed early and forced himself to sleep; after the telephone conversation with Max he did not wake again until Ada, who was supposed to be sleeping in her own hotel, suddenly arrived and crept into bed with him. It was as if she had had a premonition of his deceit and wanted to make it invisible, like putting a layer of paint over the primer. That alone deprived him of the right to demand an abortion—even if he had wanted to.

For Ada too, beside him, the darkness had filled with that last evening. She had no reason at all to think that she would become pregnant by Max, because she was on the pill; but during their night drive back to Havana, when scarcely a word was spoken, she was beset by a feeling of uncertainty for which there was no basis but which she could not shake off.

She was exactly at that time in the month when she would be fertile if she were not using the pill. Suppose the pill-maker had dozed off! She had read somewhere that it happened once in every so many million times: that would be just her luck. All her life she had been unlucky like that. On the other hand, she hoped that it would happen—not because that would mean it was Max's, but because she wanted a child; she would be out of musical circulation for a few months, but her place would be kept open.

It was four or five days since she had been to bed with Onno—neither of them were as sex-mad as Max—and if fate had struck, then he must also have slept with her during her fertile period. Not just because there must be a possibility that Onno, whom she wanted to stay with, was the father, but also because in that case she would not know which of the two of them was the father. She could then truthfully say to Max that she didn't know. She had gotten out of the car at the Habana Libre. She had said that she wanted to spend her last night with Onno, whom she had not seen all day—and because most delegates were in the Sierra Maestra, she was admitted, thanks to the mediation of Guerra. On the twenty-second floor Max had pointed out Onno's room to her, after which he had suddenly grabbed his head in his hands and disappeared into his own room without a word.

Both of them were remembering that night, when they had lain next to each other just like now. Ada had said that she had missed him, and asked what it had been like in church. Onno had said that it had been very interesting, full of middle-class folk who had fallen on hard times, and that he had missed her, too. They had never made love so passionately, not even the first time. It was as though only on that night did they taste true, pure love . . .

"So it happened then," said Onno. "I know exactly when."

"So do I."

Ada did not know that Onno was lying in the darkness feeling just as ashamed as she, and Onno did not know that the same was true of Ada. Perhaps, he thought, true pure love, like all flowers, flourished best with its roots in muck and mud. Perhaps that was a law of life that held everything together: the day, which was day only by the grace of the night. But if the day was defined by the night, then wasn't there an element of night at the heart of the day? Was the day really the true, pure day? Was there a black cuckoo at the heart of the sun? He must put that to Max sometime. If that were the case, and true purity did not exist, the only consolation was the realization that night was not pure night either—and hence death might not be absolute death. If death was inherent in the nature of life, then wasn't life also inherent in the nature of death?

"I should have known that that time would produce a child," he said.

Ada had felt something of the kind, just as she had a few hours earlier with Max. Perhaps having such an experience twice canceled out the effect of the pill, just as a minus times a minus made a plus. Perhaps it also meant that she was pregnant by both of them—and hence by neither. Was that the line she should take? Was she pregnant by the friendship between the two of them?

"You're going to be proved right after all with your plans for our side room," she said.

He nodded, although no one could see him.

"You're right. The best thing in emergencies is to keep your feet on the ground. We'll have to buy a crib and a playpen and a rattle. This business is going to be pretty expensive. Later, of course, she'll want a hi-fi system. It doesn't bear thinking about. What will your parents say?"

"They'll be delighted. My father, at any rate."

"Why not your mother?"

"My mother's mad."

"You've got a cheek. You've been a kind of mother yourself for the last five minutes, and suddenly you know it all. Why is your mother supposed to be mad? In my opinion, your mother's not mad at all. *My* mother's mad."

"I don't know your mother."

"But I know your mother."

"You think so. Shall I tell you something about her?"

"That depends. Not if it's going to embarrass me when I bump into her at our fairy-tale wedding."

"I've never told anyone."

"Not even Max?"

She shrugged her shoulders. "He was never really interested in me."

If there had been a light on in the bedroom at this moment, she might not have told Onno either; but because of the darkness enveloping her, she lost the sense of where she herself stopped and the rest of the world began.

They were having dinner in the room behind the bookshop, braised steak with potatoes and endives; her father was telling them that as a boy he had had a friend who wanted to become a great chemist, whom he was allowed to help in preparing experiments. The boy had a laboratory in his attic, read popular biographies of great chemists like Lavoisier and Dalton and Liebig, and one birthday he was given a real white lab coat with a stand-up collar. In their bedroom his parents had a wardrobe with a full-length mirror in one of its doors, in which you could see yourself the moment you entered the room. When they were out, he would sometimes go downstairs to their bedroom in his fascinating coat, where he would rush to meet himself with his hand extended—like the great chemist, able to spare just a minute or two for his visitor, who had come all the way from America to consult the Nobel Prize winner.

"And did he become a great chemist?" Ada had asked.

"No, he didn't. But he did become a great businessman. He's a divisional director with Philips now and drives around in a car with a chauffeur. It's all a question of attitude."

"That's right," her mother had said. "Just look how far *your* attitude has gotten you. First a drab little museum keeper, and then an even drabber dealer in secondhand books, all stinking of death."

Brons looked at his wife as if he had been struck with a whip—and when

Ada saw the look in his eyes, she had dropped her knife and fork and had flown at her mother. She grabbed her wrists and forced her back against the wall.

"Apologize!" she had screamed. "Apologize at once!"

Ada's chest was heaving. A chink had opened up, she said, which had revealed the true nature of their marriage. Her father was still playing the same role in it as he had with his friend the great chemist.

"If you ask me, she's really a lesbian but doesn't know herself."

"Horror, horror!" cried Onno, pulling the blanket up to his chin. "You dared to force my daughter's grandmother up against the wall! And how did it end?"

"She looked at me as if she would like to murder me. My father intervened. I went to my room, and there was never another word said about it. I think that afterward she pretended to herself that it never happened."

"Then she has an enviable gift. It's the key to a long life."

Outside there was now a dense silence, floating on the scarcely audible hum of airplane engines—perhaps very high up, or a long way away, on a runway at Schiphol.

"Perhaps you shouldn't tell Max until we know for certain," said Ada after a pause.

"Of course not." Again he remembered that without Max not only would he not have met Ada, but he would not have had this child. In some way or other something like this had been in the air from the first moment. He remembered the dark green sports car coming toward him along the Wassenaarseweg, signaling and pulling over to the side of the road in a rapid movement. He almost had to kneel down to see that clown's face at the steering wheel. It was less than a year ago. "What shall we call her?" he asked.

"I haven't given it any thought yet," said Ada with a little laugh.

"What about Elisabeth?" she asked a little while later. "Then we can call her Liesje."

"Now, that's the most idiotic custom of all," said Onno, "giving your child a name that you've no intention of using. If you're going to call her Liesje, you should christen her Liesje. Of course Elisabeth is nicer—it's the name of the mother of John the Baptist. But I think that our child should have as symmetrical a name as we have, and we can achieve that by changing Onno, according to Quist's law of phonology, into Anna. That's a good religious solution too, because it's the name of the grandmother of our Lord and Savior. On his mother's side, that is; little is known about his paternal grandmother—at least I've never heard anything about the mother of God. The feminists will have to work that one out. Come to that, Freud's daughter was also called Anna. It's what great men call their daughters."

"And what if it's a boy, after all?"

"Then we shall change Ada, via the transposition of alpha and omega, into Odo."

"That sounds a bit like a knight in a boys' book."

"Good point. We won't do that, then. Anyway, we don't need to think about it, because it won't be a boy. It's going to be a girl—with wonderful long ringlets. If it's a boy, we'll think up an impossible name." He gave her a kiss. "Thanks very much. I'm very happy with your present."

22

What Next?

Once science had duly confirmed intuition, Onno phoned Max in Leiden and asked him if he had any plans for that evening. It surprised Max a little, because Onno usually gave only ten minutes' warning before dropping in. At nine o'clock the sound of his stumbling footsteps resounded through the stairwell, and on the threshold, with clumsy elegance, he assumed the pose of a classical god, an Apollo Belvedere: arms outstretched and head slightly averted.

"Noble simplicity, silent grandeur," he said. "You see before you a personage beside whom you sink into total insignificance."

"You have a supernatural beauty," said Max. "It can only be that the spirit has been poured out into you."

"You have no idea of everything that's been poured out."

Onno sat down in his chair and said, "Brace yourself, Max." And when Max joined in the game and grabbed hold of the grand piano, he continued, "I'm going to be a father."

Max kept his hands on the smooth black varnish and looked at him. "It's not true."

"True, true, infinitely true!"

The full implications of those few words had not yet gotten through to Max, though he had had an immediate sensation like at the launch of a ship, when the bottle of champagne smashes fizzing against the bow and the ship slowly starts to move. It was as though his hands had stuck to the grand piano; his attitude belonged to a game that was suddenly no longer being played. He stood up.

"How long have you known?"

"We've known for certain since yesterday. A frog was crucified for my child. You'll see in eight months if you don't believe it. To your astronomical mind, which is totally focused on eternity, the infinitely tender creation of a new life means nothing, of course, but you're still the first person to hear about it—for reasons that are too disgusting to refer to."

Max felt sick. Had Ada told him what had happened in Varadero? That was surely impossible! And when the memory of that night in the sea came back to him, as he made a lightning calculation, a much more awful possibility suddenly dawned on him: whose child was it?

He went over to the cupboard where he kept the glasses and asked: "What do you mean?"

"Let's say that you introduced her to me. What did you think I meant? What's wrong with you? You look green around the gills, my friend."

Max realized that he was starting to panic. "It's a shock," he said, putting the glasses down. "I'm sorry. It may be because I occasionally thought of children when I was with Ada and that's now out of the question for good."

He went to the kitchen. That was another lie—Onno would tell Ada, and she would know that that was not the reason for his alarm, but she wouldn't tell Onno. Hands shaking, he took a steaming ice tray out of the freezer compartment, held it under the tap for a moment, and pushed the ice into a bowl. He had to get his thoughts in order, weigh everything carefully, see what he had to do, and at the same time he had to go in and have a conversation with Onno, which would not be about what it was about. He had destroyed the palace of their friendship, which Onno thought was still standing, without realizing that it had become a mirage.

"I had no idea," said Onno.

"Of what?"

"That you wanted a child with Ada."

"It's not exactly like that, but she was the only woman in my life with whom the thought of a child didn't immediately scare me to death. Forget it. Things are as they are."

"If things were other than they were, something very strange would be going on in the world."

Max put a rum-and-Coke down next to Onno, poured himself a glass of wine, and sat down opposite him. He forced himself to look at Onno. "Had she stopped the pill?"

"The pill! Don't talk to me about the pill. She could just as well have swallowed a peanut every day. Medical technology is still obviously in its infancy—just as my child will be shortly. But I have no regrets. I reacted very differently than I thought I would. I would certainly never have decided to have a child of my own accord, but now that it's been taken out of my hands by a quack manufacturer, I've discovered I'm a born father. That warm, profoundly paternal element in me must have often struck you too. Or didn't it?"

"Of course," said Max, having difficulty in adjusting to Onno's tone, which had not changed but for him already belonged to the past. He took a sip and said, "If my arithmetic is right, it happened in Cuba."

"In Havana, in the headquarters of the revolution, on that night of the eighth to the ninth of October, A.D. 1967, at about two in the morning. You two had gone to the beach that Sunday. I was unfortunately prevented from going by some religious-phenomenological field research."

They looked into each other's eyes. Max nodded; he knew that Onno knew that he was now remembering their telephone conversation, in which he had called himself a "moral wreck" and a "necrophiliac." But whatever had happened, one thing that was certain was that Ada—after what had happened between her and himself—had seduced Onno that evening: that was why she had wanted to sleep with him instead of in her own hotel. She had taken everything into account, and quite rightly, as it now appeared. Quite deliberately, she had contrived to make the paternity of an extremely improbable but not impossible child uncertain. Did her cunning know no bounds? He had never known her like this, nor had Onno. But one day the moment of truth would arrive, because who would the child begin to resemble? In alarm, he allowed the question to sink in. Now, if he had himself looked a little like Onno, then no one would hit on the idea that the child was not Onno's, if it was his—but what did Onno and he have in common?

As Onno sat there on the green chesterfield with his big, heavy body, alongside which his own elegant figure was almost ethereal—and particularly with his straight, classical nose and, beneath it, the curved lips of a small restrained mouth, which was indeed a little like a Greek statue's. From an art/historical point of view, his own face belonged more in the period of Mannerism, with his predatory nose and his rapacious mouth. In a certain sense his head would be better suited to Onno's body, and vice versa. Fortunately they were both dark blond with blue eyes. Just imagine if one of them had been Chinese, or black . . .

"My daughter," said Onno, "will be the incarnation of the revolution. A second Rosa Luxemburg—or, rather, something like that woman in that painting by Delacroix, *La barricade:* leading the working masses with breasts bared and a rifle and the fluttering *tricolore.*"

Of course, it might also turn out to be a girl—then Ada's share might predominate; but it might be better if it didn't turn out to be anything at all.

"And are you sure you want it?"

"Basically," said Onno, letting the ice cubes clink in his glass, "I'm in favor of abortion up to the age of forty, and euthanasia from the age of forty on. I shall do my utmost to have that included in the party program. But in this particular case I want to make an exception. I knew you would allude to abortion. You'll never have children, because you haven't got a father. But I've got a father, and not just any old father, and this is my chance of giving him a devastating blow on his home ground, because soon I shall be his equal and then he won't be able to tell me what to do anymore. I'm going to perform an abortion, yes! But on the son that I am, if you follow my meaning. I'm going to get rid of myself!" he cried with an exalted look in his eyes.

Max was becoming increasingly distraught. In the past he would have delighted in every word that Onno said; now it was as though he were being forced to drink champagne at a deathbed. It couldn't go on like this— something had to happen. He would have preferred Onno to leave now, so that he could collect his thoughts, but he had only just arrived and would stay for hours, until he had taken the status of paternity into the highest regions, reigned over by God the Father, who no longer had any authority over him, either.

"And what about Ada? What will happen to her musical career?"

"No problem at all, because I shall go into labor. Yes, don't give me that stupid look. In darkest Africa, which has retained its links with the primeval roots of humanity, it's generally accepted. The mother-to-be works the land in the scorching heat, singing as she goes, while the father-to-be lies groaning on the bed in the shadow of the hut. Confinement is a short incident. Ada will pick up her cello again, and I will push the baby carriage around the Vondelpark, sit on a bench, and talk with a retired civil servant from the Housing Bureau about the old days, while I rock the carriage to and fro with one hand. Later I'll take the toddler to the sandbox and talk to young mothers about diaper rash and baby powder, while our little darlings try to dash each other's brains out with stones. In the evenings when Ada plunges into the thundering depths of Mahler in the Concertgebouw, I shall have the impulse to throw the screaming child out the window; but when it finally falls asleep I shall wake it up because I'm frightened it's dead. In short, I shall merge completely with the imbecilic eternity of the elemental."

"And what about politics?"

"I've been delivered from that, too. While Holland sinks rudderless into chaos without me, I will penetrate to the ultimate philosophical insight that is given to only the few: the father *is* the mother!" He took a large swig and said, "Maybe eventually I'll start wearing dresses, and earrings that reach to the ground."

Max got up to do something at his desk, where there was nothing to be done. He arranged some papers that didn't need arranging and asked: "Are you planning to get married?"

"Yes, what did you think? That I was going to go on living in sin? It's already bad enough that our child will start doing arithmetic one day and won't arrive at nine months between our wedding day and its birth, in July next year. What on earth will it think of us!"

The naming of that date gave Max a new shock. It was now November—and time would continue, week after week, through winter and spring to summer, until that day of days irrevocably dawned.

"Yes," he said, not knowing what to say.

"I'll tell you something else," continued Onno. "We are announcing the engagement this afternoon. Our wedding will be in two weeks. The twenty-seventh."

"That's my birthday."

"I know, but that's the date they had free at the town hall. Perhaps you can arrange to take the day off. Of course you're going to be a witness."

Max felt as though he were being tortured. A machine had started that could not be stopped but which could not continue in this way. Something must happen—but what?

"Very honored, I'm sure."

"I say, you don't give the impression of being very edified by the fact that the urge to found a family has taken hold of your friend. Are you really paying attention?"

"To be honest, Onno," he said, sitting at his desk, "not completely. In

Leiden we're busy processing some important measurements from Dwingeloo, which keep running through my head. Would you mind if I give a colleague of mine a call?"

"If you consider the universe more important than my wedding, then you must phone now. Obviously you've lost all sense of proportion."

Max smiled and dialed his own number, which turned out to be engaged.

"Hello, Max here," he said to the stupidly repeating tone. "Is there any news yet? You can't be serious—a polarization of forty percent with a wavelength of ten centimeters?—That's sensational! But if that's right, then . . . Of course. Of course . . ." He didn't know what else to say. He was saying whatever came into his head. "And what if it consists of two double radio sources? Yes, why not? On the one hand the structure of the magnetic field is virtually uniform, but on the other hand if you take account of the Faraday rotation . . . What did you say? Yes, that's a bit difficult," he said with a hesitant look at Onno. "I've got a visitor. But . . ."

"Okay, okay, I'm going," said Onno, putting down his glass. "Off you go to your polarization."

"I'll be right there. I'll be in Leiden in twenty minutes."

However, he did not go to Leiden. He took Onno to the Kerkstraat in his car and then parked not at his apartment, but one street farther on, so as not to be caught out in case Onno and Ada went for a walk. So things had gotten this far! With a feeling of self-loathing that he had never experienced before, he went up the steps again and, without turning on the light, he continued pacing deep into the night following the set diagonals and perpendicular bisectors, now and then glancing at Onno's glass, which he had not completely emptied.

The following morning when he awoke, it immediately took hold of him again and did not let go for the whole day. From minute to minute the embryo was growing in the darkness of Ada's womb; thousands of new cells were being added and organizing themselves into a dreadful threat. Although important data from the Computer Institute were in fact coming in, he kept going over to the window of his office in Leiden with his hands in his pockets and looking out over the Botanical Garden, where the Dutch autumn had descended on the tropics.

For some time he had been repeating the same thoughts over and over. There was a 50 percent chance that it would be his child—that was a dreadful risk—and even if it turned out eventually not to be his child, he would still live for years in fear of an emerging likeness. As far as he knew, there still was no method of determining paternity at the pregnancy stage. But suppose that his paternity were to be evident on the day of birth, from his spatula-shaped thumbs. What would happen then? Or if gradually his own nose—that is, his mother's—appeared under a replica of Ada's eyes. What would happen then? Shouldn't he emigrate within eight months? Accept the fellowship in California on Mount Palomar after all? Hang himself? What would he do in Onno's place? Perhaps he would murder him.

He rubbed his face with both hands. Was it conceivable that he had wrecked his own life? How could the dignity ever return to it? *He* was now the moral wreck, up to his neck in lies and betrayal. He thought back to that night in the sea: what in heaven's name had possessed him? How could he have ever been so crazy! Onno had asked him to be a witness at his wedding in two weeks' time: that was as impossible as a refusal would have been. He was caught in a trap. There must be a fundamental change in the situation this week, tomorrow rather than the day after—but how? He would have preferred to be honest and confess his faux pas to Onno, fall at his feet, take his foot and put it on his neck and await his fate. Or perhaps he should do it in writing, in a more cowardly but more accurate way.

He sat down at his desk, took a sheet of squared paper, sharpened a pencil over the wastepaper basket, and began writing without much conviction:

Dear Onno,

    I'd give many years of my life not to have to write this letter. Our friendship, which has now lasted for nine months, was the most precious thing I possessed. I'm not even sure whether "friendship" is the right word. Lots of men are friends, without my having the impression that it has much to do with our relationship; I too had plenty of "friends," of course, but that was always a completely different kind of thing. "Spiritual affinity," then? I don't think that word touches the core either, because what two souls are more different than ours? Perhaps, I've sometimes thought, we should think more of the affinity of lightning and earth, sometimes with me as the lightning, and sometimes you. I can't speak for you, but when I met you I often felt like a thundercloud that couldn't discharge. Or rather: after I'd met you, I realized that I'd felt like that. I'm aware that so far this sounds like a love letter, and in a certain sense it is. But of course it won't escape you of all people that I'm using the past

tense. In a way that I will never forgive myself for, I have forfeited the
right to say we are still friends. It's almost impossible for me to admit
what has happened; most of all I would like to go on writing to the end of
my days, simply to postpone it. Onno! The child that Ada is expecting may
be mine.

The moment he had written this, he realized that he could obviously never send the letter. He had no right to reveal this on his own initiative, without consulting Ada. In that case he would, again for his own convenience, in a certain sense be doing the same to her as he had done to Onno. He was dependent on her; without her he couldn't do anything. So the first thing he must do was talk to her. But again that must be done behind Onno's back— whatever he did would drag him further and further into the mire. And apart from that he must manage to persuade her to abort her fetus. It was all equally disgusting, but doing nothing was also impossible. If he couldn't get her to come around, she might say that *he* must marry her in two weeks' time and act as the father—with a 50 percent chance that it would be Onno's child. That would also mean the end of the friendship, but if that was what happened, he wouldn't hesitate. He simply had to accept it as his fate. For that matter, if he hadn't seduced Ada that evening, she would not in turn have seduced Onno—so that even if it was Onno's child, it would not exist without him. Moreover, deep inside he felt a kind of acceptance of the fact that in that case he would have a child of Onno's.

But what would Onno do in that case? He was looking forward to his child and was preparing for his wedding. Perhaps he had already talked to his family about it. Suddenly everything would be taken away from him. That was also inconceivable. On the other hand it wasn't inconceivable that Onno would react in a similar way and be prepared to accept a child of *his,* though at the same time terminating their friendship. No, that was improbable—unless he really had slept with a woman that afternoon in Havana, when he himself had gone to Varadero with Ada. "I can't face myself anymore. I'm a moral wreck. I've spat in the holy-water font." In that case he would be caught up in a similar situation, and perhaps reason that without that escapade none of it would have happened, and that he would now have to pay for it with his friend's child. But no, for Onno there was perhaps something even more powerful at issue: for him his child might have to be first and foremost a *Quist,* a continuation of the dynasty—but for that of course it had to be really a Quist and not in fact a Delius. He himself did not have that feeling, and it required little effort for him to understand why not.

A young female colleague, who worked on polarization but looked more like a champion swimmer, poked her head around the door of his room and said that there were still problems with 3 C 296.

"I'm studying it too," said Max, tapping the letter with the eraser end of his pencil. "What would you say if it were to consist of two double radio sources? In that case the smaller one might coincide with the optical mist. Think of Centaurus A."

She stared at him for a moment, then raised a forefinger and disappeared.

This was the second time he had blurted this out for something to say, but it now dawned on him that it was probably true: at first sight it explained everything. Perhaps he had made an important discovery, on which he should start work immediately before it was taken out of his hands—but he wasn't in the mood for discoveries. First he must get to talk to Ada. He took the letter and tore it in two five times over; then he tore each half once more, after which he carefully mixed the clippings with the other rubbish in his wastepaper basket.

23

Heads or Tails

She was playing not for the audience but for her child—the sounds from the instrument between her legs, she thought, must penetrate deep into her abdomen and surround the little creature inside with beauty. After the last heroic bar, while the Czech guest conductor stood hunched up, as though he had had a sudden attack of colic, there was a moment's silence in the auditorium—and then the applause erupted, with hurrahs and, here and there, enthusiastic whistles. Slowly the maestro freed himself from his cramp; with a broad smile, shaking one hand with the other, he thanked the orchestra, his gaze meeting Ada's for a moment. With a flourish he took his handkerchief out of his breast pocket and mopped his brow ceremoniously, and only then did he turn his back on them, look at the balcony for a few moments with a triumphant snort, after which his head slumped forward as if he had been shot in the neck.

The audience rose to their feet and acclaimed him as though he were Franz Liszt himself—although a troublemaker like Mazeppa would be immediately arrested by the police in Amsterdam in the present circumstances, with a great degree of approval from the same audience. Tapping the side of her cello softly with her bow, Ada waited for him to turn around and, with an imposing gesture, baton in one hand, handkerchief in the other, make them rise like puppets. When she was on her feet, she realized that she wasn't looking into the audience but was staring over their heads, straight through the back wall to a point in the infinite distance.

In the orchestra's room under the stage she put her instrument to bed in its case; because there was a rehearsal the following morning she didn't take it home with her. Her friend, the clarinetist Marijke, asked if she was going along to the pub. In fact she would have preferred to go straight home, as she was feeling tired, but it was the kind of suggestion that only the strongest characters could refuse.

"Just for a bit then," she said when Marijke persisted.

Max was sitting on a collapsed red sofa next to the gas stove and reading the paper. He stood up in surprise.

"What a coincidence!"

Ada was not so sure it was a coincidence—on the contrary. Of course, he had looked in the listings to see when the orchestra's next performance was. He was still tanned from Cuba. They kissed each other on the cheek. She took off her wet coat and sat down next to him, while Marijke was swallowed up by the rapidly swelling crowd.

Now came what could no longer be put off. When Max heard that they had performed *Mazeppa* after the intermission as a kind of encore, he said that Prokofiev had obviously also listened closely to that highly romantic symphonic poem, because it always reminded him of the passage from Prokofiev's *Romeo and Juliet* that had been playing in the street in Havana, with Michelangelo's *Creation of Adam*. The two compositions merged in Ada's memory, and she heard what he meant. These days Onno could also explain everything to her about the Pythagorean comma, or about *il diavolo in musica,* or why the Mixolydian and Aeolian scales were each other's mirror image, but he would never be capable of an observation like Max's.

"Together," she said, "you and Onno know everything about music. But I sit there in front of a score counting and have to play the strings. That's something else."

Max nodded and looked at her. "Only the three of us know everything."

She realized immediately what he was alluding to. Head bent and looking at her hands on her lap, she said after a few seconds: "Maybe not even then."

Max bent one knee and turned ninety degrees to face her on the sofa. "Listen, Ada," he said softly. "Since Onno told me that you're pregnant, I've thought of nothing else. This is an absolute disaster."

"I'm very happy about it."

She could see that he was in a panic; but whatever he said, she knew that she wasn't going to budge an inch, and perhaps he sensed that. He made a few uncoordinated movements with his head and one hand.

"Of course, you're a woman, you're pregnant, you're expecting a child, and of course you identify completely with that child. I understand that. It's probably something like an artist who's pregnant with a symphony, or a novel; they're not going to let anyone or anything get in their way, either. But at the same time that's the difference—because a work of art has only a mother, while your child has a father too. After all it wasn't an immaculate conception!"

"I'm assuming it wasn't—although I was using the pill."

"It was more of a doubly maculate conception. But who's the father? You don't know."

"And I don't want to know. You and Onno are the father. You two are such a unity after all, aren't you?"

"Ada, you're crazy! It will all come out one day who it is, Onno or me. I hope to God that it's Onno—then it will be all right, that is . . . all that will happen is that we'll have been living in fear for years, or I will at any rate. But supposing a duplicate of me is born, what will happen then? What will we have done to Onno then? How are we supposed to go on? That will be an inconceivable catastrophe, won't it!"

"These things were sent to try us," said Ada, folding her arms. "I'm quite aware what you're getting at, but you can save yourself the trouble. I'm not having an abortion."

Max moved slightly closer to her. Other people were now sitting at their table too: an untidy man with a gray beard, who had clearly decided to have a wild old age and was trying to impress a young girl with a story from the war, while her boyfriend listened rather uncomfortably. Now and then all three of them had to bend forward under the pressure of the throng behind them. The smell of wet hair and coats mixed with smoke and beer formed a gas that no one would have been able to stand for more than a minute at home; amid the screaming and laughter Max and Ada need have no fear that they were being eavesdropped on.

"But for God's sake, can't you see that there's no other way out! You can tell Onno you've had a miscarriage—and after a few months you'll be pregnant again if you want to be."

Ada took a sip of her white wine, which had been brought by a waiter who had become as thin as a pencil stroke from having been mangled by bodies evening after evening.

"No, I won't be."

"What do you mean?"

She put down her glass and looked at him. "I won't get pregnant again."

"And why not?"

"I have a presentiment."

"Based on what?"

"I don't know."

"Do you mean because of the abortion, perhaps? Listen, obviously we won't have it done by an old lady with an enema—I'll make sure of that. Maybe we can even have it done in the Academic Hospital in Leiden."

"It's got nothing to do with that, but I know for certain that this is my only chance of having a child."

She felt sorry for him. Perhaps he was the father of her child, perhaps not; in any case he had a dreadful time ahead of him. Everything that Max had thought of she of course had thought of herself; but even if the sky were to fall in, she was determined to have her child. Everything would sort itself out somehow in the end, even if the child was Max's—if necessary at the cost of her marriage and Max and Onno's friendship: that was all of secondary importance. Perhaps Max would want to spend the rest of his life with her in that case, perhaps not; perhaps she would have to cope by herself—it didn't matter. She would face that when she came to it: as long as her child was born. The source of this determination was a mystery to her. In the past she had only known it in regard to her musical career, but when a world-famous young cellist of her own age had recently performed with the orchestra, in the Elgar concerto, with a Stradivarius, she hadn't thought for a moment: I'd like to be sitting there.

"But that's completely irrational, Ada. Countless women have had abortions and had children afterward."

She looked at him. "If you're so rational, why don't you simply tell Onno the truth?"

Max emptied his glass helplessly. "I started writing him a letter, but I tore it up."

"Why?"

"I felt I couldn't do it behind your back."

"Well, now I'm in the picture."

"Do you think I should do it? What do you think the consequences will be for you? You didn't tell him, either."

"No," said Ada. "And not just because I felt I couldn't do it behind *your* back. I'm prepared to take the risk. The truth's a toss-up: heads or tails. If we tell him, everything will be wrecked for certain."

"Unless *we* get married."

She put her hand on his for a moment and smiled. "Even then. In that case we'll only get into a new quagmire."

"Exactly," nodded Max. "*Quagmire*—that's the word. *Morass.* Whatever we do it will be a disaster. And even if we do nothing and it turns out to be Onno's child, even then our relationship with him will be all wrong. Like when you know someone has cancer but they themselves think they're healthy."

"And that will be just as true if I have an abortion," said Ada. "And that's another reason why I am not doing it. My child is the cause of everything, but at the same time it's the only ray of hope. Eventually we'll all be dead, and then all our problems will have disappeared, but he'll still be alive somewhere, and his children and his children's children."

"How do you know it's going to be a boy?"

She shrugged her shoulders. "Onno thinks it's going to be a girl. He's even thought of a name."

"A name?" repeated Max in dismay. "Is he already thinking of names? But in that case it's already there!"

Marijke squirmed her way between the bodies and set down two glasses of wine in front of them.

"Are you okay here?"

Ada glanced at Max, who sighed and gestured.

"We're doing the best we can."

The man opposite them, leaning aside for someone trying to take his coat off, complained that these days the trams in Amsterdam were always as full as this in the rush hour; you couldn't use public transportation anymore.

"So what are we going to do now?" asked Max.

Ada shrugged her shoulders. "Nothing."

"Have you met his family yet?"

She nodded.

"And?"

"He's presented me to his parents very officially. We've been to tea. It's wheeled in on a cart by a housekeeper, after which the lady of the house pours the tea herself."

"And how did they react to you?"

"I couldn't really make it out. They were cordiality itself, but I don't know how much of it was sincere. According to Onno I went down well. He himself was as nervous as if he were making his first visit. His mother didn't strike me as exactly a genius, and his father was a bit intimidating. He didn't say much. He was very friendly, but behind it there was something completely different. When I said so afterward to Onno, he said that I'd seen that he's a politician. According to him they're glorified street fighters, with brains that are really muscles—people who know how to settle scores with their enemies."

"And then he said," added Max, "that it was characteristic of him too, that he would also crush his enemies to the last man." He remembered the way Onno had settled accounts with Bart Bork in the park in Havana. His eyes began stinging a little. Onno was completely a part of him, but it was an Onno that would no longer exist for him.

"Very possibly. I can't remember."

Ada looked at her watch. She wanted to go home; Onno was waiting for her. Just like that afternoon in The Hague, she experienced her presence in the crowded pub as in the kind of portrait that you can have taken of yourself at the fair: behind a pasted-up, life-size photo of the queen, with a crown and ermine mantle with the face cut out and you having to stick your own through the hole. Deep inside she felt the presence of something else—not only localized in her womb, but even more in her whole self. At the same time it was still completely part of her, as Max had said: it was her and not her. Her personality contained a part of herself as something else, which was nevertheless completely herself, just as on the platform her part belonged to the indivisible orchestral sound.

24

The Wedding

When Max had found the wedding invitation in his mailbox, in which Onno Matthias Jacob Quist and Ada Brons announced their forthcoming marriage—both sets of parents had been passed over, which must have been a severe blow, particularly in The Hague—a great sense of resignation came over him. Untruth had now gotten its hooks into his life and would always remain there. His life had broken irredeemably in two: a white section up to that evening in the Bay of Pelicans, and a black section afterward. It had never occurred to him that such a thing could happen—and now it had happened, not in the form of an illness or a disaster that was no fault of his own, but because of his own actions: in a certain sense he was the very opposite of a murderer, but the remorse came down to the same thing.

In the past he would wake up like a trapeze artist falling into the safety net: he would leap out of bed and survey the day stretched out before him. Now he made a sound as though wanting to vomit and would have preferred to stay under the covers. Regularly there were girlfriends under there with him, but less frequently than in the past; after all, that insatiability had been the cause of everything. The harmonious triad he had formed with Onno and Ada had changed once and for all into a dissonant chord by a composer of the Darmstadt school.

Onno thought it very discreet of him that as a former boyfriend of Ada's he preferred not to act as a witness at his wedding: "Your noble character throws a pleasant light on my capacity to choose my friends."

The wedding day, Max's birthday, brought a melancholy reminiscence of summer; it was windless and the sun shone mildly from a cloudless pale-blue sky. In the afternoon Max, without an overcoat, walked to the town hall, which had been hidden away in the center of town on a seedy side canal full of whores after the monarchy had driven the republican citizenry from its proud municipal palace on the Dam. There wasn't an obvious entrance; only Amsterdammers were able to find the obscure brick gateway to the inner courtyard. Here the continuation of the Dutch nation was in full swing: a bustle of wedding parties coming and going, black limousines with white ribbons on their side mirrors turned in and out of the gate; all around were young petit bourgeois in rented morning coats, with brown shoes, collars that were too large, and gray top hats, only wearable by people who had attended the Ascot races for generations, brides in white carrying bouquets, sometimes accompanied by stumbling bridesmaids, posing for photographers, while handfuls of confetti were scattered over them with shrieks of laughter. Everywhere there were groups of people huddled together, and after a quick inspection he had located the one belonging to Ada and Onno.

Actually, there were two groups. One consisted very obviously of Onno's family, which he was seeing for the first time: ten or twelve distinguished-looking people, ladies with hats on, pearl necklaces, and lots of bright-red and navy-blue with white polka dots. They looked with skeptical amusement at the working-class Amsterdam goings-on. One of them was undoubtedly a brother: as large and heavy as Onno, with the same face, but everything transposed into the well groomed and well adjusted. The much smaller, slightly stooping but sturdy old gentleman with a hat and walking stick, who now took a watch out of his waistcoat pocket and glanced at it, was of course his father; it was already obvious from the way in which the others grouped around him. His mother was a strapping woman, taller than her husband, with white hair and a straight back.

Taking off his hat, a chauffeur held open the door of a recently arrived car, from which an unmistakable Quist also emerged and joined them with his wife: obviously Onno's eldest brother, Diederic, the provincial governor. He now also suddenly saw Ada's parents: they stood next to the group, looking rather out of place without merging with it, like fat rings in soup. The other group, alongside but some distance away, was obviously the group of apostles of the New Left: giggling men of his own age, though perhaps still somewhat intimidated by the physical proximity of one of the icons of the old Holland, reaching back into the sixteenth century, the Holland that they wanted to abolish.

Max hesitated. Whom should he join? He had met Ada's parents on only one occasion, and apart from that he knew none of them—while no one had had a more intimate relationship with the bride and bridegroom than he had. He slowly strolled in their direction and when he caught something in passing about "the Cypriot syllable sequence," he realized there was a third group, comprising Onno's linguistic colleagues. And there was even a fourth one—he suddenly saw Bruno and then Marijke too. There were the musicians. He greeted Bruno, whom he hadn't seen since they said goodbye at Havana airport.

"Do you still think of Cuba occasionally?" asked the pianist with a deadpan expression.

"Every day."

"I had hoped that Ada would get fed up with Onno there so I could be the bridegroom here today. Now I'm a witness."

"I'm not even that," said Max, while thinking: *just imagine if she'd been to bed with him too.*

"It's a black day for us."

A little later Onno turned into the gateway: on a bike, with Ada on the back. To applause he slid from the saddle, as triumphantly as a circus artist jumping off his nine-foot-high unicycle, and acknowledged the applause with a bow.

"Forgive us for being a little late, but we had to buy a bridal outfit first. Doesn't she look marvelous, my bride-to-be?"

Ada was wearing a simple black dress with a gold lamé jacket over it, which was not a perfect fit but gave her the look of a precious jewel. Onno himself looked as he always did, with a red tie; according to Max, he hadn't even washed his hair.

"Can I?" asked Marijke. She took hold of Ada's lower arm and bit the price tag off the sleeve.

After Onno had locked his bike, he cried: "I'll introduce you all to each other soon. Right now we have to tie the marital knot and be quick about it!"

The dark, paneled wedding room was actually too small for the marriage party. Max stood at the rear looking at the backs of Ada and Onno. Besides Bruno, Ada had her father as a witness; Onno had a woman who was probably his younger sister, and one of his political friends. A fellow party member of theirs, the alderman for public works, acted as the registrar for the occasion. He announced that at the request of the bridegroom he was not going to read the normal text but that of the Batavian Republic, which had not been used since 1806. He took a brown parchment off the table, glanced over his semicircular glasses at the Calvinist patriarch in the front row, and read:

" 'Ceremony, *as used at Weddings at the Municipal House in Amsterdam since the joyful Revolution of the nineteenth of January 1795. Bridegroom and Bride! Since we assume that you have not made a rash choice, are uniting with honorable intentions, and have obtained the blessing for that union from Him, to whom you owe everything; we also make no objection to complying with your lawful request by setting the seal of the Law on your mutually declared love and promises of faithfulness. Before doing so, however, we shall briefly remind you of your duties.'* "

There was some hilarity in the room. The Social Democrat rebels tried to read something in Quist's face, but it remained as impassive as a stone; likewise, the provincial governor, the public prosecutor, and the professor of criminal law, whom they of course knew by sight, gave no sign of life. After the alderman in true patriot fashion had urged them to industry, honesty, good behavior, modesty, obedience, and thrift, and had warned them of the corrupting influence of being too forbearing to their children, he asked:

" '*Dost thou, Bridegroom, take thy Bride, here present, as thy Lawful Wedded Wife?*' "

Onno threw back his head and cried with pathos: "I do!"

Not everyone in the room began laughing, but most people did. The alderman, too, found it hard to keep a straight face.

" '*Dost thou, Bride, take thy Bridegroom, here present, as thy Lawful Wedded Husband?*' "

"I do," said Ada softly.

There was something in her voice that silenced everyone. Max felt an unexpected catch in his throat. He had difficulty in controlling himself, and would have preferred to leave the room, but that was of course unthinkable. Ada and Onno had to take each other's right hand, and as they stood there, the language of the revolutionary past continued:

" '*Do you therefore now admit, in the presence of an omniscient God, and in the hearing of your Fellow Citizens gathered here, that you have accepted each other in marriage, and, following the duties presented to you, will live together until death do you part?' "*

"I do."

"I do."

" *'May God, who is love itself, make you keep your promise; may He protect you from domestic displeasure, may He crown your union with the greatest of his blessings; and be with you in all the circumstances of your life!' "* The alderman looked up, took the glasses off his nose and said, " *'Be mindful of the Poor.' "*

"Fantastic," whispered one of Onno's political friends. "Be mindful of the Third World."

Max was overwhelmed with emotion: wasn't he the poor fellow they should be mindful of? But no one was thinking of him, or must think of him, except for Ada perhaps. He saw Onno put a wedding ring on her finger; when the alderman waited for Ada to do the same to him, he said gruffly:

"Men don't wear rings."

They signed their names, and after the formalities had been completed they shook hands with the alderman, after which there was an opportunity to congratulate them. Max waited until the first crush was over. Without a word, he kissed Ada three times on her cheeks. When he shook Onno's hand, he realized that this was the second time: the first had been in his car, that first evening, as they were passing Leiden and introduced themselves. The hand was white and warm and dry.

"Congratulations, Onno."

"Thanks very much, Max. Happy birthday."

"Thanks very much. How do you feel?"

"Determined. I shall become the most narrow-minded of heads of family. All your fault."

In the evening there was a dinner for close friends, but before that everyone was welcome in a pub next to the town hall, where tables had been reserved and champagne was waiting. There, too, the groups did not mix. The musicians clung together, as did the scholars, while the politicians ignored the tables and mounted the bar stools, where they ordered beer; Ada sat with her parents, who had detached themselves from the Quists.

When Onno saw Max, he took him to the corner at the back, where his family had nestled. "Now you must finally come and see what fate has allotted me."

At their table he pointed to Max with his forefinger, like an auctioneer, and said: "This is my friend Max Delius."

"Oh, so you're him," said a lady approaching fifty, who a little while later turned out to be Onno's eldest sister, married to the public prosecutor. She had something large and formidable about her that seemed endemic in that family; there was something rough about her face, something masculine, that frightened him a little.

"Yes, Trees, that's him," said Onno in annoyance. "All it needs is for you to peer at him through your lorgnette." He gave Max no opportunity to shake hands, because now he pointed out his parents, his two brothers and their wives, and his youngest sister and her husband. He called her Dol, and she was the only one for whom he had a kind word. Then he left Max alone with them.

There was a rather charged atmosphere. The Amsterdam style with which everything was being done here—the bride and bridegroom on a bike, the reception in a pub, artists everywhere, freethinkers and Reds, no sign of a clergyman; instead, a revolutionary document from the Napoleonic period—and now they were saddled with the son of a war criminal from the German occupation: their dismay was not entirely incomprehensible. Such things did not happen in The Hague. Of course everyone at this table knew who his father was, but hence also who his mother had been. People here knew everything—except who he was. Onno's brother Menno, the Groningen professor of law, about ten years his senior, offered him a chair with a friendly smile, and when he sat down among them he felt the weight of the family. He himself had no one in the world—family for him was something from a distant past—but suddenly here a power was assembled that helped him understand Onno better. This here was what he was reacting against, but with the strength of that same family of which he was irrevocably a part.

"Well, Mr. Delius," said Diederic, the governor, folding his arms and leaning back. "Did you find the ceremony edifying?" He was in his early fifties; Antonia, his wife, also a fairly formidable matron, appeared to be approaching sixty and could almost be Ada's grandmother.

Max realized with dismay that a new phase of ambiguity and secretiveness had begun—how could he ever simply be himself again, without being reminded at every turn of something he could not say?

"I thought that text from the Batavian Republic was an original idea of Onno's. Particularly if you take the current political situation into account."

"The only problem is that the marriage of course will be completely invalid in that form," said the public prosecutor. He was thick-set and a little bloated, with thin, lank hair and sharp blue eyes. "That alderman will probably have to resign."

"Don't be so silly, Coen," said Dol. "Stop making a laughingstock of yourself."

She wasn't at all like her gangling sister, Trees. She was on the frail side, with an open, attractive face; obviously Mendel's law had ensured the reappearance of some refined ancestress. Max realized at once why she was Onno's favorite sister.

"Resign," growled Coen. "Resign."

"How about another glass of champagne," suggested Dol's husband, Karel, a brain surgeon at a Rotterdam hospital, as Max knew from Onno. He too looked out of place, with his sharp, gaunt features, which gave him the appearance of a diabolical scholar from the Frankenstein family, obsessed with destroying the world, though that was not what he wanted.

"Resign," repeated Coen once again, prompting Menno's wife, Margo, to burst out laughing.

"It's like the Council of Blood in the revolt against Spain here," she said.

"Are you a left-winger like Onno, Mr. Delius?" asked Trees. "Surely not. I hope you exert a favorable influence on him."

"Of course," he said. "I focus only on higher things. I'm an astronomer."

"Oh really?" Onno's mother leaned forward. "So you can foretell the future."

"To," said Quist. "Be quiet."

"Absolutely," said Max. "In a number of respects, at least. For example, when the next eclipse of the sun will be. But in other respects, no."

"What respects?"

"For example, whether or not a letter will arrive telling you you are about to make a long journey."

"That's a shame."

"You're telling me."

"I'd so like to go to the Galapagos Islands one day," said Mrs. Quist dreamily, looking at her husband. "It seems they have all kinds of strange animals there. Do you remember those turtles in Surinam, Henk?"

Quist nodded. "That was back in 'twenty-seven."

"They'd completely lost their bearings. After laying their eggs on the beach, they didn't return to the sea, but went farther and farther inland, where they were put into baskets by little Negro boys."

Max looked at her. She had Onno's classic straight nose. Until he was four, she had made Onno walk around in pink dresses and ringlets. Whose grandchild was she going to have? Her own, or that of a Jewess gassed at Auschwitz? And him, the prime minister? His own, or that of an executed war criminal?

In the little basement restaurant on the Prinsengracht that Onno had booked they ate leg of hare with red cabbage and drank Burgundy. All the relations had been packed off home and there remained a select group of mainly politicians, musicians, linguists, and a solitary astronomer. There were comic after-dinner speeches and toasts were drunk, which Onno endured with inflated self-satisfaction, putting his domineering arm around Ada's narrow golden shoulders. When someone alluded to his forthcoming fatherhood, he cried:

"I'm married to the daughter of my child's grandmother!"

"Do you think that's anything special?"

"Can't you hear it is?!"

A few times Max met an inquiring look: shouldn't he, as a bosom friend, also say a few words? But he made a slight gesture of refusal with his hand and shook his head. He must hold his tongue. If things went wrong, then anything he might have said now would be counted as extra salt in the wound. Perhaps his silence would be interpreted as evidence of good taste, because the bride was an ex-girlfriend of his, or as a sign of resentment at not being the bridegroom—he would just have to put up with that.

Even after coffee the drink continued to flow; people changed places and finally started mixing. Brittle linguists and bony politicians demonstrated that they also knew something about music, and delicate musicians that they knew nothing about linguistics and were not interested in politics; politicians assured linguists that *they* were in fact the true "linguists," since they used nothing but words, so that all things considered there was nothing left for the linguists. What were they doing here, anyway? Hadn't Onno himself realized that? Whereupon the linguists inquired if they had decided where they stood on the issue of surplus manure. As the atmosphere got livelier, the volume rose, and somewhere someone launched into "Arise, ye wretched of the earth!" in a stentorian voice, and shouted that it was better than Schubert's *Erlkönig*; Max had his first chance to exchange a few words with Ada. He had seen that she was drinking only water.

"Fine," she said, when he asked how she was feeling. "And you?"

"I feel like someone who's trodden on a land mine and heard the *click:* he knows that if he takes another step he'll be blown sky-high."

"Just wait and see. What's the point of getting so worked up? There's just as great a chance that everything will turn out fine."

"But, Ada, that wedding, all these people, this party—while only you and I know that it may all be a lie, phony, nonsense, fraud. How can you live with that?"

"I'm living with my child."

"When I think of Onno—"

"Quiet, here he comes."

A full glass of rum-and-Coke in his hand, Onno surveyed him from head to toe.

"When I see your pitiful appearance, I have to think back to the dreadful time when I was still a bachelor. What a nightmare! In my mind's eye I see a desolate landscape with a single bare tree in the biting wind, into the teeth of which a lonely, stooping pilgrim dressed in rags, with a long staff, is laboring on his way to his mournful end. And now look at me," he said, puffing out his chest. "I have just attained the highest state of human self-fulfilment: marriage! My flesh is as fragrant as the Rose of Sharon, because I am married! As the lily among thorns, so am I among the sons. My lips drip like the honeycomb, my shoots are a paradise of pomegranates, for I am married. I am a walled garden, a sealed fountain!" he cried—and, inspired by the silence that had fallen, he stretched out an arm to Ada. "Behold, thou art fair, o my bride! Thy eyes are the sun rising above the fishermen cycling palely out of town with their worms. Thy voice is the singing of the first birds in the roof gutters. Thy hair shines like oil lying in the street where cars have been parked in the watery early morning light. Thy teeth are as the milk that schoolchildren drink at playtime, your lips a scarlet pool of blood at lunchtime, recalling the lady who has been run over. Thou art all fair, my love! Thy laughter is as the gold leaf of the sirens in the ear of factory girls. Thy breasts glow like the first neon signs, unseen in the falling dusk. Thy navel is the orange fire of the setting sun in the windows of the department stores. Thy belly is hidden like the shop window behind the rattling steel shutters that the jeweler lowers to the ground over his treasures after six o'clock. Awake, O south wind, and come! Thou art as the late evening, when the actress in her tunic cries: 'Wretched one! Woe, didst thou never hear who thou art!' And thy sleep is ... I haven't a clue. Thy sleep is the wakefulness of the small boy on whom croaking madness is descending!"

Exhausted, he put his glass to his lips. And amid the applause that was his reward, Max felt the urge to pray that it would be Onno's child—but that was pointless, because it was already certain whose child it was. Even if God existed, he could do nothing to change it.

25

The Mirror

Mid-February was the first anniversary of their friendship, but Onno was too busy with politics to remember and Max did not remind him. It was a fitful winter—in Czechoslovakia indeed the "Prague Spring" broke out early—interspersed with a few extremely cold days. Sometimes the impending danger vanished from his mind for hours, but then it suddenly loomed up in front of him again like a cliff out of the fog. At work, too, he sometimes found his attention wandering from the papers on his desk and himself staring at the second hand of his wristwatch, turning with inexorable jerks, but actually advancing down a possibly infinite straight line, along which the event would take place one summer's day.

"Just wait and see," Ada had said. He thought back to the image that had occurred to him during the wedding dinner: standing on a land mine with the pin taken out. He imagined an American soldier, on reconnaissance in the Vietnam jungle. *Click.* He stopped, dead-still. One more step and he would be blown to pieces. What was he to do now? He had lost contact with his patrol, and there was no point in screaming amid the deafening screeching of monkeys and parrots and cockatoos. Nor could he fire a shot, because the recoil would set off the explosion. Beneath his feet, covered by a thin layer of earth, he could feel death: a flat iron pressure cooker, assembled by women's hands somewhere in China or the Soviet Union. He must think hard—but there was nothing to think about. He must wait. Perhaps someone would happen to see him standing there, hopefully not a Vietcong: a motionless American in the tropical forest. He thought of his life, which had suddenly come to a halt, like a film stuck in the projector. Why had he always done his homework? Everything around him was moving, but he had turned into the statue of a GI, heavily armed, with helmet and backpack. His head was still moving, his chest was moving up and down, in his body his heart was beating and his intestines were working, but the weight of all that now determined the moment of his death. He didn't dare discard anything, because that would change his weight; nor could he reach his water bottle without danger. Hour after hour went by. Sweating, bitten by insects, his tongue thick and dry like a mouthful of flour, he thought of his girl, at home in Oakland, on the bay—night fell with scarcely any transition, his legs began trembling gently with exhaustion. If they gave out, or if he fell asleep, it was all over for him. Should he turn his submachine gun on himself, or was there still hope? Had he been wrong, perhaps? Could it have been the mating sound of some giant beetle or other? Was he not standing on a land mine at all, perhaps, and should he simply walk on?

Max in his turn had forgotten that the twenty-seventh of February was the day of their joint conception.

"We have to celebrate that," said Onno on the telephone. "Anyway, I need to get away for a bit and talk to a normal human being for a change."

"Do you mean me?"

"You see how warped I've become."

"Where shall we do that?"

"What would you say to the Reichstag in Berlin? Or do you have a better idea?"

"I can think of nothing better," said Max, looking in his diary. "Trouble is, I shall still be in Dwingeloo for the whole of that Tuesday. What would you say about coming to Drenthe on the train? Then I'll collect you from the station in Wijster and show you the works, so that you can make yourself popular with a large subsidy when you're in power."

"On the contrary, drastic cuts are needed. Mirrors, mirrors, nothing but mirrors; you're all just like the military. And what is the social use of all those mirrors?"

"Nil, thank God."

"I'll have someone work out how many nurseries could be built for the price of one mirror."

"So you'll be left holding the babies," said Max, immediately thrown by the ambiguity of that remark.

"If you ask me, they're just distorting mirrors, and you're all killing yourselves laughing all day long at the stupid government."

"Please don't tell anyone. Come and have a look on Tuesday—you'll kill yourself laughing. If you like, you can stay over in the guest room, then we'll drive back together the following morning."

"Agreed. Of course you don't mind if I bring Ada with me? I scarcely see her anymore; if things go on like this, my marriage will also be on the rocks. I see the same thing all around me."

"All three of you are welcome."

It had been abnormally warm all week. That afternoon, as Max sat waiting alone on the open platform of the country station, it was oppressive, without a breath of wind. The sky was overcast, and there looked to be a storm on the way. With the middle finger of his right hand he stroked the small bald patch on the back of his head, which he had discovered to his alarm a few weeks ago. It was oval, just under half an inch long, and invisible under his hair; the fear of suddenly going bald had stayed with him for days, but when the spot did not increase in size, it had gradually lessened.

He looked at the slowly approaching short train. A yellow caterpillar. It contained what he loved most in the world and what threatened him most. When Onno gave Ada his hand as she got out, with a carryall in the other, Max saw for the first time that her belly had grown larger. She was wearing an ankle-length black dress, with strips of white lace around the high collar and the long sleeves. Below the waist she suddenly expanded, because her center of gravity had shifted, causing her to lean slightly backward.

Onno looked contemptuously around him.

"So you think you can plumb the depths of the universe in this hole." He cupped a hand behind his ear and listened. "I can't hear the echo of that Big Bang of yours at all. All I can hear are stupid cows in the distance, wanting milking."

"So you can actually hear it," said Max.

The hood of his car was open, and small boys were bending over the dashboard to see how fast he could go. Because of the changed circumstances, it was now Onno who had to force himself sideways into the narrow space behind the seats. They drove out of the village along a provincial road, lined by tall elms; the sky, monochrome-gray like tin, hung over the alternating farms and woods. Max pointed out the large erratic stones, from the Ice Age, which were piled into small pyramids at the entrance of every farm. They worked themselves to the surface from the depths, he told them, whereupon the farmers hit them as they plowed.

"Am I right in thinking," asked Onno, "that stones fall upward here?"

"Not once they reach the surface."

"Ah, mother earth!" said Onno with something like paternal pity in his voice.

Max was about to say he had also heard that with war veterans, bullets sometimes appeared from their backs after twenty years—but it was no longer possible to talk to Onno in this playful way. The barrier was now right next to him, under that black curve. He cast a glance in his mirror, in which he could see Onno looking around with his hair waving, obviously enjoying the ride. Behind him, still in the mirror, they were driving backward on the wrong side of the road: yes, that was what their relationship was like now.

They passed farm cottages, also with erratic granite blocks in their small front gardens, drove through a village, and after a few hundred yards signs appeared on a woodland path forbidding all motor traffic. That was because of the radio waves transmitted by the spark plugs, explained Max; the telescope was so sensitive that even such a minimal signal was enough to interfere with reception.

"And what about your spark plugs?" asked Ada.

"They're insulated."

"So it might happen," suggested Onno, "that you think you've discovered a new spiral nebula when it was simply a moped trespassing on the site."

Max made a skeptical gesture with his hand. "Okay," he said. "That might be possible. I hope you haven't got an electric razor with you."

"So that it's not beyond the realms of possibility," Onno persisted, "that what you radio astronomers regard as the universe is simply the traffic situation in the surrounding area."

Max had to laugh despite himself. "God knows."

"You've put your finger on it! The earth is flat and the stars are tiny holes in the firmament, through which the light of the Empyrean, the abode of the blessed, shines. And anyone who maintains anything different, like you, is on the slippery slope."

Suddenly a portion of the mirror became visible above the trees: a gigantic framework twenty-five yards in diameter, a transparent parabola of gray steel, as out of place in the rural environment as an oath in a sermon.

"It's not an eye at all," said Onno. "It's an ear."

At a complex of low-rise service buildings, Max turned off his engine and an unrestrained silence descended upon them. The birds in the wood simply made it deeper; from the other direction, where it was more open, came the scent of heather.

Ada got out, took a deep breath, and looked around. "How marvelous it is here."

"Yes," said Onno, lighting a cigarette and inhaling deeply. "That's the marvel of numbness. Nature is the sleep of the intellect. Only in the city does the spirit awaken."

"I wouldn't mind living here, though. If necessary, with a little less intellect."

"Shame on you! Nature is for children."

"That's what I mean."

With a groan Onno had also clambered out of the car and gave her a kiss.

"You're a darling, but you're making a terrible logical error. For her own safety, our daughter must become a real city child. You can tell that from all those children from the provinces. At the age of fourteen they sneak off to Amsterdam and then walk into every trap at once. They know which toadstools are poisonous and that they mustn't walk through the tall grass barefoot, but they haven't a clue about the vipers in the city. If they've grown up in the city, they know exactly what they have to be careful of. And believe me, in fourteen years' time it will be a lot more dangerous in Amsterdam than it is now, because everything always gets worse. Could you live here?" he asked Max. "Nothing was ever thought of in the country, was it? After all, you think up in Leiden what you test out here."

Max had listened to him in desperation. What he had said about that "daughter" was of course a game, but as a real father he had obviously already thought about the best environment for Ada's child.

"Really live here all the time? I'd prefer to give up astronomy. I'd feel like a banished criminal. I won't say a word against Drenthe, but of course it's the Siberia of the Netherlands." He looked at the sky. "I think I'll put the top up."

With the help of Onno, he pulled it up, and after securing the handles and press studs, he took them to the guest suite, where he had asked the caretaker to reserve a bedroom. In the communal living room, furnished with wicker chairs and plywood sofas, he introduced them to a young colleague from Sydney, who was too fat for his age and was sitting working at the dining table. Max told them in English that he was here to combine the Australian data on the distribution of neutral hydrogen in the Milky Way with that of the Northern hemisphere, thus producing a complete map.

"Something like this," he said, pointing to one of the papers, on which was a diagram that, according to Onno, looked like a Rorschach test but in Ada's opinion was like a view of the brain from below.

"What do you know about brains?" asked Onno. "That's my specialty."

"I once saw a photograph of one."

After they had unpacked their bags in the bedroom, they went to the low hall in the main building, where astronomers, technicians, administrative personnel, and students working their way through college had gathered around a cart carrying tea and biscuits. Some of them knew Onno and Ada from their visit to the Leiden observatory—that was the very first day, Max suddenly realized, when he had plucked Ada from the "In Praise of Folly" bookshop. He saw her sitting at her cello again, *musicienne du silence,* her father with paint on his face—and later: "Be careful, don't hurt me . . ."

He showed them his office, as tidy as the one in Leiden, the metrological department, the instrument-making workshop, and the other workshops, where the lights were on, after which they went outside through the back entrance. A hundred yards farther on stood the colossal telescope, silently focused on a point in the dark sky. Max himself still felt a mysterious effect emanating from the instrument, which he knew so well—not comparable with any other technical structure. The wind had come up somewhat, and while they walked toward it along the path, he said that the wind was, of course, because of the contact with the most distant and earliest things in the universe that was taking place there. On the edge of the heath, which extended to the horizon, the reflector towered above them, as transparent as a fallen leaf in winter, in which only the veins had remained. The monster rested on feet, between which was a service hut; the whole construction was supported by four wheels on a circular track.

"If you ask me, those are kitchen brushes," said Ada, pointing to the brushes, which had been tied provisionally with string at the front and back of each wheel to keep the rail smooth.

"From the household store in Dwingeloo," said Max, nodding. "It ultimately comes down to that kind of thing. That's how it is in science, but no one must know."

"It's just the same in politics," said Onno. "All improvisation and making do. People believe in masterminds and devilish plots, but if they were to hear how policy is actually made, they'd get the shock of their lives. It's just the same as at home. I think it's the same everywhere when you look behind the scenes. It's a miracle the world still goes around."

In the service hut, where a couple of observers were sitting at the panels, he inquired what was being observed, or eavesdropped on, at the moment.

"I think they're calibrating," said Max. "What are we doing, Floris, 3 C 296?"

A man of his own age, perhaps a little younger, said without taking his eyes off his meters: "Yes, but there's interference from somewhere. It's probably one of those bloody weather balloons from Cuxhavn, with its thirty-eighth harmonic. Why don't we call the air base at Leeuwarden and get them to shoot the damn things down?"

"They cause just as much interference."

That really was the problem, said Max; Onno was right about his moped. Once you had the information on punch cards, you had to first work out what you'd really measured and make sure you'd gotten the astronomy out of it.

"Excuse me, but I think that I'll have to lend a hand. Why don't you two take a walk across the heath, and I'll see you at about dinnertime. I've reserved a table at what you might call a gourmet restaurant in the village. And remember, if a storm starts, you must lie flat on the ground and crawl back. That's the kind of thing you don't know when you are a city person."

But the moment he said this, he was struck as though by lightning by the realization that this would be the solution to his problem: if Ada were to meet her end in that way—and he wanted that thought to be immediately burned out of his head.

It hadn't been necessary to reserve a table; because of the bad weather they were the only ones in the restaurant. In the dark, primitive space, full of vague paintings and prints and iron pots on the walls, they chose a table as far away as possible from the windows, against which gusts of rain blew now and then. Max lit the candle and listened to Onno's argument about the difference between rotten weather in the city and rotten weather in the country. In Onno's view you got wetter from the rain in the country— weather didn't belong in the city at all; on the other hand people in the country became depressed because of it, while in the city it was simply inappropriate.

"You don't give me the impression of being depressed at the moment, though."

"No, not me of course, because I'm above all that. I dwell in the regions of pure reason, on which the weather conditions have no influence. But you—you seem depressed to me. Is there something wrong?"

"Of course not," said Max. He looked uncertainly at Ada, whom he had just now wished dead. "What could be wrong with me?"

"That's what I'm asking. Perhaps you come here too often. What's going to happen to you when that installation in Westerbork is finished?"

"I'll see about that nearer the time."

"How far have they gotten?"

"The twelfth mirror will be finished this year."

"That's sure to be a fantastic sight," said Ada. "One of them is already impressive enough."

"I think so too."

Onno looked at him searchingly. "Do you mean you've never been to see them yet?"

"No. I mean, yes. I've not been to look yet."

"Isn't it near here?" asked Ada.

"Fifteen miles farther on."

"Very close, then."

Onno placed his hand on hers for a moment, and Max could see that this was not only a gesture of tenderness but also an instruction to be quiet. Obviously she didn't realize what Westerbork meant to him: he had never told her; but probably she had been told by Onno meanwhile and had simply forgotten the name. It wasn't exactly pleasant to find himself treated with such circumspection, like a patient.

"But I know the site backward. I have all the plans in my head, and I can take you to the parade ground or the punishment barracks blindfolded."

It looked increasingly as if he were going to become telescope astronomer in Westerbork—that is, the astronomer who worked regularly with the technicians on the spot—and he would see what happened then. Perhaps it was best to put it off until there was no alternative, just as one shouldn't first feel how cold the water was with one's toe but simply dive in. Perhaps it had been obscured for the last few months by the problem he had inflicted on himself.

Not even the neat black suit could change the coarse face of the waiter, whose grandparents had probably been born in a turf hut. But he opened the champagne expertly, without making the cork pop. Max tasted it, waited until he had poured the glasses—with Ada putting her hand over her glass—and then proposed a toast.

"To our simultaneous conception!"

Ada looked at him in astonishment. Had he told Onno about this? "What on earth do you mean?"

He realized immediately what she thought he meant—but before he could answer Onno said:

"I told you about that, Ada, but you weren't listening. You thought: yes, yes, I'm sure that's true. That's what we're celebrating here; the silent, holy night of Van der Lubbe, the most influential Dutch politician who ever lived."

While they studied the menu, he told her again—and he described the occasion on which Max had worked it out for him. "Mrs. Hartman, can Onno come out to play?" Max had already almost forgotten. It was a year ago, but it seemed something from the distant past.

"How is Helga?" he asked. "Have you seen her again?"

"Never. She's sitting dutifully at the Art Historical Institute keeping the catalog up to date."

They ate wild boar, and Onno expanded on his domestic political adventures, while Max and Ada listened politely. A Great Leap Forward was being made, he said, in which what his father and his friends had prevented in 1945 was finally being achieved—that was, going hand in hand with a rabid wave of democratization, which was not devoid of plebian features: no one was allowed to achieve any more than anyone else—and if you simply promoted that and meanwhile you yourself aristocratically achieved what no one else achieved, then you were assured of power to the end of the century.

"Machiavelli did not live in vain," said Max.

"Oh, Machiavelli!" cried Onno. "A name that is mentioned too rarely!"

After coffee Onno asked for the check, but the waiter said that everything had been settled.

"You're my guests," said Max, getting up. "I'll have a meal on you sometime in Amsterdam."

26

Fancy

It was still pouring rain, and now there was a strong wind. They rushed to the car. Driving down the dark, abandoned roads they reached the observatory in ten minutes. The lights were still on everywhere. Observations were still being made, and the Antipodean was still sitting at the dining table in the guest suite. It was ten-thirty and Max asked if they wanted to go to bed yet—if not, he still had some wine and rum-and-Coke in the kitchen. Ada said that she would have a glass of cola, even if it might not be a good idea for a pregnant woman; but Onno thought alcohol was deadly to harmful bacteria and therefore extremely good for growing embryos. It was as though Max could see the colorful pile of books on pregnancy and childbirth that was of course at Ada's bedside.

Outside, the storm was getting worse and worse and they sat comfortably around the open hearth, in which there was no fire. Onno now made a distinction between "large weather" and "small weather": the weather could be so bad that it fell below zero and became good again. Thunder and lightning, breached dikes, floods—you couldn't say that they were "bad weather"; Max then told them that Dickens gave a dinner for his friends every Christmas Eve, in which a hired tramp had to stand outside in the snowstorm under the window and shout every few minutes, "Brr! How cold it is!"—so that the people inside enjoyed the warmth and the goose even more.

"What a bastard," said Ada.

"Not at all," said Onno. "That's perfectly all right dialectically. It shows that in his way of living, he was a great writer."

"You two have strange ideas of greatness."

"So what is the mark of greatness according to you?"

"Modesty."

"Ada!" cried Onno, grabbing his head in despair. "Anything but that!"

"I mean it. If you ask me, Bach felt very small compared with music."

"But meanwhile he did write one masterpiece after the other. Very modest. Anyway, what is 'music'? Without Bach and the other composers music would not even exist. Or do you think that 'music' is something that is simply floating up in the sky somewhere?"

"Perhaps, yes."

"All women are Platonists," said Onno, shaking his head.

"And what about Max, then, with that telescope here?" asked Ada, turning to him. "Don't you feel small when you look at that enormous universe?"

"I think," said Max cautiously, "that you're confusing two different things. Einstein was also a modest man, you always read, but meanwhile he did tell us how the universe is made. Onno's right: how modest is that, actually? You may say that he didn't brag about it in his everyday life, but it wasn't necessary. But then you are seeing modesty only as a psychological category—"

"And psychology is *always* uninteresting," interrupted Onno. "Anyway, how modest was Freud? Read the documents and tremble."

"To be honest," said Max, "as a boy I never understood how anyone could feel small compared with the universe. After all, man *knows* how overwhelmingly large it is, and a few other things besides—and that means he is not small! The fact that man has discovered all this precisely proves his greatness. The amazing thing is rather that this insignificant being can contain the whole universe in the tiny space under his skull—and, what's more, can reflect on it, as we are doing now. That makes him in a certain sense even *greater* than the universe."

"Yes," said Onno to Ada with a smile. "You should listen to that closely."

The flue of the open hearth was humming like an out-of-tune organ pipe in the storm.

"Of course you can imagine," said Max, pouring another glass, "someone saying that man must feel small compared with his own greatness, since he has it from God."

"But that makes him a masochist," interrupted Onno. "And he's over-looking the fact that God is a product of mankind."

Max studied the deep red color of his wine and was silent. *The Ego and His Own.* He was occupied with extragalactic research—the signals of cosmic events that had occurred billions of years ago in the young universe; but those paled into insignificance alongside the event that perhaps awaited him, on a small planet in an insignificant solar system, on the periphery of one of the scores of billions of galaxies. But that awareness did not lead him in any sense to something like "a sense of relativity." On the contrary, the birth of a human being was not an insignificant event in the measured immeasurability of the universe but rather an event of metacosmic proportions—even without God. Especially without God.

Floris came in dripping wet, and with disheveled hair.

"We shall have to secure the telescope, Max, otherwise we'll have to hunt for it on the heath tomorrow. It's gale-force ten, and according to the meteorologists in De Bilt, it's going to get worse—they're expecting gusts of wind of nearly a hundred miles an hour. It appears to be the last remnant of a hurricane from the Caribbean that's been roaming the ocean for a couple of months. Can you come and lend a hand? We've already positioned it with its back to the wind."

Onno and the Australian put their coats on too. Ada said that she was going to bed; she had her score of *Das Lied von der Erde* with her and was going to work on it for a bit.

"Right!" cried Onno when they got outside.

In the howling storm trees were waving and swishing, as if wanting finally to shake themselves loose of their chains.

The rain pelted in their faces, and they bent forward as they walked down the path toward the telescope, where the beams of flashlights were moving about and ten or twenty people were at work. The mirror was slowly turning into the horizontal position. Blocks were being lugged up and clamped to the wheels; someone shouted that the azimuth motor must be turned off; someone else screamed that Floris must now go up top to turn off the elevation motors. The whole procedure went by the book, which provided for such contingencies—and half an hour later people looked with satisfaction at the reflector, pointing immovably at the zenith, like a majestic sacrificial bowl.

Everyone assembled in the laboratory, drenched to the skin, to talk things over and to listen to the director's speech of thanks.

"Look at my brand-new chestnut-brown suedes," said Max, and pointed to his muddy black footwear.

"Serves you right," said Onno.

The caretaker's wife had made hot chocolate, which she poured out of a huge gray enamel kettle into thick white mugs, which gave everyone the hilarious feeling of being back home with Mom and Dad after a well-spent day.

"I'm going to become an astronomer, too," said Onno with pleasure. "There's real human warmth here."

At that moment a girl called: "Is there a Mr. Quist here?"

"Yes?" said Onno in amazement.

"Telephone for you."

"This can't be true," said Onno, getting up.

Max didn't believe it, either. It was nearly midnight—who would want to reach him here at this hour? Perhaps there was something wrong with his father or his mother.

A little later Onno came back. From his face Max could see that there had indeed been bad news.

"Ada's father has had a heart attack. That was her mother. It seems to be fairly serious, and she asked if we can go straight to Leiden. He's been admitted to the Academic Hospital as an emergency case."

"There are no more trains," said Max, and also got up. "Let's go. I'll drive."

They went through the building to the guest suite. Ada was already asleep, with her face on one side, her forefinger in the closed score. While Onno woke her, Max went to his own room to pack his things. He thought of Ada's father, whom he could scarcely remember, felled by a blow to his chest on a stepladder in front of his bookcases. Obviously anything could happen at any moment; everyone lived from day to day in a sort of blind faith that everything would remain as it was, and then suddenly it all changed. He quickly fetched the punch cards for the Computer Institute and went to the lounge with the two bags, where a little while later Ada and Onno also appeared.

"Christ, Ada," Max said, kissing her on the forehead. "What a mess. Has he had heart trouble before?"

"I think he has, but he didn't want to admit it. Men are always so tough, aren't they? Let's get going."

None of them had an overcoat. Outside, Max ran through the storm to his car, which he drove close to the door of the guest suite. Because the top was up, Onno now had to fold himself behind the two seats to a quarter of his size; Ada offered to change places with him, but he wouldn't hear of it. The rain pelted on the cloth top, and with his headlights on high beam, Max turned onto the sandy road.

The wood moved as though made not of plants but of animals; everywhere there were branches that had blown down in the mud, which he had to avoid. Hunched over his steering wheel, occasionally wiping the mist off the windshield with his forearm, Max peered at the road. The path gave way to an asphalt road, on which the cloudburst produced myriads of dancing mice: thick bubbles with feet, a largely absurd polka, since he could register only a fraction of the bubbles. The lights were off in virtually all the houses in the village; on the pavements there were large puddles that the drains could not cope with and which he caused to shoot into front gardens with a sound of sharpening knives. When they passed the restaurant he suddenly had a quick vision of the interior: the waiter and the cook had gone home, the lights were out, but in a fathomless dark abandonment the tables and the chairs and the pots on the wall were still there.

On the provincial road, where no lights were on at this hour, he had to grip the steering wheel tighter to keep control of the car. The asphalt gleamed from the water, but fortunately the car was weighed down by the weight of Onno on the rear axle, and by Ada, who counted for two. It was raining so hard that the wiper had virtually no effect on the curtain of water hitting the front windshield. Immediately correcting for each gust of wind, Max tried to keep the white line in the middle of the road in view, which his headlights changed into cones full of dazzling pearls.

"I'm sorry," he said, glancing at Ada. "I have to drive slowly."

"Look out!" she cried.

Right across the road lay an uprooted tree, which had fallen across the road from the left. He braked but immediately felt that the tires were losing contact with the asphalt. He declutched and swung the wheel; while Ada grabbed his shoulder, he came to a halt with his front wheels in the right-hand shoulder, a few feet from the towering scene of havoc.

"Good God" he said. "That was a close shave. We'll have to go back."

He shifted into reverse and tried to get off the shoulder, but the front wheels had sunk too far.

"We'll have to push, Onno."

He turned the engine off and opened the door, which was immediately almost wrenched out of his hands. He tipped the back of his seat forward to let Onno out.

"Should I help?" asked Ada.

"For God's sake, stay where you are," said Onno.

"And we have to hurry," said Max, shutting the door, "before another car comes along."

In the howling pandemonium they went to the shoulder and in the light of the headlights grabbed the bumper. Now sinking up to his ankles into the mud in his new shoes, Max counted to three—but at the same moment a second thing happened. Out of the din of the storm and the pouring rain a new noise emerged: a dark wheezing, which turned into deep cracking and rustling. Max looked around, up, and then suddenly saw a dark crown coming toward him from the other side of the road, like a giant hand. He grabbed hold of Onno and pulled him to the ground with his own weight. With a thundering crash, the tree hit the road and the car, which absorbed the impact for them.

Although the tumult did not subside, it was as though a total silence had suddenly fallen. The headlights had gone out; branches hung over him. Max groped for Onno.

"Onno!"

"Yes, yes, I'm okay—but Ada!"

They struggled to their feet and looked aghast as they saw the tree trunk lying across the white top of the car, still visible under the bare branches.

"Christ, no . . ." said Onno "This isn't true . . . Ada!" he screamed.

As quickly as they could, slipping, hurting themselves, they extricated themselves from the tangle and tried to reach the doors by clambering up, but it was impossible.

"Ada!" Onno screamed again.

There was no answer. Everything was twisted, of course. Half lying, Max squeezed his arm through the branches and tried to pull down the car's top but couldn't get a grip anywhere.

"We need help!"

Gasping for breath, he looked around. A hundred yards farther on, in the fields, there was a farmhouse where some lights were on. Just when he was about to go in that direction, there was the light of a flashlight on the other side of the ditch and a voice called:

"God Almighty! That's the second one within ten minutes! Is there anybody there?"

"Hello! Would you please go and get help!"

"The police have already been phoned!"

"We need an ambulance at once!"

The light of the flashlight swung around and moved in leaps and bounds toward the farmhouse.

In despair, using all his strength, Onno tried to force a way through the branches, but it was hopeless: the car was caught as if in a cage.

"Christ Almighty!" he roared. *"Ada! Our child!"*

Max stiffened. Her child . . . For the second time that day, that monstrous thought rose up in him—he tried to suppress it immediately, but it was already there, and now not because of a joke about lightning, but when she was perhaps already really lying dead there under that mountain of wood. He felt as if a shiny black cloth were being laid around him, following all his contours, like a second skin. At the same moment he had to be sick. He turned and vomited up the wild boar. When he stood up, he saw that Onno was leaning over the branches with his face on one arm, sobbing.

A fire engine approached from the direction of Dwingeloo, with its siren sounding and its red revolving lights, followed by a police car with a blue revolving light. A little later a bright searchlight flashed and suddenly men in oilskins were swarming everywhere. Red-and-white tapes were stretched across the road; shortly afterward there was the screech of electric saws, which sliced through the branches like knives through bread.

No one asked Max and Onno anything. Onno looked at what was happening, but at the same time he walked to and fro in a daze, in a loop like a caged tiger. Max helped pull away the branches and wanted to say something to him, but didn't know what; in his mouth he had the bitter taste of vomit. The luggage compartment was dented; the punch cards could probably also be written off. The three revolving lights remained on. The pulsing signals modulated into a cruel pattern, which expressed exactly what he felt. There was still a storm and pouring rain, but it seemed to be abating a little.

As the inside of the car was uncovered, he saw Ada doubled up under the flattened top, which had provided no protection at all—motionless, her face on her knees; the trunk had not landed on her place but right next to her, on his. He looked for no longer than a second—he immediately averted his gaze—but Onno staggered forward and leaned over the hood, at which a policeman grabbed him roughly by the shoulder.

"Please get out of here. Are you enjoying it?"

Obviously, they were being taken for curious locals.

Onno turned around, trembling. "It's my wife."

The policeman let go and took hold of him in a different way, with two hands on his shoulders.

"Come on."

"Is she still alive? Ada! Can you hear me?"

"Come on, sir."

While the fireman carefully pulled away the top and laid blankets over her, an ambulance, with screaming sirens, dazzling headlights, and revolving lights approached at high speed from the opposite direction. Two paramedics jumped out, and one ran to the back to get the stretcher. The other leaped over the branches, crouched down beside Ada, and put a stethoscope in his ears.

"She's pregnant," said Onno.

The paramedic glanced up, took off his stethoscope, and got to his feet. "She's alive," he said.

Max took a deep breath and put his hands over his eyes. A moment later he looked into Onno's dripping, filthy face and hugged him.

Ada did not regain consciousness even in the ambulance. Max had sat next to the driver, who refused to say what he thought; when he got out at the hospital in Hoogeveen, he saw that Onno's relief too had given way to a new concern. Ada was quickly wheeled inside, and they were taken by a nurse to a washroom, where they could clean up a little. In those light, silent, immaculate surroundings, they were shocked at how they looked in the mirror: clothes torn, drenched through, and covered in mud and green stains from the tree bark, their faces and hands covered in blood and scratches. It looked not as though they had just come from a catastrophic storm but somehow from a different time.

"I hope it's going to be all right," said Onno. "What an absurd mess. The fact that we were in the exact spot where that bloody tree fell. What's the sense of it all?"

Max rinsed his mouth out and didn't answer at once. He realized that Onno was now experiencing for the first time in his own life the absurd mess of existence. The fact that anything could happen at any time was for him as axiomatic as the fact that the weather was good one day and not the next. That's how things were on earth. It was much less the case in the heavens, where much stricter rules applied: the sun always rose, and not sometimes not, or only a day later—which one could not even say in that way—but always exactly at the moment predicted. There was no danger from that direction. But they had nothing to do with life on earth, and perhaps that was why he had made a profession of that inhuman reliability.

"On the other hand," he said, "if she had been sitting in the back, in your place, she wouldn't have survived."

Onno splashed water in his face with two hands—and suddenly he stiffened. He slowly stood up and looked at Max in the mirror wide-eyed.

"Max . . ." he said softly, almost whispering. "Ada's father . . ."

Max's mouth dropped open. "Christ! I didn't give it a moment's thought."

They looked at each other in astonishment.

"That's all we need" said Onno. "What are we going to do now?"

"You have to call."

"Call? Imagine the woman. Her husband has a serious heart attack and has to go into the hospital. The telephone rings and she gets the news that her pregnant daughter has had an accident and is in a coma. She won't survive it."

"What are we to do, then?"

"You've got to go there and tell her carefully. I'm staying here, with Ada, that's for certain."

"And how am I to get there?"

"In a taxi. At my expense."

"It'll cost a couple of hundred guilders. Do we have that much with us?"

"If not, we'll borrow it here."

Max looked at his watch. "It's a quarter past one. We should have been in Leiden about now. It'll be nearly three before I get there. But okay, of course I'll do it."

They went to the waiting room, where they pooled their money and got someone to call for a taxi. The driver of the local firm was already in bed but would be there in about twenty minutes. While they waited, a blond young man in a white coat, who turned out to be the duty doctor, appeared. They couldn't say very much yet. She was still unconscious, but it looked as if she had not broken anything; blood pressure, pulse, and breathing were good. Everything seemed to be okay with the child too.

"Thank God," said Onno.

"We now have to wait for the neurological examination."

"And when will that be done?"

"At once. We've got the neurologist out of bed."

Because the taxi was still not there, Max went to the ward. Ada's head lay on the pillow; her eyes were closed. A drip had been attached to her arm. The curve of her belly under the blanket was like a tidal wave. There was something about the expression on her face that struck him, that seemed familiar to him, that he couldn't place. But a moment later he suddenly realized: it was the expression she had when she played, when she lost herself in the music.

27

Consolation

When the taxi driver saw Max, he said he wouldn't dream of taking him like that.

"You can walk, friend. I just got new seat covers."

Perhaps he thought Max had been in a fight. Only when Max had gotten the local paper from the porter and put it on the backseat was the man prepared to drive him. Max was shocked at his rudeness, but on the other hand he was glad, because now he didn't have to sit next to him out of politeness and make conversation, no doubt about soccer, of which he didn't even know, or want to know, the rules.

Again the rain and the high wind. He still couldn't really take in what had happened. When the car turned onto the highway, he closed his eyes to allow it to sink in: the tree suddenly across the road . . . the shoulder . . . Ada's head on the pillow, her black hair on the white linen . . . the dazzling searchlight in the raging night, the sirens and the revolving lights . . . the mud, the branches . . . he is cycling along the Rapenburg and a woman in a summer dress draws alongside on her bike. She asks where the tram stop to Noordwijk is. Very close, he says, first on the left. Is the tram cheap? It's easiest to go on the bike; it isn't far. But perhaps I'll have a long wait at the bike shed? It'll be okay. It's hot, but he has his raincoat on. *It's already twenty-five past four.* In the Botanical Garden he is struck by the first trees coming into leaf: the top half of their crown is covered by a thick pack of snow, dazzling white in the summer sun. Look! He cries, and stops, but it doesn't seem to interest her; she cycles on to the beach, completely self-absorbed . . .

He woke with a start. Through the car window he caught a glimpse of the terrace of the Capitol in Havana—which immediately afterward shrank to become the entrance to the Academic Hospital in Leiden. His clothes were still clammy and damp. It was raining, but the storm had died down, or perhaps there hadn't been a storm here; he paid the bill and went inside without saying goodbye.

The night porter, who surveyed him suspiciously from top to toe, had a message for Mr. and Mrs. Quist—and asked who he was. Once he decided to believe Max's story, he said that Mrs. Brons had gone home ten minutes ago. She was going to wait for her daughter there.

"And Mr. Brons?"

"He died at about twelve-thirty."

Max turned away, looked at him again, turned away again, and looked at him again.

"Would you be kind enough to call the hospital in Hoogeveen for me?"

He realized that the formality of that sentence helped him control himself.

The porter did as he had been asked and handed Max the receiver.

It took a little while before he got Onno on the line.

"Mother?"

"No, it's Max. I'm here in Leiden at the hospital." He hesitated for a moment. "There's worse to come, Onno." And when there was a silence: "Ada's father is dead."

"You can't be serious!"

"It's as if none of this is real."

"My God, I'm going mad. It's unbelievable! The poor guy, is he really dead?"

"It seems it happened at about twelve-thirty, apart from that I don't know anything, either."

"And what about my mother-in-law? How's she coping? Have you already told her what's happened to Ada?"

"I haven't talked to her yet. She waited for us, but now she's at home; I'm going straight there. How is Ada?"

"She's with the neurologist, they're taking X rays."

"I'll be off, then. Take care. Try and get a bit of sleep tonight."

"Yes, they've made up a bed for me here in Ada's room. I'll make sure she's transferred to Amsterdam tomorrow."

"Your mother-in-law will be calling you shortly."

"Thanks a lot, Max. It's fantastic what you've done for me."

"Shut up, you know I'm glad to do it."

Max handed the receiver back to the porter, who hung up.

"Can I make a note of the number of that hospital?" When he'd done that, he asked, "Would you order a taxi for me? I'll wait outside."

"You take care, too." said the porter, picking up the receiver again.

On the terrace Max took a couple of deep breaths. What a night! But now it had hit *them,* and on other nights other people were the victims, and tonight countless other people were being struck too—there had never been a day or a night or even a moment when something like this was not happening to someone, for as long as humanity had existed. Doom roamed the earth constantly, like a swallow through a swarm of gnats, with sharp twists and turns, its beak wide open.

When he got out of the taxi at "In Praise of Folly," the rain had finally stopped. There was a light on in the shop. Somewhere farther off in the silent town there was the sound of students coming from their club celebrating noisily; all through those hours they had been bawling away in their ravaged, oak-paneled domain. As soon as he rang the bell, Sophia Brons appeared at the back of the cave of books. Her face was taut, but her eyes showed no sign of redness.

When she opened the door and saw him, she seemed to be alarmed for a moment. She looked quickly left and right down the street.

"You look a sight! What's happened? Where are Ada and Onno?"

"We had an accident on the way here, but don't be alarmed, everyone's alive."

"An accident?" she repeated. Her cold, dark eyes looked at him in a way that made him feel immediately guilty. "And her child?"

"All fine. They're in Hoogeveen hospital. I came by taxi. I've just been at the Academic Hospital, and heard the terrible news about your husband. How awful for you."

She looked at his scratches and ruined clothes again.

"Everything comes to an end," she said with a taut mouth. "Come in."

Onno did not know his mother-in-law very well: this was not the kind of woman who needed to be treated with kid gloves and would be devastated by a telephone call. He followed her through the labyrinth of legibility to the back room. Poetry. Technology. Theology. On the low table he saw an opened photo album, and next to it a pair of black reading glasses. Above the brown corduroy sofa hung a large portrait of the writer Multatuli, which he hadn't noticed the last time, in the Romantic, conquering pose of a Bavarian king, a coat with a cape attached over his shoulders like an ermine mantle, focusing on truth with watery eyes.

"A cup of coffee?"

"I'd like nothing better."

While she poured the coffee, he told her what had happened. When he mentioned with concern that Ada was still unconscious, she stopped stirring her cup and said:

"Still? For more than three hours?" She thought. "Fortunately she's still young. I've known patients who were in a coma for days or weeks, without permanent effects."

He looked at her in amazement. "Were you in nursing?"

"Ages ago. In the war."

"Anyway, I don't know what things are like now. I just called Onno from the hospital, and the neurologist was with her. Shall I call Hoogeveen for you? I've got the number."

She pointed to the telephone. "Go ahead."

"Onno knows about your husband," he said as he dialed the number. "He was very shocked, and he said that he would make sure that Ada was transferred to Amsterdam tomorrow." When he got through, Max handed the receiver to Sophia.

"Mrs. Brons here," she said. "Thank you very much—thank you, Onno. I don't know. I'd gone to a lecture on Thoreau and Gandhi. When I got home, he was on the floor in the kitchen, unconscious.—Yes. Yes, don't worry.—So I heard. He's here now.—Yes.—Yes.—Yes.—Yes.—Of course.—Yes.—Oh.—Yes.—Yes.—Yes.—Let me know what happens.—Fine.—Of course.—I'll see you tomorrow."

She put the receiver down.

When she sat down again and said nothing, Max asked: "Well?"

"The X rays are good. No fracture of the base of the skull or anything like that. We'll have to wait. Tomorrow she'll be admitted in Amsterdam, probably at the Wilhelmina Hospital. They'll do an E.E.G. there."

Max nodded. He didn't know what else to say and asked: "How old was your husband?"

"Forty-seven."

"And a fatal heart attack, though he led such a quiet life here among his books."

"No one knows the kind of life a person really leads."

Max nodded. "You could be right about that." He was silent for a moment. "There are also people who are constantly under terrific pressure who live to be a hundred. What were his last words?"

" 'That rain just goes on pelting down.' " With her arms folded, Sophia looked straight ahead for a while, as though she could see him again. "He'd been feeling nervous and anxious all day. He thought it was the weather."

They continued looking at each other. Max wanted to ask if he had had much pain, but that didn't seem appropriate. He bent over the photo album and saw the family at the base of a statue. At the foot of it was a giant-size winged lion; in a burst of high spirits, Ada had laid her head on a step, under a bronze claw, while her father shrank back with feigned alarm. Her mother was looking up at the statue, which was not visible on the photo.

"Venice?" he asked, and looked up.

"Two years ago."

"All three of you are in it. Who took the photo?"

"Someone who happened to be passing by."

He leaned back and looked at the shop through the open dividing door. In fact he wanted to leave, but he had the feeling that it wasn't possible yet.

"What will you do about the bookshop now? Are you going to continue it?"

"I don't want to think about that yet. First we have to get the funeral over with."

Max nodded. "Will you have to cope on your own, or does he have relatives?"

"I have a mother in the old people's home and a brother in Canada, but my husband has two sisters who could help. Anyway, Onno said that he'll involve his family tomorrow morning."

"You can rely on him for that. If I can be of any help to you in the next few days, I am always at your disposal," he said formally, getting up. "Well, Mrs. Brons, I won't keep you any longer."

She looked at him questioningly. "Where were you thinking of going? It's past four. Surely you're not going to take a taxi to Amsterdam?"

"I can go to the observatory. The director lives on the premises—he'll have a bed for me. Otherwise I'll sleep at the caretaker's."

Sophia got up. "What nonsense waking those people up. You can sleep in Ada's room. Why don't you go upstairs now and start by having a shower."

Yes, why not? He'd been frightened of finding a distraught widow, crying despairingly over the body of her husband; but it was as though his death had made her even more steadfast. He, too, hated the idea of having to go straight back into the street. And perhaps she would prefer not to be alone in the house tonight.

"Well . . . If I'm not being a trouble to you, I'd like to."

She turned off the lights and, upstairs, pointed out the bathroom to him—a small room with a washbasin, a folded ironing board against the wall, and a tall laundry basket. He would have preferred to take a bath, but there was only a separate square shower compartment with a white plastic curtain. He quickly took off his clothes, which were still not completely dry, threw them in a heap, and stood on the springy, zinc floor of the shower compartment; an attempt to clean it, obviously with some acid or other, had left white corrosion marks in the metal. But the modest jet from the shower was warm and filled him with a blissful feeling of rebirth, as though he hadn't been subjected to enough water today. An egg-shaped piece of pink soap hung from a rope, and with it he was able to finally wash everything away—not only the dirt, but also somehow the closeness of what had happened. When he opened the curtain, a bath towel was lying over the edge of the washbasin, and a folded pair of pajamas.

They were Ada's father's, of course. The legs were too short, but the flannel was soft and pleasant. In Ada's room, at the back of the house, her mother was making up the bed; the window was open. She glanced briefly at him.

"That makes a difference."

He had never been in here. Of course Ada had taken most belongings to Onno's, but her girlhood things had remained. Dolls and stuffed animals on the low bookcase filled with girls' books; small things and knickknacks, boxes, bottles, on the wall a large poster of a melancholy bloodhound, but also a framed photo of Stravinsky; a bent music stand with a woollen rabbit. Everything looked neat; obviously, the room had been painted not long ago.

They said goodnight and he got into bed. Next to him there was a cord against the wall; the switch near the ceiling was the same kind of parrot's beak as in his own childhood room, at his mother's. It made the same click and immediately the darkness overwhelmed him. Outside there was deep silence. He put his hands under his head and closed his eyes. Had it really been today that he had met them from the station? The crown of the tree came swishing down . . .

He woke when she slipped in beside him under the blanket. At first he thought he was dreaming, because this was impossible. He wasn't dreaming. Suddenly he felt Sophia's arm around him and her warm body next to him, shaking with sobs. Her hair was loose. Yes, of course this was the impossible, completely unthinkable!

"What is it?" he asked.

"I'm sorry," she sobbed and buried her face in his neck. "Don't send me away. It's because of the way you looked with all those scratches and those ruined clothes. It's exactly how Oswald looked the day that I met him in the war, after a bombing raid . . . On the very day that he died. Of course he was an old fogey, but . . . And then Ada . . . perhaps it's better that he won't have to go through that now . . ."

He was alarmed by her words. Might it be fatal after all? In confusion, he in turn put his arm around her, both in fatherly consolation and seeking help, and under a thin rucked-up nightdress he felt her soft back, her full hips. What was happening? His body fitted exactly into the curve of her body, her breasts, her belly, like a musical instrument in its case. Unwittingly, he stroked her large naked buttocks, which were not those of a girl but of a mature woman, in her mid-forties—and as though his hand were seized and dragged down by a whirlpool, it slipped between them and landed in another tropical world of damp, hair, living flesh, that seemed to envelop it suddenly and completely in the darkness.

He began to shiver and kissed her. She pulled down his pajama bottoms and he disappeared into her unaided, as though her opening were everywhere. She kept her tongue out the whole time, right out of her mouth, while a dark growl came from her throat, and in the depths of her belly something seized the head of his penis each time—what was that secret? Her cervix? He thought of her husband for a moment, stiffening on his trolley in the morgue, who must have felt this too when he sired Ada, but he didn't think very much; the snapping soon took him to a climax, as though he were being pumped up. He caught his breath, and with a loud scream the whole scene exploded, and with a second and third and fourth scream he emptied himself into her. Sweating and breathless, he slumped back beside her, and before he had even realized it, she had got out of bed. He was just able to hear the door close.

He hadn't seen her. He groped for the cord of the switch and, dazzled by the light, closed his eyes. What had just happened was impossible! It must have been a hallucination, provoked by all the emotion and exhaustion! He felt his penis: still half erect and soaking wet. Perplexed, he wondered whether he had really slept with the grandmother of his child—in the bed of her daughter, who had just been in an accident, dressed in the pajamas of her husband who had just died. Those last two facts were certain in any case.

How could they look each other in the face tomorrow morning? Who had seduced whom? She had seduced him, of course! For the first time in his life he had been seduced. Perhaps she hadn't been to bed with her husband for years. Shouldn't he get up now, leave a note and go? But how should he start that letter? *Dear Sophia? Dear Mrs. Brons?* They were equally impossible. No heading at all? And it was as though the thought that he would have to put his damp clothes on again, and walk to the observatory through the Botanical Garden after all, was the final sign for his body to put an end to things for today. He had just enough strength to pull the cord.

He woke at a quarter past nine; the memory of the previous night immediately filled him with frenzied uncertainty. He cracked the top joints of his thumbs. He quickly got out of bed and drew the curtains. It was calm weather; only a few branches that had blown down and fragments of roof tiles recalled what had happened. His clothes were hanging over a chair: everything had been cleaned, dried, and ironed; even his shoes had been polished. In the bathroom Brons's shaving things were still on the washbasin, but he did not touch them. When he entered the room downstairs, Sophia was on the telephone. Her hair was up again; she nodded to him and pointed to the coffee pot, which was on the table.

While he poured himself a cup, he could hear that the conversation was about mourning and the funeral. She had behaved naturally to him; her eyes again had the look of the abbess, as though nothing had happened. If that was the attitude she had chosen, she was making things easy for him.

Or had nothing really happened? Had he dreamed it, perhaps? He sneaked a look at her. Was that the woman who last night had stuck her tongue out so far? Only now did it strike him that she had a good figure, fuller than Ada's, but in good shape everywhere; nowhere were its contours blurred with fat. There was a clear transition from her firm calves into slim ankles.

"That was Dol," she said, putting the receiver down, "Onno's sister. She's taken all the formalities off my hands. Did you sleep well?"

"Very well. And thank you very much for tidying up my things."

Onno had also already called. There had still been no change in Ada's condition; he would be coming to Amsterdam in the ambulance in the course of the morning. She herself would be going there that afternoon.

"Did you say that I'd spent the night here?"

"Yes. You did, didn't you? Would you like a fried egg?"

"Yes please, Mrs. Brons."

When she had disappeared into the kitchen, he thought: the woman's split into two completely separate halves. There was a daytime Sophia and a nighttime Sophia, who had nothing in common—a cool, unfeeling person, and a second one brimming with emotion. He remembered how Ada had sometimes talked about her as a disgusting bitch, but had she really known her mother? It fascinated him—but it was also clear to him that he mustn't make any allusion to what had happened last night.

He thought about everything that he had to do today. Of course he had to call Onno, then he had to go to the observatory: prepare everyone for the news that a week's observation material might have been lost. He had to call Dwingeloo; Floris must contact the police. He had to call his insurance company, and his garage. The car was not a write-off, there was probably nothing wrong with the engine, but he never wanted to see the thing again; they would have to clean it up and sell it. He took out his diary and was going to make a few notes, but the point of his pencil had broken off. While he was sharpening it, the shop doorbell rang.

"Would you go and see who it is?" called Sophia.

He walked to the front of the shop, up little flights of stairs and through the caverns. At the cash register stood a tall, thin man with a short black beard, who stared rather wildly into his eyes.

"Have you got anything on metempsychosis?"

Metempsychosis—that sounded like madness. Max looked around.

"Perhaps in the psychiatry section . . ."

"I mean the transmigration of souls," said the man, still staring at him.

It was on the tip of Max's tongue to say that they didn't have anything on migration, but Sophia had already appeared.

"We're closed. We're closed because of a bereavement." To Max she said, "Your egg's ready."

28

The Funeral

On the evening of that day, on his way to Keyzer's, where he had arranged to meet Max at seven o'clock, Onno looked in alarm at the Concertgebouw: he had completely forgotten to phone the orchestra! They were due to give a subscription concert shortly! When he asked the porter at the stage door whether anyone from the administration was there, Marijke came past with her clarinet. When he told her what had happened, the color drained from her face and she clutched the case to her, like a child in need of protection. She would pass on the message and visit Ada the following day.

"You needn't bother," said Onno. "At the moment she's not aware of anything that's happening around her."

"How do you know that? Anyway, I want to do it for myself, too."

He gave her the room number, pressed a kiss on her forehead, and went across the street, to where the restaurant was filled with dining concert-goers.

Max was sitting at a small table against the wall. "What's the news?" he asked immediately.

"Not too good."

Onno had been told by the neurologist that afternoon that Ada's electro-encephalogram was fortunately not "flat," as he called it, but did show a "diffuse, seriously slowed pattern."

"I know those kinds of terms from my own subject," nodded Max.

"He said that for the time being they couldn't make any predictions. Only if it continues like this for two or three more weeks may they perhaps be able to call it an irreversible coma."

"And if you've got a flat E.E.G. . . . ."

"Then you're a vegetable."

They sat opposite each other in silence.

"But suppose . . ." Max began hesitantly. "Ada's now in her fifth month . . . and if it takes—"

"It doesn't seem to make any difference to the child."

Suddenly Max realized that at the moment he was the only person who could still say what had happened in the Gulf of Mexico. But even if that remained the case, it still wouldn't help him. Even if she had not had an accident, Ada would never have talked about it.

"What then?" he asked cautiously.

"Yes, then there will be a problem. But there's no question of that for the time being. It only happened last night, do you realize? Her mother was there this afternoon—she used to be a nurse; she also said that she'd known cases of unconsciousness that lasted for weeks."

Onno could hear himself saying this—and at the same time he saw Ada's motionless face on the pillow, the horrible catheter in her nose, and himself sitting in their silent house that afternoon for minutes on end looking at her cello, like at a tombstone.

"In any case," said Max thoughtfully, "it seems there's no threat to the child."

"Everyone agreed about that."

The waiter handed them the menus, but Onno waved him away and said he wanted four rissoles and two glasses of milk. Max would have preferred to eat nothing at all, and ordered only a plate of vegetable soup. He had the impression that Onno was more optimistic than he was; he himself did not trust it—and of course that was because of what the same Sophia had said, last night.

"Off you go again," said Max, "with your milk and your rissoles."

Onno sighed deeply. "To be quite honest . . . but of course you must never tell anyone . . . this is not the worst thing. I'm the stock comic type of the married bachelor."

Max smiled. He was about to say that in that case he, who was Onno's opposite in everything, was probably the tragic type of the unmarried husband—but that was too ambiguous for him to manage to say. For his part,

Onno had of course immediately had the same thought, and he also knew that Max was thinking that, and he appreciated the fact that he didn't want to slip into their usual tone now.

Max spread the napkin over his lap. "How did your mother-in-law react when she saw Ada?"

"Incomprehensible. She looked at her daughter as though she were just any patient. No feeling at all, even though her husband has just died too. I ask you. No, what a mother to have. I never wanted to believe Ada, but now I've seen it with my own eyes."

"She was very nice to me, though," said Max, without looking at him, "I can't say any different. She gave me shelter for the night, pressed my trousers, and fried an egg for me. Perhaps she has difficulty in showing her feelings."

"Yes, yes. I could tell you a few of Ada's stories about her, but I won't. Maybe you know them too, for that matter. Anyway, Brons is being cremated on Monday—you'll be getting an invitation. Will you be coming, or will you be back in Dwingeloo?" His voice faltered. "What's wrong? You suddenly look as if you've pooped in your pants."

Max's eyes had widened in dismay. He noticed that, at the prospect of seeing Sophia again, he was getting an erection under his napkin. What in heaven's name did that mean? Did it mean that he, like Ada and Onno, had not only never understood her, but not even himself?

Max drove from the observatory to the crematorium near The Hague in a Volkswagen borrowed from his garage. He really ought to have been in Dwingeloo, but when he had mentioned the accident, someone had filled in for him.

Here all hope went up in smoke. Just like three months ago, at Onno's wedding, it was rush hour here too—but now in order to undo something the foundations of which were constantly being laid in the town halls. The same black limousines, now without white ribbons on their side mirrors, drove in and out of the gate, and now not accompanied by confetti and laughter but, in a leaden silence, filled only by the soft crunch of ground-up shells under the tires. He breathed in the sea air deeply. Here too there were groups of people standing everywhere, but he saw no one that he knew. At the gate a man in a black suit, with a hat in his hand, asked him for which deceased he had come; because of his profession his face expressed such a boundless, universal, almost syllogistic sorrow at the mortality of all human beings, hence also of Socrates, that no one could match it with their individual sorrow. The service for Mr. Brons was in the small hall. The cortege had not yet arrived.

He walked down the wooded path, past the columbaria. In the niches of the brick walls the urns stood like in an eighteenth-century pharmacy; but at the same time it made an Asiatic impression on him. There was something Chinese about it, something from a culture that had been submerged for thousands of years. He would never have himself cremated; it was far too final for him. He and Onno had once come to the conclusion that you had to decide for yourself whether after your death you wanted to return to your father or your mother. If you wanted to return to your father, then you must go into the fire, because that was spirit; but your mother was of course the earth, the body. Since that conversation, Onno had known for sure that he would have himself cremated.

The sun shone low over the tops of the trees—and when the crematorium loomed up he saw above the low flat roof, against the dark background of the wood, thin pale blue smoke drifting slowly upward, like from a cigarette. He decided to walk around the building first before going in.

Around the back he stopped. Not because of the container of rubbish, which was standing there, because rubbish was inevitable everywhere; or because of the drivers, who stood laughing and talking by their parked hearses, since everyone had a job to do; but because of the square chimney that he recognized from Birkenau. Now too there was no smoke coming out of it, only scorching heat. At its base there was the hum of ventilators from a grille. He couldn't see it, but at the same time he did see it: how stokers under the ground took the coffins out of the descended elevators, carried them across a tiled floor in neon light, and pushed them, flowers and all, into the white hell: not thousands a day, true, two or three an hour, but that was what was going on down below.

In the waiting room of the small hall a small company had gathered. Onno's parents were there, and his youngest sister's husband, Karel, the Rotterdam brain surgeon. The others—friends and acquaintances of Brons's of course, freethinkers and anarchists, perhaps even teetotalers—he had never seen before. He could only remember Ada's father vaguely, but in some way they were like him: slightly shabby, like Social Democrats, but without their petit bourgeois air and plus a certain intellectual clarity, in the way they looked at things. They had read books—even if they were probably books that only they still read. They looked shyly now and then at the Calvinist prime minister, who had read mainly one Book.

Apart from that he knew only Bruno. The pianist had seen the announcement of the death and asked how Ada had reacted to her father's death.

"She didn't," said Max. After Max briefly told him what had happened, Bruno asked in shock whether she was still unconscious, but Max didn't know. He excused himself and said hello to Onno's family. They also took it for granted that they would talk not about Brons but about Ada. The brain surgeon confirmed hesitantly that even a long coma did not necessarily mean brain damage, but he would prefer her to wake up sooner rather than later. At least her brain stem, where the breathing center was located, was not damaged.

"Poor child," said Onno's mother. "And expecting, too. Isn't it appalling?"

"One doesn't talk like that, To," said Quist with granite authority. "God moves in mysterious ways."

"Yes of course, but . . ."

"In the eyes of Providence there are no 'buts.' "

She was intimidated and fell silent.

"It was more as if the devil had a hand in it," said Max. "We had to stop for a tree that had fallen over, and just afterward a second tree fell on precisely the same spot."

Quist shot him a short glance, which he couldn't quite place: on the one hand it said that the devil was something for idolaters, or for Roman Catholics, which in practical terms amounted to the same thing; on the other hand there was a hint of something like sympathy, because Max had come to his wife's aid in a Manichean way in her Theodicean dilemma. Perhaps, thought Max, it was really true that you could only believe in God if you believed in the devil as well. If you believed only in God, you got into difficulties. In that case where did the gas chambers come from? Why did that tree have to fall exactly where it fell? Why was God's creation so faulty that later on a Messiah was necessary, too? "And God saw that it was good"—but it wasn't good at all. It was all wrong.

The doors of the hall were slowly opened by an attendant, who, despite his youth, was also completely shattered by grief. Max was the last to enter. The coffin, covered in flowers, was centrally placed in front of them, like a missile about to be launched. In the front row he saw Onno, his sister Dol, and Sophia with an old lady who must be her mother; the others were of course Brons's relations. Dol had had the idea of having them play the second part of the Dvořák cello concerto, which made Ada more present than if she had actually been there. It seemed to Max that the music was the only thing that moved in the room. He looked at the white-haired back of Ada's grandmother's head, the hair in a knot. Was that perhaps the great-grandmother of his child sitting there?

When the music had slowly ended, the broken young man took a step forward, and said, again with a hat in his hand:

"Mr. A.L.C. Akkersdijk will now say a few words."

Pulling papers out of his inside pocket, a graying man stepped forward and stood at the lectern. He folded them open, looked fiercely at those assembled, and said with great determination:

"Oswald Brons is dead."

This was someone who knew no such thing as doubt. Now he outlined Brons's contributions to the cause of free thought and the triumph of reason over all obscurantism, of scientific atheism over the dogmatism of the churches of all denominations, particularly in the Leiden chapter, where Oswald had given of his best. Max could see from the back of Onno's head that he was thinking of his father, who was now forced to endure this, too. He looked around. The clear hall with its brick walls was as clean and bare as a stream of cold water from the tap—it wasn't the functional architecture of modern death. But was the true architecture of grief perhaps still a dark church full of incense, with columns and statues and dark alcoves, in which candles were burning by dim paintings, executed gods and sacred accoutrements? Wasn't that much more functional emotionally? That had obviously been forgotten by the vegetarian iconoclasts of the Bauhaus and De Stijl.

To conclude his address, Akkersdijk quoted a bitter aphorism of Multatuli's, with his voice changing as if into that of a vicar reading a verse from the Bible. He folded his manuscript, and somewhat in conflict with his ideology, he looked at the coffin and said gruffly:

"*Au revoir*, Oswald."

Music again took over the space. After half a minute Max wondered what they were waiting for now—then he suddenly saw that the coffin had almost disappeared into the ground. The flowers were disappearing too, and slowly two doors slid shut. They were now setting to work in the basement, sweating men with beer bellies and cigarettes between their lips; he would have liked to go outside to see smoke suddenly coming out of the chimney. He thought of Ada. While her father's body was being destroyed, she was lying in bed unaware of anything. Or was there such a deep, subterranean bond between a daughter and her father that it still registered in some way or other? Perhaps the same kind of bond as that between herself and her unborn child—or between a son and his mother?

When the process in the underworld was obviously complete, the young man again took a step forward and beckoned toward the family; at the same time double doors opened at the side, and the smell of coffee immediately spread like the incense of the realm of the living. The family stood in a row and Max was the last to give his condolences. Without saying anything he squeezed Sophia's hand, aware of her warmth; but although she must be able to see that on his face, she did not react at all. She introduced him to her mother, who, resting on a stick, looked at him with the same cool eyes and said:

"You were driving, I hear. How terrible it all is."

He nodded without saying anything. Brons's mother was in tears, and because of that his father could scarcely keep control of himself; but as the generations progressed, grief became more bearable: the youngest nephews and nieces, at the end, were in an unmistakably cheerful mood.

Behind him, the line had broken up and he asked Onno how Ada was today.

"The same." He excused himself, he had to go to his father and mother to make up for the havoc that A.L.C. Akkersdijk had wrought. "What I am putting the pair of them through . . . I shall be severely punished for it one day. Besides, we're going back to the Statenlaan shortly, to my parents' place, but that's only for close family. I can't really invite you."

"Of course not. I'll call you tomorrow."

He took a coffee and a cake from the buffet and wandered into the crowd, exchanging a few words now and then. Sometimes he cast a short glance in the direction of the widow, but she did not look at him. Of course not. He was making a great mistake, and he must put it out of his mind. It had been an isolated incident; under the pressure of disaster she had let herself go for once and now she was back under control. She was again the unattainable woman that she had always been. Maybe she had by now really convinced herself that it had never happened.

Nevertheless, when people were about to leave, he made sure that he happened to be in her vicinity.

As she was helping her mother up, she asked him: "Haven't you missed your pencil sharpener? You left it behind last week."

"Oh, was it at your house!"

She looked at him coolly. "See you again sometime. Thank you for coming."

"Goodbye, Mrs. Brons."

Max would have liked to get back his pencil sharpener that same evening, but that was of course not possible. His thoughts constantly wandered the following day: from system 3 C 296 to Mrs. Brons's greedy internal biting. It had of course been a disguised invitation! "See you again sometime." Or was he fooling himself? Perhaps all she was thinking about was indeed that pencil sharpener. But did one really mention something as trivial as a forgotten pencil sharpener immediately after the cremation of one's husband? If it had been a fountain pen, or a very special pencil sharpener. But it was an ordinary gray thing costing a few cents, which he had not even missed and of which he had five or ten at home, as he did at the observatory.

The fact that he did not visit her the following evening, either, but forced himself to get into his car and drive to Amsterdam, was because he could not yet comprehend what he might be getting himself into. Hadn't he gotten himself into enough of a mess already by now? The first time it was Sophia Brons who had taken the initiative, under extraordinary circumstances; in a certain sense it had never happened. But on the second occasion the initiative would be his. That would be a new beginning, and if it was effective, then everything would change. Then there would be a third time too, and a fourth. How much of a secret could it remain? Imagine Onno getting to know about it! Moreover, her daughter might shortly have a child that looked remarkably like her lover; what then? Then it would be a double disaster, and perhaps not entirely devoid of danger. And as a man of science he could not completely exclude the chance of an even further compounded disaster: that Sophia would become pregnant by him.

But there was no stopping it. The memory of the greedy biting and the thrilling circumstances of that night, now a week ago, had destroyed any interest in other women for him. Like someone who had stopped smoking and thought of nothing but cigarettes all day long, he wandered through the observatory, went into the garden, came back, paced up and down his room, went for a coffee, had conversations that he immediately forgot, and when most people had already gone home, he went for a meal at the Indonesian restaurant, where he had often been with Ada. He drank three carafes of sake and at nine-thirty he went to the telephone and dialed the number that he had in his diary under Ada's name.

"Mrs. Brons speaking."

"It's Max Delius. I'm calling about my pencil sharpener."

"It's here on the table."

"Would you mind if I dropped by to pick it up? Or is it too late?"

"It's not all that late."

"Then I'll be right over."

Trembling, he paid the bill and drove to "In Praise of Folly." He parked his car half on the curb and determined not to take any initiative, as was his usual custom; he would see what happened.

Sophia opened the door with the black reading glasses low down on her nose.

"Hello, Max."

"Hello, Mrs. Brons."

He followed her through the bookshop, which gave the appearance of being open for business again. In the living room the television was on, with the sound turned off. In a square, in Rome by the look of it, the police were beating up demonstrators.

"What's going on?"

"Oh, that. I don't know, I wanted to see a Greta Garbo film that's on in a moment. Have a seat—or do you have to go right away?"

While she made him coffee in the kitchen, he turned the sound up and sat down on the sofa. Since Ada's pregnancy, politics had actually passed him by; of course he read in the paper about everything that was happening, and there was plenty, but he read it like he read the advertisements or the economic news: it didn't penetrate the area that he had inhabited almost exclusively since then; and it did not do so now, either. As Sophia came in with the coffee, the opening titles of *Anna Karenina* appeared.

At home he had a portable set, with an extendable, V-shaped indoor antenna, but it was seldom on; he couldn't remember once having watched television with Ada. But now, in this back room behind a bookshop, in deepest secrecy, that most petit bourgeois of all pleasures suddenly revealed an unknown, exciting side, like an innocent boot to a shoe fetishist.

Sophia sat cross-legged in the small armchair, stirred her coffee, and watched the unfolding drama. They did not speak. He had read the novel about ten years ago, but he didn't have the impression that the film had any more to do with the book than the photo of the disaster with the disaster it-self. Palaces, dazzling uniforms. The impenetrable face of Garbo, the de-spairing sing-song note in her voice. He looked at Sophia now and again out of the corner of his eye, at her beautiful, slim ankles. The function previously performed by the stove, around which the family sat, he reflected, was nowa-days fulfilled by the television set. Television was the modern fire. He was go-ing to say that to her, but he had the feeling that he must hold his tongue.

When the whistling and hissing of the fatal locomotive and the lugubri-ous clouds of steam gave way to the news, Sophia turned off the set and asked if he would like anything more to drink. "A glass of wine perhaps?"

"If I'm not keeping you . . ."

"I never go to bed that early, but you have to go to Amsterdam."

"I can be there in half an hour. It's quiet on the road at this time."

Was she playing a game—or precisely not? After she had poured him a drink from an opened bottle of Rioja, they talked about Ada. She had been to the hospital again that morning: there was no change in the situation, and the doctors had become noticeably more gloomy. Because she had made no secret of the fact that she was a qualified nurse, they talked to her differently than to just any relation. She was given details of laboratory results, exami-nation of motor functions, eye reflexes. Only weeks afterward could a more or less accurate prognosis be given, but there was still hope and there would continue to be for the time being. In medical literature there was even a case known of a forty-year-old man who had been in a vegetative state for a year and a half but nevertheless woke up and began speaking again, although he was largely paralyzed and completely dependent on other people.

Max nodded. Of course, she was now thinking the same as he was: how things were to go on should Ada not regain consciousness. He wanted to broach the subject, but did not dare. In answer to his question as to how the bookshop was going, Sophia said that it was open in the afternoons, but that it could not continue for very long; when someone came and browsed and wanted to buy a book, she sold it at the price that her husband had written in pencil on the flyleaf. But when someone took a pile of books out of a bag to sell them, she didn't know what to do and sent them away.

There was a silence.

"What was Ada like as a child?" asked Max.

Sophia glanced at her hands.

"Should I tell you? Once, just before Oswald and I had to go somewhere, I had an argument with her. She was about eleven or twelve. She had been spreading a terrible story about me: that I had put the cat in a box used for books and drowned it in the Rapenburg canal—when we didn't have a cat at all. Oswald was allergic to cats. When we got home in the afternoon, we found a note here on the table that said she had run away from home and that she was never coming back. The day before we had pancakes for dinner, and as you know you always make too many pancakes; all the leftover pancakes had disappeared. We didn't think it would be too serious, but when she hadn't come home by dinnertime, we began to get alarmed. We called everybody she knew, and later that evening Oswald went to the police with a photo. Of course we stayed up, and in the middle of the night Oswald couldn't stand it any longer. He was quite beside himself, and he got his bike and went to look for her. Even after he had gone a few streets away I could still hear him calling out her name. But half an hour later I suddenly had a strange feeling—I don't know what it was. I went up to the loft and opened the door of the lumber room. She was lying there asleep, with her coat on. Next to her were the pancakes, in a knotted tea towel."

"And your husband cycled through Leiden for an hour calling out her name?"

"Yes. By the time he got home, she had long since been put to bed. She hadn't even noticed that I'd undressed her."

"And the next day?"

"We didn't talk about it anymore."

There was not a sound outside. Max emptied his glass—and on an impulse he decided no longer to be the first to say anything. He poured another glass for Sophia and himself and looked at his pencil sharpener, which was lying on the table. *Fairy Tale.* There he was sitting in that back room where he had seen Ada for the first time, and a little later her mother.

Time passed, and silence enclosed them like a warmer and warmer bath. At the edge of his field of vision he could constantly see her figure, with the secret deep in her lap. For a few minutes he glanced at her, and for a second she looked back at him, but without expression. He gave no sign of understanding either; he knew for certain that if he had smiled now, he would have destroyed everything.

After the silence had lasted for ten minutes or a quarter of an hour, he was certain that he was going to lose. He had met his match. She would sit there in her chair saying nothing until the following morning.

With his heart pounding, he glanced at his watch and said: "It's getting late. I'll think I'll be going."

She also looked at her watch. "Do you have to be back in Leiden tomorrow morning?"

"I'm afraid so."

"And you've been drinking. If you like you can stay over here."

"Well . . . if I'm not disturbing you . . . "

Brons's things turned out to have disappeared from the bathroom.

29

Irreversibility

In the weeks that followed, he visited Sophia every few days. Each time, he called up first to announce his arrival, because even making a date seemed too intimate; and every morning he thanked her formally for her hospitality. They talked a little, read a little, or watched television; when it was finally really too late to go to Amsterdam, it was all the same to her if he stayed over. And then each time the door opened in the dark and she crept under the covers with him; after letting herself go completely, she disappeared again without him having seen her. Since that first time she had not spoken again, which was also the sign for him to say nothing more in bed. He had never experienced anything so mysterious, but in some way it answered a deep wish of which he had never been conscious. He had attained the unattainable woman!

No one must know; he must never speak to anyone about it—first and foremost not to her. If he once gave an indication that he knew, it would be over at once. She must remain the two women that she was, the daytime Sophia and the nighttime Sophia—if he were to link the two, a short-circuit would immediately disable the mechanism. He must not even use her first name until she had invited him to. Psychiatrists would find it perverse, he considered—Freud would have found it hilarious—but because her mystery was absolutely complementary to his, like a nut to a bolt, he became completely addicted to the situation—quite apart from her long tongue, and the glowing, subterranean biting. If in other cases his desire for the same women always decreased exponentially, it now seemed to be growing even more intense each time after a month. He no longer looked at other women—which had the incidental advantage of a considerable gain in time.

Onno had already asked him a few times where on earth he had been for the last few weeks—he seldom got any answer when he called the Vossius-straat—to which Max replied that there were regular evening meetings on the program of the new telescope in Westerbork, which was due to be inaugurated that same year. Onno was quite prepared to believe him; he himself did little else but attend meetings anymore. After Berkeley, Amsterdam, and Berlin—where Rudi Dutschke had meanwhile been shot—the students had now revolted in Paris, too. That immediately had another, more serious dimension, in view of the fact that there it was taking place in a revolutionary tradition; the revolt promptly spread to the workers, who occupied their factories, and suddenly things began to get serious in Europe. *L'Imagination au pouvoir!* A new epoch was about to begin, and in the Netherlands too the new guard must be ready to take over power. In mid-May, in order to bring himself up-to-date, Onno went to Paris for a few days with some comrades-in-arms, where in the crowded cafés around the occupied Sorbonne he saw various activists he knew from Havana, orating with Cuban authority, the illuminated look of victory in their eyes. But, as he told Max after his return, he didn't make himself known to them in the presence of his Dutch friends: they did not need to know precisely what he had been up to in Cuba in order to be able to use it against him one day.

"Nice profession you're in," said Max.

"You're telling me. Politics are conducted by glorified gangsters, and I'm the meanest gangster of them all. Not a job for gentle-natured, unworldly spirits like you."

But world events were passing Ada by. Max had not seen her again since the night of the accident; he felt a resistance to visiting her, and because he didn't have to feel guilty on her account, he didn't feel guilty anymore. Sophia never inquired whether he had been to the Wilhelmina Hospital yet; but when Onno called up one Sunday morning and asked if he would go with him, Max could not refuse. And an hour later they were walking through the streets of the extensive complex of somber buildings, which dated from the last century. Even outdoors in the windless spring morning there was the smell of Lysol, mixed with that of oranges.

She lay in a remote wing with six other coma patients in a ward painted a dirty yellow. It was visiting time, and silent or whispering relatives were already sitting by every bed; most patients had bandages around their heads. A male nurse was sitting reading at a table, under a monthly calendar with a large photo of the pyramid of Cheops. Ada was lying on a sheepskin; her head, with a catheter in her nose, was turned slightly aside on the pillow. She was breathing peacefully, eyes closed, as though she were asleep—and at the same time one could tell in some way that it wasn't sleep. The expression on her face had changed, but it was difficult to say in what way: there was something eternal about it, as though it were slowly making way for an image of itself. Her arms lay next to her body, the hands motionless. What had unmistakably changed in any case, grown, risen, was the wave under the blanket. She was now in her seventh month, and what was growing there inside her was no image, but a creature of flesh and blood. It was as though she only continued to exist to give birth to that, like a helpless queen bee kept alive by drones.

Max and Onno, standing on either side of the high, tightly tucked bed, looked at each other.

"The statue gives birth to a human being," said Max softly, immediately sensing that he was going too far.

Onno shivered. That expressed exactly what he had been feeling all those weeks. She had been reduced to an oven, which was different in kind to the bread that was rising in it. Would the moment ever come when she opened her eyes? Today again nothing had changed, and a short while ago he had virtually lost hope, but he did not want to admit it to himself; and the problems that probably lay in store for him, he only wanted to think about when it was certain. He had the vague feeling that by assuming this he was in some way bringing the irrevocable closer.

"Everyone is convinced," he said, "that the people in those beds can't hear anything, and yet everyone is sitting whispering."

"So that they won't hear," Max added. "So perhaps they can hear something."

"Do you really think so?"

Max shrugged his shoulders. "I don't know. We're whispering too, aren't we? Why are we here, for that matter? Perhaps deep down we're convinced that those patients here can take in everything but simply can't express it." Onno opened his mouth, but closed it again—whereupon Max said, "Yes, I know about that E.E.G. too, of course."

Marijke had also said something like that, Onno remembered, but of course that was utter nonsense. He was going to counter by saying that in that case the dead also obviously heard everything, because people whispered in rooms where someone had died too; but Ada's presence prevented him—so that perhaps it was not such an absurd notion after all. Moreover, he knew that Max would immediately push his theory to the limit, just as he always pushed everything to the limit, and would also be ready on this occasion to widen the border area between life and death into an expanse of no-man's-land. From what Onno knew of him, with his rather homosexual tendency to symmetry, he would take a postmortem period of nine months—thus immediately explaining the deeper reason for the period of mourning.

Max, for his part, didn't really believe his theory either—but he too was quite sure that he would not dare to whisper in Ada's ear, "Your father is dead, and I am having an affair with your mother." He read the card on the flowers that stood next to the bed:

"From Bruno." He looked at Onno. "An absurd gesture. Waste of money."

"He did it for himself."

"Worse still."

When Onno realized that Max's answer implied that he was sure that Ada would never wake up, he said: "Or perhaps he hoped that she would come to and immediately see his flowers."

There was a silence in the ward. The motionless patients, with the visitors looking at them: the living dead.

"It's like a museum in here," whispered Max.

At the same moment as Onno, he took Ada's hand in his: Onno the one with which she had controlled the strings, Max the one with which she had held the bow. They both felt that the hand, although warm, had become a thing. Here and there rust erupted through the white paint of the bed.

"Let's go," said Onno after a few moments.

They laid the hands back in place, Onno pressed a kiss on Ada's forehead, and they went to the door. As Max put his hand out toward the handle, it moved downward and a doctor in a white, open jacket appeared, letting Sophia through. They stared at each other in surprise.

"Good heavens," said Onno. "Hello, Mother."

"Hello, Onno. Hello, Max."

"Hello, Mrs. Brons." Max shook hands with her, knowing for sure that no one could tell anything by looking at either of them.

The doctor, a small, balding man, was wearing a pair of glasses with double lenses, the front pair of which was turned up, so that he seemed to be looking at right angles into the sky. After Onno had introduced him as Ada's neurologist, Dr. Stevens, they returned to the bed.

Max had a strange feeling. Suddenly all four of them, or in fact all five of them, were together. But who were they? Onno simply thought he was in the company of his friend, his mother-in-law, and the mother of his child. But at the same time he was in the company of the mistress of his friend, who himself was perhaps the father of the child that his wife was expecting and who could therefore no longer be rightfully called his friend, and nor could his wife be called his wife. Sophia knew a little more than Onno, but not everything, as Max himself did.

Sophia ran her hand through Ada's hair and then loosened the sheet a little at the foot end.

"She'll get club feet like that," she said, without looking at Stevens. And then with an impassive face, "The news is not good, Onno."

Onno looked at the neurologist in alarm.

"Well . . ." said the latter, glancing at Max.

"Go ahead, I have no secrets from my friend."

"We've just been talking about it. The E.E.G. has deteriorated seriously in the last few days, and there are other indications that you must be prepared for the fact that your wife is in all probability in an irreversible coma."

Onno stared at him, then glanced at Ada and left the ward. Max hesitated, but then followed him into the corridor, where Onno was staring out of the window across the bleached roadways of the hospital site.

"I knew it," he said. "I knew all along. We all knew. What in heaven's name are we going to do now?"

In his eyes Max saw complete, unbearable despair—which at the same instant seem to leap across to him, like a summons, a demand!

When Onno phoned his youngest sister that same afternoon to give her the bad news, she told him that members of the family had been telephoning and talking things over for days, discussing what was to happen if Ada were to remain in a vegetative state. That immediately irritated him beyond measure: he would decide for himself. But on the other hand the solution must come from that direction; he understood that too. "Family is forever," he was in the habit of saying—and when Dol suggested organizing a family council, he agreed. In the evening she called back with the message that their father wanted to invite the vicar along too, to which Onno replied that in that case he wanted it called off.

Of course everything had been prearranged by the clan. It would only seem to be a consultation; it was clear to him at once how it would turn out. In the immediate family there were only two couples with small children: that of Diederic's oldest son, Hans, and that of Trees's oldest daughter, Paula. He had never been very interested in those secondary branches; he occasionally saw their offspring at parties, but they had always grown and changed so much that he couldn't remember who was who, and he didn't really care.

His nephew Hans, at present first secretary in the Copenhagen embassy, with whom he had never exchanged more than a few words, was on the threshold of a promising career in the diplomatic service; partly by virtue of being a Quist, he was predestined for ambassadorial posts in the most awful countries, possibly eventually achieving the highest state of diplomatic bliss: London. He was married to a banker's daughter from Breda, whose father had the notion of calling her Hadewych. His niece Paula, whom he didn't really know either, had chosen a freight-shipping magnate from Rotterdam, Jan-Kees, who had brought three children from a previous marriage: a clumsy, jovial man approaching forty, who had a loud voice and smoked cigars.

Two days later a heavyweight delegation had assembled at his parents' house in The Hague. With the light behind him, next to the lectern with the Authorized Version of the Bible on it, old Quist sat in his winged armchair and surveyed his children and grandchildren. Women were in the majority. Diederic and his Antonia were not there—they were paying an official visit to Indonesia—but their Copenhagen Hans and his Hadewych were; since Hans had to visit the Foreign Office anyway, he had taken the opportunity. As Onno had expected, Paula and Jan-Kees had also turned up. Like Hadewych, Paula was Ada's age, perhaps a little older, and expecting her second child. Only Sophia did not belong to the immediate family circle. After Coba had served tea and gingersnaps and had left the room, Onno assumed that his father would open the meeting, like the chairman of the cabinet—but it was his mother who said:

"The poor child. I didn't sleep a wink last night. Is there really no hope, Onno?"

He shrugged. "Nothing seems to be a hundred percent certain in medicine, but according to the doctors we must assume that things will stay as they are. You can ask Karel."

"I phoned the Wilhelmina Hospital yesterday," said his brother-in-law the brain surgeon. "I'm afraid that's how it is. And perhaps," he said, with a quick glance at Onno, "this may be the lesser evil. A protracted coma like this would be bound to have dreadful consequences, such as complete loss of memory or complete change of character."

Complete loss of memory. Complete change of character. The words sank into Onno like bullets. No one had said that to him before—not Karel and not the doctors in the hospital; obviously everyone had been *hoping* recently that she would not wake up.

"It's dreadful for you, too," said Mrs. Quist to Sophia. "First the death of your husband and now this dreadful fate befalling your only child."

Onno looked at his mother-in-law. Since he had once turned up at the ward and had seen her filing Ada's nails, which were no longer bitten, he had softened his harsh judgment of her. It was obvious that she felt ill at ease in this company, but she sat up straight and held her ground.

"I've always known that life is a bit like the weather. It can change completely at any moment."

After these words, which did not testify immediately to Christian sentiments, there was a moment's silence. From the distance, where there was roadwork going on, came the sound of jackhammers. Onno hoped there wouldn't be some soothing quotation from the Heidelberg catechism; fortunately, everyone turned out to have enough of an instinct to avoid this. Anyway, he reflected, it applied mainly to weather conditions in the Netherlands and not those in the Sahara; but he kept that to himself.

"Things are as they are," he said—with the feeling that this tautology contained the ultimate wisdom. "Perhaps we shouldn't talk about our emotions this afternoon but about the question of what we are to do next. If everything goes well, our child will be born in two months, in July. And according to the people who should know, there's no reason to suppose that it won't go well, as far as that's concerned. But after that?"

"Of course," said Trees, his eldest sister, adjusting her silk scarf, "no one expects you to start washing diapers."

Onno heard the unmistakable silent addition ". . . while you're still in diapers yourself"—but he let that pass, not only because this was not the moment to get prickly, but also because he didn't entirely disagree. He would put the safety pins not just through the diaper but also through the baby, be lost in thought and let it fall off the chest of drawers, pick up the telephone and meanwhile let it drown in the bathtub.

"Of course not," said her husband. "That's women's work. These days you hear different opinions, but the fact is that women have children and men don't. They only have it on hearsay. So let's keep it simple. Onno's child is due shortly, he can't look after it himself, so who is going to look after it?"

In saying this, Coen had reduced things to their essentials—probably he had lots more to do this afternoon. With raised eyebrows, the public prosecutor looked around the circle, so the first one to raise a finger would be assigned the child by right, and the matter would be settled; they would go on discussing the weather, be given another cup of tea by Coba, and then they would simply head off home.

"We haven't got any children," said Dol, "and I'd like nothing better than to take on yours, Onno. I'm almost forty, so it would still be possible. We've had a long talk about it, but we finally think that it's better for the baby to have younger foster parents. Isn't that right, Karel?"

The surgeon sat with the tips of his outspread fingers touching; he took them apart for a moment and allowed them to return to the original position. That gesture made him look more than ever like Count Frankenstein.

"Of course it would be best to be brought up in a family with other young children."

Onno nodded and looked at Sophia. "It seems right to me."

"It must go where it has most chance of developing its full potential," said Sophia.

That sounded fairly obvious, but Onno also heard a distant echo of Solomon's judgment "Divide the living child in two, and give half to the one, and half to the other." He looked at the two couples, Hans and Hadewych and Paula and Jan-Kees—but first Margo spoke, the wife of his brother Menno, the professor, who had been prevented from coming himself because he had to account for his actions at a student meeting. As always her eyelids were swollen and red-rimmed, as though she had been crying, but actually she was good-humored.

"Ours are already in high school, and to tell you the truth, I can't bear the thought of having to wash diapers again. And from what I know of Onno, he wouldn't want his child to grow up in Groningen anyway. Isn't that so? To you that would be the depths of the provinces, and it would also be too far away for you."

"No one has to apologize for anything at all here," said Onno. "I'm not asking anyone for anything."

"Right," said Jan-Kees. "Then we'll offer it to you." He put his cigar in the ashtray, stretched his legs, crossed his legs, and put his hands at the back of his neck. "I've already got a house full of children, so yours won't make any difference. We live in a place in the country near Rotterdam, with quite a nice garden because I've got a transshipment company that makes a bundle. I may be right-wing, but I look after my workers, and anyone who doesn't play ball gets the boot. We will bring up your child completely in your spirit, you can leave that to me, because before I belonged to high society, I was a Socialist myself. And it won't cost you a penny. Well? Have we got a deal or haven't we? Your turn."

This was business Rotterdam-style. There was a slightly embarrassed silence, but Onno liked what he heard. Of course Jan-Kees was being provocative, maybe out of embarrassment; he was pretending to be what he ultimately was; but the fact that he was pretending to be like that meant that at the same time he was not.

"You're being terribly tactful again," said Paula, smiling apologetically at Onno.

"Yes, don't you think?" said Jan-Kees.

"Very," said Coen, his father-in-law.

"But we mean it, Uncle Onno. We'd like to do it," said Paula.

The fact that his child would grow up in a reactionary environment was no problem for Onno—the same thing had happened to him; many of his progressive friends also came from more or less well-to-do circles. But Jan-Kees was of course a vulgar money-earner, devoid of any cultural interest; he also had something unmistakably animal about him, with his pointed teeth and his heavy, dark beard, which came bursting out of his face. On the other hand his Paula made a sweet, defenseless impression, sitting there with her fat tummy in her ankle-length black, gold-embroidered Afghan tent dress. Physically, she wasn't anything like her formidable mother Trees, but she was probably the boss at home. There had to be something of a lion-tamer in her.

"We're also prepared to help you," said Hadewych.

The second bid was on the table.

"Not all at once!" laughed Margo, dipping her gingersnap in her tea. She immediately put her hand to her mouth and looked around in alarm. "I'm sorry," she said.

Perhaps Hadewych had been supernaturally predetermined by her name, perhaps she had modeled herself on it, because in any case she did indeed look like a medieval mystic. Her face had the dark complexion that the Spanish troops had left behind in Brabant four hundred years ago, with two large brown eyes, which seem to shine with ecstatic illumination.

"We haven't got a villa in Kralingen," said Hans, "nor have we got a garden with a swimming pool, but we do have a comfortable flat in Copenhagen. That is, for as long as it lasts. Of course, I don't know what our next post will be. I can imagine that being a problem for you. It will always be farther away from Amsterdam than Groningen."

He was the opposite of Jan-Kees in everything. He had satin-soft blond hair combed to the side and light blue eyes, was twenty-six or twenty-seven and already fitted out from top to toe in the uniform of the foreign service: in a suit of the correct shade of gray, not too dark but most of all not too light, a blue striped shirt, a dark blue tie with modest white polka dots, and black brogues. But he made a pleasant, intelligent, albeit rather wan impression— and he had immediately indicated the fundamental problem: his nomadic existence.

Lost in thought, Onno looked around the circle. Trees turned and looked at Coen, who was moving his left wrist very slowly out from under his shirt and looking down without moving his head to see what time it was. His mother sighed deeply and with a slight shaking of the head looked at Sophia, who, impassive as ever, was moving her forefinger back and forth through a loop of her coral necklace. The two couples, who had made their offers, seem to be avoiding each other's eyes, like people applying for the same job.

Suddenly Onno gave a start. "I don't have to decide now, I hope?"

Immediately everyone started talking at once.

"No question of that."

"Just imagine."

"Of course not."

"The very idea!"

"Just think about it calmly," said Dol. "You've got at least two months."

"Basically, yes." Karel nodded.

Finding himself suddenly dependent on the good offices of his family,

Onno had difficulty in finding words of gratitude. He felt particularly weighed down by the awkward position of rivalry in which the families of Hans and Jan-Kees had placed themselves willingly for his sake. Just imagine if he had had no family, like Max—what would he have done then?

"I've often behaved badly to you all," he forced himself to say. "I apologize for that."

He meant it, and at the same it disgusted him to hear himself talking like that. Heads were shaken and dismissive gestures made; but his mother's face began glowing, and to set the seal on Onno's genuflection his father said:

"Right. Let us pray."

There was silence, cigars were put away, heads were bent, hands folded. Even Onno caught himself inclining his upper body somewhat. Only Sophia did not change her attitude; but she stopped playing with her necklace. In the silence Coba opened the door to come in and pour some more tea; she paled, and quickly closed it again.

With eyes closed, Quist said:

"Lord God, Heavenly Father, Thou seest us gathered here together in Thy sight in our wretchedness. This life—which is nothing more than a constant death—has become even darker to us because of Thy unfathomable decision on Ada's fate. But we know that Thou can do all things and that none of Thy thoughts can be cut off. Give us Thy blessing and lighten our hearts. Pleading for Thy fathomless mercy, we pray Thee, Almighty and Eternal God, to give strength and wisdom to our prodigal son, who has been found again. Amen."

30

The Scaffold

Max knew about the meeting and waited restlessly for the report. He would have preferred to contact Onno or Sophia immediately, but it didn't seem wise to show too much curiosity. The following day Onno phoned him in Leiden and announced that he would be coming that evening.

Whereas Onno usually sank immediately into the green armchair, he paced constantly to and fro in Max's room, telling him how things had gone, and that he had finally abased himself, humiliated himself, for which he had been immediately rewarded by being commended to God.

"What kind of dishonorable, slavish religion is that? How was that seedy character from Nazareth ever able to defeat proud Jupiter?"

"But those dishonorable Christians have offered to take your child."

"Do you mean that wouldn't have happened among the heathen Romans? That has nothing to do with religion—it's tribal. You know nothing about it, because you have no family, but it even happens in the animal kingdom. It's blood ties."

"No, I have no family," said Max, looking at him. "I know about it to the extent that I was once also taken in by Christians, though I did not belong to their tribe."

As he said this, he realized that this would also perhaps apply to Ada's child in turn, if it were not of Onno's tribe. When Onno returned his glance, he realized that he had made a blunder.

"Right," he said with a generous gesture. "Unselfish love of one's fellow men exists, let's leave it at that. It's just that when I woke up this morning, I still didn't know what to do. How in heaven's name do I choose? Each option is as bad as the other. One option is worse than the other, and the other is worse than the first. According to narrow-minded spirits, that's logically impossible, but that impossibility is true in this case."

"So why don't you say that one is better than the other and the other better than the first?"

"No, because neither of them are good. At least not good enough. Take Jan-Kees and his Paula. They live in Rotterdam, in a huge house, where I can go every Wednesday afternoon to pick my child up and take it to the zoo. In a way I like them, but they're not my type, or Ada's; I don't want our child brought up there. Hans and Hadewych are better in that respect, but they can be transferred from Denmark to Zambia at any moment, and then from Zambia to Brazil, and then from Brazil to the Philippines, with our child being dragged from one international school to the other and having to say goodbye to its friends every four years. On the other hand, of course, it would see a bit of the world and learn lots of languages, but I would be bound to become a stranger to it: a kind of uncle in faraway Holland. It would only be here for a few weeks in the summer vacation—I don't care for that, either. Now, if Jan-Kees had been in the foreign service and Hans and Hadewych lived in Kralingen, I'd know what to do; but life doesn't seem to be as benevolent as that. So what am I to do now? There's no other option. What would you do if you were me?"

He sat down and Max got up. With his hands in his pockets, he went over to the window and looked out into the dark evening without seeing anything. He knew that the back of his head and his back were transmitting the message that he was thinking calmly, but his heart was pounding and he felt torn. What would he do if he were Onno? Perhaps he *was* Onno—that is, Onno himself did not know who he might be. How long must it go on like this? Wasn't it time to cut through this knot of lies and deceit once and for all? Shouldn't he turn around, now at this moment, and finally say, "Onno, the child that Ada is expecting may be mine . . ."—the words that he had once wanted to write to him, had written but not sent. The thought that he could not do it without Ada's knowledge no longer applied. Nothing happened without Ada's knowledge anymore, since everything happened without her knowledge. It was just that he couldn't bring himself to do it anymore; he had let things go too far. And yet he couldn't simply wait and see and trust that everything would come right. Something had to happen!

Suddenly he made out his reflection in the dark glass. He straightened his tie and ran his hands through his hair, and was reminded of an evening when he had gone to the theater with Onno, to see *Oedipus the King*; during the intermission, as they were drinking a cup of watery coffee in the foyer, Onno had asked, "Are you always looking in the mirror, you vain sod?"—to which he had replied, "Yes, I always look in all mirrors: in order to calibrate them."

He turned around, put his hands back in his pockets, and sat down on the windowsill.

"You could employ a housekeeper, a full-time help."

"Me have my child brought up by a housekeeper? And then find myself probably lumbered for twenty years with an unfortunate woman who sits in the kitchen crying every evening? I wouldn't dream of it. Anyway, how much do you think that would cost? As you know, as a result of my noble character I devote myself solely to scholarship and the public good, so I earn virtually nothing; I live on a small allowance from my inheritance. But anyway, I could do something about that. For example, I could go out to work, although it goes against the grain. Teaching third-year students the alphabet. I could get a job at some university right away, maybe even in Holland."

"But it needn't be longer than the first five or six years, need it? After that it could go to a good boarding school."

"A good boarding school! Is my child really to be thrust from security into insecurity at the age of six so that for the rest of its life the whole world will be insecure? The English method? Is that really what you'd do in my place?"

Max rubbed his face with both hands.

"No," he said.

"Of course," said Sophia, when Max phoned the following afternoon and asked if it would be okay if he dropped in for coffee after dinner. "You can have dinner here if you like."

That was new.

"Are you sure I'm not disturbing you?" As he heard himself saying that last word, he had the feeling that he was taking things too far, but that turned out not to be the case.

"You know how it is yourself. If there's food for one, there's food for two, and if there's food for two, there's food for three."

"That's true. If there's food for a hundred, there's also food for a hundred and ten. It's hard to understand why there's still hunger in the world."

He took a bottle of Chianti with him and, seated opposite each other at the kitchen table, they tucked into their steaks. While he listened to her view of The Hague family council, he was again seized by the excitement that the situation always aroused in him: an audience with the unattainable Mother Superior, the bride of Christ, soon about to change in the darkness into voluptuous, vociferous Circe.

He had repeatedly asked himself how the transition took place. He tried to imagine what was going on inside her: she hung her clothes over a chair, washed, got into bed, and turned out the light. Was that the moment? Was it the falling darkness that changed her from the one into the other? Or was there no moment of transition at all—was it simply a malicious game, the effect of which she had once discovered with a certain kind of man, like Brons and himself? But what did he have in common with Brons? Well, perhaps susceptibility to this game, but there ought to be a few other shared characteristics—and there were not. With Brons, of course, it had not happened like this at all; it only happened like this with him, and it wasn't a game.

He was convinced that in some way her nocturnal existence really didn't exist for her during the day, just as one couldn't remember one's dreams in the daytime. He was her dream and so he must remain. If he were to say to her during the day that they had had another exciting night, then perhaps she might really not know what he was talking about and throw him out with his weird talk. Her go to bed with him, her daughter's ex-boyfriend— where did he get that idea from? He should act out that kind of male fantasy with the whores!

He listened to her and nodded, wiped his mouth, took a sip of wine, and looked from her moving mouth to her eyes and from her eyes to her moving mouth. He was listening more to the timbre of her voice than to what she was saying—because he already knew that from Onno; for the first time he heard something of a sob in it, a despairing undertone, which might have nothing to do with emotion but only with the structure of her vocal chords. She told him that after the meeting was over she had taken the train with Onno. Between The Hague and Leiden she had said to him that of course she could also take care of the child.

"I said that's the traditional role of the grandmother, after all. If the parents have to go out, a grandmother is called to come and baby-sit."

Onno had said nothing to him about that conversation. He thought of his own mother for a moment, who might have been the other grandmother of Ada's child—the union of life and death.

"And how did Onno react?"

"He was noncommittal, but I could see that he didn't think it was an ideal solution, and it isn't. I'm nearly forty-five, so you can work it out: by the time the child is fifteen, I'll be sixty. It might be possible, but despite all his progressive ideas, Onno suddenly becomes very old-fashioned about that: he believes that there should be a man in the family. Apart from that, I get the feeling he doesn't like me very much. Nevertheless, he'll have to decide quickly."

She had gotten up and was clearing the table. Although Max knew exactly that following a conception on October 8, 1967, nine months meant a birth at the beginning of July 1968, he asked casually: "Yes, in about two months, isn't that right?"

"No," said Sophia. "Probably much sooner."

"Much sooner?" he repeated in surprise.

As she was putting the plates on the draining board, she said without turning around: "Haven't you talked to Onno yet today?"

"Yesterday was the last time. Has something happened?"

"He phoned shortly after your call. I don't know exactly what's happening, but there seems to be a risk attached to Ada's condition. According to the neurologist, her E.E.G. gives scarcely any reading. In any case the doctors are considering delivering the baby by cesarean section very soon. They would have had to do that anyway, because of course she can't give birth anymore. I'm going straight there tomorrow; they're making a decision."

Max stiffened. Suddenly it was there: the moment of truth. Of course he had known for all these months that the moment was drawing irrevocably closer; but without being clearly aware of it, he'd constantly had the feeling that it would never be reached—just as in Zeno's paradox there was always a portion of the way still to travel: first half, then half of the second half, then the first half of the remaining quarter . . . so that there would always be some time left. But now the leap had suddenly been made.

"Do you want coffee, too?" asked Sophia, holding the whistling kettle under the tap.

He stood up in confusion. He had the feeling that nothing was what it had been anymore, that he'd already made a decision but he was not letting it sink in yet.

"No," he said. "Thank you . . ." He searched for words. "I have to go."

She turned around. "What's the matter all of a sudden?"

"I don't know . . . I have to think. I'm sorry, it's rude of me but . . ." he put out his hand. "Thank you for the meal. I'll call you tomorrow. I need to be alone for a while now."

"Of course. As you like."

Sophia saw him to the door and he got into the Volkswagen, which he had finally bought. He drove off aimlessly. He wanted to think, but he only wanted to think when there was no one else around. No one can force themselves to have thoughts, but if they do have them it's possible to hold them back. The same applies to mental processes as to the metabolism. A line of Rilke's kept running through his head, like a dam holding back his thoughts:

You must change your life.

Night had already fallen, and on his way to Amsterdam, he took the turn-off to Noordwijk on impulse. He drove down the dark road through the dunes to the lighthouse, where he parked the car.

He turned off the engine and got out: the clunk with which he shut the door was like the period at the end of a sentence. The rush of the surf rose up like the first letter of the next sentence—audible silence, through which the beam of the lighthouse swept like something more silent than silence. There was a chilly sea breeze blowing; stars appeared and disappeared between black, scudding clouds. He breathed the salt air in deeply and went down the path to the deserted beach.

When he reached the sand, conditioned by countless summer days, he felt like taking his shoes off, but he turned up his collar, thrust his hands deep into his pockets, and walked straight toward the water. Reaching the harder, damp sand left behind by high tide, he stopped for a moment and looked at the dark horizon, indicated by the cone of light that swept over it every few seconds at once slowly and quickly. Head bent, he began walking southward over the shells.

Cesarean section! It was obvious: he must sacrifice himself. *He* must bring up Ada's child—together with Sophia. Only by doing that could he really do something to atone for his previous act. Should it emerge, God forbid, in some way that the child was not Onno's but his, it would cause endless suffering and Onno would disappear from the picture, but at the same time he would understand what he, Max, had done—namely, that he had taken responsibility for the child at a time when he was *not* yet sure who the father was, and had taken the risk of organizing his life around a child that was not his. If it really did turn out not to be his, Onno would never know what had gone on. It would still not mean that nothing was wrong, because betrayal of the friendship could never be undone: the lie would be between them for all eternity—although only he would know that—but he would at least have done what he could. He suppressed the thought that the surgical delivery might perhaps go wrong, which would mean that everything was solved—but he suddenly found himself feeling that it might be a disappointment.

The cross-shaped beams of the lighthouse moved constantly across his face, like helicopter rotor blades that kept the earth airborne in the universe. He must put his proposal to Sophia tonight, he thought, or at the latest tomorrow; if she agreed, then he would immediately tell Onno. If Onno agreed too, then he must leave Amsterdam and his life there as quickly as possible, give up the tenancy of his flat and go to Drenthe, look for a house around Dwingeloo and Westerbork for himself and his strange family: with a wife who is not the mother but the grandmother of his child, who might not be his child. Or had he gone mad perhaps? Would he be able to stick to it? Yes, he would be able to stick to it, because of course he wasn't sacrificing himself completely—calling it "sacrifice" was just another lie, and Sophia would know that, but this was an opportunity of giving his clandestine relationship with her a lasting form; the way things had been up to now could of course not continue without becoming ridiculous.

What would she say? After all her own life had reached an impasse, too. What was she to do there in Leiden, with a bookshop that she could not handle, and which was bound to fail? On the other hand, when the child was fifteen, in fifteen years' time, she would already be sixty, as she'd said, but he himself would only be fifty. Only? He was shocked by the thought. Would he be fifty in fifteen years' time? But by then everything would have changed, and he would wait and see what happened.

He thought of an anecdote that Onno had once told him during one of their walks through the town. At the beginning of the last century the second-rate German dramatist Kotzebue, who was in the service of the czar, was murdered by the nationalist student activist Sand; the student was sentenced to death and beheaded by the executioner Braun. However, Braun subsequently felt such remorse at having executed such an exalted person that he built a hut from the planks of the scaffold, where the student activists secretly met to honor Sand, to kiss the bloodstains and sing anti-Semitic songs.

The shells crunched under his shoes and a kind of intoxication took hold of him—not from the wine but from the complete change that was suddenly imminent; he felt like someone deciding from one moment to the next to emigrate far, far way under threat of war: to a country designated not by pointing his finger in any particular direction, but simply by pointing vertically downward toward the nadir, to the Antipodes: as far away as possible, to where trees grew downward, people and animals were stuck to the earth upside down, and stones fell upward.

Again it was as if he wanted to hold back his thoughts as he did in bed when approaching orgasm, because that increased the pleasure fourfold. He suddenly felt the need to visit his foster mother. He had lived with her and her husband for ten years, until 1952, after which he had moved to a rented room, working his way through college in Leiden. At the end of the 1950s they had moved to Santpoort, where his foster mother became a nursery school teacher; his foster father, once a geography teacher, was already seriously ill. Gradually he had visited them less and less; first every few weeks, then every few months, later only at Christmas, and finally not even that. Every visit meant a return to the war, which weighed more and more heavily on him the further the war receded. He had not been in touch for years.

He peered at his watch—in a flash of light from the lighthouse he saw that it was nine-thirty. What time did she go to bed? It was about twenty miles, so he could at least give her a call.

A little farther on, at the edge of the dunes, stood Huis ter Duin, a large brightly lit seaside hotel with a Mediterranean air, as though it were on the Boulevard des Anglais in Nice instead of near a sleepy village on the cold North Sea coast. He toiled up through the loose sand, found a door to the terrace that was not locked, and emerged into the middle of an exuberant party awash with gin, beer, and carnival songs.

On the stage sat a brass band in peasant costume, with black silk caps on the musicians' heads and red kerchiefs around their necks, and the worst bit of all was in progress: a "polonaise" with the merrymakers moving in a snake under the decorations, hands on each other's shoulders. As he stood there, still blinking at the light and noise, someone yanked him into the singing and dancing line, and before he knew it he was part of the ceremony. He had seldom felt so out of place, but with an indulgent smile he allowed himself to be carried along; if he were to protest, he might be slaughtered on the spot and thrown into the frying oil, among the sausages. He managed to slip away when they came to a door, and went to the reception desk in the lobby.

Heavy sofas and armchairs covered in linen material, with red-and-blue-flower prints, indicated that England lay across the waves. In the telephone booth he dialed her number in agitation. Was she still alive?

"Blok speaking," said a man's voice.

"Excuse me, isn't this Mrs. Hondius's number?"

"She doesn't live here anymore."

For the last year she had been in an old people's home in Bloemendaal, Sancta Maria. He gave Max the number. With his finger on the dial, about to dial the last digit, a 1, he hesitated. She had not notified him of her change of address. Obviously, she had given up on him after he failed to appear at her husband's deathbed. That awareness filled him with such shame that he did not dare to go on dialing—but he also knew that he would never see her again if he did not move his finger through those last ninety degrees. He jerked it down until it reached the steel rest.

The porter in Bloemendaal put him through and a moment later he heard her voice.

"Yes, who is it?"

"It's Max." There was a moment's silence.

"Really?" She asked softly. "Is that you, Max?"

"Were you asleep?"

"I never sleep at night. It's not something serious, is it?"

"I'm in Noordwijk, and I'd like to drop by for a moment. Can I?"

"Right this minute?"

"Is it a bad time?"

"Of course not, it never is for you. I'll wait for you downstairs in the lounge."

"I'll be with you in half an hour, Mother Tonia."

He walked quickly back to his car across the deserted promenade. As he drove toward Bloemendaal, taking a shortcut through Haarlem, he considered whether he should say anything about his scandalous absence when her husband was dying; but perhaps she understood without being told that he found the death of parents difficult, even when they were foster parents.

Sancta Maria, surrounded by an iron fence, built in dark brick in the somber aristocratic style of Dutch Catholicism, was on a quiet avenue opposite a wood. He parked the car on the paved forecourt, and as he opened the front door he was immediately eye to eye with the mutilated body of the founder of the religion—attached to the cross in the same attitude as Otto Lilienthal to the flying machine in which he had made the first glider flight. *Consummatum est,* thought Max; the engineer had not survived his experiments, either. The porter looked up from his paper in annoyance, glanced at the clock, and motioned toward the entrance of the lounge with a jerk of his head.

In the wave of social change, a modern interior designer had created a successful impression of impending purgatory with harsh neon lighting and dreadful furniture in garish plastic. Everyone had obviously retired to bed. His foster mother sat alone at a table by the window and waved to him; he was seeing her without his foster father for the first time since he had moved out of their home. The only other person was a heavily built man of about sixty in a wheelchair, which was at a completely arbitrary angle in the room, as though someone far away had given it a push, after which it had come to a halt swerving and turning; there was a black patch over his right eye.

"Max! What a surprise!" She had stood up; she kissed him, her eyes moist, and held him away from her in order to be able to take a good look at him. "You've become more of a man, a real international gentleman."

He had to laugh at the compliment. "And you're the same as ever, Mother Tonia."

That was not completely true. She had grown smaller, with a more rounded back; her features were now more sharply etched than in the past, with a faint, refined smile in the corner of her mouth. But she still wore the same chestnut-colored wig, which left a narrow strip of dark shadow around her head: mysterious ravine between skin and wig, which as a boy had fascinated him more than the ravines in the books of Karl May. For as long as he had known her she had worn wigs and he had no idea what secret was hidden underneath; and since then he was convinced that he could always tell if someone was wearing a wig—until one day Onno had told him that he could only see it when he saw it and not when he couldn't. He had always called his real mother Mommy.

He sat down opposite her and she took his hands in hers. She stroked his spatula-shaped thumbs for a moment and looked at him.

"Your hands are just as cold as ever."

"That's always the way with hotheads."

"Tell me, how are things with you?"

"Good," he said. "Good."

Good? It was obviously out of the question to tell her about the fix he was in and how he was thinking of solving it; he didn't know how things were himself, and perhaps that was the reason he was here now. She wasn't really old yet, perhaps just turned seventy—his real mother would have been sixty now—but she was sitting here in this dreadful place waiting for death, her thoughts focused only on the past, while his concerns were only about the future. He told her about his work in Leiden, and said he would probably be moving to Drenthe in the near future, where a new telescope was being used.

"You in Drenthe? Max! A *bon viveur* like you stuck out in the fenlands? You're not going to tell me that you've gotten married in the meantime, without letting me know?"

"When I get married, you'll be a witness," he said, reflecting that he might even be having a child without letting her know. "No, I'm sacrificing myself for science. It's a very special telescope."

"I can still see you sitting in your room with your celestial map. 'I'm going to lay bare the secret of the universe,' you said at the table once."

"Did I?" He smiled affectionately. "They put that kind of thing out of your head at the university. The first thing they destroy there is the impulse that made you want to study a particular subject. The really great geniuses, like Einstein, are all amateurs—and not only in the natural sciences."

"It's better to be happy than a great genius."

"Perhaps. But the annoying thing is just that Einstein was probably happy as well."

"And you?"

"It would be nicely symmetrical if I were both not a genius and unhappy, wouldn't it?"

She slowly shook her head. "You haven't changed at all, do you know that? Who on earth gives an answer like that?"

"You're right."

He thought it over. Of course it was nonsense to say that he was happy, but did that mean that he was not? Logically perhaps, but psychologically? For the last few months he had probably been really unhappy, or at least hopelessly caught in the trap that he himself had built. *Happy, unhappy . . .* those were not the terms in which he was used to thinking about himself:

that was more something for girls, to use Onno's expression. But from the moment that he had made his decision tonight, though everything had remained the same—ruined for good, that is—it had also suddenly changed, turned on its head to become its opposite, like when a marathon runner derives strength and perhaps even something akin to pleasure from his deathly exhaustion. He may even have become a marathon runner because he is addicted to the pleasure of exhaustion.

"God knows, yes, I suppose I'm happy."

His foster mother drew back her hands and looked down. "That bloody war," she said.

The remark astonished him, but he did not react to it. He took hold of her hands in turn.

She looked at him. "We haven't seen each other for so long, Max . . . Why have you suddenly come this evening of all evenings?"

"Because I've made an important decision tonight, Mother Tonia, which may determine the rest of my life. But you mustn't ask me what it is, because it may not happen at all. When I'm sure, of course I'll let you know. I don't know . . . I suddenly wanted to see you again. Of course I should have done it long ago, I've failed you, but—"

"Don't say any more."

He was silent. At the next table there was a chessboard with an unfinished game on it. Doubtless it would be continued the following morning by two old men, who were now lying in their beds thinking about their next move, leading to a devastating checkmate with the knight and the queen, who would transmit their lines of force across 666 squares to the opposing king like deadly rays. The man in the wheelchair did not move; he had bent his head and was looking at his white hands, folded in his lap. In some ways he also resembled a castled king, waiting to be checkmated.

In the doorway, under the crucifix that was also hanging in here, a young woman appeared and said that it was the children's bedtime. She was tall and slim, in her late twenties; two blue eyes looked at Max from beneath thick, dark-blond eyebrows—and at the same moment he realized that he could take her into the woods across the road later if he wanted. He also saw that she immediately saw that he knew that—but he didn't want to. That was over. As if he had known her for years, he gave her something like a wink with both eyes by way of apology. She blushed a little and went over to the wheelchair.

"Are you coming, Mr. Blits? Time for beddy-bye."

Max and Mother Tonia got up.

"Come with me to my room for a moment," she said. "I wanted to show you something, but I couldn't find it immediately."

As they passed the wheelchair and Max exchanged another melancholy look with the nurse, Mr. Blits fixed him with his one eye and said: "Swine!"

"Ho, ho, Mr. Blits, what's this? Are we going to get silly?"

"Mr. Blits is quite right," laughed Max. "I'm a bad sort."

They took the elevator, and as he entered the small apartment he had a shock. He knew everything from their house in Amsterdam, and later the one in Santpoort, but here it had been reduced to its essence, like a concentrated extract. Immediately on the right was a kitchen the size of a tablecloth, leading to a tiny living room, which was linked to an equaly modest bedroom by a curving hallway.

On the sofa covered with that unforgettably hard, stiff material and dating from the 1920s or 1930s, he had read his first book on astronomy, a translation of Jeans's *The Mysterious Universe*; two vague pieces of material lay over the threadbare arms. Above it hung the reproduction of Brueghel's *Fall of Icarus*, every detail of which had penetrated his very soul: the immense space of land and sea, the plowing farmer, whose red shirt had now faded to a gentle pink, the shepherd leaning on his crook as though nothing were happening, with his back to the event on which everything hinged and which was taking place like a futile incident: an insignificant leg barely protruding from the waves. On the low table in front of the sofa was the cut-glass bonbonnière, which he had never thought of since, but which was more familiar to him than most of what he had at home; in the small bookcase were the familiar spines. *Everyman's Encyclopedia*.

A fairy-tale feeling came over him, like an archaeologist who has suddenly uncovered a classical site: suddenly all those antique things were gathered together, in these few square feet in Bloemendaal. There were things in his life that were still more ancient: from the plundered royal tomb of his parents' house—which he could only vaguely remember and which perhaps also still existed somewhere in the house of the thieves who had followed in the footsteps of the murderers, or in those of their widows or their children; but those would never come to light.

On the television set there were two framed photographs: one of his foster father and one of himself. For all those years, during which he had made no contact, his portrait had stood there and Mother Tonia had looked at it? Hondius, in waistcoat and watch chain, looked at him sternly. *Why didn't you come, Max?* He turned away in embarrassment. His foster mother, down on one knee in the bedroom, was looking for something in a cardboard box, which she had pulled out from under her bed.

Against the wall he saw the mahogany chest with the two opening doors, the symmetrical grain of which still formed the frightening head of a gigantic bat. On it, next to a sewing basket, was another head, of smooth wood, with no face, like in a De Chirico painting. It was clearly not intended for his eyes, since she obviously put her wig on it at night; perhaps it used to be in a box, because he had never seen it before. But who did she have to hide anything from here? Above the door, Christ on the cross again, dressed in nothing but a diaper.

"Yes, I've got it," she said. Supporting herself on the edge of the bed, she struggled to her feet and brought him a large, bent, dog-eared photograph, torn here and there around the edges. "Is this familiar?"

"It's them!" he exclaimed.

There they were, arm in arm: his father and mother. Incredulous, open-mouthed, he looked at the couple. The yellowed black-and-white photo, more a formal portrait, must have been taken before he was born, by a professional photographer, perhaps on their wedding day in 1926. In a tailor-made suit of chiseled perfection, his father was looking into the lens, now replaced by his son's eyes, which immediately recognized his own; he had not put down the cigarette in his right hand. On his left arm his wife, age eighteen, sixteen years younger than himself, close to him, a hand on her hip, the dark hat on her head, and beneath it two indescribable eyes, the color of which he did not see and which he did not remember, combined with his own nose and mouth. He looked up and put his finger on the photograph.

"It's them," he said again, not yet recovered from his surprise. "This is the first time I've seen a photo of them."

"I suspected as much. You're like both of them."

The thought that his child would be as like him as he was like his parents entered his mind only momentarily.

"How did you come by this?"

"I found it among my husband's papers, when I had to clear up before I moved here. I saw at once that it couldn't have anything to do with his family; they were not such worldly people. That photo must have been among the things that we were sent after your father's death."

"Why did your husband never show it to me?"

"I don't know. Perhaps he didn't want to confront you with what had happened and was going to give it to you later, which he was never able to do . . ."

She fell silent. Did she perhaps mean that Hondius had meant to give him the photograph on his deathbed? Max did not take his eyes off the photograph.

"May I have it?"

"Of course."

It was a mystery to him. So this photograph had come from his father's cell, which meant that it was one of the few things he had taken with him when he was arrested—why? He had driven that woman there on his left arm to her death, which had brought him in front of the firing squad, him, the Mortal Ego. So why should he have a photo of someone who didn't exist and hence could not die? Did that mean she did still exist for him? So had she died after all? How explicable was a human being? How explicable was he himself?

31

The Proposal

The following morning Max woke up in his own bed with the memory of something glittering and glowing. He kept his eyes closed for a moment and saw that it was Mother Tonia's silver scalp, which was hidden by her wig—and for a moment the boundless halls of his dream of that night, with their corridors and chambers, their momentous messages and dizzying vistas, opened up again and then immediately closed forever, as if the country of a departing traveler were not only to disappear below the horizon but to cease to exist . . .

He opened his eyes. Everything was in its place in the soft light that shone through the orange curtains. Nothing had changed, and at the same time everything had changed: somehow it had lost its permanence, which allowed it to be the same tomorrow as today and the same the day after tomorrow as tomorrow. It was as though he no longer lived here, as though his soul had already departed. Ten o'clock. Because it was Saturday he had not set his alarm; he did not have to go to Leiden. He got out of bed, opened the curtains, and dialed Sophia's number. She was on the point of leaving for Amsterdam, to go to the hospital.

"I've got my coat on."

"Is Onno coming too?"

"I think so. Why?"

"I have to speak to you for a moment, but without Onno. It's important."

"Has something happened? You disappeared so suddenly yesterday."

"Yes, something has happened, but I can't tell you over the telephone."

"Where shall we meet?"

The obvious thing for him to do would have been to invite her to his flat, ten minutes' walk from the Wilhelmina Hospital, but he had the feeling that that would be crossing a forbidden boundary.

"How about the station buffet? That may be easiest for you."

"But I can't possibly say exactly what time I'll be there."

"I understand. Don't hurry, I'll be there from one o'clock onward. We can have a bite to eat."

"See you this afternoon, then."

On his desk lay the photograph of his parents. He looked at it for a while and decided to have it framed later. He ran a bath and in the hot water tried to think about the future, but there was not much point until he had spoken to Sophia. It was not impossible that she would look at him in astonishment and ask him if he had taken leave of his senses; that would probably mean an immediate end to their secret relationship. But perhaps things might be different, and in that case he must take immediate steps to ensure his appointment in Westerbork and his living accommodations. Although ... ultimately everything depended on Onno. He must decide. It concerned his wife and what was at least officially his child; he was under pressure from his family, and there was some doubt whether he could come to terms with a scheme that he might be inclined to class as surrealistic. Max was aware that he must rely on the very friendship he had betrayed.

At about twelve-thirty, with the photo in a folded newspaper, he went downstairs, took the morning paper out of the mailbox, and walked in the direction of the Central Station. In the window of a photographer's on the Leidsestraat was a shot of a car crash from the 1920s: a yellowed little snap of two cars that, absurdly, had collided in what was still a virtually car-free world, enlarged by technical wizardry into a large, shiny photograph that looked as though it had been taken yesterday. In the shop a girl offered to transform his damaged photo in the same way; but what mattered to him was not only what was depicted but the object itself, that original paper, that substance, which had been in the possession of his father and mother. There must be traces of molecules from their hands on it.

He walked down the Damrak to the Central Station, which blocked off the harbor front like a dam. It was as if the town council of Venice had hit on the idea of building a station on the Molo, behind the two pillars on the Piazzetta, which would have obscured the view of the lagoon. Amsterdam, he thought, might be the Venice of the North, but Venice was fortunately not the Amsterdam of the South. Ever since he'd had a car, he'd only been in the station once: when he'd made his trip to Poland. Just as he always used to, he glanced to the left before going into the station concourse: at the ramp for goods traffic, along which the 110,000 Jews had been driven to the goods wagons.

The gigantic, semicircular roof of steel girders—so constructed in order to absorb the smoke and steam of locomotives—had always felt like the inside of a Zeppelin, but now it reminded him of the ribs of a whale that had swallowed him up. He felt something akin to stage fright. In the buffet, with its dark paneling and carving and murals, he sat down at a table by the window.

Because the station blocked the view of the wide world, like a seal set on Holland's vanished maritime power, it had a magnificent view of its own; the busy square branching out in all directions, with churches, hotels, and seventeenth-century gables reflected in the water, on the other side affording an almost obscene view deep into the city. As he looked at it he had the same kind of feeling as this morning when he woke up: perhaps it was no longer his city. Apart from his scientific work, everything had happened there, from his birth up to the conversation that he was shortly to have.

He ordered coffee from a waiter in a white full-length apron and opened his newspaper. In Paris, de Gaulle had made a statement that he would remain in office as president, whereupon riots had broken out again in all French cities, with several deaths and thousands of casualties. He read only the headlines and the leads—not because he was unable to concentrate, but because it still didn't interest him. Since he had been in Cuba, he was preoccupied solely with his personal problems, which he had caused, and with those of radio sources in the distant past of the universe—everything in between, like the war in Vietnam and the revolution in Europe, was less and less real for him; he left that to Onno. He read an article about the rapid development of the silicon chip, in which he was later to be involved, with the constant squeaking of the restaurant door in his ears, shrill guards' whistles filling the belly of the whale, the thundering of arriving trains, reducing speed with reluctant grating. Now and then an incomprehensible voice blared from the loudspeakers.

"Have you been waiting long?"

Sophia was standing looking down at him. He got up, said hello, and took her coat, which was cold on the outside and warm on the inside.

When they were sitting opposite each other, she said: "Well, it's been decided. Next Thursday at the latest they're going to get the baby out."

He nodded. "Did they say why?"

"They don't say everything even to me, particularly when Onno's there. They discussed it at length; they say they're doing it to be on the safe side, but I don't know what that means. You can imagine that all kinds of things have gone haywire in that body of hers. She's also getting bed sores. She has to be turned every three hours, iced and blow-dried."

The way in which Sophia said *that body,* when she herself had given birth to it, sent a chill through him. Turned. Iced. Blow-dried.

"But can she survive such a severe operation?"

Sophia looked at her hands. "Who can say? We've just spoken briefly to the surgeon, but of course he's not giving anything away. He says that there needn't be any risk to her life. In any case there's no problem at all for the child: it's already over seven months."

Max reflected that it might be best if Ada did not survive, and that Sophia was probably thinking the same thing at that moment; but he didn't have the courage to say it.

"What about Onno?"

"He understands that there's a risk, of course, but he said that he'd rather be a father sooner than later."

Max could hear him saying it: with an expansive gesture, to which the surgeon had no reply, though he knew more about it than Onno. He always created misunderstandings; the doctor probably now thought that he lacked seriousness.

"If all goes well," he said, "it will mean that the child will need a roof over its head in a few weeks' time. Has Onno made his mind up yet?"

Sophia looked at him in bewilderment. "It's as though you never see him anymore. Is there something wrong between you?"

"No," said Max, returning her look. "Why should there be? The last time I spoke to him was the day before yesterday." He looked down and folded the newspaper.

"We were just talking about it in the tram," said Sophia, "but he still hasn't decided. He asked my advice."

"And what advice did you give him?"

"In my opinion he shouldn't let the child be dragged around the world by civil servants; he should choose his niece Paula in Rotterdam. Besides, one day he'll meet someone else and then he can still take it back."

Max had not considered that possibility. Yes, even that was of course conceivable; but it wouldn't happen. He remembered what Onno had said to him the very day after the accident: that he didn't find being alone the worst thing about it, since he was the classic comic type of the married bachelor. He would certainly meet another woman one day, but he'd never live with anyone again; for him that had been an incident, like when a miser who once buys shares then loses his money, after which he puts his capital on deposit forever, even though his speculative friends tell him that saving with a bank is pouring your money down the drain. For Onno it was once bitten, twice shy.

"Did you tell him that?"

"Of course not."

Max shook his head. "From what I know of him, he'll stay a bachelor for the rest of his days—that is, live like a bachelor."

A waiter was standing in silence by their table looking from one to the other, with his ballpoint pen and notepad in his hand. Used to such rudeness, they both ordered a small open sandwich, even though that would probably be equally unsavory. With his fingernail, Max drew bars across a stain that had not been properly washed off the tablecloth.

"But what if," he said slowly, without raising his eyes, "you and I were to do it . . ."

"Do what?"

"Take care of Ada's child."

It had been said. Suddenly it was there, like a thing, a meteor that had penetrated the atmosphere. He looked into her eyes and tried to read from her face the effect his proposal had had, but he saw no emotion at all.

"Us look after Ada's child? You and me? And how do you picture that?"

It was on the tip of his tongue to say "In heaven's name let's stop this play acting, Sophia. It's gone on long enough; I'm crazy about you, I can't live without you, and you know that; even when I take your coat, I'm thinking of the dark ritual of our nights in Leiden, and the same goes for you." But supposing he'd said that, and she'd then said, "Yes, of course, you're right, we must put an end to this pretense"—would he still have wanted her to move in with him with Ada's child? Of course not. He knew perfectly well that it was precisely the incomprehensible secrecy to which he was wedded heart and soul: that which they not only kept hidden from the world but from each other, and she perhaps even from herself.

"Since your husband's death," he said, "you've been running 'In Praise of Folly,' but if you ask me that won't last. I will probably have to move to Drenthe shortly—I'm going to be appointed telescope astronomer, in Westerbork. Next Thursday your daughter is going to give birth to my best friend's child. These are the facts, aren't they? Ada is no longer of this world, Onno has to find a home for his child, I don't like the thought of living alone in the provinces, and there's nothing left for you in Leiden. All five of us are alone—so let's throw in our lot together. You told me that the grandmother is traditionally the one who looks after the children, and that you had offered yourself to Onno in that capacity, but that he felt that there should be a man in the family. Well, that'll be me. It won't be your average family, but it will have some features of one. In a higher sense it might be even more of a family than normal families."

What he meant by this last remark was not immediately clear even to himself, but that might come later. Sophia turned her head away and looked outside. Her remorseless profile suddenly reminded him of that of a woman in a painting by Franz von Stuck, *Sphinx*, of which he had once seen a reproduction: a nude lying on her belly, with a raised upper torso, and fingers curled into claws, in the attitude of a lion, on the shore of a dark mountain lake into which a waterfall is plunging. He could not see what was going on inside her, but at least she had not dismissed it out of hand.

She looked at him. "Do you know what you're saying?"

"I don't know always what I'm saying, because then I'd never say anything important; but what I've just said I've considered from all sides. I know it would completely change my life, and yours too. But we owe it to Ada. Or perhaps we don't owe it to her, but in that case we have to do it although we don't owe it to her." He put the paper aside and stretched his back. "That's what I wanted to say to you. Of course everything would have to be arranged at short notice; I must find a house with sufficient room for the three of us, some old vicarage perhaps. You should wind up the bookshop, but that's all solvable. My salary isn't that fat, but there are families who have to live on less; and anyway everything is cheaper in the country, particularly when you get it from the farm." He made a gesture with his hand. "I can imagine that it's come as a big surprise and that you'd like to think about it calmly for a day or two, so—"

"I don't have to think about it," she said, and looked him straight in the eye.

"Because?" He looked at her tensely.

"For the last few months my life . . . I mean . . . if Onno agrees . . ."

He had an impulse to take her hand in his, but controlled himself. For the first time he saw something like a chink in her armor. "Is he at home now?"

"I think so."

"Then I'll drop by to see him in a moment. I'll let you know at once how he reacts; I think it's better if I go alone." He saw how he surprised her with his decisiveness. "You must always make big decisions quickly, otherwise you'll never get around to it." He laughed. "Onno will be very surprised—even by the fact that I'm dropping by to see him. It's never happened."

Unlike Max, Onno had the gift of being able to switch his attention completely from one moment to the next, like someone going from one room into the other and closing the door behind him. The news that his child would be delivered in five days' time and that he must now reach a decision quickly had preoccupied him until he put the key in the lock. He agreed with his mother-in-law that the choice of Hans and Hadewych would be the worse one, but because he wanted to make not a less bad but a good choice, he still could not bring himself to cut the Gordian knot. Once inside, in his study, his eye was caught by the party papers, in which shortly afterward he was immersed.

When the bell rang, he got up automatically and opened the door, without interrupting his thoughts. When he saw Max on the step, he came to himself in amazement.

"This is very unusual," he said.

"Thank you for the heart-warming reception. I know that you don't belong to the species host, but I need to discuss something with you."

"*Salve.*"

Max followed him to the basement, which after a short period of modest tidiness had again succumbed to the second law of thermodynamics. The chaos caused him almost physical pain. Lost for words, he looked at the mess. He himself could spend minutes carefully arranging the instruments at the edge of his desk, the magnet, the compass, the tuning fork, to the millimeter—here, there was not even the beginning of an awareness that there was such a thing as order.

"Are you really human?" he asked.

"Yes, it leaves you speechless, doesn't it? Only the very strongest can live like this. Upstairs it's a little tidier, but I only go up there to sleep these days."

That he was probably human, after all, was apparent from Ada's cello: the case lay on two upright chairs, standing facing each other next to his desk, like a body on a bed. Onno led the way to the back room, where his bed had once been, and cleared a corner of a sagging sofa; books, newspapers, a pair of gray socks, a toaster, were pushed aside, and in a flash Max also saw the book on Fabergé, which he had given Ada that first day.

"I was at the Wilhelmina Hospital this morning. It's going to be on Thursday, at four-thirty. Oh you don't know yet: the doctors—"

"I do know. I talked to your mother-in-law. That's why I'm here."

Onno had sunk into a small armchair, which dated from his student days and which he bought from a secondhand shop; at the sides there were stripes and scratches in the brown leather, perhaps from a long-dead cat that had once sharpened its claws on it. Had Max talked to his mother-in-law?

He looked at Max with raised eyebrows. "You talked to my mother-in-law?"

Someone may know someone else for years, but if he's asked what color the other person's eyes are, he often doesn't know, because people don't look at someone's eyes but at them. For the first time Max saw that Onno had a brown ring around his blue irises.

"Yes."

"We're listening."

Everything depended on the right tone. Max had not prepared what he was about to say, because then he would have to remember what he had prepared, when it was not a matter of remembering the right things but of saying the right things in the right way.

"Listen, Onno, I won't beat around the bush. The day before yesterday you told me about your dilemma, deciding who the child should live with. Because I had the feeling that I might be able to help you in some way, I contacted your mother-in-law yesterday. She told me two things—first, that the child is going to be delivered next Thursday by cesarean section, because Ada's condition may become critical."

"Which might be the best for everyone. And second?"

"Second, that she had also offered to look after the child herself. But you didn't want it to go to a single woman."

Max waited for a moment to see whether Onno had already realized, but there was no indication that he had.

Onno listened to him with the slightly unpleasant feeling that he was being intruded upon, even if it was by his best friend. Not only in his immediate family were they talking about him behind his back, about things that directly affected his life. He hadn't the faintest idea what Max was getting at.

"That's right." He nodded. "So?"

"I arranged to see her and I've just met her, in the station buffet. I've come straight from there."

What in heaven's name was going on here? Onno sat up. "Isn't that slightly odd? She didn't tell me anything about having arranged to meet you."

"You weren't supposed to know." Max struggled for words. Now he was about to say it for the second time. "Brace yourself, Onno. I suggested to her that she and I should look after your child."

Onno stared at him numbly. What he had just heard could not be possible. "Say that again."

"It's now more or less certain that I'm to become telescope astronomer in Westerbork, and in the foreseeable future I will probably move to Drenthe permanently."

"What on earth are you saying? I remember you saying that you'd feel like an exiled criminal in Siberia there."

"Things have changed for me, Onno. Your mother-in-law is prepared to move in with me, so that your child would be in good hands."

Onno felt as if he were seeing a city collapse and subsequently rise from its ruins in the shape of another city—Amsterdam changing into Rome, the palace on the Dam into St. Peter's. Once before he had had such a sensation. Years ago one winter evening, snow had deadened every noise and every sound in the city and he sat bent over his photos of Etruscan inscriptions: suddenly he saw everything shift into a new constellation, turn on its head, flip, and suddenly his discovery had been made. The sudden metamorphosis of his friend into his child's mentor and that of his mother-in-law into Max's house companion hadn't yet entirely sunk in, but wasn't it the ideal solution? Goodbye to all those cousins and their spouses!

Or was it complete madness, too crazy for words? Max with his dreadful mother-in-law in Drenthe. Surely that would be impossible. He, the frenzied satyr, under one roof with the icy Sophia Brons—what had gotten into him? How had he hit upon the idea of effacing himself in that way? Had his past caught up with him, as a foster child himself? But he had offered it to him; he was sitting there waiting for an answer. Was it perhaps simply friendship?

"Max . . ." he began—it was as though the resonance of his voice sent tears into his eyes. "I don't know what to say . . ."

"Then don't say anything. Or rather say it's okay, and then we'll have it over with."

Onno got up and went out of the room. At the basin, he threw water over his face with both hands. While he was looking for a towel, which was not there, he asked himself whether he could accept the offer. Could he be the cause of such a radical change in Max's life? Maybe Max felt partly responsible, since he, Onno, would never have met Ada without him. Or was the accident involved, because Max had been at the wheel, although he was entirely free of blame? He wiped his face on a sleeve and went back in.

Max had stood up too and was looking at the sheets of squared paper with linguistic diagrams on them that were pinned to the wall; the Phaistos disc was obviously not yet out of Onno's system.

"My ears are still buzzing," said Onno. "Are you sure you're not letting your sense of humor run away with you?"

Max burst out laughing. "I don't think I've ever been as serious as today."

"Perhaps it's been staring us in the face all along, but please help me understand. What's gotten into you? I couldn't stand one day with that creature. What am I to make of it? Is there something going on between you and her, perhaps?"

"Ha, ha," laughed Max. "Don't make me laugh."

"You're capable of it, but probably there are limits even for you."

"I imagine," said Max with great control, "that I shall live there like a vicar with his housekeeper and her grandchild. She'll cook my food and iron my shirts, collars never toward the point but always away from it. I'll get by sexually somehow—I'm sure to bump into someone."

"But why should you do all that for me?"

"Not just for you. I've had enough of the kind of life I've been living up to now myself. I don't have to go to Westerbork if I don't want to, do I? But I'm going to turn over a new leaf in my sex life too; anyway, it's a practical impossibility to live like a beast in the country. Let me put it like this: in a certain sense it suits me very well. I want to work with that telescope, and otherwise I would have been on my own, in rooms with the local lawyer. Commuting from Amsterdam every day would of course be crazy, certainly in a Volkswagen; and anyway, there are often things to do at night. I'll start an affair with the surgical nurse at Hoogeveen Hospital and then with the German teacher at Zwolle High School. I can teach her a thing or two. And eventually something beautiful will develop between your mother-in-law and the antiques dealer in Assen."

"But supposing you do meet someone, someone you want to start a family with?"

"Then of course I'll take your child with me. But I can't see that happening. Anyway, the unexpected is always possible—even your cousins Hans and Jan-Kees could get divorced."

"Dear God," cried Onno, raising his hands. "You've reminded me. My family! How am I going to tell my family?"

That was it.

"Does that mean that we're going to do it?"

"*Of course* we're going to do it! I'm sure that Ada would have thought this was the best thing too."

That remark had a big impact on Max. He hadn't thought about it yet, but there could be no doubt about it; it was as though he could see her, nodding with eyes closed. He put out his hand, and Onno looked at it for a moment before shaking it.

"Champagne!" said Max. *"La Veuve!"*

"I wish I had." Onno shook his head gloomily. "I don't even have any beer here. I've sunk completely back into barbarism."

"Let's go out for a drink, we have to celebrate this. It's my treat."

"You go on. I need to be alone now. I need to stare numbly into space for a long time to get over the shock. And then the three of us must meet as soon as possible; there are bound to be all kinds of snags, but we'll solve them. The child is being born one and a half months prematurely, and according to the doctors it will definitely have to stay in the incubator for four or five weeks. Plenty of time to settle everything."

32

The Dilettante

When Max had gone, Onno went upstairs and dropped onto his bed. Suddenly the mists had cleared and a future again lay in front of him like day after night. Max had convinced him, but it was still not completely clear to him; after all, bringing up a child was a matter of about seventeen years—that meant Max was basically tying himself down until the year 1985, when he would be fifty-two. Fifty-two! Good God! By that time life will be more or less over; his own, too. At least perhaps not over, because why shouldn't someone live to ninety, but certainly changed from afternoon into evening. And meanwhile Max would be doing other things besides bringing up a child—namely, scientific research; bringing up a child would help him in this, since it brought order into his existence.

His child was perhaps precisely what Max needed in order to do really important astronomical work, since otherwise he would waste a large part of his time charming another thousand women out of their panties—which would be all well and good if you could remember it, so that you could look back on it all with satisfaction on your deathbed. But of course you forgot; all that would be left will be an enormous pile of laundry, in which one pair of panties was indistinguishable from the other. Apart from that, when you were ninety, what good to you was the knowledge that you had lain on top of countless eighty- or seventy-year-olds? Or on centenarians? You would sit dribbling on a park bench and an old woman would come by, her body

327

twisted into a rheumatic angle, talking to herself, supporting herself on a black lacquered stick, and you would think: I was once in the sack with that girl. Terrific triumph.

But perhaps Max didn't want to remember it at all; perhaps he wanted to leave and forget women continually because he had once been left and forgotten. At any rate it would never happen to him, Onno himself. He had been to bed with eleven women, all of whom he remembered exactly: Helga had been the ninth, Ada the tenth, María from Havana the eleventh; and since the accident there had been no one else.

However, now that Max had reached this point, he reflected, there were of course other conceivable ways of changing his life—without Sophia Brons.

Max was taking her as part of the bargain; he himself could not bear the thought of having that woman around him the whole time, but Max obviously didn't feel intimidated by her. However much of a bitch she might be, he was also giving back meaning to her life. No, Max was trying to represent his offer as an act of egoism, to make it easier for him, Onno, to accept; but it was and remained first and foremost an unselfish act of friendship, for which Onno would be grateful to him all his life. He could now devote himself to his activities with a clear conscience, without wrestling at the back of his mind with the doubt whether he had done the right thing. The club of rebels had recently put him up as a candidate for the party executive, and a decision was due soon; if that went ahead then he would have to concentrate fully on his responsibilities.

Suddenly he jumped off his bed, went to the telephone, and dialed his youngest sister's number. He wanted to make it definite immediately, so that there would be no way back.

"Dol? It's Onno."

"Just a moment, I just got in. Let me give the dog some water.—Yes, I'm here now."

"Listen carefully, Dol. I know I'm taking you by surprise, but I want to get it off my chest immediately. My friend Max has just been here—you know, my best friend, Max Delius—and he's offered to bring up my child together with my mother-in-law. I just wanted to tell you."

"Good heavens, Onno, wait a moment, not so fast. What on earth are you saying?"

"That my problem has been solved. Max is getting a job at the new radio telescope in Drenthe, and he's going to live there; my mother-in-law is going to move in with him as housekeeper, and there'll also be room for my child. It couldn't be better. It's all wrapped up."

Stuttering, Dol tried to say something. "But Onno . . . wait a moment . . . you can't just . . ."

"Oh yes I can!"

"Don't be so idiotic. You can't decide this in the blink of an eye."

"I already have."

"How do you see it working? Have you thought through all the implications? Are you sure that you won't regret it? Anyway, I don't think this is something to discuss on the telephone. Can't you—"

"There's nothing further to discuss, I'm just letting you know. Hans and Paula will both get a nice note from me, thanking them for their offer—and I can't see what other implications this solution is supposed to have. I can't see into the future, but why should I regret it?"

There was a few seconds' delay before Dol replied. "Because . . . I don't really know how I'm supposed to say it . . . it's not what I think, but I can imagine someone thinking . . . look, of course I can't say anything against your mother-in-law, but—"

"Well against who, then?" he said, feeling himself getting angry. "Or rather, against who else? Out with it—say what you mean."

"Well, I don't want to offend you, Onno, but your friend Max . . . he struck me as a very interesting man, good-looking too, but . . . he isn't one of us, is he?"

"*Et tu, Brute!*" cried Onno in fury. "You mean that he's the son of a Jewess and a war criminal, the son of everything that God forbade and not the son of decent Christian folk who plundered the colonies for centuries! That's what you mean! And that a fellow like that isn't eligible to bring up a Quist! No, but now I am absolutely sure. I'm glad you said it. Thanks a lot for your help."

The following morning, Sunday, he was sorry about his outburst and called her again. His brother-in-law came to the phone; Dol was taking the dog for a walk. He accepted Onno's excuses on her behalf; with hindsight she had understood. Anyway, he began, yesterday evening they had been over to the Statenlaan . . . but because Onno realized at once that Karel was trying to bring up the question of Max again in that roundabout way, he interrupted him and said that he didn't care what his parents had said, because his decision had been made: this was what was going to happen and nothing else—it was pointless coming back to it. The family would simply have to learn to live with it. Next he was on the phone to Max and Sophia, and they agreed that he would come to Leiden in the course of the afternoon with Max; Max would pick him up from the gate of the hospital.

Why he visited Ada for a moment every day—recently usually outside official visiting hours—was not completely clear even to Onno himself. He did not need to do it for Ada's sake: it was more a visit to a grave than to a sickbed. However, paradoxically, in that grave a dead body was not slowly but surely starting to decompose, but on the contrary an unborn body was taking shape. As he stood next to her with his arms folded, the ward nurse came up to him and said that Dr. Melchior, the surgeon, had asked whether he would drop by; he was in his room, in the wing opposite.

"By the way, now I'm talking to you: can we have your permission to cut Ada's hair a little shorter? Up to now we've left it more or less as it is, but for reasons of hygiene . . . Given the circumstances it will soon grow again."

Onno realized that he could not refuse, just as he could not demand that she should be made up every morning. He nodded, pressed a kiss on Ada's black, silky hair, and left the ward without so much as exchanging a glance with the nurse.

He wondered what Melchior wanted from him; he had spoken to him only yesterday. On his way there he again noticed that the staff looked at him in a special way: everyone knew by now who he was and the state his wife was in. It was as though some of them wanted to see how someone felt in his situation, while most of them gave the impression that they wanted to help him by looking at him.

With his fleshy, round face, his hump, and his deformed leg, the little surgeon came out from behind his desk and shook Onno's hand. He was wearing a white short-sleeved gown.

"Have a seat," he said. "We can keep it short. I wanted to speak to you alone for a moment, without your mother-in-law." He folded his large hands on the top of his desk and looked penetratingly at Onno, while he obviously carefully weighed his words. "Yesterday you inquired how risky next Thursday's operation would be."

"I understood from you that the chances were quite good."

Melchior nodded and allowed another silence to fall, during which he did not take his light-blue eyes off Onno. Onno looked back at him in bewilderment, getting the feeling that those pauses contained the real message rather than his words.

Slowly, the surgeon said: "In general that is the case. But complications can always arise, which may be fatal."

"We're aware of that," said Onno. "My mother-in-law perhaps most of all—she was in medicine herself. There was no need to keep that from her."

"So I've heard." Melchior again inserted a silence. "But you know, a mother . . ."

Suddenly Onno felt the blood draining from his face. Was he understanding him correctly? Was the man prepared to pull the plug? If he were to say to him now that an unexpected fatal outcome might ultimately be the best for everyone, first and foremost for Ada, to the extent that there was still such a person as Ada, would the required complication occur on Thursday? Some hemorrhage, or a cardiac arrest, with fatal consequences? Thursday was the day when that would be possible; if it didn't happen, then the opportunity would have been missed and her body might remain in its present state for months and perhaps years, before it died a natural physiological death.

It would be a long time before that would change in the Christian-dominated Netherlands, without someone risking a prison sentence and being struck off the medical register; that was another reason for changing society. He got up and went to the window, where he looked out without seeing anything. He was now in conversation with the doctor, but he must not indicate with so much as a word that this was happening; if he were to utter the word *euthanasia,* Melchior would dismiss that suggestion in alarm and the operation would proceed faultlessly. If Ada were to die on the operating table and suspicions were to arise so that people like his brother-in-law Coen could take him to court, on the basis of laws that his brother Menno taught, then everyone could swear under oath that there had been no question of terminating a life. The judge might have his own opinion, but the upshot would be acquittal, acclaimed by the enlightened section of the nation.

What was he to do? He now suddenly had to decide on her life. He couldn't possibly do it! He felt the responsibility weighing on his back like the sack of anthracite on that of a coalman from his childhood. But was her life "her" life anymore? Was there still a subject called Ada lying fifty yards away from here on a sheepskin? The day before yesterday he had asked the neurologist if her E.E.G. was completely flat—to which Stevens had replied that it was indistinguishable from a flat E.E.G. But he also thought of the conversation he had had a week ago with Max at Ada's bedside, when they had said that everyone, despite all the E.E.G.'s, instinctively whispered at all those bedsides.

He turned around. Melchior was leafing through a pile of large index cards, which had been bound into a temporary notebook with tape; he gave the impression that he had already forgotten the topic of conversation. Onno looked at his watch.

"I'm sorry," he said. "Someone's waiting for me at the gate. Shall we continue this conversation another time?"

"As you like. There isn't that much to continue."

"What's wrong?" asked Max. "Why aren't you saying anything?"

Surrounded by tentative gray-haired Sunday drivers, they were making their way along the highway to Leiden.

Onno groaned and looked sideways at him. "Can I trust you?"

Max laughed uncomfortably. "Is it conceivable that I should say no?"

"Then swear you'll never tell anyone what I'm going to tell you in deepest secrecy."

"I swear."

"Not my mother-in-law, not my child, or anyone else—even later. Raise two fingers of your right hand and repeat it."

Max took his right hand off the steering wheel, raised two fingers, and said: "I swear."

Onno then told him what had just happened. Max, too, was shocked by the sudden emergence of extreme seriousness. Deciding on life and death—like Onno he had never dreamt that it might become an issue in his life. That was something for doctors, military people, politicians, not for astronomers; so it was still more Onno's territory than his.

"When I said that we might continue our conversation another time, he said there wasn't much to continue. Of course he wasn't talking about our conversation, but about Ada's life. He looks like Quasimodo, the bell-ringer of Notre-Dame, but I know from my brother-in-law that he's a top man at his job. What would you do in my position?"

Perhaps Max was in his position. Suddenly his brain was operating quickly and efficiently. "I'd want to find out," he said, "whether the neurologist and the surgeon are really one hundred percent certain that Ada is brain-dead, that there's not one ounce of individuality left in her. Because even if there's just a tiny bit left, it's murder. I'm inflexible on that point. Suppose there's only as much left as a one-year-old child; then you can't do it. You can't murder babies, either. But if there's really nothing left at all, zero percent, just a vegetable, then it means nothing. Then you can."

"You talked differently last week. I got the impression that in your view not even the dead should be killed, so to speak."

"That was fantasy." Max nodded.

"But how can I find out what Quasimodo really thinks? I can't just ask him, because then the whole thing would be called off at once. And I can't approach that neurologist Stevens, because Melchior didn't inform him, of course."

At that moment Max had an idea.

"Do you know what we'll do? Ask casually if Ada is going to be given a local or a general anesthetic. If he says he won't be anesthetizing her since she has no perception left, then that would settle it, but if he says 'local' or 'general,' you'll know the score."

"This marks the exact scientist!" Onno exclaimed. "But if I ask him he'll probably smell a rat anyway, because he doesn't strike me as stupid. Perhaps it'll be better if I involve my brother-in-law on some pretext—he's a brain surgeon as you know; all these butchers know each other. Or maybe not," he said, shaking his forefinger. "He may say that a cesarean section is never carried out under local anesthetic, that he doesn't need to ask the surgeon. But he'll have been immediately alerted, because everyone has obviously considered that possibility, certainly good old Karel, who in terms of character might be persuadable, if he weren't such a holy Joe. No one else must be involved!" He looked sideways again. "I know a better way. You must find out."

Max glanced at him, then looked back at the road. "How do you see that happening?"

"You must get friendly with the surgical nurse a day before and find out from her if they're going to use an anesthetic—if necessary in bed, without regard of persons. So that disgusting promiscuity of yours will finally have some point for a change."

Max smiled. Now that promiscuity might have some point—even though Onno was only half serious, of course—it no longer existed. "Success doesn't strike me as guaranteed."

"Bashful all of a sudden?"

"Listen, she may be a lesbian; you never know with nurses. I could tell you things. . . . There has to be a surer way of getting a result. Suppose I read up a little on the technical side of the anesthetics business—"

"Anesthesiological. Anesthetics are the substances."

". . . so that I can see whether equipment is switched on and that kind of thing. Then on Thursday I'll simply wander into the operating room by mistake a quarter of an hour beforehand. Things like that are always possible in Amsterdam. Then I'll let you know; as the husband, you'll accompany the stretcher to the door of the operating room, where they won't let you through. Then you can ask to see the surgeon for a moment and privately give an indication of your decision."

Onno looked pensively at the little imitation three-wheeled car ahead of them that would not budge from the outside lane.

"Right," he said. "That's what we'll do, *compañero*. What would I do without you?"

"Nothing, it seems."

When the three of them had met for the first time that afternoon in the back room at the bookshop, with tea and biscuits, Onno's main problem was in getting used to their new status: Max as foster father, Sophia as foster mother, himself as a grass widower. He felt embarrassed by the situation, but Sophia was businesslike as always; she seemed to have adjusted completely to the changed circumstances, like someone who had simply changed jobs. But Max was aware that only she and he knew that the relationship they were entering into with each other was a facade, hiding a completely different relationship; and that too was in turn of course a facade, behind which there was nothing but chaos and uncertainty. Now that plan they had hatched on the way here had been added to that awareness; he felt as if he himself were falling under something like an anesthetic. What he would have liked most was to stay over at "In Praise of Folly," in order to sink into the arms of the nighttime Sophia, but of course that was out of the question now that Onno was there.

"Goodbye, Mrs. Brons."

" 'Bye, Max."

The next conclave was on Tuesday evening at Onno's, but there really had not been that much more to discuss. They had soon reached an agreement on the financial side of things, and the sale of the bookshop had meanwhile also been agreed upon. Onno had not had to think very hard: from the inexhaustible reservoir of his family a second cousin had emerged who had always been a bad sort but who was now the director of a large real estate firm. Onno had called and told him to get an extortionate price for the premises without charging a commission, as otherwise he would report him to the police. And as far as accommodation in Drenthe was concerned, Max had talked to the director of the observatory, who had smiled mysteriously and said that he might know of something nice. That sounded promising, at least not like a two-bedroom house in a new development. It also meant that his appointment as telescope astronomer was virtually settled.

Afterward, Sophia did the backlog of cleaning, vacuumed, and put on the washing machine, which reminded Onno of Ada's first visit: she was more like her mother than she realized, or had realized. While Sophia busied herself upstairs, Max suggested that they really ought to tell Onno's mother-in-law about their anesthesiological plan. In the first place she knew about these things, and in the second place it concerned her daughter. But Onno felt that was precisely why she should be kept out of it: as a mother she would never have a hand in the death of her child, even if there was nothing left of that child. Max was not so sure, but he could not give away the fact that he knew her better than Onno. The main reason why she should remain ignorant—and on this point Max agreed—was that Melchior's position must not be jeopardized in any way: he was the only one who was sticking his neck out and was ready to break the great taboo, and he had made his veiled proposal precisely in the absence of Sophia.

On Wednesday morning—after staying the night in Leiden, since it was ridiculous driving back to Amsterdam again—he went to the Academic Hospital. He had devised the plan of presenting himself as a writer of medical novels doing background research who would like a look at the operating room, where he would be given an explanation of how the anesthetists' equipment worked. But once on the terrace he remembered that disastrous night three months ago, and his courage suddenly failed him. He decided to go to the medical faculty library first.

While next to him two students whispered about the Carré theater in Amsterdam, which was probably going to be occupied tomorrow after a musical performance—led by the writer and the composer whose paths he had already crossed a few times and who, it seemed, had just returned from the rebellious ferment of Paris—he leafed through manuals of anesthesiology and studied illustrations of equipment. Then he asked a surly lady with her gray hair worn up in a bun and a pencil behind her ear to point out where the literature on obstetrics was.

While he immersed himself in the techniques of cesarean sections and looked at the gory insides of wombs, where infants were being retrieved from damp, dark caverns, apparently against their will, he was struck by the mirror-image similarity between the work of surgeons and his own. Just as he, starting from his own body, looked into the depths of the universe, where everything became increasingly incomprehensible, they took the opposite direction and penetrated that same body, where they encountered similar mysteries, culminating in enigmatic neurons and DNA molecules, whose operation was perhaps ultimately determined by quantum processes. The fact that the dimensions of the human body were almost exactly halfway between those of the universe and those of the smallest particles was in line with that fact. Man was the axis of the world—that was not a theological dogma: you could measure it.

However, he encountered an unexpected problem. The cesarean section, a routine operation lasting no more than half an hour, was usually carried out under general, but sometimes under local, anesthetic; in the latter case only the lower half of the body was anesthetized, with a lumbar injection. That meant that even if the equipment was not switched on, no conclusions could be drawn from it. If the red lights were not on, that meant that on Thursday he would have to locate within a few seconds a particular hypodermic syringe among scores of other syringes, scissors, hooks, clamps, forceps, scalpels, and whatever else might be ready to ensure that everything went according to plan. That was of course impossible. Nor was there any point in finding out on some pretext or other whether there was an anesthetist in the operating room. Of course there would be one; it was inconceivable that he would get a telephone call telling him that he could stay home today, since the patient couldn't feel anything anyway. Blood pressure and heart function all had to be monitored, whether anesthetic was administered or not.

Max closed the book with a bang, which earned him an icy look from the librarian. She had of course seen long ago, over the top of her glasses, that it was a layman struggling there with the Anglo-Saxon folios bound in red and blue linen, with gold lettering. Of course hypochondriacs regularly came here in order to self-diagnose their imaginary illnesses. He felt ridiculous, like a general practitioner who imagined in the observation room in Dwingeloo that he could see at a glance whether the mirror was being used for espionage purposes.

A ten-minute conversation with an expert in the Academic Hospital would make everything clear; but if it went wrong and got into the newspapers, then that person might report to the court and give an affidavit on that strange conversation the day before the fatal operation that had caused an uproar in the whole of the conservative Netherlands. Murder! He would be traced—because the librarian had once seen him coming out of the observatory while out walking with her friend through the Botanical Garden—and Melchior would wind up in jail. There was simply no way of finding out quickly without a risk. Unless he were to immediately take a plane to a distant country, Italy for example, and introduce himself in the hospital in Rome as a German writer working on a short story about a pregnant woman in a coma, who . . . No, even that was probably too risky. Such a spectacular case might even make the world press.

33

Cesarean Section

Onno and Sophia had seen it before, but when the three of them entered the ward the following afternoon, Max stopped on the threshold in shock. Ada's hair had been cropped. She looked like the girls and women whose hair he had seen cut off by men, foaming at the mouth, because they had consorted with Germans: "Jerry's whores" in the eyes of the mob, who until the Battle of Stalingrad had had a much cozier arrangement with the Germans, apart from cheerfully taking off their panties. The rectangular frame around her face had disappeared and had revealed a round, defenseless head, which only now seemed to have departed finally into the realm of inaccessibility.

At a quarter to four, two nurses appeared to wheel Ada, bed and all, to the operating room. The previous evening Max had called Onno and informed him about his medical fiasco, whereupon Onno had immediately concluded that the uncertainty about Ada's mental existence remained and that she should therefore remain alive. Max pressed his lips to her forehead and wondered how he would have felt if the decision had been different.

Onno, too, was relieved that it had gone like this. Looking back on it, he doubted whether Melchior had actually meant it all as he had interpreted it, though he would never dare to say that to Max. Perhaps he had had him carry out an absurd mission. While Max and Sophia went to the lounge, he accompanied Ada through the corridors and in the elevator upstairs, with one hand on her belly. In a room outside the operating room proper, a man of his own age was washing his hands; he was wearing a green short-sleeved smock, with a cap of the same color on his head. Onno introduced himself and asked if he could speak to Melchior for a moment.

"Can't you tell me?" asked the man. "My name is Steenwijk. I'm the anesthetist."

Onno looked at him in shock. He had a walnut-colored complexion, which was a little darker around his eyes. Onno realized that he was suddenly in a situation where he might yet find out what he wanted to know.

"Anesthetist?" he repeated. "Are you putting my wife under an anesthetic?"

"Of course."

"But I understood from Dr. Stevens that she can't feel pain anymore."

With a vague smile Steenwijk shook his head.

"That's a separate matter. The sensation of pain is a matter for the cerebral cortex. But what we must avoid in the interest of the child during the operation are possible reflexes from the brainstem. And that is intact, as you know; after all your wife is breathing. Anyway, my instinct also tells me that we have to do it."

Onno looked at him for a moment and then nodded. At one fell swoop all the nonsense had been dismissed. Steenwijk's last sentence about his instinct echoed in his head. Did that mean that in his view, too, something of Ada still remained?

Although he was no longer certain that Melchior had actually alluded to euthanasia, he said, feeling ridiculous: "Please tell Dr. Melchior that he must remember his Hippocratic oath and do everything to save my wife's life."

Steenwijk similarly did not answer immediately. Had he understood?

"I'll tell him, although it really ought to be unnecessary." He looked at Onno with a slightly melancholy expression and said, "You have my sympathy. You can wait next door."

"My friends are downstairs."

"As you wish."

Max and Sophia were sitting at a round bamboo table with a glass top in wicker garden chairs, surrounded by patients in bathrobes over striped pajamas and nightgowns, their bare feet in slippers. Some were playing cards, others were reading illustrated magazines, doubtless from months or years ago, but most of all they were smoking; with the blissful absorption of prisoners who were finally allowed into the fresh air, the smoke was inhaled into lungs, so that the tips of the cigarettes glowed red. On a cupboard stood a television set that had been switched off.

Calmly, as though she were waiting for a train, Sophia was also leafing through a magazine; beside her chair was a carryall. Max looked at his watch: four o'clock. Although he too was outwardly calm, inwardly he was trembling with fear. He suddenly felt as though time were a hollow cone, within which he had for months been driven from the base, which was as wide as the world, toward the point, which he must soon pass through—and perhaps he also realized that image was an echo of the usual space-time diagram in relativity literature: the "light cone" of an event. Within an hour the catastrophe might be a fact, if somehow it became immediately apparent that he was the father.

Onno joined them and said: "I've just spoken to the anesthetist."

Max looked up with a jolt, but immediately realized that he must control himself so as not to let Sophia know what they had been talking about.

"And?" asked Sophia.

Without looking at Max, Onno reported the conversation to her, but actually of course to Max as well—after which Max suddenly realized that he had behaved even more absurdly with his research yesterday than he already suspected. He felt like a little boy who thought that the station-master's whistle set the train in motion and was now having it explained to him in a few words that it was not really like that. He was ashamed—not so much as a friend in Onno's eyes, because he had other reasons for that, and Onno had also seen some merit in the plan, but particularly as a man of science: just imagine if his colleagues were to hear about this. How had he taken it into his head to research a question of life and death in a few hours on his own initiative, in a completely unknown field, which other people studied for ten years! Were the tensions getting too much for him? Perhaps he should start being a little more careful.

A nurse asked if they would like a cup of tea; only Max refused. Sophia thought that Ada would have a general anesthetic, administered by drip; under normal circumstances, with a local anesthetic you had to sit up and bend forward with your head between your knees, which in her condition was of course impossible; it could also be done lying down, on one's left side. But she still did not think they would do that. Onno said that the most important thing was that there was nothing wrong with the baby, and he wasn't completely sure about that, even though the doctors maintained there was no reason to worry. Sophia assumed a pediatrician would be present—at least that had been the case in her day, but that was long ago. Now and then their conversation flagged. They were aware that Ada was now lying on the operating table under a huge lamp and was being opened up.

"Everything is about to change," Onno suddenly said solemnly. "The child will change from an embryo into a human being, Ada from a daughter into a mother, you from a mother into a grandmother, and I from a son into a father." He looked at Max. "You're the only one who won't change. Just like you."

Max nodded. He had an impulse to pray that he would remain as unchangeable as a stone.

"Every thirtieth of May from now on," said Sophia after a while "we will celebrate a birthday. Wait a moment, that means that it will be a Gemini."

"A *Gemini?*" repeated Onno with horror, and looked at her in disbelief. "You can't be serious."

"What do you mean? The end of May is Gemini, isn't it?"

"The end of May is Gemini . . ." repeated Onno again, with sarcastic emphasis. "You're not going to tell me that you believe in that nonsense? You're like my mother; she combines astrology with Christianity, and you obviously combine it with humanism. Astrology as an overarching world religion. But okay, go ahead, it's all excused because of its ancient roots. Max's profession wouldn't even exist without astrology."

"Our ancestors, the astrologers." Max nodded. Gemini, he thought—and at the same moment he remembered Eng and Chang, but he kept that to himself. Imagine if Siamese twins were really born upstairs—or nonidentical twins. In a sense one would be Onno's child and the other his own; was such a thing possible?

"And you," Onno asked Sophia, still with a sardonic tone in his voice. "What 'are' you?"

"Virgo."

"That's what I like to hear, Mother. That makes a totally respectable impression on me."

Whenever Onno said "Mother" to Sophia, Max felt sick, as though that made him something like Onno's "father."

"I don't believe in it at all," said Sophia, and pointed to the astrology column in the magazine on her lap. "I just happened to see it here."

A step at a time an emaciated, aristocratic-looking gentleman in his fifties came in; the plastic tube hanging from his nose was attached to an upturned bottle on a tall stand on wheels that he pushed along beside him like a bishop pushing his crosier. Although it was as though his body were filled only with a rarefied gas, he didn't give the impression that he intended to die—rather, that he had something better to do and that he was mainly annoyed by this stupid delay in the hospital; that probably seemed to him something more for the bourgeoisie. His dark-blue dressing gown, obviously silk, was edged with white braid; a white handkerchief protruded from the breast pocket. Without deigning to look at anyone, he put on the television and sat down at the table next to theirs. A woman in a harsh pink bathrobe and a huge plaster over one ear, like Van Gogh, said that there was nothing on at this hour. As though he had received a compliment, the gentleman made a slight bow, calmly lit a pipe, which contrasted strangely with his catheter, crossed his legs, and looked expectantly at the screen. Heraldic coats-of-arms had been embroidered in gold thread on his blood-red slippers.

Max and Sophia, who were sitting with their backs to the set, were talking about the war, about the improvised situation in those days in the hospital in Delft.

But then Onno suddenly said: "Be quiet for a moment."

Charles de Gaulle had appeared in a special broadcast. The awkward-looking general, lumbered with his colossal body, which was somewhat like Onno's, looked straight into the camera and addressed the French people. Despite the bloody events of the last few weeks, he said, he would not resign as president of the republic; he declared the Assemblée Nationale dissolved and announced general elections; if the riots continued, then very forceful measures would be taken. It was a live broadcast without subtitles; a soft woman's voice gave a simultaneous translation—but in Dutch it was no longer the same: France speaking to France, in French. It was as though that language were the only real presence, on the one hand crystalized as the general, on the other the French people. Perhaps, thought Onno, the fact that the speaker in all his monumentality at the same time had something of a small boy about him, who was allowed to put his father's suit on for a short while—the suit of the King of France—as though under the table little Charles was still wearing his short trousers, with bare knees covered in scabs from healing wounds.

"Right!" said the man at the table next to theirs, and got up.

The speech had lasted no longer than five minutes.

Onno gave Max and Sophia a perplexed look. "Shall I tell you something? It's over. At this moment the whole of right-wing France is taking to the streets. The party's over."

Max had not been following it; he was less able to concentrate on politics at this moment than ever, and he listened without interest to Onno, who said that in his view a new age had dawned with those few sentences, because by nature of his profession he had an infallible instinct for that kind of thing; the 1960s were over, imagination had been ousted from power, and from today on the world was going to be a less enjoyable place. But they themselves had the same kind of memory as the previous generation had of the 1920s—and it was doubtful whether the next generation would have such a thing.

"Speaking of the next generation . . ." said Sophia "Do you remember why you're here? You're going to be a father."

With a jerk, Onno returned from world politics to the lounge. He looked at his watch. "Let's go. We can wait upstairs too."

A huge iron service elevator, obviously not intended for visitors but for stretchers and coffins, took them slowly to the second floor. In a narrow space next to the operating room a varnished wooden bench had been screwed into the wall; on the opposite wall hung a poster with a sunny Greek coast: deep blue bays between foam-edged rocks, behind which Ada was now being operated on.

They sat awkwardly next to each other, Sophia in the middle, her carryall at her feet.

"What is it that you're lugging with you everywhere?" asked Onno.

Without saying anything, she opened the zipper and with one hand took out a tiny white gown and a pair of tiny socks.

"In the incubator it won't be necessary for the time being, but if everything goes okay, I'll put the things in Ada's bedside cupboard shortly. That's what she would have done herself."

"You're fantastic," said Onno, opening the gown between his fingers and looking at it like a biologist at a newly discovered species of animal. "Fancy your thinking of that . . ."

The sight of the microscopic wardrobe reminded Max of the shadow that in B-movies was cast by the approaching villain, of whom only the feet, wearing shiny shoes, were shown.

"Well, well—*les boys!*"

In the doorway stood the journalist who just over a year ago had been pulled across the table in the pub by Onno for attacking his friend.

"I don't believe this!" said Onno. "What are you doing here?"

"I'm doing my job. I've got an article to write on what's going on here."

"How do you know what's going on here?"

The journalist shrugged his shoulders. "Where does a newspaper get its information from?"

"For God's sake, beat it. Publicity is something I can do without. Of course you were called up by some male nurse anxious to make a few guilders on the side."

"There's no point in asking me, Onno. I'd rather be sitting in the pub too."

"I'm not Onno to you."

"Okay, Dr. Quist, let's keep calm. I can understand that you're a bit overwrought. What's going on inside you at the moment?"

"The uncontrollable desire to smash your face for hour after hour! And if you don't clear off this minute I'm going to do just that."

When Onno made to get up, with the smock still in his hands, the journalist shrugged his shoulders.

"Okay, I'll do it without you," he said, turned on his heel, and disappeared.

Onno threw the smock furiously into the carryall. "Those sensation-seeking scum . . ."

"Don't get excited," said Max. "The fellow has already been sufficiently punished by being who he is."

Suddenly Sophia put her hand on both their arms. "Quiet a moment . . ."

There was the scarcely audible sound of a child crying on the other side of the wall.

A little later a nurse put her head around the door and said with a smile: "The stork has been here! An angelic little boy! Mother and child are doing fine!"

The fact that it was a boy was hidden by a diaper—but establishing the sex meant little. They stood speechless in front of the incubator while doctors, assistants, and nursing staff looked over their shoulders. No one had ever seen such a baby. Newborn infants tended to look like boxers at the end of the final round: swollen, eyes puffed and closed, reeling from the violence they had been through—but what was lying there in the sealed glass space was really like a precious museum piece in a display case, more like a *putto,* such as could be seen in Italian Renaissance paintings: all that was missing were the wings.

It was not balding and wrinkled in the way some infants immediately prefigured their old age, but had strong black hair with a deep mahogany glow, which covered its whole scalp as though it had just come from the hairdresser's; its skin was firm and seemed bathed in the light of the full moon. Nor did it have the bloated monstrousness that could be found beautiful only when seen through the eyes of maternal and paternal instinct; its cheeks were full, and in the thighs and at the wrists there were slight folds of skin, which in an adult would indicate obesity. But there was no trace of endearing chubbiness; everything was perfect, like a work of art worthy of the name. At the same time this caused it to radiate a certain aloofness, as though it did not need anyone. The small nipples, the slim fingers and toes, looked as if they had been engraved with a fine etching needle; although it had been born a month early, not only the ears but the nose and mouth too had already developed into more or less their final shape.

However, most striking of all were the eyes. They were wide open, and the space between the dark lashes was completely filled with lapis lazuli, a color blue that none of them had seen before in a human being. It reminded Max of the color of the Mediterranean—but only at a particular moment, when after driving for days through Belgium and France he caught the first glimpse of it, between the scorching hills near Saint-Raphael: *Thalassa!* The incredible blue of that moment; he now saw it in two places in that pale, strange face. His fear of an immediately evident likeness had immediately disappeared—he could obviously relax for the first few years. He had looked immediately at the nose and the thumbs, but there was nothing of himself to be recognized in them, either. There was no discernible likeness to Onno, either, and from Ada it had only the black hair and the black, sharply etched eyebrows and eyelashes, which made the blue of its eyes even deeper.

"What a beautiful child," said Sophia. "That's going to cause him problems in the future." Suddenly she turned around and asked the faces behind her, "How is my daughter?"

"She's still in there. Everything is going according to plan, but it will be a little while yet."

Onno and Max were not thinking of Ada.

"What's his name?" asked Max.

Onno looked at him proudly. "You must know the story of the man who said to a colleague of yours that he understood how astronomers could determine every possible property of the stars with their instruments—but how had they discovered their names?"

"That is indeed our most brilliant achievement." Max nodded.

"Quinten," said Onno.

DE PROFUNDIS

out out

·   *is*

no stay

the waves

·   *black*

liesje   *·*

help

get up   to school

bring yourself   ·

daddy

·

la valse

horror horror

·   *not   the hooblei*

·   *a girl?*

delius max

for God's sake stay   you stay

·

want to get out

·   *close lid*   *·*

where are you?   *score*

PART THREE

THE BEGINNING
OF THE
END

Second Intermezzo

—*Congratulations! That must have been a satisfying moment for you. So there he was, our envoy—after years of hard work.*

—Only for a moment, though. After that, it was like it always is: once you've achieved what you wanted to achieve, it's no longer what you wanted to achieve, but simply what you've achieved. You've come to take it for granted. What you win you lose, all things considered. What's more, when you see the havoc you've had to wreak to achieve it, it takes away the satisfaction. But anyway, I'm a professional, an old hand. Only the end matters.

—*I take it you're thinking of the friendship between those two. But that tree that blew over . . . was that coincidence, or were you behind that, too?*

—I was behind that, too. There were two trees, by the way.

—*What was the point of that? It was a very risky course of action, wasn't it? Suppose she hadn't survived, or had had a miscarriage. I know you don't care for this kind of question, but perhaps you'd like to answer anyway.*

—If I couldn't make trees blow over exactly as I want, I wouldn't make any trees blow over. We know the position and force of every molecule in the air and, moreover, the elasticity of every point in the tree and its roots— it would gratify Laplace if he could see our aerodynamics division handling that kind of thing.

—*Laplace? I expect he's one of those French intellectuals with a dirty scarf around his neck and a shawl over his shoulders.*

—I don't know if they did that in his day. At any rate, a great man, a colleague of Max Delius's. But also an incorrigible optimist. A demon who knew all the world's preconditions at a given moment, he claimed—would not only be able to reconstruct the past precisely, but also work out the future with certainty.

—*Definitely someone from the eighteenth century. Even we can't do that.*

—We do very well at the level of trees being blown over.

—*Tell me, why did that poor child have to have such a dreadful accident?*

—Because otherwise the mission couldn't have been accomplished. In everything I did, I had only one thing in mind: the return of the dictate.

—*All right, I can understand your not wanting to answer. Obviously it's a matter of your professional honor, and I respect that. I expect it will be clear to me in retrospect.*

—To you, yes. In the past things were easier for us.

—*What do you mean?*

—When we simply used to address people directly as the need arose.

—*But we stopped doing that after the creatures got the idea that it was not our voice they were hearing but their own inner voice. Of course, we couldn't stand for that kind of pickpocketing. It's undeniable that technology is increasingly taking the place of theology on earth, but psychology shouldn't get any big ideas on that score.*

—It's still a shame it happened like that. The fact is that heaven and earth are only linked by means of the word—the present operation has precisely made that clear yet again.

—*Exactly. This operation was the period we put after that conversation.*

—It would be nice if people were scared to death when they hear what has happened—namely, that the testimony has been returned—and the shock brought them to their senses.

—*No one will ever know. And anyway: senses? Don't make me laugh. Did you really think that brood would give up anything at all? Come now. What they once have, they want to keep. That wretch Lucifer knows exactly what he's doing. With each new invention, people have stolen a piece of our omnipotence and in so doing have demonized their own reality step by step. Under the terms of the contract he has turned them into vampires, who are sucking us dry under his patronage. With their rockets they are already traveling faster than the wind, sound even, and one day they will approach the speed of light; with their television they are in fact already virtually omnipresent—they can see in the dark, they can look into the insides of a human being without opening him up; with their computers they have a complete operating and monitoring system, in which they're already vying with your department; they can observe elementary particles, and they already know what happened ten to the minus forty-third seconds after our explo-*

sion of light. Beyond that limit their theories have failed up to now; for the time being all their calculations result in infinity, and let's hope that they never realize the deeper meaning of that; but by now I'm not sure of anything anymore.

—I've something to tell you about that in a moment.

—*If they want, they can even destroy the earth. Excuse my saying so, but that power really was our prerogative. Meanwhile they're busy destroying the planet without meaning to, and to be on the safe side, they're already walking on the moon as a jumping-off point for the rest of the universe. In the foreseeable future they will have mastered our absolute privilege: the creation of life, as a pendant to its wholesale extermination. A virus to begin with, then a microbe, then a worm,* Caenorhabditis elegans *probably, and one day they will produce people in their own image—and these days that's often as vacuous as a doll: instead of an expression, they have things, like cars. Of necessity they will become peoplelike things. Human knowledge doubles every twelve years—now, in their 1985, they know and can do twice as much as in their 1973, and as omnipotence draws closer, literally everything becomes possible down there.* Knowledge itself is power—*who do you think thought up that aphorism? That damn Francis Bacon again, of course. Knowledge is power sure enough, and not just over nature, but over people, and us too. The earth has changed once and for all into his doomed House of Solomon and people no longer need us—we've become fairy stories to them, curiosities, literature ... Do you remember that string of questions that the Chief once fired at Job—whether he could raise his voice to the clouds, and whether he could shut out the sea with doors, and heaven knows what else? No, he could not, only the Chief could do that, and now just look at everything our Job can do. There are some things that are brand-new even to our Chief. Lucifer has won, and there's no use in beating around the bush any longer. Through his devilish move with the treacherous viscount, he has proved the stronger—there's no getting away from it. Less than five years after Bacon's death, Galileo and Descartes wrote their fundamental works, the* Dialogo *and the* Discours de la méthode, *the beginning of the modern age, which set us off along the fateful road to Auschwitz and Hiroshima and the decoding of DNA. Old Goethe had foreseen that course of events, although he gave it a worthily positive twist: he has his hundred-year-old Faust end up as a technocrat who subdues the sea with dikes and canals—that is, he turns nature into a human creation.*

—A kind of Dutch polder engineer from the Ministry of Transport, in fact, who shuts out the sea with doors. Perhaps Goethe was thinking of Leeghwater; he was very famous as early as the seventeenth century with his *Book of the Haarlemmer Meer.*

—*Maybe, but I can't concentrate on literary historical reflections at the moment. You're distracting me from my argument—what was I talking about?*

—About the general downfall of everything.

—*Yes, and especially our own. Because that was what Lucifer was after from the very first day: our complete humiliation and destruction. In the last analysis human beings leave him cold. And for that matter don't forget that the damn technology also has all kinds of pleasant aspects. Not only the construction of polders, but take medical technology for example. Think of local anesthetic, to mention one small thing. Did you think that anyone at all would want to go back to having a tooth pulled without anesthetic? And can you blame them? How dreadful to have teeth! No, take it from me—that it's hopeless. Via people's bodies, Lucifer has gotten a grip on their minds. Our greatest mistake is that we have always underestimated him. We thought things wouldn't be that bad, because who could challenge the Chief? Well, he could. Sometimes I think—it's a shame to have to say it—that he knows people much better than the Chief. The Chief is an idealist, a darling, who wants the best for people without knowing what he has taken on. But Lucifer knows that they would prefer to let heaven and earth go under rather than get rid of their car. He has ensured that their salvation now resides in things. He knows that they'd sooner get rid of their own legs. So heaven and earth will go under. And there will be nothing left to be lost in that* Twilight of Humankind, *because it has been devilishly betrayed, sold and melted down to make machines. A motorist is not a pedestrian in a car but a totally new creature, made of flesh, blood, steel, and gasoline. They are modern centaurs, griffons, and the actual mythical creatures are the only thing that will ultimately remain, because they have been created at the cost of nature, human beings, us and the Chief. With every new technological gadget, human life has automatically become more absurd. And our world will finally contain only that triumphant Negative in the ice-cold flames of its hell, with in heaven the eternal agony of the Chief as the flickering ember of a great Light. Looking back on it, it's all been for nothing. What was I actually going to say? I've totally lost the thread. Yes, I'm getting more and more confused. I can feel the decay and exhaustion in myself, too. Go on. I'm listening.*

34

The Gift

"Healthy baby born to brain-dead mother," reported the morning paper the following day; Ada survived the operation without complications, and the weeks following—during which Quinten had to remain in the incubator—brought new changes.

The director of the observatory kept his word: he had made an appointment for Max with an old friend from his student days, a Baron Gevers, who lived a few miles south of the radio observatory at Westerbork and, as he had informed Max, had a place to rent. It was a sunny June day when Max drove there from Dwingeloo, with the caretaker's description of the route in his head. On his right, the sun flickered like a strobe light between the alder trees along the provincial road as they flashed by, which meant he had to resist something like a threatening hypnosis; as always he glanced at the space on the left of the road where there were two trees missing.

After driving along the main highway for a few miles, he took a turn-off into a winding woodland path by a collapsed barn. There were still fallen trees everywhere, their crowns forever in their bare wintry state, their roots, which had been torn out of the earth, already dried out and whitish. To his amazement he suddenly saw a group of Indonesian boys creeping through the bushes, in improvised battle dress, as though there were a war on—a moment later he had the feeling that he had dreamt it. And now and then the wood gave way to meadows with a farmhouse, fields, maize plantations, the path crossed an unmanned level crossing—and at the moment he saw the house looming up, he thought of what Goethe had once said, according to Onno: "Humanity begins with barons."

The low, white, quite small country house, from the look of it dating from the beginning of the last century, lay at the end of a lawn and radiated restrained distinction. At the same time it also looked like the center of a working farm. Next to it there were stalls, a haystack, sheds for agricultural machinery. It was called Klein Rechteren. The drive was flanked by large erratic stones and was strewn with gravel, which crunched feudally beneath his tires and forced even the Volkswagen to the slow sedateness of a Bentley. Because his intuition told him that he couldn't park his car right outside the door, he parked it opposite. When he got out, he saw a peacock sitting on the eaves.

The door was opened by a boy of about twenty with Down's syndrome. He looked up at Max with bewildered beady eyes.

"Mommy!" he shouted at once in a hoarse voice, without taking his eyes off Max.

A slender lady of about sixty appeared in the hallway. Max introduced himself and then also shook the warm, broad, motionless hand of her son, who turned out to be called Rutger. In the conservatory at the back of the house, where the doors to the terrace and the vegetable garden stood open, he was given a cup of China tea.

"I'm expecting my husband any moment. How is our Jan getting on? We haven't seen him for quite a while. He occasionally stays here when he has to come to Dwingeloo."

She was talking about the director. Although the director had of course explained exactly Max's own circumstances to them, she did not allude to them. That might have been discretion, but also something else; he felt a little uncomfortable with the cool politeness of her conversation, and he had the impression that this was the intention. Should he come to live here, he must be quite clear from the outset that this was no charter for familiarity.

Next to her stood a round table with framed family photos on it; also a photo of a white horse. Max looked at Rutger now and again with fascination. He sat in a wicker chair, the back of which spread to enormous dimensions like a throne, fiddling about, with his tongue hanging out. To his left a ball of violet wool lay on the ground; by means of a reel, with three small nails in it, he was weaving a woollen thread into a rope, which must by now be hundreds of feet long and lay in a colorful heap at his feet.

"Make very big curtain," he said when his eyes met Max's.

Max nodded at him in encouragement and looked at his mother.

"He's been working on it for about ten years, that very big curtain. I cut a bit off now and then, otherwise eventually we won't be able to get into the house anymore."

"And he doesn't notice?"

"Not if he doesn't see me doing it."

"Perhaps," said Max, "he has no sense of the length of that thread because he has no sense of time."

The baroness looked at him with an expressionless face. "Maybe."

Max had the feeling that he had gone too far: whoever talks about time is also talking about death.

A tractor approached down the path at the end of the vegetable garden, driven by a heavy figure in workman's clothes; only his sand-colored hat, the brim of which was turned up on one side and down on the other, indicated that this was not a simple farmer. He came into the conservatory in green boots and introduced himself with a hard, callused hand, without coming in. There was something severe, but not unfriendly, about his face; he sported a cultured, small white mustache.

"You're just in time, I've already had ten phone calls. Shall we get right off?"

For the second time Max realized that relationships must be clear, even though he had been recommended by a friend. As he went through the vegetable garden to the road next to his landlord-to-be, he became extraordinarily curious about what awaited him. Without entirely admitting it to himself, he hoped for an idyllic coach house among the trees, with a lawn in front; but to be on the safe side he prepared himself for a melancholy turf cutter's cottage on a canal, waiting motionless for drowning toddlers. It was clear that this would not happen when Gevers said that they could go on foot, because it was close by. Max told him about the Ambonese he had seen crawling through the woods.

"Those are those stupid Moluccans from Schattenberg," said the baron, "a few miles farther on. They're preparing for the liberation of their island on the other side of the world."

The Schattenberg estate: that was the present-day name of Wester-bork camp.

"I really thought I was dreaming," said Max.

The baron nodded. "The world is made of dreams. Fortunately, there are only a few left and they'll be gone soon too, thanks to the observatory."

They met two girls on horseback, who called out, "Hello, Mr. Gevers!" cheerfully—and a few hundred yards farther on, where the road curved slightly, there was a turn-off toward a large wrought-iron gate, fixed to two carved, hard-stone plinths surmounted by shield-bearing lions. A bridge over a narrow canal led to a long drive flanked by a double row of trees; at the end of it there was a second bridge, across a moat, to the forecourt of a castle.

"Groot Rechteren," said Gevers with a motion of his hand, and pushed open the creaking gate.

A castle! As they walked over the loose planks of the bridge toward the drive, Gevers told him that he had been born here, like his father and grandfather before him, but it was all getting too expensive, staff particularly, and it was no longer heatable without going bankrupt. They had moved to Klein Rechteren. The castle had been temporarily divided up into flats, which were occupied by fairly respectable people—except for one, where there was a Communist, but that was now vacant.

Looking at the large, broad castle that he was approaching step by step, Max was speechless. At the sides and in the back it was surrounded by huge trees; it made an impression of neglect and it was not particularly beautiful—obviously it had been repeatedly converted and expanded over the course of the centuries—but it was unmistakably a *castle:* a building that was as different from a house as an eagle from a chicken. The facade, probably dating only from the nineteenth century, was flat and symmetrical; at the level of the attic, in the straight pointed gable above the entrance, was a clock without hands. On the ground floor there was a series of arch-shaped cellar windows; a double staircase led to the terrace with the main floor, flanked by high windows divided into small panes; the upper story ended on the right in a large balcony. Beneath it stood a container on the forecourt, into which someone was throwing planks and all kinds of rubbish. The back turned out to be older; the pointed roof of a square tower could be seen crowned by a weather cock. Could it be true that he was going to live in this fairytale place? Perhaps there by that balcony? What had he done to deserve it?

The castle was the center of a small hamlet. On the left there were newly planted saplings, which turned into coniferous woods, but on the right there were a number of small houses, a coach house, converted stables, and barns.

On the lawn in front of what had probably been the porter's lodge, a man with a scythe was cutting the grass around a colossal erratic stone, and looked up and said, "Hello, Baron,"—which elicited a benevolent "Hello, Piet." Half visible between the buildings and hedges was an orangery, where there was also someone moving; under the trees a billy goat was trying to reach farther than the length of the rope around its neck would allow.

Everything looked occupied; there were windows open everywhere. Shaded by the colossal crown of a brown oak tree, on the bank of the moat, two black swans glided past with the majesty of a more exalted existence, while among the water-lily leaves, at the foot of head-high rhododendron bushes, a couple of ducks were making a vulgar din.

Max had the urge to walk on tiptoe. The castle lay in the water as if on the palm of an outstretched hand; the stone bridge over the moat had, according to Gevers, replaced the earlier drawbridge. A couple of cars were parked in the forecourt, the bricks of which had been laid in an artistic undulating pattern, like a horizontal wall. When they were on the steps to the terrace, a refrigerator crashed with a resounding thud into the container, after which a face leered down at them over the balustrade of the balcony. It emerged, from a blue and white plate next to the main door, that the castle was a listed monument. One half of the door was open, secured with a wooden reel on the ground. Before going in, Gevers stepped out of his boots and took his rakish hat off, which suddenly made him still more severe with his bald pate.

In the hall, paneled in dark oak, a small, carefully dressed lady appeared from a doorway; Max glanced into a large room with Empire furniture, a table with framed photographs, a marble mantelpiece with a gold-framed mirror above it. Gevers introduced her as Mrs. Spier.

"Mr. Delius may be the new upstairs tenant."

She gave him a searching look. Her whole appearance was carefully groomed; not one hair of her coiffure dared to step out of line.

"Welcome, Mr. Delius. If we can be of any help to you, do let us know."

"Her husband is a famous typographical designer," said Gevers as they climbed the wide oak stairs at the end of the hall. "For that matter, it's crawling with clever people here; you'll fit in very well. As a simple yokel I'd feel quite out of place in this cultured company."

The violence in that remark did not escape Max. From the way Gevers looked around, it was clear that he didn't like coming here; of course everything reminded him of the past and confronted him with the decline of the castle. The director had told him that Gevers had played a leading role in the resistance during the war; because Holland was a small country, he might also know Onno's father. At the same time, Max realized that this probably meant he knew who his own father had been.

Upstairs there was another hall, actually more of a spacious landing, which led onto various doors; the oak formality had disappeared here. Through a large window in a conservatory the woods behind the castle were visible; on one side of the space stood buckets covered with plastic and wrapped-clay models on slender, tall modeling stands.

"An artist lives there," announced Gevers with a short motion of his head. "Theo Kern; a rather odd type. Outside on the estate, he's got a studio for larger work." He suddenly stopped and looked straight at Max.

"Bloody fine thing you're doing, Mr. Delius, looking after your friend's child. Just wanted to say that. Bloody fine thing." Before Max knew how to reply, Gevers pointed to the apartment opposite, where all the doors were open and there was the chaos of a removal. "Action Group Egg. Headquarters of the revolution in Drenthe. Moving tomorrow or the day after to Assen, in order to bring the province to a state of proletarian readiness."

The baron did not give the impression of being sad about the departure of this tenant. The man who had just leered at them was sitting with a woman and a number of friends on the floor of the balcony room, where they were drinking tea from flowered mugs. He was about thirty, had long hair; stuck in his teeth was a thin cigar, which he didn't take out of his mouth when he spoke.

"Well, comrade," said Gevers. "Having a rest?"

The man gave a brief nod, with a brief smile, but did not get up. That Gevers was a baron was obviously not a neutral fact in this company; except that it didn't add to his stature, like everywhere else, but detracted from it. Rather scornful but not unfriendly, the social worker looked at Max's blazer and club tie.

"Are you moving in here?" And after Max had made a vague gesture toward Gevers: "Congratulations. You'll never find anything like this again. Have a look around if you like." When Max met the eyes of the woman, he saw hate in her eyes—but because this would now become his apartment, perhaps. Of course she didn't want to go to Assen at all.

In the balcony room, which faced south, the ceiling was painted light blue, with white clouds in it; that would all have to be redecorated. A dividing door gave access to a large room next door, which was linked by a run-down pantry with a tower room at the back. That seemed to him to be the nursery; and because Sophia had to sleep near Quinten, but also near him, it looked as though he would be laying claim to the balcony room. On the other side, the latter room gave access to a spacious kitchen-dining room, which looked out over the forecourt; there was another large room adjoining it, which must be above the front door.

There were open shutters next to all the windows. He looked around excitedly. There was ample room for three people to live here. Everywhere was full of rubbish. Shelves had been fixed to the walls, loaded with folders, piles of newspapers and magazines, stencil machines on trestles—but his eyes overlooked all that and saw how it would be.

"Well?" asked Gevers as they stood on the balcony—which was itself as large as a room—looking out over the awesome trees on the other side of the moat. "Don't expect it's your cup of tea."

Max made a gesture of speechlessness. "A gift from heaven," he said.

35

The Move

After the apartment had been cleared two days later, Max proudly showed Sophia what a marvelous place he had secured, and she too could scarcely believe it. They spent as much as possible of the time that Quinten had to stay in the incubator on doing up the rooms, which the previous tenants had left in a sorry state. For the first few nights they slept in Dwingeloo, in different rooms in the guest suite; but in anticipation of the move, he then took some essential things of his and Sophia's to the castle in a rented van: mattresses, bedding, clothes, kitchen utensils, books. She did not get into bed with him in Dwingeloo, which was perhaps connected not only with the other guests, but also with her daughter, who had spent her last conscious night there, if one can put it like that.

Perhaps the silence was also an obstacle. The first few times that he himself had spent the night in Dwingeloo, as a city dweller he had scarcely been able to get to sleep: the silence was so deep and complete that it was as though he had gone deaf. The only thing that could be heard was his own heartbeat and the rushing of blood in his ears; outside the room the world had disappeared into nothingness. Only later had it sunk in that it was the silence of the war: then it had been as quiet at night in Amsterdam as on the heath. But the very first night in Groot Rechteren, where only the distant call of an owl occasionally broke the silence, the secret ritual was resumed. With heart pounding he had lain waiting for her in the balcony room, and when he heard her coming from the temporary mattress in the room next to his, followed by the creaking of the door handle and the squeaking of the door—it would all have to be greased—his relief was if anything greater than his excitement. Imagine if for her all this had belonged solely to Leiden and her late husband!

It was the first time that they had been in each other's company on a daily basis and formed a household, but that meant no change: he continued to call her Mrs. Brons, and unlike what happened between people who were having an affair, there were no marital tiffs between someone and his friend's mother-in-law. Awakened in the morning by the ducks, they breakfasted on the balcony, and he devoted all the time that he could spare to taking down the shelves in the front room, removing the plywood boards that were supposed to give the old handmade doors a modern look in the 1950s, and on painting, varnishing, and emulsifying.

Gradually, he was seized by a kind of frenzy, which made it almost impossible for him to stop in the evenings. Long after Sophia had sat down in front of the television with a glass of wine and was sewing curtains, he was still up a ladder moving his roller over the playful cloud formations on the ceiling. He had never done anything like this—his girlfriends had always looked after that for him—and the immediately visible result had a relaxing effect on him; what's more, he thought of his work now and then while he was doing it, but in a different way than at his desk: more indirectly, in a certain sense more fruitfully, just as he always had his best ideas when he was cleaning his teeth or his shoes, or under the shower. Actually, there was no shower—he had one put in. Because the castle was not connected to the gas network, a new heater had to be put in that used bottles of butane gas; the decrepit oil stoves also needed replacing.

When he needed fresh paint or brushes or planks, he drove in his dirty clothes to the shop in the village of Westerbork, six miles south of the new observatory and with only its name in common with the camp. He had still not been to the latter; until the mirrors were completed, there was nothing for him to do there, and he had resolved to put it off for as long as possible.

In their first few days there they had paid courtesy visits to the other occupants of the castle. Mr. Spier, the husband of Mrs. Spier, was on the point of leaving when they knocked. He was as small as she was, and as painfully correct with his carefully cut, thin dark-blond hair, in his three-piece dark-blue pin-striped suit, with a decoration in his buttonhole and a pearl pin in his tie: a little off-center, as was proper. He said politely that they were bound to meet each other frequently, after which Max immediately invited them for a glass of champagne in a few weeks' time. Mr. Verloren van The-maat, who taught the history of architecture at the Polytechnic in Delft and lived in the other wing on the ground floor, was in the habit of coming only on the weekends; at the moment he was spending the summer in Rome, in the Netherlands Art Historical Institute.

In the southern half of the loft—in a series of what were formerly servants' rooms on the northern side, where superfluous furniture of the baron's was stored—lived an English translator, that is, a translator from English: Marius Proctor, a man of nearly forty, with black hair and a rather somber expression. His wife, Clara, a provocative, cheerful person with hair dyed red and large earrings, looked like a fortune-teller; she made ghostly abstract objects from old umbrellas, which hung on the sloping walls of their rooms. Whenever she invited Max and Sophia for afternoon tea, sit-ting on their modern 1950s chairs, Proctor usually disappeared without a word through the thick padded door into what was obviously his study: the tower room above the one in which a crib and a commode were waiting for Quinten.

He earned his living by translating novels, but his real work at the mo-ment was a translation of Milton's *Paradise Lost*; apart from that, Clara said that for years he had been writing a book on a discovery he had made, which would create a stir in the literary-historical world. In any case he had the sunken cheeks and temples of the fanatic who was gnawing at himself. They had an aggressive son of about four, called Arendje, who whenever he saw Max ran straight at him and began pushing against his thighs with both hands, as though he wanted to get him out of the room, out of the castle, with his head bent malevolently forward, like a billy goat; amused words and gentle force had no effect, and when Clara finally pulled him away, Arendje tried to give him a kick in the shins. Max was not inclined to go upstairs too often. Once he tried to start up a conversation on literature, but Proctor only answered with a few vague remarks and for the rest maintained his sphinxlike silence. Sophia disliked him, but Max said that he had obviously been crushed by some insight or other, or perhaps by Clara.

They got along best with Theo Kern and his wife, on their own floor. Going to their apartment meant leaving this world and entering another. The arrangement of the rooms was the mirror image of their own, but that was the only similarity. At first sight the confusion reminded Max of that at

Onno's, but at a second glance it became clear to him that it was more the opposite, but in a different way to the calculated order in his own place.

It was orderly disorder, or disorderly order—it was a third possibility: an artistic, unplanned arrangement of countless things, which had obviously landed somewhere by chance, casually put down, forgotten, like at Onno's, but which here formed an incomprehensible, harmonious creation, just as a swarm of birds at a certain moment took on a perfect shape that had not been composed by anyone. For that matter there were birds, too. Spread through the rooms were three cages, each containing three creamy white doves; some of the cage doors were open, with the crested creatures cooing and bowing on the top.

Stands with clay models on them, tables with drawings and plants; on the mantelpieces, on the tables, and on the ground there were wire sculptures, prints, pinecones, branches in vases, stones, statuettes, tree trunks, shelves. There was no distinction between bedrooms, living room, and kitchen; one suddenly came upon the Kerns' white four-poster bed, the varnished wooden bed of their daughter, who was in a summer camp at the moment, somewhere a draining board, a fridge, an oven—everything absorbed into the whole—clear, blond, weightless, as translucent as paper.

And in the midst of all this stood the artist: small, thick-set, jovial, always barefoot, his head surrounded from crown to chin by a huge halo of graying hair, like a dandelion after its petals had fallen. Whenever Max saw him he was reminded of a gnome on a toadstool; but his heavily built wife, Selma, who in her full, long dresses that reached to the ground looked as though she were eternally pregnant, who seldom laughed and sometimes looked at her husband as though he were mad, made one suspect that there were something entirely different in the sculptor—because in Max's view the hidden side of a man was visible as his wife, just as the hidden side of a woman was visible as her husband. But it seemed more sensible to him not to mention that view to Sophia.

Mother Earth was his usual name for Selma. She had long, loose dark-blond hair and a withdrawn look; Sophia got on very well with her. Like the Proctors, they seemed to have a slight problem with the constellation of Max and Sophia and the child that was about to appear; but they got used to it. Kern occasionally came and looked at Max's efforts, helped now and then and lent him tools—his electric drill, his stapler. They ate with them a few times: large, tasty dishes with a South American feel, so that they were spared the greasy schnitzels in the country restaurant.

*

Onno had not yet appeared at the castle. Whenever Max had dropped Sophia off at the Wilhelmina Hospital—where she went to visit her daughter and grandson—they arranged to meet somewhere in town, once even in the canteen of the party headquarters, which was around the corner from Max; spiritually he himself was no longer living in his half-dismantled flat. But their conversations were only about practical things and never lasted longer than half an hour. With a few friends, Onno had been elected to the party executive on behalf of the club of rebels by a party conference; as a reaction, a right-wing schism was approaching, which according to Onno every Social Democratic party in Europe envied them for, because in left-wing circles only left-wing schisms were the tradition, which meant that those parties were becoming more and more right-wing.

Because of all this, he was busier than ever; sometimes, to his own alarm he realized in bed at night that he hadn't thought of Quinten and Ada for the whole day. Meanwhile his second cousin, the real estate agent, had sold Sophia's place for a reasonable price for conversion into a snack bar, the stock of "In Praise of Folly" had been taken off her hands by colleagues, superfluous effects had been collected by an auction house, Brons's wardrobe by the Salvation Army. Once the moving was complete and they had furnished the rooms at Groot Rechteren, Max and Sophia drove to Amsterdam one warm July morning, where Onno was waiting for them at the hospital.

The staff were very reluctant to part with Quinten. He had been laid in bed next to Ada—as he had been for the last few days, since he no longer needed to be in the incubator. They looked in shock at the angelic child, with his wide blue eyes, next to Ada's motionless, almost marble face with its closed eyelids. The tidal wave under the sheets had broken, and Max felt the sight sinking deep into himself, as something that would never disappear from his memory. The moment a nurse pulled the sheet aside and picked up Quinten, everyone here realized that something irrevocable was happening, like a second birth, a second farewell. Ada, too, was shortly to leave the hospital; they were looking for a nursing home near the castle.

"May I have him?" asked the nurse with Quinten in her arms. "I've never known such a marvelous child. Do you know that he hasn't cried once since his birth? How much do you want for him?"

In the car Sophia sat in the backseat, with Quinten next to her in a travel bassinet. Little was said. Like Max, Onno was thinking of their fateful journey in February, of which this journey was in some senses the pendant, but neither of them mentioned it.

When Onno got out on the forecourt of Groot Rechteren, he looked around him, puffed out his chest, and said: "Right! This is a suitable environment for my worthy son! It's true that nature of itself is cretinous, and feudalism is completely out of keeping with the character of a simple man of the people like me, who as a Socialist through and through thinks only of the welfare of the low-paid, but in this special case the party executive will overlook it."

When Sophia took the travel bassinet carefully out of the car and was about to take it inside, he said, "No, Mother, I'll do that. That is my privilege." He put the handles of the bassinet over his arm like a shopping bag, raised one hand, and as he mounted the terrace began reciting solemnly: *"In nomine patris, et filii, et spiritus sancti!"*

In the tower room Sophia laid Quinten on the chest of drawers to change his diaper, and Max showed Onno the apartment. In Sophia's living room-cum-bedroom he recognized the corduroy sofa and the low table, but here, with a view of the moat and the wood, everything had taken on a completely new look. The portrait of Multatuli had obviously been given to the house clearer. When he saw all this, he wondered what had really possessed Max, but the time to raise the subject had now passed.

Mixed with other things of Sophia's, Max's belongings were mostly in the larger room at the front: the green chesterfield armchair; the grand piano; his books. On his desk again was the row of small instruments, transformed into symbols through their combination and precise arrangement. Although he knew all those things, they too had changed character here. Onno asked whether the rent wasn't astronomical, but Max said that it was scarcely half what he had paid in Amsterdam.

Onno stood at the mantelpiece, on which were the books in the "shelf of honor." Kafka had disappeared from the row, and in its place he now saw a copy of Turgenev's *Fathers and Sons*. There was also a photo of Ada and him, taken last year by Bruno in Havana. Next to it a second, framed old photograph. He had seen at once that they were Max's parents. Without saying anything he looked at Max.

Max nodded. "Risen from limbo," he said.

"Where has that suddenly appeared from?"

Max told him about the visit to his foster mother, without going into the circumstances.

Onno bent forward and studied the couple. "You've got the top half of your face from your father and the bottom half from your mother."

"Do you remember that you said something like that about my face before—the day we met?"

"No," said Onno, "but I'm sure I hit the nail on the head."

"Of course."

"Are you coming?" called Sophia.

She was sitting under a sun shade on the balcony over which Max had spread two bags of fresh gravel, giving Quinten a bottle. Both Max and Onno were struck by the unity that she formed with the child, as though she were really the mother. Both fathers saw a completely happy woman, who seemed never to have had a daughter.

Kern and his Selma also appeared.

"Max has already told me about you," said Onno, after he had introduced himself with a click of his heels, perhaps as a commentary on Kern's bare feet.

Kern gave the impression that he had not heard. With one hand, covered in clay and stone dust, he gestured toward Quinten, who, as he lay on Sophia's lap drinking, fastened the deep-blue pools of his eyes on the orange stripes of the sun shade.

"Whoever saw such a creature? This is completely impossible!"

"You've either got the gift or you haven't," said Onno proudly. "There are artists who create beauty in a dogged struggle with spirit and matter, like you, but I do it in a lascivious moment with flesh." As he spoke these words he suddenly felt a chill go through him, as though Ada's presence on the balcony were suddenly penetrating his body.

Perhaps because he could not bear Quinten's gaze, Kern had left shortly afterward. In a cooler covered in condensation stood a bottle of champagne, and after Max, with ballistic satisfaction, had made the cork prescribe its parabola into the moat—where the ducks made a beeline for it, flapping and half running over the water, before ducking and waggling their tails and turning their attention to more serious things—the Proctor family appeared. Clara behaved like a woman behaves when she sees a baby for the first time; but when the gloomy translator saw Quinten, something in his face changed: it lightened as if a veil had been removed. The effect of the child on Arendje was even more strange. As Max poured the glasses, he kept a wary eye on the little rascal, who ran to Sophia—in order to be able to intervene at once in case he tried to plant his fist on Quinten's nose.

Instead of that, he hugged him, kissed him on the forehead, and said: "Doesn't he smell nice."

Little Arendje tamed! Proctor looked back and forth between Quinten and Onno—and then said something that made Max's heart leap:

"He looks like you. He's got your mouth."

He couldn't have given Max a greater present. And yes, perhaps that was the case: perhaps he did have the same thin, classically arched lips. It was as though the last remnants of his doubt were washed away by those words like the dirty scum by a jet of water after one had washed one's hands.

After sufficient chairs had been pulled up, the company split into two by sex, with Quinten in the middle of the women. While the latter group swapped experiences with infant care, Onno told Proctor that his wife had been a cellist. He assumed that Max had told him about the accident and said:

"I was first going to call my son Octave in honor of her: after the simplest, completely consonant interval, on which all music is based. Have you already plumbed the Pythagorean mysteries of that simple one-to-two relationship?"

Max had told Onno about Proctor's withdrawn nature, and he could see that Onno was trying to find a way to get through to him.

Proctor made a vague gesture. "I know nothing about music."

"Who does? Music transcends all knowledge. But when I hear the name Octave in my mind's eye, I see a type that I wouldn't want to see as my son. More an elegant, rather effete philosopher on stiltlike heron's legs with a flower in his buttonhole and not the robust man of action that my son must become, as I am myself so signally according to everyone. So I moved from the completely elemental to the cunning two-to-three of the dominant. The pure fifth!"

That was new for Max, too.

Meanwhile, Proctor's brain had also been working, because he said: "The octave consists of eight, and God is also eight."

It took a couple of seconds to get through to Onno. "God is eight? How did you work that out?"

"You know a bit about languages, don't you?"

A bitter laugh escaped Onno. "To tell you the truth I don't really know anyone who knows as much about languages as I do. That's the reason why I couldn't call my son Sixtus. Not because that's a pitiful interval of three-to-five, but because the name derives not from *sextus,* the Latin word for 'sixth,' as everyone thinks, but from the Greek word *xystos,* which means 'polished.' "

"So you also know what the tetragrammaton is?"

"Please continue, sir."

Next Proctor reminded them that God's name *Yod He, Wau, He* was Jehovah. Because Hebrew, as Mr. Quist of course already knew, had no separate figures, those four letters also had the numerical value 10, 5, 6, and 5. Adding them together gave 26. If, following the rules of Gematria, you added the 2 and the 6 together, you got 8.

"You stagger me!" exclaimed Onno. "You are a gifted cabbalist! But if God is eight, what is five?"

"Of course it can be an infinite number—" Proctor began, but the last word was lost in a rattling cough that suddenly took hold of him.

"Not infinite," Max corrected him. "Very great. Although ... perhaps an infinite number, yes."

"And what is significant in this connection," continued Proctor after taking a deep breath and wiping his mouth, "is the number of letters in the alphabet."

"Of course." Onno nodded with an irony, which only Max noticed. "Twenty-two."

"In Hebrew, yes. But our alphabet has twenty-six." He looked at Onno with an expression that said he had unveiled the final secret.

"Ah-ha!" said Onno with raised eyebrows, and lifted an index finger. "Ah-ha! The same number as the numerical value of God! Dutch as a divine language! By the way, Mr. Proctor, you mustn't say 'Jehovah,' but 'Jahweh,' with the accent on the *e.* 'Jehovah' is a bastardized Christian word from the late Middle Ages. It's even more sensible not to speak the name at all, because otherwise you might come to a sticky end. It would be better to say 'Adonai,' with the letters *alef, daleth, nun, jod.* At least if that has an acceptable numerical value, but it's almost bound to have."

"One plus four plus fifty plus ten," said Proctor immediately, "makes sixty-five."

"Makes eleven, makes two." Onno nodded. "Seems fine to me."

While Arendje counted Quinten's toes when he heard all those numbers and cried "Ten!" Kern appeared on the balcony again, now accompanied by Mr. and Mrs. Spier.

With a friendliness that did not reveal whether it was pretended or real, they fulfilled their social duties.

"What a darling," said Mrs. Spier.

Mr. Spier looked intently at Quinten, stroked the soft spot on his fontanel with the tip of his ring finger, and then said, as though one could see by looking at him: "His initials are Q. Q."

"Qualitate qua," nodded Onno.

"That is rare. The *Q* is the most mysterious of letters, that circle with that line," he said, while he formed a slightly obscene gesture a circle with the manicured thumb and index finger of one hand and the line with the index finger of the other, "the ovum being penetrated by a sperm. And twice at that. Very nice. My compliments."

Like Proctor, he was obviously aware that Onno had a relationship with written characters. Max felt a little shiver go down his spine at his words, but Onno made a clumsy and at the same time elegant bow. Spier too gave a slight bow and took out a silver watch from his waistcoat pocket. Unfortunately they had to leave immediately—the taxi was already waiting for them on the forecourt to take them to the station: they were going on holiday to Wales, to Pontrhydfendigaid, as they did every year.

Kern had meanwhile sat down astride an upright chair and against the back of the seat in front of him had placed a thick piece of cardboard to which a sheet of paper was fastened with a clip. Without taking his eyes off Sophia and the child on her lap, he made large sketching movements, gliding over the paper with just the side of his hand. In his fingers he had a stick of charcoal, but it was not yet given permission to leave a trace. He was obviously waiting for an order from the world of the good, beautiful, and true, telling him that the moment of irrevocability had come.

36

The Monument

A man who was free, Max reflected one afternoon in autumn as he looked at the yellowing trees from his balcony, could not imagine that he could ever be imprisoned, just as a prisoner could never really imagine freedom. The slowness of the masses found its pendant in the slowness of spirit: anything that was not the case at a particular moment had the character of a dream. The result was that history was to be found in books but scarcely anywhere outside them—and what were books? Little things, seldom larger than a brick, but lighter, and almost irretrievable amid the myriads of other things that covered the surface of the earth, and on their way to becoming more and more insignificant in the electronic world, which was rising faster and faster out of abstraction.

Everything was progressing, and everything that had happened could just as well not have happened. Dreams were remembered for a few minutes after waking up—and a little later they had been forgotten. Where was the battle of Verdun now, except in barely traceable and in any case unread books, and in the memory of a handful of old men, who in twenty years time would also be dead and buried, with nightmares and scars and all? Where was the battle of Stalingrad? The bombing of Dresden? Hiroshima? Auschwitz?

In the winter of 1968, six months after they moved into Groot

Rechteren, Max went to Westerbork camp for the first time. All twelve mirrors were now ready, as were the computer programs; a start had been made with experimental observations. His arrival was not really necessary, but in Leiden—where he still had to go regularly—even the director had already asked him in surprise whether he hadn't been to take a look at his new workplace yet. It finally happened on the day that he showed Sophia the observatory at Dwingeloo. During the furnishing of Groot Rechteren she had spent the night there a few times, but she hadn't viewed the observatory on those occasions; technical things didn't interest her. One bright, cold morning he persuaded her to wrap Quinten up warmly and come with him. Why he wanted her to, he didn't know himself. While he showed her the buildings and the mirrors, he thought constantly of that day with Ada and Onno, now nine months ago; but he did not refer to it, and she didn't ask about it. Not much had changed since then—except that there were now unused electric typewriters all over the floor with the cables wound around them, while computer screens had appeared on the desks.

Quinten sat earnestly on Sophia's arm during the tour, and to everyone's delight he looked around with his blue eyes like a personage that was not displeased with the course of events. He was now seven months and had never yet cried, but had never yet laughed either—in fact had scarcely uttered a sound. Sophia was sometimes worried that he had suffered damage in the accident, but the doctor said that he was obviously an extraordinary child; there were no indications apart from that, that he was not normal.

During the coffee break, while all the staff gathered in the hall of the main building around the trolley with the shiny urn, Max talked to an electronics engineer who was responsible for the wiring of the synthetic radio telescope; soon he would have to go Westerbork on the shuttle bus, because there had been new teething troubles. He spoke with such a soft, modest voice that Max could scarcely hear him in the hubbub. On an impulse he offered to take him there in his own car, seeing that he had to go there himself. He had suddenly said it: this was the moment, with Quinten and Sophia. Over the months, during the long evenings at the castle, he had told Sophia more about his life than he had ever told her daughter—possibly because their formal relationship somehow made it easier for him than an intimate one.

Three quarters of an hour later they were driving along the provincial road. Sophia, who was in the backseat with the child, perhaps suspected that the accident had happened somewhere here; but when they passed the spot Max only glanced at it quickly out of the corner of his eye. The open space where the trees had been was now filled with two young alders, supported by wooden poles, to which they were attached by strips of black rubber, obviously cut from car tires, in the form of a figure eight. They did not speak. The engineer leafed through a folder of papers on his lap, Quinten had fallen asleep, and suddenly Max was reminded of his walk through the clammy Polish heat, from Auschwitz I to Auschwitz II—as though that were a counterpart of the route from Dwingeloo to Westerbork. A feeling of nausea seized him, which not only issued from that memory but mainly from what lay behind it. He did not think of it for weeks or months, but it always suddenly reappeared in an unchanged state, without the decay to which even radioactive material was subject.

"You have to turn right here," said the engineer when they were at the village of Hooghalen.

"Sorry, it's the first time I've been here."

"You can't be serious."

"But it's true."

"Are you really interested in astronomy?"

"Maybe not."

He saw a sign pointing to a neighboring village of Amen—as though the whole area had been prepared for centuries for what would one day happen there—and suddenly there was a sign to the Schattenberg estate. He drove down a woodland path, flanked on the right by rusty train rails. Now and then they passed Ambonese in traditional ankle-length Indonesian dress, supplemented for the Dutch winter with woollen scarves and woolly hats; sometimes whole families, whose members walked not alongside each other but one behind the other, with the father at the head, and the youngest child at the back. A moment later Max realized with a shock what the rails along the road were: laid by the Germans and ending at Birkenau.

He stopped at a barrier in the barbed-wire fence, got out, and looked at the camp with bated breath. From the plans and blueprints, which he had looked at repeatedly in Leiden and Dwingeloo, he knew that it was a trapezoid approximately a third of a mile long and a third of a mile wide.

What he saw was a large forest-framed space, the freezing air filled with minute icicles that gleamed in the sunlight; there were rows of dilapidated huts, set carefully at right angles like in Birkenau, as if they were still on the drawing-board—an inhuman pattern that seemed to have served as a model for postwar housing developments. Smoke still rose from some chimneys, but most of the huts were obviously no longer occupied; a few had burned down, and here and there huts had disappeared. Children were playing; somewhere someone was cycling along who undoubtedly would have a great deal to say about what went on in Indonesia during the Japanese occupation but knew nothing of what had taken place here.

Straight in front of him the rails continued to the other end of the camp—and parallel with them, farther to the right like . . . yes, like what?—like a vision, a mirage, a dream over a distance of a mile, the procession of huge dish aerials, entering the camp on one side and leaving it on the other. His eyes grew moist. Here, in this asshole of the Netherlands, they entreated the blessing of heaven like sacrificial altars in the total silence. At the same moment he felt the pressure that had weighed on him for the past few years lifting: the pressure of having to work in this accursed spot. Suddenly he could think of no place on earth where he would rather work than here. Wasn't everything that he was gathered together here, as in the focal point of a lens?

Without looking at Sophia, he got back in the car and drove slowly to the new low-rise service building, suddenly unable to stop talking. Agitatedly, occasionally half turning around, he told them that the camp had been set up by the Dutch government in 1939 for German Jewish refugees—the first Jewish camp outside Germany—but that the cost had been recovered from the Jewish community in the Netherlands. So that when the Germans arrived, they had the refugees neatly collected in one place. Subsequently, over a hundred thousand Dutch Jews were transported to Poland from this place—proportionately more even than from Germany itself. After the war Dutch fascists, of which Drenthe was full, were imprisoned in it. For a while it was a military camp, then Dutch citizens expelled from Indonesia were accommodated in it, and finally the Moluccans, who were now, reluctantly and with regular police intervention, being forced into more or less normal housing developments. In order to prevent their return to the camp, everything was deliberately being allowed to fall into disrepair. By establishing the observatory here, the government hoped that the name Westerbork would lose its unpleasant connotations.

When he had once said this to Onno, Onno had said that his eldest brother, the provincial governor of Drenthe, was bound to be behind it.

"Imagine the Poles setting up a conservatory in Auschwitz so that the name Auschwitz would sound less unpleasant! It would be hilarious if it were not so sad. You sometimes wonder if people really know the sort of world they're living in. Did you know, for example," he asked the engineer, "that Westerbork council sold a lot of those huts to neighboring farmers and sports clubs? All over Drenthe young soccer players are getting changed in those huts that once inspired terror. Business is business! But the things are Jewish property, and I've not read anywhere that the proceeds were transferred to the Jewish community. They are still being ripped off!"

He banged his steering wheel excitedly, and the engineer turned and exchanged a short glance with Sophia.

In the control building, on the other side of the line of telescopes, it was warm and there was the smell of fresh coffee. Smiling with surprise, the director of the installation, a technical engineer who had once worked for an oil company, appeared.

"We thought we'd never see an astronomer here." His dark-brown eyes met those of Quinten. "Well, well, the daughter of the house has come too!"

It took a while for Max to explain that Quinten Quist wasn't a daughter but a son, and not his but his friend's, and that Sophia Brons was not his wife or the mother of the child but the grandmother.

The director made a gesture indicating that it made no difference to him, and led them into the computer area. Sophia took off Quinten's coat and cap and handed him a little doll, which he haughtily ignored. Max shook hands with the technicians, who were sitting around at the monitors and whom he knew from Dwingeloo. He was shown his office and went with the director to the reception area, humming and groaning with the ventilators, isolated in a Faraday cage. When they returned to the central terminal, he stood for a while at the large semicircular window with a view of the mirrors and the huts.

When he remembered Sophia's presence, he turned around, pointed to the telescopes, and asked: "Do you know how they work?"

"I won't understand anyway."

"It's dead simple."

The row of reflectors, he explained, was aligned precisely from west to east, a hundred and forty-five yards apart, exact to within a fraction of an inch. Beyond that, however, it was a true straight line: over the distance of a mile the curvature of the earth had also been compensated for. Just imagine! And that accuracy was necessary, because the twelve mirrors had to be seen as one gigantic circular telescope with a diameter of a mile, the largest in the world. The idea was that because of the rotation of the earth, seen from space, the row of mirrors after a quarter of a day would be at right angles to its original position and after half a day in the reverse position; so by observing a radio source for half a day, you could achieve the synthesis that you wanted.

"Surely a child can understand that."

"I can hear everything you say, but it doesn't mean anything to me," said Sophia, while she held Quinten's wobbling head and wiped his mouth.

Max took a radio map off a desk and asked the technician: "What's this?"

He looked at it absentmindedly. "M 51."

"Here," said Max, and held it in front of Sophia. "This is what it looks like. The whirlpool nebula in the constellation of Canes Venatici. Thirteen million years ago."

But it was Quinten who took the paper in both hands and subjected the pointed mountains of waving lines of intensity to a close inspection.

"I'm curious to know what he's going to tell us," said the director with raised eyebrows.

When Quinten had given back the sheet, without crumpling it up or rubbing it on the ground in an uncoordinated way, Sophia put her arms around him and cuddled him and said: "What a strange child you are. You're just like your father."

The way in which she had behaved with Quinten from the first showed a completely different side of her nature, which had amazed Onno during his sporadic visits, but which Max recognized from the way she behaved with him at night—but then without saying a word. Quinten didn't like the hug and freed himself from it with dignity.

Max watched and, lost in thought, said: "I'm going outside for a while."

He put on only a scarf, stuck his hands in his pockets, and wandered onto the site. The air was still full of magically floating, glowing splinters. He needed to be alone for a few minutes, so that he could allow the change that he had just undergone to penetrate through him. There was a vague smell of Indonesian food; in an arid garden behind a hut a boy was repairing a bike. He remembered from the plans that a line of hospital huts had been demolished to make way for the mirrors. The camp was already no longer what it had been during the war, but even if everything were to disappear, it would still be the spot for all eternity. The house by the barrier, where he had just gotten out, had been the house of the camp commandant. It was still occupied; there were curtains and plants on the windowsill. Across the road along the railway line, which was once called Boulevard des Misères, he walked in an easterly direction. When he had told Sophia just now about the exact west-to-east alignment of the instruments, his father's Polish triangle of Bielsko-Katowice-Krakow triangle with the same angles occurred to him, which also pointed directly eastward, with Auschwitz at its center. None of it meant anything, but that was how it was. And now he suddenly saw the map of Drenthe in front of him: an isosceles triangle with Westerbork camp at its center.

Here, on this road, perhaps on the spot where he was now walking, his mother had gotten into a cattle truck under the watchful eye of the camp commandant, after which the door was slid shut and the bolt fastened. Here her last journey had begun. He tried to reconcile that awareness with what he could see; but although the event had taken place on this spot, the two things remained as different from each other as a thought and a stone. The road was deserted, but the rails were empty, it smelled not of Jewish cooking but of *nasi goreng*. It was time, he thought, that tore everything to shreds. He looked around: the silent, majestic entry of the mirrors into the camp. From somewhere came the hammering of a woodpecker. He was sure of it—he belonged here; here was where he must spend his life.

He walked on, to the other end of the camp, where the rails ended in a decayed bumper. He crouched down and put his hand on the rusty iron, stood up and looked again at the row of antennas, all pointing to the same point in the sky. And suddenly he thought of the yellow star that his mother had had to wear on her left breast during the war. A star! Stars! All those tens of thousands here had worn stars; they had been forced into the wagons with stars on their chests, on their way from the small trapezoid to the great square. He remembered from the papers discussions on the question of whether there should be a monument to the deported in Westerbork. The survivors had been against it; everything should now be forgotten. But it was there anyway! What was the synthetic radio telescope finally but a monument, a mile in diameter, to the dead!

37

Expeditions

While life continued in Groot Rechteren and Dwingeloo in rural and astronomical calm, in Amsterdam Onno had embarked upon a lightning political career. Sometimes he had the feeling that the way in which it was happening was not connected solely with his qualities but also with the fate that had befallen him: as though all his political friends felt that he deserved it after his wife's accident—or in any case that they could not decently obstruct him too forcefully. At the beginning of 1969 he had been elected to the city council, and shortly afterward he became alderman for education, arts, and sciences.

"During my period of office," he had whispered to the mayor after his appointment, at a dinner in the official residence, "education will be principally geared to producing spineless yes-men. With Plato in mind, I will put poets mercilessly to the sword, and I shall bring science completely into line and put it in the service of my personal ambitions. I shall make myself hated like no previous Amsterdam alderman. While your statue is decorated daily with fresh flowers, my name will be spoken even centuries afterward only with the deepest revulsion."

Whereupon the gray-haired mayor had taken his hand from his ear and said: "Yes, yes, Onno, take it easy."

Everyone was worried that he would harm the party with his big mouth, but things went surprisingly well: he had found his bearings in a few weeks, and in the council chamber he took a completely different tone—namely, the measured tone that he knew was the only effective one in Holland. A new life had begun for him. University administrators who refused to see him had to cool their heels in his waiting room; the chairman of the arts council was summoned; in The Hague he argued for Amsterdam interests at the ministry, he lobbied his party colleagues in the Lower House of Parliament, he made decisions, mediated, intervened, dismissed, appointed, joined battle with the students. Suddenly he had power, a secretary, civil servants who danced to his tune and a car with a driver, who took him from the town hall to the Kerkstraat in the evenings.

But there was no one there any longer. When he had closed the door behind him, he was greeted by a silence that seemed to emanate from two boxes: Ada's cello case in his study and the Chinese camphor chest in his bedroom, in which he had stored her clothes. But the thought of her and of Quinten was quickly buried under the dossiers that emerged from his outsize briefcase—partly because he knew that Quinten lacked for nothing and Ada was being well looked after in a nursing home in Emmen, although he had not been there more than twice. Measured by his interest in the cryptic signs on a certain plate in the museum of Heraklion, his interest in the content of those dossiers was minimal—after all he could just as well be in charge of a different portfolio. But he had resigned himself to the fact that his life was evidently to be determined by brilliant beginnings, which were suddenly frustrated—in his family life just as in linguistics.

He knew people for whom being an alderman in Amsterdam would be the pinnacle of their life's achievement. He himself was happy with it because it at least gave him something to do. He had decided to make the best of things. He had abandoned the illusion that he could change Holland or even Amsterdam after just a few months—and if he were honest with himself, he didn't really think it was necessary. Where in the world were things better than in Holland? In Switzerland, perhaps—but that was more corrupt and, worse still, more boring. If he could grasp the light-hearted changes that had been brought about in the second half of the 1960s from below and stabilize them, he would be satisfied; but now, as the 1970s approached, he saw imagination being drowned in a morass of constant, embittered meetings, which seemed to be out to achieve something like a merciless, totalitarian democracy. No one did anything anymore; everyone simply talked about the way something ought to be done, if anyone did it. He had once talked in an interview about "the self-abusive reflection," which had caused softening of the brain and weakening of the bone marrow in students.

His front door was daubed with red paint and in the middle of the night he received a threatening phone call: "We'll get you one day, you bastard!"

But before he was able to say, "Is that you, Bork?" the caller hung up.

Since the accident he had lived in celibacy. Not that he forced himself, but because it did not occur to him to take up with a woman. There would be no trouble: he had soon discovered that power had an erotic effect; and if anyone wanted to get into his bad books forever, then they should ask him why he didn't get divorced, which would be a legal formality.

The fact that his rooms were tidied up every morning by a municipal housekeeper, who also made up his bed and did his laundry while he himself was at the town hall, was of course connected with this. That had been organized by Mrs. Siliakus, his secretary, without whom nothing would have gone right, either with his work or with his life: she supplemented exactly what was missing in him. "Together we make a human being," he was once to say. But Mrs. Siliakus was already in her fifties and for twenty years had shared a flat with a lady of her own age. "If you didn't have such an offensively unnatural nature," he confessed to her in an intimate moment, "but were as utterly normal as me, then I'd know what to do."

Until, one Sunday evening in July, Max had called him on his new, unlisted telephone number and had asked if he knew that that evening the first man was to set foot on the moon.

"Of course you'll be watching? It's all on television."

"What time, then?"

"At about four."

"To tell you the truth I wasn't intending to. The moon? You must be crazy. It plays absolutely no part in municipal politics. Tomorrow morning at half past nine I've got to address the chancellor of the University of Leningrad, in Russian. I'm working at it now."

"You absolutely must watch. The fantastic thing is not that it's happening, because Jules Verne predicted that, and Cyrano de Bergerac, and Kepler as well in fact—"

"And what would you say to Plutarch? And Lucian? And Cicero? *Somnium Scipionis!* Of course you've never heard of them. That takes us before Christ. Don't get any ideas."

"Let me finish for goodness' sake! What I'm trying to say is that one thing never occurred to anyone: that everyone in the world will be witnesses when a man steps onto the moon, without even getting out of their armchairs—even though the moon is not visible in the sky to them at that moment. That's the really inconceivable thing. If anyone had predicted that, he'd have been branded as a madman."

"Will you always be twelve years old? If I understand you correctly then I have to watch because it's something that can't really be seen: an idea. For you everything is always different. You yourself, indeed, are more or less looking at the Big Bang there on the heath. But okay, I'll listen to you again, although I have the feeling that it won't do me much good. Tell me, how is Quinten Quist getting on? Has he said anything yet?"

"No idea, I can't understand it anyway. You would probably have to know what language he's babbling in. It may be the same one that you were looking for before."

"Yes, just you go on opening old wounds, born sadist that you are. Perhaps I shall have to resign myself to being the father of an illiterate. It always happens: Goethe's son was thick as a brick, too. Great men always have imbeciles for sons—which of course implicitly proves that my father wasn't a great man. Anyway, perhaps we should be glad that his lordship is at least prepared to crawl."

"We sometimes have the impression that he understands things."

"Let's hope so. How is my esteemed mother-in-law faring?"

"Fine. Come and see us soon."

Onno replaced the receiver, but held on to it and sighed. Since Quinten's first birthday, two months ago, he hadn't been back in Drenthe; so many Quists with their retinue had appeared, and fellow tenants of the castle, and even the mother of his mother-in-law, that he had scarcely had an opportunity to spend any time with Quinten. He had had to spend that thirtieth of May mainly massaging his family, who had seen for the first time how a Quist was being brought up by his grandmother and his father's friend.

With his hands still on the receiver, he looked at his watch. It was eleven o'clock. The five hours still separating him from Max's lunar moment seemed insurmountably long to him. Hearing Max's voice had done him good; it had suddenly torn him away from the drudgery of his work. Of course he could just go to bed, Max would never know, or wasn't there someone who could keep him company? Couldn't he look someone up?

At the same moment he knew he who he was going to ring—but the brainwave gave him such a shock that it took him a couple of seconds to get over it. He still knew the number by heart.

"Helga?"

"Yes, who's that?"

"How awful. Don't you even recognize my voice anymore?"

"Onno! What a surprise! How are you?"

"Well, I expect you heard a bit about all of it. Uh, a lot has happened."

"Awful. I wanted to write to you, but I didn't know what kind of tone to take. Is there any change in her condition?"

"No."

"And your son? How old is he now?"

"Just over a year."

"Does he live with you? How do you manage? Aren't you an alderman at the moment?"

"I live alone. He's being brought up by my mother-in-law and by Max—you know, the chap you were so crazy about. They live in Drenthe."

"Isn't that a bit odd?"

"A little, yes, but it's the ideal solution. Of course he's got some new girl-friend there already, but we don't talk about that kind of thing anymore. And what about you? What are you getting up to?"

"At this moment? I'm sitting reading."

"What?"

"You'll laugh: the council report in the paper."

"You're sitting reading the newspaper? Haven't you read what's going to happen in a few hours?"

"What?"

"Tonight a man is going to set foot on the moon."

"So what? As long as he doesn't slip over. Is that why you're calling? Since when have you been interested in that kind of thing?"

"Since five minutes ago. Max called and said that I had to watch."

"And so you're going to."

"Helga, the shrill note in your voice is not escaping me. I don't give a damn about celestial bodies, including the earth; but I'm glad he did so, because that gives me a chance to ask you to receive me, so we can watch it together."

"I don't know if I want to, Onno."

"And, of course, I'm the one who determines what you want?"

"No, not for some time. How do you know that I haven't long since found another boyfriend, who is now lying languidly on the sofa?"

"Because I know that no grass can grow where I once stood."

"Onno, have you really not changed at all?"

"I'll be with you in a quarter of an hour—and if you don't open the door, I shall abolish the Art Historical Institute tomorrow. First thing in the morning."

"Of course all you want to do is bring your dirty laundry."

"Listen, dear Helga. Do you know how the Habsburgs were buried?"

"I beg your pardon? The what were buried?"

"The Habsburgs. The Austro-Hungarian monarchs."

"How they were buried?"

"Surely you know?"

"What in heaven's name are you getting at?"

"Listen. The cortege of the coffin arrived at the Kapuzinergruft in Vienna and then the major domo or someone knocked three times on the door with his staff. From inside you then heard the trembling voice of an old monk, asking, 'Who is there?' And then the major domo said, 'His Imperial, Royal and Apostolic Majesty, emperor of Austria, king of Hungary' and another five hundred and eighty-six such titles. Afterward there was a silence inside, after which he knocked three times on the door again and rattled off the same list. And after he had knocked for the third time on the door and the monk had again asked, 'Who is there,' the major domo answered, 'A poor sinner.' And only then did the doors slowly open."

"And what do you mean by that?"

"Do I have to make myself clearer? With my tail between my legs, I'm telling you that I've had enough of playing outside—if that still means anything to you."

✱

After first appropriating the rooms of the apartment, Quinten had broadened his world to the whole castle with the result that he kept getting lost every day. From the wonderful baby who had teethed after three months, a toddler had emerged who delighted everyone with his beauty. Selma Kern said repeatedly to Sophia that her husband was addicted to QuQu's appearance. He was often called QuQu, since Mr. Spier consistently addressed him as Q—moreover to point him to the door just as consistently, since he did not wish to converse with someone who didn't say anything back. "You learn Dutch first, Q."

However, at the Kerns' on the other side of his own floor, he was always welcome; if the artist was not carving in his studio in one of the coach houses, he could not take his eyes off the child. Martha, his ten-year-old daughter, a skinny blond girl, was also crazy about him and had resigned herself to the fact that he could not speak. With her legs crossed, she sat with him on the ground and handed him a pinecone or a shell to study, or pointed the white doves out to him. Once when a dove alighted on his crown and stayed there cooing softly, Kern spread his arms out in pleasure, as though he wanted to fly himself, and remained in that attitude looking at Quinten, who did not move either and in turn didn't take his eyes off Selma, in her black dress.

"This is just out of this world!" he exclaimed.

A large folder already contained scores of drawings of Quinten, in which the eyes became bigger and bigger, made vivid blue with the tip of the middle finger with methylene powder; he also appeared subsequently with a scepter and an orb in his hands, seated on a voluptuous cushion, or as pope with a tiara on his head. According to Selma, Kern's daughter had never inspired him in this way. He had asked Max whether Onno would agree to him exhibiting the series one day; whereupon Max assured him that he could probably persuade Onno to open the exhibition, but then he would have to be prepared for the latter to claim all the honor for himself as father. Undoubtedly, he would dream up some kind of structure in which there was nothing left for the artist but the stupid duplication of reality— that is: the proof of his complete superfluousness.

"He would probably call that the 'parrot principle' or some such thing," said Max—again realizing how Onno had become part of his own being.

Upstairs, at the Proctors', among the gruesome black umbrellas, Quinten looked at the electric train—saw how when the train was approaching the curve, suddenly little Arendje pulled the handle of the transformer right over to the right with a jerk, so that the train derailed and fell on his back, and he convulsed with laughter, thrashing his legs in the air with demonic pleasure. Quinten looked at this with the same expression he had used when looking at the train.

Then he went exploring in the northern part of the attic. One room there was always locked, and invariably that was the first one whose handle he rattled. When that had no effect, he clambered around in the baron's musty, crammed storage room, over rolled-up carpets, books tied with string, among upturned chairs and tables, fallen chandeliers, cupboards, boxes, and piles of clothes, on which he sometimes fell asleep—and where he was finally found by a relieved Sophia or Max:

"I've got him!"

On his second birthday he still could not speak, or at least he had not yet said anything comprehensible; what he did do was display more and more strikingly that strange combination of curiosity and aloofness. He did not wish to be hugged, although he allowed himself to be occasionally, by Sophia; the toys Max bought for him did not interest him any more than a potato, a screw, or a branch. He could look for minutes at the flow of water from a tap, at that clear, cool plait that kept its form and glow although it was made up of constantly new water.

No one knew what to make of him. He was too beautiful to be true, seldom cried, never laughed, said nothing; but no one doubted that all kinds of things were going on beneath that black head of hair. Once he stood motionless on the balcony looking at the balustrade, at the gray stone banister on the wooden amphora-shaped pillars. Max squatted down beside him to see if there was perhaps an insect walking along them; but only when Quinten carefully put his forefinger on a certain spot did he see that there was a tiny, fossilized trilobite, from the Paleozoic period, about 300 million years old. At the same moment he realized that the creature that Quinten had discovered had lived at about the moment that the extragalactic cluster in the constellation of Coma Berenices—"Berenice's Hair"—had emitted the light that was *now* reaching earth.

Quinten looked at him.

"That's a trilobite," said Max, "a kind of silver fish. What would you like? Shall we free it?"

He took a file out of Sophia's manicure case, placed the point at an angle beside the little fossil, and gave it a slight tap with a pebble, so that it flew up and disappeared into the gravel. But Quinten bent down and already had it in his hands.

"When you're grown-up," said Max, "you must become a paleontologist."

When he was lost, he might also be in the cellar. On his way there he always first tried the handle of the door of Mr. Verloren van Themaat, downstairs in the paneled hall, opposite the Spiers' apartment. But the door only opened on the weekends, and during holidays. The art historian was about sixty, a tall, thin, rather stooped man with thin gray hair and fine features; behind a pair of metal-rimmed glasses, he usually looked withdrawn, as though he were sizing you up, but suddenly he burst into exuberant, almost manic laughter, in which all his limbs participated. His wife, Elsbeth, was probably scarcely forty—in any case about five years younger than Sophia; they had no children. Max was a little intimidated by the professor: an academic intellectual of the severe Dutch kind, who overlooked nothing.

Once, with Onno, Max had divided intellectuals up according to the Catholic monastic orders: he himself soon turned out to be an unscrupulous Jesuit, while Onno first maintained that he was a coarse Trappist, since he always just did his duty in silence; but finally he joined the cultivated, well-behaved Benedictines, who devoted their souls to God after a successful worldly life. In that spectrum Themaat was a strict Carthusian, who Max felt saw him as an intellectual libertine where astronomy was not concerned.

But when Quinten appeared in the doorway, on tiptoe, his hands still above his head on the door handle, something changed in the stiff professor, too. When he was sitting reading in his rocking chair—he was al-ways reading—he put the book away, folded his pale hands on his lap, and looked at the approaching child. Unlike the Spiers' apartment, where everything was furnished with precious antiques, the room here had the character of outgrown student quarters, up to and including the worn Persian carpets, the old desk, the worn brown leather armchairs, and even a half-disintegrated hockey stick in an umbrella stand. Although it was a second house, the long wall opposite the windows was covered with bookcases up to the ceiling. Here and there were framed architectural drawings, most of them a little lopsided, but Quinten's first port of call was always a large, framed etching, which was on the floor against the bookshelf.

Once Themaat had knelt down beside him and told him that it was an obelisk:

"Say it after me: *obelisk.*" And when Quinten said nothing: "You must regard it as a petrified sunbeam. It's in Rome, near the Lateran, that palace here on the right, the place where the popes resided in the Middle Ages. Can you see all those signs that have been carved in the shaft? That means that they are actually chiseled into light. Can you see all those birds? They're Egyptian hieroglyphics. I think your father can read those—at least he *could* before he started wasting his time with politics. You take after your father, Q. The emperor Augustus had wanted to take that monster to Rome, but an unfavorable augury prevented him from doing so. Three hundred years later the emperor Constantine didn't bother about that; he was the man who introduced Christianity. Look, there's almost no pavement. That print was made in the eighteenth century; today it's a very busy place, with hundreds of scooters and honking cars. In that building behind is the former private chapel of the pope, the Sancta Sanctorum, and also the Scala Santa, the holy staircase of Pontius Pilate's palace in Jerusalem, up which Jesus Christ walked. At least so it's said. There are still bloodstains on the steps. You're only allowed to climb it on your knees."

"What on earth are you saying to that little mite?" asked Elsbeth, looking up from her magazine. "You must be out of your mind."

"A person is never too young to learn."

Then Quinten was off again. Via a door next to the staircase, he went to the cellar, which extended on either side of a low passageway under the whole castle. There was suddenly an even deeper silence than above—perhaps because it was emphasized by the echoing sound of drips, which, somewhere far off, at long intervals, fell into a puddle.

The musty passageway was almost completely dark; scarcely any light penetrated into the compartments through the small, high windows, almost black with dirt. Some of them were still half full of coal, which was no longer used; others were packed with hundreds of empty bottles, discarded furniture and gardening equipment, broken carriages, bicycles without wheels. Washrooms, rinsing rooms, pantries, larders—everything full of the debris of decades. The great kitchen, where for centuries staff had bustled about, until they dragged themselves exhausted up the back stairs to the attic late at night, and lay desolately in the deep gloom.

Cracked draining boards, disconnected water pipes, and tiles that had been prised up. The kitchen dumbwaiter to the dining room, where Mr. Spier's living room now was, had plunged to the bottom of the shaft with its ropes broken.

Quinten crept into it, wrapped his hands around his knees, and stared into the darkness.

38

The Grave

A few weeks before Quinten's third birthday, which in 1971 fell at Whitsun, there came a proud moment for Onno. At the insistence of Helga he had found time to pay a visit to Drenthe—in an official car, although that was not entirely proper; he had picked up Helga from her home. There was no question of them living together; neither he nor she wanted that. He had resumed his visits to the Unicorn, although now without plastic bags full of laundry, and it sometimes seemed to him that his episode with Ada came from a novel he had once read, in which Quinten was also a character.

The high point of his friendship with Max also belonged to the vanished 1960s; it too was bathed in the melancholy light of memory. He had the beginnings of a middle-age spread and wore a dark-blue suit, but with dandruff on his collar and mostly with a tail of his shirt hanging out of his trousers, so that a segment of his white belly was visible. He always had an inappropriate tie and socks that were too short—all those disasters that Max called his "Social-Democrat lack of style."

They were approaching forty now, but they no longer celebrated their joint conception on the day of the Reichstag fire, because that was also the day of Ada's accident and her father's death. Helga sometimes accompanied Onno to official receptions or dinners, although she usually did not feel like it, so he had to pester her first. But that endeared her to him; it proved that she did not care about the dubious glamour of his position but about him.

Sophia's mother was also at Groot Rechteren. Onno had greeted Quinten by putting his hand on his crown, raising his eyes heavenward, and saying, "A wise son gladdens his father's heart." Precisely because he in fact no longer thought of Quinten when there was no reason, he did not really know what sort of tone to take with him. During lunch in the kitchen— fried eggs with ham, milk, fruit, everything local—Max sat like a pater- familias opposite Sophia at the short end of the table; on his right sat old Mrs. Haken and Onno, on his left Helga with Quinten. The driver had also been invited, but he preferred to stay on the forecourt and eat the sand- wiches he had brought.

"A Christian Democrat who knows his place," Onno had said. "The real mechanisms of oppression are not outside human beings but in them—and that's just as well. Recently far too many of them have disappeared, and we shall pay for it yet."

"Well, well," said Max. "Strong language for a progressive politician."

"External behavior without inner behavior is not possible. That cannot be replaced by the police—you'd need two policemen per individual for that: one for the day and one for the night. But who would guard the police, then?"

"What would you say to God?" asked Max, laughing. And then he said to Helga, "Is your companion really becoming such a reactionary?"

Before she could answer, Onno said: "It's all far more hopeless than you lot think. But please don't let's talk about it, because then I'd prefer to go."

Suddenly Max heard a tone in his voice that he didn't recognize.

"Are you leaving already?" asked Mrs. Haken. "You've only just come."

"No, Granny. I'm staying for a little while."

Helga inquired about Max's work. He knew that she did this out of po- liteness; he still had the same stiff relationship with her. Obviously she would never forgive him for the role that he had played in her life—first when without realizing it he had broken up her relationship with Onno, and then when he had restored it, again without realizing it. When he had first heard that they were back together again, thanks to the landing on the moon, he had a momentary feeling that nothing had changed; but he only had to look at Quinten and Sophia to see that this was not the case.

Westerbork, he said, was operating better than expected; all his colleagues throughout the world envied him the research he was able to do. In reply to a question from Onno, he said that after all kinds of violent evictions and conflicts with the police, the last Ambonese family had gone; there were scarcely any reminders left of the Schattenberg estate, and hence of the transit camp at Westerbork. In order to prevent their return—that is, the return of the Moluccans—all the huts had been demolished; the barrier had also gone. Against his will, by the way, but the survivors wanted it, so what else could he do? Even the rails had been removed; only a rotten buffer was still there. He had, however, thought of something for the last Day of Commemoration, on the eve of the fourth of May; a couple of hundred visitors always came then. He had devised a small computer program that caused all twelve mirrors to bend meekly toward the ground, which happened down to the thousandth of a second at eight o'clock; they stayed in that position for the two minutes' silence and then turned heavenward again.

"One does what one can," he said, and lowered his eyes for an instant. "Only the house of the former German camp commandant is still standing. Strange, isn't it? The widow of the military commandant from shortly after the war still lives there. Would you like to hear a nice story? A few weeks ago there was a sudden power cut, so we immediately switched over to the emergency generator; a little later we heard her trotting up to the terminal. She had a package in plastic wrap in her hands: she asked if she could leave it in our fridge for a while. It turned out to be her husband's evening meal—beefsteak, roast potatoes, and peas—that she had made for him twenty years before, that he had not been able to eat, because he had suddenly died of a heart attack."

"Right!" cried Onno to Helga, shaking his knife over his head. "That is love! Take a leaf out of her book."

Quinten knelt on his chair and looked at his father open-mouthed as if at a fireworks display.

When Onno saw the expression on his face, he said: "Yes, my son, it leaves you speechless. Even if love can no longer find its way to a man's heart through his stomach, it still transcends death! Why don't you say something, you scamp? When I was your age I was already reading Tacitus."

"Onno . . ." said Sophia reproachfully. "He understands more than you think."

After lunch, while Helga stayed behind with Quinten, they went to see Ada—Onno, being the largest, sat next to the driver; Max was wedged between Sophia and her mother on the backseat, with arms folded. On the way Mrs. Haken asked when they were going to tell Quinten what had happened to his mother.

"Maybe never," said Onno at once, without turning his head. Whereupon he turned around after all and said to Sophia, "I'm sorry."

"There's nothing to be sorry about. Don't worry, one day he'll suddenly be able to talk, I'm sure of it." And to her mother: "Of course he mustn't be allowed to think for a moment that I'm his mother and Max his father. He must know how things stand immediately. Isn't that so?"

"Of course," said Max. He now saw clearly the gray hairs that had appeared here and there in her hair. He was sitting closer to her than he ever did during the day, and at night it was dark. "Just imagine."

"And when do you plan to let him see Ada for the first time?" asked Mrs. Haken.

"Onno must decide that."

"No, you must decide," said Onno. "You know him best. It all depends on what kind of boy he turns into, because it will be a dreadful shock of course. When he's six? Ten? What do you think, Max?"

"I think we'll know precisely when the moment comes."

"Probably true."

"By the way, do you know," asked Sophia, "who still visit her a couple of times a year? Marijke and Bruno. They got married."

No one said anything else. Everyone sensed the same thought in the others: would she survive for years? Would she have to go on living for years? And if she suddenly died—should Quinten never have seen her, even if she was doing nothing but breathing?

The nursing home—called Joy Court by sardonic civil servants from the health department—was in a new building in a new street on the outskirts of Emmen. It was built in the same modern nonstyle as the room in which Oswald Brons had descended into the flames, with brick interior walls that looked like exterior walls, so that although one was inside, one constantly had the impulse to go inside.

"Even architects leave people out in the cold these days," said Max.

Onno agreed with him: "It's hopeless. Architects are peace criminals. The end is nigh."

Ada lay in a small room on the second floor, with a view of a paved courtyard. They gathered silently around the bed; a chair was pulled up for Mrs. Haken, whose eyes filled with tears. Here they were, thought Max:

Quinten's great-grandmother, his grandmother, his mother, and his father, too, in any case. Ada had changed again, but it was difficult to say what had actually changed. It was like when you had bought a new book and put it in the bookcase unread: when you took it out for the first time after a few years, it wasn't new anymore, although nothing demonstrable had changed. It had not *renewed itself;* it had not moved with the times. There she lay, her head turned to one side on the pillow, and she did not even know that she had a son with unworldly blue eyes, let alone that the Russians had occupied Prague, that the Americans were now destroying Cambodia too, and that her husband was an alderman for Amsterdam.

Even a cat knew more than she did, thought Onno; maybe she still had the consciousness of a mouse. But with mice you were allowed to spread poison or set a trap . . . he was shocked by his own thoughts and glanced guiltily at Sophia, who had taken Ada's hand in hers and was looking at her daughter with an imponderable expression in her dark eyes.

Back at Groot Rechteren they drank tea in the front room, but no real conversation started up again. In the kitchen the driver was reading the newspaper. Mrs. Haken went for a nap on her daughter's bed, and Sophia showed Helga photos. While Onno made a few telephone calls at Max's desk, Max, with his arms folded, looked at a point in the bookcase and thought of the plans to install movable thirteenth and fourteenth mirrors in Westerbork, which would improve the resolving power of the instrument by a factor of two; but The Hague felt that the radio observatory had already cost enough.

The windows had been pushed up and from the direction of the coach houses came music that sounded like the Rolling Stones; now and then there was a dull thundering sound to be heard as a car drove over the loose planks of the bridge over the outer canal. Onno turned and said that politics consisted of telephoning; you wondered how Julius Caesar had done things. He sat down in the green armchair, where, lost in thought, he took an astrophysics magazine off the table.

In the distance was the faint rumble of a train, passing the unmanned level crossing. A little later Max saw Quinten lying on his tummy across Onno's feet, half over the still-unpolished shoes with the threadbare laces. That was very unusual; he had never done anything so intimate with him—Quinten was not very close to him. The sight reassured Max. His fear of fatherhood had receded over the years, like the bald patch on the back of his head; but unlike that spot, it had never disappeared entirely—just as someone who had recovered from cancer or a heart attack never felt a hundred percent sure and would never forget that he had once fallen prey to it, although he sometimes didn't think of it for months: for the rest of his life there was a monster lying in wait somewhere in a dark cave. He knew that now—for as long as Ada was alive, he might be able to determine paternity by means of a blood test: if Quinten had certain genetic factors that were lacking in both Ada and himself, then Onno was the father; if they were lacking in Onno, then he was. He could have his own blood analyzed very simply, and with a little thought he would be able to secure blood samples from Ada and Quinten, but how could he get hold of Onno's blood? Anyway, it could not be completely ruled out that there were no factors missing; either in his own blood or in Onno's. Indeed, that wouldn't surprise him. In the future it might be different, but for the time being tests couldn't give a conclusive answer in all cases.

Quinten tried in vain to turn the lid of a tin box, in which something was rattling. Onno didn't notice what was happening at his feet; with his eyebrows raised skeptically, he leafed through the specialist journal, as though it were a publication of the Theosophical Society. Only when he felt Quinten's warmth penetrating through the leather of his shoes did he put it down and bend forward.

"Can't you turn it? Leave it in there. It's much nicer when you don't know what it is. What would you say if the two of us went for a walk?"

"Are you sure?" asked Max. "It'll mean venturing out into nature."

"I shall give nature a dreadful shock."

"Look after your father, Quinten," said Helga as they walked hand in hand to the door.

In the forecourt, Onno was undecided about which way to go. Only now did he see the flowering rhododendrons beside the coach houses: huge violet explosions that hung heavily over the water and from beneath which some ducks swam, like the faithful emerging from a cathedral. The decision was made by Quinten. The warm hand pulled him along over the bridge and down the path by the moat; they were walking under the shade of the majestic brown oak and past the side of the castle. The flat, weathered stones of the lower part, which rose at a slight angle from the water, were obviously still from the middle ages.

Onno realized guiltily that it was the first time that he had been alone with Quinten. He was a degenerate father; he left everything to Max as if it were the most natural thing in the world—and on what basis? The little hand in his reminded him of his own in his father's large hand when he had walked with him along the pier at Scheveningen. They had bent over the railings together and looked at the large oblong nets that were winched squeaking and creaking out of the waves on which ten or twenty innocent fish were thrashing about. He was still wearing the curls and pink dresses that his mother liked to see him in. The memory shocked him: was Quinten perhaps the kind of creature that his mother had looked for in himself and that she had brought into being through him? He stopped and looked at Quinten. Yes—if you didn't know, he might just as well be a girl, even without a dress or curls.

"Take a lesson from your wise old father, Quinten," he said as they walked toward the pinewood through the young saplings. "The new is always the old. Everything that's old was once new, and everything that's new will one day be old. The oldest thing of all is the present, because there's never been anything else but the present. No one has ever lived in the past, and no one lives in the future, either. Here we are walking along, you and me, but I in turn once walked just like this with my father along the pier at Scheveningen, which was blown up by the Germans in the war. He told me about the miraculous catch of fish, and that the Lord of Lords had called the apostles "fishers of men." Thirty-five years is an unspeakably long time ago for me, but for your foster father thirty-five years ago is yesterday. For him everything is yesterday. And the war is not even yesterday, but this morning, a moment ago, just now. I don't get the feeling that you're very fond of him, though, or am I mistaken? Tell me honestly. If you ask me, you understand me perfectly well, although you can't understand a word. True or not? Or are you making fools of all of us? Do you understand everything, perhaps, and simply don't feel like talking? Do you get out of bed at night and secretly read the *Divina Commedia*? Yes, that's it, I think. Of course you're annoyed at the corrupt translation that Max has in his bookcase, and you can't find anything by Virgil. Isn't that it? Admit it."

Quinten did not reply, but obviously he knew exactly where he was going. As they passed, the trunks of the precisely planted pinewood produced geometric patterns with turning and changing diagonals and verticals till they merged into an overgrown park, where there were bare, uprooted trees everywhere, in various directions, felled by various storms. Where the wood became somewhat lighter a wall of exuberantly flowering rhododendrons appeared. Quinten let go of his hand and went in as though there were no resistance to be overcome, while Onno had to force his way with his hands through the unyielding bushes, which were taller than himself.

"Where in heaven's name are you taking me?" he cried. "This is not meant for human beings, Quinten! People belong on pavements!"

But when he had gotten through, even he experienced the fairy-tale nature of the spot. They were at the edge of a large, capriciously shaped pond, enclosed by mountains of violet flowers; in complete silence two black swans glided between the water lilies. In the distance there was a glimpse of the tower of the castle between the trees—obviously the pool was linked with the moat. But it was too distinguished here for the ducks. The aggressive black coots, with the wicked white patch on their heads, obviously didn't feel at home here either.

Yet they had still not reached their objective. Quinten began walking along the water's edge under the branches. Holding on, complaining all the while, blowing petals out of his face, and once slipping and cursing and getting one shoe wet, Onno followed him to the other side. Once he had gone through another wall of flowers, he was standing at the edge of an open space, thickly overgrown with deep-green stinging nettles that reached to his waist.

"Not through there, surely?" he said.

But Quinten took him to a narrow, winding path that consisted of flattened, but in places already reemerging, stinging nettles. Because he himself was smaller than the devilish brood, he made Onno lead the way. With a sigh Onno tucked his trouser legs into his socks, picked up a branch, and with his squelching shoe went down the path, swiping furiously and with real hatred at every nettle that could threaten them.

"What are you doing to me?" he cried. "If only I'd never married!"

After thirty or forty yards they were suddenly confronted with a square gravestone at the foot of a small, pointed conical pillar.

"What on earth is this?" said Onno, perplexed. He squatted down so that his scratched head was at the same level as Quinten's. His forefinger passed over the carved letters in the stone: DEEP THOUGHT SUNSTAR. He looked at Quinten. "Shall I tell you something? There's a horse buried here. That's what they call racehorses." He got up. "Who on earth buries a horse? Horses go to the knacker's yard, don't they?"

And then something happened that after a moment's speechlessness moved him to hold Quinten in his arms and to run back with him through the stinging nettles in triumph, and through the flowers and past the geometrical dancing of tree trunks to the castle: Quinten extended his finger toward the pillar, leaned back a little, and said with a laugh: "Obelisk."

39

Further Expeditions

Just as in Noordwijk the light of the lighthouse swept in all directions, so the four seasons swept over Groot Rechteren each year in great waves. In fact Max only knew the changing of the seasons from Amsterdam: one day in February or on March first, the indescribable scent of spring when he came into the street in the morning, as indefinable as the decimals of   ; the stuffy summer, when the city was filled with tourists, equally suddenly changed into the damp, bitter autumn; and then the pale winter in which the cobblestoned streets and the walls suddenly seemed to express the inaccessible nature of the world—but really only in passing, noticed in short intervals between going from one interior to the next.

If in the city nature was soft background music, in the castle he was in the midst of a thundering concert hall with Quinten and Sophia. Spring and autumn came with a huge show; the summers were hotter and drier, the winters colder and whiter. The constant change, he had once said to Onno, was of course the source of all creativity; the monotony of nature between the tropics also led to cultural stagnation—the tropics were a constant steambath, always green, just as the polar regions were always white—but the temperate latitudes with their four seasons were hot and cold baths, which kept people awake. That was true in the city too, of course, but only in the country had it become clear to him. Onno had countered by saying that in the country it was perhaps a little too clear, since that annually repeating four-part pattern in turn retained a certain monotony, so that real creations always took place in town. He had seen that Onno refrained from inquiring whether his own creativity had increased in the countryside; but although he had no complaints about his work, he did not broach that topic of his own accord.

In Drenthe not only was the darkness deeper, the silence more silent, storms more violent, and the rainbow more vivid than in Amsterdam; even the rain was different. When there was a walk through the woods with Quinten on the program, it did not occur to Max to wait until it was dry, let alone take an umbrella with him. All three of them put on their green boots and their oilskins, pulled the hoods over their heads, and waded through the mud, while the shots of the baron and his friends rang out in the distance.

Once, when it was no longer raining, and it was still dripping from all the trees, Max said: "When it stops raining, the trees start raining."

"They're crying," said Quinten.

"So you're not a tree, then," said Sophia.

Quinten waved his arms, jumped with both feet into the middle of a puddle, and cried: "I'm the rain!"

When Onno was told of this pronouncement by Max one Saturday afternoon in Amsterdam, in the reptile house at the zoo—while Quinten was looking at a motionless snake, coiled like a rope on a quayside—he said that this might cause problems at school. Everything suggested that he undoubtedly had a more brilliant mind than the teachers, just as had been obvious in his own case.

Since Quinten had communicated his first word to Onno, together with his first laugh, it was really as though he had been able to speak much earlier but had not seen any point. Less than six months later there was no question of any backwardness; grammatically, he seemed to be advanced for his age. When he meant himself, he didn't talk about Quinten, or about Q, but said "I." He called Onno Daddy; Sophia, Granny, or Granny Sophia if he had to make a distinction with Granny To; and Max, Max.

He did, though, remain more silent than other children. General toddler's chatter, tyrannical orders, whining about what he wanted to have, chattering what he had just done or what he wanted to do: there was none of that kind of thing. Nor had he any need for playmates; it did not really give him any pleasure when Sophia took him to the playground or the swimming pool. Before he went to sleep he allowed himself to be read a fairy tale. Apart from that, he was satisfied with the castle and what was going on there; since he had deigned to speak, he was even welcome at Mr. Spier's.

He was never bored. He sat for hours in his tower room and looked at pictures—not pictures from children's books, let it be understood, but particularly the illustrations in a book that Themaat had let him take upstairs, Giuseppe Bibiena's *Architetture e prospettive*. As though Quinten knew what the eighteenth century and the Viennese court were, Themaat had told him that the book had been made in the first half of the eighteenth century at the Viennese court. Particularly the etchings of imaginary theatrical sets fascinated him: grand baroque, superperspectivist spaces with colonnades, staircases, caryatids, everything laden with ornaments. He would like to walk through those places.

When he was four, Sophia wanted him to go to the nursery school in Westerbork: that would be good for the development of his personality; in her opinion he was becoming far too solitary like this. Onno and Max had never visited such an institution—it was not usual in the 1930s—and they were not very keen; but Sophia had her way. On his way to the observatory Max dropped him off at the nursery on the first day, and that very morning another toddler bashed Quinten's head with an earthenware mug. When this happened he had not cried and just looked at his attacker with such an astonished look in his deep blue eyes that the other child had burst out crying.

Afterward the teacher, who had not seen anything of what had happened in the dolls' corner, had told Quinten off because he had obviously done something to the little boy, since otherwise he would not be crying like that. Quinten had said nothing. When Max picked him up, bustled by mothers and their screaming offspring, the teacher had told him what had happened. Of course she did not want to say that Quinten was underhanded or spiteful, but perhaps he should be watched a little. Sitting in the backseat of the car, Quinten told him what had actually happened and Max believed him; at home Sophia also discovered a small wound under his black locks. After a telephone call to Onno, having been put through by Mrs. Siliakus, they decided to remove him from the institution immediately.

"You don't have to go there anymore," said Max. "Is that all right?"

Quinten nodded. He stood by Max's desk, twisting the small compass slowly and looking at the wobbling needle, which seemed not to be attached to the compass but to the room.

"Don't you worry," said Sophia.

But it was something else that was troubling him. He focused his eyes on her and said: "All the children were picked up by mommies."

Max and Sophia looked at each other. There it was. Suddenly the fundamental question had been asked. Max didn't immediately know what to say, but Sophia knelt down to him, put an arm round him and said:

"I'm your mommy's mommy, Quinten. Your mommy is much too tired to pick you up. She's lying in a very big house with very nice people, sleeping in a bed, and she can't wake up anymore, that's how tired she is. She can't hear anyone and she can't talk to anyone."

"Not even me?"

"Not even you."

"Not even for a little bit?"

"Not even for a little bit."

"Really not even for a little tiny bit?"

And when Sophia shook her head: "Not even to Daddy and Auntie Helga?"

"Not to anyone, darling."

Thoughtfully, he put the top on the compass. "Just like Sleeping Beauty."

"Yes. Just like Sleeping Beauty."

"What about the prince, then?" he asked, looking up.

Like Max, he saw that Sophia's eyes had grown moist. Max had never seen such emotion in her before. Quinten wiped away Sophia's tears with the palm of his hand and did not ask any more questions. Max went to the mantelpiece and gave him the photograph of Ada and Onno.

"This is Mommy when she was still awake."

Quinten took the photograph in two hands and looked at the face in the square of black hair. "Beautiful."

"That's why you're so beautiful too," said Sophia.

Max expected that he would want to have the photograph, but he gave it back and went to his room. When they were alone, Max wanted to hug Sophia, but that was of course unthinkable.

"That was to be expected," he said. "And what now?"

"We must discuss it with Onno. I don't think we should return to the subject ourselves. I think that what he doesn't ask about he can't cope with."

Max nodded. "One day he'll give another sign."

Sophia brushed real or imaginary crumbs off her lap. "A few weeks ago I read him that fairy story of Sleeping Beauty, and I was halfway through before I realized what it was really about, but by that time I couldn't go back."

"Surely you don't feel guilty about it now?"

"Guilty?" she repeated, and looked at him. "Why should I be guilty about anything?"

The attack in the nursery class had of course also been provoked by Quinten's beauty. He already had his new teeth by the age of four. Theo Kern had had to open a second folder for his Quinten studies; he hadn't managed an exhibition yet, probably because he really wanted to keep them to himself. But not everyone was as jealous. Despite the sign saying NO EN-TRY, ART. 461, CRIMINAL CODE by the gate with the two lions on it, cars regularly appeared in the forecourt with newly married couples, who had themselves photographed against the background of the castle, the women in long white dresses, the men in rented suits, gray top hats in their hands, since otherwise they would come down over their ears. Their faces were mostly tanned, halfway across their foreheads a sharp line where there was clammy white, where their caps usually reached.

A couple of times Quinten had already caught the photographers' eyes, after which they had rung the bell and asked Sophia if they could take a series of photos of this astonishingly beautiful boy—for advertising purposes, which would of course pay well.

The fact that he had not cried when he was hit on the head did not surprise Max and Sophia. In fact he had only really cried once. During a heat wave, in July, Sophia had put an inflatable round white plastic bath on the forecourt; when she couldn't find the air pump, she blew it up herself and half filled it with the garden hose. She lifted Quinten into it, called to Max that he should keep an eye on things, and went off to get eggs at the farm.

Half an hour later Max heard him crying. There had been a plague of flies all summer, but now the hot stones of the forecourt were suddenly covered by a black, seething carpet, which gave off a gruesome singing sound, like hundreds of cellos. Surrounded on all sides by the devilish brood, as if on an island, Quinten was standing up in the water, naked, his hands over his eyes, whining and shivering with fear. At the same moment the sight unleashed in Max a rage of an intensity he had never experienced; he himself had only a pair of swimming trunks on, and before he knew it he was running through the swarming, buzzing mass, feeling how he was crushing hundreds of flies under his bare feet, dragging Quinten out of the water in

one movement and taking him to safety on the other side of the moat, in the
shade under the brown oak tree.

By about his fifth birthday, in 1973—the year in which Max and Onno
turned forty and Sophia fifty—Quinten had extended his territory to the
whole of the wooded area. Every day he visited the former coach house
where Theo Kern carved his large pieces. In the tall space full of stones and
dust and tools, plaster carts, tables full of sketches, discarded furniture, and
the constantly bubbling coffee machine in the corner, where everything was
focused on work, he felt even more at ease than in Kern's apartment in the
castle, in Selma's presence. He would sit on a lump of stone for hours watching the sculptor extracting heavily built female figures and ornaments for
government buildings from the blocks, walking around over the sharp
splinters in his bare feet like a fakir.

Now and then something alarming happened to him. He would suddenly stop, half close his eyes, bare his teeth to the gums, and raise his hands
high in the air, shuddering, as though he had to defend himself against the
image with a supreme effort. Then the good-natured gnome was suddenly
changed into a ravenous beast. A moment later his face relaxed completely
again, as though nothing had happened. Quinten saw that he himself no
longer remembered behaving so strangely.

According to Kern, sculpture wasn't an art—anyone could do it. All you
had to do, he said one day, was to remove the superfluous stone. "At least
that's what Michelangelo used to say."

"Who's Michelangelo?"

"Someone like me, but different. He made that over there,"—he pointed
to a photograph pinned to a wooden beam with a drawing pin: a statue of a
man with a wild face, a long beard, and two horns on his head.

"Is that the devil?"

"What makes you think that?"

"Well, those horns of course."

"Yes, I don't understand those either. But in any case it's Moses. Someone
from the Bible."

"What's the Bible?"

Kern's mallet came to rest. "Don't you know that? Hasn't your father
ever told you? A whole book of stories, which lots of people think really
happened."

Quinten remembered the huge book that stood on a lectern in his granddad's house in The Hague from which he sometimes read aloud. That was the Bible of course.

Kern looked at the photo with a sigh.

"I couldn't make anything like that, QuQu. I get commissions from Assen Council, but he got them from the pope. You have to know your place. I myself don't really like color very much, but he could paint beautifully too. For example, he painted the Sistine Chapel—not bad at all. That's in the Vatican: the pope's family chapel."

"Who's the pope?"

"The head of the Catholics. Those are people who believe in God. And now I expect you're going to ask who God is?"

"Yes," said Quinten. He was sitting on a block of dark-blue granite, hands between his thighs, and nodded three times.

"He doesn't exist, but according to those who believe in him he made the world."

"Max says the world started with a bang."

"Then I expect that's right. In the Sistine Chapel you can see God: he's floating in the air and he's got a beard, like Moses."

"And you."

"But his isn't nice and white like mine. When you're older you must go and have a look in Rome. There's plenty more to see there, for that matter."

"How on earth can you paint someone that doesn't exist?"

"You make something up. Or you use a trick. Michelangelo simply painted some old chap or other who came into his street every day selling pizzas; he made him float in the air and then everyone said it was God. If I had to make a sculpture of God for Assen Council, then I'd simply be able to carve my own head."

"And yet," said Quinten, "you could make a sculpture of God himself perfectly easily if he doesn't exist."

"You'll have to tell me how you're supposed to do that."

"Well, you take a block of marble and you carve it until there's nothing left."

He looked at Quinten perplexed, and then burst out into a thundering laugh. "Then I take it to Assen. 'Here it is,' I'd say. 'God! Do you see! Nothing!' Do you think they'd understand? And pay me? No way! They wouldn't even pay for the marble. They're as thick as two planks."

"Who's the devil, then?"

"Christ, Quinten! Who's the devil? Why don't you ask the lady vicar. The devil is the archenemy of God!"

"Doesn't he exist either, or does he?"

"No, of course not."

"Well then, I know how you can make a statue of the devil too."

Kern lowered his mallet and chisel and looked at Quinten. "How, then?"

"You've got to fill the whole world with marble."

Quinten could see that he was confused.

"Where on earth do you get things like that from, QuQu?"

"Just like that . . ." Quinten didn't understand what he meant, but he had the feeling that he should go now. He glanced at Moses; under his arm he had some large thing or other, a kind of map, which was obviously slipping out of his hands and threatening to fall on the floor, which he was just able to prevent. In real life he would probably have been a gardener or something. "Bye," he said.

Whenever he came out of the studio, there was the house in front of him. Seen from the castle, the group of outbuildings on the other side of the moat looked rather small and insignificant; the house itself, looked at from there, made a powerful, inaccessible impression. He always stood and looked at it for a few moments. He didn't think of anything—or, rather, what he thought coincided with what he saw: the castle, self-absorbed like his own thoughts, the clock with no hands above the door. Sometimes it was as though it suddenly became invisible for a split second.

To the right of Kern's studio was a smaller stable that housed the workshop of Mr. Roskam, the caretaker of Groot and Klein Rechteren, who did repairs; the door was usually locked. At the side a covered staircase led to the second floor, where different people lived every few months: sometimes a blond woman, then a man with a black goatee. He had no contact with them, but he did with Piet Keller, who lived on the other side.

On either side of the gravel path, which led to his front door past the large erratic stone, one could see the top halves of cart wheels. At first sight it looked as though someone had buried them up to the axles—but Quinten knew better. It was the other way around: they weren't sticking in but out of the earth; they weren't the top halves but the bottom halves. In fact the cart was under the path, the coach, the golden coach, which he had once seen on television: but upside down, pulled by eight horses, the coachman with the reins up in the box, all upside down in the ground, and there wasn't a queen in it but a much more beautiful woman, the most beautiful woman in the world—and the coach was standing still because they'd all fallen asleep . . .

When Piet Keller had once asked him why he never simply walked down the path but always around the wheels, across the grass, he had said: "Just because."

Keller was in his fifties, a skinny man with a stoop and an unhealthy complexion, usually dressed in a short beige dust coat. His wife sometimes suddenly made strange jerky movements with her whole body, which made Quinten a little afraid of her; his daughter and two sons, all three of them a head taller than he was, had reached an age at which they probably scarcely noticed Quinten. In an adjacent barn he had his workshop, and Quinten was in the habit of watching him, too, for hour after hour. He repaired old locks, which had been sent to him from miles around, not only by individuals but also by antiques dealers and museums. All around were boxes containing thousands of keys in all shapes and sizes, tins full of levers, locks, bars, tumblers, bolts, stops, and other components whose names he had taught Quinten. Countless skeleton keys hung on large iron rings.

"I've got every key," he had once said with a wink, "except musical keys and St. Peter's."

On a trestle table illuminated by a wobbly light, fixed to the wall with wire, lay the locks that he was currently dealing with; next to it was a set of shelves with countless compartments full of screws, nuts, pins, and other small items. There was also a heavy bench with a lathe and drilling and grinding machines. When Quinten was there, Keller usually accompanied his work with a mumbled, monotone commentary: not didactic, simply reporting on what he was doing and what he was thinking. Occasionally, when he was working on a heavy medieval padlock, as large as a loaf, which was locked and of which the key was missing, lyrical notes crept into his reports.

"Look at that, isn't it an angel? We call this a sliding padlock. Can you see those H-shaped grooves? That's where you have to put the key. I'm going to make it in a while. Inside there's a barrier of very strong springs; the ends are now relaxed, making them lock the shackle in the body of the lock."

"How do you know? Have you looked inside?"

"No, and I'm not going to. At least not now. First I'm going to do something quite different." From one of the storage boxes he fished out a couple of long, steel pins, which fitted in the H. Back at his bench, he lubricated them with oil and began sliding them slowly inside, with his eyes looking up, as though that was where the inside of the lock could be seen. "Yes, now I can feel the first curve in the spring blades . . . yes. That's right, yes . . . a little further . . . now they're compressing . . . yes . . . it's difficult, it's rusty in there . . . perhaps a little careful help with the hammer . . . and now a couple more taps and one more, that should be enough . . ." There was a stiff click from inside, and he pulled the stirrup out of the lock.

He looked at Quinten with a smile. "Yes, QuQu, I could earn my living in a much easier way. But 'Thou shalt not steal.' Just ask the lady vicar."

He pulled out the pins and pushed the shackle back in again, which made a second click.

"What are you doing? It's locked again now!"

He put the monster down in front of Quinten. "You can already pick ordinary locks a bit, but try this one. Perhaps you can take over from me one day—I can't talk my own sons into it."

The lady vicar, Ms. Trip, the head of the Calvinist congregation in Hooghalen, was unmarried and lived twenty yards farther on, with her black cat, in the former gardener's house, which had a large conservatory built on. She had little contact with the other residents of Groot Rechteren—only the Verloren van Themaats occasionally had tea with her; she was a friend of the baroness's. Although she was no older than Sophia, her hair was already snow-white. When she sat on her terrace reading—Karl Barth, or a nice novel—or tended the flowers in her garden, which sloped down to a tributary of the moat, Quinten sometimes stopped and looked at her from the gate. She would give him a friendly nod, but she never waved to him, and he did not think that was necessary. She must know an awful lot, perhaps almost as much as his father, because everyone always said, "You must ask the lady vicar about that" when they did not know the answer themselves. It was mostly about God, or Jesus Christ, but he had never asked her anything. Usually he ran straight on toward the bridge.

Sophia had forbidden him to go across it: it was a very romantic, dilapidated, wobbly construction, with planks missing and which for some reason always reminded Max of a Schubert song: *"Leise flehen meine Lieder durch die Nacht zu dir . . ."* On the other side, in the shade of tall beech trees, was the orangery: a low, long building with large windows, where Seerp Verdonkschot lived with his friend. He not only lived there with his friend but also had his antiquities room there. There was scarcely ever another visitor when Quinten went in. For Verdonkschot himself was not there usually either; he worked for the post office—a gruff man, according to Max, embittered because he wasn't taken seriously as a scholar, either by the university in Groningen or by the Provincial Museum in Assen. Perhaps that was because he also put his antiquities up for sale.

His friend, Etienne, a man of about forty who was on the corpulent side, always put his head around the door and said: "Hello, beautiful, are you back? Don't pinch anything, you hear?"

On the wall were colored maps showing the extent of the Beaker culture in Drenthe, and Verdonkschot's prehistoric finds were displayed in two rows of showcases: dozens of stone arrowheads, five thousand years old, hand axes, rusty hairpins, potsherds, half-decomposed pieces of leather. It was not the objects themselves that fascinated Quinten; they didn't really appeal to him. It was the atmosphere in the brightly painted room: the orderly silence, with those dirty old things in it, which belonged deep in the earth and were now lying in the light like the guts of a fish at the fishmonger's in the village.

It was mysterious because it was really forbidden. And the strangest thing of all was the idea that all those things were lying under the glass even when no one was looking at them—at night, too, when it was dark here and he himself was in his bed. That was impossible, of course, because then they'd scream with fear and he'd hear from his bed; but he never heard screaming coming from the orangery at night. Just the call of an owl sometimes. So they only existed when he saw them.

Outside, he always climbed straight onto the erratic stone, which had appeared there too. He sat down and waited until Verdonkschot's goat Gijs came toward him with lopsided leaps. If Gijs had been able, he would definitely have given him a butt with his horns, but the rope was just too short for that.

Then Quinten would talk to him: "Why are you always so rotten to me?" He put out his hand to stroke the goat's head; but that was always refused with an abrupt movement. "I haven't done anything to hurt you, have I? I like you. I think you're much nicer than Arendje, for example—he bangs into people with his head down like that sometimes too. I think you're just about as nice as Max, but not nearly as nice as Daddy. Daddy's the nicest person in the world. When we go for walks he always tells me lots of things. He can speak every language and read hieroglyphics. Do you know why I can't go and live with him? Because he's so busy playing boss. That's why he hardly ever comes. He's the boss of at least a million million people. Auntie

Helga doesn't live with him either. I've never been to his house, but he lives in a castle in Amsterdam. When I'm grown-up I'm going to see him there. Then you can come too. Do you know who I think is nicest of all? Mommy. Mommy's really tired, Granny says. Mommy fell asleep. Do you know what made her so tired? I bet you don't. But I do. Shall I tell you? But you mustn't tell anyone, do you hear? Because it's a secret. Do you promise, Gijs? It's because she always had to wave to everybody in the gold coach."

40

The World of Words

Meanwhile, Onno had gotten busier and busier playing boss. Late one evening, during the closing stages of cabinet formation, after he had been to see Helga and had drunk a couple of rum-and-Cokes on his way home, the man charged with the task of forming the cabinet called and asked if he wanted to be minister of state for science policy.

"Since when has that been a matter for the person forming the cabinet?"

"I'm ringing on behalf of your minister."

"Can I think about it for a little?"

"No."

"Not even for five minutes?"

"No. The whole business has to be completely sewn up within twenty-four hours—the whole damn fuss has been going on for more than five months. There are rumblings in the land."

"To what do I owe the honor, Janus?"

"Indirectly to the suggestion of a friend of yours, a certain pub-crawler from your town: the new minister of housing."

"And my own minister? Does she know that I'm extraordinarily ill-disposed toward science?"

"Yes, yes, Onno. I'm sure it will get you into difficulties in the cabinet. Come on, I've got plenty else to do. Yes or no?"

"If it's a matter of the national interest, everything else must be put aside. Yes."

"Fine. I'll expect you sober at General Affairs in The Hague tomorrow morning at ten o'clock. We're going to do a good job. Goodnight."

That had suddenly changed everything. He was not unhappy being an alderman, which he had now been for four years; although government had less and less influence every year, in a number of respects his job had more direct power than being a minister of state, who was hidden behind a secretary of state. In local politics he had direct contact with people; in national politics that would no longer be the case. For precisely that power sometimes filled him with disgust, as though he had suffered a defeat; exerting power was necessary to make society function, but at the same time there was something unmistakably plebeian about it.

There was also the advantage that as an alderman he worked in Amsterdam and not in that stuffy lair of civil servants The Hague, from which he had once fled and to which he would now have to go every day—it was a blessing for Amsterdam that the seat of government was not in the capital. But with a feeling of shame, he also realized immediately why he had said yes: to please his father and to put his eldest brother's nose out of joint. They would know immediately that he was going to be a minister one day: the highest state of political happiness.

Still looking at the telephone, he was suddenly amazed that in response to the question "Yes or no?" uttering the short sound *no* wouldn't have changed a thing in his life, while enunciating the equally short sound *yes* had changed a lot—while the spectrograms of the two sounds could only have been identified by experienced phoneticians. And if he had said *ken,* nothing would have changed either, although that also meant "yes," but in Hebrew. It was all obvious, bread-and-butter stuff to him, as easy as ABC, but suddenly it disturbed him, while at the same time he was really disturbed about being disturbed.

After saying yes, he had even less time for visits to Groot Rechteren: from then on Quinten saw him more often on television than in real life. By now he was in the first grade at the elementary school in Westerbork; and on one of Onno's sporadic visits—in a large dark-blue official car with two antennas, after he opened an institute of technology in Leeuwarden—Quinten told Sophia proudly that he knew how to read.

"Show Daddy what you can do," she said, and gave him the book.

" 'Pim is in the wood,' " read Quinten, without using his forefinger. But before Onno was able to praise him, he looked at the newspaper lying on the ground and read the headline: " 'Cambodian President Lon Nol extends special powers.' " In the astonished silence that ensued, he said, "I didn't learn it at school at all. I've been able to do it for ages."

Max was the first one to say anything. "Who did you learn it from, then?"

"From Mr. Spier."

He could not understand what was so special about it. In Mr. Spier's immaculately tidy study, with the sloping drawing board, which looked out onto the woods behind the castle, his new letter designs were pinned alphabetically on the wall: twenty-six large sheets of squared paper, each of them with a capital and small letter, which he called "upper case" and "lower case." Mr. Spier—who was always immaculately dressed when working, with a tie, coat, and pocket handkerchief—had not only told him everything about "body of type," "serif," "flag," "tail," but for a couple of days in succession had taken him by the hand and conducted him along the wall step by step, pointing to letter after letter and speaking it, and making Quinten repeat it after him. That way it was as easy as pie! At the letter *Q* Mr. Spier had always raised his forefinger meaningfully. He had called his new typeface Judith, after his wife. He also designed postage stamps and banknotes, but he only did that at the printer's in Haarlem, under police guard, because that was of course top secret. Inside it always made him laugh a bit, he said; in the war, when he had had to hide because Hitler wanted to kill him, he himself had forged all kinds of things: German stamps; identity cards.

"Who's Hitler?"

"Isn't it wonderful that there are once again people who don't know. Hitler was the head of the Germans, who wanted to kill all the Jews."

"Why?"

"Because he was afraid of them."

"What are Jews?"

"Yes, well lots of people have been asking themselves that for a long time, QuQu—the Jews themselves as well. Perhaps that's why he was frightened of them. But he didn't succeed."

"So are you a Jew too?"

"You bet."

"But I'm not frightened of you." And when Mr. Spier smiled: "Am I a Jew?"

"Quite the opposite, as far as I know."

"Quite the opposite?"

"I'm just joking. Jews often do that when they talk about Jews."

"What's wrong, Quinten?" asked Sophia. "What are you thinking about?"

"Nothing."

Max could still not understand. "Why did you never tell us you could read?"

Quinten shrugged his shoulders and said nothing.

"His lordship confronts us with new mysteries every day," said Sophia.

"He has a congenital defect of being highly gifted." Onno nodded. "Shall I test him again?" And then he said to Quinten, "Can you see anything funny in the name Lon Nol?"

"There's a mirror in between," said Quinten immediately.

"You can't believe your ears!" cried Max—with double joy: there could no longer be any doubt who had contributed the hereditary factors here!

"Just like . . . ?" Onno went on.

Quinten thought for a moment, but didn't know.

"Me," said Onno. He was going to say Ada too, but he didn't; anyway it wasn't quite right: the *d* in the middle was not itself symmetrical.

"Of course!" said Quinten, laughing and covered the two *l*'s with his two forefingers. "You're in it!"

"I'm in Lon Nol . . ." repeated Onno. "If my party leader should hear, it will harm my career."

"That rhymes," said Quinten, "so it's true."

Max burst out laughing. "At last someone who takes poetry seriously."

"A while ago," Onno told them, "I was also asked to read aloud. By the P.P.S."

"What's the P.P.S.?" asked Sophia.

"*Who* is the P.P.S.? The permanent parliamentary secretary, the top official in the department who outlasts all the politicians—the representative of eternity."

"What did he want you to read?" asked Max.

"Everything, the whole time. Of course I wouldn't have dreamed of reading something from a piece of paper in Parliament, like the honorable members almost all do—I've always spoken my shattering truths impromptu. But he said that created bad blood, and that by doing it I was confronting them with their own bungling and they would take revenge. In his view oratorical talent was undesirable in Dutch politics—and what do you think? Since then I have deigned to put some papers in front of me, sometimes blank sheets, so that the chamber at least has the impression that I am reading from notes. Doesn't it make you want to hang yourself?"

And when Max laughed, he went on:

"Yes, you're laughing, but I'm sinking farther and farther into the morass of decline. In politics everything hinges on words. It's a disgusting world of words."

"Well, to me," said Max, "a world of words seems just the place for you."

"But not in this way. When I used to decipher texts in the dim and distant past, that consisted of *actions,* which were separate from the text even though I was only substituting one word for another. Can you follow me?"

"Even when everyone else has long ceased to follow you, Onno, I shall still follow you."

"But in politics the words themselves are the deeds, and that's something quite different. When you're sitting there in Westerbork and listening to the rustlings from the depths of the universe, I listen to words from early in the morning to late at night: at the ministry, in Parliament, in the coffee lounge, at party headquarters, during committee meetings, on the telephone, in the car, at cocktail parties, at dinners and receptions, and on working visits, from people who whisper something in my ear, who thrust information at me in notes, even if it's only 'Be careful of that guy' or some such thing. And I myself keep on saying all kinds of things to everyone on such occasions, and at press conferences or interviews in the paper and on television. I try to persuade, influence people. That's politics, power: it's all verbal, a continuous blizzard of words. But it's not just speaking, it's making statements. It's action; it's doing something without doing anything. Of course it's wonderful if you can change and improve things—I won't say a word against that—but the realization that it all happens like that is beginning to gnaw at me."

"Why? What could be nicer than *doing* things with words? Does a writer do anything else? And what about God?"

"Yes," said Onno. "Let's take God. That can never do any harm. 'In the beginning was the Word, and the Word was with God and the Word was God.' "

"Is that from the Bible?" asked Quinten.

"It certainly is! So according to St. John, the creator coincided with the word of creation, and according to the psalmist that was at the same time creation itself: 'He speaks and it is there.' God, Word, World—they're all identical. Nothing more political than Christian theology is conceivable."

"You can also turn it around, and say that it means politics are a religious matter," said Max.

"Do you know whom you're talking to? 'Government is the servant of God armed with a sword': I imbibed that with my mother's milk. It's just that the Christian dogs have never looked at it from the point of view of the philosophy of language. Anyway, that applies not just to politics. When I once said 'I do' at the town hall on your birthday, that was more of an action than a statement, or when I called that strange creature there Quinten. But I wasn't cut out for God, like you perhaps. There's a bad smell about doing things verbally without doing anything. Something that I don't like about it is a certain—how shall I say . . . immoral dimension."

"Immoral dimension . . ." repeated Max. "That doesn't sound too good." He had to force himself not to look at Sophia—suddenly he had the feeling that Onno was really speaking about his clandestine relationship with her, but of course that was nonsense.

"The emperor Napoleon beautified Paris," said Onno, and was suddenly silent. Max nodded and waited for what came next. "King Solomon built the first temple in Jerusalem."

"I expect that's from the Bible too," said Quinten.

"Everything is always from the Bible."

"And what about Napoleon and Solomon?" inquired Max.

"The thing is that in the whole of his life King Solomon never once put one brick on top of another. So he didn't build it. He commissioned his architect to build a temple, but he didn't build it, either. It was built by anonymous workers. What right has the person who has least to do with it to take the credit for it?"

"Because it would not have been built without him."

"And it would have been built without the architect? And without the workers? And yet Solomon is of course the sole builder of the temple—the grounds of his power and a deed consisting of three words: 'Build a temple!.' Or rather two: *'Tiwne migdásch!' Build* obviously means saying 'Build.' Isn't that indecent?"

"Exactly," said Max, who suddenly felt criticized in some way. "And having a temple built is still something noble, but take the example of being given an order to do something criminal." He turned to Sophia. "Tell him what you heard yesterday—about that cap."

Sophia looked at the paper pattern that she was pinning to a piece of cloth. Max and Onno could see that she had to concentrate for a moment: these kinds of conversations tended to pass her by. Probably, she thought it was all boyish nonsense.

Yesterday Mr. Roskam, the caretaker, had been invited to coffee, and he had told her about his father, who had been gardener under the father of the present baron. When Mr. Roskam was the same age as Quinten, he had once gone with his father to the orangery, which was still in use as a winter garden. On the threshold the old Gevers had stood, also with his son, also about six at the time, and he had glanced at Mr. Roskam's father's cap. "Fetch a spade, my man." His father had fetched a spade. "Dig a hole." His father had dug a hole. "Throw your cap in. I want that filthy thing out of my sight." His father had buried his cap and stamped down the earth with his clogs, while the two boys looked on. Fifty years later Mr. Roskam still trembled as he talked about it. His father had thought that he would be given a new cap, but that hadn't happened.

"Mr. Roskam?" asked Quinten, who had listened open-mouthed.

"Right," said Onno. "When I hear something like that I remember why I'm left-wing."

"As you say," said Max in an agitated voice, "the immoral thing is that commands like that are *possible*. 'Build a temple!' 'Bury your cap!' Take Hitler. He once gave Himmler his very personal order: 'Kill all Jews!'—of course only verbally. But he himself never murdered a Jew, nor did Himmler or Heydrich or Eichmann; that was finally done by the lowliest foot-soldiers. And in Auschwitz it was even more idiotic; there the Zyklon-B had to be thrown into the gas chambers by Jewish prisoners. So there you had the spectacle of the actual murder not being committed by the murderers but by the victims. Whoever did it didn't do it, and whoever didn't do it did it." He met a look from Sophia and suddenly checked himself. So as not to burden Quinten with the past, he never talked about those things when he was there—and actually, not even when he wasn't there.

"That's what I mean," said Onno. "*The Führer's orders have the force of law*. With Hitler you always find everything in its purest form. If words become deeds, deeds evaporate and the hell of paradox opens up and engulfs everything. There's something completely wrong with the world, and at the same time it can't be any different than it is. Perhaps it's my midlife crisis, but on rainy afternoons, toward dusk, I gaze out of a window at the ministry sometimes and already look forward to the day when I leave politics. Everyone in The Hague precisely wallows in that immoral constellation, but I will be happy when I can talk just as I normally do—like now. If I want to do something, I want to do it by doing it—like all decent people. Just now I opened an institute in Leeuwarden: with words, which were a deed; and afterward I had to do something else, namely pull a curtain off a statue. So that was a deed that wasn't a deed but a symbolic act. That's an ignoble existence! And if the day is even gloomier, I sometimes think of the queen in her deathly quiet palace: Her Majesty has to perform such nonacts day in day out, all her life, never being able to speak her own words, only ours. One ought to abolish the monarchy out of pure politeness."

He got up and stood at the window. "Politics," he said after a while, "harms everyone's soul. In politics your potential archenemy is always in the first row of the auditorium. That's why I have to distrust everyone—my friends first and foremost; and that in turn means that I constantly have to despise myself."

No one said anything else. Max looked in alarm at his hands, Quinten at his father's powerful back, while the words that he had heard swirled through his head like a swarm of bees.

After a while Onno turned around and said to Max: "Of course you were intending to lobby for your toy again, weren't you? Those completely superfluous thirteenth and fourteenth telescopes. I realize I've now made that virtually impossible for you. But because I would be playing politics again by using that, I shall in my infinite goodness not do so."

With relief Max realized that Onno's remark about friends he could not trust was not addressed to him.

" 'Build two mirrors!' " he said in the same tone in which Onno had quoted Solomon. "I don't know how you say that in Hebrew."

"*Tiwne shté mar'ot!* I regard it as wasted public money, social relevance nil, but I can tell you that I've meanwhile found a gap for it, at the expense of a couple of institutes abroad, which won't thank me. King Onno—builder of two mirrors in Westerbork," he said in an august tone. "When I can't even grind a pair of lenses, like Spinoza. What a wonderfully good person I am." He looked around. "What's happened to Quinten?"

"You never know with him," said Sophia.

⋆

Quinten had gone outside. In the forecourt stood the car with the two aerials—which one moment was standing still and next could be traveling at eighty miles an hour. The chauffeur was smoking a cigarette on the balustrade of the moat and gave him a friendly nod. Quinten thought the car was nicer than Uncle Diederic's, the governor's. He walked pensively across the bridge and glanced at the two wheels by the path to Piet Keller's door. The queen was sitting in her deathly quiet palace and wasn't allowed to say anything. Now he as quite sure: the queen was his mother. Otherwise his father would surely not be in the government and not have such a beautiful car, with a chauffeur; and his uncle was her governor in Drenthe, in that fancy house in Assen, looking after him. But his father had kept it hidden from him too, because of course it was a secret.

Perhaps they knew about it at school, otherwise they wouldn't be so rotten to him. They were jealous, because they themselves all had ordinary mothers, with flowered dresses and curls, and they lived on farms or in funny little houses that were stuck together. He could understand the children in his class, but they spoke differently from him, and their faces were different. Their hair was sometimes almost white and their eyes were like fishes' eyes. The boys liked soccer, which went against the grain with him, being the queen's son. Such a lovely round ball—who would think of kicking it? You might just as well kick people. You didn't do things like that as the queen's son. But the Jews all had to be killed, said Hitler, in gas chambers—Max had been talking about that again.

Perhaps he was a Jew himself; he must ask him. Max got very excited when he started talking about Hitler. What a rotter: wanting to kill Mr. Spier. . . . When he thought of "Hitler," he saw a huge muscular figure in front of him, a cannibal with long blond hair waving in the wind, who slept in a giant's bed on the heath at night.

"Watch where you're going, QuQu!"

He looked up. Selma Kern cycled past in her enormous dress. The statue his father had unveiled today might have been carved by Kern. You only had to take away the superfluous stone, and then a cloth. Perhaps Mr. Kern sometimes pulled that frock off Mrs. Kern, so that she suddenly stood naked in the room. He started laughing. What a sight! And maybe Max did that with Granny—when she crept into his bed at night, because she was cold; but he didn't want to think any more about that.

He looked at Kern's studio: he wasn't there; the padlock was on the door.

The door of Mr. Roskam's workshop was open—he could see him shuffling around in the dark. His father had had to bury his cap. Just imagine, his father had to bury his cap on the orders of the baron. He'd never do that! Anyway, he didn't even have a cap. I wonder if Mr. Roskam ever talked about it to the baron—I'm sure he didn't. He was obviously very ashamed, or perhaps he'd forgotten about it.

He walked past the lady vicar's house to the orangery, where Etienne was just driving off in his car. He turned down the window and said: "You can't go in now, beautiful. I have to run to the village. Come back tomorrow."

Once he had heard the loose planks of the bridge bumping, he carefully considered the situation. Mr. Roskam and his father had come out of the gardener's house, where the lady vicar now lived, and the old baron had stood with his son there on the threshold. So the Roskams must have been standing more or less on the same spot where he was now. But the ground was hard here; you couldn't dig a hole here. He looked around to see where he would dig a hole if he had to. He took a couple of steps from the hardened section to the start of the soft forest ground, which was now covered with fallen leaves. He took a stone and put it on the spot where the cap must be. Then he ran back to Mr. Roskam.

He was already old. He was trying to twist a nut off a tap with a pair of pliers, but didn't really have the strength anymore. When Quinten looked into his sad eyes, he wanted to say right away that he'd found his father's cap, but he preferred to surprise him.

"Well, QuQu, on the warpath?"

"Can I borrow a spade from you?"

"Buried treasure?"

"Yes," said Quinten.

"They're over there. Take the small one. But bring it back, mind, and not too late—it's getting dark earlier again."

Back at the orangery he moved the small erratic stone aside, brushed away the leaves with one foot, and stuck the spade in the ground. How deep would the cap be? No more than a foot or two. In order to increase the chance of finding it, he decided to dig a trench about a yard long, then he was sure to find it. Carefully, so as not to damage the hat even more than it already was after fifty years, he began shoveling the earth away. A few inches down he struck a stone, which he threw aside. A little later another stone appeared. He started to get worried that the cap was farther back, or to the side, but of course he couldn't dig up the whole area. It was just as well he hadn't said anything to Mr. Roskam. It was already growing dark. Suddenly there were four arrowheads on his spade, just like those in the orangery in Verdonkschot's windows. Antiquities!

He made a much bigger find than a cap! Wouldn't Etienne and Mr. Verdonkschot be pleased! He looked again at the two stones that he had thrown aside. No doubt about it! Hand axes.

Excitedly, he stuffed the finds in his pockets, filled up the trench, stamped down the ground, and brushed the leaves back in place so that no one else would have the idea of coming to look for prehistoric remains here. He was also glad that Gijs was in his shed and couldn't have seen him working. He decided not to say anything to Mr. Roskam, because he might ask him why he had started digging there; and what was he supposed to say then?

The light in the workshop was on, but the nut still wasn't loosened.

"Well?" said Mr. Roskam without looking up, when Quinten put back the spade. "Did you find any?"

"Yes."

"Good."

Fortunately he didn't ask anything else. But the chauffeur had gone and sat in the car, from which soft music was issuing. The engine was running almost inaudibly; he had obviously gotten cold. Upstairs at the front there was no light on, but when he came in everyone was sitting in the same places in the dusk.

"You've been up to something," said Sophia.

"I've been looking for Mr. Roskam's father's cap."

There was a silence, which was only broken after a considerable time by Max: "Mr. Roskam's father's cap . . . you've been looking for it . . . ?"

"Yes."

"Well?" asked Onno.

"I dug a trench and look what I found."

He emptied his pockets on the table and put the light on. All three of them stood up and bent over the artifacts.

"Fantastic!" cried Max. "Quinten! Unbelievable!" And to Onno he said, "This is unbelievably ironic. God knows all the places that man goes digging, and it's right outside his door."

"Yes," said Onno thoughtfully, holding an arrowhead close to the lamp.

"Such is life," said Sophia.

"Perhaps it's not that odd," speculated Max. "The fact that there's been a castle here for centuries might well indicate that this place was already inhabited in the Stone Age."

"So were all those things in a line?" Onno asked Quinten.

"Yes."

Onno blew on the arrowhead, moistened it with a little spit, and studied it closely again. Then he looked at Max and said: "I'm not an archaeologist, but from my previous life I have some experience of a certain kind of archaeologist. Shall I tell you what I think? That gentleman there in the orangery. . . . What's his name?"

"Verdonkschot."

"That Mr. Verdonkschot made these things himself and put them in the ground, where he lets them go prehistoric for a few years and then sells them for a bundle. I'd swear to it. That whole collection of his is fake, of course."

Max looked at him flabbergasted and then sank back on the sofa. "Of course!" he cried. "Of course!"

"Okay, you can laugh," said Onno, "because you always laugh. But we've still got a problem. One fine day those con men are going to realize that something's missing and that they've been found out."

"Shall I put them back?" asked Quinten.

"Can they see that you've been digging there?"

"I pushed the leaves back on top."

"Very good. It's October now, and by the time the ground is visible again it'll be February or March next year. And all the traces of your digging will be gone. The stuff will have just disappeared; that's their problem. Perhaps they only dig up their goods after three or four years, because if you ask me they don't look nearly old enough yet. No, there's probably no problem. Throw that rubbish straight in the dustbin."

"What villains!" said Quinten indignantly. "Shouldn't we report them to the police?"

"Absolutely," said Onno. "Legally that's our duty, in fact. But I suggest not doing it, because it's not pleasant work. Naturally it's shameful that I should say so as a minister, but the police can't blame us for not having the idea that we had immediately, of course."

Obviously, the police had other channels for discovering the truth, because a year later a blue police van suddenly appeared at the orangery, policemen in sweaters without hats on threw the contents of the display cabinets into plastic garbage bags, and, under the silent gaze of almost all the residents, Etienne and Mr. Verdonkschot were arrested. Quinten shivered when he saw them getting so helplessly into the van. He looked up at Sophia and whispered, "Daddy's always right"—at which she put a finger to her lips. Just imagine, he thought, that this had happened because his father had reported them. Etienne gave him a wave from behind the barred window.

The following day it was even in the national papers. This made the position of the two friends at Groot Rechteren untenable, and the baron immediately gave them notice to quit. Piet Keller's wife looked after the goat for another week, but after their move it disappeared too and the orangery remained uninhabited.

Quinten missed the animal most. Weeks later he sometimes sat down on the large stone and saw Gijs leaping toward him in his lopsided way—but he wasn't there. The sky was empty, and the emptiness and the absence so unfathomable and complete that he could scarcely bear it. It was as though the whole world were affected by it—the woods, the castle, everything was filled with Gijs's impossible absence in that spot, so everything that was there in some way wasn't there, actually couldn't be there, or wouldn't be there. Who was he going to talk to now? Once he had burst into sobs on the stone, and decided not to go there anymore.

He had a similar feeling when at the end of the summer there was a plague of wasps. There were screens over all the windows, but it was as though they penetrated the thick walls. There were scores of them buzzing in every room on the ceilings with their black and yellow bodies: that nasty color combination, with which they proclaimed that there was no mercy to be expected from them. Actually that was pretty stupid of them, thought Quinten; if you were a villain, you didn't flaunt it, and you really ought to clothe yourself in soft blue or pink. But of course it was to frighten off greedy birds. No one understood where they suddenly appeared from; apart from that, it looked as though there were more wasps inside than outside, so the screens were probably having the reverse effect.

One afternoon when he was wandering through the back attic he suddenly stopped and cocked his head to one side as he listened. He was aware that the whole time there was a scarcely audible trembling in the air, almost more a feeling than a sound. Here too there were wasps buzzing close to the beams, but the sound was coming from somewhere else: from the direction of Gevers's storage rooms. He stopped at a closed door. He knew that it led to a small room, really more a cupboard, where the washerwoman had perhaps once slept, but which now contained only a few rusty bed springs. Cautiously, he pushed down the handle and slowly opened the door. He froze. It was as though he were seeing something holy, that he was not allowed to see.

The wasp's nest hung from the ceiling like a huge drop from another world—slightly off-center but completely in accordance with the Golden Section, which Mr. Themaat had taught him. It seemed to be made of dusty gold. Hundreds of wasps were walking over it, slipping in and out of the opening and flying back and forth through the room, almost without buzzing, as if not to disturb the queen who was laying her eggs there in the dark interior. Suddenly they no longer seemed dangerous, just modest and charming. The window was closed. When he gently closed the door it was as though the vision of the secret had nestled deep inside him, as though he had swallowed it. In the front loft he met Arend—who was now in sixth grade and didn't want to be called Arendje anymore. When Quinten told him about his discovery he went there in disbelief, opened the door ajar, and cried, "Christ Almighty!" quickly closed the door, and fetched his father. "Very good, QuQu," said Proctor, and immediately took steps.

Half an hour later, to Quinten's dismay, the farmhand from a neighboring farm appeared in the stairwell with a spray of pesticide on his back. When he got upstairs he asked for a broom, opened the door, and immediately knocked the nest off the ceiling, took a couple of quick steps backward, and for ten or fifteen seconds sprayed a thick mist of poison gas inside, after which he aimed particularly at the fallen nest, made another sweeping movement through the whole room, and nodded to Proctor with a smile, indicating that he could close the door. After that everyone had looked in astonishment at Quinten, who had suddenly gone pale and had to be sick.

Because the farmer had said that it would be best if everyone kept out of the room for a week, Quinten was the only person who still thought about the nest. Because he had blurted out the secret with such fateful results, he felt he had something to make up to them. Meanwhile the wasps had disappeared from the castle, and from the stuffed bottom drawer of the kitchen cabinet he had taken a plastic bag. When he got upstairs, the stuffy room had lost its enchantment. Around the shattered nest the floor was strewn with dead, dried wasps. The whole state had been wiped out—

he had heard from Piet Keller that the population of wasps was called a state. The nest was now pale, like old packing paper; it felt like it too. He took it in both hands. It was very light—it had almost the opposite of a weight, like a gas-filled balloon. He put it carefully in the plastic bag. Outside, he borrowed a spade from Mr. Roskam, buried it under the brown oak tree, and marked the mass grave with a stone, which he could see from the castle.

41

Absences

Quinten was seven when Max suddenly lit a candle twice in two weeks. First Quinten heard that his great-grandmother, old Mrs. Haken, had died; and then that his grandfather Hendrikus Jacobus Andreas Quist, prime minister, Grand Cross of the Order of Orange, Grand Cross of the Order of the Dutch Lion, Grand Cross of the Order of Orange-Nassau, etc., etc., had passed away peacefully at the age of ninety-four. In the three-column announcement of his death, followed by ten more in which he was mourned, among the long list of members of the family was the name Quinten Quist, Westerbork. Max showed it to him, at the same moment regretting that he had done so: it might lead to a difficult question. But it didn't come; it had obviously not occurred to him. When he'd gone to bed, Max spoke to Sophia about the fact that Ada Quist, née Brons, Emmen, had not been listed in the notice. She thought that this was right, because her daughter no longer existed. Onno had called her about it—she'd forgotten to say; she had agreed with him.

Quinten did not attend the cremation of Sophia's mother. Max agreed that he should not be burdened with sadness about someone of three generations ago, whom he had scarcely known; but there was no question of his staying away from the funeral of Onno's father. He had been to see his grandparents in The Hague a few times, and he saw the rest of his family too, incidentally, at birthdays and parties. Occasionally, a cousin of his came to stay at Groot Rechteren, but he did not have much affinity with them. The family too, for its part, seemed to regard him more as a kind of corresponding member: if Onno was already something of an odd man out among the Quists—although somewhat less so the last few years—Quinten, brought up by his grandmother and a total stranger, was from a different world in their eyes. Moreover, his beauty was "un-Quistian," as his aunt Antonia put it: Quists were not beautiful. In fact beauty was inappropriate for respectable people.

In order to spare sensibilities Helga did not attend the funeral, and Max's instinct also told him that he did not belong there. He took Quinten and Sophia to The Hague, to the ministry, where they were received by Mrs. Siliakus, whom Onno had kept as his secretary; Max himself drove on to Leiden, to the observatory.

Onno sat at his desk, above his head a portrait of the queen, and was talking to a civil servant.

"Alone in the world!" he cried with feigned despair when they came in—but it was less despair that he was enacting than the artificial nature of that despair.

After he had put his signature—which looked like a lion tamer's whip at the moment of the crack—to a few things, had had one last telephone conversation, and had put his head around the door here and there in the silent corridors, they drove to the Statenlaan in his car. Behind closed curtains, scores of family members and close friends were assembled and were conversing in muted voices. Coffee was poured for them by Coba, and they were taking gingersnaps from a large dish.

It was apparent in all kinds of ways that Onno was now in the position of highest authority in the clan: compared with the deceased, of course, a mere nothing—a lowly minister of state—but the deceased was dead. People moved aside, the governor shook his hand, the public prosecutor looked deep into his eyes. He kissed Dol and put an arm around his mother's shoulders as she sat in a wheelchair. She began crying when she saw him. Then, holding Quinten by the hand, he went into the front room, where candles were burning and there was the stifling smell of piles of flowers. The old Quist, after a life devoted to queen and fatherland, lay in state next to the lectern with the huge, open Authorized Version.

Quinten started. He was actually lying in a *box*—they had put Granddad in a *box*! His face, which lay on the satin cushion, had changed beyond recognition. He remembered the full, heavy, powerful face, which still had something good-natured about it. Now suddenly the marble statue of a bird of prey was lying there, a fanatical hawk, like he had seen a few times swooping as the flapping doom of a field mouse. There were strange blotches on the skin of his forehead and temples; something was gleaming between his lips, as though they'd been stuck together with glue.

"Is that really Granddad?" he whispered.

"No," said Onno. "Granddad doesn't exist anymore."

On the other side of the coffin, his sister Trees shot him a reproachful look. "Granddad has left this earthly life for eternity," she said to Quinten.

He looked agog at the motionless contents of the coffin, without understanding what he saw. Something impossible was lying there. Everything that he had seen up to now in his life had been possible, because it was there; but now there was something lying there that couldn't possibly be seen and that he still saw. It was Granddad and it wasn't Granddad!

Trees suddenly began reading quietly from the open Bible: " 'And he saith unto him: Verily, verily I say unto you: hereafter ye shall see heaven open, and the angels of God ascending and descending upon the Son of Man.' "

Quinten looked at her in astonishment, and at the same time saw the thin, winding line of ants climbing and descending up the doors of the sink when sugar had been spilled.

Onno had to control himself not to snap at her that she herself definitely preferred the social ladder to that of Jacob; that insufferable reading aloud was of course only apparently intended for Quinten.

A little later six men in black appeared, with a *lid*. Quinten saw Granny To, supported by Uncle Diederic, place a last kiss on Granddad's forehead, after which the lid was lifted over the coffin. He saw the shadow fall across Granddad's face and bent his knees a little to catch the very last glimpse; at the moment that it disappeared in the darkness and wood struck wood, he heard a deep sob escape from Onno's breast, like an animal that had been imprisoned and was now finally set free. He looked at him and took his hand—and when Onno felt the small hand in his, it was as if he were his son's son.

Quinten shivered for a moment when he suddenly saw the long line of large, black limousines all waiting outside. Across the street neighbors with their arms folded watched who came out of the mansion; the police had also appeared. Two motorcycle policemen at the head of the cortege, one boot on the road, looked coolly ahead with engines running as if they owned death.

The coffin was slid into the first car, the flowers and wreaths into the following two cars. On the instructions of a balding man with papers in his hands who was leaping back and forth, Quinten was allotted his place in the third following car, on a folding chair opposite Sophia, Diederic's son Hans, now ambassador in Liberia, and Hadewych; Onno had sat next to the chauffeur. They drove to Wassenaar at an otherworldly pace, with saluting policemen at every junction. At a church in the center of the village, where spectators were kept at a distance by crowd barriers, there were many large cars already parked; except for a television news team, photographers, chauffeurs, and large numbers of police, there were in fact few people to be seen. Organ music sounded from the open doors, but shortly afterward stopped.

When Quinten went inside, he was overwhelmed by the fullness and at the same time silence. Everyone in the packed church had stood up. The first two rows were empty; as he went to the pew the man with the papers directed them to, in the middle of the second row he saw the gray-haired queen standing in the middle of the third row. Not only had she turned her gaze on him, it was as though everyone were looking at him; but he had gradually gotten used to the fact that the whole world found him beautiful.

With the queen just behind him and Granny To just in front in her wheelchair, he heard the vicar and the psalms and songs, but he didn't listen. He hadn't thought about it for quite some time, but the queen was of course not his mother, because not only was she not sleeping, she was also far too old; apart from that, she had not given any sign of recognition. On one side of him sat Granny Sophia, on the other side Rudy from Rotterdam, the same age as himself. With one finger Rudy kept an elastic band pressed against his thigh which he kept stretching and letting go of with his other hand—until Paula, his mother, suddenly took it from him.

When it was finally over and he was walking behind the coffin between Onno and Sophia, along a narrow path between the graves, Quinten suddenly asked:

"Daddy?"

"Yes?"

"Why wasn't Mommy in that big advertisement in the paper?"

Onno looked at him and didn't know immediately what to answer. He had thought long and hard about it and talked to Helga and Dol about it. Both of them thought that Ada should be included, even if she was unreachable; but in his view she was not "unreachable," because that implied the possibility of her being reached, and that simply didn't exist. Could you say of a vegetable that it was "unreachable"? His sister had called that "playing with words," but he had retorted that he obviously had a different view of both words and play. Only his mother-in-law had agreed with him; no one had thought of Quinten. Flustered, Onno glanced at Sophia. It was the second time in his life that Quinten had said something about Ada.

"We mustn't disturb Mama at all." He heard it coming from his own mouth, realizing at once that it contradicted his real motive.

"Will she wake up otherwise?"

Onno looked at Sophia, appealing for help.

"No, darling," she said. "She can't do that ever again."

Quinten nodded without saying anything.

The old village cemetery was far too small to fit everybody. When they stood in a semicircle around the grave, the queen now hand in hand with Granny To, the stationary line still wound its way back along the paths into the church. Many people were carrying bouquets—still more flowers: why flowers, of all things? Wouldn't stones be far better? While the prime minister outlined the inestimable services the deceased had rendered to the country, Quinten looked at the coffin with his hand in Onno's. It was flanked by the six men in black; against the wall of the cemetery, four ancient gentlemen stood in line, each with a colored ribbon in his buttonhole. Between the pine branches he saw the darkness of the hole into which Granddad would soon disappear forever.

"Daddy?" he whispered, when the prime minister had finished. He looked up: only then did he see that Onno's cheeks were covered in tears. He did not dare ask anything else, but Onno said in a hoarse voice:

"Yes?"

"I'd really like to see Mama."

Onno closed his eyes and nodded in silence.

At the age of four he had first said something about his mother; now he was almost twice as old. He did not even know anything about the accident; he also appeared to have forgotten that Ada's photograph was on the mantelpiece—no one had ever seen him looking at it. Everyone agreed that he should only go to see his mother accompanied by his father. A week later Onno got Mrs. Siliakus to cancel an appointment with Philips Laboratories; then she called the nursing home and on behalf of the minister of state requested that the drip feed be removed from Ada's nose temporarily the following afternoon. Although he still had very little time, he picked up Quinten from the castle, after which they drove at a hundred miles an hour down the provincial highway to Emmen. He still had a discussion with the management of the gas union in Groingen on his schedule; that evening he had to attend a state banquet in The Hague in honor of an African president whose name he had forgotten—without Helga, because concubines were not welcome at court.

They sat together on the backseat, but they still said nothing about Ada. When Onno asked what he had been up to, Quinten said that he had recently been in Theo Kern's studio. The sculptor had been working on some memorial stone or other; the letters that were supposed to go on it, he carved not from left to right, as you would think, but from right to left; he said that it was easier: he held the chisel in his left hand and the hammer in his right, so it was easier to work from right to left.

Quinten demonstrated and asked: "Could that be connected with the fact that people used to write from right to left? Because most people are right-handed?"

Onno opened his eyes wide for a moment and sighed deeply. "Yes, Quinten," he said. "Yes, that's probably a lot to do with it. From a political point of view too."

"I thought so."

"And who told you that people used to write from right to left?"

"Mr. Spier."

Onno suddenly had the feeling that one day he might be able to learn something from his son. Then he fell silent when he thought of the fact that he was contributing scarcely anything to his upbringing—even less than someone like Mr. Spier and the other residents of the castle. Of course, he could again resolve to devote more time to him, but again nothing would come of it.

When they were approaching Emmen, the driver looked in his mirror and said: "The police are after us."

Onno turned around. It was a small patrol car with a large light.

"Faster," he said.

"But, Minister . . ."

"Faster! That's an order."

The driver accelerated to a hundred and twenty. Behind them a siren began wailing, and at the entrance to Joy Court, the police car cut across them, as though it had overtaken them. Two excited policemen leapt out and a moment later realized who they were dealing with.

"Was that *you*, Mr. Quist?" said one of them flabbergasted.

"I wasn't sure you were genuine," said Onno. "I thought it might be a kidnap attack, here, with all those Moluccans and those train hijackings . . ."

"Oh, is that what it was," said the policeman, though with a rather suspicious look in his eyes. "Of course, excuse us, that changes matters."

"Doesn't matter, officers," said Onno magnanimously. "I expect you enjoyed the burn-up?"

"In one way, yes. But it was quite dangerous."

When they went inside, Onno said to Quinten: "That could have become very unpleasant for me."

Quinten was trembling a little with tension: that he would be taken to see his mother so suddenly was something that he hadn't expected. After that chase, the wheelchairs in the brick-lined hall seemed to be going even slower than before. The administrator of the hospital stood waiting for them, but Onno indicated that he preferred to be left alone; he knew the way.

The large elevator took them upstairs, and with his hand on the door handle he said: "You needn't be afraid."

Quinten saw his mother. There she was: exactly there in that place in the world, and nowhere else. Her black hair had been cut short. He stepped across the threshold and looked at the motionless sleeper—only the sheet moved slowly up and down. She was going a little gray around the ears.

After a while he asked: "Can Mama really not wake up anymore?"

"No, Quinten, Mama was already asleep when you were born. She can't hear anymore or see anymore or feel anymore—nothing anymore."

"How can that be? She's not dead, like Granddad, is she? She's breathing."

"She's breathing, yes."

"Is she dreaming?"

"No one knows. The doctors don't think so."

"How do they know?"

"They say they can measure it, with special instruments. According to them you can't even say that Mommy's sleeping."

"What, then?"

Onno hesitated, but then said anyway: "She doesn't exist anymore."

"Although she's not dead?"

"Although she's not dead. That is," said Onno, pulling a face, "Mama is dead although she's not dead . . . I mean, what's not dead isn't Mama. It's not *Mama* who's breathing."

"Who is it, then?"

Onno made a helpless gesture: "No one."

"That's not possible, is it?"

"It's absolutely impossible, but that's the way it is."

Quinten looked again at the face on the pillow. The eyes were closed; the black, semicircular eyelashes looked like certain paintbrushes, which in Theo Kern's place stood in a stone mug and which in turn looked like Egyptian palm columns, which he had seen in a book of Mr. Themaat's. Her nose was small and straight, at the side a little red and inflamed, the mouth closed, the lips dry. So could something be still more incomprehensible than his dead Granddad, last week in the coffin? In the bed lay a breathing, living woman—and they were going to see his mother, weren't they?

Why else had they driven here? So was it his mother or not? And if it was his mother and at the same time not his mother, who was he himself? His thoughts spun around—and suddenly it was as though, like with a dynamo, a soft glow lit up in his head when he suddenly saw the light of the Easter bonfire behind the trees: the towering bonfire of dried twigs collected by everyone in the area, which the baron lit every year on a field near Klein Rechteren and which hundreds of people came to look at.

"Mama's locked up," he said, thinking of Piet Keller for a moment.

Onno gave him a chair and sat down himself. He was suddenly bitterly aware that his family had been reunited for the first time: father, mother, and son, and no one else.

Quinten looked at him across the bed. "How did it happen, Daddy?"

Onno nodded and told him the whole story in broad outline. Almost the whole story—he left out the fact that Ada had first been Max's girlfriend. He told him about the friendship between himself and Max, how they had gone around together day and night, so that Quinten should understand why Max of all people had become his foster father. He told him about Ada's musical gifts, about her playing in one of the best orchestras in the world. When he came to their visit to Dwingeloo and the accident in the stormy night, the memory suddenly came back with full intensity, so he had to fight to control himself.

"After that you were in Mama's tummy for three months. That was very strange—it was even in the papers afterward."

Quinten looked at the white outlines of Ada's body under the sheet. "Was I in *that* tummy?"

"Yes."

Pensively, hands on knees, he rocked back and forth with his upper body. "But if I was in there, then I wasn't really in *Mama's* tummy anymore?"

Onno made a helpless gesture and did not know what to say. The paradox made everything true, so that nothing was true anymore. "Don't try to understand, Quinten. It's impossible to understand."

While everything looked so ordinary in the room, Quinten felt surrounded by mysteries, of which he himself was a part. It was as though in that body, inside, there was a boundless space.

"Can I touch her?"

"Of course."

He laid both his hands on hers and—for the first time since his birth—felt her warmth. Could she really not feel it? He looked at her face but it remained as motionless as that of a statue in Kern's studio.

"I'd so like to see her eyes, Daddy."

Her eyes! Onno sat up in bewilderment. He hadn't seen her eyes for eight years, either: should he fetch a nurse, or could he lift up an eyelid himself? With a feeling that what he was doing was right, he leaned over the bed, put the tip of his middle finger on an eyelid, and carefully raised it. Together they looked at the deep brown, almost black, eye that saw nothing—as little as the eye that seems to form in the sky in a total eclipse of the sun.

That evening Quinten could scarcely keep his eyes open at dinner, and immediately afterward he went to bed and found himself in the dream that was never to leave him . . .

Suddenly there are buildings everywhere: the universe has been transformed into a single architectural complex, without beginning or end. Nowhere is there a living being to be seen. Completely alone, but without a feeling of loneliness, he wanders around through a limitless series of rooms, colonnades, staircases, galleries, alcoves, pillars, footbridges, doorways, vaults, which extend in all directions—past pompous facades covered with statues and ornaments that reveal themselves as interior walls, through cellars that at the same time are lofts, across roofs that at the same time are like foundations. Because the interior has no exterior, no daylight can penetrate anywhere; but even though there are no lamps lit, it is not dark. And although he does not meet anyone and it is not clear either where he has come from or where he is going, wandering through the dimly lit world edifice fills him with happiness: all that material built, joined together, piled on top of itself, spreads out and envelops and encloses him like a bath filled with warm honey. Everywhere there is a total silence; only now and then is there a momentary swishing sound, which reminds him of the wingbeats of a large bird. Suddenly he is standing in front of a closed double door made of ancient wood, decorated with diamond-shaped patterns made of iron. It is bolted with a heavy, rusty sliding padlock, as large as a loaf. The menacing look of that device overwhelms him with dismay. It is as though the door is looking at him, and at the same moment he hears a hoarse voice saying:— *The center of the world.* The words sound calm, like when someone says "Nice day today"—but at the same time they flood him with such a sulfurous fear of death; he knows there is only one way of saving his life: waking up . . .

Trembling, bathed in sweat, he opened his eyes, but the terror did not subside. He sat up and did not know where he was. The complete darkness surrounded him as if the universe suddenly contained nothing else but him. He put out his hand and felt a wall after all; he got out of bed. Breathing heavily and groping around, he found a door, but on the other side it was just as dark and silent; at his wit's end he took a couple of steps, brushed a wall with the palm of his hand, bumped into something, felt it without recognizing it, left it, and turned on his heel. Where was he? Again he took a couple of steps. He stubbed his toe on a threshold and stopped with his eyes wide open. Suddenly, without wanting to, he gave a loud scream.

Immediately afterward, he heard Sophia's voice in the distance: "Quinten! What's wrong? Did you have a nightmare? Wait, I'm coming . . ."

After she had closed the bedroom door behind her, a strip of light appeared under the threshold. Max folded his hands under his head and stared up into the darkness. This was the end. It was bound to happen one night: and here it was. She would no longer appear in his bed. In itself there was no reason, because why should a grandmother not have an affair with her son-in-law's friend? But Quinten must not know, because then he might mention it to both of them during the day, and that was of course unacceptable.

He listened to the voices in Sophia's bedroom. Quinten was of course in bed with her now, and a great sense of calm came over Max. In fact he had expected it much earlier. He was now almost forty-two; she, fifty-two: it had lasted seven years—a long time. Their affair had had the character of a mystery, a completely new alternative alongside the classical family of father, mother, and child, without displacing the family.

During the day he had been the only man in the world who was the head of a family without quarrels, consisting of his friend's child and mother-in-law, to whom he was bound by no sexual ties; but at night he was her lover. Depending on the position of the sun, everyone was someone else—except the child. He remained simply his friend's child—although he had even doubted that for a long time. "For you everything is always something else," Onno had once said to him. Nothing in his life was what it seemed. Even the fact that he "studied stars" actually meant something different to him since he had been working in Westerbork.

What were they going to do now? The foundation of his relationship with Sophia had been removed, but the task he had undertaken of course remained unchanged: there was no question of his leaving as long as Quinten was in the house—and that could be another ten years. By that time he would be fifty-two.

42

The Citadel

For Onno, too, a moment came when everything suddenly changed again. In March 1977 the coalition government fell and new elections were held, in which his party was the great winner: that probably meant there was a ministry in prospect for him. But at the eleventh hour, after the longest political birth pangs ever known in Holland, nine months, the Christian Democrats opted for the Conservatives rather than the Socialists as partners, and overnight he was out of a job.

After handing over his powers at the ministry to his successor and receiving his decoration, he was offered the opportunity of being taken home one last time in the official car, but declined. "Decent people travel on the train," he said with insolent dignity—but when he stood in the street that cold winter afternoon it turned out not to be so simple, because since he had been in the government he was in the habit of not carrying money with him. The doorman was prepared to lend him twenty-five guilders, and sitting in the tram on the way to the station, he found himself whistling. He was free! Goodbye to The Hague! Farewell to ponds, avenues, chancelleries, cocktail parties, blue-striped shirts, poker faces!

When he left the station in Amsterdam it was already dark. He walked whistling into the lighted, messy city and for the first time in years he suddenly saw everyday life again without ulterior motives and policy initiatives, like when a window is opened after the party and the fresh night air streams in. With Christmas approaching, the streets were crowded and the shops and pubs were full; men from the Salvation Army were standing singing on the pavement around a jar in which one was expected to put money; a girl was sitting on the curb playing a guitar; a man leaned out the window of his car and swore at a cyclist.

Everything was as it was—crowded, noisy, chaotic, and at the same time with something eternal about it, something that had been exactly the same in the Middle Ages, or in imperial Rome, or in present-day Cairo, or even farther away or longer ago. There had been periods in which it had been different—like during the German occupation—but since for unfathomable reasons good ultimately always triumphed in the world, this was the real face of the eternal city. Onno felt completely happy. Since he spent little, he could if necessary live on his inheritance from his father until he died; and the automatic transfers for Quinten's upbringing were in no danger. For that matter, there was still more to come from his mother's side, and she had been in the hospital for the last few weeks; in addition, he would receive a generous severance payment for a number of months. In fact a man, he thought, should spend his life doing nothing except wandering the streets, or if he could afford that, do something real. Perhaps the real man was the craftsman.

In a telephone booth, the floor of which was covered with the pages of a telephone directory that had been torn to pieces, he called Helga. They arranged to meet in a Greek restaurant.

By the light of a candle, intended to give even the toughest cut of lamb the look of a noble *tournedos,* he told her that his dismissed colleagues and the party bosses were now gathered together bitterly in the party's room in Parliament but that he had spared himself the wake. He was celebrating his regained freedom: it was only a month since he had turned forty-four—he had a whole life in front of him! And finally he'd have more time for Quinten.

"Who do you think you're kidding?" inquired Helga. "Me or yourself?"

Onno fell silent and sighed deeply. "What an insufferable woman you are. Of course I'm kidding myself. But couldn't you have allowed me a little more time to do so?"

"I know exactly when you'll pick up the telephone and call your embittered comrades."

"And that will be?"

"When you get home in a little while and see the yellowed papers of your disc hanging on the wall."

He looked at her severely for a few seconds. "Do you think it's decent to know someone so well? It's not at all what's needed between man and woman. Between man and woman there should be nothing but misunderstandings, so that they can be overcome by physical intercourse."

"Forgive me."

He took her hand and planted a kiss on it. "Where would I be without you?"

And a few weeks later he sat on a bench, which was in fact too small for his bulk, in the Lower House as a member of Parliament and groaned as he listened to the government's policy statement.

The Phaistos disc had driven him back to The Hague. Just like most of his colleagues from the previous cabinet, he could have applied for a job outside politics—he might have become director of the Foundation for Pure Scientific Research, or mayor of a municipality like Westerbork, before receiving the sarcastic congratulations of his eldest brother; but he did what according to him befitted a politician in his circumstances: he joined the opposition, which was now led by the ex-prime minister.

Apart from that, none of those social functions accorded with his character. He had never felt like a real politician; but real politicians had in common with him the fact that in the last instance they were bohemians, street urchins, not to say street fighters, marginal figures, adventurers. And he soon realized that in a certain sense he was more in his element as parliamentarian than as a member of the government: he was better at caustic interruptions than wise policy. He created a political squabble in the blink of an eye. In response to developments in left-wing Holland, the two most important Protestant parties had merged with the Catholic party into a general confessional party; but in fact the Catholics had simply annexed the Protestants—the iconoclasts had finally been subdued by the idolaters—which prompted him to go to the microphone during the annual debate on government policy and say to the new ultra-Catholic prime minister that the revolt against Spain, out of which the nation had been born, had obviously been fought in vain. In saying this he had cut Holland to the quick, obliquely involving even the royal family, and the observation created a commotion in the papers and on television for weeks.

But when he saw the face of the prime minister stiffen, he felt disgust. Not because he was doing something to him—because his opponent was precisely a master of that style—but because again it was the words that were doing things. Now that he was a monitoring member of Parliament with no power, his world in fact turned out to be even more rarefied and abstract than it had been when he could still make decisions. That had an immoral dimension, as he had put it to Max—it was acting without doing anything, but at least it led to results. Now his speaking was on the one hand no longer action, on the other hand still not normal speech, but a hybrid, bastardized activity—in the chamber of the house, in committee rooms, and all those other forums of verbal conjuring in Parliament light-years removed from reality. It all happened in a glass bowl, which only Max might one day see thanks to his thirteenth and fourteenth mirrors, which Onno had long since been able to secure for him and which were now under construction.

"Do I really have to go on doing this for four years?" he asked Helga reproachfully as he sat on her sofa. "And perhaps for another four years after that? I'll be fifty-two by then! How long can you be a democrat with no power?"

"Who knows," she said. "Perhaps there'll be another crisis soon, or something unexpected will happen that will change everything."

"Oh Lord!" he exclaimed. "Make all things new!"

There was no interim crisis, and for the four years that the despicable, scandalous right-wing cabinet was in power—as the counterpart of the Spanish-Catholic-Habsburg tyranny in the sixteenth century—he saw Quinten even less than before—no more than a couple of times a year: on his birthday, at Christmas, at Granny To's funeral—partly because he no longer had a chauffeur-driven car, and not even one without a chauffeur, because neither he nor Helga had a driver's license: driving, in his opinion, was for chauffeurs and not for passengers like him. Increasingly, Quinten became an incident from the past for him.

But at Groot Rechteren life went on even without him. Since Quinten had appeared at the door of Sophia's bedroom that night, she had, as Max had expected, no longer appeared in his room. After seven years of clandestine faithfulness, which at the same time had been thrilling deceit, and after a few weeks of celibacy, he had started an affair with a secretary at the observatory in Dwingeloo—Tsjallingtsje Popma, a tall blond woman of about thirty, with a good figure but also with a severe rural Christian appearance.

She looked like a sculpture by Arno Breker, Hitler's favorite sculptor. Whenever she saw him, in his elegant, worldly outfit, a look of deep revulsion and contempt had appeared in her eyes; that had left him indifferent, although he had interpreted it from the very beginning as a declaration of love, because of course one did not look like that at someone one scarcely knew. But with the help of his self-denial she began to excite him more and more each day. The very first evening after he had proposed going to see the new moon with her, in the thundering silence on the heath her virtuous revulsion turned into struggling lust and loud cries of "Oh God! Oh God!" which frightened the grouse and heath frogs, so that with his trousers around his knees, he stopped with a laugh and listened to hear whether any alarmed astronomers were approaching.

But afterward: blood and tears. He had deflowered her.

"I'm so ashamed, I don't even know you . . ."

"Well, we have that in common."

She lived in a rented room in Steenwijk over a little stationer's, which also sold postcards and photo albums. One of the things that made him grow fond of her was the touching, girlish interior, with a little collection of old tin toys; because it had gotten too expensive for her in recent years, he occasionally bought her a colored wind-up bird when he was in Leiden.

They did not talk much, least of all about him and his life: they listened to music, he unfolded his radio maps, she made a cable-knit sweater for him that he would have to wear, and after taking a shower he went home. Although she had once asked him, he never took her to Groot Rechteren—although it was not primarily out of consideration for Sophia. Since after all there had never been anything between Sophia and him during the day, after a few months he had told her casually in the kitchen:

"Oh, by the way, I should tell you something, Sophia. I've got a girlfriend."

"How nice for you," she said, without looking up. "I can smell that you occasionally use a different soap."

"Respectable woman—a vicar's daughter from Enter," he added, but she didn't ask anything more; nor did she indicate that she would like to meet her.

They never talked about it after that. But it was mainly Quinten who prevented him from introducing his sturdy, affectionate Tsjallingtsje. Groot Rechteren was first and foremost Quinten's domain, which Max must not disturb with his private frivolities; apart from that he was a little frightened of the look Quinten might focus on her. Nor did he discuss her with Onno.

As he grew up, Quinten became increasingly incomprehensible to everyone. He had no friends. Usually, he sat reading in his room, or wandered through the surrounding countryside—occasionally with his recorder. As Max and Sophia sat on the balcony, they sometimes heard pastoral sounds coming from the woods, from his favorite spot by the pond with the rhododendrons. That sound, mingling with the song of the invisible birds, touched Max more than the most moving performance of the most beautiful symphony by the best orchestra, and he could see that Sophia too was thinking of Ada at those moments, but it was never mentioned.

When he was ten, in 1978, Ms. Trip stopped Sophia on the outer bridge one afternoon.

"Has Quinten told you?"

"Told me? What do you mean?"

The previous day she had been walking in Klein Rechteren with the baroness in the rose garden. As he frequently was recently, Quinten was with Rutger. In general the baroness was not very keen on unannounced visits, but because Rutger obviously perked up when Quinten came, he was always welcome. Suddenly she heard heart-rending whines coming from the direction of the terrace. They rushed toward it and saw Rutger sitting on the ground crying, with his arms around Quinten's knees—around those of his torturer, as appeared a little later.

Quinten was busy cutting Rutger's cat's cradle into pieces—the most beautiful thing he possessed, his endless creation that he had been working on for years. His mother also regularly took the scissors to it, but of course never when he was there. They had been too flabbergasted to intervene; moreover, they had the feeling that something was happening that must not be interrupted. They were also paralyzed by the strange beauty of the scene:

the wonderfully beautiful boy with that misshapen imbecile twenty years his senior at his feet, while in the vegetable garden the peacock looked at them with a fan of fifty eyes.

"Yes, calm down," said Quinten as he went on cutting the thread into yard long lengths. "Wait. We're going to make a great big curtain. You'd like to do that, wouldn't you, make a great big curtain?"

"Yes," sobbed Rutger. "Don't do that, don't cut . . ."

"But if you want to make a great big curtain, you've got to do that. Then you mustn't just go on making one thread the whole time. You've got to weave. Look, like this . . ."

Then he'd sat next to him on the ground, took a large needle out of his pocket, and picked up the stiff, coarse-meshed base a yard square that he had brought with him and which he had turned out to have bought with his pocket money from the fabric store in the village. While he threaded a length of yarn through it, explaining what he was doing the whole time, Rutger stopped crying and looked breathlessly, chest still heaving, at what was happening.

"Now your turn," said Quinten, giving him the needle. "And when this one is completely full, we'll buy a new cloth. And when that's full, then we'll sew it onto this one and then we'll buy another one— until," he said with a sweep of his arm, "the curtain is as big as the whole world!"

"Yes!" Rutger laughed, dribbling.

"And if you make another curtain after that, then we'll hang it on the sun and the moon!"

"Yes! Yes!" Rutger bent over to him and gave him a kiss on his cheek. No one had ever had the idea that it was possible to intervene in Rutger's senseless activity, let alone that anyone would have had the courage to carry it through.

"How did you get that brainwave?" Max asked him that evening in awe. "How did you dare?"

"Well, I just did . . ." said Quinten.

Max looked at Sophia and said: "That boy has an absolutist streak in his character."

The nurturing architectural dream that had appeared after his visit to his mother turned out to recur every few months. But it never ended in a nightmare, although the fortified door with the padlock on it at "the center of the world" must still be there. Whenever he had wandered around the limitless construction, through the labyrinth of rooms, past the decorated interior facades, along the galleries, he lay still for a moment after waking up, cracking the top joints of his thumbs as he did every morning, and tried to retain the memory—but always the images took their leave after a few minutes, like in the movies when the end of the film became invisible if the lights went on too soon. He gradually began to wonder where that building was. It must actually be somewhere, because each time he saw it clearly. But since he never met anyone there, he was certainly the only person who knew of its existence—and that meant a lot, because it was secret and he mustn't speak to anyone about it: of course not to Max, but not to Granny either; not even to his father, the few times that he saw him. For that matter how could it simply be somewhere in the world when the whole world was not built up? Perhaps it was in another world. He had also given it a name: the Citadel.

Sometimes he did not think of the Citadel for weeks. If it presented itself again, he sometimes went to Mr. Themaat's to see if there were illustrations of anything like it in his thick books. The professor had retired and now lived permanently at Groot Rechteren, so his library had expanded still further. Quinten was always welcome. Occasionally it happened that Mr. Themaat was in his rocking chair without a book on his lap. His face suddenly changed unrecognizably, as if it had been turned to stone, and that stone looked at him with two eyes expressing such total despair that he went away at once. It was as though Mr. Themaat in that state no longer even knew who he was. For a few days he did not dare visit him; but when he came back there was suddenly no trace of the stone.

"What are you looking for, for goodness' sake, QuQu?"

"Just looking."

"I don't believe a word of it. You're not just looking at pictures."

Quinten looked at him. He must not betray the secret, of course, because then the dream might not come back. He asked: "What is *the* building, Mr. Themaat?"

Themaat gave a deep sigh. "If only my students had ever asked me such a good question. What is *the* building?" he repeated, folding his hands behind his head, leaning back in his rocking chair and looking at the stucco of the ceiling. "What is *the* building . . ." While he was still thinking, his wife came in. He said, "QuQu has just asked me the question."

"And what is that?"

"What is *the* building?"

"Maybe this castle," said Elsbeth.

"Yes," said Themaat, laughing at Quinten. "Women usually look less far afield, and perhaps they're right. Wait a moment. Perhaps I know," he said. "*The* building of course doesn't exist, but I think the Pantheon comes a good second."

A little later they sat next to each other on the ground looking at photos and architectural drawings of the Pantheon in Rome: the only Roman temple—devoted to "all gods"—that had been completely preserved. Quinten had seen at once that it was not like the Citadel at all. It was not a maze, but precisely very simple and clear, with a portico like a Greek temple facade at the front, as Mr. Themaat called it, with pillars and two superimposed triangular pediments; behind them, a heavy round structure that from inside consisted of a single huge, empty, windowless rotunda, with a large round hole in the middle of the cupola, through which the light entered—a little like the fontanel in a baby's skull.

On a cross-section drawing Mr. Themaat demonstrated with a compass that if you continued the line of the cupola downward, you produced a pure sphere resting on the ground. According to him, you could see the temple as a depiction of the world.

That meant, Quinten reflected, *this* world—and that was obviously not what he was dreaming about. But nevertheless it was connected with the Citadel, perhaps through the opposition of the decorated front and the closed back. In any case it fascinated him—also the carved letters on the architrave, which announced through a number of abbreviations, that AGRIPPA was the architect. The emperor Hadrian had magnanimously had this inscribed after it had been completely rebuilt, Themaat told him—and at the mention of the name Hadrian he suddenly stopped and looked at Quinten—the deep blue of his eyes between the dark eyelashes, the lank black hair around his moon-pale skin.

Themaat made a gesture in his direction and said to Elsbeth: "Antinous."

She smiled, glanced at him, and nodded.

Quinten didn't understand what was meant, but he didn't care.

One day, when he started talking about those letters to Mr. Spier, in fact just for something to say, Spier immediately became enthusiastic:

"That's the Quadrata, QuQu, the most beautiful capital there has ever been! How did you find out about that?" Then he told him that it was also called "lapidary" from the Latin *lapis,* meaning "stone." "That letter forms the perfect balance between body and soul."

"How is that possible? A letter isn't a human being, is it?"

"Of course it is!"

"Well how can letters have a soul?"

"They speak to you, don't they?"

"That's true." Quinten nodded earnestly.

"Like everyone, a letter has a soul and a body. Its soul is what it says and its body is what it's made of: ink, or stone."

Quinten thought of his mother. Was she just a couple of ink spots, then? Or a stone with no letters on it?

"A letter doesn't have to be made of anything," he said.

"Oh no? I sometimes dream of pure letters, floating through the air, but that's impossible, just like a soul without a body."

"And what about those letters in the Pantheon? They're not made of stone, precisely not stone. The stone has been carved away: I've seen Theo Kern doing that sometimes. They're made of nothing. So you sometimes do have a body without a soul in it, don't you?"

He was now in the sixth grade, and according to the teacher he should gradually start spending more time on his homework. His marks were not bad, but not good either; what naturally interested him, he mastered immediately, even if it was difficult; all the rest, even when it was actually easy, required lots of effort. But instead of learning his geography, or doing arithmetic, he preferred to find his way toward the Citadel with Mr. Themaat.

Sometimes the professor showed him examples of modern architecture from the first half of the twentieth century, by Frank Lloyd Wright or Le Corbusier or Mies van der Rohe, of which he was quite fond himself. Sometimes Quinten thought it was nice, but that was all; because the cool objectivity of those matchboxes in no way reminded him of the Citadel, he lost interest.

Classical buildings came closest, centrally the Roman Pantheon, which, with its circular, windowless central section, added something somber and threatening to the pure light of the Greek temples. The Athenian Parthenon, which Mr. Themaat showed him, might be perfect, even as a ruin, but to his taste it was too rarefied and transparent. According to Themaat, the Romans had in fact never invented anything themselves from an artistic point of view; they had taken that sense of circularity and somberness from Etruscan tombs, *tumuli,* as could still be seen in Rome in the mausoleum of Augustus, or the tomb of Hadrian, the Castel Sant'Angelo. He should go and see all those things one day, later.

Under the direction of Themaat, who once talked of him to Max as "my best student," Quinten had soon found his way to the Italian Renaissance. There he was most fascinated by the churches of Palladio, who again showed that combination of brilliant classical facades and introverted brick walls. Themaat praised him for his good, albeit not very progressive, taste but that compliment was lost on him; none of it had anything to do with taste.

In the baroque, he had a vague feeling of recognition in the exuberant ornamentation, and neoclassical buildings from the nineteenth century fascinated him because they reminded him of those of Palladio in the sixteenth century. In any case they were all exteriors: magnificent exteriors, but he was precisely not interested in exteriors, only interiors.

Running the risk that he was revealing something of his secret, he decided one afternoon to ask a crucial question:

"Is there a building that has an interior but no exterior?"

Themaat stared at him for a couple of seconds before he was able to answer. "What made you think of something like that?"

"I just thought of it."

"Of course that's impossible, just like a building with an exterior but no interior."

"That's perfectly possible."

"How?"

"If it's not hollow inside, but of solid stone. Like a sculpture."

"There's something in that," said Themaat with a laugh. "And perhaps an interior without an exterior is possible too."

While he looked in his bookcase, he said that he himself had been brought up with the idea that the Renaissance was old-fashioned, and to tell the truth he still thought so; but when he heard Quinten so preoccupied with it, he had the feeling that there was something like a "re-Renaissance" coming. Then he showed him photographs of Palladio's Teatro Olimpico in Vicenza, his architectural swan song.

From the outside it was an ugly brick box, but inside it showed indescribable magnificence. The back and the side walls were made of inlaid marble facades, exuberantly decorated with Corinthian columns, statues in luxurious window frames, with triangular and segment-shaped pediments; there were other sculptures—on pedestals, ornaments, scrolls, reliefs, inscriptions, behind the sloping benches of the semicircular room more pillars and sculptures—all made of wood and plaster, but you had to know that. That was also an exterior without an interior, said Themaat, because it was a piece of decor, and at the same time it was an interior without an exterior. Quinten understood that, but it was only partially a depiction of the Citadel.

"For that matter, do you remember that book by Bibiena that you used to like looking at so much?"

No, Quinten had forgotten, but when he saw it again a vague memory awakened in him. Themaat explained to him that those decor drawings showed the inside of buildings that had no outside. Obviously pleased with his explanation, the professor looked at the perspective drawings a little longer. Then he suddenly said: "Wait! Perhaps I have something even nicer for you."

From the case where everything was in perfect alphabetical order, he looked a little farther on from Palladio, Pantheon, and Parthenon—a large book of reproductions of Piranesi's *Carceri*.

When he opened it, it gave Quinten a jolt. Almost! It was almost there, his dream!—the same rooms continuing endlessly in all directions, full of staircases, bridges, arches, galleries; the deep shadows without sources of light; everything filled with the same still air. But in these etched prison visions it seemed chilly and dank, while in the Citadel it was warm and sweet. Except for him, the Citadel was empty, but here there were figures to be seen everywhere; the pillars and the massive, decorated facade were also missing. Only in combination with the decors of Palladio and Bibiena would it have really resembled the scenario of his dream.

"Now I'm gradually getting a vague idea of what you're looking for," said Themaat. "But in that case we'll have to look at a completely different kind of book than we have up to now. You don't want existing buildings but architectural fantasies. By the way, do you know that Piranesi is also the man who made your favorite print over there?"

"My favorite print?"

Themaat pointed to the framed etching that stood on the floor against the bookcase.

Quinten looked at it in astonishment. For years the print had merged with the other things in the room, he had never noticed it: the obelisk next to the building with the Scala Santa, the Sacred Staircase.

43

Finds

In the early summer of 1980, the two new movable mirrors were inaugurated in Westerbork—not by Onno's successor, but by the minister himself. Onno and Helga drove with Max from The Hague and were welcomed by Diederic the governor, who was shortly to retire. Apart from that, everyone from Leiden was there—at the center the old director, now eighty, but still upright, as if he were the axis around which the globe of heaven turned. The whole of Dwingeloo had also naturally appeared, even Tsjallingtsje, but that was because she wanted to see Sophia and Quinten at last. Quinten had initially not wanted to go, but when he heard that his father would be there, Sophia and he had naturally come, too. When Max saw them all together in the control building, with a glass of champagne in their hands, he was reminded of a certain kind of thriller, in which all the suspects were finally gathered in the lounge of the hotel, where after an acute reconstruction the detective singled out the culprit, whom one would never have thought capable of doing it.

After the speeches and the ministerial finger on the button, a large part of the company, including Tsjallingtsje, walked to the thirteenth and fourteenth mirrors, which were a mile and a half away; some of them were still holding their glasses of champagne. Floris, who knew how far they had to walk, had put a bottle in his pocket. Sophia stayed behind with Helga in a circle of astronomers' wives, who had seen enough, while Max, Onno, and

Quinten walked into the grounds. Onno, who was in Westerbork for the first time, had put a hand on Quinten's shoulder and was listening to Max. Only the villa belonging to the camp commandant was still standing; the huts had given way to a broad, innocent-looking expanse of grass with an occasional tree, surrounded on all four sides by woods. As they walked along the former Boulevard des Misères, Max tried to give Onno a picture of the scenes that had taken place almost forty years before; looking at the boy he controlled himself, but Quinten suddenly asked:

"Are you a Jew?"

Max and Onno glanced at each other.

"My mother got on the train here and never came back," said Max.

"And what about your father?"

"Not him."

"Is he still alive, then?"

"Not for a long time."

Quinten was silent. Since he had talked to Mr. Spier about it, he hadn't thought any more about the Jews—it shocked him that Max, too, was connected with those things: his mother had even been murdered by Hitler! It did not concern him, but it gave him a vague feeling of guilt that he had never known about it. What did he really know about Max? Last year he had heard him say that he had to go to Bloemendaal, to his foster mother's funeral; he had not asked any more about it, but now he understood why Max—like he himself, in fact—had had foster parents.

At the buffers the rails and sleepers had been left, neatly framed by a kind of curb. Max showed them that the buffer was new; the old one was close behind it, almost completely forgotten. The end of the rails had been bent upward by an artist, as though in that spot the last train had gone to heaven.

"It's all gone for good," said Max, letting his eyes wander over the site.

In the distance the cheerful group of worthies and astronomers walked past the majestic row of parabolas, pointing at the blue sky like the rails; their laughter resounded faintly across the plain. While neither Max nor Onno knew what to say next, Quinten looked back and forth between the mirrors and the rails, which reminded him of the antennae of a grasshopper.

"If you ask me," he said, "one day you'll be able to see here very clearly what happened during the war."

Max and Onno looked at him in alarm.

"May one ask what you mean, Quinten?" asked Onno.

"Well, it's quite logical. Max once told me that we see the stars as they used to be. So on the stars they see the earth as it used to be. If the people on a star that is forty light-years away from here look at us with a very powerful telescope, then they must be seeing what happened here forty years ago, mustn't they?"

"Is that right?" Onno asked Max.

Max shivered. "Of course."

It amazed him that he had never had that idea: the image of Westerbork as a transit camp was now rushing at the speed of light through space between Arcturus and Capell A, like that of Auschwitz with its fire-belching chimneys. "In theory it ought to be always visible somewhere in the universe. Except that doesn't mean we can see it."

"But it will be reflected back, won't it?" said Quinten.

"Reflected back?"

"With those telescopes over there you can look at a star that is twenty light-years away from here, can't you?—so you can see your mother getting into the train forty years ago, can't you?"

And getting off somewhere else, thought Max.

"You're right again. Perhaps you should think more of distant planets or moons, at least if such things exist outside our solar system, but then we first have to discover a completely new principle."

"But when that's been discovered in a hundred years' time, it will be possible to see it from a planet or a moon, which is fifty plus twenty light-years away from us."

"I can't argue with you."

"I don't feel well," said Onno. "Quinten! What's gotten into you? What kind of person are you?"

Quinten shrugged his shoulders. If you asked him, it was all pretty obvious.

While Sophia and Helga were busy in the kitchen, as in Onno's view befitted women, the gentlemen went on talking about the subject of "historical astronomy" founded by Quinten. Proctor was also there. He had dropped by to borrow some eggs. Clara and Arend were spending the night with his mother-in-law. Sophia had invited him to join them for a meal.

That everything that had ever happened on earth was still to be seen somewhere in the universe was obviously a very seductive idea of Quinten's; but according to Onno, it could never be realized. It was true that satellite photos of the earth could be enlarged down to the smallest details, at least if it was cloudless when the photo was taken—at the Defense Ministry they knew all about it—but what would be left of such an image after a journey of scores, hundreds or thousands, of years through the universe? Moreover, how was it to be reflected back? After all, planets and moons were not made of mirror glass. They were strewn with stones and dust and, besides that, convex instead of concave: the last remnants of the image would be immediately dispersed.

"And that's as it should be," he concluded. "The past is sealed for eternity, and whoever tries to break those seals—would that he had never been born. Only the Lord of Hosts sees everything."

"Of course," said Max, "your optical knowledge is astonishing, but that's what people have always said. Just imagine a boy of twelve saying to his father a hundred years ago that within a hundred years not only would man set foot on the moon, but that everyone on earth would have been able to witness it at the same moment—"

"Yes, yes, we know all about that," Onno interrupted him. "I vaguely remember your saying that eleven years ago." He gestured toward Helga, who was setting the table. "Thanks again."

Helga glanced around, and Max made a polite bow to both of them, and then continued:

"If you go on thinking of an optical image, of course it would never be possible—that's obvious. But in radio astronomy we don't work with optical images, do we? Do you have any idea how weak the signals are that we receive in Westerbork? What makes things so misleading there is that when you've got large instruments and machines, you automatically think of large forces: a large dam produces enormous quantities of energy; a huge cannon has an enormous range. But with the synthesizing radio telescope it's precisely the other way around: there, the large is intended for the small. Shall I tell you something? A bicycle lamp uses more energy in one second than all those fourteen dishes receive in a hundred years."

"Really?" asked Quinten.

"Really. And as far as that's concerned, we're getting quite a long way. In other words, in a practical sense it may not be totally impossible, but some Einstein or other would first have to find an entirely new principle, just as was necessary for television."

"If he says it," said Onno, "it's probably right. Okay, so there's a nice branch of science for you—as long as you know that Quinten has a right to share the Nobel Prize."

Quinten did not like Max contradicting his father; on the other hand he was flattered by his support, and he thought it was nice of his father to allow himself to be convinced. He also thought that it was nice that they talked for a long time about the idea that had occurred to him.

"If there's a possibility," said Max, "I think it will be even more difficult than the key to your disc. After all, you also assumed that messages from the distant past could be read on it, didn't you?"

"Dr. Quist's unforgettable *Narration from A to Z*," said Helga, glancing at Onno as she left the room.

Onno sighed deeply.

"Do you know what that woman is? My scribe, like Eckermann was to Goethe. She never forgets anything you've ever said. God knows, perhaps the principle may be on that wretched Cretan thing, who knows? If one day I'm ousted from power because of an excessive intelligence that forms a danger to the state and am driven shamefully over the frontier by the royal military constabulary, I may give it one last try—but I fear that I shall need precisely that historioscope in order to decode the principle on which it's based. Probably by that time I would have been murdered by some secret service or other, or by agents of the pope, because imagine what it would unleash: photographs of everything that's ever happened or what precisely didn't happen . . ."

"Or film," said Quinten.

"Or film, of course! First silent films, then talkies, and then in color as well! We focus on the Star of Bethlehem and we zoom in on the Mount of Olives. Is someone ascending into heaven there? No. Is someone receiving the Ten Commandments on Mount Horeb? Alas. No, I would be quite rightly eliminated; the world would descend into chaos."

"A great spring cleaning," said Max, "that's what it would be. All nonsense and fraud would be brought to light; mankind would be liberated and would finally possess the whole truth!"

But as he spoke, to his dismay he suddenly saw another astronomical documentary before him: the bay at Varadero—himself bobbing up and down in the waves, cheek to cheek with Ada, her legs spread wide around his hips in the blood-red light of the rising moon. . . . So hadn't it disappeared—not even in himself?

Onno was going to ask him what event he would photograph first, but he could tell from his look that it would probably be something dreadful, perhaps his father's execution—so he turned to Proctor:

"What about you? What would you focus this historical camera on?"

As befits someone who has just come to dinner, the translator had not taken part in the conversation, but now he leaned forward and said: "At a deathbed in a certain house in Stuttgart in the old center, which was devastated in the Second World War. In the year 1647."

"Of course. For that purpose of course we screw the X-ray lens on the camera, which can penetrate through all walls. And whom do you want to see dying there?"

"Francis Bacon," said Proctor, and looked significantly from one to the other.

"Francis Bacon?" repeated Max. "In Stuttgart? In 1647? Are you sure you're not wrong?"

Proctor gave a short laugh with a bitter undertone. Of course, official scholarship had thought for centuries that he had died in London in 1626, but new facts had taught them otherwise—that is, people with an open mind who were able to let go of old ideas. Of course, he knew all about the nonsense that the Baconians were wont to spout, for example that Shakespeare's work was actually by Bacon, but he did not take any notice of that nonsense—even though it had respectable adherents, like old Freud. But it had always intrigued him why such rubbish was attributed precisely to Bacon. And then years ago he himself had discovered something unprecedented. He looked back and forth between Max and Onno. Could they keep a secret?

"Our lips are sealed," said Onno, folding his arms.

Bacon had been present at the birth of Vondel's *Lucifer*. That tragedy had its first performance in Amsterdam on February 2, 1654. Vondel had worked on it for six years—that is, he had begun it in the year of Bacon's actual death. Proctor had collected hundreds of textual proofs for his thesis, that the idea of writing a play about the downfall of Lucifer derived from Bacon. The eighty-six-year-old Bacon had whispered it to the sixty-year-old Vondel on his deathbed.

"Do you also have proof," asked Onno, having exchanged a short glance with Max, "that our national prince of poets was in Stuttgart in 1647?"

"He must have been. That is implicitly proved by my other evidence."

"Of course."

"I keep finding new proofs."

"Name one."

The usual code from the seventeenth century, Proctor told them, numbered the letters of the alphabet from one to twenty-four, with the *I* and the *J* having the same number, 9, and the *V* and *W* the figure 21. The sum of BACON came to 33 and that of FRANCIS to 67, totaling 100. Now, if you took Lucifer's first speech in Vondel and looked for the thirty-third word, then you found: *this*. Meaning, "This is Bacon." Or, "This should really be attributed to Bacon." If you went on counting to the hundredth word, then you found *extinguished*. That is, "This man is extinguished. Francis Bacon dies."

There was a moment's silence, after which Max said to Onno: "If you ask me, there's no answer to this."

"We have absolutely no answer to this. But," inquired Onno cautiously, "if you want to focus that deathbed there in Stuttgart with Quinten's telescope, does that not mean that you're not a hundred percent certain of your case, which to me personally seems so completely plausible?"

"What makes you think that?" said Proctor, almost indignantly. "All I want to do is hear *why* Bacon wanted to see a play about the downfall of Lucifer written. I imagine he told Vondel. What had he, as an Anglican, to do with a figure like Lucifer? Perhaps that may be connected with all those absurd legends attaching to his person; but I shall get to the bottom of that."

"Of course." Onno nodded. "That's necessary. And why did Bacon choose Vondel, of all people?"

"That's obvious! As a Catholic, Vondel had a relationship with devils and angels—there was no point in Bacon tackling a Protestant like Gryphius about it. Vondel was at that moment the only great dramatist who came into consideration for his project—except for Corneille, perhaps, but one couldn't permit oneself such fantastic extravagances in the Paris theater as one could in Amsterdam."

"Why fantastic?" asked Quinten.

"Listen," said Proctor. "It had never been shown in literature before: a play set from beginning to end in heaven. If that isn't fantastic, then I don't know what is."

"What a beautiful ring you have on," said Quinten suddenly.

A little disconcerted, Proctor looked at it. "It's a sapphire. Also a symbol of heaven."

"I expect it's very expensive."

"I should say so. A five-carat stone costs a good five thousand guilders. This is one gram."

Max too leaned forward. "Can you see that stone is exactly the color of your eyes, Quinten?"

"Are you coming to eat?" asked Sophia. "We've got hot pot with rib of beef."

Even though he only understood half of them, Quinten never forgot conversations like that. But what he heard at his high school in Assen, where he had to go on the bus every day from the end of the summer onward, he could only retain with the greatest effort. Moreover, the fact that *Gallia est omnis divisa in partes tres* he was prepared to believe; but the fact that in his book it was printed in lower case, and sometimes even in italics, he found idiotic: the Romans hadn't known those letters at all! They should be capitals, preferably the Quadrata. According to Mr. Spier, that typeface had originated in the Middle Ages and the Renaissance—like the Greek minuscule: the ancient Greeks, too, had written only in capitals. When Onno once called up from Parliament to say that he was terribly sorry that he was tied up again, Quinten had complained to him too:

"Can they just change it just like that? It's the same as if you were to depict Caesar in a denim suit instead of a toga."

Whereupon Onno had exclaimed: "Well done, Quinten. You're a son after my own heart! Fortunately modern theater doesn't appeal to you at all. Until the Heaven and the Earth shall pass away, not a jot or tittle of the Law shall pass you by, until everything shall be accomplished!"

Of course that was from the Bible again, but he had no idea what it referred to. Since the evening after the inauguration of the new telescopes, he had looked up to his father even more. At dinner he had asked him what kind of disc it was that Max had talked about, and for the first time it had dawned on him that his father had originally not been a politician at all, but a linguistic genius, who had interpreted Etruscan. Something quite different from that strange father of Arend's, who only concerned himself with sterile abracadabra, as Onno told him afterward. He himself, he had said, could prove in a trice that Bacon had written Genesis, or the novels of Nabokov: all you had to do was look at the first five letters of his name and you could see that it was an anagram of "Bacon," and if you had to remember that the *c* in the Cyrillic alphabet was the *ka;* and the ending *ov,* of course, stood for "of Verulam"—that was obvious.

Max sometimes told him fascinating things, too—for example that it didn't matter which way you looked: the most distant object was always yourself; or about the mystery of why it was dark at night and not much brighter than during the day, with that indescribable number of stars, which altogether should really form one gigantic sun, one infinite light, that should constantly light the whole firmament ... but when all was said and done Max was not his father. His foster father's connection with the war, with Hitler, who had murdered his mother, was in an alarming world, which Mr. Spier also inhabited, but in which he, fortunately, was not involved.

His interest continued to focus on things that were not taught in school. As in elementary school, he made no friends; he had never yet met anyone of his own age with whom he could talk about the things that concerned him. But it was not something that caused him pain, nor did it surprise him, because he did not even have the *feeling* that he was different from his classmates—it was so self-evident. In the breaks he talked and laughed with them, but a little like an actor playing his role; after the performance, when he was himself again, the character disappeared completely from his thoughts. For the same reason he did not feel superior, because it did not occur to him to compare himself with them.

In a heavy wrought-bronze box that he had found in the loft among the baron's things, he kept the sketches that he made of the Citadel of his dreams. Because the Citadel was infinite in all directions, he was obliged to limit himself to fragments, cross-sections, ground plans, which could not form a whole but did all relate to each other. The double-folded papers were in a thick beige envelope from the Westerbork Synthetic Radio Telescope, on which he had written in his first high school Latin and in his most beautiful Quadrata *Quinten's dream:* SOMNIUM QUINTI.

In his search for "the" building, Mr. Themaat had meanwhile put him on the trail of the classicist revolutionary architecture that flourished around 1800—at least in designs, because very little of it had actually been built. Again neglecting his homework, Quinten studied the drawings of scores of architects from that school, but he kept returning to the megalomaniacal fantasies of Boullée. They really exceeded all bounds, said Themaat, and that boundless quality was precisely what fascinated Quinten. Gigantic public buildings: a palace of justice, a necropolis, a library, a museum, a cathedral—each of them of such Cyclopic dimensions that one needed a magnifying glass to be able to distinguish the people, who swarmed like ants over the staircases and between the towering columns. Also a gigantic temple, which according to Themaat you had to imagine as the Colosseum, crowned by a cupola like that of the Pantheon. It was built over an inaccessible, dark ravine, which led into the center of the earth; the entrance to the cave stood a statue of Artemis Ephesia, the goddess with the many breasts. Quinten stared at them shyly. Did perhaps the world of the Citadel begin in that black abyss? He was reminded of his mother for a moment, but immediately put it out of his mind. He scarcely ever thought of his mother, because he had learned from his father that it meant he was thinking of nothing; he had never visited her again since that one time, because how were you to visit no one? Fortunately, Granny never asked him if he was going with her to Emmen.

He was just as fascinated by Boullée's extreme designs for a Newton monument. He knew who Newton was from Max: the Einstein of the seventeenth century, with whom modern science had begun, and who—so Themaat told him—was worshiped in the seventeenth century as a kind of messiah, since he had been the first to understand and calculate the work of the world's architect.

The cenotaph would have consisted of a colossal globe more than six hundred feet across, held up to its equator in three staircaselike, windowless cylinders, planted with colonnades of cypresses, the trees of death par excellence. Within, in the deep twilight, the empty sarcophagus stood on a dais, illuminated only by the small holes·in the globe, causing the sunlight to be transformed into the night sky full of stars. When Quinten saw the tiny coffin in the enormous space, the thought of his mother occurred to him willy-nilly. A drawing of the building in the moonlight exuded an ominous threat, as though the globe were a dreadful bomb that could explode at any moment and devastate the whole world—and one day he imagined that a smoldering fuse was sticking out of the top of the ball. Even while he was telling that fantasy to Mr. Themaat, he immediately saw something else: the bomb with the fuse was at the same time an apple with a stalk.

"If you ask me, that building is actually the apple that fell on Newton's head."

"No one has ever seen it like that," said Themaat, laughing. "Up to now we always thought of the universe."

"And now I know exactly what kind of apple it was that fell on Newton's head."

"Is it a secret, or can you tell?"

"The apple that Eve picked in Paradise."

"From the tree of the Knowledge of Good and Evil!" added Themaat, and suddenly he went into one of his strange, exaggerated fits of laughter, in which even his long arms and legs participated, so that his rocking chair threatened to tip over. "Help! You did it again, QuQu! And in order to prove your assertion," he said, getting up, "I'll immediately show you something else."

As he hunted among the piles of magazines that were lying on the bottom shelves of his bookcase, he said that Quinten would have of course noticed the similarity between Boullée's Newton cenotaph and the Pantheon: that windowless round globe, which in both cases depicted the universe. "But as the founder of modern science also sat beneath the Tree of the Knowledge of Good and Evil," he said, "what do you think of this?" Slightly triumphantly, he put a photo of a nuclear reactor on the table. "Talking of your bomb. Do you see that this thing fits exactly into the stylistic tradition of the Pantheon and of Palladio and Boullée? The fantastic thing is that the factory wasn't at all designed in an aesthetic tradition, but purely functionally, by architectural engineers from a government institute. Goodness gracious, QuQu. I'm inclined to think that what you say is true. And if you know that the creation of atomic energy, therefore also of the atom bomb, is due to Einstein, the second Newton, then Boullée may have actually designed an Einstein monument."

"That's why it wasn't built then." Quinten nodded.

"Because it's only relevant now, do you mean? Yes, why not? Although . . ." he said, making a face, "there are still a few snags. Not technical, because we'd be perfectly capable of building it nowadays, but something that is actually connected with your apple of paradise."

Then he gave Quinten a lecture about the gigantic. It was always connected with death. The Colosseum had been built with the intention that human beings and animals should die in it; the gigantic, circular Castel Sant'Angelo, also in Rome, had been built by Hadrian as a mausoleum for himself and his successors. That gigantic scale originated in Egypt, where the whole of life was oriented toward the kingdom of the dead. The pyramids, those denials of time, were nothing but graves with a sarcophagus in them; and what Boullée had achieved, at least in imagination, was a link between that necrophiliac monumentality and its opposite, Greek harmony and moderation.

He showed Quinten a sheet with a design for a necropolis: a pyramid, in the base of which a semicircular hollow had been cut, wedged in it, like a mouse in a trap, a Greek temple facade with columns and the decorated architrave. That portico in combination with that arch were again of course reminiscent of the Pantheon, but at the same time that joyful Greek element was overshadowed and crushed by the mass of Egyptian style above it. And that architectural representation of the fragility of life, suddenly obviously threatened by the power of a colossal death, returned 150 years after Boullée as the depiction of direct mass murder: in the designs that Albert Speer had made for Adolf Hitler.

Quinten started when he heard that name: there was that villain again! Actually, that name should never be spoken again. Mr. Themaat showed him photographs of the models for "Germania," as Berlin was to have been called after the final victory, as the thousand-year world capital. Series of unbridled buildings, with as their Germanic climax the Great Hall, which surpassed everything that had ever been imagined.

On Speer's own testimony this monster, too, issued from the inexhaustible womb of the Pantheon: a neoclassical facade of pillars with a round space behind it, topped by a cupola. But that cupola was now twice as high as the pyramid of Cheops; on top of it was a cylinder-shaped lantern, surrounded by pillars to admit light, which was itself already many feet taller and wider than the whole Pantheon, which in turn was larger than Michelangelo's cupola in St. Peter's. On top of that, like the fuse of Quinten's bomb, stood an eagle with the globe in its claws. The hall could accommodate 180,000 people, reduced to the status of fleas; the possibility of cloud formation and drizzle had to be allowed for. The project was based on a sketch that Hitler himself had once made—originally Hitler wanted to become an architect, Mr. Themaat told him, but on reflection he preferred to go into the demolition business, because after his suicide, scarcely one stone was left standing in Berlin. Even the models had finally been burned.

"So now you've got everything together architecturally, QuQu. Hiroshima and Auschwitz. The gigantic triumph of science and technology in the twentieth century!"

If he wanted to read without being disturbed or to play his flute, Quinten sometimes went to sit by the side of the pond when the weather was fine. There, surrounded as though in the tropics by the tall rhododendron bushes and usually in the company of the two black swans floating on their own reflections, he felt protected and at peace. He had built a hut of branches, which he was proud of and which protected him against rain that was not too heavy. But if something was worrying him or if he had to think about something, he usually sought out a different spot: a couple of hundred yards outside the estate, behind the baron's fields.

Although scores of people came past every day, he was certain that he was the only one who had recognized the place, because he never saw anyone looking at it specially. In fact there was nothing much to see about it. It was the site of the annual Easter bonfire: a small, oblong field, enclosed on three sides by tall trees, on the fourth by a narrow country lane. In the summer a red cow grazed there; she looked up attentively when he sat down in the ditch and put his arms around his knees. Perhaps it was also connected with those two trees, which seemed to have escaped from the dark edge of the wood and were standing separately in the grass, each in a perfectly good place, where they gave the space structure, as did the three large erratic stones—but that did not explain the mystery that hung about the place. It was as though it were warmer and quieter than in other places where it was just as warm and quiet.

He let his eyes wander over the enclosed domain and thought of the previous day. Because his father had again not found time to come to Groot Rechteren for a couple of months, Quinten had been to visit him in The Hague with Max, where to his satisfaction they had gotten lost in the Parliament building. In the party offices, a lady who worked there said that he was in the chamber of the house; and after having listened to a long set of directions, by the end of which they had forgotten the beginning, they set off through the maze of narrow corridors—upstairs, downstairs, to the left, to the right, past lines of portraits of deceased members of Parliament, libraries, committee rooms, girls using copiers, talking loudly, obviously slightly tipsy journalists, politicians conferring in window alcoves: everything repeatedly converted, improvised, with walls knocked through. But only after they had asked the way twice more did they open a door and suddenly find themselves in the public gallery.

In the beautiful oblong room, full of red, brown, and ochre, which was smaller than Quinten had imagined, a minister slumped in his chair behind the government table was listening to the argument of someone at the lectern, or at least pretending to; on the countless benches there were no more than four or five equally bored members of Parliament. Onno was standing talking to the Speaker of the House, but he saw them immediately and gestured them to come to him.

"Thank you for releasing me from the most dreary of lion's dens," he said, and took them to the coffee room. And there, while Quinten ate his open sandwich, he had asked him, "You're twelve now—do you know what you want to be yet?"

When he didn't answer at once, Max said: "An architect, if you ask me."

Quinten was annoyed that Max had said that; it was an intrusion. Apart from that, he didn't want to become an architect at all.

Preceded by four young dogs, a young woman now ran across the country road, dressed in a long white dress, with rings on all her fingers and hung with chains and bracelets; she came from the farmhouse a little farther on, where a commune of Amsterdam artists lived—dropouts, who had had enough of life in town. She raised an arm cheerfully and he returned her greeting absent-mindedly.

He looked dreamily at something that could not be seen but that was still coming toward him from the quieter than quiet field with the cow, the three boulders, and the two alder trees in it. The question of what he wanted to be had never occurred to him. He was what he was, surely—so what was he supposed to be? But of course his father meant some profession or other, like one boy in his class, who was always announcing that he wanted to be a doctor. It was just that he could not imagine ever practicing some profession or other, not even architecture. That interest was only connected with the dream of the Citadel, but Max could not know that. Perhaps everything would always remain the same.

44

The Not

Onno might have been just as unsure what he wanted to be, but the following year, in 1981, after the new elections, he was put forward by his party leader as minister of defense. The center-right coalition of the previous four years gave way to a center-left coalition, in which the Christian Democrat prime minister was obviously not subject to change; only the conservative vice-premier left office with his cohort, to be replaced by the new Liberals and the Social Democrats of the last cabinet but one, who had been duped four years previously and now wanted to be in government again at any price—bearing in mind the adage that politics did not wear out those in power but those not in power.

Toward the end of the cabinet formation, one Sunday in August, twenty or thirty of the principal players gathered for a boat trip on the IJsselmeer. That had been organized months before by an enlightened, stubborn banker, who not only promoted the arts but did not let even his opinions be determined by his interest, because his wealth did not prevent him from being more or less left-wing; and because, besides being more or less left-wing, he was also a rich banker, and moreover the scion of an old patrician family, no one ever had a reason to refuse an invitation from him.

However, the trip now became an appropriate opportunity for the new political friends to conclude their squabbling over the portfolios undisturbed; the leaders of the Conservatives, who had previously also been invited, had understood that unfortunately it would be better if they were otherwise engaged. Their place was taken by a number of ministers-designate, like Onno. Usually he stayed over Saturday night at Helga's, but now he had gone home so as not to wake her the following morning; she had herself had a ticket for a late showing of the old film *Les enfants du paradis*.

Before they went aboard, the groaning politicians, still half asleep, drank coffee in Muiden castle, but by eleven o'clock the first empty whiskey bottles were already landing in the crates. It was an oppressive day; the bank's seagoing motor launch, manned by a graying captain-cum-navigator and two ladies in white aprons who attended to those on board, made its way through the water, which was as gray as the sky. In the afternoon they were to drop anchor in Enkhuizen, where an organ program by the Social Democrat party chairman was planned; then there would be a crossing to Friesland, to Stavoren, where a hotel had been booked. For those not wishing to spend the night there, official cars would in the meantime have arrived.

In a circle on the rear deck, with a rum-and-Coke in his hand, Onno was explaining to the banker why he was considered by everyone so excellently suited to become minister of defense.

"I owe it to my big mouth. Even in my own party they're frightened that a Social Democrat won't be able to stand up to the generals. But they know that I will line up that bunch in my room on the very first day and say, 'Gentlemen, if any of you should ever feel the necessity to threaten resignation, then he can regard himself as automatically dismissed.' And after I have had them swear allegiance unto death to my person, I will wipe the Soviet Union off the map with a fearsome first strike."

The banker had an infectious asthmatic laugh, which resonated in the sounding box of his overweight body. He was sweating and with a newspaper was constantly brushing away the myriad tiny gnats that were accompanying the boat. For that matter they were not the only accompaniment: about a couple of hundred yards away, somewhat behind them, was a patrol boat of the national police. A company had also formed on the foredeck, but the important business was being conducted in the cabin, which no one entered without being summoned. Through the open door at the bottom of the steep stairs Onno could see them at the drawing room table—the prime minister and the two other party leaders with their intimates. Someone regularly went to the bridge to make a phone call.

Obviously something was wrong, because they'd been together for an hour. Everyone called everyone else by their Christian names, but the staff were addressed as "sir" and "madam." Why was that? Onno wondered. Why was it that this handful of people called the tune in Holland? How was it possible that it was possible? Obviously, there were indeed two different kinds of people in the world. He emptied his glass, looked around the circle, and was going to ask whether there shouldn't actually be a god on board as well, but controlled himself.

The first signs of drunkenness were becoming noticeable. In the forecastle an interim minister had been shouting for sometime "Steady as she goes!" at the helmsman, who each time nodded with a smile. A veteran politician in an over-thick sailor's jersey said threateningly to a serving lady, "Tonight I shall count your hairs." The radar aerial revolved slowly and superfluously. They passed Marken, and when they had left Volendam and Edam behind them, the coast slowly sank below the horizon. Although the boat was in the middle of nothing but water, it was becoming more and more oppressive. Everyone had become convinced that things were not going according to plan in the cabin: something was wrong. While Onno discussed with the minister of internal affairs the delicate matter of the crown prince, who in all probability would become liable for military service under his regime, his party leader came out of the cabin. His tie was loose and his shirt was hanging out of his trousers at the back; with clumsy, uncoordinated gestures he took Onno aside behind the sloop. It became quieter on deck, and immediately Onno knew that something was seriously wrong.

The leader with his bald pate, prime minister of the cabinet in which Onno had been a minister of state, vice-premier of the coming cabinet, two heads shorter than himself, waved a sheet of paper and looked up at him.

"Things have gone to pot, Onno. Were you in Cuba in 'sixty-seven?"

That was it.

"Yes."

"When you were there did you take part in . . ." He put on a pair of reading glasses with heavy frames and looked at the paper, but Onno immediately completed his question:

"*La primera Conferencia de La Habana?* Yes, but actually not."

Lost for words, the leader took off his glasses and stared at him. "And at the conference you were actually on the first committee—that of the armed struggle? I can scarcely get the words out."

"Yes, Koos."

Koos revolved on his own axis in astonishment and looked out across the water; on his neck, his slightly too long white hairs came together in a series of points, like shark's teeth. "What in God's name is the meaning of this? Do you really think that you can take over Defense with something like this in your CV? Why did you keep it from me?"

"I didn't keep anything from you. I simply didn't think about it anymore. It was fourteen years ago. For me it was a silly incident that meant nothing."

"Does your stupidity know no bounds, Onno?"

"Apparently not."

"Do you realize what you're doing to the party? The whole cabinet formation may now be in jeopardy. Tell me, who are you? Did you have guerrilla training there as well, perhaps?"

Onno ignored that remark and asked: "Is that an anonymous letter?"

"Yes."

"Then I know who wrote it."

"Who?"

"Bart Bork."

"Bart Bork? Bart Bork? That ex-Communist student leader? Were you at that conference with him?"

"On the contrary—he couldn't get in. But he had a score to settle with me, and it seems as though he's got what he wants."

"Would you now please tell me at once what actually happened?"

"I would appreciate doing that with the prime minister present."

"That's fine by me."

"Was that addressed to you?" asked Onno as they went toward the cabin, followed by the silent glances of the others.

"No. Dorus suddenly put it on the table just now. Goddamnit, Onno, I won't let him have the pleasure."

Onno knew that the prime minister was the bane of Koos's life. When Dorus had been minister of justice in his own cabinet, he had become thoroughly irritated by the bigoted zealot, who could not ignore a single abortion—to say nothing of euthanasia—but who ordered the security forces to open fire without pity when the Moluccans hijacked trains in Drenthe; in the last cabinet formation Koos had been eliminated remorselessly by him—as leader of the opposition he had not gotten a hold on him—and now he had to serve under him again. Politics was the continuation of war by other means, in which you could win or lose; the problem was that you got used to winning but never to losing. That meant that when you lost, more went through you than when you won; that when you lost, you lived more intensely, which in turn resulted in some people ultimately preferring to lose than to win, because winning bored them. Onno would have liked to say to Koos that this destructive tendency was a much greater enemy of his than Dorus, but he had never dared.

Meanwhile Dorus had also appeared on deck, where he was applauded by everyone when he did a handstand to relax. Onno saw that Koos, who was fifteen or twenty years older than Dorus and who could scarcely stand up properly, was extremely irritated by this. Like Onno, he came from a Calvinist family.

A little later in the warm cabin the atmosphere was icy. Apart from them, only Piet, the new Liberal chief, was at the table.

"We're listening," said Dorus. He was in shirtsleeves, his hair combed with excruciating care. His appearance had something fragile and boyish about it, but his shaded eyes, which were focused on Onno, and his fleshy, slightly pursed lips in his expressionless face with its pointed nose, talked a different, a more remorseless, language.

Onno was surprised at his own calm. Without feeling that it really mattered, he explained what had happened fourteen years before: his meeting with Bork after the political and musical demonstration in Amsterdam, where Bork had announced that Onno would become a beachcomber on Ameland after the revolution—and that it was precisely that ominous remark that had finally made him decide to go into politics. Then the Cuban invitation to his wife, the misunderstanding at the airport, and the explosive conference in which he had found himself. He said nothing about the role of Max, who had persuaded him to go. Finally, he told of his meeting with Bork in the park in Havana, where he was exchanging money on the black market, where he had gotten even with him.

"And now it's his turn again," he concluded. "But it was an interesting conference, from which I learned a lot. It's just that looking back on it, it might have been more sensible if I had enrolled as a press representative."

Dorus tapped the tips of his outstretched fingers against each other and looked around the circle. "We believe you."

"At least I do," said Piet, with the astonished, innocent look in his blue eyes that won him so many votes.

"Moreover," continued Dorus, "I appreciate your honesty. There are also photocopies of the conference administration enclosed, in the name of a certain Onno Quits, and you could have said that was someone else or that they're forgeries. As long as there's no photograph on which you can be seen in the company of the formidable Dr. Castro Ruiz, you could have risen very high."

"I'm not lying, Dorus, because I have nothing to hide."

"But as things are at present, what's the good of us believing you? Will the chiefs of staff believe you—or want to believe you? It's like that naughty bishop who's found in the brothel and who proclaims, 'In order to be able to fight evil, one must know evil.' What's happened to your authority? Because I assure you that the generals will also be in possession of these documents within twenty-four hours. This epistle," said Dorus, putting his narrow, well-manicured hand on it, "was not addressed to me but to the American ambassador, who had the politeness to send it to me by courier last night. Well, that means that the CIA now knows about it, that our own armed forces will soon know about it, and that they will know about it in Brussels, at NATO headquarters, under the archpatriarchal leadership of our inestimable countryman. Mr. Bork has done his work thoroughly. And you can rest assured that our American friends will not wish to run any risks, however small, that a pro-Fidel lout will ever have authority within the treaty organization over the forces on the north German plain, nor that this individual should be informed of vital military secrets, so that the Cold War might have been fought in vain."

With this the open account of the Eighty Years' war that had been fought in vain was settled. Politics, thought Onno, was a profession in which everything was settled down to the last cent. "It's hopeless, Onno," sighed Koos, without taking his thin cigarillo out of his mouth. "You're finished. For that matter, I don't mind you knowing that even in my time some generals had strange ideas: *I* was already going too far for them. What's more, certain monarchist groups from the former resistance have been hoarding caches of weapons since the beginning of the 1970s, just in case the New Left came to power. They know that we know who they are and where they've buried their stuff, and as minister of defense you'd also be informed of that."

"That is," observed Dorus, "we know what we know, but we don't know what we don't know."

"It won't be as bad as that," said Koos. "Most of them are okay people, although there are a few generals among them. It's just to give you an impression of the atmosphere."

With a mixture of numbness and relief, Onno said: "It goes without saying that I am withdrawing."

"And if our feathered friends of the press inquire for what reason?" asked Dorus. "Your name has been circulating in the newspapers for some weeks."

"Because you in your unfathomable wisdom decided on a different distribution of portfolios, which unfortunately left me high and dry. Or think of some illness for me. Say I've had a slight brain hemorrhage."

"Nonsense," said Piet. "Why should you have to lie because you don't want to lie? Apart from that, Bork may still make the matter public. If anyone asks anything, you simply tell it like it is and in a year's time you'll become mayor of Leiden."

"The job of beachcomber of Ameland," said Dorus, with a deadpan expression, "appears to have been already allocated."

"Dorus!" cried Piet reproachfully, but also smiled.

"Just tell us what you want," mumbled Koos.

"And who will get Defense now?" asked Piet.

"Without the shadow of a doubt you have a *sweet prince* on board for that exceptionally responsible post who is dear to all of us."

"Just a minute!" said Koos indignantly, sticking up an index finger, the top joint of which was deformed. "That means that we—"

"Undoubtedly," Dorus interrupted. "With his crystal-clear intelligence, old Koos has immediately hit on the essence of my spontaneous brainwave."

Onno had gotten up and said that he felt superfluous here. They agreed that for the time being he would say nothing to the others; God willing, they might have solved the problem before they arrived in Stavoren. Onno promised that he would not jump ship in Enkhuizen.

When he sat down again in his chair on the afterdeck, everyone in the circle looked at him in silence, but no one asked anything. Only Dolf, the badly shaven Catholic minister of economic affairs, put a hand on his shoulder as he passed. What he would have preferred, Onno reflected, would be to be fired by cannon from the ship onto the shore, because he no longer had any business here. While the conversations were resumed, he realized calmly that once again he did not know what he wanted to be.

From one minute to the next, everything had changed. He did not feel at all like simply remaining in Parliament; and a job as a mayor did not come into consideration, or becoming director of the Foundation for Pure Scientific Research, or anything in "Europe"; it was now a fact that he was definitely leaving politics. It had begun with Bork and it was ending with Bork. That his life should be forever linked with Bork's filled him with disgust. He saw Bork's leering eyes and felt as if a disgusting insect had crawled over him; he rubbed his face with both hands to shoo it away. Then he thought of Max, who ultimately had all the turning points in his life on his conscience, but did not bear him any malice. The only person whom he begrudged his fall was his retired elder brother—fortunately his father did not have to experience it. And as far as Helga was concerned: she'd probably be just happy that it had gone as it had.

The few citizens of Enkhuizen who saw them walking through the quiet old streets from the marina to the church stopped and were sure that they were dreaming: it wasn't just the prime minister walking there but *everyone*. That was of course impossible, because all those faces belonged on television and not in their little town: if it was really true that all those in power were now in Enkhuizen, then great danger probably threatened them.

The mayor and the local police were also in the dark; only the vicar and the sexton welcomed them. Giggling like a class of schoolchildren, the visitors distributed themselves across the wooden pews in the nave. In order to stretch their legs, Koos, Dorus, and Piet had joined them, but they immediately withdrew into a side chapel, where they continued their deliberations under a painting of St. Sebastian. The church still smelled of incense from the morning mass. The minister who had just now kept shouting "Steady as she goes!" suddenly mounted the stairs to the pulpit, undoubtedly to preach a Calvinist fire-and-brimstone sermon, but was prevented from doing so by his minister of state. Meanwhile, the Social Democratic party chairman, who had begun as a Protestant theologian, had vanished—and shortly afterward Bach's equally invisible variations on the choral *"Vom Himmel hoch da komm' ich hier"* came thundering out of the motionless pipes.

Onno glanced around: the front of the organ reminded him of the opened jaws of a whale, attacking him from behind. He felt completely out of place, both in this Catholic church and in this company. He thought back with embarrassment to his inflated words of just now, that he would line up the generals and threaten them—he would be jokingly reminded of this one day, when people happened to bump into him.

Feeling a certain stiffening in his body, he looked at the crucifix on the altar and listened to the music. Bork's observation at that time may have been decisive in his decision to go into politics, but there was a deeper motive behind it: his failure with the Phaistos disc. Now the wheel had obviously come full circle, shouldn't he try and go back to the disc?

Four years ago he had still been able to take the escape route of becoming a member of Parliament; now everything was much more final. Perhaps it was because of Bach, but suddenly the prospect attracted him. Of course he would have to get back into it again—he hadn't kept up with the specialist literature in the intervening fourteen years. The only thing he knew for certain was that it had still not been deciphered, not even by Landau, his Israeli rival, because Landau would certainly not have deprived himself of the pleasure of informing him personally. He sighed deeply. Who knows, perhaps all those years had been necessary to allow the solution to mature deep inside him: perhaps he might very shortly have the liberating insight!

The sexton came out of the sacristy and asked something of someone in the front row, who turned around, scanned the church, and pointed at him. Onno looked up inquiringly, whereupon the sexton made a turning movement next to his ear.

Onno got up in astonishment, while two things went through his head at once: how could anyone know that he was here—and how was it possible that the gesture for "telephone" was still determined by the mechanics of a piece of equipment that had not existed for fifty years and could only be seen in Laurel and Hardy films?

The sexton took him to the sacristy. The telephone stood on a table with a dark red cloth on it; in a wall cupboard with its sliding doors open hung long mass garments, like the wardrobe of a Roman emperor.

Onno picked up the receiver. "Quist speaking."

"Are you Mr. Onno Quist?" asked a woman's voice.

"Yes, who am I speaking to?"

"Mr. Quist, this is the central police station in Amsterdam. We managed to find out where you were via the prime minister's office. We're sorry, but you must prepare yourself for some shocking news."

Onno felt himself stiffening and immediately thought of Quinten. "Tell me what's happened."

"We know that you are a friend of Ms. Helga Hartman's."

It was as though those two words, *Helga Hartman,* penetrated his body like bullets.

"Yes, and what about it?"

"Something very serious happened to her last night."

Onno suddenly could not speak anymore; his breath was stuck in his throat like a ball.

"Mr. Quist? Are you still there?"

"Is she dead?" he asked hoarsely.

"Yes, Mr. Quist . . ."

Was this possible? Helga dead. *Helga dead?* His eyes widened in dismay; he felt as though he were emptying, in the direction of Amsterdam, where her dead body must be.

"Really completely dead?" he asked, immediately hearing how idiotic the question was.

"Yes, Mr. Quist."

"Christ Almighty!" he suddenly screamed. "How in God's name did it happen?"

"Are you sure you want to talk about it on the telephone—"

"For God's sake tell me! Now!"

She must have been attacked in the early hours of the morning, when she was opening the front door of her house. She was dragged inside and in the hall attacked mercilessly with a knife, probably by an addict; after her house had been ransacked, she was left to her fate. There was no trace of the culprit. Because her vocal chords had been cut, she could not call for help; but bleeding heavily, she managed to open the door and crawl to the telephone booth on the other side of the canal, with some change in her hand that had been left in her emptied bag.

Obviously, she wanted to call the emergency number, and if she had been given immediate help, she would probably have survived, but the telephone had been vandalized. Probably only an hour later, toward morning, she was found by a passerby; by that time she had already died from loss of blood. She was in the morgue at Wilhelmina Hospital.

Onno did not rejoin the others, but went out into the street through a side door. A small crowd had meanwhile gathered by the closed church door, but nothing from his surroundings got through to him anymore; without looking where he was going, he wandered into the town along a narrow canal.

Helga was dead. A desert had been created in him. He would have liked to cry, but he felt dried up inside. They had slaughtered her senselessly. She no longer existed. In an Amsterdam cellar her mutilated body was lying under a sheet, and at this moment her murderer was in a state of heroin bliss. Perhaps he would see him one day in town, rummaging in a dustbin—how could he ever go out into the street again?

He had to get away, away from Holland for good. First Ada, now Helga. Everything had been razed to the ground. Had he loved her? He'd never really understood what other people meant when they said that they loved someone, but at any rate Helga was a part of himself that was now dead. Why weren't addicts cleaned off the streets, on the basis of the Mental Health Act? Perhaps he might yet be caught—but what about the vandals who had wrecked the telephone booth, as a result of which she had bled to death? Without them, she would still have been alive. They would never be caught, or even hunted for. If they happened to be caught in the act, they'd be back on the street half an hour later, with a reprimand. Robbery and murder could be combated by the police, but vandalism could only be prevented by despotic authority, or by God in heaven, in whom no one here believed any longer. He did not exist, but as long as people believed in him and his commandments were valid, no public telephones were vandalized for fun.

Helga was dead. So was a lie necessary, since the alternative was despotic authority? Neither in Moscow nor in Mecca were the telephone booths vandalized. Was the choice perhaps between being misled and despotism? He no longer wished to be involved in a world where things were like that. Did he have to choose between theocracy and worldly tyranny? Could society only function properly on a basis of fear? Did human beings have to be given a built-in policeman from above? Were they intrinsically evil, and did they only become good when circumstances were bad? So should their circumstances be made worse out of humane considerations? Was Rousseau the greatest idiot of all time? In Holland people had never been so humane as in the winter of 1944–45, when thousands of people were dying of hunger and the shots of the execution squads were exploding around them. It was hopeless. Helga was dead. His colleagues in the church, his former colleagues, would simply have to see how they got on with their tolerance—because they refused to choose, all that was left for them was anarchy. Fidel had his own optimistic design, with the ideal of the New Man in the role of God, and Che in that of his murdered son—Fidel had his blessing, but for him it was over. He was opting out.

Helga was dead. No more politics; no more girlfriends. Perhaps all that was left was the Phaistos disc. He did not want to be anything anymore. He was devastated. What day was it? He looked around, at the well-behaved Sunday gables. Probably, he had never been in Enkhuizen, nor Helga. But she wasn't not there in the same way that she had been not there before; her death had planted a completely different, permanent

NOT in the world and in himself. It was over. His decision was made: he was going to disappear. In other civilized countries it was not a bit better than here, but there at least no one knew him, because he himself didn't want to know anyone from now on—not even Quinten. He'd become a stranger to everyone, in the first place to himself. He wasn't going to stay a day longer in Holland than was necessary.

45

Changes

The last time that Max, Sophia and Quinten saw him was at Helga's funeral, which many politicians and journalists had also attended. The press had treated him with compassion; the impression had been created that he was declining the ministerial post because of the death of his companion. Everyone considered that it was best to leave it at that. Of course he had made a dull, depressed impression, but nothing indicated that he intended to give up everything, not even when he said goodbye. A week later each of them received a handwritten letter, mailed from Amsterdam, which they read at the same time at the breakfast table on the balcony.

Dear Max,

We probably won't see each other again. I'm going away and not coming back. I've been pushed over the edge. Hopefully you'll understand that without my having to explain, because I can't explain. All I know is that I have to make myself invisible, a bit like a dying elephant. The person I was no longer exists, and everything that may yet happen in my life is actually already posthumous. I don't have to tell you that there are people who have endured unspeakably worse things and still don't react like me, but they are different people from me. There are also people who hang themselves over much less. I don't know if what I want is possible, namely that I don't want anything anymore, but I must at least have a try. All I want to do is think a few things through. The fact that I'm cutting loose from those I love best, like you, and of course Quinten and my youngest sister, instead of coming closer to you, is a mystery to me too; but what attitude can a person take in order to solve the riddle that he is? Perhaps the fact is that I've always wanted to escape from everything.

Between Ada's accident and Helga's murder there is my political career, which has now also come to an end. My life isn't conceivable without yours. Up to last week you determined its course to a greater extent than you yourself know. I realize that this may sound mysterious, but let it remain so. However many things we discussed, particularly in those first few months, what was essential always remained unspoken. What was it between us, Max? Gilgamesh and Enkidu? Do you remember? The "mentopagus"? I have forgotten nothing and I will forget nothing; the memory of our friendship will remain with me to my dying day. The fact that you've been prepared to take pity on Quinten—denying your previous joie de vivre in a way that, to tell the truth, still astonishes me—is something that not only fills me with deep gratitude, but also and perhaps with an even greater feeling of guilt. In fact from the very start he was much more your son than mine. Look after him well for the few years that he will still be with you. All the practical and financial matters have been settled with my bank; that will of course simply continue as usual. Sometimes I have the impression that he knows everything already, but should he want to go to university, there will be an allowance for him.

I have given my notice in the Kerkstraat and my things are in Dol's loft for the moment; should any of you want anything from them, then they can collect it. Except for my lawyer, Hans Giltay Veth (the son of your father's defense lawyer after the war, by the way), no one knows how I can be reached, not even my family. If there's something really important, you can turn to him. May it go well with you, Max, in your scientific work too. Unveil the Big Bang! I shall always think of you as someone who knew the answer to a question before it was posed.

Yours,
Onno

Dear Mrs. Brons,

Any other opening would sound just as idiotic, so let's leave it like that. Max will let you read my letter, telling him that I'm going to disappear. That may look as though I've made a difficult decision, which I have thought over for a long time, but that's not how it is. As soon as I heard what had happened to Helga, I was certain that nothing else could be done. As I am now, I've become unsuitable for any social tie. In the background, of course, Ada's fate is intimately connected with all this.

It's difficult for me to write these lines. Although we've never had any disagreement, neither have we had any real contact with each other. You didn't choose me and I didn't choose you; but because Ada and I chose each other, we had to deal with each other, while in fact we've remained as alien to each other as creatures from different worlds. Obviously nature only deals in short-range psychology, and we shall have to resign ourselves to that. But that doesn't detract from the fact that your daughter is my wife . . . or was—that twilight world of conjugation expresses exactly the depth of the disaster. Our five lives are interwoven for good: yours, mine, Ada's, Max's and Quinten's.

Ada will never know how splendidly you have taken over her task for the last thirteen years, but I know and I wish I had the ability to express my feelings. Sadly, I can't; but I console myself with the thought that someone who can probably doesn't have those feelings. Let me put it like this: in a number of respects I'm more grateful to you than to my own mother. Ada is flesh of your flesh; should decisions need to be made about her, then of course you must have the last word.

Please forgive the formal tone of this letter. Farewell. May things go well with you.

Your son-in-law

My Dearest Quinten!

You will have probably realized for yourself that in life things are constantly changing—usually that happens gradually and almost imperceptibly, but sometimes suddenly and very drastically. When you cycle somewhere not much is happening, but if you fall and break a leg, then suddenly a whole lot is wrong. War is something like that, but not just war. Mama and I lived very quietly together, but when she told me one day that you were going to be born—that is, at that moment of course we didn't know that it was going to be you, or even if it was going to be a boy or a girl—from that moment nothing was really the same again. Of course that was a nice change, but when Mama had that accident, everything was completely different in a terrible way. In the meantime you've also stood at Granddad's and Granny To's graves. They were very old, and when you're very old you simply die; but a few days ago we also buried Auntie Helga. Can you understand that suddenly I can't take it anymore? Perhaps you hadn't expected that of me, and perhaps you think I'm a wimp; I can't help it. It's like a match: you can break it twice and the halves are still attached, but the third time it breaks in two. In some countries you have little wax matches—you can bend them backward and forward as much as you like and they never break; but I'm not one of them. Anyway, they're rotten matches that you always burn your fingers on.

My writing this letter means a change like that for you. By the time you read this, I shall have gone. I've gone underground, as we called it during the war. Then, people went underground to avoid the Germans. I've gone underground to escape life itself. Perhaps you may find that odd for a talker like me; perhaps one day you'll despise me because of it and perhaps you already do—but that's how it is. I have gone for you, just as I've gone for myself. You'll scarcely miss me, because not much will change. I've never been a real father to you, always a kind of distant uncle. Max is your father, just as Granny is your mother. There are fathers and sons in the world, and I've always been more of a son than a father. Perhaps you're more of a father than I am. Try and forget me. All I want to do is to think a bit. Just see me as a hermit who's going into the wilderness for the rest of his life.

Forgive me and don't look for me, because you won't find me.

Your Prodigal Father

Quinten looked up and met the eyes of Max and Sophia, who had also read each other's letters. In the morning sunlight, the first wasps had already alighted on the remains of the honey.

"What's a hermit?"

"A recluse."

"Has Daddy gone in the same way as Mama?"

Max had a constant line running through his head: *I have lost the world—* it was as though Onno's message were hidden beneath it, so that it couldn't really get through to him. He was also alarmed by the sentence in which Onno said that his life had to a large extent been more determined by Max than he himself knew—but from what followed it was apparent that this could not refer to Quinten. In confusion he looked at Quinten and looked for an answer to his question.

But Sophia said: "Of course not. He's simply somewhere, but he doesn't want to talk to anybody anymore. He's mourning Auntie Helga very deeply and that's why he's saying all that. I think that . . ." Suddenly her words were lost in the ear-splitting roar of a formation of jets flying low overhead; she waited for a moment until the noise changed over the woods into the boom of a distant storm. "Time heals all wounds. It wouldn't surprise me if he's back in a few months."

"I'm not so sure about that," said Max. It didn't strike him as completely impossible, either, but he didn't feel any false hopes should be awakened in Quinten. "In that case he would simply have hidden away somewhere for a while; but when someone writes letters like this, something else is going on with them. Can we read your letter too, Quinten?"

"Not now. I have to go to school."

"I'll call and say you'll be a bit late."

Reluctantly, Quinten handed the letter over, after which he read those of Sophia and Max. He did not understand everything, but he again formed an idea of the bond of friendship there had been between his father and Max. In that letter to Max, it also said that Max was actually his father, but that was of course in fact precisely not the case: the man who had written those farewell letters was not *not* his father, but his father. Max was only his father in a manner of speaking, just as Granny was only his mother in a manner of speaking.

He looked up. "Can I have Mama's cello in my room now?"

"Of course," said Max. "When I have to go down to that part of the world next, I'll collect it from Auntie Dol."

Quinten sighed deeply and stared across the moat toward the trees and the coach houses. He felt the absence of his father around him much more intensely than he had ever felt his presence; it seemed as though he was now far more present than when he had been there.

What did it all mean, Max asked himself a few months later, late in the evening after returning from Tsjallingtsje's, while he intended to drink a glass or two of wine in the silent castle but had emptied the whole bottle, when times suddenly changed? In the 1960s the students in Berkeley revolted; shortly afterward the Provos appeared in Amsterdam; and then the universities were occupied in Berlin and Paris too. There might still be a causal link between those things, but how come it also happened in Warsaw, on the other side of the Iron Curtain? And why was it that at the same time the Cultural Revolution took place in China, also something that involved young people? There was no connection, and yet it happened simultaneously. Imperial Japan had nothing to do with Hitler's Germany, and yet at the same moment it became just as aggressive.

Did Hegel's World Spirit perhaps really exist, and was humanity as a whole subject to the ebb and flow of mysterious undercurrents that paid no attention to political differences? That was the kind of question to which there was no answer, but on a small scale something comparable was now happening in his personal circumstances. "When troubles come they come not single spies" said the insufferable cliché; but since he was approaching fifty, he began to realize that clichés were simply truths. Although it was entirely unconnected, it seemed in retrospect as though Onno's departure had also heralded the end of their stay in Groot Rechteren.

When after a long illness the baron had nevertheless died unexpectedly, as the death announcement said, it had in the first instance a gratifying consequence. As Quinten's guardian, Max received an invitation from a lawyer in Zwolle, where he was informed that the deceased had included Quinten in his will. In an imposing paneled room, which a silent lady entered now and again, to adjust something among high piles of documents folded lengthwise, the slightly emaciated official read him Gevers's testament. It had not escaped the deceased that Quinten regularly cleared the grave of Deep Thought Sunstar of stinging nettles: as a reward, therefore, he was leaving him ten thousand guilders. He was to receive thirty thousand guilders for the fact that he had made the life's work of his son, Rutger, possible: Rutger's "very big curtain"—by now measuring thirty feet by thirty. Forty thousand guilders—that was a lot of money, said the lawyer, and the family was probably not happy about it, but all in all it amounted to the restitution of rent since 1968. They had had free accommodation for all those years.

"By the way, if it interests you . . ." he said as he was accompanying Max to the front door, "I can tell you that the heirs plan to dispose of Groot Rechteren shortly. You can buy it if you like. You can have it for five hundred thousand, minus the park and Ms. Trip's house, but including the coach house and the other outbuildings. Ridiculously cheap."

"Where would I get half a million from?" laughed Max. "I have to get by on a scientist's starvation wage."

"Have a chat with your bank. And if it's too much for you alone, you could consider setting up a cooperative association with your fellow tenants, which can act as buyer. You never know what might happen otherwise.

Once ownership passes to a third party, you can be given notice after three years, and you'll never get anything like that again. I'm always available for advice. But don't take too long deciding—there are already sharks about."

This heralded a period of confusion and uncertainty, but the first result was an increase in solidarity. They had never gathered together so often in the castle: at Max and Sophia's, among Theo Kern's cooing doves, on the immaculate Empire furniture of Mr. and Mrs. Spier, occasionally also up-stairs, at Proctor and Clara's, among the umbrellas; but usually in the library of Themaat, who had not been doing well recently.

Because no one was wealthy, they got the lawyer to draw up the draft statutes of a tenants' association; with an eye to restoration grants, he very shrewdly reserved a seat on the committee for an outsider, such as the Foundation for Drenthe Castles, or the National Forestry Commission. But when finance came up—the mortgage loan, people's own resources, rates, property tax, the mutual division of all those expenses—the first problems appeared.

Those with the nicest accommodation would of course pay most, that could be assessed; but Kern, who in any case had nicer accommodation than Proctor and moreover had the use of the coach house, began to have cold feet. Everyone had a fixed income and a pension, except for him; he was an artist. He was already well into his sixties, and if he fell ill tomorrow, not an-other cent would come in, and Selma would have to go and scrub floors at the baroness's; and anyway, how long would he still be physically able to sculpt, so that he could meet his obligations? His share of the lawyer's bill was already costing him an arm and a leg. But anyone who didn't become a member of the cooperative, the same lawyer had stipulated, had to agree to the loss of his residential rights.

Next Max also began to have doubts. He had let himself be carried along by the first flush of enthusiasm, but when things stagnated, he wondered what he actually wanted. In five years' time at the most, Quinten would be leaving home—was he to stay living here with Sophia? The task he had undertaken would then have been completed, after which nothing would tie him to her except memory.

One evening, when he was slightly tipsy, he suddenly plucked up courage to raise the subject: "Listen, Sophia, something else about the castle. In a few years' time, when Quinten—"

"Of course," she immediately interrupted him. "Then our ways will part."

Using the alibi that they could not simply abandon Theo, who after all had lived longer at Groot Rechteren than all of them, he was able to convince the others simply to let events take their course and to hope that the new owner would leave things as they were.

All this passed Quinten by. He also took Gevers's substantial bequest for granted: looking after Deep Thought Sunstar's grave and teaching Rutger how to weave a carpet were perfectly natural, after all!

Because he knew that he was going to be kept back a grade this year, he did even less schoolwork than usual. In the evenings, in the total silence, a little dazzled by the light on his open books, he stared at the tall black window in his room, in which he could only vaguely make out the transition from the dark sky to the even darker wood.

His father was somewhere out there in the night now—far away, perhaps in America, or even on the other side of the world, in Australia. But in any case not infinitely far away, like his mother. And anyway perhaps he was close by; perhaps he only implied that he was leaving Holland so that no one would look for him there: perhaps he was simply living with a farmer nearby. But if you didn't know where someone was, that really made no difference. What was he doing at this moment? He'd wanted "to think something through," he had written to Max. What was that? What did he mean by that? He took his father's letter from the bronze box, in which he also kept the secret maps of the SOMNIUM QUINTI. He did not need to read it again, because he knew it by heart: he carefully brushed with his fingertips the paper on which his father's hand had rested. The idea that he would really never see him again seemed just as impossible as the idea that the sun would not rise tomorrow.

He locked the box with the antique padlock that he had been given by Piet Keller; he hid the little key between the loose bricks behind the oil stove. After placing his hand on the case of Ada's cello for a moment, he went to the window to look at the spiders again.

They looked awful and he hated them, but they fascinated him. Because the light in his turret room attracted the insects from the wood, five or six large spiders had realized that they should spin their webs in front of the glass. He didn't understand them. On the one hand they were ingenious, subtle architects, who wove gossamer-fine webs patiently, and in a material that reminded him of the stuff that for the last few months he had even found in his pajama bottoms when he woke up in the mornings: that had always been preceded by a blissful dream, which he could never remember and which had nothing to do with the Citadel. But when their work was finished, they emerged as equally patient but gruesome murderers, who pounced mercilessly on their prey, bit it to death, spun the wings so that they were crushed together, and sucked it dry. How could those things be reconciled—that architectural sophistication and that savage aggression?

There were spiders that waited at the edge of their web until something wandered into their fatal silver trap, but there were also spiders that sat in the middle. And one evening he suddenly saw that the lucid structure of their webs in a certain sense was a geometrical representation of their repulsive bodies, with the eight hairy legs—a kind of transparent extension of it, just as algebra is the abstraction of mathematics. He had to know more about this, and he decided to put it to Mr. Themaat.

"Do you know what's wrong with you, QuQu?" said Mr. Themaat the following day, with the resignation of someone who had met his match. "You . . . anyway, leave it. I don't know what's wrong with you."

Then he told Quinten that for the umpteenth time he had hit the bull's-eye. He spoke more slowly than he used to; his exuberant fits of laughter no longer occurred, either. It was as though his head had grown into a motionless extension of his trunk; his wide-open eyes stared out at Quinten from a practically expressionless face. Quinten had heard from Sophia that it was because he had to take so many pills—they made you like that. He looked like a wax image of himself, like at Madame Tussaud's, but it was clear from what he said that his intellect had not been affected.

Via the spider's web, he said, Quinten had hit upon the "homo-mensura-thesis": Protagoras's argument that man was the measure of all things. In Roman antiquity, Vitruvius had said that temples should have the ideal proportion of the human body, as had been the case with the Greeks. In the Middle Ages that prescription had been linked to the Old Testament notion that God had created man in His own image, which gave human measurements a divine origin, with as a New Testament addition of course the central fact of Christ's body. In architecture that had led to churches and cathedrals in the form of a Latin cross, that is, the rough scheme of the human figure; but only in the Renaissance did those views evolve into a sophisticated philosophical architectural system.

"Lie down on the ground," order Mr. Themaat.

Quinten looked at him in astonishment. "Me?"

"Yes, you."

When Quinten did what he had been told, Themaat rose from his rocking chair slowly, as in a slow motion film, and asked Elsbeth if she had any string in the house.

"String?" she repeated suspiciously. "What on earth are you planning to do, Ferdinand? Are you going to tie him up?"

"Just give me it."

She took a ball of white wool out of a basket. "Will this do?"

"Even better."

Themaat said that Quinten should put his ankles together and spread his arms. Crawling on his knees, he then put the thread on the carpet in a pure square bordered by Quinten's crown, the tips of his middle fingers, and his heels. Then he had to move his feet slightly apart and his arms slightly upward, whereupon Themaat draped a second white thread in a circle along the soles of his feet and the tips of his fingers. Quinten got up carefully and looked at the double figure. The circle was resting on the lower side edge of the square; to the side and at the top, it circumscribed it. Themaat took a guilder coin out of his pocket and put it carefully in the middle of the circle which coincided with that of the square.

"And that spot marks your navel," he said, "which linked you to your mother."

A little alarmed, Quinten looked at the coin, which through Themaat's words was suddenly transformed into a shining mystery.

That linking of the "homo circularis" and the "homo quadratus," Themaat told him, had been described before Christ by Vitruvius in his treatise on architecture, but in the fifteenth century Leonardo da Vinci made a famous drawing of it. He took a book out of the case and showed it to Quinten: a proud, naked man in a square and a circle, with thick locks of hair down to his shoulders and four arms and four legs, surrounded by a commentary in mirror writing.

"I expect it's a self-portrait," he said. "And good God, he's like a spider in a web too—and he's got eight limbs as well! What does that mean?" He glanced sideways at Quinten, who had also seen it right away. "Aren't you frightened that you're gradually venturing into areas where no one can follow you anymore?"

"How do you mean?"

"I don't know."

Quinten looked at the figures on the carpet again and said. "It also looks a bit like the ground plan of the Pantheon."

Themaat exchanged a glance with Elsbeth and said with a solemn note in his voice: "The awareness that the divine body is determined by two perfect, elementary mathematical figures placed man in the center of cosmic harmony. You can understand that this was a colossal discovery for those humanist architects, like your great friend Palladio."

Quinten did not take his eyes off the white square and the white circle, the guilder in the middle. Might that configuration also be the essence of his Citadel? Was this the last word? He was reminded of what Max had once said to him: that in the limitless universe the circumference was nowhere and the center everywhere—but also of the hoarse, blood-curdling voice in his dream, which had said that behind the bolted door was "the center of the world."

He looked at the guilder and suddenly saw his mother in front of him in her white bed: but that was oblong. Did the oblong go a step farther than the square? But the circle would then of course automatically become an ellipse, with two centers: the orbit of the earth around the sun!

At that moment he felt fingers in the hair at the back of his head, slightly to the right of the center. It was Mrs. Themaat.

"Quinten! Did you know that you were getting a white hair here? Just here, in this spot!"

46

The Free Market Economy

Within a few months it had become clear that people fought over castles just as they had done in the Middle Ages. It was a fight that took place in the black of night, between virtually invisible parties, which the residents had no part in but which would probably end in their expulsion by the victor. The longer the war lasted, the better it was for them. The first purchaser was a rich poultry farmer from Barneveld, the lord of life and death of millions of chickens. When he appeared one day at Groot Rechteren in order to survey his new property, which he had acquired unseen, he looked exactly as one imagined such a person: a large, heavy man with a harsh voice, a cigar, and an excellent disposition, who never appeared again. He left it to his estate manager, a graying gentleman of noble extraction who had also adapted his appearance to his title—but, Max felt, with something just a little too measured and aristocratic about his knickerbockers, green socks, and highly polished brogues, since he was, after all, the servant of a vulgar poultry farmer.

The new owner had not made any statement about the use to which he wanted to put Groot Rechteren, but according to the manager he was definitely not going to live there; he had a splendid villa in Lunteren. In the village, rumors began circulating that the castle was going to become the main building for an anthroposophical center for the mentally defective, with three units in the park taking sixty pupils each—which was supposed to have been sold to a pension fund. That was supposed to have been a precondition of the baroness's for the sale, although the lady vicar said she knew nothing about this.

Because it had been he who had frustrated the tenants' association, Max felt obliged to do something to resolve the uncertainty. He was completely absorbed in the preparation for an exciting international research program on a new wave band on quasar MQ 3412, from which the condition of the early universe could be studied—but nevertheless he regularly sat wasting his time in the town hall in order to get some clear idea of the plans. But the alderman and the officials, who of course were fully in the picture, and who were undoubtedly pleased to see the name Westerbork linked to a medical facility, proved even more impenetrable than the horizon of the universe to which he had now come so close.

Six months later, the anthroposophical lunatic asylum suddenly vanished from the scene. The rent had to be transferred immediately to a different bank account, in the name of someone who did not even deign to view his acquisition. He lived in a large country house in Overijssel, in the middle of the woods, where Max visited him. He looked like the postage-stamp clerk at the post office counter; his skinny wife was slightly hunchbacked; and on the lawn a hollow-eyed gardener with a scythe gave him a bloodthirsty look. It was all as menacing as in a Gothic novel, and Max could not even find out what the new landlord did for a living, let alone what his plans were. According to Mr. Rosinga, who lugged the oil drums upstairs in the winter, people were now telling each other in the village that Groot Rechteren was going to be converted into a luxury hotel-restaurant, but Piet Keller had heard that it was going to house a police training school.

None of this went ahead, either, and the owners continued to succeed each other. Now there was mention of an auction house that wanted to set up shop in the castle; now a recreation center for overworked managers. Meanwhile, nothing more was done about maintenance. Mr. Roskam had cleared his workshop, and no one knew whether or not he had followed the baron underground, into the domain of his father's cap.

Cracks in the external walls became visible; there were leaks; plaster fell from the lath ceilings; and in the corners of the rooms mildewed wallpaper began to come loose from the latching, exposing rough, centuries-old masonry. Autumn leaves blocked the gutters, so the rainwater streamed down the walls and flooded the cellars, which led to a plague of gnats in summer. It was as though the castle had cancer. It deteriorated month by month, and a stubborn spirit of resistance seized everyone: they weren't going to be driven out by the capitalists!

Eighteen months after Gevers's death, in 1983—Max had meanwhile turned fifty, Sophia sixty—the first breach appeared in their community: Keller agreed to let himself be bought out. At that time the owner was a good-natured-looking man in his forties, according to the vicar a Jehovah's Witness, whose wife ran a sex club in Amersfoort. He called himself an "antiques dealer," which meant that he drove to Spain with a "partner" in an empty van every month and came back with a load of peasant chairs, tables, and cupboards, which he stored in the dilapidated orangery. Keller's house was intended for the partner, who gave more of the impression of a lackey who would go through fire for his master.

According to him, no one need have any worries about taking advantage of their protected period of three years; after that the castle would be thoroughly restored, with a link-up to the natural gas network and central heating. The present residents would of course receive the right of first refusal, though they would have to take into account the fact that the rents would then be many times what they were at present. According to Mr. Spier, it would amount to a gigantic brothel under the patronage of the Supreme Being.

But suddenly it turned out that he had in turn also sold the castle. He had kept only the buildings beyond the moat—and when Max and Sophia saw the new lord of the manor, they knew immediately that things were going to be very different.

There was no doubt about it. There was the victor—the exalted market mechanism had finally achieved its worthy goal: a small, self-satisfied man with a bald head and a short beard called Korvinus, the owner of a demolition company. He had obviously decided to shorten the three-year notice period dramatically by means of harassment, because he immediately began poking his finger in everywhere. When Quinten, counter to the new regulations, had put his bicycle on the forecourt again, instead of in the bicycle shed, Max received a registered letter the following day asking him in emphatic terms to prevent this happening. Kern was informed that the communal upstairs landing was not part of his property and could not be used for the storage of goods. Clara was informed that she must no longer put her laundry out to dry on the roof, as was usual in slums. The stone demolition ball, which his workers hurled at house walls with cranes, was in some way or other in his head too.

Every week he was there for one occasion, by common consent solely in order to think up new tricks—but obviously that wasn't enough for him. He needed a jailer. The former storage rooms of the baron's, in the loft, were converted into an apartment, and one day its occupant appeared: Nederkoorn.

Max started when he saw him for the first time, and every time after that. A huge fellow of his own age, with a hard face, always in black riding boots, which he struck with a plaited whip, invariably accompanied by an Alsatian. Max would have most liked to empty a submachine gun into him immediately, but perhaps that would have been precisely more in the spirit of his new fellow resident. He had not introduced himself, never said hello, and spent hours training his dog, Paco, on the lawn opposite Piet Keller's former house. He shared his life with a plump young woman, much younger than he was and three heads shorter, who to Max's astonishment was obviously in love with him and put an arm around his shoulders when they drove off in their jeep.

But Sem Spier did not limit himself to murderous fantasies.

"I'm going," he announced a few days afterward with a tense face. "I can't live under one roof with that fellow. I'm sorry, that person makes me physically ill. It reminds me too much of something."

Everyone saw that he was serious, everyone begrudged Korvinus his victory, but everyone respected his decision and understood that the last phase had now begun.

The departure of Piet Keller had been something like that of Verdonkschot and his friend for Quinten: more an astonished observation of the fact, which his father had written to him about: that not everything remained the same. Keller's children had long since left home, just like Kern's daughter Martha for that matter, and he had helped him load up the keys and locks and the other things from his workshop, which he had played with so often. When he had asked if the two cart wheels along the gravel path shouldn't come too, Keller had hesitated for a moment and said that he had no room for them in the terraced house where he was going to live. When the hired van had disappeared bumpily over the loose planks of the outer bridge, he had the feeling that Keller—from whom he had learned so much—had never existed.

But he couldn't bear to watch the departure of Mr. Spier. He remembered that when he was a little boy, Granny had always come to tuck him in and turn off the light; after she had given him a kiss and gone to the door, he pulled the blanket over his head and squeezed his eyes tight shut—if he opened them afterward then it must remain just as dark as when they were still shut. There mustn't be any difference any more between open and shut. If the light on the other hand was still burning, because she was clearing something up in his room, that was a disaster; then in some way or other the night was ruined.

Inside at the Spiers' everything was already packed in boxes and gray horse blankets. When the moving van turned onto the forecourt that early afternoon, he said goodbye to them on the terrace. Mrs. Spier had tears in her eyes and couldn't say anything; she just hugged him to her and kissed him five or six times.

But Mr. Spier shook hands with him firmly and said: "We're sorry we won't be able to see you every day anymore, QuQu. You've become part of our life—in fact you were always something of our child. I hope that things will go well in your life, but I don't really have any doubt that they will. As long as you look after yourself. You promise me that you'll look after yourself?"

"Yes, Mr. Spier."

"Come and visit us in Pontrhydfendigaid when you're in England—or in Wales, I should say."

Quinten went to the pond with his recorder, to the embrace of the rhododendrons. He left the instrument unplayed in his lap all afternoon; he sat in front of his hut until it began to grow dark. It was an overcast spring day; there was no wind, and the oily, gleaming water was only occasionally crossed by the reflection of a bird flying overhead.

Now Mr. and Mrs. Spier had also disappeared from his life. The Judith. The Quadrata. Pontrhydfendigaid . . . Was his father there too perhaps? He felt sad. Why was there actually something, and not nothing? And if everything passed anyway, what point was there in its ever having been there? Had it really ever been there? If there were no more people one day, no one who could remember anything anymore, could you then say that anything had ever happened? That was, could you *now* say that *then* you could say that something had happened, when there would be no one else to say anything? No, then nothing would have happened—although it would have happened. He knew that he could talk to Max about this; but because he couldn't talk to his father about it, he didn't want to talk to Max about it either.

He was reminded of the Remembrance Center that had been opened at the Westerbork camp the previous year, which he had gone to with Max and Granny. In the large photographs and also in a film you could see people getting into cattle trucks, supervised by people just like Nederkoorn, being transported to their deaths. He had seen that Max leaned forward to inspect all the faces closely—obviously in the hope that he would discover his mother by chance. There were also women, of whom one could see only the backs of their heads. All dead. Surely that could never have happened! Max had told him that there were admirers of Hitler nowadays, who maintained that all those films and photographs were fake, that none of it had ever happened—but why did they admire him? They were saying that actually Hitler was a failure who had not managed to do what he had proclaimed. Fine sort of admirers they were—Hitler would have put them up against a wall straight away. But still ... those people could *say* that it hadn't happened, although it had happened—that would be proved by the historioscope—but if one day there were no more people left so no one else could say that it *had* happened, how could it *not* not have not happened?

That fish there, poking its nose out of the water, creating an expanding set of circles, like an ever-expanding halo—had it really done that forever? And he himself; he was sitting here now. Was it possible that he had never sat here? Was he actually sitting here now, properly speaking? Did anything really exist? Perhaps you should say that the world existed and did not exist. A bit like the Citadel. And he himself: he existed and he did not exist. That was completely wrong, then. What was he to do in such an idiotic world? What was the point of his being here?

When he got back, Mr. and Mrs. Spier had gone. Korvinus was already walking through the empty rooms with a yardstick, and month later he was living there himself. From that moment on it was as though the castle were keeling over, like a torpedoed ship.

No one dared to go and look, not even by accident, to see how Nederkoorn was living up in the loft. According to Max, he slept under a swastika flag, with a portrait of Himmler above his bed. On Max's own floor, which he shared with Kern, everything was unchanged at first sight; but below, Spier's Empire interior had been replaced by oak furniture, so massive—and probably reinforced with concrete on the inside—that, according to

Kern, Korvinus could count himself lucky that everything did not crash through the floor and plunge down into the cellar.

He, too, had a wife who was obviously devoted to him; but because he had obviously forbidden her to fraternize with fellow residents, it was impossible to discover whether she was attached to him because of or despite the stone ball in his head. They had two sons of the same age as Quinten and Arend Proctor. Quinten had nothing to do with them, but Arend made friends with the elder, Evert—probably against Korvinus's will. It was obvious that he wanted the whole castle to himself, and links of friendship with the enemy made his war of nerves more difficult.

When Paco was not cringing at Nederkoorn's whip and orders, he lay in the forecourt on a chain under a room of Themaat's, where he barked continually. Invoking her husband, who was ill and could not stand it, Elsbeth had complained about it a few times, but from Nederkoorn she could only count on the kind of glance one casts at an object. Once, at her wits' end, she had phoned the police, but they could do nothing.

"The police can almost never do anything," Max had said afterward, "except pick up Jews—they were very good at that."

The dog itself was unapproachable: if anyone came closer than three yards, it began leering and bared its teeth with trembling lips, without giving the impression of laughing. Only when it saw Quinten did it immediately stop barking; it laid its ears flat into its neck, wagged its tail, and allowed itself to be stroked. When Nederkoorn had first seen that, he had erupted into rage.

"If you so much as lay a finger on that animal again, you'll have me to deal with!"

Quinten had never stroked him after that—not because he was frightened of Nederkoorn, but because Paco would of course have to pay for it. But he did, when he had the chance, take his book and sit below Mr. Themaat's window, so that the dog would at least be quiet for a little while. He had learned so much from Themaat that he was prepared to do that for him. He did not go to the pond anymore anyway, since his hut had been destroyed. As far as his chain allowed, Paco crawled toward him and would lie down with his snout as close as possible to him and with his golden brown eyes focused on him. He looks just like me, thought Quinten, but he doesn't know that he's got eyes. Once Korvinus had appeared on the terrace and had ordered him to go away—the forecourt wasn't a slum where the rabble sat in the street; but immediately Sophia had opened the window above and said calmly:

"It begins to strike me that you talk a lot about slums, Mr. Korvinus. Why is that?"

That had helped—but how long was this to go on?

One evening, lying on the sofa, Max tried to work a little, but he was constantly disturbed by thoughts of the situation at the castle. He got up in irritation and went to Sophia's room. She was sitting in her dressing gown on the edge of her bed and giving herself the daily insulin injection that she had needed for years.

"I'm sorry to disturb you, Sophia," he said, and looked at the needle in her thigh, "but I'm angry. I can't concentrate anymore, and what does it really have to do with me? Since the days of feudalism are over and the bourgeoisie now rule the roost, I spend hours every day thinking about the fact that we are living here. But you live somewhere precisely so that you can do something else. When you're walking, you don't think the whole time about the fact that you're walking—except when you've just broken your leg. I've got other things to think about—at present I'm involved in the most interesting project in my whole career. Do you remember that I once explained to you that the mirrors in Westerbork are actually a single huge telescope? But nowadays, with those computers, we're able to link up all the mirrors on earth, so shortly we should have a supertelescope with a diameter of over six thousand miles, as large as our whole planet. So what's in it for me not to be outwitted by this rabble here at the castle?

"What are we actually talking about? Do I really have to dig my heels in over this? If you ask me, there's a great risk of one's messing up one's whole life over this. Take those Moluccans who used to be in Westerbork. Schattenberg estate, do you remember? They were in the Dutch East Indies army, collaborators who had to leave after the independence of Indonesia. Here they were also thrown out of everywhere too, but they were certain that one day they'd be able to return to a new republic of their own, Maluku Selatan. That's why those suckers didn't want to leave those rotten huts—because that would mean they had resigned themselves to the situation. Their sons began hijacking trains in the name of the ideal, and now they're in prison. What's more, they believed the Dutch government still owed them back pay—two thousand guilders or something. They fought their whole life for that with petitions and demonstrations at the houses of Parliament, and finally they were given it, but by that time their lives were over. They couldn't even buy a color television with it. And now they are old men, who still raise the flag on a country that doesn't exist. Shouldn't we learn from their experience and get out of here as soon as possible?"

Putting a piece of cotton wool on the small wound in her left thigh, Sophia looked up. "I don't like it when you just come wandering into my bedroom, Max."

47

The Music

To protect himself against Paco's barking, Verloren van Themaat now usually sat in the side room during the day, below Sophia's bedroom. That was Elsbeth's domain, where they also ate. One stuffy, overcast Sunday afternoon in the autumn of 1984, Elsbeth had asked Quinten if he would visit Themaat again. He would really like that, she said.

Mr. Themaat lay with his hands folded on a sofa in front of the window that overlooked the moat. The view was the same as upstairs, but from a different angle, so that at the same time it was not the same: the water lilies and the ducks were closer; the trees on the other side, taller. Because the sky was dark, a light was already on inside and there was the faint sound of music, some violin concerto or other, perhaps to drown out the distant barking. Mr. Themaat was in a bad way. Quinten could not imagine that this sick old man was the same person he had known. He sat down, and because he had not come with a question, he did not know what to say; he had never just talked to him. He looked at Mrs. Themaat's antique secretary. In the symmetrical grain of the mahogany he saw a devilish, batlike figure; its head with two great eyes on the top drawer, its outspread wings on the closed writing surface, its claws on the two doors below.

It seemed as though Mr. Themaat also found the situation difficult. There was something strange about his eyes: he blinked not very quickly, like everyone else, but kept shutting his eyes for a moment and then opening them again, as though he were dead tired.

"Well, QuQu . . ." he said. "Times change. How old are you now?"

"Sixteen."

"Sixteen already . . ." He focused on the oak beams in the ceiling. "When I was sixteen, it was 1927. In that year Lindbergh was the first person to fly nonstop across the Atlantic—I can remember precisely. I was living in Haarlem then, close to the flea field, as we called it; I used to hang around there a lot with my friends. It was an extended grass field opposite a great white pavilion from the end of the eighteenth century, with columns and an architrave and everything that you're crazy about." Quinten could see that he was seeing it again, although he could only see the ceiling. "It was so grand, it didn't fit into the bourgeois surroundings of Haarlem at all." He looked at Quinten. "I myself was much more interested in the New Architecture, in the de Stijl, the Bauhaus, and so on. I always find your preference rather strange for such a young boy, but shall I tell you something? You're really modern with your Palladio and your Boullée and those people."

"How do you mean?"

Mr. Themaat raised his hand for a moment, perhaps to brush his face, but a moment later he dropped it, trembling.

"I haven't kept up with the literature for quite some time, but after classicism and neoclassicism, all those classical forms are coming back for the third time. By the year 2000 the world will be full of them—you mark my words, you'll see. At the beginning I thought it was just a whim of fashion, but it goes much deeper. You'll be proved right, and I'm not sure if I'm pleased about that. In the visual arts and literature and music, it might be the end of modernism, and in politics as well. Gropius, Picasso, Joyce, Schönberg, Lenin—they determined my life. It looks as though soon it will all be in the past."

"Freud and Einstein, too?" asked Quinten. At home he had always heard those names in that kind of list.

"It wouldn't surprise me. The last few years I've felt like a champion of the Gothic must have felt at the rise of classicism. All those magnificent cathedrals had suddenly become old-fashioned. Are you still interested in that kind of thing?"

Quinten had the feeling that Themaat was not quite sure who he was talking to. It was though he were regarding Quinten as a retired professor, like he himself was.

"I've never been interested in that way."

"In what way, then?"

Quinten thought for a moment. Should he tell him about the Citadel of his dreams? But how could you really tell someone about a dream? When you told someone about a dream, it always sounded stupid, but while you were dreaming it, it wasn't stupid at all—so when you tell a dream precisely, you are still not telling the person what you dreamed. Telling someone about a dream was impossible.

"Well, I was just interested," he said. "I don't know. I think you've told me everything that I wanted to know."

Themaat looked at him for a while, then turned his legs laboriously off the sofa and sat up, with his back bent, two flat white hands next to his thighs.

He closed his eyes and opened them again. "Shall I tell you one thing that you may not know yet?"

"Yes, please."

"Perhaps you'll think it's nonsense, just the chatter of a sick old man, but I want to tell you anyway. Look, how is it that that ideal Greco-Roman architecture and that of the Renaissance could turn into the inhuman gigantism of someone like Boullée? And how could it later, with Speer, even degenerate into the expression of genocide?"

"You once said that it had something to do with Egypt. With the pyramids. With death."

"That's right, but how could it have had anything to do with that?"

"Do you know, then?"

"I think I know, QuQu. And you must know too. It comes from the loss of music."

Quinten looked at him in astonishment. Music? What did music suddenly have to do with architecture? It seemed to him as though a vague smile crossed the mask of Mr. Themaat's face.

The humanist architects, like Palladio, he said, were guided in their designs not only by Vitruvius's discovery of the squared circle, which determined the proportions of the divine human body, but also by a discovery of Pythagoras in the sixth century before Christ: that the relationship between the harmonic intervals was the same as that between prime numbers. If you plucked a string and then wanted to hear the octave of that note, then you simply had to halve its length—the harmony of a note and its octave was therefore determined by the simplest ratio, 1:2. With fifths, it was 2:3 and with fourths, 3:4. The fact that the fantastic notion 1:2:3:4, which was as simple as it was inexpressible, was the basis of musical harmony, and that the whole of musical theory could be derived from it, gave Plato such a shock 150 years later that in his Dialogue "Timaeus" he had a demiurge create the globe-shaped world according to musical laws, including the human soul.

Fifteen hundred years later, that still found an echo in the Renaissance. And in those days the architects realized that the musical harmonies had spatial expressions—namely, the relationships of the length of strings, and spatial relationships were precisely their only concern. Because both the world and the body and soul were composed according to musical harmonies by the demiurge architect, both the macrocosm and the microcosm, they must therefore be guided in their own architectural designs by the laws of music. In Palladio that developed into an extremely sophisticated system. And subsequently that Greek divine world harmony also became connected with the Old Testament Jahweh, who had ordered Moses to build the tabernacle according to carefully prescribed measurements—but he could no longer remember the details. He'd forgotten.

"The tabernacle?" asked Quinten.

"That was a tent in which the Jews displayed their relics on their journey through the desert."

"Did it have to be square or round?"

"Yes, you've put your finger on it. That was precisely the obstacle to reconciling Plato and the Bible. There were also squares involved, if I remember correctly, but nothing round. The whole tent must be oblong."

"Oblong? Greek and Egyptian temples were oblong too, weren't they—like beds?" Quinten's eyes widened for a moment, but he wasn't given the opportunity to pursue his thoughts, because Themaat came to a conclusion.

In the sixteenth and seventeenth centuries, he said, at the birth of the new age, when modern science originated, it had all been lost. The view that musical theory should be the metaphysical foundation of the world, of body and soul and architecture, was rejected as obscurantist nonsense—and that led directly to Boullée and Speer. The harmonic relationships of course did not automatically change when the elements were enlarged a hundredfold; but the dimensions of the human body, as the measure of all things, remained unchanged—that is: it became proportionately a hundred times smaller, thus ultimately disturbing all harmony and eliminating the human soul in an Egyptian way.

Slowly, as though he were lifting something heavy, Mr. Themaat raised an index finger. "And what you see at the moment, QuQu, is the unexpected return of all those classical motifs, all those stylobates and shafts and capitals and friezes and architraves—fortunately on a human scale again, but also in a totally crazy way. It's just as though somewhere high in space the classical ideal exploded and the fragments and splinters are now falling back to earth, all confused, distorted, broken and out of their equilibrium. Here," he said, and took hold of a large, thick book, which he had obviously laid out ready. "Catalog of the Biennale in Venice. Four years ago there was an architecture exhibition there, which made me first see what was brewing. 'The Presence of the Past' was the theme. Look," he said, and opened the book where he had laid a bookmark. "The Acropolis in a distorting mirror." With half-closed lids, he handed the book to Quinten.

Was it a view of the Citadel? Quinten's eyes began to shine. How splendid! They were photos of a fantastic street, indoors, consisting of a covered hallway: huge pieces of scenery consisting of gables, designed by different architects, all the gables differing totally from each other and yet belonging together, while each gable also consisted of elements that didn't belong together and yet formed a whole. While Themaat said that Vitruvius would have a heart attack if he saw that and that Palladio would kill himself laughing, Quinten looked at a paradoxical portico with four standing columns very close together: the first was a bare tree trunk, the second stood on a model of a house, the third was only half built—the upper half, which floated in the air and still pretended to support the architrave—the fourth was a hedge cut in a form of the column; the architrave was indicated by a curved strip of blue neon. Everything had a fairy-tale paradoxical quality, the disharmony as harmony. Mr. Themaat might meanwhile maintain that it was classical language, but with all the words wrongly spelled and the syntax turned into an Augean stable, such as toddlers wrote, it gave him an overwhelming feeling of happiness.

"I thought you'd like it, QuQu," said Mr. Themaat, dabbing the corners of his mouth with a handkerchief. "For me it's an end, a kind of fireworks to conclude the great banquet, which once began in Greece. But then you had the balanced world view of Ptolemy, with the earth resting in the center of the universe; according to humanism you got that from Copernicus, with the sun resting in the middle; afterward you got the infinite universe of Giordiano Bruno, which no longer had any center at all. All those universes were eternal and unchanging, but recently we have been living in the explosive, violent universe of your foster father, which suddenly has a beginning. Then you get a postmodern sort of spectacle; then everything bursts into pieces and fragments. Everything's exploding at the moment, up to and including the world population, and that's all because of the crazy development of technology. Suddenly a whole new age has dawned, which fortunately I won't have to experience."

Quinten looked out of the window thoughtfully. "But a beginning is also some kind of fixed point isn't it? What is more fixed than a beginning? You really ought to see that as progress after the previous universe, which had no center anymore."

"Yes," said Themaat. "You could look at it like that."

"Anyway, I suddenly remember what Max once said: that human beings are smaller than the universe in approximately the same proportion as the smallest particle is smaller than the human being."

For a few seconds Mr. Themaat fixed his great staring eyes on him. "So is it true after all? So is man in the middle after all? They should have known that."

"Who?"

"Well, Plato, Protagoras, Vitruvius, Palladio—all those fellows."

Groaning a little, he lay down again, and there was a moment's silence. "For the last few weeks I've found myself thinking of music all the time, QuQu. The Platonic harmony of the spheres has disappeared from the world since Newton, and harmony disappeared from music itself with Schönberg, in Einstein's time. But just like those wretched columns in that catalog, tonality is making a comeback at the moment—except that in the meantime music has become a bane instead of a boon. Here it's still relatively quiet—here it's just dogs barking—but in the city there's no escaping it anymore. There's music everywhere, even in the elevators and the bathrooms. Music comes out of cars, and on the scaffolding every building worker has his portable radio on as loud as it will go. Everywhere is like it only used to be at the fair. But all that harmonic music now together forms a cacophony, compared with which Schönberg's relativist twelve-tone system was nothing. And that ubiquitous cacophony is what the new-fangled cacophonous architecture expresses. That bomb that you once talked about,

Quinten, has exploded. That's what I wanted to tell you, but perhaps you should forget it again at once. Anyway, I've gotten tired. I think I'm going to close my eyes for a minute."

The talk had affected Quinten deeply: it had sounded a bit like a testament. Suddenly he'd heard so many new things that he couldn't take it all in. While he went up the stairs in the hall, he reflected that there was still more to know in the world than he knew. Of course you couldn't know everything, and that wasn't necessary either, but lots of people probably didn't know what there was to know. They lived and died without anyone ever telling them that there was this or that to know that they might have liked to know. Except, once you were dead, what difference did it make? You might just as well never have been born. Anyway, most people didn't want to know anything. They simply wanted to get very rich, or eat a lot, or watch soccer or that kind of thing. Or kiss each other.

In his room, he stood indecisively and looked at the black case with his mother's cello in it, upright against the wall. He had never opened it; he had always had the feeling that it was inappropriate to do so out of mere curiosity. But if ever the moment had come, it was now. Perhaps it was the first time for sixteen years that the light would shine on it again. But no, of course his father had looked at it occasionally. He laid the case carefully on the ground, knelt down, clicked the two locks, and slowly opened the lid.

Although he knew that the instrument was inside, the sight of it was still a shock to him. It lay dull and dusty on its back in the dark-red velvet, the edges of which had been gnawed by moths. It had the form of a human being, with broad hips, a waist, and a torso with shoulders; at the end of a long neck the peg box and the scroll formed a small head, like that of an ostrich. The symmetrical sound holes on either side of the bridge looked like footprints. Carefully, he took it out of the case—on the bottom the lining had been virtually completely eaten away—and he solemnly carried it over to his bed. He sat down next to it, as if next to a human being, and sat looking at it in silence. Perhaps it was more like his mother than his mother now was. He looked at the strings, over which her fingers had glided, at the side edges that she had held between her thighs—all of this retained more memories of herself than she did herself.

After a while he got up and went to the front room. Sophia was busy polishing the glass of the framed photographs on the mantelpiece, and he asked her if he could borrow her measuring tape; when she said that she had lost it some while ago, he went to Theo Kern and borrowed a yardstick. Then he carefully measured the length of the A string, from the nut to the bridge: twenty-four inches. Now he had to strum it, but the fact that he was going to make sound on that cello after all this time was an awareness that he first of all had to overcome. He pulled the string with the nail of his index finger and listened to the singing sound. He frowned. According to him, it was a semitone too low. He checked with his recorder: he was right; it was an A flat.

Although it didn't matter, he tried to tune the string; but the peg would not budge. Then he determined the middle of the string with the yardstick, twelve inches, put his index finger on that point, and struck it again. When he heard the same A flat, which at the same time was not the same A flat, he sat up and looked around with an ecstatic smile. It was true! Pythagoras! Plato! He had picked up a sound from the center of the world!

Suddenly, he left everything where it was and ran downstairs into the hall. Downstairs Korvinus tore open his door and snapped that there were other people living there and couldn't he be a bit quieter, but Quinten did not even look at him. He ran across the forecourt—where Nederkoorn was teaching Evert Korvinus to drive in his Jeep, with Arend on the backseat—over the two bridges and then into the rectangular, tree-enclosed field behind Klein Rechteren. There he flopped into the ditch and, panting and sweaty, looked at the red cow, which with grinding jaws returned his gaze and then resumed its meal in reassurance. The sky was still overcast, but now with strange, hectic, scudding clouds, dark purple in the middle, but light at the edges; it looked as though they were coming up vertically from the depths. Yet it was windless and oppressive where he was sitting.

He looked with excitement at the dark trees that fringed the field, at the grazing cow between the two alders, and at the three boulders that lay in their perfect positions, like in a Japanese garden. He suddenly knew for certain that he was predestined for something awesome—it was as though he had received a message, a mission to do something that only he was capable of! But what was it? How was he to find out? Did it have something to do with that completely different time which, according to Mr. Themaat, had dawned? At that moment a deer appeared on the other side between the trees. It stopped and looked out across the field. Immediately afterward—no one would believe it—suddenly a strong wind began to blow in Quinten's face, so that from one moment to the next the whole wood started rustling and roaring like the sea, and between the trunks high undulating leaves suddenly rolled onto the meadow, whereupon the deer bounded into the darkness and disappeared.

48

Velocities

When at the beginning of December Ferdinand Verloren van Themaat was admitted to a psychotherapeutic clinic in Apeldoorn for an indefinite period, Elsbeth finally took the plunge and also moved to that town, whereupon Korvinus immediately incorporated their flat into his own. From then on Paco was no longer chained up in the front courtyard. The year 1985 approached.

The demolition contractor now occupied the whole of the ground floor, with the result that the other occupants could no longer use the front door: he didn't want people traipsing to and fro through his part of the house. From then on they had to use the former tradesmen's entrance at the side, through the bicycle shed, the cellar, and the former staff staircase at the back of the villa. Like the cellar, that stairwell had for decades been crammed with rubbish, rusted buckets, broken chairs, rolls of carpet; if they didn't like it, then all they had to do was to clear it up, and anyone who didn't like it could clear off. On the way to the attic only Nederkoorn was allowed to go on using the old, now partitioned-off stairs to the first floor.

Proctor was driven to distraction by this measure. Up to now it had seemed that the domestic upheavals had actually passed him by, of course because his mind was occupied with his great book on Vondel's *Lucifer*; but now he suddenly came charging down the stairs one afternoon with an ax and, with a roar, began hacking at the new partition door. It took Clara, Sophia, and Selma an hour to pacify the shuddering translator somewhat. He wasn't going to be forced to use the back door, he kept on repeating as he drank a glass of water; he'd been using the front door for twenty years, and a brute like that needn't imagine that he could direct him to the back door. He wasn't staying here one day longer!

Everyone expected a dreadful response from Korvinus, but he reacted with astonishing restraint; the same day he had the door repaired and didn't say another word about it. According to Max, the explanation was that he saw himself getting closer to his goal step by step and had to do less and less in order to undermine their morale; it was enough to turn off the electricity or the water without warning from time to time. Quinten assumed that he was also inhibited somewhat by the friendship between Arend Proctor and his son Evert, who were inseparable.

"The two of them also smashed up my hut," he said.

"How do you know it was them?" asked Sophia.

Quinten shrugged his shoulders. "I don't, but it was."

Although Marius Proctor had announced that he wasn't staying a day longer, he did finally stay: those blows with the ax had obviously sapped his willpower. He left only after the police had rung his bell on the terrace on New Year's night. There had been a serious accident. After having drunk too much in a disco, the two boys had stolen a car, skidded on an icy country road, lost control going around a bend, and crashed into a tree. Evert Korvinus, who was at the wheel, had been very badly injured but might perhaps survive. Arend Proctor was dead.

The news shook Groot Rechteren to its psychic foundations. For the whole of New Year's Day, Sophia and Selma supported Marius and Clara, neither of whom could handle their despair. Max had been conscious from an early age of the inescapable fact that anything could happen at any moment, but even he was beside himself for the whole day: it suddenly brought back the memory of another car accident, seventeen years ago. There was no sign of Korvinus. His wife—who suddenly turned out to be called Elsa—tried to make contact with Arend's parents via Sophia; but Proctor shouted at Clara that he would kill her if she spoke to the woman. Arend was dead, but her own son was alive, and, what's more, she had a second son! Quinten heard him screaming, with his voice breaking, that life was a dung heap, that there was no point to it all, that existence was one senseless mess!

As he stood listening in the hallway, Quinten wondered how one could say that. Perhaps you only said such things when someone died, or when you yourself died; but was it right or, on the contrary, quite wrong? Was there an ultimate truth in death or in life? If you found life absurd, shouldn't you find death precisely meaningful? It seemed as though Proctor were confusing everything. If he found Arend's death senseless, then surely he should find life meaningful! Anyway, what did it matter that Arend was dead? Why was he screaming like that? Perhaps it depended on the kind of person you were. His own father, from whom he had heard nothing for three years, had perhaps understood just as little of what it was all about. He himself was reminded of his mother's accident, and of the death of Aunt Helga, but apart from that, what had happened left him unmoved: they shouldn't have destroyed his hut.

That night he couldn't sleep with all the wailing going on above his head. He got out of bed and went to the window. The frozen moat lay beneath the icy light of the stars. Suddenly the roaring and commotion in Proctor's study assumed absurd proportions; a little while later he saw papers fluttering past his window, followed by umbrellas and still more papers, sometimes whole packs of them, which disintegrated in the air.

Once the Proctors had left, a week after Arend's funeral, Nederkoorn expanded into their flat. From then on Max's and Theo's flats were sandwiched between those of the rabble as if between the jaws of a serpent. But Max and Sophia agreed that out of solidarity with Theo and Selma, they could no longer go. Evert Korvinus, it transpired, had a lesion of the spinal cord and was paralyzed from the waist down and for the rest of his life would be confined to a wheelchair, Sophia heard from his mother. The demolition contractor would therefore be a little quieter for a while and would not try to sour the last year of their protected tenancy—if only because Elsa Korvinus had now, in addition, broken the rule of silence.

Max, completely absorbed by his work on quasar MQ 3412, which turned out to be behaving in an increasingly mysterious way, looked forward to the prospect of a year of peace and quiet—but that was not granted him. For months Ada's condition had been gradually deteriorating. First she had problems with her digestion; then she developed a chronic pelvic infection, as a result of her bladder catheter. But on an arctic day in February, when the oil stoves in Groot Rechteren could not warm their rooms even at the highest setting, Sophia came back from Emmen with much more serious news. She had gone to the director to talk about the mold in Ada's mouth; she had been told that Ada would probably shortly have to be transferred to the hospital. Hemorrhages had begun occurring even between her monthly periods, and according to the doctor in charge, it looked as though she had cancer of the womb.

While she was telling him this, her face again assumed that masklike expression that Max knew so well. The fact that Ada—that is, her poor body—had gone on having her periods every month all through those seventeen years shocked him more than the news of her illness. The latter, on the contrary, was something hopeful: the upbeat toward the end of her absurd existence.

He looked at Sophia in silence. After a little while he asked: "Do you suppose this is the moment of truth?"

Since Onno and he had embarked on their crazy campaign, at the time of Ada's cesarean operation, they had never talked about euthanasia again. He had never once spoken to Sophia about it, although it of course preoccupied her, too.

She did not reply, but he could tell from her eyes that she felt the same way.

Ten days later, in the car on the way to Hoogeveen hospital, they did not discussed it, either. When he closed the door and looked about him in the crunching snow, it amazed him that everything here was just the same as that evening of the accident, that calamitous February 27 when Onno and he had celebrated their common conception in Dwingeloo. Suddenly he also remembered the taxi driver who had refused to take him to Leiden, where Sophia had become a widow. The fact that Ada had now been admitted here for the second time gave him the sense of things having come full circle—and full circles always signaled radical changes. He was happy that he had made a date with Tsjallingtsje for that evening.

Kloosterboer, the doctor who had invited Sophia to come, confirmed the diagnosis. They sat next to each other facing his desk and looked at the young gynecologist, who with his short blond hair and bright-blue eyes looked more like a tennis coach.

"How far has it gone?" asked Sophia.

He nodded. "It's spread. There's no point in operating anymore."

"Well, well," said Max.

The doctor focused his eyes on him. "How do you mean?"

"Of course you're not going to operate on a woman who has been lying in a coma for seventeen years and living like a vegetable. Even if there was any point, there would still be no point."

Kloosterboer folded his arms. "Let's understand each other from the start, Mr. Delius. If there were any point, we would go ahead."

Max and Sophia looked at each other for a moment.

"And now?" asked Sophia. "Chemotherapy, radiotherapy?"

"Not that, either."

"And pain-killers?" asked Max. "I'd be interested to know if you are also giving her pain-killers?" He saw that Kloosterboer did not know what to make of that question, because there was not an immediate answer. "I mean, if you aren't giving her any pain-killers, what actually is your position? How can you reconcile the two things?"

The doctor's face stiffened. "I can quite understand your views, and your situation, but I cannot discuss the matter with you at all. You must understand my position, too."

"We do," said Sophia, and stood up.

Kloosterboer rolled his chair back. "I'll take you to your daughter's room."

"Don't bother. We'll find the way."

As they walked along the corridors, Max said that Kloosterboer was obviously a Christian fundamentalist, however much a man of the world he looked.

"Perhaps he's just young," suggested Sophia, "and frightened for his career."

Yes, of course. She knew the medical world better than he did. Out of the corner of his eye he glanced at the upright, graying abbess at his side, of whom he still understood nothing. She was starting to look more and more like her mother. So they would now finally have to talk about it.

He slowed down. "Tell me, Sophia, what do you think should happen now?"

"Ada's husband must decide."

He shook his head. "Ada's mother must decide. Anyway, I remember that Onno wrote as much to you."

"What did he write, then?"

"That Ada is your flesh and blood, and that you have the last word if decisions have to be made about her. He can't have meant anything but a situation of the kind that we have now."

She stopped and looked him straight in the eye. "They intend to let her die slowly, but I think a stop should be put to it. Very positively—with a morphine injection. But we shouldn't bank on that. At most there will be a staff meeting about this, or they will withdraw—"

"Withdraw?"

"Stop feeding her. But they won't do that, because what happens then is terrible for the staff to see. She will slowly dehydrate, until she's just skin and bone."

Max shuddered. "In other words," he said, "she must be taken away from here, to a more enlightened hospital, where they are not so frightened that it will get into the papers. In Amsterdam."

"If they let her go at least, if they don't make it a matter of honor. Don't talk to me about hospitals. Anyway, she doesn't even have to go to a hospital. Any reasonable GP will do it—anyone knows that, the public prosecutors too, but no one talks about it."

He looked at her. "Do you mean that we should simply take her to the castle?"

"Of course not," she said immediately. "With Quinten . . ."

"And what shall we do with him? Should he know what's going on?"

Sophia looked at him uncertainly. "What's the point of burdening him with that?"

In the lounge, patients and nurses were watching a broadcast of a chess game; someone showed them the ward where Ada was. Max no longer remembered when he had last visited her, perhaps four or five years ago, perhaps even longer—but what he now saw, by the window, hidden behind a screen, he saw for the first time. He stiffened.

In the whiter-than-white, snowy light her head reminded him of a cut-open coconut that, years ago, when he was still in Amsterdam, he had once forgotten to throw away and which was still in the dish on his return from holiday. Her stubbly hair had gone gray, deathly gray, framing her gaunt, blotchy face, her nostrils were red and inflamed by the feeding tube. One could scarcely see any longer that there was a body under the sheets. Her desiccated white hands were like a bird's claws; the tips of all her fingers were swaddled in bandages.

"You never told me about this," he said in dismay.

"You never asked."

He found himself thinking that a stop should be put to this at once—in the next five minutes. He looked at the tarnished remains in the iron bed, while yellowing images rushed through his memory like autumn leaves blowing past: in her parents' house in the upstairs room, the cello between her legs, her fingertips on the strings, naked and cross-legged opposite him on his bed, her legs around his hips in the warm, nocturnal sea. . . . With ribs heaving, he turned away and looked out of the window at the blinding snow, with the sun shining on it.

He had never been so absorbed by his work as in the past eighteen months. In the mornings, when he was not yet fully awake but was no longer asleep, precisely on the borderline, MQ 3412 immediately appeared in his brain—but in the shape of a chaotic tangle of data, diagrams, spectrums, radio maps, satellite X-ray photographs, absurd interpretations, whimsical fantasies, all hopelessly confused and entangled, like a ball of wool that the cat had been playing with and, moreover, surrounded by a halo of doom: it was all wrong, he was on completely the wrong track, it was pointless nonsense.

However, he'd gradually come to understand that waking depression in himself. It had begun when he had got into the habit of drinking a bottle of wine every evening—recently sometimes even two—and when he went to sleep he was on the contrary convinced that he was on the threshold of a earth-shattering discovery. Over the years he had learned not to take any notice of all this. By the time he had cracked the joints of his thumbs and thrown off the blankets, the worst of the gloom had already receded.

The same thing happened on Monday, March 11, 1985. That morning the first data from the VLBI, Very Long Baseline Interferometry, the telescope as large as the whole world, were due in. A number of young astronomers from Leiden had spent the night watching in Westerbork with the technicians; but he himself did not even call. At breakfast he first leafed through the morning paper, in a bad mood. Chernenko was dead; within four hours the Central Committee in the Kremlin had chosen a successor, a certain Gorbachev, but of course he wouldn't change anything, either. Nothing would ever change; the Cold War was forever. The remnants of a dream were still haunting him—an image of Ada: her organs were floating in the air outside her body, like in certain kinds of cross-sectional diagrams of the inside of engines, so that at the same time it looked like a still photograph of an explosion.

"I'm going to have dinner at Tsjallingtsje's tonight," he said, getting up with a slight groan.

"Will you be coming home?" asked Sophia.

"Maybe, maybe not," he said. "I'll see." He ran one hand over Quinten's shoulders and said: "Do your best."

As he drove through the hazy spring morning to Westerbork, he listened to Schubert's Unfinished Symphony, conducted by Böhm. It was still indestructibly beautiful, but he did know every note of it, as by now he did of almost all music.

Once he was in the busy terminal his depression lifted and he looked with the same curiosity at the computer printout that Floris gave him as he would have when he was half his age—except that there were not yet any computer printouts then. As far as his enthusiasm was concerned, it was as though time had stood still. On the other hand, one thing that was governed by the passing of time was the quasar—and he saw at first glance that something was completely wrong.

"Good luck," said Floris sarcastically. "You might just as well throw it in the wastepaper basket."

Because Quinten had discovered the historioscope at the age of twelve, Max had once sketched the portrait of a quasar for him: a mysterious, superheavy object at the limits of the observable universe that emitted as much energy as a thousand galaxies of 100 billion stars each, while the quasi-star was much smaller than even one galaxy. Probably there was a black hole in it, the most monstrous of all celestial phenomena. The most distant known quasar, OQ 172, was over 15 billion light years away; so that you could see from it what the universe was like 5 billion years after Big Bang, when it was only a quarter of the size it was now. A contemporary of his from Leiden— who now worked at Mount Palomar in California—had discovered that distance in four-dimensional space-time through the red shift in the hydrogen lines in the optical spectrum. When a jet plane approached, Max had explained to Quinten, the sound of its engines became higher, and after it passed over you, it became lower: first it retracted its sound waves a little, making them shorter, and afterward it stretched them, making them longer. The fact that the strongest spectrum line of OQ 172 had moved a long way from ultraviolet in the direction of the longer wavelengths of red, into the middle of the visible spectrum, meant that the thing was moving away in the expanding universe at over 90 percent of the speed of light.

Quinten had shown only moderate interest—in the last analysis, Max reflected, he was still a real arts man, just like his father. Moreover, MQ 3412 refused to conform to the pattern of the almost two thousand quasars now known. And the VLBI now turned out to have a serious teething problem, probably a defect in the incredibly sensitive communications between the hundreds of mirrors in scores of countries on different continents; or perhaps there was something wrong with an atomic clock somewhere, so that the things had not been put into the computer with absolute synchronicity. Max looked at the calculations as though at an unbelievable juggling trick for which one would actually prefer not to know the explanation. This time MQ 3412 had decided to move at infinite speed, as appeared from the desolate radio spectrum.

"In other words," said Max "our tachyonic friend is at all points on a line simultaneously with an energy of zero."

"A. Einstein would have raised his eyebrows at that," said Floris.

Max spent the rest of the day in meetings, telephoning as far as Australia, reading and sending faxes and discussing things with the engineers. One of them suggested that the mistake might be theirs. Gas was being extracted from the earth beneath Westerbork, which may have caused minute subsidences, so that the mirrors were no longer absolutely perpendicular; a few months ago a small earthquake had been recorded near Assen, with a force of 2.8 on the Richter scale. It was decided to recalibrate everything and to contact the gas board in Groningen. It struck Max as remarkable that an event deep in the earth, in the perm, might have disturbed one's vision of the edge of the universe.

Toward evening he withdrew into his little office in order to look at the data at his leisure, but he couldn't make head or tail of them. It was though a monkey at a typewriter had tried to write a sonnet. But he was also reminded of a revolutionary experiment that had been conducted three years before in Paris. It related to a fundamental conversation in the 1930s between Einstein and Bohr—that is, between the theory of relativity and quantum mechanics, which had never gotten along very well.

Einstein's putative experiment was tested in 1982, and it turned out that Bohr was right. Even then there seemed to be instantaneous, infinitely fast signals—that is, faster than light; since no one doubted that this was impossible, it indicated something in reality that no one had foreseen. Could it be connected with this? But how? Maybe the solution would only come with the VLBI in space, dish aerials on satellites, enabling a telescope to be built with a cross-section of 62,000 miles—but that would take ten years, and by that time he would probably have retired.

Around him there were tables, cases, and shelves overloaded with piles of papers; as usual with his things, though, the order among them was immediately visible. One wall was taken up by a green blackboard, on which formulas and diagrams were written in different-colored chalks—not scribbled down higgledy-piggledy in brilliant frenzy, with carelessly erased sections, but in a harmonious composition, as in a work of art.

He put the papers into a folder, rested his chin on his hands, and looked out the open window. On every side his view was blocked by the giant black skeleton of a mirror. They were calibrating. In the complete silence he heard at short intervals the soft hum of the mechanism with which the rotation of the earth on its axis was being compensated, in order to keep the observed object in focus. What kind of sinister irony was it that under the former Westerbork concentration camp it turned out that they were extracting gas?

Dusk was already falling, but in the distance visitors were still walking around the site—not looking at the telescopes, but at something that was no longer there. If those directly involved had wanted nothing more to do with the camp, in the new Jewish generation voices had recently been raised in favor of restoring it to its original state. The barrier was back in its old place and a watchtower had been restored by the buffers. There had even been a case made for ousting the observatory. If they really persisted in this, he would write a letter to the editor of the *New Israel Weekly*, extol the synthesis radio telescope as a "Jewish observatory," and argue that it could only be destroyed if after the complete restoration of Westerbork camp the ninety-three trains also appeared at the Boulevard des Misères, to bring the people back from the gas chambers.

49

The Westerbork

Over the years Max's relationship with Tsjallingtsje had assumed the calm character of a marriage. While she still cried out "Oh God!" when she came, the stationer's above which she had lived had been taken over by a large publishing firm, which needed her rooms for storing cut-price English art books. He had arranged for her to move into a rustic Hansel-and-Gretel-type house on the edge of the village of Westerbork, where a shy electronics engineer from Dwingeloo had entertained young farmhands until he retired.

At the same time, Max had had the end of Groot Rechteren in mind and the moment when Quinten would leave home, after which Sophia and he would go their separate ways. At the bottom of the overgrown garden a wooden shed took up the whole width, was in fact much too large for this spot, but it could be turned into a studio for him; even now he sometimes sat there when he wanted to work undisturbed. He had never talked to Tsjallingtsje about it, nor had he suggested anything in that direction; but because she knew that he had promised to bring up the child of his friend, who, moreover, had disappeared four years ago, she of course knew that a new situation would arise afterward.

In Dwingeloo she had heard about the fiasco with the VLBI, and obviously to console him, she set the table for a special meal; there was even champagne in a cooler. She was wearing a bright red ankle-length robe, making her look even bigger, and although she was the same size as he was, she embraced him like a larger person embracing a smaller one: she with her arms around his neck, he with his hands on her high hips, which immediately resulted in a change in his chemical balance.

"At least you know what becomes a disillusioned researcher," he said, taking off his coat. He sank onto the sofa and with a glass of pink champagne in his hand he told her about the worldwide astronomical debacle, which had cost hundreds of thousands of guilders, perhaps millions. "In fact isn't it wonderful that it's possible? Thousands of toddlers' playrooms could have been built, and if the experiment had succeeded, it would still have been no good to anyone. The fact that that's still possible, reconciles me a little with mankind. It means that *Homo sapiens* still hasn't grown out of his curious childhood. Only when shortsightedness finally takes over and the importance of things is seen as a function of their proximity will things be really going the wrong way. Listen to me: I'm speaking as though I'm writing."

"You mean that people should look farther than their nose is long."

"In my case, that's actually scarcely possible."

Perhaps it was the way she burst out laughing that attracted him to her. He couldn't remember ever seeing Sophia laugh so genuinely, or Ada; but Tsjallingstje's stern face was always ready to change into something completely different from one moment to the next, as though a light were switched on in a dark room. Perhaps a talent for laughter was true wit, more so than the ability for intellectual *tours de force*.

While she was busy in the kitchen, he looked down at the evening paper, which was lying next to him. He read the headlines about the changes in Moscow. There, too, it was obviously a question of something like a red shift—or rather the reverse, a violent political shift: something was approaching humanity at great speed, since the expansion of the political universe had suddenly changed into contraction. He felt tired. He put his legs on the sofa, and when he closed his eyes for a moment he again saw the absurd measurement results. Perhaps it was because of the champagne, but for some reason he suddenly had the feeling there was nevertheless a meaning hidden in them.

At the table, too, it struck him that Tsjallingtsje had spent over her budget. There were oysters, with which they finished the champagne;

when she then came out of the kitchen with venison steak and gave him a bottle of Volnay to uncork, he was certain that something else was going on.

"Out with it, Tsjal," he said, clinking glasses with her. "What is it? Have I forgotten a date?"

She looked at him over her glass. She gulped; he could see that it was an effort for her to say what she wanted to say.

"I hope you won't get angry with me, Max, but I'd really like there to be a date that we wouldn't forget.".

"You're talking in riddles."

"I want a child by you."

He looked back at her without moving. The words ricocheted through his head like a burning arrow that had flown in through an open window. He had suspected previously that this was on her mind, but he hadn't expected that she would come out with it so directly and with such determination. Even before he knew what his reaction was to the statement, he got up and knelt down beside her, his arms around her waist and his face hidden in her lap. Tsjallingtsje began to cry. She took his left hand and pressed her lips to the palm, while she ran her other hand through his thick, graying hair. Max's head was spinning. Of course! That's what must happen! It was as though in the tumult a voice was constantly saying "Everything will be put right. Everything will be put right." He wanted to think, create some kind of clarity in himself. What he would most like to do would be to go into the garden through the open doors; but he couldn't simply abandon the festive meal.

He looked up. "Tell me honestly. Are you pregnant?"

"Of course not, what do you take me for? Do you think I'm black-mailing you? But I want a child of yours, even if you don't want one. I'm thirty-six, and every year it gets more and more critical, as you may know. If I wait a couple more years, all I'll be capable of having are Down's syndrome children."

"Oh, I know a very nice mongol, though." Because the hard coconut mat was beginning to hurt his knees, he sat on his haunches. "So it's a child with me or without me there, but in any case a child."

"Yes."

"And if I hadn't wanted to, what then? Would you have found someone else?"

She looked down. "I don't know. You mustn't ask me a thing like that."

"And you realize of course that I'll be seventy when your child is eighteen?"

"No more ideal father than a grandfather—everybody knows that."

"Well, that's settled then." He got up, put his arms around her large body, and kissed her. "Have your coil taken out tomorrow. Then I expect, of course, you'll want to get married."

"I couldn't care less. I don't have to."

"And your father, the vicar?"

"If you ask me, he hasn't believed in God for a long time."

"What kind of world are we living in?" cried Max, with a feeling that he was quoting Onno's tone.

He emptied his glass in one gulp, the same way that one drinks water, then poured another one for himself. While they ate they discussed the consequences of their decision. If everything went well, Quinten would take his university entrance exam next year and perhaps go somewhere to study, although he hadn't given any indication of such an intention; at the same time their stay at the castle would come to an end. Sophia hadn't said either what she intended to do afterward, but from what he knew of her, she'd known for a long time what she was going to do.

"Don't drink so much," said Tsjallingtsje, putting a fresh bottle on the table.

"Of course I drink a lot. In fact I intend to drink far too much this evening. Do you realize that I will be a father for the first time if we succeed?" He rubbed his face with both hands. Suddenly the world had changed. All those seventeen years he had spent with Sophia and Quinten suddenly seemed to have blown away like a sigh of wind. Everything began anew, but now in an honest, unambiguous way. He got up and tottered slightly.

"Don't you want some coffee?"

"Excuse me, but I have to be alone for a moment. I'm going to the shed."

"To the shed now? You're drunk, Max. Why don't you go and sit upstairs?"

"Now, leave me alone."

He gave her a kiss on the forehead, opened the conservatory doors, and went into the garden with the bottle and his glass. Night had fallen; above the trees the moon was in its third quarter. Halfway down the winding path between the bushes, he rested the bottom of the bottle for a moment on the gigantic erratic stone, which had worked its way out of the earth there and which came up to his waist; when he had controlled himself again, he turned on the unshaded light in the shed and sank into the worn wickerwork chair with a sigh. He left the door open. Once, the large space had been used for storage of some kind or as a workplace; perhaps a carpenter had once lived in Tsjallingtsje's house. At head height there were a couple of small windows.

He poured himself another glass and was amazed at the mysteriousness of existence. It was as if Tsjallingtsje's six words that she wanted a child of his had given his existence a new impetus, like a crack of the whip gave to a spinning top when he was a child. Since he had lived with Quinten and Sophia at Groot Rechteren in Onno's service, his personal life had been in past perspective; it was now as though she had turned him around 180 degrees, so that he was suddenly facing the future— where although he couldn't make out anything concrete, since it didn't yet exist, there was nevertheless something like a dark space-time full of teeming possibilities.

At a stroke she had put an end to the tangled situation in which he had lived for seventeen years. Like a baby in a playpen. Quinten's playpen must still be somewhere in the storage room, folded up, like a dismantled bed. It was as though the prospect of a child, which would undoubtedly be his, now finally made Quinten Onno's son. In the paper he had read that a short while ago it had become possible to determine paternity unambiguously by means of DNA testing, but his former fears had long since receded. In appearance Quinten didn't look like either of them, only like Ada, as she had once been; and the arts-oriented nature of his interests pointed much more in Onno's direction than in his. The fact that music meant little to him simply confirmed that; he didn't even have a hi-fi in his room. Perhaps the incomprehensible boy didn't resemble anybody who had ever lived.

When the motionless, gradually disintegrating horror in the hospital bed appeared before him, he rubbed both hands over his face, as though the image were sticking to his skin. He took a swig and had the feeling that he would be capable of putting an end to the existence of that living dead person with his own hands. But how? With a knife? And why not with a knife? Why, he wondered would a cry of horror go up in the world if it turned out that in some hospital other terminal patients were taken to the cellar, where they were beheaded by guillotine? Or where they were given a shot to the back of the head in a courtyard? Simply because of the association with executions? Or because of that it wouldn't become clear that killing was killing and not anything else, such as "falling asleep"?

Perhaps it was ultimately all a question of words. *Endlösung* was what the Germans had called the mass murder of Jews. What was more beautiful than the "final solution" of something, the definitive result, the decisive result of the division of zero? It almost something like the physicists' Theory of Everything. With half-closed eyes he looked at the rusty red in his glass and thought of Onno. He'd like to talk to him about that—language as a way of disguising reality. Probably Onno would dismiss it as a hackneyed topic, over which only adolescents racked their brains, but then go on to say a few unexpected things about it. Where was Onno? What was he doing at this moment? Was he perhaps also thinking of Max? Perhaps, but perhaps not. Perhaps he'd banished him completely from his consciousness. Not just him but Quinten, Ada, and Sophia as well. Perhaps he wasn't even alive anymore. Perhaps he'd crawled into a cave somewhere on Crete, where his bones would be found in fifty years' time, and would be initially taken for those of the writer of the Phaistos disc, until it was discovered by using the C14 method that this could only be a Dutch politician, probably of Calvinist origin.

Max could see through the open door that Tsjallingtsje had turned on the TV without switching on the light; the image flickered through the room as though there was a constant succession of small explosions. He had the feeling that he shouldn't really leave her alone now, but he wanted to think for a bit—or at least float on his thoughts, like on an air bed in the sea. At home Sophia was now also sitting alone in the room, just like Quinten was undoubtedly doing in his. Everyone was sitting alone in a room.

Recently he had been getting a little worried about Sophia: sometimes she sat motionless on a chair for hours, staring ahead of her with her hands in her lap; when he said anything about it, she started and looked at him as though she weren't aware of it herself. From his earlier vacations he remembered French and Italian families, in the evenings at long tables under pathetically twisted olive trees, themselves trees, with ancient great-grandfathers and great-grandmothers and all their branches of children, grandchildren, great-grandchildren, nephews, nieces, and innumerable in-laws, down to infants at the breast, the tables covered with food and wine: he knew none of that. Only Onno's family tended a little in that direction. But those vacations were long ago, from the time of his fatal sports car. Since he had lived with Quinten and Sophia in the castle, they'd seldom gone abroad. Every other year, occasionally to the south of France or to Spain on a sudden impulse, when the weather gave them cause; anyway they could never have it better than at Groot Rechteren. He himself had no need for travel. Every year he had to go to a conference somewhere in the world for his work, and he was always glad when he was back.

Maybe that was also connected with the fact that he'd never been able to penetrate to the real peak of international astronomy. True, he knew everyone and everyone knew him and respected him for his work, but at the official closing dinner he never sat at the top table with the mayor or the minister, like his colleague Maarten Schmidt from CalTech.

As he refilled his glass—with one eye closed, in order not to fill a glass that wasn't there—he thought of the first time he had been to the south, a couple of years after the war, the overwhelming impression the light there had made on him, the color of the Mediterranean, which he had later seen again in the blue of Quinten's eyes.

In his student room in Leiden he sometimes saw those colors in his mind's eye, just after waking up but before he opened his eyes—when he opened them, then it was displaced by the gray Dutch morning. When he had been to the Riviera for the second time, he had thought of something to make up for that shock. When he woke up there, with his eyes still closed, he imagined that he was back in rainy Leiden and that the memory of the Mediterranean scene would be dispelled when he opened them. But then he opened them and it was really there! The sea the color of lapis lazuli, a blissful miracle! Instant displacement, faster than light! The sea ... At night the sea was black—but he didn't want to think about that anymore. What was her name again? Marilyn. Her submachine gun. God and the invention of central perspective; the vanishing point, which since the fifteenth century nothing had been able to wriggle through, neither from one side nor from the other. She must be about forty by now, and of course she'd gone back to the United States long ago, to some provincial niche, where she had become a teacher of art history and the mother of three children, married to a well-behaved lawyer, who would have a fit if he heard about her revolutionary past.

Suddenly, in an even more distant past, he saw his mother's bedroom: the open drawers and cupboards, her clothes in a pile on the ground. That would never stop. As Onno was wont to say: "family is forever." Tsjallingtsje knew nothing about any of those things; perhaps he should tell her something about the grandmother and grandfather of the child that she wanted to have by him. What was it to be called? Octave? Octavia? After Onno's one-to-two ratio of the simplest perfect consonant interval? It seemed that nowadays you could determine sex during pregnancy by using an ultrasonic echo—in fact as new a principle as Quinten needed for his "historioscope." He looked at the house through the open door. The television was off; there was a light on upstairs in the bedroom. She was reading in bed, *The Brothers Karamazov*, which he had prescribed for her, and was waiting for him to come up.

Gradually, his head sank back and his eyes closed for a moment. He came to himself with a start and sighed deeply a couple of times. The smell of tarred wood. He poured himself another glass and sank back again; with his head against the chair he stared through the shed. It was though he could feel his life like a large object that he could put his arms around, like a dog that was much too large on his lap. Everything kept increasing, becoming more and more complicated, just as an acorn gave birth to an ethereal, symmetrical plant, which grew into a gnarled, twisted oak that retained nothing of its almost mathematical origin. And yet it had once had that form. How could one have been transformed into the other? And if that couldn't be explained, how could that transition have taken place? The problems, he considered, consisted not in what happened, because that was simply what happened, but in how what happened was conceivable. The universe had emerged from a homogenous origin—then how, in that case, could it look as it looked now, with a division of the solar systems as it was and no other way? Why hadn't anything remained homogenous? Why was the earth different from the sun? And the sun different from a quasar? How was it possible for a chair to be here and a rake there? How could he himself exist and be different from Onno? How could he now be thinking something different than he had just been thinking, and shortly something different from now? What had happened meanwhile? Or had the origin perhaps not been homogenous? Of course he knew the theories, on initial quantum fluctuations, but did they really explain the difference between him and Onno?

He looked at the planks of the shed. They resembled each other, but that's how they'd been made. Moreover, they weren't exactly the same; one of them was a little wider than the others, a little darker, a little lighter, and something appeared to be carved in one plank. He screwed up his eyes, but he couldn't see what it was. Because he felt he should know, he got out of his chair with a groan and went across to it. There were letters and figures, thin and almost illegible; he leaned against the plank with one hand and put the other over one eye.

Gideon Levi. 8.3.1943.

He put the other hand against the plank and dropped his head, exhausted. The shed came from Westerbork. Forty-two years ago a boy had carved that there with his pocketknife. After he had succumbed to the gas, someone had bought the hut and put it here in his garden. Through the small window, which he now also understood, he looked at the house. He wanted to tell Tsjallingtsje what had happened and that the shed must be demolished the very next day; but the light in the bedroom had gone out. Pale moonlight illuminated the front of the house. He looked around. The space was too small to have served as a barracks; perhaps it had been a school, or the sewing room. Perhaps his mother had been put to work here. Supporting himself on the planks, he found his way back to the chair, which he sank into with a flourish, and upturned the bottle over his glass.

After that he must have dropped off to sleep for a moment. He woke because it had become cold and damp in the shed; but he still did not stand up to shut the door. It was past twelve. He knew he was drunk and that he ought to go to bed, but he had the feeling that either beneath or beyond his drunkenness his brain was still working—perhaps less inhibitedly than when he was sober. With his eyes closed, rocking back and forth a little in his chair, he thought back to the computer printouts of that afternoon. Was the result really so absurd? He saw the sheets very clearly in front of him, as though he were really looking at them. And suddenly it was as though a great light were turned on in him: he understood everything!

In a split second everything had come together—but what was it? He knew the answer, but it seemed as difficult to unravel as the question. The so-called infinite velocity of MQ 3412 was not an error, as his colleagues all over the world thought, but revealed a constellation that had not occurred to anyone! It was like the discovery of penicillin by Fleming: his assistant had put away a petri dish with a staphylococcus culture in it to throw it in the wastebin, because it had gotten mold on it; but Fleming himself had another look and saw that it wasn't the bacteria that had attacked the penicillin, but the penicillin that had attacked the bacteria—which subsequently saved the lives of millions of people and won him the Nobel Prize. The Nobel Prize! There was no Nobel Prize for astronomy, but there was for physics. His thoughts wandered to Stockholm, where he would be standing on the platform in a tailcoat, on that circle with the inscribed N, in his hands the gold medal, received from the hands of the king—or at least he could expect an honorary doctorate too, in Uppsala . . .

He put aside these fantasies and forced himself as far as he could to think through his discovery. The supposed infinite velocity pointed to a distortion of perspective! It was like with the vanishing point: at the horizon the rails met, so that no train could get through, because it would be destroyed at that point—and on the other side of it there was nothing else. And yet trains passed through it, both from one side and from the other. Quasar MQ 3412 wasn't a quasar at all! Or perhaps it was a quasar but everyone regarded it as something that it wasn't, since another object in a geodetically straight line was behind it, still farther away, which was covered by it. Perhaps that was not a black hole but the primeval singularity itself: the point in the firmament where the Big Bang could still be seen!

Perhaps last night the VLBI had received signals from the other side right through that vanishing point, which had tunneled right through from that vanishing point—or rather: through the vanishing point! Black holes too, from which theoretically no information could emerge, turned out on closer inspection to leak like sieves. In a negative space-time suddenly all those infinities had become visible, those which theoreticians invariably encountered in their mathematical descriptions. Shorter than 10^{-43}th second from the zero moment, Planck time, the hypermicroscopic universe was a theoretical madhouse; for the zero-moment calculations arrived at a paradoxical universe with a circumference of zero, hence a mathematical point, and at the same time with infinite density, infinite curvature of space-time, and infinitely high temperature. There, both the general theory of relativity and the quantum theory collapsed.

Everyone agreed that a new, overarching theory was necessary to be able to continue the discussion; the occurrence of infinities was always regarded as a sign that something was fundamentally wrong with the theory—but they really existed then; they'd been observed twenty-four hours ago! It was just that no one thought of interpreting it like that: the whole of cosmology was the victim of an optical illusion! And wouldn't it in fact be idiotic if the beginning of the universe were *not* linked with infinities. If something emerged from nothing, then that was of course an infinitely different matter than when something emerged from something else—the incomprehensibility was precisely the *esssence* of the fact that the world was there and not not there! He sat up. Now he must go to sleep and tomorrow immediately work this out and publish it as soon as possible, before someone else hit on the idea.

Instead of getting up, he held the bottle over his glass once more. When nothing more came out of it and he was about to put it down, it fell from his grasp. He put out an arm to pick it up but got no farther. As he let his arm hang down, his chin dropped onto his chest. Suddenly it occurred to him that in the last few months a similar new theory was causing excitement in physics, since it could perhaps finally reconcile quantum mechanics and the theory of relativity: the great unification—the long-sought-after Theory of Everything! This summer a large conference was going to be devoted to it in Bari—shouldn't he go? Up to now elementary particles, like electrons, had always been regarded as pointlike, zero-dimensional, which of course also meant that their energy in that point was infinitely great, and hence also their mass; strangely enough no one had ever worried about those infinities, but by now he was no longer surprised about that bungling and selective indignation: it was no different in science than in politics. The new theory suggested that elementary particles were not zero-dimensional but uni-dimensional: supersmall strings in a ten-dimensional world. Not only all particles, also the four fundamental forces of nature and the seventeen natural constants, could be explained by the vibration of otherwise completely identical strings. Strings! The monochord! Pythagoras! Had science arrived back where it had begun? Was music the essence of the world?

The image of Ada appeared before his eyes, the cello between her parted legs. "All things are numbers," Pythagoras had said. For him ten was the sacred number, which you could count on your fingers, like the Ten Commandments and the ten dimensions in the superstring theory. Ten was the "mother of the universe," and from long-forgotten boyhood reading he suddenly remembered Pythagoras's mystical tetractys, the four-foldness, the symbolic depiction of the formula "one, two, three, four," with which his pupils swore the oath:

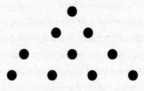

As a true Greek, thought Max, Pythagoras of course rejected complete infinities, although in his famous thesis he had encountered irrational numbers—but Max himself needed them in order to interpret the observations of the VLBI, that is, the origin of the world: the Big Bang as infinite music! Suddenly he lifted up his head and opened his eyes. Because the light dazzled him, he got up unsteadily, turned off the lamp, and sank back into the chair.

Was it possible that the mathematics already existed for this? When Einstein needed a non-Euclidian, four-dimensional geometry for his curved space-time, it turned out to have been created decades before by Gauss and Riemann. If the world was first and last a realized infinity, then he himself might be able to turn to Cantor, the founder of set theory. Cantor! The singer! As a student he had occupied himself for a while with Cantor's shocking theory of transfinite cardinal numbers, the infinite number of complete infinite numbers, but that had been a long time ago. He remembered the vertigo that had overcome him on his visit to the Orphic Schola Cantorum: its alephs, $\aleph_0$, $\aleph_1$ . . . his Absolutely Infinite $\beth$. He must immediately immerse himself in it again, but at the same time watch his step, because it had also driven Cantor mad. Because he was interested in the man who had ventured into such regions, he had read a biography of him, which he remembered better than the mathematics. Cantor was regularly admitted to the asylum; originally he had wanted to become a musician, a violinist, but on his own testimony, God Himself had called him and revealed his theory.

As for Pythagoras, mathematics for him was also metaphysics: all numbers were things. He was paranoid and suffered from severe depressions, was interested in theosophy, freemasonry, the teachings of the Rosi-crucians, and wrote a pamphlet in which he demonstrated that Christ was the natural son of Joseph of Arimathea, while he also gave lectures about Bacon and demonstrated irrefutably that Bacon had written the plays of Shakespeare . . .

In the dark shed Max now had his eyes wide open. Again and again he brought the empty glass mechanically to his lips and put it back again; it was as though in the darkness the mists of alcohol cleared, but at the same time he knew that this was not the case. He suddenly saw an enervating drawing from a still more distant past, while he remembered immediately where it came from; from the translation of a popular book by Gamov, *One, Two, Three . . . Infinity*, which he had read when he was seventeen and which had played a part in his decision to become an astronomer. Gamov, he had later learned, had first made the Big Bang theory scientifically acceptable and in 1948 had predicted its echo, the cosmic background radiation observed in 1964, which finally established the theory. His hand-drawing in the book showed a topological distortion of a man walking on earth and admiring the starry sky: everything was turned inside out. If in reality the organs were all enclosed in the body, which was surrounded by the universe—with the only access to that outside world via the mouth, the alimentary canal, and the anus—now the internal had become the external: his intestine stretched out limitlessly like extestines, while the universe, full of planets and stars and spiral nubulae, had become the interior of the man, where he was still walk-ing inside out on the earth and which his eyes were still looking at. Who was the wretched man? Himself, looking through the vanishing point into the negative space-time to the far side of the Big Bang? God? Or was it perhaps a woman? Was it Ada, in her womb the tumor that had taken the place of Quinten? Or was it his own mother, with him in hers? The mother of the universe . . . Ada and Eva . . . Women . . . only women . . .

Again he had fallen asleep. When he woke up he felt tired and happy. He was now in his fifties and he was still preoccupied with the same things as when he was seventeen. Had anything really happened in his life since then? There was no break, as there was with Onno; the boy he had been had no need to be ashamed of him. He got up and again thought of the child that Tsjallingtsje wanted by him. Of course: Octavia! He couldn't make the child tonight—he was too drunk for that; what's more, the coil was still in place. He opened the door and with the handle in his hand he stopped.

Where was Onno? Who had Onno become? How was it possible that he could deny his child so completely? And poor Quinten himself—who was farther away for him now, his mother or his father?

The house was dark, the garden lay silently in the moonlight. Janáček, he thought. *Fairy Tale.* Forcing himself not to stagger, he walked down the path to the erratic stone, on which he sat down to have a break. The March night was cool and damp. Was it all nonsense that he had thought up? Had the VBLI really seen the primeval singularity, perhaps seen right through it, into another, timeless world, which was therefore larger than the universe? Wasn't he forgetting something? How drunk was he, actually? How was it possible to demonstrate that none of this was the case?

If something like that were possible, then at least an enormous red shift must have taken place—so great that it did not occur to anyone. The maximum that had been measured up to now, in OQ 172, had a value of 3.53; the lyman- -line had found its way into visible light. For MQ 3412 they were now looking somewhere between 4 and 5, but perhaps you should look around 20, or 50. Or 100! No one in his right mind would look there, not even Maarten. What would such a shift be good for? He tried to calculate, but he was no long capable. Somewhere on the shortwave band, probably. Perhaps some radio ham had once received a singular voice: "I am the Lord thy God!"—after which he had turned the dial in boredom because he thought he was dealing with a weirdo on the air! Obviously not a second Moses!

Max raised his arms, threw back his head and began laughing loudly.

The thunderous impact with which a white fireball, like a rocket from the sky, hit the stone on which he was sitting scorched all the trees and plants in the garden. It shattered the windows of Tsjallingtsje's house, the curtains caught fire, and the explosion woke up the whole village. Everywhere dogs began barking, cocks crowing. For miles around, lights went on in panic and out of the windows people began shouting to each other that it must be a gas explosion. The following day even the erratic stone seemed to have partly evaporated.

That was how Max finally made the world press—not because of his cosmological hunch, which remained unknown, but because of the unbelievable coincidence of his being in the place where he was. As far as was known, the only person who shared his fate was a seventeenth-century

Franciscan monk in Milan. The direct hit had left nothing more of the unfortunate Dutch astronomer than is left of an ant when two flints strike.

Experts assumed that the meteorite had been the size of a fist. Only tiny fragments had been recovered, from which it could be deduced that this was a stone meteorite, an achondrite, over 4 billion years old, probably originating from the area between Mars and Jupiter.

In accordance with international custom the celestial body was named after the nearest post office: the Westerbork.

50

The Decision

Four days later, at the funeral in the churchyard of Westerbork—to the strains of Janáček's *Fairy Tale*—Quinten did not dare ask himself what was in the coffin that was descending into the earth. Surrounded by astronomers and technicians, he glanced at Sophia, who stood arm in arm with Tsjallingtsje. Was there anything in it? But what had happened only got through to him with a jolt a month later.

Sophia and he had been invited by Theo and Selma Kern to dinner for Easter. Sophia had provided the wine, and around a great dish of *pot-au-feu* with horseradish they were talking about the gigantic Easter bonfire that the baron used to light every year on the grounds near Klein Rechteren—a tradition that had not been continued after his death. According to Kern, the reason was that there were no other country noblemen living in the area; they were more to the south, in Overijssel and Gelderland. Gevers had been the northernmost nobleman. Since the old baroness, together with Rutger and his hundred-square-yard curtain, had recently moved in with her daughter in The Hague, who ran a flourishing beauty salon for a select clientele, the rabble would shortly appear in Klein Rechteren too and destroy it.

"I'm a simple man of the people," he said. "My grandmother was a water-and-hot-coal seller in Utrecht, with sand on the floor, but if I have to choose between the nobility and the rich rabble, then I don't have to think for very long. Of course the aristocracy is also rabble, everyone is rabble, but they at least have style."

"You're getting old, Theo," said Selma.

"You're telling me. And just as well."

Quinten looked at him. The sculptor sat on his chair like a gnarled, snow-covered pinecone; his bare right foot was lying on a white linen pouf, the ankle swollen and the skin purplish, as though he had stepped in a jar of blackberries. Did the aristocracy have style? Quinten was reminded of Roskam's father, who had had to bury his cap on the orders of Rutger's grandfather. Yes, perhaps that was style—but a particular kind. On the other hand, the baron had left him lots of money because he had looked after the grave of Deep Thought Sunstar and had taught Rutger to weave. Perhaps the thing was that the aristocracy really thought there were two kinds of people: on the one hand themselves, with the queen at the head, and on the other side ordinary bourgeois people—in the same way that there were men and women. He would like to talk to his father about that, but he had disappeared.

"Do you remember the Easter eggs that you and Arendje always hunted for under the rhododendrons?" asked Selma.

How could he forget something like that? Again he could feel the branches on his back as he crawled over the ground, over the damp, withered leaves, between which a suddenly a bright color glowed, completely formed, like when he had a liberating brainwave while he was thinking about something. The troubling thought that Arendje would find more eggs than he did . . .

"I always kept the most beautiful ones," said Sophia. "Shall I get them?"

When she had left the room, Theo said to Selma: "Do you know what Max once said to me? 'A chicken is the means whereby an egg produces another egg.' I don't know in what connection, but I've never forgotten."

"Poor Max . . ." sighed Selma.

A little later Sophia put a large, old-fashioned candy jar with a wide neck and a screw top on the table. While she told them that the jar came from her mother's bequest, Kern stared at the colored contents and it was as though he could scarcely control his emotions.

"All of those were painted here in this room, QuQu," he said, "while you were tucked up in bed. By all of us here at the castle."

After Selma had cleared the plates away, Sophia carefully laid the eggs on the table one by one. Quinten did not know that she had kept them all, but he recognized his finds almost without exception. She arranged them neatly in four rows of eight. Kern took his foot off the pouf, put on a pair of steel-rimmed reading glasses, and bent forward.

"Can you see who painted what?"

Carefully putting one sort with another, Quinten began to change the places of the eggs. Suddenly he had the feeling that they should actually be in eight vertical rows of four rather than in the four horizontal rows of eight. There were Kern, Max, Proctor, Themaat, and Spier and their five wives—that made ten people; but Elsbeth Themaat and Judith Spier would probably not have joined in—they never came upstairs. It would be nice if there were four eggs from each of them, but there was only one from Mr. Spier: on the otherwise unpainted white shell there was an elegantly red painted *A?* on one side, and a blue *Q?* on the other. The capital italics obviously referred to *Arendje,* but now he was suddenly reminded of *Ada.* He assigned three eggs to Themaat, with pale geometrical patterns: diamonds, circles, triangles. The somber, dark-brown ones, sometimes black with zigzagging lightning bolts, were of course by Proctor, while it was probably Max who had limited himself to plain, bright colors, which now in some way contained his death. There was no mistaking Kern's work: expertly painted clown's faces, flowers, and animal heads. Clara had also made it simple for him by depicting umbrellas in all states of openness. He had more difficulty with Selma and Sophia. The remaining eggs were all abstract in design, with dots, stripes, and bands. He decided that the beautiful ones were by Selma and those with the clashing colors by Sophia.

The others looked in silence at what he was doing. After he had finally arranged the eggs by person, Kern said:

"You don't have to say any more." He glanced at it for a moment, then looked up and said to the two women, staring at the constellation on the table, "That's what's left of our community."

At the same moment Quinten realized that this was the truth. After the death of Max, only these three old people were left, of whom his grandmother, at sixty-two, was the youngest. Upstairs was Nederkoorn, below Korvinus, and soon it would be completely over. What was there to keep him here any longer? Everything around him had been destroyed, everyone was dead, had left, was inaccessible; even Kern's dovecotes had been empty for six months. Suddenly he got up and went to his room without saying anything.

He put his bronze box on the table. Because the key of the padlock had disappeared one day from between the loose bricks behind the oil stove, he had straightened a sturdy paper clip and, according to Piet Keller's lessons, had made a skeleton key with it. He carefully unfolded his father's letters and looked at the last sentence, although it was just the same as he remembered: *Forgive me and don't look for me, because you won't find me.* So it was something of a last wish that Quinten should not look for him! In fact it didn't say at all that he didn't want him to—just that he should save himself the trouble, because it would be to no avail. He looked at the case with his mother's cello in it. Now he was certain. He was going away. He was going to find his father.

"But where are you going to look for him, then?" asked Sophia the following morning at breakfast. "He could be anywhere. Do you know how large the world is?"

"In any case he's on earth. That excludes lots of other places."

"That's true," said Sophia. A smile appeared on her face, and she looked at him with a shake of her head. "You've virtually already found him, haven't you?"

"Yes." Quinten nodded and looked back at her, but without a smile.

They were sitting on the balcony. For the first time this year it was a mild spring morning. In the moat below, the ducks were noisily celebrating the change of season.

"But what if you find him and he doesn't want to have anything to do with you? Are you aware of what's happened to him? He's become a different person. I thought that it would turn out okay too and that he'd turn up again, but he's been gone for four years. He knows where he can reach you, doesn't he, and he hasn't done so, has he?"

"If he sees me and he still doesn't want to have anything to do with me, then I shall know. Then he'll really have become a different person, as you say, and a different person doesn't interest me. A different person isn't my father. Then I'll be finished with it."

"And your school," asked Sophia, without looking up from the apple she was peeling. "What'll happen to that?"

"I know enough. And anyway, the most important things that I know, I didn't learn at school."

"But, Quinten, you're almost there. Another year, and you'll have your high school diploma. Aren't you afraid that you'll be terribly sorry if you don't finish high school? That'll change the course of your whole life. You do want to study, I assume?"

Quinten looked at the bare trees on the other side of the moat. He could still look right through the wood; soon it would again become an impenetrable wall. In the distance a car was driving along the road to Westerbork. His father had once asked him too what he wanted to "be." "An architect," Max had said—but the idea of doing this or that for the rest of his life, and nothing else, still seemed idiotic to him. He wasn't born to gain certainty; he could leave that to others. Something completely different was waiting for him—that was the certainty that had come to him six months previously in the field near Klein Rechteren.

"I don't think so," he said.

Sophia tried again. "You won't be seventeen until next month. Keep at it for another year, then you'll be eighteen; and afterward you can do what you like for a year. Or two years. Then you can still always decide if you want to study or not. But if you stop now, you'll have decided once and for all."

"I'm going to look for Dad," said Quinten.

He was sorry for his grandmother. In order to keep up appearances she got up, brushed the crumbs and remains of bread into her other hand, and threw them over the balustrade, which immediately unleashed a flurry of quacking down below. She too was alone. Her daughter had been struck down by a terrible accident, her companion killed by a meteorite, and now she was being abandoned by her grandson, too. What else was there to do? Moreover, in a few months' time she'd be out in the street—with all her things, those of her daughter, and those of Max.

He went over to her, put his hands on her shoulders, and gave her a kiss on her forehead; a strange, sweet-and-sour smell penetrated his nostrils. Immediately afterward, she pressed her crown against his breastbone for a moment, which reminded him of Gijs, Verdonkschot's billy goat. When she raised her face, it was wet with tears. It was the first time that he had seen her cry.

"Granny!"

"Don't worry about that. When did you want to go?"

"As soon as possible." Only when he said this did it become final for him.

Again Sophia controlled herself. "But where on earth are you going, Quinten? In which direction? You can't simply just get on the first train that comes along."

"Perhaps that's a method too. First I'm going to see Dad's lawyer tomorrow. He knows where he is, doesn't he?"

"But he won't tell you. He's got his professional code of ethics."

"I can at least try. Perhaps he'll let something slip out, or something will slip out that I can use. And mightn't Auntie Dol know more than we think, too? Anyway, perhaps it's best if I go to see her first."

Sophia looked at him red-eyed. Suddenly she could no longer restrain her tears; her face contorted, she sat down, put her hands over her eyes, and said in an almost sing-song voice: "Quinten . . . something dreadful's going to happen when you've gone . . ."

He had never seen her like this before. Helplessly he sat down opposite her. "What makes you think that?"

"I don't know . . ." she whispered, with her shoulders heaving, "I feel it."

"What nonsense! No one knows what's going to happen. Perhaps I'll be away for a few months, and then I'll keep you posted about everything. And after that I can always go back to school again. Otherwise I'll take the state examination."

He himself did not really believe that, and he saw that Sophia didn't believe it either. Holding a napkin to her eyes, she got up and suddenly went inside, with her face averted.

Quinten looked at the apple peel on her plate: one long uninterrupted spiral, like she always made. You could make it as long as you wanted, he thought—infinitely long if only you peeled thinly enough. He breathed in the mild air deeply. It was over; in fact, he was not there any longer. But at the same time it seemed as though through that awareness everything struck him more intensely than ever before, just like at Christmas the burnt-out, guttering candles on the tree flared up once more and then went out, with the floor covered in colored wrapping paper and unwrapped presents.

Max had always told him to stay in his room on *Heiligabend* until the Christmas tree had been decorated and the candles lit. "Come on!" From the harsh electric light of his room into the warm candlelight—a dark world from the distant past. . . . He got up and went over to the stone balustrade. Deep in the wood an owl croaked. On an artificial island on the other side, the pitiless coots had built a new nest, around which everyone else swam respectfully. Fancy his unemotional grandmother suddenly becoming so tearful! But was he to stay here because of that? Would he have to look after her, as she had looked after him for all those years? His decision was made. He was going. He was going to look for his father. Deep in himself he felt the unshakable certainty that nothing and no one could stop him.

"Quinten?"

Via Max's bedroom, where Max's made-up bed had already frozen into an untouchable museum exhibit, he went into Sophia's. She was kneeling on the floor, in front of the open bottom drawer of the chest of drawers. In her hands she had a tiny compass. Much smaller than the one on the edge of Max's desk, it was no more than three quarters of an inch across.

"Take this with you," she said, and gave it to him, with the cool, distant look in her eyes again. "It belonged to your granddad. He always carried it when we went walking on the heath, in the years after the war. It was still big in those days."

The needle was fixed, but after he moved a pin at the side, it wobbled into motion: it still worked. A black leather shoelace had been threaded through the ring. Without saying anything, he allowed Sophia to put the instrument around his neck. He realized with relief that she had resigned herself to his departure. He had never known Granddad Brons; for Quinten, he belonged more to history than to himself, like most things in the crammed drawer. Although it was not locked, he had never rummaged in it; nor did he want anyone to poke their nose in his own things. He bent down and took out a yellow card from the chaos of photos, letters, folders, dolls, girls' books, a woollen rabbit.

"*Certificate of Report,*" he read, "*As required under Article 9, first clause, of Decree No. 6/1941 of the Reichskommissar for the occupied territory of the Netherlands, regarding compulsory reporting of persons of wholly or partly Jewish extraction.*" He turned it over. "*Haken, Petronella. Number of Jewish ancestors in the sense of Art. 2 of the decree: one.*" He looked inquiringly at Sophia.

"That's my mother's," she said. "Her grandmother on her mother's side was Jewish."

"That means—" Quinten began.

"Yes, that you've also got Jewish blood in you."

"You never told me that!"

"It wasn't worth mentioning. Work it out."

"My great-grandmother was a quarter, you an eighth, Mommy a sixteenth, and me a thirty-second." He put the card back and said, "No, it's not much. Did Max know about this?"

"To tell you the truth, I never thought about it."

*

His aunt and uncle could only repeat that they did not know where Onno was, either. Dol was the only person in the family to have had a letter from him, and since then she had not heard anything either; nor had he tried to get hold of his stored things in any way. Only on one occasion—already eighteen months ago—had Hans Giltay Veth written to them; Onno wanted the certificate of his honorary doctorate returned to Uppsala. They had done that, although they did not know the reason, nor did the lawyer.

It was their last day in the suburb near Rotterdam. They were just able to receive him in the midst of their moving. Uncle Karel, the surgeon, had finally laid down his scalpels, and they were going to move permanently to their second home on Menorca, where Quinten had stayed a couple of times during summer vacation.

In the dismantled front room, as they sat with plastic cups of mineral water on nailed-down boxes, the conversation that he had had with Sophia repeated itself: about interrupting his studies, and if he was so sure that what he was doing was sensible, and about where was he going to look. He had the feeling that Onno had almost disappeared from their lives. His things had already been collected a few weeks ago by a storage company; they were now in a warehouse in the docks. Sophia had been informed about it, but she had obviously not wanted to burden him with that message. While he waited for the train to Amsterdam on the platform, the expression that his uncle had used for his father constantly echoed through his head: *dropout.*

In the lobby of the lawyers' office building behind the Rijksmuseum the name J.C.G.F. Giltay Veth, M.L. stood among a long list of other names. The bearer of it came to see him himself: a fat, kindly man in his early fifties, with a small pair of reading glasses on the tip of his nose. In the elevator up to the top floor he told Quinten that he had known his father since they were students together. Although Onno could say terrible things, Giltay Veth had seldom laughed so much as he had with him. His room looked out over the entire center of town. He pointed out the palace on the Dam in the distance to Quinten, with Atlas carrying the globe of the world on his neck—like someone, thought Quinten, who was himself outside the world.

When a black girl in a white coat put down some tea, they sat down opposite each other at a long table, half of which was taken up by piles of folders and dossiers.

"I must extend my sympathies on the death of your foster father," said

Giltay Veth. "I read about it in the paper. It's scarcely credible, something like that." Lost for words, he shook his head for a moment. "Of course I had nothing to do with it, but are his affairs properly sorted out, as far as you know?"

"You should ask my grandmother about that. I believe there are problems, because he had no family at all."

"Please tell your grandmother that she can always contact me if she needs help. It won't cost her a penny. I know that I will be acting in the spirit of your father."

Quinten looked straight at him. "Didn't you tell my father, then?"

Giltay Veth held a lump of sugar in his tea and waited until it had absorbed all the tea. "No." He let go of the lump. "I can only contact him in extreme cases."

"So he doesn't know at all that Max is dead?"

"I couldn't tell you. Perhaps he's read about it in the paper somewhere, too."

"So he's not in Holland?"

The ghost of a smile crossed Giltay Veth's face, but it immediately disappeared; he stirred his cup seriously for a few seconds.

"I know what you're getting at, Quinten. To tell you the truth, I expected your visit much earlier. I knew that you'd be sitting here opposite me one day; I said as much to your father at the time. But if you want to know from me where he is, I can't tell you."

"I swear I'll never tell anyone that I heard it from you. Surely I can bump into him by accident somewhere, as it were, can't I? Coincidences like that do happen, don't they? My foster father was hit by a meteorite; surely that's a much greater coincidence?"

"Absolutely." Giltay Veth nodded. "Except that it's not a question of my knowing and not being able to tell you; I really don't know. I haven't the faintest idea."

"How can that be? In his farewell letter to Max my father wrote that he could always be reached by you in emergencies."

"That's true, but only in a roundabout way. There are two other addresses in between. The first is that of a colleague of mine—abroad, yes, you got hold of the right end of the stick there. But he knows only of a post-office box in another country. That might be Holland, but just as easily Paraguay. Suppose you managed to get me to tell you where that colleague is—which won't happen. Even then that gentleman won't help you out, because he knows nothing about you. Quite apart from the fact that the only thing he knows is that post-office box number, in another country." He put one hand on top of the other and looked at Quinten. "Forget it, lad. Your father has covered his tracks thoroughly. Something dreadful has happened to him; you must assume that he's not alive anymore. I know all about your situation. I know of the dreadful fate that befell your mother, I know what happened to your father and recently to your foster father, but you must resign yourself to it. There are boys whose fathers have been murdered, or have been killed in a plane crash. It's all equally horrible, but that's obviously how life is. Try and put it out of your mind. Don't let your life be scarred by it."

Quinten made an awkward gesture and said: "If I knew that my father was really dead, there would be nothing wrong. But he isn't dead. He's somewhere in the world and is doing something or other at this moment. Perhaps he's sitting reading the newspaper, or drinking a cup of tea." He faltered. "That means . . . are you actually sure that he's still alive?"

Giltay Veth nodded. "If it were otherwise, I would know and so would you."

"Then I'm going to look for him."

The telephone rang, and without waiting to see who was on the line, the lawyer said: "I don't want to be disturbed." He put the receiver down, folded his arms, and leaned back. "No one can stop you. But have you asked yourself whether you're acting in accordance with your father's wishes?"

He had been talking the whole time about his father's *spirit*. Quinten took Onno's letter out of his pocket and read the last sentence aloud. When he had explained his interpretation—that it wasn't a ban on looking for him but just a statement of the pointlessness of doing so—a smile crossed Giltay Veth's face.

"You'd make a good lawyer, Quinten."

"It says what it says."

"There's no arguing with that. But it also says that you won't find him. How were you planning to go about it?"

"I don't know yet. I'd hoped that you would put me on the track, but I'll find something else."

Giltay Veth raised his eyebrows. "Is that why you came here?"

"Yes, why else?"

"I thought you might need money for your search."

"I've got plenty of money."

"Have you?"

"I inherited forty thousand guilders."

"Forty thousand guilders?" repeated Giltay Veth, taking off his reading glasses. "Who from?"

After Quinten had told him what he had done to deserve it, Giltay Veth looked at him reflectively for a while.

"A lot's been taken from you, but a lot's been given to you. God knows, perhaps you really will be able to find your father, although it's a mystery to me how you're supposed to do that."

"Perhaps the age of miracles hasn't yet entirely passed," said Quinten.

The drizzle was so fine that the drops seemed to be stationary in the air and made his face even wetter than a real shower. The two alder trees, the three boulders—everything in the field behind Klein Rechteren was dripping with water, which did not seem to be coming from anywhere. The red cow was not there. Was that a good or a bad omen? A good omen, of course, because otherwise she'd be there. Now he had to decide what direction to look for his father. Slowly, with his eyes wide open, he turned clockwise around his own axis and tried to register whether he felt something special at a particular moment.

He felt nothing, although in a particular situation he must have been pointing exactly in the direction of his father with a hundred percent certainty. That seemed incomprehensible to him. He tried again, even more slowly and with his eyes closed, but again with no result. What next? He unbuttoned his shirt and took out the small compass. Again he made a slow rotation of 360 degrees, keeping his eyes constantly fixed on the needle. It wobbled across the dial from north to west and through south to north, without suddenly behaving unusually.

He gave up in amazement. It was mysterious, but it wouldn't work like that. He put the compass away and looked out across the meadow, feeling his inner certainty suddenly wavering. Was it impossible, then? Perhaps he should try it the other way around. Where would his father definitely *not* have gone? Probably not to Africa, certainly not to the Eastern bloc or to China or anywhere in Asia. That already made a difference, but in any case that still left the whole of Europe and North and South America. He spoke all languages, so that was no problem for him. Perhaps he was in a monastery, from where he would never emerge—he had written that he was a hermit, hadn't he? Or in a hand-built hut on a desert island, covered in palm leaves, or somewhere in a cave in the mountains. On Crete, perhaps, where the Phaistos disc came from? So should he go to Crete, then? But even if he knew that he was in New York, even then he wouldn't be able to find him. He didn't know where to begin. But what was he to do, then?

Tomorrow was the end of Easter vacation—so should he simply go back to school? That was also inconceivable—too much had happened to him in the meantime for that: you couldn't expect a stone that you'd let go of to return into your hand halfway, like a yo-yo.

As wet as if he had worked up a sweat, he looked at the edge of the wood, and suddenly he began to shiver. Perhaps there was a method whereby, conversely, he could lure his father to Holland: by pretending in some way that he'd been abducted—by going underground and sending letters with stuck-on characters. Then perhaps his father would appear with the ransom, somewhere by a concrete pillar under a viaduct . . .

It was as though the dream of being able to find his father had suddenly been swept away by this diabolical brainwave. He turned around and began to walk slowly back toward the castle. Of course it was impossible that he would play a trick like that—but he was going to leave here anyway, on a journey. That was all he could do now. Why didn't he go to Italy? He'd never been there. To the Veneto. Finally see the architecture of Palladio with his own eyes. Plenty of money. Of course he must take his sketches and plans of the Citadel, the SOMNIUM QUINTI, with him. Who knows what he might be able to add to them!

DE PROFUNDIS

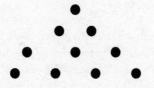

PART FOUR

THE END
OF
THE END

Third Intermezzo

—*I thought we were never going to get there.*

—I told you at the outset that the mission had been accomplished, didn't I?

—*It's probably because of your compelling narrative. That's inevitable with a good story: you don't experience it as a report in retrospect; it happens in the telling, as it were.*

—In my case there isn't that much difference.

—*Yes, you are those people's destiny, and to tell you the truth, I've been really astounded on occasion. What a disaster! Take the end of Max Delius—wasn't that a very draconian step?*

—What do you expect? He was on the point of discovering us!

—*He was on the threshold; I won't deny it. He was peering through the keyhole, as it were—but he was drunk. The next morning, he would have dismissed the whole thing as colossal nonsense. He was a specialist, after all, not an inventor of science fiction!*

—That's just the reason. I felt we couldn't take any risks. Suppose he had taken himself seriously and possessed the same persistence as his son. He didn't have a huge reputation to lose in astronomy; he might have been ready to go for broke at that turning point in his life. And after all, the last straw we cling to is people's belief; the moment our existence becomes a matter of knowledge, they'll abandon us completely. They'll shrug their shoulders and say "So what?" Besides, they always get dangerous when they discover different kinds of beings, or what they imagine to be. When they discovered the Indians, they were very enthusiastic about it for a while, but after that they lost interest and exterminated them. Or think of what they're doing with animals to this day.

—*Stop it. They've virtually reached the "So what" stage anyway. And they've also been busy exterminating us for some considerable time, without realizing it—for about as long as those Indians. Did you really not suspect that Delius would present you with a surprise like that one day?*

—Of course. After all, he was singled out to be the father of our agent, and given the laws of heredity it was obvious that he too would possess exceptional gifts. In a certain sense he owed them to his son.

—*The triumph of the* causa finalis *over the* causa efficiens.

—That's one way of putting it, although not everyone would immediately understand. Moreover, his death was necessary to get our man out of Holland at last. All that demolition was needed for that, too.

—*Yes, Holland is a unique country, but even apart from our envoy, enough is enough at a certain moment. Sometimes I wonder if it's still part of reality. In the human year 1580 a certain Joannis Goropius published a book in which he demonstrated that Adam and Eve had spoken Dutch in the Garden of Eden—and certainly Holland is the world's ideal of paradise. Every country would love to be like it, so peaceful, so democratic, tolerant, prosperous and orderly, but also so uniform, provincial and dull—although that seems to be changing a bit in the last few years.*

—Think of what happened to Onno Quist, for example.

—*I always think of everything at once, my dear friend. Now, for example, I'm thinking of the fact that you made it happen to him of course. I even suspect that you allowed that rotten environment to emerge in Amsterdam that made what happened to Helga possible.*

—You'll soon see the necessity for that. I only intervened when it was strictly necessary. I always use my resources as sparingly as possible, but I simply had to work with the tough rubber that people are made of. If it was still our habit to address them, everything would be a lot simpler—but you've already touched on that: since those dreamers have fooled themselves that it didn't come from on high but from their own depths, we've stopped.

—*Reluctantly.*

—You were talking just now about the *causa finalis*. We too started out of course from the simplest way in which our aim could be achieved in theory—namely, that our man would go where we wanted him to be and do what we wanted him to do. But as we calculated back, more and more new obstacles appeared, which made that aim more and more difficult to achieve—until, by improvising, we found the complicated route of efficient causalities, which turned out to be the only possible one. It was not nearly as complicated as our efforts to get him into the spirit and the flesh, but still complicated enough. In my department we sometimes compare it with the course of a river. The simplest way for the Rhine to go from its source in the Alps to the Hook of Holland is of course a straight line about four hundred miles long; but in reality it's twice as long, because the landscape forces it to be. In the same way, our man's route through the human landscape was strange and twisting and now and then quite violent—for example, exactly what happens in Schaffhausen; but—to change imagery—you can't appoint someone as a carpenter and at the same time forbid people to cut down trees. Wait a moment. We're not going to have the same conversation again, I hope?

—*The same conversation about the necessity of evil in the world will be conducted forever and ever—that awesome question of the theodicy, on which mankind has been breaking its teeth for centuries. But yes, the grain simply has to be threshed, so that it can be changed into sacred bread.*

—These days it's also done with combine harvesters. They're monsters, sometimes twenty feet wide, with six-cylinder diesel engines, which crawl across the fields like prehistoric grasshoppers. At the front of those combines the stalks are swallowed up, after which the grains are shaken loose in the revolving threshing drum; then a compressor separates the chaff from the corn with compressed air. It works pretty well.

—*You've put your finger on it. But it's precisely the machine itself that represents the much greater, radical, evil. That technological Luciferian evil is not in the optimistic service of the Chief in the best of all possible worlds, like the providential havoc that you must wreak, but it feeds on it; it eats it away and takes its place, like a virus usurps control of the nucleus of a cell: a malicious putsch, an infamous coup d'état. Cancer! Royal assassination!*

—Don't get so excited all the time. This is just how things are. We have failed. We underestimated human potential, both the strength of man's intellect and the weakness of his flesh, and therefore his receptivity to satanic inspiration—but ultimately he is our creature, and so what we've really underestimated is our own creativity. What we made has turned out to be more than what we thought that we had made. So ultimately in our failure there is a compliment to us: our creativity is greater than ourselves!

—*Your optimism is indestructible too, just like Leibniz's. What you are despite all your competence is obviously ultimately an irresponsible bohemian, an artistic rake, who thinks: Here goes! But you might ask yourself whether it isn't precisely the reflection of the Chief that makes our creativity greater than ourselves.*

—Ha ha! But if that's the case, then our successful failure isn't our responsibility either, but the Chief's—including man's susceptibility to the devil and hence the downfall of the Chief himself, as you have just so eloquently outlined to me. Then with mankind he has dug his own grave.

—*This conversation is starting to take a turn I don't like at all. I very much hope that your closeness to human beings and your manipulation with evil hasn't also brought you closer to Lucifer-Satan.*

—I wouldn't be making such efforts in that case. But if I can be honest: I do feel a bit sorry for him. Ultimately he's a poor sucker too, who can't be any different than he is. The fact of the matter is that we are playing with white, and he with black. If there is anyone who is condemned to hell for infinity, then it's him.

—*He'd like nothing better!*

—Yes, that too. That's hell within hell.

—*Come on. It's as though someone on earth were to claim that he whose name I won't mention was also a poor sucker and himself actually his most pitiable victim.*

—It isn't for people to claim that kind of thing. Them least of all.

—*I'm glad that you are saying it, because your post was suddenly hanging by a thread.*

—I had the feeling it might be.

—*Let's leave it at that, before things get out of hand. Of course it's sad that things had to reach this stage, but at the same time I'm dying of curiosity to hear how you finally managed it. Go on. I'm listening.*

51

The Golden Wall

In order to make the decisive event possible, it was necessary to mellow Onno Quist's frame of mind after all those years of solitude—and so I sent to him a stray young raven from the hills. One sunny day around noon it suddenly descended into the open window, shook its feathers, folded its wings, turned once around its axis, and walked in as though it lived there.

Onno looked up from his notes, perplexed.

"What do you want?" he asked. Not having said anything the whole morning, he cleared his throat.

The raven fixed him with one eye and croaked.

"Cras?" repeated Onno. "Yes, of course you're speaking Latin. 'Tomorrow'? What about tomorrow?"

The bird jumped off the windowsill onto the table, stirred through the chaos of papers a few times with its tail feathers, left some droppings, and then went over to a plate on which there were a few remnants of bread. With a loud tapping of its beak, as blue-black as fountain-pen ink, it devoured them and again looked at Onno, as if wanting to know if that was all. After it had eaten its fill, it jumped onto the windowsill, spread its wings, and disappeared—but the following afternoon it was back, at the same time.

In this way something resembling a friendship had begun. Onno had never had anything to do with animals before; they did not feature in his thinking. He had been brought up to believe that they had no souls, but after just a few days he found himself becoming anxious when the bird was late. Although he had not worn a watch since leaving Holland, he always knew what time it was thanks to the church bells. When on one occasion the raven missed a day, he could no longer concentrate. He looked mournfully at the untouched plate of birdseed and leaned outside every ten minutes to scan the sky.

"You don't treat people like this, Edgar," he said the following day with a reproachfully wagging index finger. "Not even as a bird. You don't stand your host up with the food. I trust it won't happen again."

While his pitch-black visitor scratched about around the room, over the chairs, among the rubbish under the bed, it constantly croaked and squawked, and Onno had the impression that it stayed longer if he himself talked a lot, too. From then on he made a habit of speaking while it was there. At the beginning he found it difficult; except for a few words in a shop, a restaurant, or in his bank, he had said nothing for four years. But one can no more forget how to speak than how to ride a bike or swim, and he of all people would be more likely to forget how to ride a bike than how to speak; he could not swim.

"Of course you're wondering what I'm doing here, Edgar. I'll tell you. I'm working on a letter to my father. But it's a rather strange kind of letter, because even when I get it down on paper I won't be able to send it. Kafka wrote a letter to his father too—Max read it to me once, long ago, in far-off innocent days—but poor Royal and Imperial Franz-Josef never dared mail it. My own problem is more serious, because what's the address of a dead person? Perhaps you know, being a black bird; unfortunately you won't be able to tell me. But I want to do it precisely because it's absurd. Since everything is ultimately absurd, the whole of life and the whole world, conversely only the absurd makes any kind of sense. Can you understand that? If everything's absurd, then within that absurdity only the absurd is not absurd! True or not? Have you ever heard of Camus? He was the philosopher of the absurd, and he died in an absurd car accident. For many people that was a confirmation of his thesis that everything is absurd. But for the philosopher of the absurd, an absurd death is of course an extremely meaningful end! Think hard about that. Everything is far more absurd than even he thought. Now of course you're curious about what I'm trying to tell my dead father in my absurd way. It's about the nature of power. In the last few years I've thought of a few things, on which I want his impossible judgment. It's rather sinister, and in political terms you must translate the word *sinister* not by 'left,' but rather by 'right': then you get *dexter*. Another difference with Kafka is that I'm not able to get my ideas into order. They're not in an orderly succession; they're still chaotically juxtaposed. In the past when I wrote an article or a speech, academic or political, it was always as if my thoughts were numbered in some way and I immediately knew the sequence of the sentences. But I've lost that priceless ability. Now I feel as if I have to complete a jigsaw puzzle as big as the room, while all the pieces are plain white—or, rather, as black as you, Edgar. Look over there. Thousands of notes. Very personal, about Koos and Dorus and Bart Bork, but also very general ones, about the question of how power is possible and heaven knows what else. The mountain grows higher every day, but do you think that means I'm any closer to my goal? Each note takes me farther away from it! This stuff is like a tree, constantly branching, sprouting, growing, precisely when I'm trying to locate the trunk and the point where it comes out of the ground. Each time I start on my letter, I have to go through all those notes again, to build up momentum, but it never leads to a first sentence, just to new notes. In the meantime many of them have become illegible—because they've lain in the sun, or because I've spilled coffee or cola over them, or because they're stuck together with jam, or because you've relieved yourself on them with your leaching excreta, which are as white as you are black. I don't mind. Don't worry about it—that's nature."

A few weeks later the situation had reversed itself: Edgar no longer came to visit once a day, but occasionally left the house. Changed from a guest into a lodger, he generally slept in a corner of the room among the clothes lying on the floor. The first time the tame animal fluttered onto his shoulder and held onto his ear with its beak, Onno's reflex was to try to push it off, but he was glad that he hadn't, because there would have been no second opportunity. And now Edgar was given fragments to hear every day, sometimes these, sometimes those—and suddenly Onno had the feeling that reading them aloud was bringing him close to a structure, enabling him to make a start on sifting and organizing.

"Listen," he said, sitting at his desk with his reading glasses on his nose. "Take this. This is very important. Perhaps my patriarchal treatise should begin with this. *The Golden Wall* is the title. *In front of the Golden Wall it's an improvised mess; people teem around in the noisy chaos of everyday life, and the reason things don't go haywire is due to the world behind the Golden Wall. The world of power lies there like the eye of the cyclone, in mysterious silence, con-*

trolled, reliable, as ordered as a chessboard, a sort of purified world of Platonic Ideas. At least that's the image that the powerless in front of the Golden Wall have of it. It is confirmed by the dark suits, the silent limousines, the guards, the protocol, the perfect organization, the velvety calm in the palaces and ministries. But anyone who's actually been behind the Golden Wall, like you and me, knows that it's all sham and that in there, where decisions are made, it's just as improvised a chaos as in front, in people's homes, at universities, in hospitals, or in companies. I've never had that impression more strongly than in the archaeological museum in Cairo. Once when I was a minister of state I was given a guided tour by my Egyptian colleague. We looked at the treasures from the grave of Tutankhamen—all those wonderful things that were reverently displayed there. But there were also a couple of large photographs of the state in which the tomb had been found. All the things were piled on each other, like old rubbish in a loft, and the mess had not only been caused by robbers. The wooden shrines that housed the sarcophagus had also been crudely and wrongly assembled; the granite lid of the sarcophagus did not fit and had been broken in two when it had been lowered. The same spectacle was presented by the pitiful human remains that had emerged from beneath that indescribably splendid golden mask of the pharaoh's. All politicians, some civil servants, and some journalists know that it's just as pitiful a junk shop behind the Golden Wall as in front of it, but almost none of the powerless citizens know. Should anyone discover how a policy is made—which is virtually impossible—he will spend the rest of his life with a fundamental feeling of insecurity. So it's a miracle that things don't go haywire behind the Golden Wall too: it points to a much higher power. For you that's no problem; for you that's God. But for me unfortunately not even the functioning of society is a proof of God's existence. How can it possibly have functioned up to now? You won't believe it, but I know. It's because of the existence of that very Golden Wall. The Wall itself is the highest power. Wait a moment. Of course—this is where that quote from Shakespeare belongs, from the opening of one of his sonnets. Where is it? Here: *From what power hast thou this powerful might?* It's about love, but the Golden Wall is connected with love, too. Look what we've got here: *What is the nature of the Golden Wall? The powerless think that it consists of the congealed majesty of the mighty, who in some cases are even worshiped: the Liberator, the King, the Leader. But in reality it is not a product of the mighty but of the powerless themselves: it's the crystallization of their own reverence, awe, and fear. But if the powerless are hence in fact worshiping nothing but their own worship, are in awe only of their own awe, and are afraid only of their own fear, which at the same time excludes them from power, what is left for the pow-*

erful? What are they? Once someone has penetrated the Golden Wall, what does he see? Nothing special. Just ordinary people going about their business, no more interesting and no different in kind than the powerless. They exercise power not in some 'powerful,' inevitable, so to speak mathematically, certain way, as the powerless believe, but in just as messy and improvised a way as every powerless person manages his affairs. Dorus and Frans formed a cabinet over lunch; Churchill and Stalin carved up the Balkans over a drink. And yet . . . they must have something extra, which the powerless experience, because not everyone can penetrate the Wall by acquiring power. That means, Edgar, that the 'powerful might' of Shakespeare's Dark Lady was also in a certain sense not her quality, because she didn't possess it for all men. So her answer to his question, where she got it from, must therefore be 'From you yourself, Billy.' He gave her that power over him—although . . . yes, I'm saying it again: although . . . and yet . . . what does that something extra consist of? Not of intelligence, because there have always been some unspeakable idiots in power . . . : there are also always superintelligent people who never rise to power, although they would like to despite their intelligence. That something extra isn't the 'will to power,' because there are countless people who want it and will never succeed in achieving it, just as there are people who come to power who never wanted it but who, to their own amazement, are impelled toward it. So political instinct, you may say: there are lots of people with political instinct who never rise above the level of alderman in a country municipality. 'Charisma,' then? That's simply a Greek word that means gift, 'grace': that doesn't answer the question but asks one. No, something's involved that no one knows about, except me. Now I must write this down, before I forget: *Of course the whole of society is as saturated with all forms of power as a sponge, between man and woman, in education, in business, over animals, nowhere is there no power—but what is political power? Political power is the fact that someone can achieve things that he knows nothing about; that he is in a position where he can decide the fate of people that he doesn't know—sometimes on matters of life and death, and frequently beyond his own death. The powerless see the powerful one, but he does not see them. That applies not only to Caesar, Napoleon, Hitler, or Stalin but also to our own good old Dutch rulers, to Koos and Dorus, and to you of course, and to myself a little too.* I don't know what it's like among ravens, but in any case that's what it's like among people. Political power is an abstract, which only becomes concrete outside the field of vision of the powerful person. But what is that something extra that enables them to be in power? What does Dorus have in common with Hitler; what has Koos in common with Stalin? I'll tell you a secret that will make you sit up. In my own days in power I once had dinner at the Élysée; seated opposite me was a French professor of sociology. After Giscard d'Estaing's speech he told me that during the election battles, a couple of his students had hung up the posters with the portraits of Giscard and Mitterand on them in some backward country village in Thailand. The population had never heard of them and no one could read what was on the posters. On the day of the presidential elections they got them to vote, and what do you think? The results corresponded exactly with those in France. That made us laugh at the time—the professor regarded it as a good joke, and I don't believe that he was ever able to draw the dreadful conclusion from it; but I was suddenly reminded of it when I realized what power means. Listen to this: *As a boy I identified power with property. My books were mine, but then in a higher degree yours, and in a still higher degree the mayor's; after that everything was yours a second time, as prime minister, but ultimately everything in Holland was the queen's. As an alderman, I thought that political power was simply the power of the word. Whoever had the best ideas and could express them best had the greatest power. Now I know that it's only in the third place a matter of ideas and words, and only in the second place a matter of who expresses them, the person. Most people find even that extremely undemocratic, but it's much worse. Power is the power of the flesh. Power is purely physical. No one has dared face up to that. No one attains power by what he says; his political program is incidental, and so is who he is: someone else may come along with the same program and nothing will happen. Someone gains power solely because he has the physical constitution of someone who gains power. If he were to say something different—the opposite, for example—in another party or movement, he would still gain power. He would always obtain power, Father, even with the Catholics, or the Communists. The powerful person is someone who gains power because he has a physical secret that makes other people say, 'Yes, that's our man'—or woman, of course. The something extra is solely that one thing: the body.* I mean, politics isn't a branch of economics, as Marx thought, or theology, as my father thought, or sociology, as other people think, but of biology. That was proved scientifically by those yokels in Thailand. I virtually never read a newspaper, Edgar. I have no idea what's going on in the world anymore—I don't have television, radio, or even a telephone—but when I see a photo of Margaret Thatcher, who appears to be in charge in England at the moment, at a newsstand, then I know immediately: shrewd eroticism. A bourgeoise Cleopatra. Of course, she's intelligent and energetic and what have you, but so are other Englishwomen, who never get any further than head buyer at Harrods. Why is that? Take Hitler. Freud demonstrated that illness must not be understood in terms of health, but health in terms of illness. Similarly, you mustn't try to understand Hitler's absolute power in terms of more or less normal power structures, because you'll never be able to; you must do it the other way around. You can explain Margaret and Dorus through Hitler, but not Hitler through Margaret or Dorus. Suppose Hitler had never existed but someone else had said and done the same things as him from his birth in Braunau— and there were such people. Do you think things would have gone as they did to the bitter end? Of course not! How long could that other person have kept it up? At a certain moment at the beginning of the 1920s Röhm or Strasser would have rounded on him with: 'Why don't you shut your trap!' But he wasn't anyone else—he was the dark man with that dogged face and the 'basilisk's stare,' as Thomas Mann once called it, with a pale forehead, those fanatical cheekbones, those smooth cheeks and pinched lips. That appearance accounted for 33 percent of his effect, and all the neo-Nazis are still in love with it. And Salvador Dalí once said, 'I love his back.' You can dismiss that as a surrealist observation by a Spanish lunatic, but it also indicates a sense of all-determining physicality. And what do you think of a remark that Heidegger once made to Jaspers, who wondered how such an uncivilized creature as Hitler could rule Germany. Heidegger's answer was, 'Civilization has nothing to do with it . . . just look at his wonderful hands.' Apart from that, he had a voice that went right through you, which made everything he said different than if someone else had said it. A second 33 percent of the oratorical impact of his words on the masses can be attributed to that sound. I once saw an X-ray picture of his skull in a book somewhere, and it was observed that he had exceptionally large sinuses, with extraordinary resonance. And the third 33 percent of his power was due to his incomparable body language. On the one hand his terrifying outbursts of rage at the lectern, on the other hand his perhaps even more terrifying silence: his masklike face, the precision of his pose, the tension in even the smallest movement. The way he saluted at a parade, with that slight curve of the wrist, the position of his thumb, the way he brought his hand back to his belt: all of it had bewitching power. All rehearsed in front of the mirror, of course; there are photos of that. Some conductors have the same thing, that absolute control, like a hummingbird hovering stationary in the air and keeping its proboscis fixed motionless in the pistil of a flower. A *fleur du mal* in this case. Look, you don't feel left out by my mentioning a little bird?

Anyway, I've got something here that fits: *Through his total physical discipline, Hitler was able to penetrate people's minds with the equally total chaos of his thinking. And his physical discipline continued in his monstrous parades and processions, all of which he directed himself and which were no more than reproductions of his body. He was actually a movement artist, a dancer, a ballet master of death. The choreography of those great fascist dances of death derives less from Prussian militarism than from expressionism, from the theater of Piscator, from the ballet of Mary Wigman, the teacher of Leni Riefenstahl, who immortalized the gruesome fascination of his Nuremberg rallies in her equally gruesome, fascinating film* Triumph of the Will. *It was the marriage of classicism and expressionism, Apollo and Dionysus:* the realized tragedy, *in Nietzsche's sense. Never, for as long as mankind has existed, has the beautiful form been so misused and put in the service of evil. Hitler himself was the real 'degenerate artist.' And the effect of all those creations was ultimately not aesthetic but erotic, like that of Hitler himself.* What he had to say, his political aims, all those scandalous things, were no more important than the remaining 1 percent of his power. But the fact that it all happened, that it was all carried out by people who weren't basically any worse than any other people, the fact that 60 million Jews died, and 50 million others, including 8 million of those who had cheered him and paraded in front of him—that was because of that physical 99 percent. That was the enormous extra something he had; it was his unique body that made his power absolute. That's why it's impossible for him ever to be portrayed by an actor; even if only his back is shown in a film, it's completely wrong. Perhaps that's the best proof of my argument. But behind his Golden Wall even this envoy of Providence sat slumped with a cake and coffee in a flower-patterned armchair and spent the evening and half the night talking endlessly, as we know from the memoirs of his architect, Albert Speer. And he should know, because everyone was in love with Hitler; but Hitler was in love with Speer—probably even more than with Eva Braun. The German people thought that this *Übermensch* with his triumphant will was working tirelessly for the good of the nation, but he did almost nothing; he slept a good part of the day and, to the frustration of his ministers and generals, hesitated endlessly before making a decision. But in the meantime! Speer tells us that in the second half of the 1930s the bohemian's mood was starting to darken; during receptions at his country estate in the Alps he began to cut himself off and stared out across the mountains from a corner of the terrace, which made Speer think: As long as it doesn't mean war. Just imagine! One individual's mood darkens and it may mean war! And dammit, there was a war. How in heaven's name is it possible? Because of his body, Edgar, because of the accident of his body and nothing else. It was a natural phenomenon. All the powerful are natural phenomena and in that sense 'supermen'—but that 'super' resides in their spirit, not in their flesh. It has nothing to do with beauty. You can just as well be small and have a pot belly, like Napoleon, or be a semi-invalid like Kennedy, or have a face like Dorus; but it has to be there, that indescribable physical odor, they all had it and have it to a greater or lesser extent: Stalin more than Trotsky, Reagan more than Carter, and on and on in all countries and ages, all those Dark Ladies of power. People want to touch them, feel their flesh. Isn't it horrible? It's the same as with cult leaders and all other seducers. And it's even more horrible that there's no other way, and that it has to be like that. Because, listen: *Dominance is indispensable because it is the axis of life itself. Power is exerted in every cell: by the DNA molecule in the nucleus. It contains the genetic material that calls the tune. From the first living cell, via animal communities to today's states, power has retained its physical quality, because only then is it possible: the condition of physicality is power and the condition of power is physicality. That's why for a long time power was hereditary. The first capitano of a dynasty himself had the physical presence of power of somebody like Hitler, Stalin, Mussolini, Churchill, Fidel Castro, or Napoleon; that was why it was sufficient to be flesh of his flesh. (In our case it runs in the family, too, for that matter.) In Holland the portrait of the queen hangs in the offices of all ministers and mayors, but you and I know who hangs in the queen's study: William of Orange. Come to that, those founders of lines are called 'born' leaders in many languages. For centuries, wars were dynastic wars, like with the Mafia, concerned with the interests of princely families, and hence with physicality—just as republican wars originated in the physicality of new rulers. Where the royal families disappeared, continuity was ensured only by the civil service, which originated from the court and has existed without interruption since Babylon and ancient Egypt. Civil servants are eternal—they survive pharaohs, kings, and presidents—but it's no good without a leader. Civil servants without a leader are clothes without an emperor. That might well be the fate of a unified Europe. More important than the competence of a leader is the fact that he is there. With an incompetent leader things go badly, but without a leader everything sinks into abstract arbitrariness, from which a new leader irrevocably emerges—because despite the optimism of the anarchists, that is the fundamental DNA principle.* Anyway, that principle governs not only life but everything that exists. The first living cell is preceded by the first atom, which also has a nucleus, with quarks and nuclear forces. The solar system also has a nucleus: the bright sun dominates the dull planets with magnetic attraction. There's no arguing with that, Edgar. But if the same thing therefore applies to inanimate as to animate matter, I suddenly realize, to everything in short, should we perhaps see the Big Bang as the 'nucleus' of the universe? I discussed that with Max in the past. I'm talking about Max again—I'll tell you another time who that was. Another seducer in any case. And now this: *Everywhere the 'Führer principle' prevails: there has to be power, even in democratic societies, and that power can only be physical. In religion that's been known for a long time, and the first to formulate it was John: 'The Word is made flesh.'* Do you know what Jesus Christ said: 'Take, eat, this is my body.' *Hoc est enim corpus meum.* If you eat it, then you're eating God and you're saved: that superleadership goes much further than Hitler's, but the principle is the same. Think of sacred relics, which are worshiped by the believers, the faithful. A hollow tooth of St. Peter's in a golden shrine! A toe-nail of St. Paul's! Body, body, body! But power can only be power by the grace of a Golden Wall. In order to consolidate his power, the representative of the naked Christ finally had to withdraw in full regalia as pope behind the Golden Wall of the Vatican. And that's where the problem begins. For the first time in the history of mankind, the Golden Wall is beginning to give way. Once, at the dawn of history, it was erected by the powerless with the material of their own adoration, awe, and fear; now it's beginning to show ominous cracks, like a medieval castle, through which everyone can peer inside. *In your time you were still 'His Excellency the Prime Minister, Professor H.J.A. Quist,' now you would be 'Henk' to everyone—which you weren't even for us, only for Mother.* Because they can see that the chambers of the castle are as big a mess as everywhere else, the powerless rapidly lose their veneration for their own veneration, the awe at their own awe, and fear of their own fear, which at the same time undermines the authority of the powerful and makes the power of their physicality descend toward the ridiculous. In so doing, the powerless blow all the built-in fuses. What the hell does it matter to us anyway? Why shouldn't we smash that public telephone over there to pieces? Yeah, why not? What a laugh. Any police anywhere? No, nowhere. Not even in ourselves. Right, so we'll wreck it. A joke. Why do we think it's such a joke? Just because. Why has that suddenly happened, after all those eons? Perhaps it's something to do with technology—I don't know; at any rate, technology is the only thing that is suddenly developing just as fast. I don't understand the connection, and I'm confused by the fact that the telephone is also part of technology; but if that's the case, then the future looks grim. If it goes on like this, the whole social contract will crumble and the whole of society will gradually be smashed to pieces. Then everything will start to sink into anarchy without a nucleus, which contradicts the nuclear principle of being. Moreover, virtually no one in the West believes in a God of vengeance anymore, and it won't last very long in the East, either, and in twenty-five years' time not even a dog will believe in Allah, when they all have a fridge and a car over there. How can we avoid an invasion of fascist tyrants, who will lodge in the empty nuclei like cancer viruses? I've written down the answer here, Edgar. I scarcely dare read it aloud, and it's just as well that my father will never see it. *As a boy—in a time that was still yours—it once happened that my ball rolled onto the grass in the park. Because walking on the grass was forbidden, I waited for a good five minutes until a certain moment when there was no one else to be seen; only then did I dare to step over the low fence, with my heart pounding, to take the few steps across the grass and to jump back again as soon as I could. That inhibition, that pounding heart, that's what it's about. Did I feel unfree? Not at all. It was simply forbidden to walk on the grass. At the moment I don't feel unfree, either, because I'm not allowed to kill anyone. That's simply not allowed. How do you prevent everyone killing everyone else without a pounding heart one day? How can we get that heart pounding again? Only by forcing respect. I say 'respect'—not fear as a result of some dictatorial regime or other, but respect for respect's sake: a new Golden Wall for the sake of the Golden Wall. This can only be done by means of the authoritarian rule of an enlightened despot—with the emphasis on 'enlightened.' Someone whom everybody knows, who puts the interests of his fellow citizens first, therefore making him the complete democrat. Someone like Pericles, in short. But how can you institutionalize that? How do you know in advance that the despot is indeed enlightened? Even Plato wrestled with that problem, but within twenty-five years it must be possible to select him by means of DNA analysis—and that brings us to the way in which in Tibet the new Dalai Lama is tracked down among the babies in the villages. The question is simply: how do we get through those last twenty-five years without accidents? I have a presentiment of changes without end, followed by dreadful disasters. That democratic institutions will not have to function for long, a century perhaps; afterward, based on the Ten Commandments, everyone can be incarnated genetically as a reasonable human being and the government will consist of a computer network, with a mongoloid or a stone as dominus mundi. Once the king is ruler by the grace of God, then technology will personify divine omnipotence. By that time no telephone booth will be vandalized and no one will walk on the grass anymore—not even if a ball is there. Probably, no one will even play with a ball. Isn't that awful? It's just as well that my son will never see this.* Yes, Edgar, I had a son too. Quinten was his name. Shame you'll never meet him. I'll tell you about him too. But first of all my letter. It isn't completely clear yet, but how about simply beginning with: *Most Honored Father!*' "

Wings flapping, Edgar jumped onto his shoulder.

"*Cras. Cras.*"

52

Italian Journey

On May 11, 1985, as a pope was flying to the Netherlands for the first time, beneath him on the ground Quinten was traveling south by train. Under the ground, actually, through Alpine tunnels, beyond which Italy suddenly unfolded: blue and green and descending, like at Groot Rechteren when he emerged from of the chilly cellar into the warm sun on the forecourt. Sophia had taken him to the station, hugged him with a stony face, but as soon as he had said goodbye she had disappeared from his thoughts. On the way he had not read or slept, but simply looked out the window the whole time, at all those countless towns and villages in Germany and Switzerland where his father might be.

However, while he was looking for his connection in Milan in the throng on the platforms, even that had receded and gradually an exciting feeling of freedom took possession of him, which became more and more intense when near Mestre he traveled out to sea along a railway embankment and saw Venice on the water in the distance; a vague blue phantom, as though on the horizon the sky had been lifted up a little and a glimpse of another world came through the crack. Was it a mirage? Was that where the Citadel was?

Emerging from the station with his blue-gray nylon backpack, he stopped. On the wide stairs of the terrace and on the square in front of the station hundreds of young people were sitting in the sun. On the other side was a white church. Between, it looked as though the water of the Grand

Canal was being stirred by giant, invisible white bird's feathers: everything was moving, it was as though the light itself were undulating and waving and glittering in the sun—gondolas, *vaporetti,* water taxis, swaying and crying everywhere, everything foaming like a breaking wave in the surf. At the same time he had the impression that when he stood there, more eyes were focused on him than had ever happened at home. He went to a simple hotel nearby, in the out-of-the-way working-class district of Cannaregio, where few tourists went. On the arch above the entrance were Hebrew letters, most of which could no longer be deciphered. His window gave onto a small courtyard with flues and flaking plaster. The bed took up virtually the whole room, and the shower was in the corridor, but he didn't need any more room: he had the city for that.

After a few days Holland was so far away that it was if he had never been there. His mother's body in her white bed, Max's empty grave, his vanished father—none of that seemed to be his life anymore. He didn't get involved with anyone; he communed with things the whole day long. He wandered from morning till night through the maze of alleys, canals, bridges, dark doorways, silent squares; ate some tortellini here, a plate of spaghetti there; went into and out of churches and museums and allowed himself to get lost. If it took too long, he glanced at the little compass around his neck, with the plan of Venice in his head: those two relaxed intertwined hands, divided by the Grand Canal.

That labyrinthine quality sometimes reminded him of his dream, as did the absence of trees and plants and wheels. Behind the Piazza San Marco he also discovered a church, San Moisè, the black facade of which was covered from top to bottom with a baroque eczema of statues and ornaments; when he stood close to it and threw his head back, it might be a fragment of the Citadel. The high altar was a wild monument, entitled *St. Moses Receiving the Tablets of the Law on Mount Sinai.*

But apart from that his Citadel, where he was still the only person, was more the reverse of Venice. Not only because of the stream of people, which always moved along the same ant paths, and which he was soon able to avoid, but because it wasn't an interior without an exterior but more an exterior as an interior. Each time he emerged via a doorway or a narrow street into St. Mark's Square, it was like a bang on a drum. That gigantic marble-coated banqueting hall, with the sky as the ceiling as painted by Tiepolo with a real blue sky and feathery cloud! All that lightness and floating, whether it was Byzantine, Gothic, or Renaissance, the filigree arabesques of the basilica, the four horses that pulled it through the centuries, with the pink, newly built Doge's palace with its gallery of keys, with the teeth as balustrades, the shafts as pillars, the Gothic perforated eyes seem to carry the actual weight of the building—to think that such a thing could exist! At the end of the piazzetta, like a gateway to the great outside, the wide world, with the two colossal pillars of red and white granite, their capitals topped with the winged lion and a patron saint seated on a crocodile, between which for centuries death sentences had been carried out. Even criminals were allowed to die in beauty here: the last thing they had seen was the living water of the lagoon—and the church on the small island on the other side: Palladio's San Giorgio Maggiore.

So there it finally was—no longer in Mr. Themaat's books, but in the sun and the Adriatic sea wind. The white marble facade with the two superimposed temple fronts, as harmonious as a fugue: behind it the bare red-brick nave, with the gray cupola at the intersection. Of course he also took the *vaporetto* to see everything at close quarters and from inside, sailing across the spot where for centuries the Doge had thrown a ring into the water annually, to seal his marriage with the sea.

How could he be so fascinated by Venice when the city had so little to do with his Citadel? All things considered, Palladio's severe symmetries were completely out of place here too, because in Venice everything was precisely asymmetrical. The piazza wasn't an oblong but a trapezoid, the basilica was not on the axis; the windows of the Doge's palace did not reflect each other. Was he on the track of a law? Might it be that beauty was geometrically and musically calculable but that, in turn, perfection somehow diverged from it? Just as a straight line drawn with a ruler was always somehow less than a straight line when Picasso drew it without a ruler? Was there a difference between a dead and a living line? Should he perhaps start studying art history? But you couldn't study without your high school exams; besides, art didn't interest him at all for its own sake, but because of what was behind it.

On Ascension Day he took an excursion to the mainland, to Vicenza. With a mainly English group he visited the Teatro Olimpico, with its fairytale interior without an exterior, and all those other churches and palaces that he knew so well from the library at Groot Rechteren, under the *P* of Palladio. They were no longer framed by the silent white of the page, but turned out to be standing next to other buildings, in certain streets, full of the din of cars and scooters, where in the squares old gentlemen stood and talked indignantly to each other, and then walked on arm in arm, where fruit sellers cried and young pizza bakers tossed their spinning circles of dough in the air, to allow the laws of nature to do their work in the spirit of Galileo and Newton.

On the way back, the bus stopped at two other Palladian villas. First, just outside Vicenza, the Villa Rotonda: a vision in stone on top of a green hill, with its round central building another descendant of the Roman Pantheon, but now equipped with four entry doorways with staircases and Greek temple fronts, one in each direction—just as in families certain features suddenly recur double or fourfold.

There, walking across the marble, between *trompe l'oeil* frescos of pilasters and divine figures, making the interior look like an exterior, he first noticed the dark-blond woman in the party. While he looked at an illustration of Diana hunting with her breast bared and a black dog, he suddenly felt her eyes focused on him. In a long white dress, with her hair worn loosely up, and her head slightly bent, which made her smile and the look in her large brown eyes even more sensual, she was standing on the other side of the Rotonda, near a depiction of a swaggering Hercules. He found it unpleasant. It interrupted his concentration, and he tried to ignore it; but back in the bus, too, where he was sitting in the front seat, he noticed that she was constantly looking at the back of his head. She was fifteen or twenty years older than him, but even if she'd been young, he still wouldn't have liked it. Those kinds of things were not for him. He knew that for many boys and girls there was nothing else, that it existed mainly for Max and possibly for his father too; he was less sure about his Granny, and he didn't want to think of his mother at all in this connection. For him sexuality had as little meaning as sports—up to now at least. He felt it was something for people who wanted to reproduce, but he had no need. He was sufficient unto himself.

In the afternoon they drove from Padua along the provincial highway by the Brenta, lined with that unreal, poetic vegetation that only rivers create around themselves, which makes them sacred in innocent eyes. Not far from the river's mouth, as a conclusion to the excursion, they stopped at the Villa Foscari, nicknamed La Malcontenta. Because he felt overfed artistically, and also to escape the woman, he took only a quick look at the interior and then sat down on the grass under a weeping willow at the edge of the water.

He hadn't expected that she would come to him. Suddenly she sank down right in front of him, cross-legged, in a way that reminded him of the string puppet he had once had: when you pulled the string in its crotch, its arms and legs shot upward. She was sitting so close to him that he could smell her: a smell that reminded him of autumn leaves and which perhaps did not come from a bottle. Around her neck and wrists she had at least twenty gold chains and bracelets.

"Do you speak English?" she asked in English with a smile, but with a kind of German accent. When he sat up and nodded, she put a hand with long, slim fingers and red nails high on his thigh, no more than half an inch from his sex, and brushed her other hand through the hair on the back of his head. "Do you know how well that white lock of hair suits you?"

Before he could push her away, which he probably wouldn't have dared to do anyway, both hands had disappeared. Then her right hand came forward again.

"Marlene," she said. "Marlene Kirchlechner."

"Quinten Quist."

He shook hands with her and tried to withdraw his hand, but she kept hold of it.

"Your hand's tense," she said, still looking at him. "It's as though you don't really want to touch mine. Relax it."

At the same moment he realized she was right. He relaxed his muscles and only then felt the warm palm of her hand against his, which to his alarm produced warmth not only in his hand but in his whole body. She obviously saw what was happening, because as she let go of his hand, she leaned her head forward and looked at him with the same look as just now in the Villa Rotonda. Within a minute she had succeeded in confusing him completely. He wanted to hold her hand again and at the same time wanted not to want that. But the touching was suddenly over.

"How old are you, Quinten?"

"I'll be seventeen in two weeks."

She hesitated for a moment and looked at him. "Are you in Venice with your parents?"

"No," he said curtly. "I'm alone."

"So am I," said Marlene Kirchlechner. She lived in Vienna, she told him; she came here every year in May, to the place where she had been on her honeymoon with her dead husband—on the Lido in the Hotel Excelsior, always in the same suite, with a view of the sea. "What's stopping you?" she said as they sat together on the front seat as the bus drove across the embankment toward Venice, to the Piazzale Roma, the terminus for all motor traffic. "Come with me. There's a wonderful swimming pool; you won't find a pool in the whole of Venice. You can move in if you like. Where are you staying?"

Quinten realized that undreamt-of adventures were suddenly possible, as they were in the kinds of novels that Clara Proctor was always reading. Here was a mature, pretty, voluptuous woman, obviously also stinking rich, who wanted to take him under her wing—but at the same time he knew that it was not to be for him. He felt that he mustn't be carried away by chance meetings, although it wasn't clear what that would distract him from, because he had nothing special to do. He was simply messing around: he could just as well have been somewhere else.

When he said that he preferred to go back to his own room, she insisted on walking with him for a little while; she'd never been in Cannaregio, and she could take the water taxi back to the Lido. On the way she talked nonstop about herself, about her husband's vineyards in the Wachau on the Danube, which she now managed; fortunately she didn't ask him about his own circumstances. At the door of his hotel, under the laundry that hung like garlands from one side of the alley to the other, he was about to say goodbye; but she suggested having a drink somewhere first. A hearty Conegliano-Valdobbiadene prosecco, for instance, which went straight to your head: when you were in a place, you must always drink the local wine. Quinten never drank wine, but he was thirsty too.

Looking for a terrace, a rarity in this district, they emerged via a wooden bridge and a low, dark *sottoportego* onto the inner courtyard of the sixteenth-century ghetto, to which all later ghettos owed their name. The houses were taller than in the rest of the city and there were even a few trees, like almost nowhere else in Venice. By a round well with a marble lid they sat down on a bench. Most of the shutters were closed; in many plant tubs there were spinning paper windmills. Apart from the doves in the alcoves and on the weathered windowsills, there was not a living thing to be seen—and in the falling dusk they looked in silence for a while at the great silence that hung over the stones.

Suddenly Mrs. Kirchlechner put her cheek against his shoulder and began sobbing.

"What's wrong?" he said in alarm.

With her great eyes helplessly flooded, she looked up to him as if he were her father.

"I don't know what's got into me . . . I'm in love with you, Quinten. The moment I saw you, it was like seeing a gold coin in the mud. At first I thought it was simply an impulse—I have those quite often; but now I realize that I obviously won't see you again. I can see that it's something completely different. I don't go for young boys at all, if that's what you're thinking perhaps. It's never happened to me. My husband was twice my age, and now I'm more than twice yours. Why aren't you twenty-six or sixty-six for all I care? Sixteen! It's impossible, I must be crazy!" Suddenly she stood up, took his face between her hands, and kissed him on both eyes. "Farewell, angel . . . may things go well with you."

Before he could say anything, he saw her white figure waft across the campo, like a sheet that had freed itself from the clothespins, and disappear into the dark doorway.

He looked at the black hole in alarm. What havoc had he caused? Should he go after her? And what then? No, it was best like this of course. That kind of woman simply existed in the great wide world; you had to get used to it. While store shutters rattled in the distance as they were pulled down, he walked back to his hotel. He put his mouth under the tap and splashed water on his face with both hands. On his bed he was going to read some more of his guide, but he fell asleep almost immediately—and was visited not by the SOMNIUM QUINTI but by fire . . .

First he is living on the attic floor of a tall house, like those in the ghetto, where the square chimneys run along the outside walls. He calls out the window that the fire brigade should be summoned, at which everyone looks up and shrugs their shoulders. No problem. It'll be okay; just panicking over nothing. When the house is ablaze and all the beams have been transformed into architraves of fire, he turns out to be living somewhere in a basement. Suddenly smoke starts curling up there, too, between the slabs, and again no one listens to him, so everything goes up in flames . . .

He was awakened by hunger. Outside it had grown dark; it was ten o'clock. He cracked his thumbs and got up with aching limbs. In a small restaurant near the Grand Canal he ate a plate of ravioli, surrounded by locals and gondoliers in striped tunics, everyone talking loudly in a language sometimes reminiscent of Italian. Now and then he had a vision of Marlene from Vienna. In the Excelsior, surrounded by Sikhs, Japanese magnates, and American oil barons, she was now of course eating lobster and caviar under crystal chandeliers; but it was as though his dream had already thrown up a barrier, relegating her to the past once and for all.

Thanks to the baron he was fortunately rich himself. He allowed himself a second espresso, put a five-hundred lire additional tip on the bill, and wandered into town for a little while.

In that deserted midnight Venice, with all the shutters closed, the terraces cleared away and no life anywhere, he stopped on a bridge over a narrow canal. To the left and right, weathered house walls with rainpipes rose up out of the motionless seawater; a little farther on, across a side canal, was a second bridge; at the end the view was blocked off by the refined back of a Gothic palazzo, which was of course really the front. He looked at the green seaweed-covered steps, which everywhere led down to the water from dark arches with barred gates and continued underwater. The complete silence.

Had his mother ever been here? His father? Max? Suddenly the silence filled with a scarcely audible rustling, and a little later a gondola appeared under the bridge he was standing on, the gleaming halberd on the prow. Three silent Japanese girls appeared, and then the gondolier, straightening and with the merest push steering the gondola slightly toward the side, where with an indescribably perfect movement—which formed a unity with the gondola, the water, the silence, the city—he propelled himself by pushing off from a house with his foot for a second to keep up speed.

At that moment Quinten saw a white glimpse of Marlene Kirchlechner on the other bridge, immediately disappearing when she realized that he had seen her. His eyes widened. While he slept she had been waiting for him all that time, had followed him to the restaurant, waited again, and again followed him. It was clear: he had to leave Venice at once—preferably this evening.

Maybe it was the sound of its name, Florence, that made him expect the town would be even more silvery and silent. But he found himself in a noisy, stinking cauldron of traffic that he had forgotten after five days in Venice. Moreover, if everything there was light and open, everything here was heavy, closed. The function of the sea, which protected Venice sufficiently, was here fulfilled by thick walls, colossal blocks of stone, bars, buildings like fortresses; the beauty was virtually only indoors, in palaces and museums. But exactly what distinguished Florence from Venice gave it a Citadel-like quality: that reconciled him a little with his disappointment. Because all the affordable hotels were full, he had to make do with a grubby hostel, where he shared a room with seven others, most of them students but also a few older men; apart from a bed he had only a chair to use, on which he could look at the crucifix above the door.

Surrounded by international snoring, he thought back for the first time to his room at Groot Rechteren. Or did it no longer exist? Had Korvinus gotten his hands on everything by now? Of course it wouldn't happen as quickly as that. He felt as if he had been away from home for months, but it was scarcely a week. He hadn't sent any message from Venice, and he now resolved to write to his grandmother as soon as possible. But not only did he not write a letter, even when he passed a stand with postcards on it—Piazza della Signoria, Palazzo Pitti, Ponte Vecchio, Battistero—an uncontrollable revulsion took hold of him, which prevented him buying one and writing even "Greetings from Florence" on it.

He did, however, buy a series of cards in the Uffizi, to put on the chair next to his bed. In the cataract of art treasures that was poured out into that exuberant museum street, he was struck by an Annunciation by Leonardo da Vinci: an angel who was approaching the Virgin Mary rather furtively, with his head bent and the guilty look of someone who knows that what he has in mind is no good. No wonder the Mary seemed to be thinking: "Who are you? What are you doing here?" Quinten had learned at high school that *annuntiare* meant "announce": the angel was going to announce to her that, at a later date, she would be impregnated by the Holy Ghost; but according to him there was something much more going on here than simply an "announcement"; this was the event itself. In a moment he was going to pounce on her. Because why wasn't Joseph there? Surely he had the right to know for certain that his fiancée had not deceived him with the window cleaner? Every woman could maintain that she had become pregnant out of pure piety. He began to look for Annunciations in the other rooms too, but in none of them was Joseph there. The sucker was obviously in the carpenter's workshop, where he was earning his daily bread by the sweat of his brow, making crosses for the Romans perhaps, while at home his bride-to-be was listening to the seductive angel patter and letting herself go with an envoy of God. Suddenly he now remembered a relief of the Annunciation on the front of the Rialto bridge in Venice. On the left-hand pillar, at the beginning of the arch, you saw the angel Gabriel, at the highest point of the bridge the dove that he had thrown up, and on the right-hand pillar Mary, waiting for the Holy Ghost in complete abandon. So that dove was no less than the angel's holy seed!

How he would have liked to talk to his father about this. Would he have agreed with him? Perhaps he would have agreed and called depictions of the Annunciation "religious peep shows"; perhaps he would have exclaimed in alarm: "The shameful thought will crush that head of yours!" He burst out laughing. The latter struck him as most probable.

Wandering among the sculptures in the Museo Bargello, on the second day of his stay, he was suddenly reminded of Theo Kern, who had of course been here too, to learn how his colleagues had removed the superfluous stone. Through the windows of the old palace he occasionally saw the Florentines in the street and in the smoky buses, and wondered how many of them had looked at these wonderful things here. Which of them knew that their city had invented the Renaissance? Perhaps the memory of most people in the world didn't extend much farther than their own lifetime; perhaps they didn't even realize that they were living a thousand years after a thousand years ago. Between their birth and their death, they were trapped in a windowless cell; for them everything was as it always had been. Of course that wasn't the case—but in a certain sense it was, because that's how it had been a thousand years ago for almost everybody, and two thousand years ago, and ten thousand. By simply living, working, having fun, eating, reproducing, they had in fact become much more eternal than the eternal masterpieces of all those unique individuals!

He stopped at an arbitrary sculpture and thought: Take that thing there. What was it? A beautiful, naked boy, with his right hand on his crown, his left hand on that of a great eagle, which was sitting at his feet and looking at him devotedly. BENVENUTO CELLINI, 1500–1571. *Ganymede*. He didn't know the myth, but that didn't matter; he knew in any case that there was an old story behind it. There was a story behind everything. Only someone who knew all the stories knew the world. It was almost inevitable that behind the whole world, with all its stories, there was another story that was therefore older than the world. You should find out about that story!

"Did you pose for that?"

He started. A tall man, who seemed vaguely familiar, looked at him and smiled, but he didn't like the smile. He was about fifty, balding, with dull eyes, a pointed nose, and thin lips; out of his sleeves, which were rolled up, protruded two pale arms with a golden chain around each wrist. Suddenly Quinten remembered who he was: he slept in the same room, on the other side of the gangway.

"No," he said gruffly.

"I saw your guidebook on your chair, that's how I know you're Dutch too. My name's Menne."

Quinten nodded, but he didn't intend to give his own name. What did this guy want? Had he followed him too, perhaps? Menne looked back and forth between him and the statue.

"You two look very like each other, do you know that? I'm sure you have little pointed nipples just like that, and beautiful legs. Except that your eyes are much more beautiful. And that little dick—I bet you've got a much bigger one than that. Am I right or not? Tell me honestly . . ." Panting a little, he bent toward him. "Have you got hair on it yet? Do you play with it sometimes? I expect you do, don't you?"

Quinten couldn't believe his ears. What a dirty bastard! Without a word, he turned on his heel and left the room.

"Don't act so offended," the man called after him. "It was only a joke. Let's go and have a cappuccino."

As soon as Quinten got to the top of the steps, he immediately went down three steps at a time, outside, and ran criss-cross through a couple of alleyways to shake him off. It turned out to be unnecessary: of course because Menne knew that he would find him again in the hostel at the end of the day. When he went to bed at eleven o'clock Menne fortunately still wasn't back. Who knows; perhaps he'd gone.

But in the middle of the night he was awakened by a hand wandering around under the blanket between his legs. The guy was sitting on the edge of his bed, stinking of alcohol and with his fly unbuttoned, with a thick penis sticking out of it as blue-white as detergent, at which he was tugging with his other hand at a speed that reminded Quinten of the rod of Arendje's locomotive when he forced it along the rails at full speed. The thing was also a little bent—because of all that jerking of course.

"Get lost, you dirty creep!" he said.

"Oh darling, darling," whispered Menne. "Let me let me. It'll be over in a moment . . ."

He tried to put his lips on Quinten's, and for the first time in his life Quinten clenched his fist, lashed out, and hit someone as hard as he could with his knuckles. His lover got up with a groan and fell forward onto his own bed, where he stayed with his back heaving. Of course he was crying.

No one had noticed anything. For a few seconds Quinten listened in astonishment to the snores around him. He realized that for the second time he was being driven out of a city. He got angrily out of bed, dressed, packed his things in his backpack, and put the postcards with the Annunciations into his guidebook. He paid the porter, who was sitting on a brown imitation-leather bench reading the *Osservatore Romano*, and walked down the cool nocturnal streets to the station. In the hall, he sat down among scores of other young people on the ground and tried to get a little more sleep.

53

The Shadow

Even when Onno went shopping in the mornings, Edgar was in the habit of sitting on his shoulder. People no longer paid any attention in the shops. In the street the bird sometimes spread its wings, took off, and after one flap on Onno's crown flew up to a gutter or disappeared behind the houses, but it always came back. Onno was more attached to it than he was prepared to admit—perhaps to protect himself against the possibility that one day it might not come back. Imagine some bastard or other shooting it! Humanity after all contained that kind of scum, who should be ashamed at what they did to animals, none of which had any knowledge of evil and for that reason had to be killed.

"Of course there are decent people too," he said to Edgar in the street, without paying any attention to the looks that passersby gave them. "I estimate them at about eight percent of mankind. But another eight percent always and everywhere consists of the worst rabble imaginable, who are capable of anything. If they get the chance, the first thing they will do is to exterminate the good eight percent. The rest are neither good nor bad; they cut their coat according to their cloth. The first and the thirteenth in every hundred are the ones to watch; the other eleven don't matter. That means the first must make sure he gets them on his side, to keep the thirteenth down, because they could just as well follow *him*. In the best possible case number thirteen finally hangs himself, like Judas, or is hanged, like in

Nuremberg, or he is put in front of the firing squad, like in Scheveningen; but always only after they have done their work, when it doesn't really matter anymore. My head's spinning again, Edgar. The grip of the first is gradually loosening; everywhere the thirteenth is probing his limits, seeing how far he can go, slashing the seat on a train here and there, then vandalizing another telephone booth. That's what's happening now, Edgar, in a world without God and with a Golden Wall that is about to collapse. I contributed to it. *Mea culpa, mea culpa, mea maxima culpa.* And when he appears in court, then a psychiatrist will probably immediately appear as devil's advocate and explain his behavior from causes. Wretched childhood, abused a lot, parents divorced. But causal explanations can never be justifications for his behavior. Man is not a machine, or simply an animal, like you—and I'm not even so sure about you. That's why behavior must be judged not causally but finally.

"Do you mind my taking a scientific tone for a moment? The moral judgment has disappeared from the causal description, and the residue is subsequently presented judicially as mitigating circumstances, resulting in a reduction in sentence. But that of course implies a denial of human freedom, and man is dehumanized by taking away his responsibility. I vaguely remember that there was something like that in the sentence on Max's father; the fellow had probably been betrayed in his childhood by his mother. Denial of punishment is inhuman punishment. Moreover, it's an unacceptable insult to people who have had an equally rotten childhood and who do *not* commit crimes. According to the same principle, they should actually be *rewarded* by the government. That would cost the state dear, but if this system is not introduced, then justice demands that psychiatrists be driven out of court, like the moneychangers from the temple. No, what the judge needs is an iron hand, like Götz von Berlichingen. Unless you have the sweetest flesh of the Messiah, you can only fight evil brutally with evil. In the service of good you must necessarily and tragically embrace evil, but that's the price you must pay. 'No one can rule innocently,' said Saint-Just before he went to the guillotine himself."

The glances cast by the passersby at the eccentric, talking to himself with unintelligible guttural sounds, did not move him. He no longer belonged among people; all he did was think about them, like an ornithologist about birds. When he crossed a busy, square piazza, with full café terraces at the foot of orange-plastered houses, Edgar jumped to the ground and mingled with the pigeons, who gave way to his black figure in alarm.

"Good idea, Edgar. Let's inspect thirteen people here in the sun at our leisure."

He sat down on the steps of a fountain and put his plastic shopping bag next to him. From the basin rose a sculptured pedestal, with dolphins spouting water, on top of which was an obelisk, eighteen feet or so high, covered with hieroglyphics, crowned by a gold star, from which sprouted a bronze cross.

"Thirteen men, that is—as a gentleman I'll leave women out of it. You know what Weininger said: 'Woman is man's fault.' Hitler was a man, but through three elections he only came to power thanks to the lovelorn women of Germany; so let's shroud that in the democratic and feminist mantle of love. Take him," and he nodded toward a carefully groomed, graying gentleman with a newspaper under his arm and his coat draped loosely over his shoulders. "Decent man, chief accountant at a medium-sized bank, manager of some department or other. Reliable, bit vain, in any case not the first and not the thirteenth. And neither is that one over there," he said, and his eyes followed a man in overalls walking past and studying some machine component or other that had to be repaired or replaced. "He's doing his job. He's too busy to murder or perform miracles. But those two talking over there—one of them I don't like at all. That smile is no good. And that face is just a bit too pale and too smooth."

The man was in his late twenties and noticed immediately that he was being watched. Instantly, his smile vanished completely, as though a switch had been turned off, and a cold, threatening expression remained focused on Onno. Onno averted his gaze.

"Dammit, Edgar, if you ask me there's the thirteenth. But don't look, because he's dangerous. He's dangerous because he can control his emotions, like someone else's car; what he uses to steer them with is itself not an emotion. Hopefully, he'll get run over by a car today. Who have we over there?" he said, looking at a boy who crossed the square diagonally, stopped open-mouthed, and took in the building opposite. At the same moment Onno caught his breath. He began trembling and slowly stood up.

✳

The Pantheon! There it was! Quinten felt as though what he was looking at was not real. The Roman temple of all the gods, twenty centuries old: gray and bare, scraped clean from top to bottom by barbarians, emperors, and popes, it stood there as something not only from a different time but from a different space—like sometimes during the daytime an alarming image loomed up from the dream of the preceding night.

M●AGRIPPA L●F●COS●TERTIVM●FECIT

The Quadrata! There they were, those wonderful, inspired letters on the architrave above the eight pillars, under the two triangular pediments, which Palladio had studied so closely: Marcus Agrippa, the son of Lucius, who had allegedly made this during his third consulate; but in reality it was the emperor Hadrian, as Mr. Themaat had taught him. He wondered how Mr. Spier was getting on there in his Pontrhydfendigaid.

To the left and right of the doorway and the round building behind with the cupola, grooves many feet deep had been cut down to Roman street level, which made the temple appear to be rising from the earth, like the erratic stones in Drenthe. At the front, he knew, the entrance steps were still buried below the asphalt. Slowly he walked along past the row of waiting horse carriages, toward the shadow of the high, rectangular portico, supported by another eight pillars—together making as many columns as he had years. A group of visitors was already waiting. A little later one of the bronze doors, over twenty feet high, was opened a fraction by two men, which required all their strength.

As he crossed the threshold, the colossal empty space took his breath away. As in the impenetrable interior of a crystal, the shadowless light hung on the blond marble floor, against the columns and alcoves and chapels, where the proud Roman gods had been replaced by humble Christian saints. The highest point of the cupola was occupied not by a keystone but by the blue sky, a round hole measuring almost thirty feet across, through which a diagonal beam of sunlight shone like an obelisk, producing a dazzling egg on a damaged fresco. The cupola with the hole in it reminded him of an iris with a pupil: the temple was an eye, which he was now inside. From outside, the hole must be black. The building was an observatory.

What had Mr. Themaat said again? That the Pantheon, though it might not be *the* building, because that didn't exist, was a "good second" and you could see it as a depiction of the world. Perhaps he had meant by that not simply nature, the earth, the moon, the sun the stars, but all the other worlds, such as for example those of numbers, geometrical figures, and music. For that matter the building was also a clock—a sundial, which indicated the time not with a shadow but with light itself. He went and stood in the middle of the space, directly beneath the opening, and took out his little compass. The entrance was due north.

He looked in the direction the needle indicated, where his attention was caught by a seedy figure by the bronze doors, who was staring at him. He was large and heavily built and was wearing a pair of dark glasses; on his shoulder sat a black crow, no, it was more like a raven. An unkempt gray beard hid the rest of his face too. His long hair had been gathered into a ponytail at the back; his grubby shirt was half open and hanging out of his trousers, exposing his navel; worn sneakers covered his bare feet. Quinten started. Not again, surely? In Venice the woman from Vienna, in Florence that sleazy type, and now a tramp—things were going from bad to worse. He felt himself turning away in irritation, but at that moment the ebony-colored bird flew off the man's shoulder, described a circle through the temple with wings flapping, sat for a moment on the ledge where the cupola rested on the rotunda, then flew up and disappeared croaking through the blue opening.

Everyone in the Pantheon watched it go. The Japanese quickly took photos, and Onno knew immediately that it would not come back. He had not intended to speak to Quinten; he just wanted to see him for a moment. He was about to call the bird back, but was frightened that Quinten would recognize his voice. Now he had not even said goodbye to Edgar—and suddenly he felt so utterly abandoned that he could not bear it.

When Quinten saw the shabby figure coming toward him, trembling and supporting himself on a stick, he would have preferred to run around him in a wide arc and dash outside; but he decided to tell him plainly that he wanted nothing to do with him—at least if he spoke French, German, or English—and then to make a dignified exit from the temple. When the man arrived opposite him, he took off his sunglasses.

Quinten felt himself changing into an image of himself. His breathing his heart, his brain, and his intestines—all came to a stop; for a moment he turned to marble as he looked into Onno's eyes, which he knew so well and through which at the same time someone completely different from his father seemed to be looking at him. Then they fell into each other's arms and for a couple of seconds stood hugging each other without moving.

"Dad . . ." sobbed Quinten.

Onno looked around, searching for something. "I have to sit down for a moment."

Hand in hand, they walked toward a wooden bench, a few yards away from the sarcophagus containing the bones of Raphael, where they stood and surveyed each other in silent astonishment. On the one hand Quinten had the feeling that it couldn't be true that his father was suddenly sitting there; on the other hand it was quite obvious that he had found him without really trying. How disheveled he was! It couldn't be from lack of money, and yet he looked completely down and out. Uncle Karel had been right: Auntie Helga's death had turned him into a dropout. Was what was happening really the right thing?

Onno, too, was completely confused. He realized that he had again undermined his whole life with his sudden impulse. By speaking to Quinten, he had done something irrevocable: it was of course impossible for him to say goodbye forever in a moment, and equally unthinkable that he should resume his earlier existence. At the same time he felt something like relief that everything was suddenly completely different from the past four years. When he had left Holland, Quinten had been a boy of twelve, and now there was almost a man sitting there. For the first time he was ashamed. He lowered his eyes and did not know what to say.

Quinten watched him and asked: "Shall I go?"

Onno shook his head. "Things are as they are," he said softly. "Quinten . . . how are you? You look well. You've grown two heads taller."

"I suppose I have, yes."

"How long have you been in Rome?"

"Since yesterday afternoon."

"Are you here with the whole class? I came here for the first time when I was in school."

"I'm not in school anymore."

Onno, who had given up so much more, realized that he was in no position to comment; the very fact that he had not known about this deprived him of his right to speak. What's more, he heard a sort of decisiveness in

Quinten's voice that dismissed all criticism in advance. He wanted to ask about Ada, but perhaps she was no longer alive.

"I still can't believe that we're suddenly sitting here, Quinten."

"Perhaps we aren't."

A smile crossed Onno's face. "Perhaps we're dreaming. Both having the same dream." He looked at him shyly. He had to inquire about Ada. "How's Mama?"

"The same, as far as I know. I haven't seen her." He didn't want to talk about his mother; he also suddenly felt irritated that his father had to ask about her. She might have been dead. Or had she died in the meantime perhaps? His granny still did not know where she could reach him. He'd want to know in a moment how Max was doing, and then he would have to tell him what had happened. To give the conversation a different turn, he asked, "Why are you using a walking stick?"

Onno put the stick on his lap and looked at it. It was a crudely trimmed, gnarled branch, with its unprotected tip transformed into a weathered brush; the curved handle had been artistically shaped into a serpent's head.

"Nice, isn't it? Found it in a secondhand shop." Slowly he turned to face Quinten and said, "I had a slight stroke, a brain hemorrhage eighteen months ago." And then he saw that Quinten was alarmed. "Don't worry, it's over now. But it happened very deep, in a dangerous place, in the thalamus, as it's called. Less than an inch farther forward, and I would have been in a wheelchair—the neurologist said I should consider myself lucky. Do you know that feeling? When you fall under a tram and lose your leg, you should be happy that you didn't lose both legs. Whenever something serious happens, you're supposed to count yourself lucky and be happy."

"Did it hurt a lot?"

"Not at all. In real life things are always different than you've imagined them. Shall I tell you about it?"

Quinten gave a slight shrug of the shoulders. He didn't really want to know, but he wanted to put off the question about Max for as long as possible.

One cold winter's day, said Onno, he was walking down the street not far from here. Suddenly he felt something hanging over his head. It was as if he were not completely there. His left hand began tingling, and a moment later his left foot. He felt as if he had a couple of stones in his shoe, but a minute later his whole left shoe was full of stones and all those stones together formed his left foot. After another minute he realized that something was seriously wrong. His whole left leg, his left side, and the left-hand half of his face had gone numb. Because it had all been on the left, he thought of his heart, but he had no pain in his chest, though he did have a little in his head, though not even enough to require an aspirin. Now and then he had to stop.

When he felt his pulse, his heart was racing so fast that he couldn't count. He tried to take off his left glove, but he never wore gloves; he realized that he was busy pulling his fingers. He tried to tell from the faces of the people who came toward him whether there was anything strange to be seen about him; but he didn't see anything special. And yet he knew they were now in a different world from him. He sat down on the edge of the pavement and a woman asked if she should call for an ambulance. He said it wasn't necessary, but she did anyway; a little later he was driven to the hospital with wailing sirens. There they pushed him into a kind of gigantic, turning oven, for taking brain scans. Three days later he was back home.

"All that happened was that I wasn't allowed to smoke or drink anymore. Well, three glasses of wine a day, but that makes you more or less a teetotaler. The left-hand side of my body is still a little numb, and I'm almost always giddy when I walk. Perhaps it will pass eventually; but as you get older, things usually don't pass. That's why I use a walking stick now. I can do without it, but I feel safer with one."

"Why did you suddenly have that hemorrhage?"

"I've a hunch about that. Do you remember I used to work on deciphering archaic script? I once published a theory about Etruscan, for which I received an honorary doctorate."

"Yes, Auntie Dol said the other day that you told her to send it back."

"Dol . . ." repeated Onno, and was silent for a moment. "How's Dol?"

"They live on Menorca now."

Onno looked in a melancholy way through the space, which was filling with tourists.

"You probably also know that after that Etruscan thing I turned my attention to the Phaistos disc, but I couldn't crack it. I went into politics to have a private excuse for not being able to work on it anymore. But things didn't work out in politics either, and when Auntie Helga died I didn't know what to do anymore. I wrote to you all about that. I wanted to go away for good—but where? Then I thought: I'm back where I started. Perhaps I won't want to do anything anymore, but you never know for sure. Nothing is final in life, apart from death—as you can see yet again now. So I thought: if ever I want to do anything else, then I must continue where I left off, with that disc. The script had still not been deciphered. Actually, my old notes were the only thing I took with me from Amsterdam, although I could scarcely understand them any longer. And since I had to go somewhere, that settled my destination. Rome. You won't find as much material anywhere else. Maybe in London, but it rains most of the time there."

"Of course!" cried Quinten. "I could have thought of that myself! I only thought of Crete."

Onno looked at Quinten. "Did you want to find me?"

"Yes, of course. Do you think that's crazy?"

Onno looked down. Somehow he must have been groggy from the blow all these years, like a boxer hanging on the ropes and being constantly pounded by his opponent, even though the referee with his bow tie occasionally stepped between them. He hadn't really admitted the thought of Quinten to himself. Since Quinten's birth he had told himself that though the boy might be physically the son of himself and Ada, he'd actually been Max and Sophia's son from day one. What a mistake! What a dreadful lie! It was as though from minute to minute more and more crusts were falling off him, as they did off a *croûte* emerging from the oven.

"No, I don't think it's crazy." He looked at him again. "Did you visit Hans Giltay Veth?"

"Of course. But I wasn't any the wiser for that."

Onno was silent for a moment—but then he forced himself to say: "Do you forgive me, Quinten?"

Quinten looked straight at him with his azure eyes. "There's nothing to forgive."

It was as though Onno were sitting opposite his father—as though his son were his superior, and he could raise no objections.

"I was telling you what may have been the reason for my hemorrhage," he continued. "Those linguistic things were lying around in my room and I never looked at them again. But one morning, about eighteen months ago, I went to the market in the square around the corner from my place to get something to eat. I bought a piece of San Pietro, sunfish, I remember exactly; I can remember the fishwife wrapping it in a newspaper with her swollen red hands. I hadn't read a newspaper since I'd left Holland, but as I was unwrapping the fish at home, I suddenly saw my own name—spelled as *Qiuts*. When you're famous later and in the paper, you'll also notice that: it's as though the letters of your name jump off the page at you. The report was about my former rival Pellegrini, who was a professor here in Rome and had never been convinced by my Etruscan theory. In the past he had even written letters to Uppsala to block my honorary doctorate, as I heard from the vice-chancellor there. And I now read that in his old age he had been visiting his son's new country house in Tuscany, somewhere near Arezzo, and was walking through the garden when he suddenly fell into a hole in the ground. And what do you think? He'd landed in an Etruscan burial chamber. He had broken his hip, but the first thing he saw inscribed on a stela was a new *bilingue*—the same text in two languages, in this case Etruscan and Phoenician. From this it emerged that *il professore islandese Qiuts* had gotten it all wrong in any case. That meant there was virtually nothing of my life left."

"Except for me, that is."

"Yes," said Onno, looking away. "Except for you, of course. But nothing else. And I also knew that no one in the field would take me seriously again if I came up with a solution to the Phaistos disc. So I threw away all my notes, hundreds of pages, the work of years. What shocked me most perhaps was a remark of Pellegrini's. When the journalist asked him how on earth he had contrived to fall into that chamber of all chambers, the old villain said, 'A question of talent.' He was right. I had no talent. The following day there was that incident in my bedroom."

"In your bedroom? You just said it happened in the street."

"That's what *thalamus* means: 'bedroom,' 'bed,' 'marriage bed.' "

Quinten looked at the dazzling egg: it had left the fresco, sunk slightly, and moved right, toward a chapel with a terracotta-colored Annunciation. The building had become crowded, but it was still just as quiet, as though the sound of the voices was being sucked like smoke through the opening at the top of the cupola.

Quinten sighed deeply. His father had been spared few things, and much should be forgiven him. Was that the same with everyone? Was that how life was? If everything finally came to nothing, what was the point of it? So was something like that waiting for him? The thought seemed ridiculous to him. Of course not! He didn't know what he was going to do, but once he had made a decision, then he would see it through to the end—nothing and no one would stop him: that was absolutely one hundred percent certain.

"Aren't you frightened that it'll happen again?"

"A stroke?" Onno shrugged his shoulders. "If it happens it happens. I'm not so worried about my body—I've always felt as if it belonged to someone else. A kind of pet." He glanced upward, at the disc of light through which Edgar had disappeared.

"And what do you do all day long?"

"Nothing. Sleep. Make notes. Think a bit. But everything I think is just as awful." He looked at Quinten. "I don't exist anymore, Quinten. I once read a story about a woman without a shadow, but I'm a shadow without a man."

That was it. Quinten could scarcely imagine it was the same man sitting there who in the past, in answer to the same question, would have shaken his index finger above his head like a prophet and cried, "I'm devoting myself to the spirit: the call of the abyss!" He wanted to ask him about the raven, which had just flown off through that blue pupil, but at the same moment Onno too opened his mouth. Quinten restrained himself and knew what was coming next.

"Is Max in Rome too?"

Quinten did not answer, but looked straight at him.

"Why aren't you saying anything?"

With a shiver, Quinten saw that Max's death was now getting through to his father even without words, like water trickling through rock.

"When?" Onno stammered finally.

"A few months ago."

"How?"

"Hit by a meteorite."

Without saying anything, Onno stared through the whispering space. Was it perhaps this news, the possibility of this news, from which he had fled four years ago, unable to bear that too? But now it sank in like a meal that he had eaten—perhaps because he had regained Quinten in place of Max? After a minute he took a deep breath and said: "Him too."

"What do you mean 'Him too'?"

"Lack of talent."

That evening in the youth hostel, unable to get to sleep, Quinten kept seeing a drawing from a book that he had once been given by Max for his birthday: one moment it looked like the outline of a vase, the next like the profiles of two faces looking at each other: space and matter were constantly changing places, matter became space, space matter. When he finally fell asleep, his father's face had disappeared, and his own too—only what was between them remained: that vase, filled with liquid air, blue water close to absolute zero . . .

54

The Stones of Rome

The following morning Quinten went to the address that Onno had given him. The Via del Pellegrino was a tall, narrow, winding street that led into the Campo dei Fiori, a large square where there was a market. In the corner near a café there was a large heap of rubbish, but it wasn't a slum; there were orange and red plastered housefronts, lots of shops with secondhand furniture alternating with displays of plastic kitchen equipment, a piano repair workshop, a small grocer's.

Opposite a shop selling clocks there was a covered passage, hung with mirrors in gold frames; flanked by two ancient weatherbeaten columns, the greater part of which must be in the ground, the gateway led to an intimate courtyard, with plants in large pots and parked scooters and motorbikes around it. Under an array of drying laundry, a carpenter was at work; from the open windows came the sound of voices and music. Quinten took it all in, wide-eyed. So this was the point on the globe that he had been looking for all those years and which had been here all the time. Now that he was here, he found it incomprehensible that he had not known before that here was where he should have gone.

Via the outside staircase that his father had described to him he reached a very drafty stairwell, filled with the noise of playing children, constantly interrupted by mothers calling out "Paolo!" or "Giorgio!" at intervals. On the top floor the door to his father's room was half open. He stood shyly on the threshold.

"Dad?"

"*Entrez!*"

Onno was leaning forward at a sink brushing his teeth, his torso bare. His long hair was loose, his beard disheveled: it was now even more obvious how much weight he had put on.

"Good morning," he said into the small shaving mirror, with white tooth paste foam on his lips. "I'd like to say make yourself comfortable, but you'll find that a problem here."

The disorder came as no surprise to Quinten. The bed also served as a wardrobe; undefined rubbish bulged out of cardboard boxes; the chaos around a gas ring in the corner of the room scarcely suggested a kitchen. Nowhere was there a telephone or a radio, let alone a television. He glanced out the attic window above the desk. A rippling sea of rust-brown tiles, television aerials, church towers silhouetted against the deep blue sky. In the distance he could just see the gigantic angel on the top of the Castel Sant'Angelo, on the other side of the Tiber. The windowsill was covered in a thick layer of bird droppings.

"What a mess it is in here. Shall I tidy up?"

"There's no point. But go ahead and throw everything away."

They said no more about Max. While Onno told him about Edgar, who had kept him company in recent weeks, Quinten cleared the table, filled two waste-disposal bags with rubbish, and gathered up the dirty clothes that were lying everywhere.

"Why did you call him Edgar?"

"After Edgar Allan Poe, of course. He wrote a famous poem called 'The Raven.'" He stood up, looked in the round mirror that hung on a nail against the wall, and said: "'*Other friends have flown before—on the morrow* he *will leave me as my Hopes have flown before.*' Then the bird said, '*Nevermore.*' But he did leave me and I've got a feeling that he won't be back. Perhaps he was frightened by the Pantheon. But I've already come to terms with it, because I have you back in his place." And in exchange for Max, he thought, but he kept that to himself.

Each felt the other's uncertainty about the new situation, but neither could find words to talk about it. They took the washing to the laundrette, a couple of houses along, and sat down on the café terrace on the corner. In the middle of the crowded, rectangular square stood a somber statue of a monk with his cowl covering his head.

"Who's that?" asked Quinten.

"Giordiano Bruno."

Quinten nodded. "Who made the universe infinite."

"Did Max tell you that?"

"No, Mr. Verloren van Themaat."

"And you remembered that."

"Yes, why not? I hardly ever forget anything."

Onno looked at the statue for a while, lost in thought.

"That's the spot where they burned him as a heretic." He pointed with his stick at the crowd between the stalls. "Do you know what all that is? All that is also what it is not."

"I don't understand."

"The world will now always also be the Max-less world."

Quinten knew that Max had meant more to his father than to him, that long ago there had been a friendship between them of a kind that he had never had or would ever have with anyone. He looked at his father out of the corner of his eye. His head had sunk slightly forward; there was something elusive about the closeness of the hairy face with the sunglasses, as if at the same time it were too far away to reach.

The waiter came out of the café and greeted Onno like an old acquaintance, calling him "Signor Enrico." As he wiped the tabletop with a damp cloth, he glanced at Quinten with slightly raised eyebrows.

"This is my son, Mauro," said Onno in Italian. "Quintilio."

Mauro shook hands with him, without the ironic expression disappearing from his face. It was clear that he only half believed it; the old eccentric had obviously taken up with a rent boy, on the Via Appia—but he didn't begrudge him that.

"Everyone knows me here as Mr. Enrico," said Onno, when Mauro had gone inside. "Enrico Delius," with a diffident note in his voice. "They think I'm an Austrian from the Tyrol."

Quinten nodded again with an expression that seemed to say that it was all quite natural. "That Mauro gave me a rather funny look." He told his father about the advances made to him in Venice and Florence, and Onno asked:

"Didn't you leave some great love behind in Holland?"

"No," said Quinten curtly.

That didn't exist for him, and he didn't want to talk about it. Onno was about to say that he should keep it that way, since every love ended inexorably in heartbreak; but he decided not to encumber Quinten with his own gloom. That belonged not to the beginning but to the end of a life. They sat in silence and looked at the swarming activity in the market.

When the waiter put down caffè latte and croissants at their table, Onno said: "I suddenly fancy rissoles again."

"I like these much better. If only Granny could see us sitting down to breakfast like this."

"Have you already let her know that we've met?"

"No. I haven't written at all yet."

"Perhaps you should keep it to yourself for now."

"Why?"

"I don't know . . . otherwise your uncles and aunts will get to hear of it, and I'm not sure I want that yet."

Quinten nodded. He was also glad to be able to share a secret with his father.

Onno rested his elbows on his knees and dipped his bread in the coffee. He still felt at a loss, but suddenly he asked: "What would you say to moving in with me, Quinten? I don't know how long you plan to stay in Rome, but it's ridiculous being stuck in a hotel somewhere when you can live with me, isn't it?" When Quinten looked up in astonishment, he went on: "Let's buy a camp bed. You can pick up your things, and then that problem's solved."

A broad smile appeared on Quinten's face. This was it at last: he was living with his father!

He had never been with Onno for so long at a stretch before. Now they went into town together every day. Entering St. Peter's Square for the first time, Quinten was struck by the obelisk in the center of Bernini's embracing colonnades, more than by the awe-inspiring front of the basilica, which also obeyed the Pantheon principle.

"Well, what do you make of that?" said Onno. "An Egyptian obelisk in the heart of Christendom. This is where they crucified Peter upside down, in the circus of Nero. You find obelisks everywhere in Rome."

"Perhaps," said Quinten, "that might be connected with the Egyptian exile that Moses liberated the Jews from."

"Who can say?" said Onno, laughing. "But that connection can only be grasped with your inimitable way of thinking."

Quinten looked at the long shadow cast by the obelisk, like a sundial, and then at the sides without inscriptions. "There's nothing on them. There should be something written on them."

Onno focused his eyes on the smooth granite, pointed at the top with his stick, and then a little lower with each word:

" *'Paut neteroe her resch sep sen ini Asar sa Heroe men ab maä kheroe sa Ast auau Asar.'* That means—"

"I don't want to know. It sounds much too beautiful for that."

Everything became new again for Onno, too. In the past he had been in Rome repeatedly—the last time as a minister of state: preceded by police outriders with blaring sirens, a government car had borne him straight through all the red lights from the airport to the Quirinal; but since he had been living there, he had not left his own district.

In the colossal basilica he helped Quinten translate the gigantic words that stood in a circle in the cupola above the high altar:

TV ES PETRVS ET SVPER HANC PETRAM
AEDIFICABO ECCLESIAM MEAM

"At first sight it seems to say: 'Thou art Peter and on this Peter I shall build my church.' But you need to know that *petra* is a Greek word meaning 'rock.' Peter's grave is supposed to be under this altar, and hence the church is built on it—not only this building, but the Catholic Church as a whole. The popes regard themselves as his successors."

They visited the Vatican museums and the precious shrine of the Sistine Chapel, where they were allowed to talk only in whispers but where the cardinals behind their Golden Wall of course screamed and shouted when they had to elect a new pope from among their number, at least to the extent that they had not nodded off to sleep dribbling. On seeing Michelangelo's *Creation of Adam*, which had emerged in bright colors from the dark-brown candle smoke of ages, Onno suddenly remembered the neon Communist version on the *Rampa* in Havana eighteen years before, when everything had begun. But he did not mention that.

"Do you think Adam had a navel?" asked Quinten, as they came back out. "He didn't have a mother, did he?"

"It's just as well you're not a Dutch vicar. They've branded each other as heretics on that kind of issue for centuries."

Quinten also took him to all kinds of places where he had never been, such as the Aventine, "to look through the keyhole." In a quiet district, on the edge of the hill that dropped steeply down to the Tiber, there was an oblong excrescence from the street with walls on three sides, shaded by cypresses and palms. The Piazza dei Cavalieri di Malta could scarcely be called a square; the space was more like an unfinished temple.

There was no one there, and Quinten was immediately seized by a shudder, whose origin he knew: the Citadel. Onno saw that something was preoccupying him, but did not ask him about it; Quinten simply said that it was a design of Piranesi's. While Onno sat down on a stone bench to allow his dizziness to pass a little, Quinten started climbing along the wall, which was twelve or fifteen feet high, glancing at his compass. On the long southern side and the shorter western side it was interrupted by obelisks, stelae, plaquettes, and mysterious ornaments in such a strange kind of style, or nonstyle, that he could scarcely believe his eyes. Lyres, globes, points, helmets, crosses, swords, wings, panpipes. Set in the northern side, the wall was the gateway to the monastery of the Knights of Malta, a broad theatrical structure that at first sight reminded him of Palladio, but on second sight was as odd as the other constructions, with its Manneristic ornaments, blind alcoves like windows, and the row of great urns on the roof.

The sacred domain exuded the atmosphere of the *Carceri,* which Mr. Themaat had shown him, Piranesi's endless dungeons, but at the same time that of his dream—and all of it now tightly compressed in an oblong pattern. He bent down and looked through the famous keyhole of the gate. In the distance, exactly along the axis of a long, carefully trimmed hedge of laurel trees, one could see the cupola of St. Peter's. Yes, of course. For many people that was "the center of the world," but not for him.

He was about to wave to his father, but when he saw him sitting there on the other side with his stick, like a homeless alcoholic who ate out of trash cans, he checked himself. The abandoned square lay in the subdued light of the spring sun. Destiny had finally brought them together, but now it had happened, it was as if he had more contact with the stones of Rome than with his father. Even in the evenings in the Via del Pellegrino they said little, and never spoke about the past; all of that was somehow on the other side of a barrier that neither of them wanted to surmount. And yet he knew for certain that they had to stay together, like two companions who were at each other's mercy.

They looked at each other. There was something remorseless about that boy, thought Onno. Something inhuman. A touch of interstellar coldness.

On the Piazza Venezia a policeman in a white helmet was directing the traffic with such fascinatingly immaculate body language that Onno was reminded of his theory of the physicality of power. But so as not to let himself be intimidated, he himself raised his gnarled stick in the air at the edge of the pavement and, laughing all the while, they made their way to the other side through the stream of speeding cars, as if through a trumpeting, stampeding herd of elephants. A few minutes later they had descended into the silent pit of the past.

The Forum Romanum, the extended strip of white and reddish-brown ruins, fragments, and pieces, weeds, pillars broken in two, boulders, holes, remains of walls, all crushed by the flat hand of time, presented Onno with a gloomy image of his own life—but it had an entirely different effect on Quinten. The area caused a strange agitation in him, such as other boys might feel at an air show, when formations of jet fighters swooped low overhead. Again it reminded him of the Citadel, but now of what remained in his memory after he awoke. He was getting close to something; somewhere, something was waiting for him! But where? What was it? By the edge of the open cellar the traffic roared along the Via dei Fori Imperiali; on the other side rose the somber, threatening slope of the Palatine, where the imperial palaces had stood; the sun revolved around the column of Phocas and for hour after hour they wandered through the delicate ruins.

After the frothy lightness of Venice, which floated like a cork on the water, and after the massive reticence of Florence, the things here were so heavy that they had sunk many feet deep into the ground. As he listened to Onno, with the guidebook of the Istituto Poligrafico dello Stato in his left hand, the index finger of his right hand on the page, the stones ordered themselves before Quinten's eyes, tugging and shifting. Comitium. Regia. An ugly, badly proportioned brick building, which obscured the triumphal arch of Septimus Serverus and definitely needed clearing away, suddenly turned out to be the Curia, the Roman senate; according to the guidebook, the original bronze doors were in the basilica of the Lateran.

"What's the Lateran?" he asked.

"In the Middle Ages the popes lived there, before they moved to the Vatican."

"We have to go there too."

"Of course," said Onno. "Anything you say. It's not far—over there, behind the Colosseum. The original palace no longer exists, though."

With each step they took along the great stones of the Via Sacra, the Holy Way, the Forum was in a different century. Every broken column, Onno told him, every fragment of brickwork, every piece of marble that lay in the sun on the dry grass had been constantly pushed backward and forward in time in thousands of publications, until it had been assigned its place in history: the beginning of the millennium, third century A.D., sixth century B.C., Renaissance, medieval. A monstrous ruin, which Quinten had taken for something from the Second World War, suddenly turned out to be the basilica of Maxentrus. The three remaining columns of the temple of Vespasian, with a fragment of architrave still on them: Onno pointed to it with his hand, and said it was the perfect logo for classical antiquity. The round temple of Vesta cut vertically in two and half blown away by time. The triumphal arch of Titus, which spanned the Via Sacra at its highest point, opposite the Colosseum.

Onno pointed out to Quinten a frieze in the tunnel of the arch, which depicted the return of Titus's triumphant troops from Jerusalem, after the conquest of the city in A.D. 70. Titus was the son of the emperor Vespasian, whom he succeeded a few years later. Despite the damage, the relief was a masterly depiction of the soldiers, marching into the Forum along the same street where they were now standing, full of movement and as if the music and hurrahs could still be heard, above their heads the trophies from the destroyed Jewish temple: the silver trumpets, the golden table for the shewbread, the golden, seven-branched candelabra.

"What's shewbread?"

"A sacrifice," said Onno. "Twelve round unleavened loaves, in two piles of six. They were replaced every Sabbath and the old ones were then eaten by the priests. You find the same thing in Christianity in a different form. Christ said that he was holy bread himself."

"Really? Did he say he was made of bread? Then I suppose he had to be eaten too?"

"That's right. It's still the climax of the Catholic mass."

"But then the Catholics are cannibals!"

"That's what your grandfather always said, but cannibals eat people, while the Catholics regard themselves as God-eaters."

"Perhaps it's something like that with cannibals too."

"Quite possibly. But because the Catholics ultimately only eat bread, not people, they're more like sublimated cannibals—or perhaps one should say transubstantiated cannibals. The strange thing, though, is that you don't find that magic eating-of-the-god figure in Judaism. That seems to derive from Egypt, from the cult of Osiris, who by the way also rose from the dead. In the temple of Jerusalem the only other sacrifices were lambs, and Christ said that he was also a sacrificial lamb. Besides that, he compares his own body with the temple itself."

"The building obviously made a big impression."

"You could say that."

If the Pantheon was an image of the cosmos, thought Quinten, the temple of Jerusalem was obviously an image of man. Together they were everything.

"And the candelabra?"

"That was the Jews' holiest object. The menorah. God told Moses personally how it should be made."

"And the Romans simply took it away with them?"

"As you can see. Though it's not quite accurately depicted here, but for some reason Israel chose this version as its state symbol."

Quinten looked at the thing, which was almost the same height as he was. "Where is it now?"

"No one knows. Probably stolen, by the Vandals in the fifth century. They were a Germanic tribe that had founded a state of its own in North Africa. That's where our word *vandals* comes from." As he said it, he suddenly felt a great surge of weariness.

Separate capitals, flagstones, worn steps, inscriptions, caves ... wildcats everywhere, stalking each other. Once this had been the center of the world, thought Quinten, to which all roads led, not only Titus's road from Jerusalem, but now his own from Westerbork too—but that was something different than the *center* of the world. Or not? He stopped on the other side of the Forum by the "black stone," Lapis Niger.

A secret! No one knew the meaning of that square block of marble down there in a hollow, as if in a navel. According to his guidebook, it might be connected with the overthrow of Etruscan domination. Perhaps it was a grave: the grave of Romulus, the mythical first king, from the eighth century B.C. The spot had been sacred since the time of Julius Caesar. He descended a few steps, further into the past with each step, and knelt down by a weathered oblong stone beneath the Lapis Niger, in which there were remnants of archaic inscriptions. He wanted to ask his father if he could read them, but Onno had stayed at the top.

"Dad?" he shouted. "Come over here. What does it say?"

Onno looked down at him, wiping his brow with a sleeve. "Probably some ritual law or other. It's very early Latin, but almost unreadable. Just that whoever defiles that spot is cursed. So come on up quickly."

"Why can't you come down for a moment?"

"I'm aware that you've inherited it from me, Quinten, but I don't want anything to do with writing. You must understand that. Let's go. I'm dizzy."

The following day, Whitsunday, the weather changed. Dark purple clouds drifted quickly over the city and in the distance there was now a faint rumbling. After breakfast at Mauro's, Quinten wanted to go immediately to San Pietro in Vincoli, rushing as though he had an appointment for which he must not be late. The medieval church stood on the site of the Roman prefecture, where Peter and Paul had been chained, on a silent, enclosed square not far from the Forum; the black entrance reminded him of a mousehole.

Although there was no service in progress, the pews were full of people absorbed in prayer. He looked around in the semidarkness—and in the right-hand aisle he suddenly discovered the figure with whom he had had an appointment for so long. Speechless, he looked at the remnant that remained after Michelangelo had carved away the superfluous marble: the horned *Moses,* which he knew so well from the photograph in Theo Kern's studio fastened to a beam with a drawing pin, full of strength and much more colossal than he had imagined, the expression on his face much more furious, his veined hand clawing agitatedly at his beard. At a stand with a telephone on it a boy and girl stood with their ears almost touching, the receiver between them, and looked at the seething figure.

"He's bloody angry," said Quinten softly.

Onno had to laugh. " 'Wrathful,' it's called, and he had reason to be."

"Why?"

Onno looked at him with something like alarm. "Do you know anything about the Bible?"

"Only a bit. Almost nothing about the Old Testament."

"Doesn't matter. That's what your father's there for, he knows it by heart—at least, he used to, thousands of hours of Bible reading by my father and at school and at catechism class made sure of that. You obviously know at any rate that Moses led the Jewish people out of exile in Egypt. After that the refugees wandered through the desert for forty years, looking for the promised land. At the very beginning of that period, Jahweh had given him all sorts of instructions on Mount Horeb—like for example about that seven-branched candelabra that you saw yesterday on the triumphal arch of Titus. Finally he was given—" Suddenly there was a flash of light in the church, followed immediately by a loud, violent clap of thunder, which rumbled away over the city like an iron ball as big as the cupola of the Pantheon. Onno looked at Quinten in astonishment and said, "That's very appropriate."

Quinten didn't seem to understand what he meant. "What was he given finally?"

"Finally he was given the Ten Commandments, which Jahweh had written on two stone tablets with his own finger. Come on, you've heard of the Ten Commandments, I hope? The Decalogue?"

"Of course. 'Thou shalt not kill.' "

"That's immediately an incorrect, Christian translation. 'Thou shalt not murder' is what it says: *lo tirtsach*. Killing is allowed, under certain circumstances. But anyway, he was gone for more than a month. The Jews thought something had happened to him and had started worshiping a golden calf instead of Jahweh. It made Moses so furious that he dashed the stones to pieces. That's the moment that Michelangelo depicted."

Quinten looked at the tablets under Moses' arm, which he had always taken to be folders, like the ones in which Theo Kern kept his drawings.

"And then?"

"Well then, of course, he had to go back up again, with two new tablets, which he had to pay for himself this time. If I remember correctly, it's not completely clear in the Bible whether God wrote the Ten Commandments the second time himself or whether he simply dictated them. Let's assume he did that. If I were a writer, I wouldn't feel like doing the same thing twice."

"And those funny horns on his head? What do they mean?"

"Another mistranslation."

"Another mistranslation?"

"When he came down from the mountain the second time, his face shone so terribly, because he'd been speaking with God, that he had to wear a veil. But the Hebrew word for *shining* can also be translated as *horned,* except that that doesn't make sense."

Quinten nodded thoughtfully and looked at the statue. "So we really ought to get rid of those horns."

Onno looked at him in alarm. "There's a look in your eyes that says you're capable of doing that."

"Yes, why not? It's a linguistic error, isn't it?"

"But it's written in marble."

Quinten felt that everything was gradually coming together, but what was it? When he looked up at that violent marble figure, he felt his father's eyes focused on him. "Why are you looking at me like that?"

"Do you believe in God, Quinten?"

"Never thought about it. What about you?"

"Not since I thought about it."

"How old were you when you started thinking about it?"

"About the same age as you are now." A scene of thirty-five years previously appeared before Onno's eyes, in his parents' house in the front room, with the Authorized Version on the stand. After he had put on his Sunday clothes, he had solemnly informed his father that he had hesitated for a long time between the sentence "I don't believe that God exists" and the sentence "I believe that God does not exist"—and that he, as a believer, had been converted to the second sentence. His father's flashing eyes, his weeping mother ... but since as an unbeliever he had opted for the first sentence, he no longer wanted to remember that past.

"And what's next on your agenda?" he asked.

The thunderclap of a moment ago had obviously been both the beginning and the end of the storm. The sun began breaking through, and now and then a burst of bright light swept through the church.

"We were going to the Lateran, weren't we?"

Onno looked at him for a few seconds. "What on earth are you looking for, lad?"

Quinten shrugged his shoulders. "Nothing. I'm just a tourist."

55

The Spot

When he got out of the taxi on the Piazza San Giovanni in Laterano ten minutes later, Quinten could not believe his eyes. Standing next to the cathedral, by the octagonal baptistry of Constantine, he looked across the imposing square with his hair waving in the wind. There it was! Piranesi's framed etching, which had stood on the floor against the bookshelf in Mr. Themaat's place! He might have known, but he hadn't thought for a moment that he would actually find it here: the towering obelisk, standing like a rocket about to be launched to the moon; a hundred yards farther on, that two-story Renaissance building, in which the Sancta Sanctorum had been incorporated, the private chapel of the medieval popes, and the Holy Stairs from the praetorium of Pontius Pilate in Jerusalem. The sandy plain had given way to asphalt, across which the traffic roared, but with its gray fragments of clouds, alternating with patches of blue, even the sky looked as it did on the print.

Onno looked up at the obelisk. He had never been here before either; with his head right back, stroking his beard thoughtfully, he peered at the hieroglyphics.

"Can you read them?"

"I'm a bit rusty, I see. It looks like a ceremonial treatise on the eternal life of Pharaoh Thutmoses the Third."

"Another Moses then."

"But a few hundred years older than the Jewish one. This," he said, pointing with his index finger, "is definitely the oldest artistic monument on European soil. I mean, approximately between three and a half and four thousand years old."

Onno explained to him that Moses was an Egyptian name which meant "child," "son." Because the pharaoh had all newborn Jewish males murdered, Moses' mother had put her baby in a rush basket among the reeds of the Nile; it was made of papyrus stalks, since crocodiles had an aversion to papyrus. Moses' sister saw him being found by the pharaoh's daughter, and then told the princess that she knew of a good wet nurse for the foundling—namely, her mother. And so it came to pass. The princess called the child "Child," so that, without anyone knowing, Moses was brought up by his own mother. More than a thousand years later, said Onno, as a mirror image of those events, Mary and Joseph fled with their son to Egypt of all places in order to escape Herod's murder of the innocents in Bethlehem—and just as Moses' foster mother was actually his real mother, so Jesus' lawful father was not his true father.

"In those circles, family relationships are often rather complicated."

"The Annunciation." Quinten nodded.

"As you say. So Thutmoses means 'child of the God Thoth.' He was the inventor of writing."

"You look as though you really believe that."

Onno shrugged his shoulders.

"An ex-cryptographer has to have a God too, doesn't he? And anyway, what does 'really believe' mean? Do you know that story about Niels Bohr, the great physicist? Max told it to me once. Another great physicist, Wolfgang Pauli or some such person, once visited Bohr in his country house and saw that he had nailed an horseshoe above his front door. 'Professor!' he said. 'You? A horseshoe? Do you believe in that?' To which Bohr said, 'Of course not. But do you know, Pauli, they say it helps even if you *don't* believe in it.' " He laughed, and Quinten could see that it was partly also because he was thinking of the way that Max had told him that anecdote. "By the way, did you know, child of mine, that the word *obelisk* was the first word that you could speak? There at the grave of that horse, at Groot Rechteren."

"Deep Thought Sunstar," said Quinten, lost in thought. He couldn't remember it, but the sudden emergence of the castle here in the square, from his father's mouth, gave him the same kind of feeling as when he drank a glass of hot milk on a winter's day. "Sometimes," he said, as they walked toward the side entrance of the cathedral, "I have the feeling that the world is very complicated, but that there's something behind it that is very simple and at the same time incomprehensible."

"Such as?"

"I don't know . . . a sphere. Or a point."

Onno glanced at him from the side. "Are you talking about stories, like the one about Moses, or about reality?"

"Is there so much difference?"

Perhaps a story was precisely the complete opposite of reality, thought Onno; but he had the feeling that he should not confuse Quinten with that.

"And that sphere, or that point, does that give reality a meaning?"

"Meaning? What do you mean by that?"

Onno said nothing. The thought that anything could give a meaning to the world was alien to him. It was there, but it was absurd that it was there. It might just as well not have been there. Quinten's sphere reminded him of that original, shining sphere, which had been polished in Los Alamos by young soldiers, who went out dancing with their girls in the evening. What was the relation between the smoldering chaos in Hiroshima and that Platonic body? One could not be understood with the aid of the other, though it emerged from it. How could a human being be understood from a fertilized ovum? How could anything be understood?

Reality wasn't a syllogism like "Socrates is a man—all men are mortal—hence Socrates is mortal," but more like "Helga is a human being—all telephone booths have been vandalized—hence Helga must die." Or like: "Hitler is a human being—all Jews are animals—hence all Jews must die." That incomprehensible logic, which controlled everything, good and bad and neutral, Quinten must find for himself. He didn't consider it his job to cloud the purity of the boy. Someone who didn't even know what "meaning" meant must keep that pristine sense for as long as possible.

A mass was being celebrated in the crowded archbasilica—"mother and head of all churches in the city and the world"—by a cardinal in purple; they walked forward on tiptoe. The cold baroque interior disappointed Quinten; there was as little left of the medieval building from the time of the emperor Constantine as of the old papal palace. Only the high altar with its Gothic canopy did he find beautiful and mysterious. At the top of the slender cage on posts, behind bars, were statues of Peter and Paul; their heads were supposed to be buried beneath it. He looked up from his guidebook.

"Were they friends, those two?" he whispered.

"Not that I know of. When you're occupied with things like they were, I don't think there's room for friendship. In the religion business, I expect it's the same as in politics."

Quinten again focused on the closed, painted part of the ciborium, where the relics were housed. He seemed to see the two skulls already lying there. "I'd like to take a look in there."

"You won't be able to do that, my friend."

There was a flash: someone took a photo of the striking pair, the tramp with the beautiful boy. With panic in his eyes, Onno turned around. A Japanese girl with a black raincap on her head; she was already walking on, as though it was allowed simply to appropriate someone's image. A little later a sexton stopped her and pointed to her camera with the shake of his head.

"Why does it make you jump like that, Dad?"

Onno made a helpless gesture. "I'm sorry, a stupid reflex. Any Dutch scandal sheet would have gladly given a thousand guilders for that photo. You get those kinds of reactions when you've hidden away from everybody for years."

"But it's not like that anymore, is it?"

"No, Quinten, not anymore. But what it's really like, I don't honestly know. We'll see." He didn't want to think about it; he would have preferred to spend his days like this forever, with Quinten in the Eternal City. "Where are we going now?"

"To the other side."

The gigantic bronze doors of the Roman Curia, which now formed the central entrance, were closed; they emerged outside through a side door. Quinten turned around for a moment and looked up. Sharply outlined against the sky, above the eaves of the basilica, a row of enormous figures stood gesticulating excitedly, as though something extraordinary were about to happen.

They crossed the busy, windy square diagonally and Quinten stopped on the terrace of the building containing the Sancta Sanctorum and looked in through the open doors. Straight ahead of him, on the other side of a high doorway, were the Holy Stairs, the Scala Santa.

A shiver went through him. With the din of the traffic behind him, he looked into a world where it was as quiet as in an aquarium. On the slowly ascending steps, less than nine feet wide, ten or twelve men and women were kneeling, praying with their heads bowed, their backs and the soles of their shoes facing him. They were as stationary as people on an escalator, but the escalator was not moving, it was standing still; now and then someone made his way laboriously up to the next step. The walls and the semicircular ceiling were covered with pious frescoes; the architect had constructed the stairwell in such a perspective that it seemed as though it were a long, horizontal corridor to the other side, with the navel of a crucified Christ at the vanishing point. The stairs were covered with wood, but small cracks revealed the marble, over which the accused was supposed to have walked.

"Now you're the one who looks as if you're being touched by transcendence," said Onno ironically, as they went inside. "Don't tell me that you really believe that staircase comes from Pilate's Citadel Antonia."

The mention of the word *Citadel*, at this moment, gave Quinten a slight jolt. "Like those people there? Not at all. Or, rather, I don't bother to ask myself if it's genuine or not. But I don't know ..." he said, and looked around. "I have the feeling that there's a story being told here."

He bought a brochure on the building from an ancient priest at a table. As he put down his money, a second old priest tapped hard with a hundred-lire coin against the glass of a ticket office and made an inexorable gesture toward a man who was planning to visit the sanctuary in shorts. He also had an emblem of a white heart with the letters JESU XPI PASSIO, crowned by a cross on the chest of his black habit.

"You mean," said Onno in a muffled voice, as they gradually ascended the staircase and stopped at an appropriate distance, "the story about 'What is truth?', washing one's hands in innocence, 'Ecce homo' and all that?"

Quinten knew that story only vaguely. He breathed in, in order to say something, stopped, and shook his head—it was as though he were not clear himself what he meant.

"I don't know, leave it. In any case a story that those people are part of too," he said, nodding at the kneeling people, "who are praying and crawling upward, toward that ypsilon."

"Ypsilon?"

"The crucified Christ on that fresco at the end. He's in the shape of a Y, isn't he?"

"Good God," said Onno. "Pythagoras's letter." He looked at Quinten appreciatively. "Well seen. Do you know that cross is also on the ceremonial habit of a bishop? Perhaps you've made a discovery."

Quinten had not been listening to him. "I have the feeling that this building itself is telling a story in some way."

"You're talking in riddles. But perhaps that's appropriate here."

"Let me read this first."

By a pillar Quinten sat down on the marble floor and opened the brochure, but immediately a broken voice told him to get up. A second priest, just as old and dressed in black like the other, was sitting on a straight wooden chair in the middle of the vestibule and moved a white index finger reproachfully back and forth. While Onno was amazed at the frenzied mood that had suddenly taken hold of Quinten, he went and looked at the statues and painting in the entrance. Meanwhile Quinten read the short text, which was concluded with twenty-eight prayers, one for each step.

After a few minutes he looked up. "Dad?"

"Yes?"

"I know all about it."

"That's a lot."

"It's like this: according to a medieval legend, that staircase was brought to the Lateran by the empress Helena from Jerusalem. She was the mother of Constantine."

"I know. He was married to a certain Fausta—that pious Christian emperor subsequently had her murdered." He looked at Quinten with a crooked smile.

"When the popes returned from exile in Avignon, in the fourteenth century, the palace was largely gutted and then they took the Vatican as their headquarters. In the sixteenth century Sixtus V had the Lateran demolished, except for the papal chapel, up there. The architect," he said, and looked in the brochure, "Domenico Fontana, then moved the staircase to here. For some reason or other it happened at night, by torchlight."

"It obviously couldn't bear the light of day."

"The steps were laid from top to bottom, otherwise the workers would have had to stand on them."

"It seems right to me."

With a wave of his arm Quinten looked around him. "Just imagine: everything gone, that enormous palace, where all those popes lived for a thousand years—all that's left is that chapel with this staircase here. The building has been put around it like a shell."

"What's so strange about that? The whole of Rome is made like that."

"But what about those crawling people? It isn't just a kind of museum, like everywhere else, is it? There's something going on here, isn't there? It's just as though it's a stage up there, on which a mystery play has to be performed. Just look, that window with those bars, under that painting of the crucifixion, which they are heading for. It's like the window of a prison cell. Come on, let's go and have a look."

"Just a moment. You don't really expect me to go up that staircase on my knees?"

"Here at the side there are two ordinary staircases. At the other side too."

While they went up the marble stairway on the left, Onno was pleased by Quinten's enthusiasm. What boy was interested nowadays in anything else except technical things, having fun, and money? He reminded him of himself when he was the same age and how he buried himself in study, which astonished his friends. No, it had never been any different. Boys like Quinten and himself had always been exceptions. But if you were such an exception yourself, it took twenty-five years for it to get through to you that not everyone was exceptional, and that awareness came as a great disappointment—while the nonexceptional people precisely thought that the exceptional ones were constantly arrogantly aware of their exceptional qualities. The opposite was the case. They didn't despise other people; they overestimated them. It was the nonexceptional people who were constantly aware of the exceptional quality of the exceptional one. It was like a misunderstanding between a dog and cat. When a dog was afraid, it put its tail between its legs, but if it was happy, then it wafted the pleasant smell of its backside toward you; but a cat wagged its tail precisely when it was afraid, since its feces stank. The dog wagging its tail jumped forward to play with the cat wagging its tail, who in turn thought that it was being attacked, and the dog got a bloody scratch on its nose—that linguistic confusion gave birth to the irreconcilable enmity between the two of them. Out of the corner of his eye he glanced at Quinten. As they climbed the stairs, his hair billowed like black satin.

While Onno stayed hesitantly on the landing, which the five steps brought him to, Quinten immediately walked on to the point where the central staircase ended, the holy spot. The believers, who were now climbing toward them from below, kept their heads bowed as they muttered, and paid no attention to him. He turned his back on them, bent down, and looked through the bars, which were thicker than a finger and which were in a marble frame.

The Sancta Sanctorum. The transition was even greater than just now from the square to the front entrance—in the dim chapel it was as silent as in a mirror, and the first thing Quinten thought of was the face of his mother in her bed. His heart began pounding. The small space was high and completely square, approximately twenty feet by twenty, exuding an overwhelming sense of everything that was *no longer* there: 160 popes, who had prayed here daily for ten centuries.

It was as though time had disappeared from here. In the middle of the inlaid marble floor, opposite the altar, was a prayer stool. The altar was behind the protruding, raised section of the back wall, which was supported by two porphyry columns. Across the whole width of the frame above the gilded capitals were the letters:

NON●EST●IN●TOTO●SANCTIOR●ORBE●LOCUS

He beckoned his father. "How would you translate that?" he whispered.

"Quinten," said Onno sternly. "You've been to secondary school for five years. You can do that perfectly well."

"There is not," Quinten tried, "at all . . . more sacred . . . world place?"

"Compelling prose. Of course you could also say: 'Nowhere in the world is there a more sacred spot.' Just because those popes were here? That seems slightly exaggerated."

Quinten pointed out to him the great icon, which stood on the altar: a triptych with opened side panels. The scene could scarcely be distinguished in the dim light, but he told his father what he had just read: the image of the most holy savior on the central panel, *acheiropoeton,* had been painted not by a human hand but by an angel. Only the head painted on silk had not been covered by gilded, heavily worked silver, but that head was not the original one; that was underneath. The panel was covered by a semicircular canopy, crowned by two gilded angels.

"Yes, Quinten," said Onno with a laugh. "We're not in Holland here." He put his hand on the bars. "To my taste it's more like a torture chamber here. Look at this, between those turned columns above the altar: there are also two barred windows. Of course from there the holy fathers were watched as they sat praying. And the bottom part of that altar itself is also all bars. Look at those locks."

Quinten looked at the padlocks, which he had not yet noticed. The top one was a gigantic iron thing, a sliding padlock, as large as a loaf—the moment he saw it, he was overcome by alarm. Where was he? Was he dreaming? Was he in his dream? He looked at his father with his eyes wide.

"What's wrong?" asked Onno in alarm. "You've gone as pale as a ghost."

"I don't know . . ." he stammered.

Was that vanished Lateran palace his Citadel? Was he there? Those steps, four times seven steps, that chapel, his mother. . . . In confusion, he turned away from the bars and for the moment met the glance of an old woman, who had mounted the twenty-eighth step, stood up groaning, crossed herself, smiled at him for a moment, and, rubbing one thigh, went to the other staircase.

"Let's go," said Onno. "It's unhealthy here. You have to eat something."

Quinten shook his head. "That's not why . . ." He could not possibly tell his father what was going on inside him, because that was a deep secret. "Perhaps it's not that chapel which is behind bars, perhaps *we're* the ones who are behind bars. . . . He looked around him wide-eyed. "I know for certain that something very strange is going on, I can't say why, but I must and I will get to the bottom of it."

Onno gave him a searching look for a few seconds. Suddenly there was a hard glint in Quinten's eyes. Onno nodded, leaned on his stick, and looked around as though he were searching for something too. His dizziness was more intense than usual; perhaps it was because of the steps.

"I don't know what you're getting at, but something strange has struck me too in the meantime."

"What then?"

"That chapel is called Sancta Sanctorum, isn't it?" And when Quinten nodded, "Precisely, and I don't really understand why."

"Why not?"

"Well, it means Holy of Holies."

"Stands to reason."

"But that expression doesn't occur at all in the Christian religion."

"In which one does it occur, then?"

"Only in Judaism."

56

Biblical Scholarship

"How does it occur there, then?"

"Let's not stand here," said Onno, "where those people can see us."

They walked back. On the left of the Sancta Sanctorum, where there was a Renaissance chapel with two small altars, named after San Silvestro, they sat down in one of the dark-brown choir pews, which occupied the three walls. Onno saw that Quinten could scarcely wait to hear what he had to say; his otherwise gentle face was as taut as a sail in a storm. He could not understand, and it alarmed him. Perhaps he should have kept his observation to himself.

"What's gotten into you suddenly, Quinten?"

"Tell me!"

Amazed that someone should not know such a thing, Onno explained to him that in Judaism the Holy of Holies was a space in the former temple of Jerusalem. That was an oblong complex, consisting of three parts—or, actually, of four. First there was the court, where no Gentiles were allowed, only Jews—that is, Jewish men. There was the burnt-offering altar. The entrance to the actual temple building was flanked by two pillars: Jachin and Boas.

Oblong? Like his mother's bed? Hadn't he talked to Mr. Themaat about that?

"Pillars with names on?" he asked, thinking for a moment of the two columns on the piazzetta in Venice. "Why was that?"

Onno sighed. "Sometimes I amaze myself with my knowledge, but I still don't know everything. But I do know how you can look everything up, and that's a very useful alternative to knowing everything. When you went in," he continued, leaving the pillars for what they were, "you entered the dimly lit sanctum via a doorway—at least if you were a priest; otherwise you weren't allowed in. In that sanctum stood the incense-offering altar and the seven-branched candelabra and the table with the shewbread on it. The back room was in the shape of a cube, with a great curtain, or veil in front of it. Inside it was always completely dark. That was the Holy of Holies. Only the high priest was allowed to enter once a year, on Yom Kippur, the Day of Atonement."

Quinten stretched his back in excitement. "It's like the setup here! Outside on the square there is that obelisk of Thutmoses, so that's the court; then there's a doorway; then the Holy Stairs, so that's the sanctum; and then the Sancta Sanctorum! It isn't a cube, but it is a square."

"That's precisely the odd thing about it," said Onno, grimacing slightly. "In Christianity the Holy of Holies is never anything architectural, as with the Jews; Christians use that concept only symbolically. For example, in the gospels it says that in the temple the veil between the sanctum and the Holy of Holies was rent at the moment that Jesus died—'split open,' it actually says in Greek—and that was explained by saying that Christ through his crucifixion and resurrection had made the Holy of Holies, that is Heaven, permanently accessible to everyone, as a kind of super high priest. For Christians it is never an earthly building."

"And in that Jewish Holy of Holies? What was in that?"

"The ark of the covenant."

A priest shuffling past glanced at them, put a finger to his lips, and disappeared through a small door between the choir stalls.

"What was that?" asked Quinten softly.

With a sigh Onno looked at him and said: "On the one hand I think it's dreadful that young people nowadays know almost nothing anymore; on the other hand I consider you fortunate that you no longer have to carry around all that ballast with you. But obviously nature will out. The ark of the covenant was a golden box, the most sacred thing that the Jews possessed: something like the throne of Jahweh. In a certain sense it was actually Jahweh himself."

"And yesterday you said that the candelabra was the most sacred object of the Jews."

"That was the case at the time of Vespasian and Titus. Come on, let me explain the whole thing to you at once, then."

Onno raised one finger of his left hand and three on his right and said that Quinten must distinguish four things: the tabernacle and the three successive temples in Jerusalem. When Moses was given the Ten Commandments in the wilderness, Jahweh also gave him the responsibility of making a tabernacle, with all its dimensions precisely noted. At that time it was only a collapsible tent, which they could take with them on their wanderings, but it already consisted of a court, a sanctum, and a Holy of Holies. Moses was also told exactly what appearance the ark should have; and it could all be looked up in the Bible. On the golden lid there were two golden angels with outspread wings, facing each other. To one side there were golden rings for two sticks so that the box could be carried with them. A few hundred years later, in approximately 1000 B.C., King Solomon built his temple in Jerusalem according to the same principle. In the Holy of Holies in it, the ark was flanked by two huge angels fifteen feet high, again with outspread wings.

"What had happened to those first two angels?"

"I don't know, Quinten," said Onno, and sighed again. "Listen a moment. The temple of Solomon was laid waste by Nebuchadnezzar, and from that moment on the ark disappeared. Later again, in the sixth century B.C., the second temple was built on the same spot, that of Zerubbabel—without an ark, that is. That building fell into disrepair; Herod demolished it and built the third temple. Jewish tradition, however, makes no distinction between the second and third temples, since the rabbis did not accord Herod the honor, because he collaborated with the Romans. For them the third is still the second, renovated by Herod into a huge monster, again on the same spot. But that temple existed for no more than a few years: it was destroyed by Titus, as you know. It appears from eyewitness reports that the Holy of Holies was empty at that time too."

"That can't be right," said Quinten, pointing with his index finger to the two small altars, behind which was the Sancta Sanctorum, "because the ark of the covenant is inside."

Onno looked at him for a couple of seconds speechless.

"That's the stuff!" he said with a laugh. "Generations of theologians, rabbis, historians, and archaeologists have confirmed that the ark has vanished since the Babylonian exile, but Professor Doctor Quist, M.L., M.E. knows better. Listen, I agree it's odd that this chapel is called the Sancta Sanctorum, but perhaps we shouldn't take it too literally."

"The chapel isn't just called that, it also says that there isn't a holier place in the whole world. There's nothing figurative about that."

"All true. But how do you explain, then, that on the triumphal arch of Titus the candelabra can be seen, and the table with the shewbread, but not the ark? If Titus had taken that, too, then surely it would have been depicted at the very front?"

"Well, there could be a reason for that, couldn't there?"

"Such as?"

Quinten shrugged his shoulders. "I don't know ... perhaps Titus and Vespasian were a little frightened of that God of the Jews and it seemed safer not to make too much fuss about the ark."

"Not such a stupid idea in itself," said Onno with a small movement of his head. "It's difficult for us to imagine—we are the heirs of that Jewish monotheism that recognizes only one God and none other; in fact that's even the content of the First Commandment. However, when the Romans defeated an enemy, they not only imprisoned their soldiers, but sometimes they incorporated their gods into their own pantheon. But suppose it's as you say, what happened then?"

"Well, it's quite logical," said Quinten. "Titus took the ark, but didn't show it in the procession. Then Vespasian hid it in the imperial palace, after which Constantine later gave it to the popes in deepest secrecy. They then hid it behind bars somewhere here. And that's also the reason why the chapel had to be spared when the Lateran was demolished."

"Not a bad solution," nodded Onno. "But in that case that architect, Domenico Fontana, must have known about it—otherwise he wouldn't have quoted the temple in this building with the Scala Santa. No, of course he knew nothing himself, but his patron, Sixtus V, did."

"Of course."

"Wasn't that terribly risky, in combination with the name of the chapel and that inscription? Wouldn't that have given someone the clue that the ark of God is here?"

"Have you heard about something, then?"

"No, it's not that," said Onno, and was silent for a moment. "It's true, some ideas are so obvious that you can scarcely believe that no one has hit on them before. For centuries everyone believed that the *Iliad* was a myth; but with Homer in hand Schliemann simply started digging and immediately found Helen's Troy. He was obviously someone just like you. If only we had that historioscope of yours, we could simply check it in the past." He looked at Quinten in amusement. "Have you any idea what it would mean if what you're saying were true?"

"What do you mean?"

Onno turned to him. "The *ark*, Quinten! The whole world would be turned on its head if it suddenly emerged that it still exists and is here in Rome. That could have some very strange consequences."

But that aspect didn't interest Quinten. Lost in thought, he stared at the wall behind which was the Sancta Sanctorum and asked: "How large was that ark?"

"I'm sorry, I can't remember off the top of my head. Moses on Mount Horeb remembered hundreds of measurements and specifications without noting them down, but even I haven't got a memory like that."

"But we can check it."

"Of course, everything can always be checked. You just say the word. It's all in the Torah."

"In the what?"

"In the Torah. The Law. The Pentateuch, in Greek. The first five books of the Bible, which Moses is supposed to have written: Genesis, Exodus, Leviticus, Numbers, Deuteronomy. I can still recite it all by heart, but of course you've never heard of them."

"I've heard of Genesis," said Quinten, and got up. "So we must manage to get hold of a Bible somewhere."

"I'm sure we'll be able to in Rome."

"Shall we see if we can walk around it?"

The medieval chapel was indeed in the center of the Renaissance building, like the core in a nuclear reactor. At the back, too, there was a sacred area; on the right was the chapel of San Lorenzo. When they got there, Quinten stopped in shock and looked at a door that also seemed to be looking at him.

The center of the world! A bronze double door from the fourth century, which gave access to the Sancta Sanctorum. In the two top panels were round decorations, like irises with a pupil. They were locked by two heavy, sliding padlocks, one below the other, as large as that on the altar, which looked like a nose and a mouth. The wide marble doorpost was crowned by two short pillars, bearing an architrave; in the space below was an inscription:

SIXTVS●V●
PONT●MAX●

Quinten knew of course that "Pont. Max." was the abbreviation of Pontifex Maximus, the papal title Great Bridgebuilder; nevertheless he looked in alarm at Max's name, which suddenly appeared here above that bronze face that he knew from his Citadel. He returned to the familiar look of the door and this time felt no fear.

Suddenly he turned to Onno. "What was in it?"

"In what?"

"In that ark of the covenant."

"The two stone tablets of Moses, with the Ten Commandments on them."

The following morning they took the bus to the Via Omero, where the Istituto Storico Olandese was located. Initially, Onno had hesitated about going there; perhaps he would have to give his name and would be recognized: in the past he had had it in his portfolio and had cut its grant, in order to release funds for Max's thirteenth and fourteenth mirrors. On the other hand he knew that an arbitrary minister of state was not only forgotten years afterward but often while he was still in office. Anyone who had been a minister of state, or even a minister, imagined that he and his family would bask in the glory for all eternity, but apart from them no one generally remembered. And perhaps that was right; because everything always repeated itself. Without people's poor memories, politics would be completely impossible. Moreover, it didn't really matter to him if he was recognized.

In the quiet reading room, where a few students sat hunched over their papers, Onno went to the librarian, an exceptionally small, graying lady, who was standing on tiptoe with a pencil between her teeth in front of an open drawer of index cards. He had to force himself to suppress the image of Helga before he could ask whether she had a Dutch Bible that they could consult.

She glanced at his untidy appearance and said: "You've come to the wrong place. Perhaps at the embassy."

"Are you sure?" asked Quinten.

She looked up at him, and Onno saw her change at the same moment, like a landscape when the sun breaks through.

"You look as though there's a hurry," she said, laughing.

"That's true."

"Wait. Perhaps I can help."

When she'd gone, Onno said: "What is it with you and women that I haven't got?"

Quinten looked at him in such astonishment that Onno thought it better to leave it at that remark. A few minutes later she came back with a small Bible, which she handed to Quinten.

"There you are. For you. It was in the bedside table in a guest room. If you ask me, no one ever looks at it, so it's going to a better home now."

"It would have been incredible," said Onno severely. "A Dutch institution without a Bible on the premises!"

In the nearby park, the Villa Borghese, they sat down on a bench. The silence among the trees and lawns, made even deeper by the distant roar of the traffic around, had an air of timelessness. The soft green veil that the spring had drawn over everything, like a child breathing against the windowpane, reminded Quinten of Groot Rechteren—and he wondered in astonishment what the connection was between nature and the things they were now concerned with.

"What kind of covenant are we talking about, actually?" he asked, while Onno leafed through the printed cigarette paper with his legs crossed.

"The one between God and Israel, the so-called Old Covenant. With Christ you later got the New Covenant, between God and those who believed in Christ. According to the Christians, the Old Covenant was thereby fulfilled and transcended."

"And how did the Jews react to that?"

"Well, how do you think? They weren't too impressed. Jesus of Nazareth was a rabbi who said that he was the Messiah, but the other rabbis considered that sacrilege. You know what rabbis are like. According to them, the true Messiah was still to come, and they still believe that." Onno laid a hand on his crown. "Good God, if only my father could hear me going on like this." Suddenly he stiffened and stared straight ahead with a look that Quinten didn't understand.

"What's wrong?"

Onno glanced at him, handed him the Bible, and said: "Hold this. I've got to put something right."

Quinten looked in astonishment as his father fished an envelope out of his inside pocket, took a box of matches from his trouser pocket, and lit the envelope at one corner.

"What are you doing?"

"I'm mailing a letter."

He turned the burning envelope between his fingers until he could no longer hold it. He ground the charred remains, which had fallen, into the earth with his heel and scattered them with his stick, until nothing more could be seen. Quinten watched in astonishment.

"Don't pay any attention and don't ask me anything." Onno took back the Bible and looked in St. Paul's Epistle to the Hebrews for the passages whose existence he remembered. "It's a long time, son, since I devoted myself to Bible study. Thank goodness it's the Authorized Version, in the language of Canaan, and not one of those new-fangled versions of the God-Is-Dead school."

While an occasional lady with a child or a gentleman with a dog passed them along the path, or a jogger trotted by, he read aloud to Quinten about Christ, who had not entered the "the holy places made with hands, which are the figures of the true; but into heaven itself, now to appear in the presence of God for us."

" 'Christ,' " he recited with a solemn voice, " 'being come an high priest of good things to come, by a greater and more perfect tabernacle, not made with hands, that is to say, not of this building; neither by the blood of goats and calves, but by his own blood he entered in once into the holy place, having obtained eternal redemption for us.' It says here that he consecrated man 'through the veil, that is to say, his flesh.' Come now, come now. And here it talks about 'the true tabernacle, which the Lord pitched and not man.' If you ask me, all that contains a prohibition against ever building an earthly Holy of Holies with human hands again."

"But," said Quinten, "over there is a Christian building that is called Sancta Sanctorum and is the holiest place on earth."

"That's what I mean."

"So perhaps it's not so very Christian at all. That is, Christian but at the same time not Christian."

Onno nodded. "I take your point, but where do you want to go from here?"

Quinten pointed to the Bible. "Look at the ark of the covenant again. I want to know how big it was."

Onno looked up the book of Exodus and did not have to look for long. It was as though when he saw all those names and turns of phrase he again smelled the smell of his parents' house.

"Two and a half ells long, one and a half ells wide, and one and a half ells high."

"And how long is an ell?"

"Well, from your elbow to the tip of your middle finger, so about eighteen inches."

"So about forty-three inches long, twenty-seven inches wide, and twenty-seven inches high."

"That's about right."

Quinten looked through the hilly park, but all he saw was the heavy padlock. "If you ask me, that's also the size of the altar in the Sancta Sanctorum."

"Let's hope," said Onno with a little laugh, "that it's a bit bigger, otherwise the ark won't fit in it."

"Why are you laughing?"

"Because everything is always right—if you want it to be. Just think of that crazy Proctor, in the castle. Do you remember? Look, I've got one, two, three, four, five, six, seven buttons on my shirt; the top one is open. So that tallies with the six days of creation and the Sabbath."

"But something can really be right, can't it?"

"Of course."

"Why else would there be such thick bars in front of that altar? And on that canopy above there are two angels with outspread wings, aren't there? We're on the track of something, Dad! *Non est in toto sanctior orbe locus*—that could also have been in the temple of Jerusalem!"

Onno closed the Bible, looked at Quinten seriously and made a gesture. "Yes."

"Well, then! I have to know what's going on here."

"Why on earth do you have to, Quinten?"

"I don't know," said Quinten with something impatient in his voice, while he was thinking of *the center of the world.*

57

Discoveries

The origin of the urge that had seized Quinten was a mystery to Onno. Max and Sophia had brought the boy up to be agnostic—he scarcely knew the Bible, and religions had never interested him, as far as Onno knew. If this was a kind of religious mania, then he could understand. But it was obviously nothing of the kind. And besides, the question of the ark of the covenant being in the Sancta Sanctorum was of course total nonsense—but Quinten's reasoning had the enthusiasm of youth and the beauty of simplicity, though Onno himself knew the traps of this kind of simple conclusion all too well.

Things were almost never like that; something always turned up that suddenly changed the beautiful simplicity into a disheartening chaos, in which one could discover an order only with the greatest effort, which then turned out to be much more complicated. But the fact that he regarded Quinten's theory as nonsense did not stop him from immersing himself in the literature for a few days—or was it precisely the obvious absurdity of the project that attracted him?: in an absurd world only the absurd had meaning, as he had said in the letter that he had written to his father.

Because most books he had to consult would be in Italian, Latin, Greek, and Hebrew, Quinten went his own way, while Onno himself started research the following morning in the Biblioteca Nazionale. He polished his shoes as well as he could with an old rag, tucked his shirt neatly into his trousers, and for the first time in years put on a tie.

The very first day, after a few hours, he realized what he had suspected: that through the centuries the writings about the temple of Jerusalem and the ark of the covenant had formed as vast a conglomerate as Rome itself, in which one thing was built on another and most things were under the ground. He couldn't restrain himself from browsing a little in the countless rabbinical commentaries, having a quick glance at what Philo had written about the ark; in the Middle Ages, Thomas Aquinas; in the Renaissance, Pico della Mirandola, Francesco Giorgi, Campanella; in the sixteenth and seventeenth centuries Fludd and Kepler and even Newton; down to the watered-down views of modern freemasons, Rosicrucians, and anthroposophists.

The existence of all those speculations made him realize even more acutely what a commotion it would cause if the ark actually appeared—but apart from that, it was all much too interesting. He knew from experience that he would never finish if he went into that any further. Via entries in Jewish encyclopedias, not only Hebrew ones, through notes, references, bibliographies, he had to follow the trail closely, trot like a police dog with its nose close to the ground, not looking up or around, ignoring everything that did not immediately serve his purpose. And that purpose was not religious or metaphysical or symbolic but very concrete: did the ark still exist—and if so, where was it?

The following morning he checked all references to the ark, closer to two hundred than a hundred, with the help of a biblical concordance; and in the afternoon he looked with Quinten's eyes at the history of the Lateran palace, the basilica, and the Sancta Sanctorum. When the library closed that evening, he had made a couple of discoveries that would surprise Quinten; but decided only to talk to him about it when he had more or less sewn things up. At the last moment he had found in a systematic catalog a promising Italian title about the treasure of the Sancta Sanctorum, and because he did not feel like going to the same library again, he first phoned the art historical institute on the Via Omero; it turned out to have a copy too, indeed in the German original. Only when he was on his way there did he realize that he had again put on a tie.

When the librarian saw him, a smile crossed her face. "Did you leave your pious companion at home today?"

"That's my son. He's wandering through the city somewhere, looking for the secrets of antiquity."

"Congratulations. I've never seen such a beautiful boy. The spitting image of John the Baptist in that painting by Leonardo da Vinci." She put out her hand and said, "Elsa Schulte."

Onno started. He put his stick into his other hand, shook hers, and was going to say Enrico Delius, but before he realized it he had said: "Onno Quist."

He realized that he had now driven a hole through his isolation once and for all, but no sign of recognition appeared on Elsa Schulte's face. The book that he had asked about was already on the reading table: *Die römische Kapelle Sancta Sanctorum und ihr Schatz: Meine Entdeckungen und Studien in der Palastkapelle der mittelalterlicheren Päpste*, published in 1908 by a certain Grisar, an Austrian Jesuit. Now he learned everything—even that the altar was about five feet long, twenty-two inches wide, and three feet high, so that the ark could have fitted into it fairly exactly. But it wasn't in it. He himself of course hadn't doubted that for a moment, and he was apprehensive about having to tell Quinten shortly.

At lunchtime he ate two *panini* in the canteen and went back to order his notes. Gradually he began to feel like a student who had to do research for his crazy professor, and who would now definitely fail his master's exam, since the results didn't tally with the exaggerated expectations. But at the same time the crazy work filled him with nostalgic memories of the days of the Phaistos disc.

An hour later an intellectual-looking gentleman came toward him. He glanced at Onno's stick, which lay on the chair next to him, and then at his ponytail. With an expressionless face he said: "Hello, Mr. Quist. Nordholt. I'm the director here."

"I know." Onno nodded and looked at him over his reading glasses. He knew because he had appointed him at the time.

"I'm pleased that you are kind enough to make use of our institute. Our budget was cut drastically a few years ago by the then-minister of state, and people have been dismissed, but I hope you find what you are looking for." With a short nod of his head he turned on his heel and disappeared.

Again a score had been settled. Onno had had no opportunity to say anything else, but what could he have said? That the director should go and have a look at Westerbork? That thanks to his financial cuts in the foreign cultural institutes the universe had become twice as big? That it had been a favor to a friend? In any case, the news of his presence in Rome would now quickly get back to Holland; perhaps Nordholt was on the telephone at this very moment, to report that Quist—you know, that one—had gone completely to the dogs. Onno shrugged his shoulders and again bent over his book, but could no longer concentrate. He took off his glasses, looked out the window for a moment, and strolled toward a round reading table in the corner, where international art periodicals were displayed, and also a few Dutch newspapers and weeklies.

As he stood there, he read that yesterday in Rome the trial had begun of a Turk, who four years previously had tried to assassinate the pope. "I am Jesus Christ," he had cried from his heavily barred cage—"the end of the world is at hand!" To think that he had to learn about this from a Dutch newspaper. He leafed on a little, sat down in amazement, and for the first time in four years filled himself in on the situation in Holland and the world.

When he looked up an hour later and realized where he was, he felt as though he were returning from the dead. Nothing was the same anymore. From political commentaries he discovered that Dorus's cabinet, in which he was to have been minister of defense, had survived no longer than nine months; after that Koos and the Social Democrats had left, or had been driven out, after which the cabinet had soldiered on for a little, and meanwhile Dolf had become prime minister. Dolf! Of course! Called a "domestique" teasingly, a term from cycling he understood, Dolf was always underestimated by Koos too. He was welcome to it; during that dreadful boat trip, the last day of his previous life, Dolf was the only one to put a hand on his shoulder. Yes, that's how things went—they had kept the front door in their sights, the gentlemen, but not the back door: the classic error. But not only in Holland had the political situation changed. If he'd become minister of defense, then he would have had to deal with massive demonstrations against the stationing of American cruise missiles; but in the Soviet Union a new secretary-general seemed to have been in control for the past few months—a man of his own age, not with the usual concrete features, but with an open, human face and a calm, determined look.

Suddenly he had the feeling that the world had begun a transformation. How was he to picture it? Was the end of the Cold War at hand? The thought was of course absurd—East and West were still armed to the teeth—but he felt as though he had just looked at the world like a chess player, who on first seeing a game played by two other people immediately saw a possible conclusion, which still escaped the two players. He closed the papers and magazines and stared out of the window. Was it conceivable that by the year 2000 the Communist party in the Soviet Union would be forbidden? Of course that was inconceivable, but was the inconceivable precisely about to happen? Was his numb left side—as the result of a right-wing breakthrough in his head—perhaps a political prophecy? He was amazed at that brainwave; was he in the process of adopting Quinten's way of thinking? At the same time that thought reconciled him a little with his discomfort. Lenin, he remembered, had had a stroke at about the same time, but he had had his right side paralyzed.

That same day Quinten had gone for the third time to the building containing the Sancta Sanctorum, which by now he knew almost as well as his room at Groot Rechteren. He did not notice the affectionate looks of the fathers of the Holy Cross out of the corner of their eyes when again he stared through the bars at the locked papal altar with his beautiful blue eyes, or when in one of the side chapels he leafed through his little Bible piously with his slim hands. The immediate proximity of a secret, which he could walk around in half a minute, but which at the same time was as inaccessible as his dream of the Citadel during the day, shut him off completely from what was happening around him. It was difficult to assess from a distance, but it seemed to him that the space under the top of the altar was large enough to contain the ark.

He realized that it was difficult to look properly at something like this. But meanwhile he had seen that behind the bars was a bronze door, again closed with a large padlock. He had never been as certain of anything else as now: something extraordinary was kept inside—he felt it with his whole being, like a compass needle feels the pull. After the priests had motioned visitors to leave with solemn gestures, he walked around the complex a few times on the piazza and looked at the square outer walls of the chapel, framed by Fontana's slightly lower new building. On the small lawn at the side some Tamils were stoking a fire; a half-dressed man with one arm stood washing himself, while someone in a parked car took a photo of him with a telescopic lens.

On his way home Quinten went back to the triumphal arch of Titus on the Forum Romanum. With his eyes screwed up, he tried to make out whether the ark had perhaps been on the relief and deliberately removed by a pope. The sharp shadows now cast by the sun made the depiction even more lively and inspired than when he had first seen it. Close by was the roaring of cars and buses—but the excitement and the noise of the triumphal entry, almost twenty centuries before, here on this spot, now resounded through it like a real storm in a theater where a pastoral scene was being played. The grim faces of the soldiers, each with a laurel wreath; above them, agitated movement of regimental standards, the captured candelabra on their shoulders, the silver trumpets, the table with the shewbread. Everyone was doing something, carrying something. Only the last figure looked a little lost; he was the only one whose head had virtually completely disappeared. The relief was weathered. There were details missing, and the exhaust gas would obviously demolish much more, but there was no sign of an ark that had been spirited away.

When he got home, Onno was lying on his mattress reading the *International Herald Tribune*.

With his hand on the door handle Quinten stopped. "Since when have you read the newspapers?"

Onno dropped the paper, looked at him over his reading glasses, and said: "I've come down to earth, Quinten."

He told him what had happened to him in the institute and that it would now soon be the end of his anonymous existence, but that in exchange he had rediscovered the world.

"I would never have thought that it would happen again. I thought I would be in mourning till I died, and without your arrival in Rome that would have happened, but obviously this was meant to be."

"At least that's how it is," said Quinten, who had sat down on the chair at Onno's desk.

Onno folded his hands on the newspaper and looked for a while at a large black feather from Edgar's wing, which was in an empty inkwell on the windowsill.

"Do you know what may be the most terrible of all sayings? 'Time heals all wounds.' But it's true. There's always a scar that may hurt when the weather changes; but one day the wound heals. As a boy of eight I once stumbled with one of those curved pointed nail clippers in my hands. It went deep into my knee, and I can still remember exactly how I screamed with pain. So like everyone else I got a scar on my knee, but I couldn't tell you which one anymore. You must have scars, too, that you can't remember how you got. There's something dreadful about that. Because it means that looking back on it, those wounds might just as well have never existed. What happened to me is a trifle compared with what has happened to other people—in the war, for example, and that wound has obviously healed—but your mother's still in a coma and Auntie Helga is still dead. There's something wrong about that."

Quinten became confused by those words, and when Onno saw that he sat up a bit and laughed.

"Don't you listen to your old father. Humanity could not exist at all if it were any different, and for animals it's no problem at all. Very soon, when we've solved all mysteries, we'll still be left with the mystery of time. Because that's what we are ourselves. That's why I'm reading this newspaper here. I don't have the feeling that you're interested in world politics, but shall I tell you what I've discovered?"

"Yes," said Quinten. "But not what you've discovered in world politics."

Onno drew a deep breath, threw the paper on the floor, and got off the mattress. "Let me get over there." Quinten stood up and leaned against the windowsill, Onno sat at his notes. "I learned a lot, but I doubt whether you'll be happy about it." Like someone about to play a game of solitaire, he spread his notes over the table in four long rows, folded his arms, and looked at them for a few seconds. "Where shall I begin?"

"At the beginning."

"Could it also be the probable end?" He picked up a sheet. "According to II Kings, verse 9, the temple of Solomon was plundered and set alight by the Babylonians, together with all Jerusalem. The general view is that the ark was also lost when that happened. You knew that already, of course. This seven-branched candelabra and all those other things were later remade, but the ark was not. If you open your Bible at Jeremiah 3, verse 16, you'll read that Jahweh had told the prophet that no one must speak about the ark of the covenant anymore, that no one must think about it anymore, that no one must look for it anymore, and that no new ark must be made. That's the last mention of the ark in the Old Testament."

"But if no one was supposed to look for it," said Quinten, "that meant surely that it hadn't gone, although it was no longer in the second or third temples."

"You could come to that conclusion. And you find support for that in a couple of apocryphal texts. For example, the so-called Syrian Apocalypse of Baruch. It says that when the Babylonians approached, an angel descended from heaven into the Holy of Holies and ordered the earth to swallow up the ark. That would mean that it's still in Jerusalem on the site of the temple. The annoying thing is that the story was not written until a century after Christ—that is, even later than the destruction of the temple of Herod by the

Romans. Perhaps a legend that I found in Rabbinical literature connects with that. After the destruction of Solomon's temple, a priest is supposed to have found two raised tiles in the floor of the ruin; the moment he told that to a colleague, he dropped down dead. So that was the proof that the ark had not been stolen or burned, but that it was buried in that spot. There was another nice story in the second book of the Maccabees. There you read that the same Jeremiah of just now took the ark on the orders of Jahweh and hid it."

"Really?" said Quinten expectantly. "Where?"

"In a cave on the Nebo. That's the mountain from where Moses saw the Promised Land on the other side of the Jordan, and which he himself was forbidden to enter for some reason by Jahweh."

"And have they never looked for it there?"

"Of course. From the very start. The people who were with him wanted to mark and signpost the way to the cave, but they could not find it again. When Jeremiah heard about it, he reproached them and said—let's have a look . . . where is it? There is only a Greek text of it left, but you can see that it's been translated from Hebrew. Here, I'll just translate off the top of my head: 'No man shall find this or know this spot until Jahweh again unites his people and has mercy on them. Then he will reveal it.' " He looked in amusement at Quinten, who was leafing through his Bible. "You might well say that the moment has now come with the state of Israel. It's just a shame that that story, too, was only written down about a hundred and fifty years before Christ."

"I can't find that book of the Maccabees anywhere."

"That's right, because it's not in there. It's also an apocryphal book, but that doesn't mean very much; it could just as well have been canonical. All that was decided fairly arbitrarily by those Church Councils. Conversely, that letter of Paul to the Hebrews, you remember, in which Christ is compared with the temple, could just as well have been apocryphal, because of course it wasn't written by Paul but by an Alexandrine follower of Philo."

"Who's that?" asked Quinten, without really paying attention. He was trying to understand what all those facts meant to him.

"A Jewish scholar, Philo Judaeus, a contemporary of Christ's, who wanted to combine Judaism with Greek philosophy. Interesting man. But let's not digress, because then we'll sink farther and farther into the historical quicksand. Right. If all that's true then, and if according to you the ark is hidden in the Sancta Sanctorum at this moment, how did the Romans get hold of it? Isn't it a little too improbable that they should have found it in that cave in the Nebo?"

"Yes," said Quinten. "That's true. But why is it called the Sancta Sanctorum? Why is it supposed to be the most sacred place in the world, then? You yourself said that that's very strange, didn't you?"

"Wait a bit, we're not there yet. The most probable answer is that the ark is not on the arch of Titus because the Romans simply didn't have it. Pompey had previously penetrated the Holy of Holies and hadn't seen anything there. And that was all confirmed by Flavius Josephus—he was a Jewish writer in Roman service, in fact a kind of collaborator. He reported the whole Jewish war at close hand, up to and including that procession across the Forum, with the table of the shewbread and the seven-branched candelabra and all those things; he mentions them in exactly the same order as they are on the triumphal arch. Anyway, in his young days he had served in the temple of Herod, and according to him, too, the *debir* was completely empty."

"The *debir?*"

"That's what the Holy of Holies is called in Hebrew. It's true that he himself never looked inside, of course; only the high priest was allowed in. Well, that's all on one side. But!" said Onno, sticking up his index finger and putting his other on a sheet of notes. "Because—and let this be your consolation—there's always a but in life, Quinten. The other side of the matter—and that will give you false hope—is a text from the twelfth century by a certain Johannes Diaconus. In it, the term *Sancta Sanctorum* occurs for the first time. But it doesn't yet refer to the papal chapel but to a treasure of relics that was supposed to be found under the high altar of the old Lateran basilica."

"That altar with the heads of Peter and Paul in the ceiling?"

"Yes, but down below. And what was supposed to be there, according to the deacon? Not only Moses' rush basket, the foreskin of Christ, and all other conceivable rarities, but also—pay attention: *arca foederis Domini.* What do you say to that?" said Onno, leaning back with the satisfaction of a generous giver. "God's ark of the covenant."

Quinten looked at him perplexed. "Why false hope? We're there, aren't we!" he asked excitedly. "Since when has the papal chapel been called Sancta Sanctorum?"

"I know that, too. Since the end of the fourteenth century."

"Well, then! That means that the ark was taken from the basilica to the chapel sometime between eleven hundred and fourteen hundred. The name simply went with it."

"In itself what you're saying is not at all implausible. In the thirteenth century the chapel was completely restored and the relics were taken out of it for those months; afterward the ark could have been added to them. Except that you're forgetting the minor point that the ark, in the best possible case, is still lying somewhere in a cave in Jordan. It's never been in Rome." With both his hands Onno made a gesture of resignation. "Realize that it's all based on a medieval legend. What do you think of that foreskin and that rush basket?"

Quinten shook his head decidedly. "That's as may be, and I don't know either how it happened, but I know for certain that the ark is there in the altar."

"And I," said Onno, who now felt like a surgeon who has to put the scalpel into the patient without anesthetic, "know even more for certain that it isn't."

"How can you be so sure of that?"

"Because I know what's in it," said Onno, without taking his eyes off Quinten.

Quinten looked back at him in disbelief. "What, then?"

"Nothing."

"Nothing?" repeated Quinten after a few seconds.

"An empty box."

"How do you know that?"

"Because the altar was opened in 1905 and emptied. Here," said Onno, and took the book that he had borrowed from the institute—giving his address, so that wouldn't stay secret for very much longer, either. "Here you find an exact description and photographs of everything that was in it. There were extraordinary things there—the umbilical cord of Christ, for example, and a piece of the cross—but no ark. On the orders of the pope, this Professor Grisar from Innsbruck took all the things personally to the Vatican Library, where you can go and look at them tomorrow in the chapel of Pius V."

Quinten leafed through it a little, glanced at an illustration of the decorated shrine, and put it back on the table. It didn't interest him now.

"And yet," he said, "that chapel is called Sancta Sanctorum. And there are two angels above the altar. And it says above the altar that there is no more holy place in the world."

"It won't let go of you, will it?" laughed Onno. "You trust your intuition more than the facts. I regard that as a heroic quality, but you can actually take it too far. I hope you don't mean to say that there's a conspiracy—that for example this whole book was only written to hide the fact that the ark is definitely in the altar."

"Of course not," said Quinten. "I'm not crazy."

"But what are you, then? A dreamer perhaps? Forget it. As far as this is concerned, your intuition has been refuted. Another time you wouldn't have been far off the mark. The last time you suggested that Vespasian may have been frightened of the God of the Jews and had therefore hidden the ark in his palace. Well, there was no question of an ark, but yesterday I read in Flavius Josephus that after the great triumphal procession through the Forum, he did have the veil of the Holy of Holies taken to his palace."

"How strange," said Quinten suspiciously. "And not those costly gold things—that candelabra and that table with the shewbread?"

"No, they were displayed in a temple. Only the purple veil and the Jewish Law."

"The Jewish Law?" Quinten raised his eyebrows. "What was that?"

"That's a name for the Torah, the five books of Moses. He's also called the Law Giver."

Quinten thought for a moment. "How am I to imagine the Law?"

"You must have seen an illustration of it at some point. A great role of parchment, such as you now see in the ark of every synagogue."

"How large?"

"I assume that the Torah roll from the temple of Herod will have been very big. Perhaps even fifty-four inches long."

Quinten nodded. "That monster was therefore also carried in that procession through the Forum."

"Of course. According to Josephus, the Jewish Law passed as the last trophy."

"Did it?" said Quinten. "And if that thing was so important to the emperor that he took it into his palace, even more important than the menorah, why doesn't it appear on the arch of Titus?"

"How are you so sure that it doesn't appear?"

"Because I've just been back there. But something else did strike me," said Quinten, suddenly hectic. "The last figure, at the extreme left, a man without a face, who in that case ought to be carrying the parchment, is standing there as though he's got nothing to do, with his arms hanging straight down beside him. Like this," he said, demonstrating. "You can't see his left hand; but if you look carefully, you can see that at least he's got something in his right hand, something heavy and oblong, that comes approximately to his elbow." He took the book from the table and let it rest on his bent fingers against his thigh.

"Shall I tell you what he's got with him, then?"

"I'd really like to know."

"Moses' two stone tablets with the Ten Commandments on them."

58

Preparations

Onno stared at him in astonishment.

"That was the so-called Jewish Law!" cried Quinten vehemently. "How large were those stone tablets?"

Onno bent over a note. "According to R. Berechiah, a rabbi from the fourth century, six *tefah* long and two *tefah* wide."

"And how long was a *tefah*?"

"The width of a hand."

"And how wide is a hand?" said Quinten, looking at his own hand. "Three inches or so? That means? Eighteen inches by six! So that's exactly right!"

"But that Mr. Berechiah never saw them."

"Everything's clear now, isn't it, Dad!?" Quinten began pacing the room passionately. "Listen ..." he said, his eyes focused on the floor. "Jeremiah took the ark with him and hid it in a cave, but that doesn't mean that he left those stone tablets in it. Or does it say in that book of the Maccabees that they had to disappear as well?"

"No."

"Right, so he took them out. And they were seen by that priest from that rabbinical legend, who thought that they were raised tiles. They were preserved and later they were placed in the Holy of Holies in the second and third temples. It would be too stupid if that had been really empty for centuries! A high priest who goes in through the curtain every Yom Kippur—and then nothing? An empty cube? Surely he'd look a fool. Just as if God didn't exist. Then that temple would have been in a kind of coma for all those centuries—like Mama."

"What dreadful things are you saying now, Quinten?" asked Onno in dismay.

"In a manner of speaking, of course. Just let me go on for a moment, otherwise I'll lose the thread. So in the Holy of Holies those two tablets were there the whole time with the Ten Commandments on them. Just as those two pillars stood in front of the entrance of the court. Flavius Josephus had simply allowed himself to be convinced by the high priest when he wrote that the *debir* was empty. They were taken from Jerusalem together with the veil. So then you had the entry here in Rome. Are there any other eyewitness accounts of that?"

"No."

"And how reliable is that Flavius Josephus?"

"Not terribly reliable."

"Well, then I think that in all that tumult and jostling he wasn't able to see everything exactly himself; but afterward when he started writing about it, he used what he heard from other people. And they said something vague about a 'Jewish Law,' which had been carried at the end of the procession; they were Romans, they had no idea about the Jewish religion. But he as a Jew thought immediately of the Torah roll from the temple. The Ten Commandments didn't occur to him, because for him they had disappeared with the ark. But Vespasian was better informed. He had plenty of gold that hadn't meant anything to him for a long time. He only had brought to his palace what was connected with the most holy—and that was the veil and the so-called Jewish Law. A parchment that was only used in the sanctum of the temple wasn't part of that; of course it was an exceptional thing in this case, but not anything unique—you yourself say that a roll like that can be found in every synagogue. No, it was the original manuscript of the Decalogue, noted down by Moses himself on Mount Horeb in the Sinai Desert. The carver of that relief was obviously better informed." Quinten glanced at his father, who was following him about the room with eyes wide open. "And apart from that, things happened as I thought they had happened with the ark. Constantine converted to Christianity and presented the two stones to the pope of his day, who hid them in the treasury under the high altar of his basilica. As a result that came to be known as Sancta Sanctorum; and that

Johannes Diaconus wrote about the *arca foederis Domini* because he had heard the rumor but didn't know the whole story. He didn't have the ark under the high altar of his church, but he did have the contents of the ark. In the thirteenth century the papal chapel was restored, and afterward Moses' stone tablets were transferred to it, after which the name Sancta Sanctorum transferred to that chapel. And when Grisar opened the altar in 1905, he simply overlooked the two flat stones, just like Pompey when he was in the Holy of Holies and just like Flavius Josephus during the procession in Rome, and just like everyone who up to now has looked at that relief on the arch of Titus. So they're still there."

With a triumphant cry Quinten suddenly leaped in the air and let himself fall back on his mattress, where he thrashed his legs in the air excitedly, suddenly got up again, ran to the windowsill with floating dance steps, sat down on it with a twisting leap, and looked at Onno with his hands held between his knees.

Dusk had fallen. The window was open, and Onno saw only Quinten's black silhouette outlined against the purple evening sky, in which the first stars had already appeared.

"A tempting line of argument," he said. "I like that kind of reasoning. Yes, it could have happened like that. But perhaps it didn't happen like that."

"You bet it happened like that!" Now Quinten's mouth could no longer be seen; it was as though his voice were higher-pitched that usual. "Those people who for centuries have been climbing that Scala Santa in that Sancta Sanctorum have been kneeling down before something completely different than they think."

Onno gave a melancholy nod. "It's as though I am listening to myself, Quinten. But I was also once exceptionally certain of a hypothesis—until one day someone fell through a hole in the ground in Arezzo."

"The fact that your hypothesis wasn't true surely doesn't mean that no hypothesis is ever true?" said Quinten indignantly.

"Of course not." Onno made a dismissive gesture. "Don't listen to me."

"Well, state an objection then."

"There aren't that many objections to be made, I think. Why were only the high priests during the time of the second and third temples allowed to know that Moses' stone tablets were in there? That knowledge would surely have been a great motivation for the Jews?"

"Because," said Quinten immediately, "Jeremiah had actually pulled the wool over their eyes. God had made him bury the ark and told him that no one must think about it again. He had said nothing about the tablets. Jeremiah took those out on his own initiative, and of course it is questionable whether that was in God's spirit. Just to be on the safe side, the high priests let that fall under the vow of silence."

"Right," said Onno in amusement. "Let's sum up. On the basis of a number of Hebrew, Greek, and Latin texts you have constructed a theory, and we'll assume that the theory is consistent. It's a big step from the literature to reality, Quinten. And that can only be checked by looking inside that altar. We can only do that with the permission of the pope, as I know from Grisar. And you'll never get that permission—not because it's you, but because no one would be given it on the basis of your theory. Suppose you write and tell the pope what you've discovered. Of course many strange letters are written to him, which he never sees—every madman always writes letters to the pope; but via Cardinal Simonis, the archbishop of Utrecht, opposite whom I once sat at a gala dinner in the Noordeinde palace, and with whom I got on very well, I could ensure that your letter actually got onto his desk. Okay. Papa Wojtyla will read your story with his shrewd eyes. You'd think that he would have known for a long time that those stone tablets are in that altar. Via the *camerlengo*—that is, the cardinal-treasurer, who is in control in the period between two popes—the popes naturally would of course all have passed on that secret to each other, just as previously the Jewish high priests did. According to your own theory, that continuity must in any case have existed up to the thirteenth century, when the stone tablets were transferred from the basilica to the chapel. But I know for certain that the present pope doesn't know, because at the beginning of the twentieth century Pius X no longer knew. Otherwise he would never have given Grisar permission to open the altar; he could work out very easily that he would inevitably be confronted afterward with Jewish claims and all the fuss that it would entail. That ignorance doesn't itself necessarily argue against your theory, because since the thirteenth century it's quite possible that a *camerlengo* will have died in the interval between two popes, or was murdered together with his holy father, thus breaking the thread. And for that matter it may be down somewhere in black-and-white, in a deed of gift from Constantine, which then may have gotten lost in Avignon, because take it from me that things are always a complete mess everywhere. But those Jewish claims, Quinten, that's the tricky point. Through the existence of the state of Israel they have meanwhile taken on a political dimension, and our John Paul wouldn't dream of sticking his head in a hornet's nest. He's got enough on his plate with frustrating communism in Eastern Europe, as I learned today. Even if he considered your theory complete rubbish, even then he wouldn't want to take the slightest risk of its being right. Why should he? He can only lose. Suppose the tablets were actually to come to light. What then? Give them back to the Jews? Such a superholy relic? The Holy See hasn't even recognized Israel. Not give them back? Then subsequently to have to hear about the Christian roots of anti-Semitism? About the weak attitude of Pius XII toward the Nazis? About German war criminals who were given asylum in Catholic monasteries after the war? Protests by the Jewish lobby in the United States? Diplomatic problems with Washington? Excommunication of the pope by the chief rabbi? Landing of Israeli paratroopers on the Piazza San Giovanni in Laterano, in order to hijack the Ten Commandments and take them back to Jerusalem? Subsequent triumphalism of ultra-orthodox Judaism vis-à-vis Islam? Driving of the Muslims from the Temple Mount? Founding of a fourth temple for the tablets? Declaration of el-Jihad—Holy War? Rocket attack by Iranian fundamentalists on Tel Aviv? Outbreak of the Third World War? No, lad, take it from me, not even the most famous and most Catholic archaeologist in the world would be given permission. In a polite letter he would be informed on behalf of His Holiness that Professor Hartmann Grisar S.J. had previously investigated the altar with absolute thoroughness and that there was nothing more in it. Forget it. That thing is not going to be opened for another thousand years."

Onno stopped speaking. Hopefully, he had finally persuaded Quinten by now. "Anyway . . . Grisar mentions that he was given permission on May 29, 1905—and I just saw in the *Herald Tribune* that that's exactly eighty years ago today."

There was a silence.

"Then I'll be seventeen tomorrow," said Quinten in astonishment. He had not thought of his birthday for a moment. Since he had left Holland, the time had assumed the endless quality of earlier summer vacations.

"Indeed!" cried Onno. "That too! The omens are favorable—and we're going to celebrate that, on the dot of twelve at Mauro's on the corner. Just say what you want, and you'll get it sight unseen."

After a few seconds Quinten's voice came from the black window, in which his contour was scarcely distinguishable from the night sky behind him:

"Your help."

"My help? What with?"

"With recovering the Ten Commandments."

"Dear Quinten," said Onno after a few moments of feigned calm. "Even as a joke I don't think that's very good. You're surely not going to tell me that you are really toying with the idea of violence?"

"Yes. That is . . . I'm not playing. And violence? No. At least . . . if everything that happens without permission is violence then yes, yes."

Onno groped over the table, found a box of matches, and lit a candle. When he saw Quinten's face, with two small flames in his dark eyes, he realized that he was serious. But that was inconceivable! Up to now he had let himself be manipulated by Quinten's enthusiasm, which was as infectious as it was inexorable, as if he had no will of his own; but this was really the moment to call a halt to it.

"That's really enough now, Quinten," he said decisively. "You must know when to stop. It's gradually beginning to show signs of an obsession. Listen, I know exactly what the excitement and the suspense of a new theory are like, particularly if you've formulated it yourself; and I don't need soccer matches or wars for that. But you're threatening to cross a borderline, and that could go completely wrong—you could wind up in prison. And I don't think I can recommend Italian jails to you."

Because his back was starting to get cold, Quinten climbed off the windowsill and closed the window. "Aren't the Ten Commandments worth the risk of prison?"

"Yes!" cried Onno, and raised both his arms. "If you put it like that—of course! Life imprisonment! The stake!"

Quinten gave a short laugh. "Tell me honestly, Dad. Do you think it's a crazy idea?"

"I don't really know," sighed Onno. "An anecdote of Max's about Niels Bohr occurs to me. When somebody once developed a new physics theory, Bohr said, 'Your theory is crazy, but not crazy enough to be true.'" He looked at Quinten ironically. "As far as that's concerned, yours is in excellent shape."

"So it's almost certainly true."

"So it's almost certainly true. *Credo quia absurdum.*"

Onno felt that he was losing ground again. He got up and started pacing around the room in his threadbare brown slippers with the worn heels, without a walking stick, looking for support as he turned around. How was he to tackle it, in God's name? Now, if it was a question of the treasure of the Romanovs or the Treasure in the Silver Lake—but the stone tablets of the Law! Did Quinten really know what he was talking about? Of course God didn't exist, and perhaps Moses had never existed, but the Ten Commandments existed: there was no doubt about that. On the other hand it seemed as if the existence of the Decalogue—the foundation of all morality—on the one hand crystallized into God, on the other hand into Moses, and in between also into those stone tablets. Was it that what was primary was not things but the relations between things? Did love create lovers, and not the other way around? Could love itself subsequently take on the form of a stone, or of two stones?

"What are you thinking about?"

Onno stopped and was lost for words. Quinten looked at him, half his face in black shadow cast by the candlelight. The calm that the boy exuded suddenly infuriated him.

"Dammit, Quinten, you must be out of your mind!" he exploded. "What are you getting into your head? How do you imagine it happening? How are you proposing to get into the chapel? And then into that altar? Were you going to saw through all the bars perhaps? Read Grisar! In the sixteenth century you had the Sacco di Roma, when the chapel was plundered by French troops, but they could only get in by forcing the priests to open the door. But they didn't have the key to the altar, and there was no other way of getting in. Otherwise even in 1905 all those gold and silver treasures wouldn't have been in there anymore. And you think you can do it? Without anyone noticing?"

"Yes."

"How, then?"

"By opening those locks."

"And you can do that?"

"Yes."

"Without keys?"

"Yes."

"While it's bristling with priests everywhere and the Holy Stairs are full of people?"

"But not at night. Of course we're going to let ourselves be locked in."

"We? Do you really think I'm going to allow myself to get involved in such a crazy undertaking?"

"I hope so."

"But there's bound to be an electronic security system!"

"There isn't."

"How do you know?"

"I checked."

"And do you by any chance know what the Eighth Commandment says?"

"No."

"Thou shalt not steal."

"I don't regard it as stealing."

"And how do you regard it, then?"

"As a confiscation."

"A confiscation—how on earth do you think up these things?" Helplessly, Onno turned half around his own axis and said entreatingly, "Quinten, don't make me unhappy. Till I suddenly saw you at the Pantheon about ten days ago, I lived here like a kind of Lazarus in someone else's grave, if I can put it like that. The only person I talked to all that time was that dear Edgar. You helped me out of that hole, and I'm grateful to you for that. But what you want now really goes beyond all limits! Letting yourself be locked in the Sancta Sanctorum to see whether the stone tablets of Moses are in there! While I'm saying it, I can't believe my own ears. Just imagine the carabinieri suddenly charging in with their pistols drawn: *Young art thief caught red-handed in Sanctum!* I can already see it in *La Stampa*."

"Art thief?" repeated Quinten. "And you yourself say that according to Grisar there's nothing left in that altar."

"Yes, just you appeal to the archaeological literature when you talk to the police. Do you really understand what the police is? Anyway, there's something on that altar, you're forgetting that for convenience: the *acheiropoeton*—Christ depicted by an angel's hand and for more than a thousand years carried through the streets of Rome in procession by one pope after another. You can count yourself lucky if they don't beat you to death on the spot. There are things in the world that it's best to keep away from."

Quinten stared at him for a moment. "Right," he said. "Then I'll do it alone." He put the light on, sat down on the edge of the table, and opened Grisar's book.

Onno realized in despair that nothing would keep Quinten from his fateful plan. What was the force that was driving him on? That iron remorselessness with which he tackled everything had in a certain sense dumbfounded Onno since his birth. What was he going to do now? If he let him do it alone, of course he would lose him—while, he suddenly realized, they had found each other thanks to the same fury. Could you reject something that you owed your life to? Moreover, he had brought it all on himself with his remark that Christianity had no architectural Holy of Holies.

It began to dawn on him that he was losing. With a groan he sank onto the mattress and put his chin on his folded hands. He couldn't handle his son. And, all things considered, what had he really got to lose? There was of course no question that Quinten would be able to pick even one of those locks. Perhaps they would be caught in their absurd attempt and indeed land in jail—what would happen then? After having expounded their theory and watched the pitiful shaking of heads, they would be released again. It would undoubtedly be in the paper. The pope would shroud himself in silence, everywhere all over the world rabbis would raise their eyebrows over all this meshuggah nonsense, and old Massimo Pellegrini would explain on television that while he had always known that Qiuts was a talentless dilettante, he had not known that he had meanwhile turned into a mentally disturbed person, who even involved his under-age son in his absurd and dangerous delusions. Subsequently, the Dutch embassy would leap into action, after which his ex-colleague at the ministry of culture would put them quietly on the plane to Holland, and then the business would be over with—but he would have kept Quinten. He decided he might as well play along, dammit.

He turned to look at Quinten. "And what if they're not there, Quinten? There is a minimal chance of that, isn't there?"

"Then nothing. Then I'll close it up and we'll leave," said Quinten without looking up. "But they're there."

"And what are you going to do, in that case?"

"Then I'll take them with me, what did you think? No one will ever know. You yourself said that the altar won't be opened for another thousand years, but even then no one will miss them, because no one knows that they were there."

Onno looked at him, perplexed. "Now I don't understand anything anymore. You make a earth-shattering discovery, which would make you immortal, and you keep it secret?"

"Didn't you yourself say that otherwise it might end in a war?"

"That's true. But what do you plan to do with them, then?"

That question surprised Quinten. He looked up in astonishment. He had not thought about it for a moment. "I don't know," he said with a helpless note in his voice. After a few seconds he jerked his shoulders back and bent over the book again. "I'll see when I get there."

The following morning—it was Quinten's birthday—they read Grisar's minute account seated next to each other at the table, examined the photographs and drawings, and ran their index fingers over the plans. Supplemented with Quinten's own observations in the chapel they constructed a plan, that, according to Quinten, couldn't fail. According to Onno, however, everything could always fail, even failure—then he leaned back and told Quinten about the phenomenon of the failed suicide: the intention was to call attention by a failed attempted suicide, but that failed because unexpectedly the suicide succeeded.

"Can you imagine anything more sad?" he asked with a laugh.

It had not been said with so many words that he would assist in Quinten's crazy enterprise, but Quinten appeared ultimately not to have any doubts—and since at his wit's end he had finally plunged into the adventure, something like a paternal frivolity had taken hold of him. The idea that the stone tablets would be in that altar was of course monumental nonsense—the whole enterprise would culminate in a dreadful anticlimax, since they would not even manage to get the first door open, and that blow would be a hard one. But who had a son with such fantastic aspirations? What did other sons want? Equipment. Money. Fun. Who had a son who wanted the Decalogue?

Because the relief in the arch of Titus was up quite high and couldn't be examined closely, in the afternoon they went to the Piazza Monte Citorio, where there was a large bookshop opposite the parliament building.

As they passed the Pantheon, Onno suddenly stopped and asked: "Shouldn't you give your grandmother a call?"

"No," said Quinten at once.

"But, Quinten! She's all by herself in that castle, and she knows that it's your birthday too. As far as I'm concerned you can say that you're living with me. Can't you imagine that she's getting worried? You've been away from home for three weeks already."

"You were away longer without calling."

That remark shut Onno up; he didn't say anything more for the rest of their walk. Quinten may have forgiven him, but he would never forget something like that. The fact that he had abandoned Quinten for so long also obliged him to collaborate in his whim.

In the art history section in the bookshop they found a bulky standard work on the monument, in which there was a series of detailed photographs of the relief. Onno studied the faceless man at the far left intently.

"Yes," he said finally. "If you want to see it, then you can see that he's carrying something flat with him."

"Didn't I say so?"

"Absolutely."

In the Via del Corso they took the bus and went to the Sancta Sanctorum, to find out the opening times and to test their plan against reality. It was as though the kneeling faithful on the stairs were the same; it was just the same, too, in the silent chapel. Onno looked with satisfaction at the huge bars and locks: what French looters had not succeeded in doing 450 years ago, Quinten would not succeed in doing now. But Quinten didn't even deign to look at the altar; obviously, he was by now so sure of himself that he was only interested in technical details.

As though he were admiring the ceiling paintings, he showed Onno that cameras had not been installed anywhere. The sanctum was obviously regarded solely as a place of pilgrimage and not a museum; the supernatural painting of the Savior on the altar might be miraculous, Onno reflected; in the art trade, of course, it was not worth a penny. When the old priests, gnarled like olive trees, saw Quinten again, a glow of affection lit up their faces; perhaps they did not even know themselves what he reminded them of.

"They're all deaf," whispered Quinten.

"Let's hope so."

When they got outside again, Onno suggested that they should say no more about it for now.

"It's just like with an exam: on the last day you mustn't do any more, and take distance from everything—so that your mind can recover. Now we're going to celebrate your birthday. I know a reasonable restaurant behind the Piazza Navona. Tomorrow you can make your criminal purchases, I'll read up on the Ten Commandments, and to kill time we'll go and collect them the day after tomorrow. Okay?"

Of course Quinten saw the ironic twist in the corner of his father's mouth, but he didn't mind.

"Agreed," he said.

59

Waiting

The evening of the following day, Friday, they found another table on a terrace opposite the Pantheon, where they went to eat. The square was full of Romans out for a stroll; young tourists in jeans formed blue garlands on the steps of the fountain with the obelisk, where Onno had left his plastic bag full of shopping ten days before. When dusk fell and the rattling of steel shutters being let down in front of shop windows rang out on all sides, it seemed as if the temple—in the sophisticated light of floodlights on the surrounding roofs—gradually began to phosphoresce from its journey through the day, through all those hundreds of thousands of sun-drenched days.

Shortly afterward a couple of small bats flapped around the ancient walls, like charred snippets of paper from a distant fire. What Quinten had never seen on the photographs and drawings of Mr. Themaat he now suddenly saw: the building looked like a weathered skull, with the cupola as the cranium, the architrave as the triangular hole of the mouth, and the columns as a row of teeth.

Although Quinten had not once asked about it, Onno assumed of course he wanted to know more about the Ten Commandments, which suddenly obsessed him so much, because he had obviously not gotten any further than "Thou shalt not kill." During the meal, while pigeons pecked at the crumbs of bread between their feet, he shared with him what he had meanwhile found out. To start with, in the Hebrew Bible there was no mention of the "Ten Commandments," but about the "Ten Words": *asereth ha'dewarim*—which corresponded to the Greek translation: *deka logoi*. On each of the two stone tablets five "words" were written.

Traditionally the First Commandment read "I am Jahweh, thy God, and thou shalt know no other Gods but me." But that "thou shalt" is not actually there in Hebrew; the first word said "Thou obviously has no other Gods but me." By taking another good look at the text, Onno told him, he had discovered that the Decalogue did not have the character of a book of law, but more a manual of good manners: "One doesn't do such things." One didn't eat spaghetti using a spoon, to say nothing of a knife. It was also significant to note that Jahweh didn't say that there were no other gods but him, but only that you didn't worship them—and in so doing he actually confirmed their existence. The second word for that matter also had a double bottom. The fact that it was not fitting to make images was only, apparently, an anti-artistic judgment, because it derived from the one who made human beings in his own image—typically the remark of an artist, who not only wanted to be the best but also the only one; and consequently he said immediately afterward that he was a jealous God. The third word, that you simply didn't just use his name, and the fourth, that you of course honored the day of rest, also referred to the relationship of man to Jahweh. The fifth, that you naturally honored your father and mother, was a transition to the words on the second stone, which dealt with the relationships between people—but it also still belonged on the first stone, because parenthood was an illustration of Jahweh's position as creator.

"At least that was the commentary of Philo, and you'll understand, my son, that I completely agree with him."

The nonchalant tone did not sound sincere—they both thought at the same moment of Ada, far away in the north in her white bed. The short waiter on platform heels, who looked a little like Goebbels and regarded the world as though he would prefer to destroy it sooner rather than later, cleared the table and put down coffee for them. The horse carriages in front of the Pantheon had disappeared and at the kiosk the newspaper racks had been brought inside; the hour of the bats had passed, and they had suddenly given way to swallows, which swooped around the temple and across the square with a sound as though small knives were being whetted: *Itis . . . itis . . .*

Quinten listened in silence to his father's exposition, but his mind was not on it. Onno was wrong in his assumption that Quinten was interested in the Ten Commandments: it wasn't they that concerned him, only the tablets on which they were written, those concrete stone things that were lying waiting for him a few miles away—till tomorrow night.

Murder, Onno continued after a while, was, according to the sixth word, not done; according to the seventh, adultery; according to the eighth, theft; according to the ninth, blaspheming; and according to the tenth, attempts to acquire other people's property. That second group of five represented in the final analysis nothing except the ancient, universal "golden rule": Do unto others as you would have them do unto you.

Onno was able to report that according to Hillel, a legendary Jewish scholar from the time of Herod, even the whole Torah boiled down to the same thing—all five Biblical books of Moses, that is—with their 613 regulations. For Judaism those ten were no more important than the other 603—they only became so for Christianity. Many of the other commandments were even forbidden at the same time, such as circumcision, which was replaced by baptism. Onno burst out laughing. He suddenly remembered, he said, his vicar in catechism class, forty years ago in The Hague. While he told them that little Jewish boys were included in the covenant with God by giving them a cut in their foreskin, he had made a short vertical movement over his breastbone. He thought that was the "foreskin"—a vicar! Imagine the kind of world that those Dutch Calvinists inhabited!

He touched his tongue for a moment with the tip of his ring finger, picked up a crumb of bread from the table, and popped it into his mouth. Since Quinten did not react to his exposition, he began to realize that he was only listening out of politeness, but that didn't stop him going on. It was a matter of honor to be only his son's technical assistant from now on; maybe he had done his duty by Quinten as a historical-theological adviser, but that wasn't going to prevent him saying what he had left to say.

When a scholar once asked Christ, he went on, what in his view was the greatest commandment in the Law, Jesus said that it was love of God; and that the second commandment, like the first, was that you should love your neighbor as yourself. Obviously, he assumed that everyone loved themselves. Knowledge of human beings was not his strong point: for that we had to wait for another Jew, from Vienna. Anyone who did not love himself, or indeed hated himself, could according to that second thesis therefore hate his fellow man to the same extent. You could murder if you simply committed suicide afterward, like Judas and Hitler. Jesus obviously had no conception of hell, and that was in fact obvious: after all he was the creature that God loved like himself. But the profundity of his answer lay in the equals sign that he inserted between the five commandments on the first stone and those on the second; one day, for that matter, he even himself formulated a positive version of the golden rule "Therefore all things whatsoever you would that men should do to you, do ye even so to them: for this is the law and the prophets."

"This is the law and the prophets . . ." repeated Quinten, while something like happiness appeared on his face.

The mysterious turn of phrase pleased him. He looked at his father. The operation of his intelligence reminded Onno of the lightning-fast swerves with which an ice hockey player passed his opponents, slammed the puck into the goal, swept past the net on screeching skates, and raised his stick aloft in defiance. He was almost his old self. In other ways, too, it seemed as though the last ten days had completely obliterated the previous four years; neither of them could actually remember how it had been all that time. Onno wondered what the point of it had been. He looked at Quinten for a moment, but immediately looked down again. He thought of the conversation that they had had at the obelisk of Thutmoses: about the sphere and the point. Even if life had a meaning, he reflected, what was the meaning of that? And if that was a play on words, didn't the same apply to the question about the meaning of life? Was that perhaps the reason why Quinten didn't know what was meant by "meaning"?

They only got up when Goebbels pulled the chairs out from under them and from the Piazza della Minerva two screeching vans from the municipal sanitation department approached, like lobsters, with spraying water and revolving brooms.

The floodlights had already been extinguished for some time, and the Pantheon had been consigned again to the gray night. They made their way home in silence through the narrow, dark streets, interspersed with abandoned squares, where bearded marble figures had frozen in their violent efforts to struggle free of gravity. Perhaps, thought Quinten, no one was looking at the Pantheon now—how was it possible then that it could exist? Shouldn't someone look at everything the whole time, to keep the world together?

*

According to plan Quinten woke only at about midday, since they wouldn't be getting any more sleep for a while; but Onno had kept waking with a start. Each time, he stared into the dark with heart pounding and eyes wide open, wondering desperately what he had gotten himself into. If someone had ever foretold this, wouldn't he have avoided the idiot for the rest of his life? That Saturday afternoon they said little to each other. It was dreary, gray weather. Onno tried to read the paper, but the later it got, the more uneasy he became. He hoped that something would intervene, an earthquake, war, the end of time, but reality had decided not to pay any heed to their proposed expedition.

Quinten on the other hand was amazed at his own calm. It was as though he would soon simply have a routine chore to perform, like taking the dog for a walk, or turning down the central heating—while at the same time he had the feeling that his whole life had been heading toward this day. The fact that this evening he would be penetrating into the center of the world, which had alarmed him so much in his dreams, did not inspire fear in him. Was the center of his secret Citadel perhaps more dangerous than reality? Like a trail of seaweed, the title of a book—or was it a play?—began floating through his thoughts: *Life Is a Dream.* . . . He also remembered that Max had once said that you couldn't prove that you weren't dreaming when you were awake, because sometimes in a dream you were also certain you were awake and weren't dreaming. So if reality could be a dream, mightn't the dream perhaps also be reality?

Toward evening he leaned with his arms folded on the windowsill and looked at the bronze angel on the Castel Sant'Angelo, which, when the sun came from behind the clouds like a beaming pineapple, suddenly began glinting like a golden vision.

"We must be off," he said, turning around.

Onno had fallen asleep.

"What, what?" he said, sitting up from his mattress with a groan. "Not yet, surely? We're not really going to do it, are we?"

"You bet we are. It's five-thirty. The Sancta Sanctorum closes in two hours." Quinten took the small bright-red canvas backpack, which he had bought yesterday and had packed hours before, off his camp bed. "Are you coming, or would you rather go on sleeping?"

"Of course I'd rather go on sleeping," said Onno gruffly, and stumbled to the tap. "I was just dreaming about an ideal world without crime, without commandments, and without boys who are far too enterprising."

After they had eaten half a French loaf with ham at Mauro's, with nothing but an espresso, and had been to the toilet one last time, Onno suggested hailing a taxi, but that didn't seem a good idea to Quinten: if things went wrong, the driver would have their description. On the Corso Vittorio Emanuele they took the bus and got off at the basilica. As they walked past the obelisk to the entrance, Onno raised his stick in the air and said:

"Ave, Pharao, morituri te salutant."

In his other hand he had the flat, sturdy gray plastic air-travel suitcase in which the stone tablets of Moses were shortly to be put.

The Sancta Sanctorum was busier than on the previous days—perhaps because tomorrow was Sunday. The grumpy face of the old priest, who was ready to tap angrily with his coin against the glass, lit up with a smile when he saw Quinten.

"You're about to rob that dear old chap," said Onno.

"I'm going to collect something he doesn't even know he has."

"And you think that's not stealing? Perhaps it's even worse. You don't do things like that. It isn't even a question of Mosaic morality, but upbringing."

"Then you should have brought me up properly," said Quinten before he knew it. He was immediately sorry that he had blurted it out. "I'm sorry, I didn't mean it like that."

Onno nodded without looking at him. "Leave it. You're right."

No, he wasn't a thief, Quinten reflected. He'd never stolen anything. After all, he didn't want those stones for himself! Once he had them, he would no more have them to himself than those priests had them now. Those same fathers of the Holy Cross would certainly understand him better—but no, they of course had only entered the order to get to heaven; they were expecting a rich reward. He himself expected nothing, and his father kept trying up to the very last moment to make him give up his plan. But if he wasn't a thief, what was he then?

In order to win the complete confidence of the priests, and in order to be able to use their piety as an argument in the event of a disaster, Quinten had persuaded Onno to go up via the Holy Stairs. They crossed the entrance and waited at the bottom stair for their turn, as though in front of a box office.

"In a moment," said Onno, "I shall sink to my knees, and from the Calvinist Heaven my father, seated at the right hand of God, will glare down at me and then fall from his chair in a swoon. All your fault." And when a place became free and he actually knelt down, supporting himself on his stick, he bent his head and muttered, "Forgive me, Father, I know not what I do. Only your grandson knows that."

It sounded like a prayer, and Quinten had difficulty in suppressing a laugh. That old mixture of jokes and seriousness that he remembered so well from the past was returning more and more. Or, rather, it wasn't a mixture; the one was at the same time the other—the jokes were serious, without being any the less jokes for that. Perhaps no one had ever understood that except Max; perhaps their friendship had been based on it.

Quinten also knelt on the first step with his hands folded. He had not gone to the lengths of learning the twenty-eight official prayers by heart, but just moving his lips for a quarter of an hour seemed equally ridiculous to him; so he began muttering his Latin declensions:

Hic, haec, hoc. Hic, huius, hoc. Hic, huic, hoc. Hunc, hanc, hoc. Hoc, hac, hoc. Hi, hae, haec. Horum, harum, horum. Horum, his, horum. Hos, has, haec. Hos, his, haec."

The wood-paneled steps were low and wide, the next two were empty, on the fourth knelt a nun and a heavy, common-looking man. The soles of his shoes, which Quinten was looking at, had thick treads with small stones stuck in them. He would have loved to take a knife out of his backpack and prise them out, which would have made them fly six feet in the air. While the nun and the man made their way laboriously to the following step, like invalids, he and Onno also clambered upward. Out of the corner of his eye he saw his father shuffling clumsily with his stick and his case. After five or six steps, each of which were kissed by the nun, he had run out of pronouns, and so started on the verbs:

"Capio, capis, capit, capimus, capitis, capiunt. Capiam, capias, capiat, capiamus, capiatis, capiant. Capiebam, capiebas, capiebat, capiebamus, capiebatis, capiebant. Caperem, caperes, caperet, caperemus, caperetis, caperent. Capiam, capies, capiet, capiemus, capietis, capient."

The higher he got, the more irregular the verbs became and gradually he sank into a light trance. How did it go again? *Deponentia, semi-deponentia . . . Volebamus, ferebatis, ferrebaris. . . .* Through a small glass window in the wood, pale-brown spots were visible on the white marble: Christ's blood of course. *Conficit, confecit, confectus . . .*

At the top, by the barred window of the chapel, opposite the altar, they got to their feet.

"If we are not crushed by the power of God's right hand now," said Onno, "that will be the ontological proof that he doesn't exist."

It was seven o'clock. For the last half hour they wandered among the tourists and worshipers through the chapels, which gradually began to empty; a priest had stationed himself at the bottom of the Holy Stairs to prevent anyone else climbing them.

"There's still time for us to leave," said Onno, without hope.

"But we won't. Let's take up our positions."

They went to the right-hand side chapel, where there was no one except an elderly couple, obviously German; they both wore green loden jackets and were looking at the fresco of St. Lorenzo above the altar. Very shortly, Quinten knew, a priest would do the rounds in order to ask the stragglers to leave with unctuous gestures. The priest himself would not wait for them, but a little later he would come back for a last check. If he were to appear before the couple had disappeared, there would be no problem: they would wait until they were alone and then quickly make themselves invisible— there was no communication between the priest above and those at the foot of the four profane staircases. But it was made easy for them. As they stood by the outside wall, opposite the bronze door with the padlocks on it, which led to the Sancta Sanctorum, the man in the loden jacket suddenly looked at his watch, said, "Good heavens!" in alarm—and hurried off holding his wife by the arm.

The moment they were out of sight, Quinten and Onno turned, pulled open the black velvet curtains of a confessional, and slipped in.

The scuffing sandals of the priest had come and gone. Five minutes later they had again come and gone, the outside doors had closed with a thunderous crash, the light has been turned off, and in the pitch blackness of their hideaway they listened to the sounds. After the lay public had been turned out into the street, the atmosphere of sanctity downstairs at the entrance gradually gave way to a flaming row in Italian.

The clerics seemed to have undergone a transformation. Onno could not follow what all those grumbling old voices were saying, but regarded the fact that this had happened as a confirmation of his theory of the Golden Wall: behind the Church's wall things were just like everywhere else—and in a certain sense that was right and proper, because in this way those impassioned old men in their black dresses proved that they were religious professionals and not pious amateurs. After about ten minutes calm returned: murmuring voices in the distance, obviously on the farthest staircase on the other side, which led to the chapel of San Silvestro; the slamming of the door there, which gave access to the convent.

Silence.

Onno sat with his stick between his legs on the priest's bench, his hands folded on the snake's head, and felt as if he were playing a part in an absurd play. This couldn't be real. Under the bench was the suitcase. He would not have felt more foolish if someone had sent him off to catch a basilisk with a butterfly net and an empty jam jar. This was where that sultry Cuban night eighteen years ago—when Ada had seduced him—had finally brought him: to a Roman confessional with his son, locked in next to the holiest spot on earth, since that, according to this same tyrant, was where Moses' stone tablets of the Law were preserved. They were no more in that altar than yesterday's paper—or perhaps they were: they would never know. The tension he felt derived exclusively from uncertainty about how their weird burglary would turn out.

Quinten himself wasn't sure, either; but he did not doubt for a moment that they could force their way into that chapel and find the tablets there. They were simply waiting for him. In his half of the narrow cupboard things were less comfortable; there was only a bench for kneeling on, on which he had sat down. Separated by a partition with a barred diamond-shaped opening, they listened to each other's breathing.

"Can you hear me, my son?" whispered Onno.

Quinten turned around cautiously and put his mouth to the grille. "Yes."

"Satisfied, now you've finally got your way?"

"Yes."

"What would . . ."—"Ada" was on the tip of Onno's tongue—"Max say if he saw us sitting here like this?"

"I can't imagine."

"Do you know what I think? He'd have died laughing."

Onno thought of Max's fit of laughter in Havana when they had discovered what kind of conference they had wound up in. There on that island not only had Quinten been conceived, but the seeds of his own political downfall had been sown. Koos's face, on the boat to Enkhuizen: "Does your stupidity know no bounds, Onno?" Helga's death the same day . . . Ada. . . . And Quinten also thought of Max, vanished so completely from the world as if he had never existed. His empty coffin in the earth. His mother . . .

"Perhaps it's because it's so dark and silent here," whispered Onno, "but I keep thinking of your poor mother the whole time."

"Me too."

"Do you remember we went to visit her together?"

"Of course. We were chased by the police."

"Yes, I vaguely remember something of the sort."

Quinten hesitated, but a moment later said: "That evening I had a really fantastic dream for the first time."

"Can you remember that too? It's almost ten years ago."

"Didn't I say that I hardly ever forget anything?"

"What did you dream, then?"

"I'm not going to tell you," said Quinten, turning his head away a little. "Something about a building." The center of the world. He thought of the deathly fear with which he had woken up after hearing that calm, hoarse voice, how afterward he had groped around helplessly in just such a darkness and silence as he found himself in now—but although he was not dreaming now, and although the fact that he was here was completely bound up with that dream, he didn't feel a trace of fear. "But at the very last moment it suddenly turned into a nightmare. I had no idea where I was. I stared screaming, I think, and it was only when Granny came out of Max's bedroom and put the light on that I saw that I was on the threshold of her room."

Onno caught his breath. Did Sophia come out of Max's bedroom at night? What did that mean? He had the feeling he really shouldn't ask about it, but he couldn't help himself:

"Did Max and Granny sleep together, then?"

"Never noticed it. Perhaps they'd been talking, for all I know. Be quiet for a moment . . ."

Far away a soft, sing-song voice resounded: probably from the refectory, where a priest was reading an edifying text, while the others sat silently eating their frugal meal and did not listen.

Onno would have liked to ask what Sophia was wearing that night, but he knew enough. Bloody lecher. He stopped at nothing—not even that frigid Sophia Brons, who was a thousand years older than him. How could he ever have believed otherwise? But had he ever believed otherwise? He'd never wanted to think about it, because of course he suspected that there was something going on between those two in that lonely castle with its long nights, but he hadn't wanted to admit it to himself. Why not? What was wrong with it? Because Max's offer to bring up his son had to be an act of pure, self-sacrificing friendship? How pure were his own motives when it came down to it? He also realized with a jolt that this meant that his mother-in-law had recently—without anyone knowing—been widowed for the second time, at the age of sixty-two.

"If we ever get out of this alive," he whispered, "we must get in touch with your grandmother immediately."

"All the same to me," said Quinten indifferently.

Everything that followed lay before him as though on the other side of a mountain, of which he could see only the summit ridge at the moment: beyond that might be the sea, or a city, or a desert, or a mist-filled abyss. He felt as if up to now he had done everything by himself, and as if he still had to do the most important thing in the next few hours—afterward, he knew with absolute certainty, events would take their own course and he would see what happened to him. He slowly nodded off, though nothing escaped his ears, like a dozing dog . . .

"Quinten?"

"Yes?" He looked at the luminous child's watch that he had bought yesterday for a few thousand lire, with a Mickey Mouse wobbling to and fro as a second hand. It was almost nine o'clock.

"Were you asleep?"

"Just dozing."

"You're completely calm, aren't you? Nothing can happen to you."

"I don't think so."

"I wish I could say the same. I'm dying a thousand deaths, and I feel claustrophobic."

"Why did you wake me up?"

"I didn't know you were asleep."

"What did you want to say, then?"

"I keep thinking of Max," said Onno. "Have you ever had a bosom friend?"

"A bosom friend?"

"That means you haven't. A bosom friend is someone you even tell something that you'd never tell anyone."

"Do you mean a secret?"

"I don't know what you mean by a secret, but I mean something shameful, something that you are so shamed of that no one must know."

"I haven't got anything like that."

"Really?"

"What sort of thing would it be? Of course I've got a secret that I'll never tell anyone, but not because I'm ashamed of it."

"Not even your mother?" asked Onno after some hesitation.

"No one."

Quinten said no more. Hadn't his father himself said that his mother was really "no one"? So precisely by telling his secret to no one, he was actually telling it to his mother. Should he tell his father this now? He'd understand immediately, but then of course he would have betrayed something of the secret. Was his mother perhaps ultimately the secret?

Again the silence was disturbed by stumbling in the distance.

"There they are," whispered Quinten.

Everything went as expected. In the chapel of San Silvestro the priests were now gathering for complines, after which they would go to bed. A few minutes later the sound of old men's singing rang out.

With eyes closed, squeezed shut by the darkness, Onno and Quinten listened to the thin Gregorian chant, which hung in the air like a silver cobweb. For Onno it exuded a desperate loneliness, a metallic freezing cold, which seemed to flow in through a chink straight from the Middle Ages— but for Quinten its harmonic unanimity evoked the image of ten or fifteen men, sinking after a shipwreck but holding each other to the last. The psalms, intended to help them through the night, were interrupted only by a short chapter prayer.

After a quarter of an hour the door to the convent was closed again.

"Quarter past nine," whispered Quinten. "At ten past ten, then."

In a quarter of an hour the fathers would be in bed and by approximately a quarter past ten they would have gone to sleep. Because Onno had remembered once reading something about the periodicity of sleep, he had looked up a study of it in a university bookshop at Quinten's insistence. Besides the fantastic periods of "paradoxical sleep"—that of the dreams, from one which one was easily awakened—sleep consisted of four degrees of depth. The first and longest period of the deepest sleep occurred twenty-five minutes after falling asleep and itself also lasted approximately twenty-five minutes. The second period came seventy minutes later, lasted no longer than ten minutes, but was followed after less than half an hour by the even shorter third and last period.

For Quinten that was enough to decide to work only during the deepest, dreamless phases, from which sleepers could be roused only with difficulty. So, over the course of the night, he had three quarters of an hour in all to play with. That ought to be enough.

60

The Commandos

"Ten past ten."

When Mickey Mouse showed the correct time to the second, Quinten stood up and silently pushed the curtain aside. Through the three stained-glass windows, the streetlights ensured that there was not quite total darkness. On the altar a red lamp was lit. Quickly and silently, he walked in his soft thief's shoes around behind the Sancta Sanctorum to the choir chapel on the other side, but the light was out there too; by the door to the sacristy he squatted down and peered around the corner: no one had remained behind in silent prayer; only a sour smell indicated that the old men had been there. Back in the chapel of San Lorenzo he saw the shadow of Onno, who was rubbing his left leg painfully. Quinten took his backpack from the confessional, gave his father the pocket flashlight, and walked between the rows of pews to the double door opposite with the two eyes in it, which gave access to the Sancta Sanctorum.

Like a doctor feeling his patient's pulse, he laid his hand momentarily on the top sliding padlock, which formed the nose of the bronze face. Then he knelt down, unfastened the backpack, and carefully spread out on the floor a chamois cloth containing ten or twelve long steel pins, in different sizes, gleaming with oil. With the lamp at its lowest, Onno lit his work.

At home he had seen Quinten busy with his preparations and they had seemed to him so ridiculous that he had found it too embarrassing to inquire about them—but what he saw now filled him with astonishment. Quinten tucked a hammer with a rubber head into his trouser belt and like a professional burglar picked up a couple of pins, which fitted into the H-shaped keyhole. While he slid them slowly into the colossal lock, leaning with one ear against the door, he averted his eyes in order to concentrate fully on what his hands felt on the inside. Suddenly Onno remembered something from his earliest childhood, from before the war: the photographer on the beach at Scheveningen. After he had taken the cover off the lens behind his tripod, he put his arms in the two black sleeves that hung down from his huge camera and performed mysterious movements inside, which must not see the light of day, while he kept his eyes focused just as blindly on the horizon as Quinten now did on the invisible ceiling paintings. While his movements became even more minute and precise, Quinten closed his eyes and parted his lips a little. Finally he pulled the hammer from his trouser belt, looked precisely at what he was doing, and gave the pins a short, dull tap. From the inside of the lock came a stiff click. He looked up at his father with a smile and carefully pulled the heavy shackle from the box and the rings on the door.

"One down," he whispered.

Onno looked at him open-mouthed. Quinten had told him about Piet Keller, the locksmith at Groot Rechteren, whom he had often visited as a little boy; but it had seemed to him impossible that after so many years it could result in what he now saw: the opened lock. While Quinten wasted no time and immediately took the lower lock in hand, Onno realized that everything had now suddenly become much more dangerous.

If they had been discovered before or afterward, they would have said that they had wanted to spend the night in the proximity of the *acheiropoeton* out of devotion; he had been convinced that after fiddling with the lock a bit, they would have gotten no farther than the chapel of San Lorenzo. But in the meantime the lock had been picked and the pins were already in the second lock. His initial lightheartedness had disappeared instantly—but at this stage there was obviously no stopping Quinten any longer. The only way of putting an end to it was to go immediately to the convent door, bang on it with his stick, and rouse the fathers from the deepest level of their sleep. But then he would have lost his son for good.

By the time the second lock had also admitted defeat with a click, things had still gone without a hitch. Quinten looked at his watch: twenty-three minutes past eleven. In the bronze of the right-hand half of the door there were a couple of keyholes in incomprehensible places; he had read in Grisar that the door was originally Roman, and hopefully they were simply separate relics from that time. He cautiously pushed against the left-hand side, and it immediately gave way . . .

The center of the world!

He took his backpack and, lit by his father's flashlight, stepped across the threshold. He would have preferred to do it more solemnly, striding slowly, like a Pontifex Maximus—but now that he had gotten here he was suddenly in a hurry: there were twelve minutes left for the first part of the operation. Was it always like this, perhaps? Did the real work lie in the preparations and was the actual achievement nothing more than a bonus?

As he went down a passageway, approximately four yards long, that led into the chapel, a Chinese fairy tale that Max had once told him came back to him: the emperor had once commissioned a draftsman to draw a cockerel, and the latter had said that he needed ten years for the work; after he had lived at the emperor's expense for ten years and had drawn a thousand cockerels every day, he went to the palace again; when the emperor inquired if he had the drawing with him, the draftsman asked for a pencil and paper and drew a cockerel with a single line, whereupon the stupid emperor became so furious that he tore up the drawing and had the draftsman beheaded.

The low, narrow passageway, the fifteen-hundred-year-old connection with the former papal palace, seemed to explode at its end into the high, square space of the Gothic chapel. Without looking up or around, Quinten went to the altar and knelt down with his tools. Onno followed him with the flashlight, and although he had not been drinking, he gradually felt as if he were becoming tipsy. *Non est in toto sanctior orbe locus.* The things that were happening now were so outrageous that he could scarcely comprehend them. Probably he was dreaming. Unlike the fathers, he was in the state of paradoxical sleep: any moment now he would wake up, bathed in sweat, as the saying went; Edgar would be sitting on the windowsill and the sun would have risen over another hot day in Rome, full of politics, tourism, and things that twenty-four hours later would all be forgotten for all eternity. He glanced back and now saw the barred window from the inside, in a dim light that came through the windows on the ground floor up the Holy Stairs.

"Hold the flashlight still," whispered Quinten in a commanding tone.

The door to the chapel was probably still regularly used, but the locks of the barred doors in front of the altar had not been opened since 1905. There were just over ten minutes left for the first phase, but he did not have to force himself to be calm, because he was calm. He'd seen that the two bottom padlocks, no bigger than a hand, were conventional in construction and proof only against force, not careful thought: from the five simple skeleton keys, which he had had made by a locksmith behind the Pantheon, he immediately selected the right one.

Without much effort the locks clicked open; obviously they had been restored in the days of Grisar, and so the same would probably apply to the monstrous sliding padlock. For the first time Quinten saw it from close quarters. He smiled and thought: what an angel. It locked a heavy iron rod, which prevented the barred doors opening across their whole length. A few minutes later, after a tap with the rubber hammer, this item had also capitulated.

With a small can he quickly applied some oil to the four hinges, put the tools into his backpack, and laid it next to him on the altar.

"Give me a hand," he whispered. Onno put his stick on the papal prayer stool—and in order not to make any noise, they carefully moved the bar from the two rings and laid it down on the worn marble step, upon which for a thousand years 160 popes had celebrated mass daily.

Quinten looked at his watch.

"Twenty-five to eleven. It's time."

After hanging back the locks of the entrance door temporarily, Quinten lay down on a prayer stool opposite the altar in the chapel of San Lorenzo and immediately felt himself dropping off . . .

The reddish-brown wall, at reading distance from his eyes, is a little darker in the middle, so it is as if he is looking into a tunnel. A little later a small tangled violet sphere, like a turning ball of wool, no larger than a marble, starts revolving; shortly afterward it sheds its skin for a moment to reveal the accurately drawn snout of a monkey, also very small, and immediately disappears, while another new little whirlpool emerges, turning into a small, monstrous mouth with sharp teeth, again just as precisely etched. Even in his semisleep he is completely conscious; he looks in fascination at the spectacle unraveling before his eyes; watches as it evaporates and is replaced by a fish, a woman's face, with disheveled hair, a strange pig, a cat, a jar, a man with a furrowed brow and a beard, each in sharp focus, like in a photograph. Where does it all come from? He's not imagining it; he's never seen the apparitions before and has no idea what the next one will be. Were they all there before he saw them? Do they still exist when he no longer sees them? They remind him of the paintings of Hieronymus Bosch—so Bosch didn't invent anything; he simply remembered everything well. But then something begins to change. The wall, about a foot away from him, suddenly becomes transparent, as he had once seen with Max and Sophia at the Holland Festival, in a Mozart opera, *The Magic Flute*—when a front-lit gauze curtain, which closed off the whole proscenium arch, was slowly lit from behind, gradually revealing an enormous space with perspective decor in the style of Bibiena . . .

Onno had not gone back to the confessional, either; with Quinten on one side of him and his stick on the other, he stared into the darkness and listened to the sounds, his legs outstretched, his hands folded behind his neck. A soft hum surrounded the building, Saturday-night traffic; far away he heard the siren of an ambulance or a police car. The Romans were going out for the evening.

Everywhere, the restaurants and the cafés and the theaters were full, the city was blossoming around them; but they themselves were sitting here, on their metaphysical commando raid, like an incredible anachronism in search of the tablets of a Law about which not only could no one care less any longer, but which most people had never even heard of. He glanced sideways at Quinten, who was breathing deeply and now descending in his turn into the deepest stage of his sleep, while the fathers of the Holy Cross began rising into dreamier regions. Onno sighed deeply. For as long as he lived he would never forget the sound of those clicking locks. Whenever anyone said to him that this or that was impossible, he would hear *click!* and laugh in the person's face.

Now and then he dozed off for a moment or two. In the convent a toilet was flushed. It was past eleven; it seemed that the sleep theory was true. He thought of the rigid way in which Quinten had drawn up his schedule, down to the minute, as though it were a matter of mathematics instead of psychology. Where did he get that scientific bent from? Not from him. He himself was convinced that nothing made sense apart from math; come to that, even in the heart of mathematics something seemed to be not quite right.

Everything was always a mess. Perhaps that impressive tendency derived from Ada, from music, which was after all in a certain sense audible mathematics. But the technical triumphs that Quinten had tasted up to now with all those locks had of course made his expectations much greater; shortly the disillusion would hit him all the harder. There was no way there would be any tablets of the Law in the altar. Emptiness. Dust. Perhaps a short note from Grisar, with greetings from 1905 . . .

Quinten looked up, cracked his thumbs, and got to his feet. Twenty to twelve. Outside the pounding of loud music rang out, obviously from a stationary car with its door open. His father was asleep; leaning forward on the next bench, his head on his crossed arms, he breathed through his mouth with a deep rattling sound. Quinten shook his shoulders.

"Wake up!"

Onno got up with a groan. "Are we still here?"

A little later he stumbled after Quinten, feeling as if he were only now beginning to dream.

At the door Quinten turned around and whispered: "Have you got the case with you?"

The case! Without saying a word Onno went to the confessional, where it was still under the bench. Meanwhile Quinten had lifted the lock off the entrance door, and back in the chapel the oil turned out to have done its work: the barred gates of the altar opened without a sound.

Now there appeared two bronze doors, with depictions of Peter and Paul on the top panels; on these two was another heavy lock. He could see it properly for the first time. It seemed to be a different type, but to his relief he saw that it was a classic key lock. When it failed to respond to any of his skeletons, he looked for a hook from his backpack and inserted it in the keyhole. After fiddling around for a bit, he pressed down on the body of the lock with it so that the locking bar was pressed against the tongues of the levers; then with a second hook he carefully took out the levers, until the bar went into the connecting grooves and the lock could move. He pulled the shackle forward out of the lock, slid it off the four bronze rings, and put it on the step, alongside the three that were already there.

"There you are," he whispered, and looked at his watch. "Two minutes left. We're on our way."

He pulled the doors open with both hands.

From the illustration in Grisar's book Onno also immediately recognized the carved cyprus-wood relic shrine. Although it was over eleven hundred years old, it looked as fresh as though it had just recently been delivered by the joiner. On its top edge it said in Latin that the box came from Leo III, the unworthy servant of God; but the text was interrupted by a wooden shield, on which was written in gold letters:

SCA

SCO RV

An extremely illiterate abbreviation of *Sancta Sanctorum*. It was obvious that the inscription had been put on later: when the relics had been brought here from the Lateran basilica and the chapel had been given that name.

Because Moses' tablets of the Law were contained in them from that moment on? Onno looked at Quinten. Quinten looked at the four square, decorated doors, which looked like the luggage lockers in a station. On each door there was a small ring to pull it open with. Everything was in turn guarded with locks, but he saw immediately that they were not locked. He pursed his lips and pulled the top left-hand door open. While the silver covering of the *acheiropoeton* gleamed on the altar, Onno focused the beam of light into it. The drawer was empty. Quinten pulled out the top right-hand drawer: empty. The lower left-hand drawer; the right left-hand drawer: all empty.

Quinten looked at his watch. Five to twelve. He stood up and said: "We must go."

When he made to leave the chapel, Onno whispered: "Shouldn't we clear up in here? We can't leave it like this, can we?"

"We're coming back in half an hour."

Onno stiffened.

"To do what? They're not here, Quinten. You were wrong. Everything has gone well up to now, let's call it a day."

Quinten put a finger to his lips—and for the umpteenth time Onno realized that there was nothing he could say.

Back for the second time in the chapel of San Lorenzo, sitting next to each other in the dark on a bench, Onno thought of the mess that they had made—picked locks, opened doors, tools lying everywhere. Imagine an insomniac father of the Holy Cross taking his prayer book and going for a walk through the building, praying as he went, and then seeing that chaos in the sanctum! But he was even more tormented by the question how he could support Quinten.

For reasons that were obscure to him, the boy had invested so much in this adventure that he could obviously not stand the fact that it all had been for nothing. How could he get it through to him that this was how things were in life? When you were seventeen, you thought that the world was made of the same substance as your own theories, so that you had control of it and could turn it to your own advantage. But one day everyone had to confront the bitter truth that it wasn't like that, that the world was soup and thought was generally a fork: it seldom resulted in a good meal. Today the moment of truth had struck for Quinten—differently than for other boys, that was true, but it amounted to the same thing.

"Quinten?"

"Yes?"

"What do you want to do?"

"Have another good look."

"We did have a good look."

"But still no better than Grisar. Or Flavius Josephus."

Onno sighed in resignation. Again he was encountering granite. He could keep his wise sermons to himself; it was as though Freud's father were to try to convince his son that the subconscious did not exist—and it was very questionable whether it existed. At the same time it gave him a feeling of satisfaction: Quinten still had the kind of unspoiled self-confidence that he himself had long since lost—if he'd ever possessed it; he wasn't even sure of that anymore. He mustn't try to talk him around at all; he had to empty that cup to the dregs. What's more, he might otherwise have to hear for the rest of his life that the tablets might have been in that damn altar after all. On their ascetic beds the fathers meanwhile rose for a short while to the second stage of their sleep, before sinking back to the fourth.

At quarter past twelve, Quinten took the flashlight and said: "Now for it."

By now they both felt at home in the chapel that they kept going in and out of. Quinten squatted down, laid the flashlight against the marble step, rested his elbows on his knees, put his hands on his cheeks, and looked intently at the shrine. He had to finish in ten minutes.

It had not surprised him that the four drawers were empty, because he knew that. But where else could two flat stones have been hidden? Actually, only *behind* the treasure chest. At the back, the altar was built against the wall; it couldn't be reached from the side. But it must be possible to take the box out: it had once been put in. In the center of the lower frame he noticed a ring, obviously intended to pull the whole thing forward; but that was impossible, since the marble pillars of the altar blocked the sides of the box. So this meant that the shrine had not been pushed into the altar but that the altar had been built around the shrine. And that had happened in about the year 800, while the tablets of the Law had only been brought here from the basilica four centuries later. In other words: they couldn't be behind the box. So? So they must be underneath.

The box was not resting on the ground; there was a narrow chink. Obviously it was on legs, but they were obscured from view by the pillars. Quinten lay down on his stomach, put his cheek on the step, and shone the flashlight underneath. Had Grisar done this too? What reason would he have had to do that? There was all kinds of rubbish that was difficult to distinguish—shards, pieces and fragments, perhaps remains of masonry work. On either side the shrine was supported not by feet but by flat stones.

Quinten looked inside numbly, feeling the blood draining from his face. From his backpack he produced a long skeleton key and put the key around the back of the right-hand stone. Helping it along with the flat of his hand, which just fitted through the gap, he tried to see if it could be moved. Scraping over the dust, the stone moved forward. It was not supporting anything!

"Dad . . ." he whispered flatly. "I've got them."

61

The Flight

When Onno saw the oblong, gray, almost black stone appearing from the crack, he remembered for an instant how as a little boy he'd sometimes stood by the mailbox when the postman came. The flap suddenly opening, the letters falling into the hall from nowhere.

He began trembling.

"You're crazy!" he whispered, while it seemed as if he were screaming. "It's impossible! Let me see!"

"Not now," said Quinten with determination. "Give me the suitcase."

"Let me see if there's anything written on it!"

"In a moment. Hurry up."

With trembling hands, Onno gave him the suitcase, and Quinten snapped open the locks. The stone was lighter than he thought, but still almost as heavy as a paving slab; carefully he laid it among the newspapers that he had put in at home—the *Corriere della Sera*, *La Stampa*, the *Herald Tribune*. When Onno saw the second stone appearing too, his head began to spin. It was inconceivable that these could really be Moses' tablets of the Law! Surely this was the most inconceivable thing of all! Of course they were simply two old flagstones. Quinten was seeing what he wanted to see—he was simply making a bigger and bigger hangover for himself!

Quinten snapped the locks of the suitcase again, collected his tools, and put them into the backpack. As he stood there with it in his hands, he surveyed the shrine, opened the upper right-hand drawer, and put his backpack into the compartment.

"Treasure trove," he said, closing the door, "in a thousand years' time."

Then he closed the bronze doors, took the large padlock off the steps, put it through the rings, and pushed it into the lock with a loud click. Next the barred gate was shut—two clicks of the padlocks and this was also barred. Together with Onno, he pushed the iron rod through the rings and put the large sliding padlock on it. When he pushed the parts together with all his strength, it produced such a penetrating sharp click that it was as though someone were striking an anvil with a hammer. Onno stopped to see if anyone had heard it, but Quinten gave him the case and pushed him in the back. "Let's go now, before someone comes." They went quickly through the narrow passage to the chapel of San Lorenzo, where Quinten closed the entry door behind him and put on the two locks, again with loud clicks.

"Right," he said, and listened. "Not much more can happen to us now."

With his left hand Onno pointed to the suitcase in his right. "If the Ten Commandments are really in here, which God forbid, then more can happen to us than you could ever imagine in your wildest dreams, my dear friend. That would be more explosive than an atom bomb."

"Only if you can't hold your tongue. No one will ever know." What did his father know about his wildest dreams? Only because of his dream of the Citadel had he been able to fetch the tablets from *the center of the world*—thus, as it were, removing the sting from the SOMNIUM QUINTI. The sting was now in that suitcase.

When everything remained quiet in the convent, they again sat down on a bench opposite the altar. They now had to wait for the following morning, Sunday, when it would become busy. Their plan was simply to leave a quarter of an hour or half an hour after the opening of the Sancta Sanctorum: none of the fathers would notice that they were leaving without having arrived—since they were leaving, they obviously had also arrived. But that they should be uncertain about the contents of the case for the whole night was an unbearable prospect for Onno.

"I have to see it now, Quinten," he whispered, "otherwise I'll go mad."

"Then you'll have to go mad. Just imagine someone coming and seeing us peering at those things with a pocket flashlight. Haven't we agreed that we're here out of piety? If anyone comes, we go down on our knees and then we'll be praying. We have to get rid of that flashlight too, for that matter. Where should we leave it? Why didn't I think of that?"

"Is there really something you haven't thought of?" said Onno with a touch of mockery in his voice; but immediately he looked uncertainly around in the dark. "For that matter I keep having the feeling that there's something missing."

"What?"

"I don't know . . ." Suddenly Onno stiffened. "My stick! Quinten! I left my stick lying in the chapel. In the hurry when we had to put that iron rod—"

Quinten had already gotten up. He grabbed the flashlight and ran silently to the barred window at the top of the Holy Stairs. He shone it inside. As if in prayer, his father's stick lay on the papal prayer stool opposite the altar—the tip on the kneeling bench, the handle against the silk cushion with the tassels. He nodded. This was irrevocable. The flashlight had now also served its purpose, and on the way back he hid it behind a confessional against the wall.

"Yes," he said when he arrived back, and sat down next to Onno again. "So that's how it is. That changes our whole plan."

"Quinten . . ."

"Forget it, it's my fault. I hurried you along. There's no point in talking about it again. So now we have to get out of here before someone discovers it."

Onno felt a drop of sweat running from his armpit along his side. "And how are you proposing to get out? We're caught like rats in a trap."

Quinten thought for a moment. "There's only one way. What time are those services that come next? What are they called again?"

"Matins. Usually at about four o'clock."

"Then we'll simply go into the other chapel and say that we fell asleep, and can we please leave."

"And what if they ask what's in that suitcase?"

"Why should they ask that? There's nothing to steal here, is there? Anyway, what of it? Two dirty stones."

"Let's pray that they really are just two dirty stones," whispered Onno. "But we're not there yet. Tomorrow morning a father suddenly discovers my stick in the Sancta Sanctorum—and what then? What will happen then? The police will see from the oil on the hinges that we've been in the altar too. They'll open it, and they'll find your backpack. Apart from that, it will be empty—but who will remember that it's been empty for eighty years. The fathers, perhaps, but they've got no interest in making that known, given the reputation of their chapel. They'll give our descriptions and tomorrow morning identikit pictures of our faces will appear on Vatican television, together with a close-up of that stick. Father and son. Desecrators. Ten million lire reward. What will Mauro do then? Signor Enrico from Tyrol! And Nordholt? He'll realize immediately why I borrowed that book, and he's got my address at the institute. He's still got a score to settle with me, but to be on the safe side he'll probably first call the embassy for advice. In consultation with The Hague, they'll tell him that he should keep in the background for the time being."

"And I'll be recognized by the locksmith who made those things for me. He gave me a rather funny look when I got him to do it."

Onno turned to look at him. "I can't see your face properly, but it looks a bit as if you're smiling."

"So I am."

"What in heaven's name is there to smile about?"

"I don't know . . . perhaps the prospect of the journey."

"Our journey, of course. Ever heard of popular religious fury? How can we show ourselves in the street, here in the lion's den? Before the Sancta Sanctorum opens in the morning, we must be out of the country—it doesn't matter where we go."

Because St. Benedict of Nursia had understood that all that dreaming in paradoxical sleep can easily entangle the monk in the snares of physical temptation, and that therefore it has to be drastically interrupted at least once a night by the thistles and thorns of prayer, the convent began to come to life at about four o'clock. Stumbling. In the chapel of San Silvestro the light went on, and the reflection also pierced the darkness where they were.

Relieved that things had finally happened, they sat up. All those hours they had discussed at greater and greater intervals what they were going to do shortly, and where they were going to flee to—but according to Quinten they would see what happened, and Onno himself had also finally said they'd better stop, because it was like playing chess: often you thought for a long time about the right move, and when you'd finally found it and made it, you knew that it was wrong. That was quite simply the fundamental difference between thinking and doing. At that Quinten had fallen silent. His experience was different. When he'd thought and then done something, it had never been wrong but always right; and the fact that the Decalogue was now in the air-travel suitcase was proof of that. And soon it would all come right. They had not said anything more about the tablets and what was to be done with them.

While in the city the music gradually stopped, even in the last nightclubs, the building was again filled with ancient Gregorian unanimity. As he listened, Quinten was suddenly struck by the sense that old works of art were always old things: old bricks, old marble, old paint—but that old music was at the same time always brand-new, because it came from living throats. Apart from that, only old stories could also be new. That was of course because music and stories existed not in space but only in time.

"We've woken up now," he said, not whispering again for the first time. He stretched with a groan. "We look around, surprised to see where we are. In the Sancta Sanctorum! Oh no! How can it have happened? We must have fallen asleep. Come on, let's go."

"I suppose we'll have to." Onno sighed.

"You do the talking. And give me the suitcase, otherwise you'll forget that too."

As they walked through the rear chapel, where it was already lighter and the singing louder, Onno felt like an amateur actor forced to go onstage at the Royal Shakespeare Theatre in the role of King Lear. They turned the corner and stopped.

In the choir stalls a dozen old faces above black cassocks turned in their direction, the nocturne on the Resurrection died on their lips. No one showed a sign of alarm; there was only mild surprise. When they saw Quinten, a smile appeared here and there.

Quinten realized that he now had to throw this weapon into the battle. With his free hand he rubbed his eyes and made as if to yawn, but immediately he really yawned: the silence was filled with the long, touching yawn of a resplendent boy.

"Forgive us, Fathers," said Onno in Italian, "for disturbing you in your nocturnal vigil. My son and I fell asleep here yesterday. The whole day we had been wandering around your very beautiful city and we sat down for a moment in a confessional to rest. And only just now—"

With his hands clasped, as other people only do in an armchair, his head cocked to one side, an old man came forward. He introduced himself in a weak voice as Padre Agostino, the rector. He separated his hands for a moment and then put them back together again and said: "The guest is Jesus Christ. Would you like something to eat? A cup of coffee?"

Thrown off balance, Onno looked at him. Such pious simplicity and goodness rendered him helpless. The fathers had been robbed, hopefully only of two worthless stones, and they would never realize that they had lost anything; but in a few hours' time they would discover that they had been lied to by two burglars who had desecrated their holy chapel. He wanted nothing better than a cup of coffee, but he had the feeling that he would only really be committing a mortal sin if he accepted; apart from that, they had to make their getaway as soon as possible. He said that he didn't want to burden them any longer, whereupon the rector made a gesture of resignation, let his left hand float over Quinten's crown for a moment, and blessed him with the right. Thereupon Onno put out his hand to say goodbye, but at that moment the rector started back in alarm, looking at the hand as though he were being threatened with a knife. Immediately afterward another father accompanied them to the door of the convent, while all the heads turned to follow them, smiling and nodding.

In the white-plastered cloister, where a portrait of the pope hung, the father said with an apologetic gesture: "Please excuse the rector. You mustn't touch him. Padre Agostino has believed for the last few months he is made of butter."

A little later they left the place of pilgrimage via the tradesmen's entrance.

Breathing in the night air deeply, they walked into the square. By the obelisk Quinten turned around and glanced back at the building as if to say farewell.

"This is now no longer the holiest place in the world," he said.

The suggestion that he himself was therefore now the holiest place in the world was so shocking that Onno didn't know what to say. He raised his hand and hailed a taxi; at that point the driver was added to the company that would shortly recognize them, but by that time they would be far away abroad. He gave his address, Quinten put the suitcase on his lap, and, enjoying their freedom in silence, they roared toward the Colosseum and over the broad Via dei Fori Imperiali to the Piazza Venezia.

As they screeched around the corner, Onno suddenly cried: "Made of butter! How in God's name do you dream up that one!"

"Do you find that so crazy?"

"Don't you, then?"

"Not at all. On the contrary, it's logical."

"Of course," said Onno with his eyebrows raised. "That strikes me as just the sort of thing that you would understand. So explain to me why it's not senile but logical."

"Because Christ said that he was made of bread."

Onno did not reply. He looked outside, at the deserted pavements of the somber Corso Vittorio Emanuele. How did the boy's brain work? Was he really human? The rector who had spread himself on Christ to make a sandwich—in what kind of a head could such a thought occur? What kind of world did he live in? Was what he said even true, maybe? Did theology have a psychological dimension, of which psychology had no knowledge, for someone like the old padre?

In the courtyard on the Via del Pellegrino all the windows were dark. They went quietly up the stairs, and when they had gotten to his room, Onno said:

"And now I want to see it at once."

Quinten looked at his Mickey Mouse watch. "We've got no time for that. You have to sort your things out. What are you taking with you?"

"Nothing. Just my passport and a few clothes."

"And all those notes there?"

"They've served their turn. I'll leave a letter for the landlord, to say I've gone traveling for a few weeks. The rent has been paid for two months in advance; and if I'm not back by then, he'll make sure that things are cleared up."

"Just as long as you hurry. We've got to be out of Italy in a few hours."

"Five minutes!"

"Then I'll quickly put some coffee on."

"Nothing that I need more in the world! And be prepared for the biggest disappointment of your life, Quinten."

Onno took the suitcase and laid it on the table under the window. "Could anything be more idiotic? Thanks to my stupidity, we now have to leave the country—and why? For nothing!" In vain he tried to get the locks open. "How do these bloody things work?"

With a paper filter in his hand, Quinten came and made the locks spring open, and immediately went back to making coffee. It was a mystery to Onno. That boy had done everything to get those things into his possession—and now he had them. On the one hand he was convinced that they were the tablets of the Law; on the other hand they seemed to leave him completely indifferent.

Onno opened the lid, pulled down the desk lamp, put on his reading glasses, and opened the newspapers.

He saw at first glance that it wasn't as easy as that. The surface consisted on all sides of a gray-caked layer, which seemed to be made of congealed time. Was there something underneath? He scratched at it with a thumbnail, causing something of the grainy substance to loosen. This was work for an archaeological laboratory, but he had understood from Quinten that the stones would never find their way there. They had more or less the dimensions that Rabbi Berechiah, without ever having seen them, had given.

With lips tightly clenched, he leaned back. Was it really conceivable that these things here were the original of all those depictions which were to be seen in every synagogue, above the ark? The tablets of the Law: symbol of the Jewish religion, just as the menorah was that of the Jewish state and the *Magen David*—the "shield of David"—of Zionism. Was it really conceivable that these things which were now lying on the table had once lain in the ark of the covenant, had been lugged through the desert year after year, had been preserved for centuries in the Holy of Holies of the three temples, and then taken by Titus. . . . Was it conceivable that Quinten was right after all? Was Moses' handwriting hidden beneath that crust? Those signs, scratched into the stone as a result of some inspiration or other? Suddenly his heart started pounding. The oldest known inscriptions in Canaanite writing dated from approximately 1000 B.C.; Moses' writing would therefore be a thousand years older still. Undoubtedly, it would be very close to Egyptian hieroglyphics—and perhaps the Phaistos disc was connected in some way? That writing came from the same period! Suddenly he thought of the sign that looked a little like a sedan chair—was that perhaps the ark? However small the chance was that Quinten was right, it had to be proved beyond doubt that he was not! But how? What was he intending to do?

Hearing a creaking sound near his neck, he looked around in alarm. Smiling, with a pair of scissors in one hand, Quinten was holding up his ponytail. They had decided on that metamorphosis so that no one at the airport would recognize them when their descriptions appeared—and then be able to say where they had gone to. Quinten pulled the rubber band off, and a few entangled gray hairs got stuck in it; but he gathered his own hair behind him and wound the rubber band around it. At the same moment Onno saw a boy changing into a man, like when in a change of scene in a film the role of a young actor is suddenly taken over by an older one. He couldn't remember ever having seen Quinten's ears.

"Drink your coffee," said Quinten. "But keep your head still."

Like a real barber, he held the comb upside down in his left hand, the thumb of his right hand through one ring of the scissors, not the middle but the ring finger through the other, now and then making rapid snips in the air. After each snip his father resembled more and more the memory that he had of him: within five minutes the tramp had largely given way to the minister who had come and fetched him occasionally at Groot Rechteren in the car. Meanwhile he glanced over his shoulder at the tablets of the Law, like a barber glances at the illustrated magazine that the customer has on his lap.

"You'll have to do your beard yourself," he said, brushing the hairs off his clothes.

When Onno went to the basin to shave himself, Quinten bent over a corner of one of the stones, where a small, gleaming spot had struck him. He licked the tip of his middle finger and rubbed it, whereupon a deep blue glow showed itself. He sat up. The two stones were sapphires. They were gems. Since one gram cost five thousand guilders, they were worth hundreds of millions, perhaps a billion. He thought it better not to tell his father. He thought for a moment and then out of his blue nylon backpack he took the beige envelope with the heading SOMNIUM QUINTI, which he had not opened for weeks, since he had not dreamed of the Citadel anymore and nothing needed to be added to the plans. He put it with the stones and closed the suitcase.

When they drove out of the city in a taxi at about six o'clock via the Porta San Paolo and pyramid of Cestius, it was already growing light. Onno was again wearing the gray suit in which he'd arrived from Holland four years earlier; he enjoyed the feel of the cool air against his cheeks and on his neck. How could a human being let himself become so overgrown! He remembered a conversation that he had had years ago during the conference in Havana with a man who had spent years in a Stalinist work camp. The conversation was about beards, apropos of Fidel Castro and his friends, and he himself had said that he would only let his beard grow if he were one day to land in prison. Whereupon the other looked at him in silence for a while and then said, "When you land in prison, you'll shave yourself four times a day."

The sky was beginning to grow red, as though beyond the horizon the lid of an oven were being slowly opened. It was Sunday; there was little traffic.

"And what if the first plane that's leaving is going to Zimbabwe?" asked Onno.

"Then we'll go to Zimbabwe. We've got plenty of money."

"It's not a matter of money, and anyway I'm paying. But surely we've got time to pick something? I'd rather go to San Francisco than Zimbabwe. Do we absolutely have to be dependent on chance?"

"I don't know," said Quinten impatiently. "I think so."

"And when we're in Zimbabwe—what then?"

Quinten shrugged his shoulders and looked outside. In the distance the cupola of St. Peter's had almost disappeared. Here and there were large postmodern buildings in the countryside, such as he had seen in Mr. Themaat's catalog. He really didn't know. All he knew was that from now on he must not intervene anymore. From now on everything had to be determined by circumstances, just as a skier adapted himself to the terrain, avoiding trees and ravines and not trying to glide upward.

As they got out of the taxi at Leonardo da Vinci airport, the sun rose above the countryside and drenched the planes on the runway with dazzling gold, which a moment later changed to silver. It was already busy.

In the noisy departure hall Onno, pulling his case on wheels behind him, said: "Look. All thieves, making off with their booty."

Quinten carried the suitcase with the stones in it; he had his backpack on his back. They stopped in front of the great board with departure times and looked up at the destinations for the next few hours: Buenos Aires, Frankfurt, Santo Domingo, London, Cairo, Vienna, Nicosia, New York, Singapore, Sydney, Amsterdam . . .

"And what if it's Amsterdam?" asked Onno.

"Then it will be Amsterdam."

At the counter where they sold last-minute tickets sat a girl with her name on a badge; ANGIOLINA. Obviously she came from the deep south. Her hair was blacker than black; there was a dark shadow on her upper lip. Onno said they had decided to go abroad for a few weeks on impulse and that they wanted to book.

"Of course," she said, rearranging her silk scarf, which Quinten thought was back to front around her neck. She picked up her ballpoint pen. "What destination?"

"We'll leave it up to you. We want to leave on the next plane that has room in it."

"That's how I'd like to live," she said with a face that showed that nothing surprised her anymore. She glanced at the clock and looked at her monitor. "You can't make Vienna anymore. It will be Cairo or Santo Domingo. Perhaps you can just catch the eight o'clock British charter flight to Nicosia."

"Two singles to Nicosia," said Onno quickly, before it became Santo Domingo.

"Nicosia?" repeated Quinten. "Where's that?"

"On Cyprus. Nice island. Lots to see."

"Your passports, please." While she began to fix the tickets, she asked, "Would you like travel insurance?"

Onno looked sideways with a smile. "Do we need travel insurance, Quinten?"

"Of course not."

"We're trusting to our lucky stars, Angiolina."

She nodded. "At twelve-twenty local time, there'll be a short stopover in Tel Aviv."

Onno looked at Quinten, who answered his look in silence. He turned to Angiolina and said: "Make that two to Tel Aviv."

62

Thither

"So we're taking them home," said Quinten, after he had been given his boarding card.

Onno made no reply. He could feel that everything was not over yet. The check-in counter was in a corner of the hall, closed off with barriers. Carabinieri with submachine guns and bullet-proof vests strolled in twos across the marble floor; other men, too, in plain clothes, leaned against the pillars here and there. Outside, close to the high window, there was an armored police car on the pavement. It was busy, mainly older vacationers bound for Cyprus, obviously in a group, as could also be seen from their bright leisure clothes; the passengers for Tel Aviv were recognizable from an absent look on their faces. After they passed the barrier, everyone was interrogated separately at a row of iron tables.

"Let's sit down here until it's our turn," said Onno. "I'm getting tired out, and my head's spinning without my stick."

Quinten looked at him in concern. Only now did he realize that he had not for a moment taken his father's state of health into account. "Perhaps you should take a few days off in a little while."

"Good idea, Quinten. Israel seems to me just the country to have a rest in. Have you thought of what we're going to say when we open the case?"

"No."

"Everything will be all right, won't it?"

"Yes."

"So when they ask us what kinds of stones they are, we'll say 'The tablets of Moses.' "

"Yes, why not? No one will believe it, and then we won't be lying."

"But once they've stopped laughing, they'll ask again." Onno looked at him with a sigh. "It looks as though we've got a choice between prison and the madhouse." That there was the slightest chance the stones actually were what Quinten supposed them to be again seemed to him completely idiotic.

"Have you got a better idea, then?" asked Quinten.

"I've always got a better idea. Do you know what we're going to say? That it's art. Artistic creations by a modern artist. No one will dare doubt that—plastic arts have succeeded in making themselves as invulnerable as—you name it . . . as Siegfried. Even the police can't do anything about that."

"Quinten looked at the patrolling policemen. "Just look: it's quiet at all the other counters, and here it looks like there's a war going on. What is it about the Jews?"

Onno nodded. "After all those thousands of years, their existence is beginning to take on the features of a proof of God's existence more and more clearly."

The remark reminded Quinten of what Mrs. Korvinus had once said. The day after Max's death, he told his father, he had heard Nederkoorn in the hall saying to Mrs. Korvinus that as far as he was concerned, all the Jews could be stoned out of the universe like that—and then she had said that they were still being punished because they had crucified Christ.

"It's just as well you've gotten away from that castle," said Onno, making a face. Because he wasn't sure that anti-Semitic platitude had not taken root in Quinten, he decided to nip it in the bud immediately. "The Jews didn't crucify Christ at all, Quinten; the Romans crucified Christ. Crucifixion was a Roman punishment for serious criminals. Over there, that Orthodox Jewish gentleman, with the beard and the black hat on the back of his head—if you say to me, 'Kill him,' and I kill him, does that make you his murderer and not me? I don't have to do what you tell me, do I? Now, if I were completely in your power, then it would be different, but I'm not. You can say so many things. The Jews cried, 'Crucify him,' but Pilate did it. He could have stood his ground, at the top of those sacred stairs, and said, 'Get lost, I wouldn't dream of it, he's innocent,' couldn't he? He was the boss, wasn't he? Yes, he was responsible for keeping the peace in the occupied area. He didn't want any problems with the emperor here in Rome. All understandable—that's how it goes in politics—but why should the descendants of those loudmouths later be persecuted and exterminated and not the descendants of the actual murderers—that is, the Italians? Peter and Paul were also crucified by the Romans, and without the Jews demanding it. But not only were the Italian people not forced into the gas chambers; until recently, Christ's representatives on earth were virtually exclusively Italian descendants of the Romans. And the popes still have their seat in Rome, just like the Roman emperors. All very strange, isn't it? God moves in ironic ways, shall we say. I also used to think that the hatred of Jews was all about Christ, but that isn't the case; it existed long before Christ. They keep thinking up new reasons for it: that they're rich and showy, that they're poor and dirty, that they pull the strings of plutocratic world capitalism, that they're revolutionaries and have communism on their conscience, that they've got no homeland, that they're reestablishing their homeland—it's all grist for the mill, as long as it's bad. The fact that one accusation contradicts another doesn't matter, because hate is primary. And the fact that hate has always been there is another proof for anti-Semites that there must be a basis to it."

On the way to the runway a taxiing plane turned its back on them and for a few seconds emitted a deafening din. Quinten waited for a moment.

"And what is it based on?"

Onno put his hand on the suitcase, which Quinten had on his lap. "On this. At least, if what you think is in there is in there. On the fact that the God of the Jews had sanctified his people by entering into a covenant with them, which no other people can boast. Obviously an intolerable thought for many people. Anyway, give me that thing. I'll do the talking if it's necessary." He got up. "Remember, you don't know a thing, you're just tagging along."

At the tables, a few yards apart, they were questioned separately by the security officials, Quinten in English, Onno in Italian. They were asked whether the suitcases and that backpack was their property. Whether they had packed their luggage themselves. If they had lost sight of it since they had packed it. If anyone had given them anything to take along. In reply to the question what he was going to do in Israel, Quinten said that he was accompanying his father and that he wanted to visit the holy places, while Onno said:

"On business."

"What kind of business?"

"I try with moderate success to make my living as an art dealer."

The official looked at the two pieces of luggage from all sides, put two red stickers on them, gave Onno his ticket and passport back, and allowed him to pass with a brief wave of his hand.

"If we check in the suitcase," said Onno as they were standing in the back of the queue at the counter, "the stones may break, and of course they sling them around on the platform. But if we take it as hand luggage, we're almost bound to have to open it. What shall we do?"

"Hand luggage."

"Of course." Onno nodded—and he couldn't resist adding with a smile, "The first set was smashed to pieces as well, after all."

Through passport control, too, in the crowded departure lounge by their gate, there were heavily armed policemen and all kinds of people whose function was not immediately clear. Bent over the screen of the detection apparatus sat a fat woman in a blue uniform; behind her, a blond girl with her arms folded watched. Onno put the suitcase on the conveyor belt, whereupon it disappeared under the rubber flaps. A little later the belt stopped. Perhaps it won't come out again, thought Quinten—slowly the X-ray picture faded and disappeared from the screen; even after the machine was dismantled down to the last screw, nothing would be found of the suitcase.

When it appeared after half a minute on the other side under the rubber flaps, the girl came forward and invited Onno with a razor-sharp smile to open the case. He could tell from her accent immediately that she wasn't Italian but Israeli. Quinten helped him with the locks, and to his amazement Onno saw a beige envelope marked WESTERBORK SYNTHETIC RADIO TELESCOPE, with an astronomical mirror as a logo. The girl put the envelope aside and folded open the newspapers.

"What on earth is this?" With her fingers wide apart, she raised her hands in the air and looked with a distaste at the gray stones. She lifted one up and asked, "What kind of material is this? Its lighter than you'd think. Lava?"

"Maybe some plastic or other," said Onno as well as he could in ancient Hebrew. "Modern art, at any rate. A creation of a promising young German: Anselm Buchwald. An atmospheric evocation of the Grail legend."

She looked up and said in modern Hebrew: "To me it looks more like an atmospheric evocation of the Third Reich."

"Who knows, perhaps it amounts to the same thing."

She looked at him piercingly with her green eyes. "You speak Hebrew like Jeremiah."

"Like Job would be more correct," said Onno with feigned sadness.

"The Lord has given and the Lord has taken away: praised be the name of the Lord!"

After they had been let through, he asked Quinten what was in the envelope.

"Secret," said Quinten gruffly.

Onno shook his head. "You mustn't do such unexpected things. As if we didn't have enough problems already."

"You see," said Quinten with a laugh when they were off the ground, "we've gotten away."

"As long as they're not waiting for us in Tel Aviv," said Onno, looking worried. "It's a quarter past eight. Those fathers have probably already discovered my stick, or else they will within an hour. Padre Agostino will turn to Gorgonzola from fright, and in two hours Angiolina will give a precise description of that strange father and son who wanted to leave on the very first flight, and they'll hear from that Israeli policewoman that there was something very strange about the pair," he said, and pointed up at the baggage locker. "In three hours' time, when we land, there will be an expatriation request waiting for us at the airport, and we'll be taken back on the same plane under guard via Cyprus to Rome, where we shall languish until we die in a dungeon of the Castel Sant'Angelo, rattling our chains and gnawed by the rats."

"Then they'd be missing something really special in the Holy Land," said Quinten. "Besides which, you're forgetting the time difference."

Onno looked at him inquiringly. "What do you mean I'm forgetting the time difference?"

"It's an hour later in Israel than in Italy, isn't it?"

"What about it?"

"That means that for that hour we haven't existed. And if you've been able not to exist for an hour, no one can find you anymore, if you ask me."

Onno watched calmly while Quinten put his Mickey Mouse watch an hour forward, then crossed his arms and glanced sideways out of the window in front of him. The plane toppled the earth and in a wide arc they reached the sea above Ostia, which glittered in the morning sunlight like an aging skin. Confronted with Quinten's invulnerability, he felt like a bird trying to open a safe with its beak. He should surrender to Quinten, just as Quinten himself had surrendered to . . . well, to what? To something that he probably didn't know himself.

"Have you decided in the meantime what you plan to do in Israel?"

"We'll see." Quinten really didn't know. All he knew was that everything would turn out for the best.

"I know a colleague there from one of my former lives," said Onno, making a final attempt without much hope. "He might be able to help us a bit—at least if he's still alive. They've got fantastic laboratories there, where they can clean the stones; on that score there's no better equipment anywhere than in Israel. All Israelis are archaeologists—every potsherd they find is a political argument to justify their state."

"And what about the Third World War?"

"Of course it would have to be done in the deepest secrecy."

"And that colleague of yours . . . what's his name?"

"I can't remember. Yes I can: Landau. Mordechai Landau."

"When he sees that he's got the authentic Ten Commandments in front of him, will he keep his mouth shut, then?"

Onno sighed deeply. "He would immediately phone the prime minister."

"Well, then."

Onno said nothing. He was giving up. It was obvious that he would never even know for certain that those two stones were *not* Moses' stones. Quinten might perhaps hide them in a cave at the Dead Sea, near Qumran, all of which had been searched scores of times and where no one would look anymore; or bury them somewhere, in the Negev, in a place where he himself wouldn't be able to find them again. Israel was small; he could get everywhere on the bus in a few hours—nowadays even into the Sinai Desert.

He could put them back on Mount Horeb and drive straight on to Egypt, thus completing the biblical circle. Then he could finally let himself be shut up in the throne room in the pyramid of Cheops, through which he had struggled on his official visit through hot, stuffy passages, and lie down in the empty, black sarcophagus. According to the pyramid freaks, there were definitely supernatural forces at work there, which would remove him from the earth like Enoch. Onno unfastened his safety belt and put his seat back a little. He must resign himself to the whole episode's taking on the character of a dream, which he couldn't even talk about decently without being considered crazy.

The breakfast that was put in front of them seemed to be of the same substance as the plastic knives and forks with which they had to eat it. Quinten helped his father open the transparent packaging—not because he wouldn't have been able to do it himself, but because he obviously didn't want to know how to do it; and the sort of rage threatened to take control of him that led him even to putting his teeth into the plastic, which could only end in defeat for his teeth.

"This kind of food is the end of human civilization," he grumbled, twisting and turning his large body behind the lowered table.

"But we're in the air now," said Quinten with his mouth full.

When their neatly ordered trays had been transformed into repulsive heaps of rubbish, which were pushed with a smile into steel trolleys, Quinten pressed his forehead against the window. Space. World. Like irregular gray-brown grease stains, the first Greek islands floated into view. Above his head were the Ten Commandments, on their way back: he felt as though he had been working toward this situation from the moment of his birth. What else could happen now? Of course something else would happen—but what then? Simply go on living? Go back to Holland and live to be eighty? Look back at this like an incident from the distant past, an unknown event from the last century? Suddenly the feeling seized him that these might be his last days on earth; but that didn't worry him.

Perhaps everyone had something special to do in their existence and then their life was fulfilled. It might be something very insignificant, or apparently insignificant—for example, helping someone without being asked, without the other person knowing it. Everyone really ought to search their past to see if something like that had already happened; otherwise they ought to think about doing it.

Down below Quinten saw a faint white comet in the blue water: a ship, itself too small to be seen, sailing in the opposite direction. Had the tablets and the menorah and all those things from the temple been taken to Rome by Titus like that, or had they gone overland? Only after he had asked Onno did he see that he'd woken Onno up.

"I'm sorry."

"You won't allow me a moment's rest," said Onno plaintively, and loosened his tie. "How the booty was transported! No idea. To be on the safe side, I'd say overland. Actually, I think you're the one who ought to know that kind of thing by now. But you don't study—you just do what you want."

"Isn't that enough, then?"

"Far too much! But you're right. Anyone can study—there are other people to do that, like me. When I was involved in politics in my modest way, I also knew less about it than the political scientists, who knew more than Hitler and Stalin put together but who hadn't an ounce of power and who would never get it. Except that in your case you go a step further. You're firmly convinced that at this moment you're taking the stone tablets of the Law back to Israel—I can still scarcely bring myself to say it—but if you ask me, you don't even know how your author got his inspiration there on that mountain in the Sinai. You've never read up on it in the Bible."

"No," said Quinten, thinking: *they're not stone, but sapphire tablets.* "What happened, then?"

"The usual things. In a volcanic production, with thunder and lightning, smoke, earthquakes, blaring trumpets, the voice of Jahweh visible in a dark cloud."

"Visible? A visible voice?"

"Yes, according to Philo that was the real miracle. Jahweh spoke visible words, in letters of light, which were not written on anything. That's what Moses had to do. That visible voice of God, Moses said later, was the greatest miracle since the creation of man."

Even after Onno had finished, Quinten felt that Onno was still looking at him from the side. Probably he really wanted to ask whether Quinten still believed that he had the stones in his possession; but he had obviously lost heart.

Quinten looked back at him and said: "So now the *Francis Bacon* is the Sancta Sanctorum."

"The *Francis Bacon*?"

"Didn't you see when we got on? That's the name of this plane."

When they were flying over the Peloponnese, Quinten became sleepy too. With heavy eyelids he looked at the large black fly sitting on the window. It had never flown as fast before without flying—how was it to get home again? Because the creature disgusted him, he brushed it away with his hand, after which it landed a few rows in front on the shoulder of the Orthodox gentleman, who had kept his hat on. Gradually his eyes closed, while the droning of the engines changed into majestic harmonies of gigantic orchestras . . .

The voice of the captain woke him from his sleep. He told them in English that Crete was down below on the right. Looking past Onno,

Quinten saw the gloomy, violet mountains in the distance, but Onno didn't open his eyes.

"Dad. Crete."

"Don't want to see it," said Onno, with his head turned to one side and his eyes still closed. "I hate Crete."

A few minutes later the sound of the engines suddenly faded and Quinten could tell from his ears that the plane was beginning to descend.

His father opened one eye for a moment, closed it again and said: "*Luhot ha'eduth* can smell the stable."

"What are you talking about now?"

" 'The tablets of the testimony.' Another way of describing the covenant."

Quinten turned away with a jerk and looked wide-eyed through the plane without seeing anything. It was as though that word *testimony* were also deep in himself, like a cut, sparkling diamond in the blue earth.

In Lod, at Ben Gurion airport, it was full of policemen and armed security troops, which reminded Onno of Havana eighteen years before, when all these men had been in their cribs playing with rattles; but no one was looking for them. The vacationers bound for Cyprus, who had applauded after the landing, had remained in the plane. Their baggage was inspected again at long tables; for the third time people were checked to see if they resembled the photos in their passports. The suitcase was opened again and Parsifal had to help again. Next to them was the Orthodox man, who also glanced at the stones without interest.

"If only he knew," said Quinten.

"Careful," said Onno softly. "Even abroad there's always a chance that someone will understand you. Certainly in Israel." When they were finally given permission to leave and he had drawn some money—shekels, according to him the currency back in Old Testament times—he asked, "Now what?"

"Well, fairly logical. We're going outside."

It was almost one o'clock. On the square in front of the departure hall it was swelteringly hot; people had scarcely any shadows coming from their feet. They walked through the throng of cars and buses toward a low, white office for tourist information and hotel reservations.

"If there's one thing I need," said Onno, "it's a civilized bath. Do you realize we haven't taken our clothes off for twenty-four hours? Don't you feel grimy?"

"I'm okay."

"*Sherut?*" shouted a man with a yarmulke on his crown, who was hastily loading suitcases into a small bus. "*Yerushalayim?*"

There were still two free seats in his shuttle to Jerusalem, and Onno had gradually realized that all they had to do was to get in. On the backseat they found themselves next to a graying lady reading *l'Express*; all the others were intellectual-looking men, Americans, in shortsleeved shirts, some of them wearing bow ties. When the driver started the engine, he turned around and asked them what hotel they wanted. The lady was going to the King David; the Americans had to get to the Hilton. When Onno didn't reply immediately, he asked impatiently: "The Hilton too?"

Onno made a gesture that they might as well go there, and a little later they drove into the dry, stone-strewn hills.

They did not speak during the forty-five-minute drive. Onno had never been in Israel, but he felt as if the metaphysical violence that had raged here for four thousand years, and was still raging, could be read from the landscape. Of course that was a romantic thought, deriving from what he knew of history, from Bible readings with his father and the vicar and from sugary catechism prints from his early childhood, with breaking clouds that let through fans of holy rays. For him, too, Israel had always been "the Promised Land," but that he should finally get to see it under these circumstances was the most unbelievable thing of all: accompanied by his son, who had a suitcase on his lap that supposedly contained the tablets of the Law.

It was as if in this scorching light, undisturbed by any Dutch cloud, time curled up like an insect in a flame. Gradually the hills became more rugged; here and there they were in bloom, and in the verge of the four-lane highway there were the wrecks of shot-up trucks and armored cars preserved with rust-colored red-lead paint. The driver told them that they were from the wars of 1948 and 1967; but they might just as well have been from the time of the Crusaders, the Romans, the Babylonians . . .

The tower of the Jerusalem Hilton, with each balcony rail bedecked with an Israeli flag, was in the western part of the city; the excavations that were going on next to it showed that it had once been different. In the cool, sumptuous lobby, surrounded by small boutiques, the Americans reported to excited ladies at a table with miniature flags and papers on it; a board on an easel welcomed delegates to the international conference on the irrigation of the Negev. At the counter Onno put down their passports and asked for two rooms. Perhaps because he saw that they were Dutch passports, the receptionist directed him in English to the hydraulic engineers' table.

"No, we're not with them."

"Why not?" asked Quinten.

"For God's sake!" said Onno, raising his arms. "Not again! You're just like Max."

"Why?"

"I'll tell you sometime."

But there were no other rooms free, all the hotels were full; there were four or five conferences being held in Jerusalem at the moment. Only in the Old City might there be still something available, but of course security was not all it might be there. When Onno said that they weren't so easily frightened, and anyway had to find accommodation somewhere, the receptionist made a couple of telephone calls and noted down the name and address of a hotel.

After they had had a bite to eat in the bar—with Quinten being refused a glass of milk with his ham roll—a taxi took them to the eastern part of the city. At the end of a wide shopping street jammed with traffic the ground sloped gradually downward, and a little later, on the other side of a valley full of vegetation, really more a gully, the massive walls of old Jerusalem rose up above them. Behind them, in a flood of sunlight, were countless towers, with a gold and a silver cupola in the center. Quinten bent deep over his suitcase to be able to see it better through the front windshield.

"Look at that," he said softly. "There it is. It really exists."

Although the Arab on his camel belonged to the same order as the heavy, sandy yellow stones of the city wall that he was riding past, the driver hooted at him to move aside, drove through the Jaffa Gate, and stopped in a small square. A little later there they were in the throng of tourists, Palestinian merchants wearing headscarves, Roman Catholic monks and nuns, Greek Orthodox, Armenian, Coptic priests in exotic robes, religious Jews in kaftans, military patrols made up of boys and girls, with Uzis and Kalashnikovs slung around them. The pealing of church bells and the cries of the merchants merged into a din that effortlessly absorbed the two dull thuds with which a jet broke the sound barrier in the distance.

Hotel Raphael, probably not mentioned in any travel guide, sat wedged unimposingly between a *bureau de change* and a grocer's, which had displayed its boxes and sacks of herbs like the palette of Carpaccio:

vermilion, rusty-brown, terra-cotta, cornflower blue, olive-green, saffron-yellow. The reception desk consisted of a corrugated wooden counter in a narrow hallway leading via a couple of steps into what was obviously the lounge-cum-breakfast room; slumped in a chair with a torn plastic back, a man in his sixties sat watching the television, which was fed by a V-shaped indoor aerial. He put his cigarette in an ashtray and got up.

"Quist?" he asked with a melancholy smile. "*Shalom,*"—and then in English—"My colleague said you were coming." He shook hands with them and introduced himself as Menachem Aron.

He had not made things easy for himself. On his head was a wig of chestnut-colored hair that was too thick and too even, out of which reddish-gray hair protruded by his ears; what's more, there was a light-blue yarmulke pinned to its crown, which in this case may not have been strictly necessary liturgically—unless he was taking account of the possibility, Onno reflected, that God could not see he was wearing a wig. Aron put two forms on the counter and asked how many nights they wanted to stay.

"Two?" asked Quinten. "Three?"

"I'm not saying anything. It's your undertaking, you must know."

"Two, then." That should be enough.

"Shower in the hall," said Aron, putting down their room keys.

"I don't know about you," said Onno, "but I'm going straight to bed. I've had it." He pointed to the suitcase. "What do you think? Shall we ask if he's got a luggage locker?"

Aron disappeared through a door behind the counter and a little later came back with a narrow iron drawer, into which a wallet fitted. When it was explained to him what was needed, he asked Quinten to follow him. In a cluttered little office, also used to store crates of empty bottles, a girl looked up from her typewriter and nodded to Quinten with a look that made him a little uncertain. Her black hair was cut very short, like his mother's.

In the corner stood a head-high green safe from a bygone age; in the center of the door was a heavy brass plate with the name Kromer on it. Quinten had seen at once that the monster had an old-fashioned letter combination lock, which had long since ceased to be used. Aron put one knee on the tiled floor and turned the knob back and forth four times, making sure that the combination was invisible to his guest. When the colossal steel door, a good ten inches thick, slowly swung open, Quinten saw that there was room for a hundred commandments.

"Heavy," said the hotel keeper, putting the case on the bottom shelf, but he asked no other questions. After he had closed the door with a bang, he struck the knob twice with the side of his hand. "All right?"

"Yes."

The girl turned around and asked something in Hebrew, perhaps just to be able to see Quinten again, with the white lock of hair in his black ponytail. But Aron stood guard over his daughter and motioned to Quinten that he could go back to the counter.

Something had happened in the meantime. Onno stood open-mouthed on the threshold to the lounge, with his eyes obviously focused on the television. With an imperious gesture at hip height, he motioned to Quinten to be quiet.

Quinten went up to him and also looked at the screen: pictures of an exalted praying and singing throng on a square, most of them kneeling, with arms opened wide, their faces raised ecstatically to heaven; dotted among them were pizza stands. He could not catch what the voice of the Hebrew commentator was saying. When the camera swung around, he suddenly saw where it was: in the Sancta Sanctorum! The crowded Holy Stairs, the chapel, through the bars a close-up of his father's stick on the papal prayer stool opposite the altar! A little later an old woman came into the shot, gesturing excitedly, talking in Italian with a breaking voice, of which he understood only the word *miracolo,* followed by a priest choosing his words and subtitled in Hebrew, but not the one made of butter. After the stick with the snake's-head handle had been shown again, the Israeli newsreader concluded the item with an ironic look at the viewers.

Speechless, Onno sank into a chair.

"Tell me!" said Quinten. "What's happened?"

"I'm going crazy. This morning my stick was discovered—by that old woman. She's the first one to go up the Holy Stairs on Sundays, and she alerted the fathers of the Holy Cross. When she saw their amazement, she began screaming that a miracle had happened, since no one could get into the chapel. Within an hour the news had spread through the city and people began flooding in from all directions. Guess what? They believe that my stick is Moses' staff, with which he struck water from the rock. This is proved by the handle in the shape of a snake's head: at the pharaoh's court, Moses once threw his staff on the ground and it changed into a snake. At the same time, they say, the serpent from paradise is now worshiping the *acheiropoeton* in the papal Holy of Holies, and that indicates the end of

Original Sin and the second coming of Christ. At the moment there seem to be jams on all the approach roads to Rome."

It took a while before Quinten could say: "But those fathers know that it's your stick, don't they?"

"So they're obviously leaving it at that." Onno nodded. "They didn't take proper care, and now it's not in their interest for it to become known. What's more, they feel that the rise in appreciation for their chapel is marvelous, of course."

"And what if Mauro recognizes your stick?"

"He won't dare say anything. Perhaps he'll accept a bribe to keep quiet. There's no turning back for anyone."

"And why didn't the rector speak just now? Could there be something else wrong?"

"Perhaps Padre Agostino will be canonized in a while. Patron saint of the dairy industry."

"Who was that priest at the end?"

"Cardinal Sartolli, the archpriest of San Giovanni in Laterano. He was being diplomatically noncommittal. He said that the Church was of course pleased by the piety of the people but that they should now wait for an official reaction from the Vatican." Onno looked up at him. "Quinten! What have we done?"

Quinten looked at him for a moment—and suddenly, as if struck by lightning, he fell about laughing.

63

The Center of the Center

"I've never seen you laugh like that," said Onno the following morning at breakfast, after he had read the latest news of the situation in Rome to Quinten from the *Ha'aretz*: by now pilgrims from all over the world were streaming to the Sancta Sanctorum; the Piazza San Giovanni in Laterano had been closed to all traffic, and, like the Holy See, the chief rabbi's office in Jerusalem was making no comment.

"Doesn't it make you laugh yourself silly? All those praying people precisely when there's nothing more to worship? Only that silly walking stick of yours."

Onno folded the paper. "Right. So we've traded the Ten Commandments for my walking stick, and you're going to take them back." He looked at Quinten over his reading glasses. "Might those two stones perhaps be just the same as that rod of Moses they're worshiping?"

"How can you think such a thing?" said Quinten indignantly. "Your stick isn't Moses', is it?"

Onno nodded and silently spooned up his egg. "But I assume that the safe in Hotel Raphael isn't their final destination."

"Of course not."

"I wasn't able to sleep too well, as you may perhaps understand, and so I tried again to put myself in your shoes ... I know that that's impossible, but why shouldn't someone attempt the impossible ... and I think you want to deliver them exactly where Titus got them from. Or am I wrong?"

"I don't know," said Quinten. He had not thought about it himself—he would see—but perhaps it was a good idea.

"That means the spot where the temple of Herod stood."

"But," Quinten added, "it must in the exact spot where the Holy of Holies was."

Onno wiped his mouth with a sigh.

"Of course, you can never be too exact. So that means some more *learning*. I hadn't thought that I'd get to know so much because of you." He pushed back his chair with an unbearable scraping sound and got up. "Shall we go and take a look at the situation, then?"

Quinten was a little surprised at the initiative his father was suddenly showing. It was as though he were in a hurry all at once; perhaps he felt that it was time they put an end to the whole affair, after what was now happening in Rome. But he himself was curious about the spot where all those temples had stood. In the doorway, Aron pointed out the narrow street that they had to take: straight ahead—that would bring them directly to the Temple Mount, Moriah, ten minutes' walk.

The heat was becoming more intense again after the cool night. The crowded street, adorned with drying laundry, like all streets around the Mediterranean, was the beginning of the souk: an uninterrupted string of tiny shops selling souvenirs, pottery, multicolored cloth, sweets, indeterminate workshops, copper smithies, a barber's, but above all of yelling tradesmen trying to offload their wares onto the tourists. And every ten yards men with headscarves forced themselves on one as guides; hearing where they came from, all of them without exception shouted the Dutch shibboleth *"Allemachtig achtentachtig!"* with its string of guttural sounds.

Onno stopped at a display of walking sticks with primitively carved wooden handles.

"Suppose I took this one," he said, pointing to a snake's head. "That would really be tempting fate."

"I'd be careful about that in Jerusalem."

"Forty shekels," said the shopkeeper, and pulled out the stick.

Since he found them all equally ugly, Onno shook his head and walked on, but the man followed them and a few steps farther the price had fallen to thirty shekels, twenty-five, twenty.

"Wait a bit," said Onno, "and we'll get it for nothing."

"If we simply go on walking, we'll automatically become millionaires," added Quinten—thinking for a moment of the disguised hotel keeper, who had no idea that his safe had been temporarily transformed into the ark of the covenant and was housing a billion guilders' worth of sapphires.

For ten shekels Onno purchased a heavy stick with an uncarved handle, almost a truncheon, helpfully fetched by the salesman from his workshop. Relieved that he again had something to lean on, he walked on. By now they had been walking for a quarter of an hour, but there was no sign of the Temple Mount anywhere. Farther on, the street was topped by arches, and a little later they found themselves in the shadows of a crowded, labyrinthine bazaar, which made it impossible to walk straight ahead.

When Quinten looked to see where they were at a street corner, he read: " 'Via Dolorosa.' "

"Yes, that's what it's like here. The way of the cross of our Lord and Savior." Onno pointed to a relief above a church door with his stick. "This is the fourth station, where Jesus met his mother. But," he said, and looked left and right, "this route leads to Golgotha, over which the Church of the Holy Sepulcher was built; and it must start from Pilate's Citadel Antonia, where the Holy Stairs come from. So we have to go that way, because the fortress, I think, is also on the Temple Mount."

At that moment Quinten grabbed his arm and pulled him into a shop selling jewels. "What's wrong?"

"There's Aunt Trees."

Behind a man holding a closed red parasol over his head, she was walking in the middle of a group of white-haired ladies, looking as alike as their flowered dresses.

Crouched in his hiding place, Onno followed her with his eyes. He felt quite moved. "How old she's become," he said softly, "the shrew. But as devout as ever. She's going to put her hand in the hole where the cross of Jesus Christ stood."

"Or did you want to meet her?" asked Quinten. "She would have recognized you too, of course."

"I don't really know." Onno stood up with a groan. "I've no idea anymore what to do with my life, but of course I can't go on acting as if everything's the same as before. You've made sure of that."

Obsequiously, the shopkeeper held up a silver chain—or what was supposed to be a silver chain—with a small Star of David on it.

Onno looked into the eyes of the old Arab, who wore a blob of fine white lace on his head. "We'll have to buy this," he said. He paid the absurd price he was asked and put the chain around Quinten's neck.

Quinten felt it and asked: "Are you allowed to wear one of these if you are not a Jew?"

"Only if you've been given it by your father. That's bound to be somewhere in the Talmud."

A few houses farther on, they bought a map at a newspaper stand, which quickly showed them the way back to the Jewish quarter. The crossing point was clearly on a kind of border, formed by soldiers, who were standing around in a bored fashion on either side of a narrow street. As they descended a wide staircase, they passed another group of soldiers shortly afterward; in the shadow next to radio equipment with a long aerial, they sat and relaxed on chairs, automatic rifles at the ready on their laps.

"God and violence," said Onno. "It's been like that here for four thousand years." The stairs made a ninety-degree turn—and suddenly they stopped.

For a moment Quinten was reminded of Venice, when he had emerged into the Piazza San Marco from the maze of alleyways. But there art and beauty reigned, full of wind and sea and with a floating lightness. Here something else very different was going on: it was not beautiful; it was crushing. He had the feeling that the scene he was watching was not only where it was but in himself, too, like a pit in a fruit—like the word *testimony* on the plane yesterday.

Hot as an oven, filled with the buzzing of voices, the sound of drums and exotic high-pitched trills from women's throats, a great square extended before them, enclosed on the far side by the massive, yellow Wailing Wall. It did not form a division between two spaces, like a city wall; it was like a cliff. On the area above it gleamed the golden and silver cupolas that he had seen from a taxi; and from there came the electronically amplified wail of a muezzin. In this city the religions not only existed side by side, they were even piled on top of one another.

"That wall," said Onno, "is all that is left of the temple complex of Herod. It stood on top of that plateau. As far as I know it's not called the Wailing Wall because people have been lamenting Jewish persecution there for centuries, like Auschwitz and the gas chambers, but because of the destruction of the temple by the Romans. It will appeal to you." He glanced uncomfortably at Quinten. "They pray for its rebuilding and the coming of the Messiah."

Quinten looked up. Here and there soldiers with rifles were sitting on the wall. "How can we get up there?"

Onno began climbing down the last few steps feeling giddy. "Now that I'm finally in Jerusalem, I want to have a look around down here first. Do you realize what all this means to *me*? All through my childhood this hoo-ha was pounded into me with a sledgehammer. It's no accident that my sister's walking around here too."

The mood at the foot of the wall was more festive than plaintive. Part of the square was fenced off and reserved for men, a smaller area for women; at the entrance they were given paper yarmulkes—perhaps folded in prisons by Palestinians—and for half an hour they mingled in the religious throng. All along the wall, out of which clumps of weeds were growing, the faithful stood facing the huge blocks, the bottom two rows colored brown by the hands and lips that had been pressed on them for twenty centuries. Orthodox Jews, in knee-breeches, with round hats and ringlets down their cheeks, were indulging in strange jerking movements, like puppets, while reading books; old men with gray beards sat on chairs facing the wall, also reading. When Quinten began to pay attention, he saw that everything related to reading. The cracks between the stones were cemented with countless folded pieces of paper, obviously with wishes written on them.

"That's right," said Onno. "Here you're in the world of the book. I come from there myself. Perhaps you should be glad you've been spared that, but perhaps not."

Here and there were tables with books on them, which people occasionally leafed through; now and then someone took a copy with him to the wall. Through a stone archway in the left-hand corner of the square Quinten took a few steps into a dark space, which for a moment reminded him of his Citadel, where there were many more books on shelves. Suddenly a small, untidy procession appeared from the caves: men in prayer clothes, with cloths over their heads, carried an opened wooden box into the light. It contained two large scrolls with writing on them.

"So there you have the Jewish Law,' " said Onno with ironic emphasis, and looked at Quinten from the side. "That's the Torah."

Of course Quinten heard the undertone in his voice, but he ignored it.

Touched and kissed as they passed, the scrolls were taken to the partition with the women's area, from which those high-pitched trills again rose. It was some kind of initiation of a boy of about twelve; men in white yarmulkes and black beards wound a mysterious ribbon around his bare left arm and a strange, futuristic block was fastened to his forehead, while a patriarchal rabbi in a gold-colored toga read from the Torah they had brought. Exuberant women and girls threw candies over the fence.

"What's in that block?"

"Text. Commandments."

Quinten felt jealous. So much attention had never been paid to him. Why that boy and not him? Just because the boy was Jewish and he wasn't? But over and against that, he had discovered something on his own initiative that the boy and all those people had never dreamed of!

"Shall we go up now?"

On the right-hand side of the wall an asphalt path led upward in a gentle curve. Passing an unbroken line of photographing and filming tourists, they came to a gate, where policemen with submachine guns over their shoulders inspected all bags. Larger items of luggage had to be left behind.

"Do you see what it's like here?" asked Onno softly as they waited for their turn. "Steep walls on all sides with guarded gates. Down below is the most sacred place of the Jews; up here for more than a thousand years the third holy place of Islam, unless I'm mistaken—after Mecca and Medina. The situation is a kind of religious atom bomb: if they clash, the critical mass will be exceeded and the whole world will explode. The Israelis understood that very well, and you'll never get through with your stones, even though no one knows what you take them to be in your infinite optimism. You can forget that so-called 'returning' of yours, because you're not dealing here with a crowd of sleepy old fathers made of butter. Unless your name is Nebuchadnezzar or Titus, you'll have to think of something else."

Quinten jerked his shoulders impatiently. "I'll see."

He felt tense. In the gate was a table where women whose legs were too bare had to put on gray ankle-length skirts; when he came out of the shadow on the other side, he stopped in amazement and looked out over the silent expanse of the temple terrace. The atmosphere of absence reminded him for a moment of his meadow of Groot Rechteren, with the red cow, the two alder trees, and the three erratic stones. Not only were there far fewer people than down below in the square, but the silence had a strange, expectant na-

ture, like the seconds that elapsed between a flash of lightning and the clap
of thunder . . . or was it simply the exhaustion of the past—of all the religion,
murder, and devastation that this plateau had witnessed over the centuries?
A hundred yards farther on, slightly to the left of the center, on a raised terrace, stood a wide sanctum in brilliant blue and green colors: an octagonal
base, crowned with a golden cupola, framed in the cloudless sky like a second sun. It was topped by a crescent. From the cypresses and the olive trees,
which rose from their shadows everywhere here, came the twittering of
birds; on one side there was a magnificent view of a green hillside covered
with churches, monasteries, chapels, and cemeteries.

Quinten glanced at the map and pointed to the poetic hillside. "That's
the Mount of Olives."

"My God," said Onno. "That too. You were right: everything really exists."

A thin elderly gentleman, conventionally dressed in a gray suit with a
white shirt and a tie, approached them hesitantly; on his cheek was a minimal tuft of cotton wool. He gave a little cough behind his hand, as though he
had not spoken for a long time, and then said hoarsely in English:

"My name is Ibrahim. I'm a poet and I've lived in Jerusalem for sixty-
three years. With me you'll learn more in an hour than without me in a
week."

Onno burst out laughing. "Since we're not tourists, you're just the man
we need."

Ibrahim went straight to work. He half turned and pointed to a great
mosque with a silver cupola, which they were close to and which Quinten
had not yet noticed. In front of it stood a group of Arab schoolgirls with
white headscarves on and with dresses over their long trousers.

"Al-Aqsa," he said.

" 'Farthest point.' " Onno nodded.

Ibrahim looked at him flabbergasted. "You know?"

"But not why it's called that. Farthest point from where? From the other
side of the earth?"

"The farthest point the Prophet ever reached. One night he was sleeping
at the Kaaba in Mecca—"

"What's that?" Quinten asked Onno automatically.

"The holiest place in Islam, but much older than Islam. A great cube
with a black stone in it: probably a meteorite."

" . . . when a horse with a woman's face and a peacock's tail transported him at lightning speed to Jerusalem. He tethered it to the Wailing Wall down below and came up the same way as you, after which he undertook his nocturnal journey to heaven."

"We assume he was dreaming?" asked Onno cautiously.

"There are scholars who assume that." Ibrahim nodded. "There are also scholars who assume that he came here physically but that his journey to heaven was a vision?"

"And as a poet, what do you assume?"

"That there is no difference between dream and action, of course," said Ibrahim with a smile. "The dreams of a poet are his deeds."

"Bravo, Mr. Ibrahim!"

"Did Mohammed ascend from that exact spot?" asked Quinten, nodding toward the mosque.

Ibrahim pointed to the building with the golden cupola. "From that spot. He didn't ascend, come to that. He climbed, up a ladder of light. And he came down that way too, and before day broke al-Buraq took him back to Mecca."

"Lightning?" asked Onno. "He went there on a horse and returned on the lightning?"

"That was the name of the horse: Lightning." Ibrahim beckoned them. "Shall we first have a look at the mosque? This Gothic gate was built against it nine hundred years ago by the Crusaders; they made it a temporary church, which they called Templum Salomonis."

Quinten glanced at the pointed arches without interest. "And the real Jewish temples—where were they?"

Ibrahim again pointed at the golden cupola. "There."

"There too?" asked Quinten with raised eyebrows. Ibrahim looked at him with his dark eyes and again cleared his throat. "Everything is there."

"That's a lot, Mr. Ibrahim," said Onno.

"You know of course what the Jews usually say: 'Jews always exaggerate, Arabs always lie.' Judge for yourself. You obviously have no interest in the mosque."

They walked past a deeply inset basin for ritual washing, surrounded by stone armchairs, straight toward the wide staircase, which led up about twelve feet to the terrace; at the top of the stairs there was a free-standing row of arcades of four weathered arches. Quinten felt the gold-domed building becoming more and more forbidding the closer it came, like a lighthouse, which is also meant to be seen only from a distance. The bottom half of the base, covered in white marble, gave way to exuberantly colored tiled ornaments, crowned at the eaves by verses from the Koran in decorative Arabic script.

Ibrahim told him that the cathedral, called The Dome of The Rock, was usually regarded as a mosque, but it wasn't one; it was a shrine, built in the seventh century by Caliph Abd al-Malik—but, thought Quinten as he took off his shoes at the entrance, according to the design of a Christian architect, because that octagonal style didn't seem very Muslim to him. The octagon was the shape that baptismal chapels had, such as he had seen in Florence and Rome; he remembered Mr. Themaat telling him that this was connected with the "eighth day": the resurrection of Christ—which had also taken place somewhere near here. But Mr. Themaat had never told him anything about this building. They entered across the carpets in their stocking feet. Quinten stopped after a few steps. He caught his breath. Could what he was seeing be true?

A stone. In the center of the dimly lit space, within the ring of columns bearing the dome, surrounded by a wooden balustrade, there was nothing except a huge boulder, as tall as a man, with a rugged surface. As he looked at it, he felt his father's eyes trained on him, but he did not return his gaze. The stone, shaped a little like a trapezoid, was golden-yellow, like the whole of Jerusalem; obviously it was the summit of the Temple Mount. How heavy might such a thing be? In the past three weeks everything had gotten much heavier: after the lightness of Venice, the somber house fronts of Florence, then the sunken Roman ruins, just now the enormous blocks of the Wailing Wall, and now he stood eye to eye with the heaviest thing of all: the earth itself—but at the same time, Max had once told him, it was actually weightless, as it orbited the sun.

It was sacred here—or was that feeling only caused by the way the spot was represented, like a jewel in a golden setting? Could you turn everything into something sacred like that? Why were there no more than two or three tourists? In the wide gallery on the other side of the circle of arcades Arab women were sitting on the ground here and there, with their faces averted, in long white robes that also covered their heads.

At one corner of the balustrade was a tall structure in the shape of a tower, in which, according to Ibrahim, three hairs from the beard of the Prophet were kept. Then he pointed to a hollow in the stone and said:

"This is his footprint as he took off on his nocturnal journey. And here," he continued, pointing to a number of wide corrugations in the side of the stone, "you see the fingerprints of the archangel, who held back the rock, because it too wanted to go to heaven. That was Gabriel, as you call him, who dictated the Koran to the Prophet."

Quinten let his eyes wander over the stone. "So were the temples of Solomon, Zerubbabel, and Herod here too?" he asked.

"So we assume."

"But surely that's easy to check? Why don't the Jews do a bit of excavating around here?"

Ironic wrinkles appeared on Ibrahim's forehead. "Because our religious authorities don't like Jews doing a bit of excavating around here."

"And so they don't?"

"Not up to now."

"You could even prove it to some extent on the basis of the New Testament," said Onno in Dutch. "Do you remember that text in the dome of St. Peter's: 'Thou art Peter and upon this rock I shall build my church'? Christ probably said it with very special accents: 'Thou art Peter and on *this* rock *I* shall build my temple.' That means," said Onno, pointing to the rock, "distinct from the temple on this rock."

Ibrahim waited politely until Onno had finished.

Quentin saw that he didn't like being excluded, and as they walked on, in a clockwise direction, he asked: "Is this where the Holy of Holies was?"

"According to some people. According to others, this was the spot where the altar for burnt offerings stood." He pointed to a glimmer of light coming out of the rock on the other side. "There's a hole in the stone there, which leads to a cave; perhaps the blood of the sacrificial animals ran out through that. In that case, the Holy of Holies would have been more toward the west."

Quinten groped under his shirt for his compass, and first felt his new Star of David. The entrance through which they had come faced due south, in line with the al-Aqsa mosque, which, naturally, pointed toward Mecca. So that west was in the direction of the Wailing Wall, east in the direction of the Mount of Olives. The chapel had doorways there too.

"But surely," he said, as they walked on, "Mohammed didn't come precisely to this spot for his heavenly journey because there were Jewish temples here?"

"No," said Ibrahim with a smile. "Things are still not like that."

"Why, then?"

"For a reason that is also connected with the buildings of the Jewish temples on this spot."

"Which was?" asked Onno. It was as though the inquisitorial manner in which Quinten was again trying to get to the bottom of things had infected him.

Rather surprised, Ibrahim looked from one to the other. "This is like a cross-examination."

"So it is," said Onno decidedly.

"There are all kinds of traditions connected with this place," said Ibrahim formally. "Will you be satisfied with four? The first is that King David saw the angel standing on this rock on the point of destroying Jerusalem. When that danger had been averted, he built an altar here. Solomon, his son, subsequently erected the first temple here."

"And the second tradition?"

"It says that a thousand years before that, the patriarch Jacob dreamed of a ladder to heaven here, by which the angels descended and ascended."

Onno raised an arm and recited the Dutch Authorized Version: " 'And he was afraid, and said, How dreadful is this place! this is none other but the house of God, and this is the gate of heaven!' " That's Dutch," he added in English.

"Nice language," said Ibrahim. "A bit like Arabic. Just as guttural."

"That's right. Your colleagues never tire of saying *'Allemachtig achtentachtig.'* "

Ibrahim looked at him reproachfully. "They are not my colleagues," he said in a voice that suddenly seemed a little hoarser.

At the same moment Onno felt sorry he had made the remark. Perhaps Ibrahim really was a poet who earned his living as a guide, and not a guide who wrote abominable poems in his spare time.

Meanwhile they had walked around the northern, narrow, side of the rock, where there were women in white sitting everywhere. With each step and with each word, Quinten was less and less in doubt that the Holy of Holies had stood here.

"And why," he asked, "did Jacob sleep on this exact spot?"

Ibrahim ran the palm of his hand over his thin gray hair. "Because something else had happened here even earlier. This is also the place where his father, Isaac, was about to be sacrificed by his grandfather, Abraham."

"Of course," said Onno, again in Dutch.

"But at the last moment he was prevented by an archangel."

"Gabriel?" asked Quinten.

Ibrahim made a skeptical gesture. "Michael, if I remember correctly. So in a certain sense there was already an altar in the rock then: for human sacrifices. That was why the Prophet came to this exact spot—or, rather, why Gabriel brought him to this exact spot on his horse. When he arrived, he was welcomed in this place by Abraham, Moses, and Jesus."

"Yes," said Onno. "We accept everything you say at face value because that's how we are. But I'm getting really curious about the fourth tradition, because I detect a rising line in the events as you are narrating them, Mr. Ibrahim." He hesitated for a moment. "What does my ear suddenly hear from my own mouth? Ibrahim? Were you named after Abraham?"

Ibrahim made a short bow. "My father did me that honor." On the eastern side, where the stone was lower and a praying woman in white sat tucked into an alcove like a moth, with her back to them, he stopped. "Of course Jerusalem is the Jewish center of the world," he said, stretching out his arm, "but from the earliest times this rock was the center of the center for the Jews."

"The center of the center?" repeated Quinten, wide-eyed.

"This rock," said Ibrahim solemnly, "not only bore the temples, but according to the Jews it is the foundation stone of the whole edifice of the world. Here is where the creation of heaven and earth began—the first light emanated from this point."

The Big Bang, thought Onno; a pity Max was no longer here to see this tangible proof of the theory—religion and religious background radiation. . . . He looked in alarm at Quinten. Something was brewing in that head again; but whatever it was, he was having no more part of it.

Perhaps because he had seen the skeptical expression on Onno's face, Ibrahim now addressed himself solely to Quinten.

"This stone is where heaven and earth and underworld meet. As long as God is served here, he will hold back the ravaging waters of the underworld, which burst forth in the days of Noah."

"But he is not being worshiped here any longer, you say."

"Not in the Jewish way."

Quinten sighed deeply. He was now absolutely certain that here was where the Holy of Holies had been. He had suddenly gone one step beyond *the center of the world*—he had gone beyond his dream. Here in the center of the center was where the ark of the covenant had stood, and later the tablets of the Law had lain on this rock. What he would have most liked to do was to climb up and see whether a recess had been carved anywhere, by Jeremiah, in which they could have lain. And at the same moment he saw the spot, nearby, at the edge of the rock, where the woman in white sat praying: an oblong hole about eight inches by twenty, into which the tablets would fit precisely.

Ibrahim saw him looking and said: "That's the footprint of Idris, Enoch from the Bible."

"Dad . . ." said Quinten, and pointed without saying anything.

Onno had understood at once and rolled his eyes in despair. "When are you finally going to stop this outrageous nonsense? Haven't we gotten into enough of a mess already?" Suddenly he became furious. "Why don't you realize that all you've brought from Rome is nondescript rubbish, a couple of old roof tiles, and that hole is more likely to be the footprint of Enoch than what you take it to be. Shoe size twenty-two!"

"Perhaps it's both."

"Rubbish, rubbish, total rubbish! I want to get out of here this instant. I've had enough. We're going," he said to Ibrahim.

"Don't you want to go to the cave, the Fountain of Souls—"

"We're going."

Onno's outburst left Quinten cold. He had the tablets of the Law in his possession and for centuries they had lain in that hole, in the complete darkness of the *debir*, completely unobtrusive, right at the side.

When they emerged through the eastern gate into the heat and blinding light on the white marble slabs of the temple terrace, he said, "I really don't intend to put them back there."

"You won't be able to anyway."

"I don't know about that, but they'd be found the very next day by the Arabs, and that might be an even bigger disaster than if they fell into the hands of the Jews."

"Do what you want. In any case I don't want to hear another word about it. But I'd be careful if I were you. If you want to be murdered by Muslims foaming at the mouth, then you should try something here. You're playing with fire, you are."

Ibrahim, who had kept politely in the background, resumed his task and pointed to a small silver dome, close to the gate, with scaffolding around it, surrounded by a fence. That was the Dome of the Chain—so called after a silver chain that King David had hung up in it, a gift from the angel Gabriel: if one lied while holding it, then a link fell out of it. Onno was no longer listening—he was no longer interested—but Quinten peeped inside through a small gap.

The supernatural lie detector was a miniature version of the Dome of the Rock, but open around the sides; the ground was strewn with fragments, broken stones, pieces and fragments, tools, dented cans, plastic bottles, and rags: in the center stood an electric masonry saw. To the north of the Dome of the Rock there were more small buildings, but Quinten too felt that he had seen enough. He joined Onno, who was standing at the top of the eastern staircase of the temple terrace in the shade of the arcades, looking out at the Mount of Olives.

Ibrahim was indefatigable. "There," he said in the tone of a proud owner, pointing to the foot of the hill, "is the Garden of Gethsemane, where Jesus Christ—"

"I know, I know."

"Over there is his mother's grave, and there on the top of it . . . do you see that small dome? That's the spot from where she ascended into heaven."

Onno felt giddy and leaned heavily on his stick.

"I hope," he said to Quinten, "they've got some official here in Jerusalem who directs vertical traffic, to prevent jams."

Quinten burst out laughing; he was glad that the fit of rage had passed. Although it might annoy his father again, he asked Ibrahim: "Do you know where Titus's encampment was?"

Ibrahim pointed to the north slope of the Mount of Olives. "Somewhere over there. The conquerors of Jerusalem always came from the north."

Quinten looked around him and opened the map. So that meant that the tablets of the Law and the menorah and all those things had been taken out of the temple along this same route, down the terrace here, and then across the valley of Kidron to the other side. He was struck by a strange gatehouse obliquely opposite, in the east wall of the plateau, surrounded by grass and trees. It was deeply embedded in the ground, with a double nave, crowned by two low towers with flat domes; both gateways had been bricked up. At the front, where the battlements were, stood Israeli soldiers in green berets.

"What gate is that?"

"Ah!" said Ibrahim raising both hands. "The Golden Gate! According to the Jews, that's the gate through which God once entered their temple to mount his throne there. It must stay closed until the coming of the Messiah, at the end of time. That is why every religious Jew wants to be buried over there on the slopes of the Mount of Olives."

Onno pointed to the soldiers on the roof with his stick.

"The Messiah would be gunned down immediately."

A crooked smile appeared on Ibrahim's face. "Not only that—the Messiah has a second problem. On the other side of the wall there are Muslim graves, and that's unclean; he mustn't walk over them."

"What a rotten thing to do," said Quinten, "putting them there."

"So you see,"—laughed Onno—"they ride rough-shod over dead bodies here—or precisely not, how shall one put it?"

"For the Christians," added Ibrahim, "the Golden Gate is a symbol of Mary, through whom Jesus came into the world and who remained a virgin before during and after his birth: closed, so to speak."

Those words made Quinten rather uncertain. He glanced timidly at the mysterious gate and thought of his mother for a moment; to hide his embarrassment he looked at the map, which he still had unfolded in his hand. Suddenly he was struck by the fact that the whole temple square had the shape of a trapezoid, and the raised terrace with the Dome of the Rock too. He showed his father.

"What's so special about that?"

"Well, that stone that we just saw is a trapezoid too."

"Yes," said Onno. "That's right."

Quinten did not know what to make of it either. Had the rock served as the model for the terrace and the square? The Piazza San Marco in Venice was in the shape of a trapezoid, too—he'd thought that so beautiful. Were all those trapezoid-shaped things connected in some way through that shape? Or all spherical objects? Was an eye connected with the sun? Yes of course, profoundly. And with a soccer ball? The sphere, the circle, the octagon, and square, the ellipse, the rectangle, the triangle, the cube, the pyramid—all those shapes with which Mr. Themaat had first acquainted him; what was their real message? What were they themselves? Did they actually exist somewhere? Perhaps where music came from too? He looked back at the map, and saw that it was not the Dome of the Rock but the Dome of the Chain that was exactly in the center of the temple square.

"To tell you the truth," said Onno, letting his eyes wander over the Mount of Olives, Mount Scopus, Mount Zion, "all this metaphysics here is starting to make me sick. Anyway, it's getting far too hot. What would you say if we got a bus and had a drink in the west, in the new city? Nothing can happen to us there, I think." He turned around. "What's happened to our poet? We've still got to pay him."

"There he goes."

Hands behind his back, his head cocked a little to one side, like a real gentleman, they saw Ibrahim just descending the northern staircase of the temple terrace.

64

Chawah Lawan?

They got off at a busy junction and crossed to a row of shops, where a table was just being vacated on a shady terrace.

"Look at that," said Onno, rubbing his left thigh. "Here we can finally have a normal conversation."

The priests and Orthodox Jews had vanished from the streets; even the tourists had largely given way to women shopping, workmen, and groups of schoolchildren. Although there wasn't an Arab in sight, there were again fully armed male and female soldiers sitting on the edge of a large container of plants.

"Why is it," asked Quinten, "that Ibrahim knew so much about all those biblical figures? Muslims have got the Koran, haven't they?"

Onno looked at him for a few seconds. "Is that what you understand by a normal conversation?"

"What's so abnormal about it? It's an ordinary question, isn't it? All these things exist, don't they?"

"All right, I'll answer," said Onno with resignation. "The Bible and Koran overlap to a great extent. According to Islam, Allah in heaven has the original copy of the Holy Scripture; the Torah and the Gospels are corrupt editions and forgeries of it; the Koran is a true copy." He nodded, looking at Quinten. "Yes, you need quite a nerve to declare your grandfather and your father to be your son and your grandson.... Right. And now could we change the subject perhaps? Or don't you have any sense of everyday reality anymore?"

"This *is* everyday reality to me."

"That's what I was afraid of. But do you never have the feeling that it might get utterly exhausting for other people in the long run?"

"But you don't get tired from thinking and learning things? I only get tired when I'm bored."

"I admit," said Onno, "boredom doesn't get much of a look in around you." He looked around. "Of course you're right, it all exists, but not everything exists in the same way. Have you ever listened to other people's conversations? Here on this terrace you can't understand them, but people usually talk about people—about their family and friends, or people at work, or people in politics and sports, and mostly about themselves."

"And what if *I* were to get completely sick of that kind of chatter? When they talk about things, it's almost always about the things you can have, like cars, money. I never talk about people, and not about myself, and not about what I've got."

"No, you talk about trapezoids, or sacred stones—and you're not concerned with those stones but with their sacredness, their meaning. You only care about meanings and connections. I admit I may have lumbered you with that—concrete things are not my strong point, either; but even I'm not as abstract as you. Did you really examine that rock just now? Do you know what kind of stone it is? Granite? Limestone?"

"Why should I examine it if it doesn't mean anything? There are so many rocks."

"Can you hear what I'm saying? If a rock means something you don't have to examine it, and not if it means nothing, either. So you really never have to examine anything. Do you belong in this world?"

Quinten did not reply. No one knew who he was—not even himself. What was "this world"? The boys playing soccer in Westerbork, they belonged in this world—but the feeling that they got when they scored a goal was what he got when something interesting occurred to him.

All these people here were sitting chattering about other people or about things that you could have, like those two white-haired ladies at the next table: none of it had anything to do with him. So would it be best if he went into a monastery? Became a father of the Holy Cross? Had a black ribbon tied around his arm at the Wailing Wall? Then he thought of what he himself possessed—the tablets with the Ten Commandments on them, which he had seen were made of sapphire; the *testimony,* which was at the same time not his possession and which today or tomorrow at the latest he would give away somehow. After that there was nothing more for him here, not even in a monastery. Yesterday, in the *Francis Bacon* . . .

His thoughts were interrupted by a girl who came to take their order. He pointed to the neighboring table, where an old lady with her back toward them had an orange drink in front of her. "What's that?"

"Carrot juice."

"Carrot juice? Never had it."

"Order that, then," said Onno. "Don't you want anything to eat? What time is it?"

"A quarter to twelve. I'm not hungry."

After Onno had ordered a cup of coffee for himself, he asked: "Shall we go to a post office in a bit and phone Granny Sophia? We were going to do that in the Holy of Holies."

"And are you going to tell her everything?"

"You must be joking! That would probably cause a short circuit in the telephone exchange. Just to let her hear from us. I don't know what else you've got in mind, but it will probably mean us eventually going back to Holland."

"Yes?" asked Quinten. "And what then?"

Onno sighed. "That's a mystery to me, too. When I saw Auntie Trees just now in the Via Dolorosa, I took it as a signal that the world is after me again. But what am I supposed to do there? For you that's no problem— you're seventeen, you can go in any direction you like; but I've got no point of reference anymore. Really, I'm just a kind of walking Tower of Babel. What's someone like that supposed to do? In our family everyone lives to be ninety; I can't go on roaming the world for another forty years." He put his stick between his parted legs, his hands on the handle, and rested his chin on them, looking at the passersby.

Quinten found that attitude much too old-looking and asked: "Can't you start something completely new?"

"Something completely new . . . Tell me something completely new."

"Or something very old," said Quinten. "What did you want to be when you were little?"

Onno put his cheek on his hands and looked at Quinten reflectively. "What did I want to be when I was small . . ."

"Yes. The very first thing you wanted to be."

"The very first thing I wanted to be . . ." repeated Onno, with a sing-song tone in his voice, like in a litany. He raised his head. "A doll doctor."

"A doll doctor?" Quinten repeated in his turn. "What's that?"

"Someone who repairs broken dolls." Onno had not thought about that for almost half a century, but now that he said it, he suddenly realized it was of course connected with his mother, who for years had dressed him up like a girl.

"Well," said Quinten, "then you must become a doll doctor!"

At the same instant Onno saw himself sitting in a small shop in the center of Amsterdam, in a narrow cross street, surrounded by shelves filled with hundreds of pink, gleaming dolls, repairing broken eyelids, installing new "Mommy" voices . . .

"I'll think about it," he said. "What would Lazarus have done after he'd been raised from the dead?"

"Isn't that in the Bible?"

"Not if you ask me. I vaguely remember a legend about him going to Marseilles, where he became the first bishop."

"Perhaps he simply bored everyone stiff with his experiences while he was dead."

"But then we'd have some information about it. As far as I know he never talked about it." He turned his head to Quinten. "Just as I shall never be able to talk about a certain experience." When Quinten did not react, he said, "In any case we will need a roof over our heads in Amsterdam. The first few weeks we can stay in a hotel, but then I'll have to rent or buy something. I'll telephone Hans Giltay Veth right away. Won't he be surprised!"

Quinten knew that he wouldn't be going with him, but he couldn't say so. What was he to say in reply if his father asked why not? He didn't know himself. Not because he didn't want to, but because it wouldn't happen.

"Aunt Dol said that your things are in storage in Rotterdam, at the docks."

"I don't want any of that," said Onno immediately, while at the same moment the dark-brown Chinese camphor box appeared before his eyes, decorated all around with heavy carving, in which Ada's clothes had lain for seventeen years.

"Mama's cello is in my room in Groot Rechteren now," said Quinten.

Onno nodded in silence.

The girl put their order in front of them. Quinten took a mouthful of his carrot juice and to his amazement it tasted of carrots—or, rather, to his astonishment the taste of carrots could also appear without loud cracking and crunching. He wanted to tell his father this, but then saw that astonishment had taken hold of him too.

"Look," said Onno, perplexed, and pointed to the dark-brown cookie with caramelized sugar and peanuts that was on the saucer next to his coffee. "A gingersnap! Do you remember? We were always given those at Granny To's. The ones that make such a noise in your mouth." He took the round brown cookie carefully in his fingers, raised it with both hands like a priest lifting the host, and it was on the tip of his tongue to say "Mother! *Hoc est enim corpus tuum!*"—but he simply cried out rapturously, "A gingersnap!"

At that the amazement spread still further. At the next table, two old ladies were about to leave. One was already waiting in the street; the other— dressed in a creamy white dress with sleeves reaching just below her elbow—was still paying the waitress and turned to look at Onno for a moment.

"A gingersnap," she said in Dutch with a strong Hebrew accent. "I haven't heard that word for a long time."

Quinten did not look at her. His attention was caught by the blue number on her wrinkled forearm—31415. When they had gone, Onno opened his mouth to speak, but Quinten asked:

"Did you see that number on her arm? I thought only the rabble had themselves tattooed."

For a few seconds Onno looked straight into Quinten's eyes. "Did she have a number on her arm?" he asked, as if he couldn't believe what he had heard.

"Three-one-four-one-five. What's wrong? Why have you got that funny look in your eyes?"

Onno began trembling, feeling as if the trembling came from his chair, from the earth, like at the beginning of an earthquake. He did not take his eyes off Quinten.

"What's wrong? Dad?" asked Quinten in alarm. "Why aren't you saying anything?"

What he had seen, and what Quinten had not seen, was the color of her eyes—that indescribable lapis lazuli, which in his whole life he had seen in only one person: Quinten. He was going to say that she had eyes just like his, but when Quinten told him about her tattoo, the numbers that people were given in Auschwitz, it immediately triggered a short-circuit in his head. Was he seeing ghosts? He didn't want to think what he was thinking; it was too terrible, too much to cope with. He tried to put it out of his mind, to grab it and crush it underfoot, like a hornet; but it was there and it wouldn't budge. He had to think about this, think it out of existence, right away; but not with Quinten there—he had to be alone. Quinten must never know what he was thinking. He got up, swaying, holding on to his chair.

"I want to go. I'm going to the hotel. You stay here. I'll see you in a bit."

Quinten got up too. "It's not something to do with your brain, is it? Should I phone a doctor?"

"There's nothing wrong with my brain—that is . . . please don't ask any more questions."

"I'm going with you."

Quinten paid the waitress, who was still clearing the table where the two old ladies had sat, and took hold of Onno's arm. At the end of the pedestrian precinct he hailed a taxi and helped Onno in. They did not speak during the short drive; he felt that his father was fighting a battle that he didn't understand. Had he had a slight stroke again, but refused to believe it? At any rate, he mustn't leave him alone. They drove past the wall of the Old City to the Jaffa Gate again and got out in the square, which was already as familiar as if they had been living there for weeks.

"Need a guide? Need a guide? Where are you from?"

Aron appeared from the office and put the keys on the counter, with a face that seemed to say that nothing in the world could surprise him anymore, since everything was as it was and would always be as it would be. Up winding stairs, punctuated by neglected corridors with steps up and steps down, they got to their rooms on the third floor, at the back of the hotel.

Quinten opened Onno's door and gave him the key. "I'll be next door," he said. "If you need me, just call."

"You don't have to stay in the hotel because of me. Go on into town, there's enough to see. I'll see you later."

"Try to get some rest."

When he had crossed the threshold, Onno turned and they looked at each other for a moment, as though each of them were expecting the other to say something else, but they did not.

*

Inside, Onno lay straight down on the bed, put his stick on the floor next to him, closed his eyes, and folded his hands on his chest. Laid out in this way, his thoughts immediately started up again.

He saw her in front of him again on the terrace, turning her head. "A gingersnap. I haven't heard that word for a long time." Those unique eyes . . . 31415 . . . How old was she? Late seventies? Almost eighty? Was the unthinkable really thinkable? Had he seen Max's mother? Eva Weiss? Could it be true that she was still alive? He tried to recall her wedding photo, which had been on Max's "shelf of honor" in Groot Rechteren, on the mantelpiece. Of course, that portrait from the 1920s was in black-and-white; all he remembered was that Max had his father's eyes and the nose and mouth of his mother. Number 31415 also had a pronounced nose, but that was nothing special around here, either in Jews or in Arabs; her mouth had perhaps retained a suggestion of sensuality. But if that was true, then he must confront the unimaginable consequence. In that case Quinten was not his son but Max's. In that case Ada had deceived him with Max. In that case Max had betrayed their friendship. He was disgusted with himself. What kind of figments of the imagination were these?

Suppose Max's mother had survived Auschwitz. Then she would have returned to Holland at once to trace her son, and she would have found him in that foster family in no time. But they were Catholics. Was it conceivable that they'd been able to keep Max hidden in those chaotic days because he would otherwise be brought up as a Jew, which would mean that his soul was lost for all eternity? That had happened a few times; once even involving abduction to a monastery. No, he remembered Max had told him that he didn't even have to cross himself before meals. Another possibility was that the Germans had told her that her son had been transported to an extermination camp, like her parents. Back in Holland, she had inquired if any of them had come back. They had not. But if her son had not come back, it was simply because he'd never been deported. Perhaps she would have found that out at the National Institute for War Documentation—the records were kept carefully during the war by the Jewish Council; but because she had lived for years in the conviction that he had been taken to Poland as well, the idea did not occur to her. After that there would have been nothing left for her in Holland, where there were only dreadful memories, and she had emigrated to Palestine.

But wait. Max's foster parents had obviously also inquired from their side whether his mother had returned, and obviously they'd been told not. How was that possible? Everything was always possible. Perhaps they'd inquired about Eva Delius, while Max's mother had had herself registered as Eva Weiss, because she could not bear to say Delius. If that was the case, it should be possible to find out at War Documentation. And everything could have happened completely differently; one couldn't reconstruct reality by thinking. He must simply find out whether that lady just now had been Eva Weiss. That must be possible—Israel was not that big. But if it really was, then she would probably have Hebraized her name and was now called Chawah Lawan. What's more, in 1945 she had not yet turned forty; such an attractive woman with such striking eyes would of course have remarried, and now she was a widow with a different name. So now he had to get up immediately and go to the Registry Office, and to that Holocaust museum, Yad Vashem, where all the millions of dead were documented; perhaps they also had the German registration numbers from Auschwitz. But he did not get up. He lay there in his hot little room without air-conditioning. Had she had another child? Probably not. Her only son was now really dead—had she really sat next to her own grandson just now? Had Quinten sat next to his grandmother?

He found himself only holding on to all those speculations to avoid the most important thing of all. With his eyes closed, he frowned for a moment. Had Max been capable of that? Of course, he was capable of anything; for women he would have betrayed even God. But Ada? He thought back to that night in Havana, almost eighteen years ago, when according to their calculation Quinten had been conceived. Her shadow in the doorway of his hotel room late that evening . . . Where had she come from? He opened his eyes. Dammit, that was it! She'd been to the beach with Max, without him, because he was deceiving her with María, the revolutionary widow—that is, he had let himself be seduced by her, just as Ada had seduced him that same night, in complete contrast to her passive nature! He sat up, and a fragment of the *Saint Matthew Passion*, in which Ada had played, came into his head: *"Was dürfen wir weiter Zeugnis?"* Had she been through a kind of repetition exercise with Max, a nostalgic episode that had turned out to be rather active, after which she'd come to cleanse herself with him—but in fact sullied herself with María? In that case Max had been the stronger: she couldn't become pregnant; she was on the pill. But his seed was as brazen as he was and had paid no attention. That would explain everything! He must have been afraid for months that the child would look like him, and his offer to bring it up had not been simply an act of friendship but a penance—and to that extent a deed of friendship in its turn. At the same time Max had saddled him with the feeling of guilt for not bringing up his own son, who perhaps wasn't his own son, and whom, moreover, he'd later completely abandoned! With his head turned to one side, Onno looked out the window at the blue sky, in which hung the invisible sound of church bells and cooing doves. What next? If that was all true, then the old lady was none other than Eva Weiss; but perhaps it wasn't true.

Had Max known that Quinten was his son? Quinten didn't look like either of them, but maybe Max had nevertheless discovered something in common between himself and Quinten. So did Sophia perhaps know about it, too? Obviously there had been something going on between those two! Or maybe Sophia had discovered that Max and Quinten had something in common, something unobtrusive, some odd trivial thing, but had not told him. And since she had not told him, Onno, she wouldn't do so now. Anyway, what good would that knowledge do anyone? Quinten least of all. For years he'd been looking for his father, while his father may have been sitting opposite him at the table every evening, and had been acting as his father in practice all along. The only person who would derive any joy from it was Chawah Lawan.

The news that her son had not been gassed at the age of nine but had become a leading astronomer, and had only just died at age fifty-one, would of course plunge her into an impossible mixture of happiness and despair; perhaps she'd even read the fantastic report of his death in the newspaper here, referring to a "Dutch astronomer in Westerbork," without mentioning his name, because he was not *that* famous. But if she survived that news, she could then look into the eyes of her grandson as if into a mirror.

Only by establishing the identity of that Mrs. 31415 could he get at the truth—and perhaps nowadays it was also possible medically. He hadn't read newspapers for years, but it wouldn't surprise him if all that DNA research had by now led to reliable determination of kinship. But in that case Quinten would also have to give blood or saliva—which would also be bound to have a poisonous effect on him, even if Onno emerged from such a test as the father. And apart from that: did he really want to know? After Ada's accident, Helga's death, and his political and academic disasters, it might be better for him not to have a son anymore. So was it not better to banish the eyes of that lady from Jerusalem from his memory? What was truth? If he did nothing, no one else would ever hit upon such misbegotten ideas and everything would stay as it was: Quinten would keep the father whom he had sought and found, and he himself would have a son like Max had had all that time, both his and not his . . .

He swung his legs off the bed, took hold of his stick, and stood up. He went to see Quinten, who was obviously still worried. He would tell him that he may have had a touch of sunstroke on the Temple Mount but that everything was fine now.

65

The Law Taker

After taking Onno to his room, Quinten had gone to his own. On his doorpost, too, there was a small white cylinder, a mezuzah, that his father had told him contained a small roll of parchment with the commandments from the Torah on it. He touched it briefly, closed the door behind him, and automatically put the small chain on.

It was hot. He undressed completely, threw his clothes on the bed, put his watch and compass on the washbasin, and freshened up. The window was open, but no one could see him; at the back of the hotel was a courtyard, surrounded on three sides by much lower houses. Without drying himself he tied the towel round his waist, knelt on the floor by the window, and crossed his arms on the windowsill.

He let his eyes wander languidly over the old city, from which rose the bronze pealing of church bells; the Temple Mount was on the other side. From the roof came the sound of cooing doves. A glance at the trembling needle of his compass told him that he was facing due northwest. He realized that on the other side of the gently sloping hills in the distance—beyond the sea, Turkey, the Balkans, Austria, and Germany—stood his mother's bed. Nothing had changed there, of course. He had been away from home for scarcely four weeks. Really? Wasn't it four years? Forty? How would Granny Sophia be getting on? Of course she was thinking that he was still in Italy wandering around churches and museums. Was Mr. Themaat, from whom he'd learned so much, still alive? If only he knew what Quinten had been up to in the meantime. What would he have said? "Well done, QuQu, you did it again!" And Piet Keller? Without him none of it would have been possible. Was Mr. Spier still living in Wales, in that place with all those strange letters in it? And Clara and Marius Proctor, and Verdonkschot with his Etienne, and Rutger with his huge carpet—where were they all? Was Groot Rechteren still there, or was the castle by now full of villains in black boots? Theo Kern was definitely still around, with his purple feet. He thought of Max for a moment too, but in a different way. Although he'd lived under one roof with him all his life, for some reason or other he couldn't recall him clearly. He had not forgotten anything—one of his oldest memories was of Max taking him on his knee at the grand piano and playing all kinds of chords to him—but it was as though everything were happening under water: visible and in close-up, but in a different element.

Perhaps that water was the war, which always surrounded Max. He knew in broad outline what had happened to Max: a different, unimaginable world, with which he had no link at all; he had little affinity with his father's family, either, but they were his own family after all. Jews and the murderers of Jews—that gruesome union was as alien to him as the history of the Aztecs, even if he was now keeping the Jewish Law downstairs in the safe. That had nothing to do with the fact that he was one-thirty-second-part Jewish, as he had discovered, because that was a very weak concentration, scarcely more than 3 percent, but with his dream about the Citadel. Max on the other hand was 50 percent Jewish. Had he ever been in Israel? Quinten wondered. Had he ever walked through the streets of Jerusalem? Once or twice a year he'd packed his bags for a conference abroad, sometimes as far away as America, Japan, or Australia, but Quinten couldn't remember ever having heard anything about Israel. Perhaps they didn't go in for astronomy here.

Max, Sophia, his mother, his father . . . it was though he were taking leave of all that. Drowsily, he let his chin sink onto his arms and looked at the dry, sun-drenched slopes that extended motionless to the horizon beyond the new city, which was at a lower level. It was as though the undulating lines, with which the blood-soaked earth stood out against the blue sky, had not been created by geological events but had been drawn by an inspired hand. He was dry. The sweltering heat that hung over the city and the countryside enveloped him again . . . and suddenly he lifts his head in amazement. There's no more sound. The church bells are silent, perhaps because some sacred hour or other has passed, or come; but no voices come from the windows around the courtyard, either. Even the cooing of doves has disappeared. It is as though the world has fallen into a deep sleep—the houses, the landscape, the sky ... what has suddenly happened to everything? Is his father asleep next door, too? Nothing is moving anymore, and the shimmering heat over the roofs has gone. He feels as if he is not looking at reality but at an old-fashioned painted panorama, like the Panorama Mesdag in The Hague, where he once went with his Aunt Dol; in that dune landscape there was just the sort of breathless silence as there is here now. Everything that he can see exists, but at the same time does not exist; only in himself has nothing changed. He hears his heartbeat and the roaring of blood in his ears.

But then something does happen. Suddenly a small black dot appears in the blue dome of the sky, like a hole—not far above the horizon, in the direction of Tel Aviv. It moves up and down a little and slowly becomes larger. But suddenly it seems to be much closer, as though it is something that is approaching: gradually it takes shape, stretches out lengthwise into a black strip, the ends of which move solemnly up and down. Is it a bird? If it is, it's a big one. He gets up in a rapid movement and his eyes open wide. Edgar! It's Edgar!

He is already above the steep valley and is making straight for the hotel. Is it really conceivable that he has followed Onno's trail here all the way from Italy? That's impossible! But no one understands birds; no one knows how they sometimes find their way half across the world. Once he's above the city wall, Edgar stops beating his wings and begins an elegant dive with wings outspread. A little later he lands on the windowsill with his claws stretched out in front of him, shakes his feathers, folds his wings, turns around once, lifts his tail, leaves some droppings, and looks at Quinten with one eye.

"You need the room next door," says Quinten, who has taken a step backward. He points to the side. "Next window."

Immediately, he's amazed at his own voice. Normally he always hears the sound from two directions: through his ears and from inside; now the words remain smothered deep in his chest, as though his ears are blocked. Edgar's arrival also took place in complete silence. Even if the bird had heard his words, he couldn't have understood them; in any case he pays no attention. With a fluttering leap, he lands on the floor and hops to the door with an unmistakably arrogant air.

"Of course," says Quinten, "as you prefer. You can go by the corridor too. What a surprise it will be for Dad."

But as he crosses the threshold he pauses. There is no hallway anymore. The wall opposite has given way to a balustrade with amphora-shaped uprights, beyond which stretches an immense space full of staircases and galleries. He turns around. Not only has the door of his father's room disappeared, but so has his own. The whole wall is gone: and on that side too in the distance, above and down below, there are endless flights of colonnades, alcoves, gateways, vaults . . . is this a dream? He is standing on a narrow footbridge, which leads to a carved windowframe with an architrave; farther on, borne by caryatids, it disappears in the shadow of a tall portico.

He looks around with a deep sigh. In all its sweet bliss, warm as his own body, the Citadel finally envelops him again. Time after time he has thought of it—in Venice, in Florence, in Rome, in Jerusalem—but now that it is there, it doesn't remind him of anything else: it is what it is, just as the sun needs nothing else to be seen. But sunlight does not surround him there, or simply moonlight, more something like the "ash-gray light," which can be seen just before or after a new moon on the lunar surface next to the thin crescent, and which is sometimes not ash-gray but more marble-gray—caused, as Max once explained to him on a winter evening on the balcony of his bedroom, by reflected sunlight from the earth, and it is brighter the cloudier that side of the earth is.

Edgar shuffles restlessly to and fro on the balustrade, looking down with his head on one side, or upward, or both at once; he spreads his wings and dives down, climbs up, soars over a row of massive buttresses, disappears in the distance behind the pillars of a brick bridge, and far below swerves around a colossal column with an extravagant capital; on the milk-white shaft are the letters XDX, one below the other. It is as though the trail of his soaring reconnaissance flight hangs in the space like a black ribbon. When he has seen enough, he lands on the end of the footbridge, turns his head back 180 degrees, and rummages among his feathers with his beak, extending one wing with outspread feathers. Quinten has the impression that he is only doing this to kill time—that the bird is waiting for him. When he reaches him, Edgar begins hopping and fluttering ahead of him like a guide. The colonnade ends in a wide marble staircase, flanked with statues leading down to a complicated series of blind arcades and narrow, sometimes covered, alleys, leading to a series of pontifical chambers.

When they in turn give way to an indoor street with immense facades to the left and right, divided from each other by pilasters, dripping with ornamentation, Quinten has lost all sense of time and direction. But he has no need of time or direction. He would prefer to follow Edgar forever, here in this deathly silent, blissful, constructed world, made only for him. At a spiral staircase around the blocks of a pillar many feet thick Edgar suddenly discovers a trick: with his claws and beak around the round rail, he lets himself slide down in an exuberant spiral, keeping his balance with his wings. Laughing, leaping down the stairs two at a time, Quinten tries to keep up with him. Having reached the bottom of the staircase after five turns, he stops with his head spinning and looks around inquiringly. What has happened to Edgar? Has he gotten playful? Has he hidden?

With a start Quinten sees where he is, but feels no fear. No, this is not a dream. All the rest is a dream—Israel, Italy, Holland. The Citadel is the only thing that really exists. Opposite him, about twenty yards away, the double door to the center of the world covered with a diamond-shaped pattern of iron bars stands wide open; the heavy rusty sliding padlock is lying on the ground. Black as the back of a mirror, Edgar sits on the threshold, like a sentry, and looks straight at him in a way that has nothing playful about it. As he slowly approaches, he sees behind him the green safe from the hotel.

Edgar turns around, flies onto the safe with a couple of short flaps of his wings, and begins sharpening his beak against the edge—but even without that Quinten understands what he has to do. He crosses the threshold with a slight shiver. The room is cube-shaped, about thirty feet long, wide, and high; although there are no openings in the walls, the same dusky light is everywhere. He kneels down by the knob of the combination lock and holds it between his fingers. He doesn't have to think about the combination— there is only one that comes into consideration: J,H,W,H. He pulls open the immense door and takes the suitcase from the bottom shelf. When he has opened the locks, the first thing he sees is the beige envelope with SOMNIUM QUINTI on it.

He picks it up almost tenderly. This is the place to bring the plans up-to-date, but at the same time it would be rather like a mathematician counting his own fingers and noting down the result. He opens the newspapers, takes out the gray tablets, and lays them carefully next to each other on the stone floor. Then he replaces the envelope, slides the suitcase back, and closes the safe door, which this time produces no sound. As he has seen Aron do, he gives the knob a final twirl with the side of his hand. Without knowing what else has to happen, he takes the two heavy stones in his hands under his outstretched arms and stands up, which is the sign for Edgar to leap onto his shoulder.

But when he crosses the threshold, another change takes place. He stops in alarm, with Edgar next to his ear, the leathery claws with their hard talons in his flesh. The masses of stone around him are losing their substance: it is as though they are turning to wood ... and then painted linen ... and then Brussels lace, which he can see right through.... Everything is crumbling and evaporating, daylight is beginning to penetrate, and a little later there is just a momentary trembling afterimage of the Citadel left—but that suddenly gives him a sense of its dimensions: a block of at least six hundred miles to the east, as far as Baghdad, six hundred miles to the west, as far as Libya, six hundred miles to the north, as far as the Black Sea, six hundred miles to the south, to Medina, and over twelve hundred miles high, as far as the first radiation belts ... he is suddenly standing outdoors in the sun with Edgar and the two tablets and sees immediately where he is: in the Kidron Valley.

Opposite him, up above, protruding above the temple wall, gleams the golden cupola of the Dome of the Rock; behind it is the Mount of Olives. The distance he has covered in the Citadel must be approximately the same as that from the hotel to here. He feels uncomfortable with only the towel around him, but the world is still as silent and motionless as just now. Is the sun also standing still in the firmament? That's impossible, of course; in that case everything would go up in flames—he doesn't need Max to realize that. Has no time elapsed between just now and now perhaps? If this is not a dream, then what is "now"?

His eye lights on the Golden Gate, which protrudes a little from the wall here. The soldiers on the roof have disappeared; the two tall gateways are open. So should he go through them and lay the Ten Commandments back on the rock? But he told his father that he didn't intend to do that, since no one must lay hands on them. For that matter, at the side of the Temple Mount the gate is bricked up. Yet there's nothing for it but to climb up on that side: he'll see. After a few steps he stops. The rough ground is strewn with stones, which hurt his bare feet, especially because he is now much heavier with the tablets under his arms. He looks around to see if there are a few old rags or palm leaves anywhere—it would be best of course if there were a pair of shoes. Then he suddenly sees something moving out of the corner of his eye. From the right, in the distance, from the north, a white horse is approaching at a gallop along the ravine past the wall, with mane waving and tail flowing. Quinten looks at the apparition in the frozen landscape open-mouthed. Right in front of him, the horse stands on its hind legs and moves its head up and down while saliva sprays around, as though it wants to confirm something. And at the same moment Quinten realizes what the horse is confirming.

"Deep Thought Sunstar!"

Something snaps in him. Sobbing, he makes as if to put his arms around the horse's neck, but he is prevented by the two stones; when he gives the creature a kiss on its nose, it kneels down like a camel. While Edgar holds on to the ponytail at the back of his head, Quinten climbs onto the sweaty back; with short, rapid movements Deep Thought Sunstar gets up and proceeds toward the Golden Gate at a walk. With his naked upper body stretched, the raven on his shoulder, the stones in his hands, Quinten looks around him with a smile at the fairy-tale hills and the approaching temple wall. If only Titus could see him now, and the pope, and the chief rabbi! A little later Deep Thought Sunstar makes its way carefully between the graves and again kneels down at the gate.

After he has dismounted, the horse stands up again and trots back into the valley; then Edgar spreads his wings, strikes himself on the crown with them, and follows the horse. Sadly, Quinten watches them growing smaller: the horse at a gallop, the raven overhead, the one as white as the other is black . . . when they have disappeared, everything is again motionless.

He turns around with a sigh and enters the gatehouse. The other side is now also open. With a solemn feeling he crosses the dim space, with a few columns standing here and there; there seems to be a soft roaring noise, like the sound of the sea in a shell. Outside, the sun receives him again and slowly he climbs the steps, which go up to the level of the terrace. There he stops and looks around. The space is about as large as that of Westerbork camp. Not a soul anywhere. Everything is just for him; the whole world is now only for him and is waiting for him. He walks across the grass to the wide staircase of the temple terrace. The row of arcades, which encloses it at the top, has five arches here; he stops again under the middle one. Straight in front of him is the small Dome of the Chain with its silver cupola, just behind it the golden Dome of the Rock: a child with its father. The restoration of the small sanctum is now complete: straight through the open space around it he can look into the dark interior of the Dome of the Rock.

He takes a deep breath and begins walking toward that black hole, without taking his eyes off it. But as he passes the center of the Dome of the Chain, surrounded by the double row of columns, the moment has finally come—I take things out of his hands. Suddenly he hears a soft rustling and stops. He looks around in amazement, but the sound is close by. It seems to be coming from the stone tablets. He rests them on his hips on either side and looks in astonishment at what is happening. It is as though the gray crust is alive, moving, melting. Something is trying to fight its way out from underneath, to free itself; a little later he sees tiny, glassy, translucent creatures appearing all over the surface, freeing themselves from the crusts of thousands of years, leaping out and swarming around him. Letters! They are letters! Letters of light! At the same moment the sapphire plates have become so heavy that he can no longer hold them—the towel also slides from his hips. They slip from his grasp and silently smash to smithereens on the marble slabs. But he does not care—he must have the letters; they must not escape! The ten words! Thou shalt not steal! Thou shalt not kill! He grabs at them with both hands, but the swarm rises in the cupola, toward the green five-leafed clover at the highest point, hovers there butterfly-like, dives down, flutters to the Dome of the Rock, and disappears through the black entrance. He chases after them in despair.

Inside, in the dim light, the letters dance and gleam up and down above the holy rock. What in heaven's name is he to do? Suddenly he feels eyes being focused on him. The woman in white, who was sitting praying in the alcove, has turned around and looks at him with shining eyes, like a doe. The cloth has slid from her head; her face is framed in a square of black hair. He stiffens. Is this a dream after all then?

"Mama!" he cries—but no sound leaves his mouth.

As he stands there, the other women still sit in the gallery and look at him with does' eyes. In one leap he is standing on the rock: Adas all around! All the women are his mother! Slowly he spreads his arms, throws back his head, and sees the arabesques on the inside of the dome: a network of countless interwoven figures-of-eight—and at that moment Moses' swarm of letters envelops his naked body with such an endless, dazzling Light that his body disappears in it like the light of a candle in that of the sun . . .

Standing in the hallway, Onno knocked on the door. When there was still no reply after a second knock, he gently opened the door; but after an inch or so it was held by the chain. Through the gap he could see only part of the washbasin, on which lay Quinten's watch and compass.

"Quinten?" he asked. "Are you asleep?" Again there was silence. He bent down and tried to look through the keyhole, but it was impossible. Then he shouted loudly, "Quinten!" and struck the door three times with his stick.

Nothing happened. What was wrong? Quinten must be in the room; the chain could not be put on from the outside. Something was very wrong! While Onno felt the blood rising to his head, he put his stick in the gap like a lever and pulled at it with all his might, so the chain flew out of the doorpost and the door banged against the wall. No one. On the bed lay the clothes Quinten had worn this morning, and his underpants. Onno looked at the open window in dismay. Had something terrible happened? Had Quinten suddenly had the same thoughts as himself about that Mrs. 31415 and in a fit of madness . . . but then he would have heard, surely! In a couple of steps he reached the windowsill, which was a little stained with bird droppings, and looked down.

In the courtyard an old woman was busy stuffing a pile of linen into large laundry bags; lying on a stone bench, a slim, ginger-haired woman was reading a book, mechanically rocking a carriage with her other hand. He looked left and right and upward along the outer wall—nowhere was there a fire escape or drainpipe down which he could have climbed. Anyway, why should he climb out naked? He looked in the built-in wardrobe and under the bed, and then stood unsteadily in the middle of the room. He must consider this very carefully. If Quinten was not here, and if he couldn't have left through the door or out through the window, then there was only one conclusion: something impossible had happened.

He had known from the day Quinten was born that he would end up doing something impossible. It was not quite impossible that he had actually taken the tablets of the Law from the Sancta Sanctorum but his own disappearance from this room had brought about something really impossible. When the impossible was surely impossible! Onno thought of the stones, which Quinten had put in the safe yesterday: did that have something to do with it? Did the impossible prove the almost impossible?

Once again he looked around, as if Quinten might suddenly have reappeared, then went downstairs. The reception area and the lounge were deserted; he pressed the button of an old-fashioned bell that stood on the counter. A little later a girl with short black hair appeared through the door behind the counter.

"Shalom."

"My son," said Onno, at the same moment surprised at the word, "put a suitcase in the safe here yesterday. Has he by any chance collected it in the last hour?"

"Sadly, I haven't seen your son today."

"And Mr. Aron?"

"My father left for Bethlehem early this morning to visit my grand-mother, who is ill. The safe hasn't been opened since yesterday. You can check for yourself if you like."

He followed her to the office, where she knelt down by the safe and turned the combination lock. She pulled the door open and pointed to the suitcase lying on the bottom shelf.

Onno looked at it for a few seconds, and then said: "Can I have it for a moment?"

She handed it over—but the moment Onno took hold of it, it was as though the suitcase were trying to fly into the air, as though he were going to throw it at the ceiling, it was so light. The stones were gone!

"What are you doing?" said the girl with a smile.

"I'm giddy," said Onno, groping around. She hurriedly gave him a chair, and he sat down with the suitcase on his lap. This was impossible too. The stones could no more have vanished from that safe than Quinten from his room. Although he knew it was pointless, he asked, "Does anyone else know the combination of that lock?"

She looked at him in alarm. "Only my father and myself. Do you think you've lost something?"

Onno shook his head. With trembling fingers, against his own better judgment, he began fiddling with the locks, whereupon she bent forward and opened them. On the envelope he had seen yesterday when the luggage was inspected at the airport in Rome he now read: SOMNIUM QUINTI. Quin-ten's dream? Was it perhaps a farewell letter that Quinten had written pre-viously? He took the papers out, but they were only architectural sketches and labyrinthine plans, with captions here and there captions like *Foot-bridge, Center of the World, Spiral Staircase*. The only explanation of the inex-plicable . . . he suddenly grabbed his head in both hands. He couldn't think about it anymore! Perhaps Quinten was not his son, or was his son; but now he was gone, gone for good, vanished off the face of the earth, no one knew where.

Quinten had deserted him, as he had once deserted Quinten—but he would never find Quinten, as Quinten had found him. He was now really in the situation that he had placed himself artificially four years ago: he had no one else . . .

"Are you all right?"

"No," he said, and searched frantically in his inside pocket. "Not at all . . . I have to . . ." With trembling hands he began leafing through a notebook. "Can I make a telephone call from here?"

"Of course." The girl took the case off his lap and pointed out the telephone on the small desk next to the typewriter. "Local?"

"International."

"Then I'll put the counter on." She pressed the button of a black box on the wall, closed the safe, and said, "I'll leave you alone."

"Sophia Brons speaking."

"It's Onno."

"Who?"

"Onno. Onno Quist."

"Onno? Did I hear that right? Is that you, Onno?"

"Yes."

"It can't be true. Say it again."

"This is Onno, your son-in-law."

"Onno! How incredible! I knew you'd show up again one day! Where are you calling from? Are you in Holland?"

"I'm calling from Jerusalem."

"Jerusalem! Is that where you've been all these years?"

"No. I realize I've got a lot to explain, and I will, but I'm phoning now because—"

"It's incredible that you should have telephoned now of all times . . . as though you felt it . . ."

"Felt what?"

"Onno . . ."

"What is it?"

"Prepare yourself for a shock, Onno. I've just come from Ada's cremation. I've still got my coat on . . . Onno? Are you still there?"

"I'm sorry, my head's spinning, it's all . . . has Ada just been cremated?"

"I think they're putting her ashes in the urn now. There's no need for us to mourn—it should all have happened a long long time ago."

"Yes."

"That poor child ... but it's all over now. After more than seventeen years—it's such a godawful business."

"Yes."

"Of course you want to talk to Quinten, but he's not here. I was the only one there just now. He's been in Italy for a few weeks; I haven't heard a word from him yet. He's had his birthday in the meantime, but I've no idea where he's gone. He doesn't know anything yet."

"Mother ... that's why I'm phoning you. About Quinten."

"About Quinten? What do you mean?"

"We met. By accident. In Rome."

"You met each other? You can't be serious! When? Why didn't you tell me? He must have been overjoyed, surely? And what are the two of you doing in Jerusalem now?"

"A lot has happened in the meantime, I can't explain it all now, and anyway it can't be explained but ..."

"But? Can't you say anything else? Has something happened to Quinten?"

"Yes."

"What? Onno! For God's sake! He's not dead too, is he?"

"I don't know. He's gone."

"Gone? Have you called in the police?"

"There's no point."

"How do you know? How long has he been gone?"

"An hour."

"An hour? Did you say an hour? You're not a bit overwrought, are you, Onno?"

"That too. I know it sounds idiotic, but ..."

"Please stop it. If he's been gone for an hour, he'll be back in an hour. I know all about that boy wandering off—he was always getting lost as a toddler. Take something to calm you down, or try and get some sleep. You must forgive me, I've got other things on my mind now. I'll tell you something that you have to know but no one else must know."

"I can scarcely hear you anymore."

"I have to keep my voice down, because these days it's possible I'm being bugged by those scum here at the castle. Fortunately I'll soon be moving in with someone in Westerbork, Max's ex-girlfriend. Of course, you've heard about everything that's happened."

"Yes."

"Listen carefully, Onno. Weren't you wondering why Ada died so suddenly?"

"You mean . . ."

"Yes. That's what I mean. In your farewell letter you wrote that Ada was flesh of my flesh and that I had the last word about her. She was in a terrible state, too awful to look at. Her kidneys had stopped functioning, she had cancer of the womb that had spread—I'll spare you the details. She'd gone completely white. It wasn't the kind of hospital where people had the last word; I had to do it myself."

"How?"

"With an overdose of insulin. I gave it to her last Saturday evening during visiting hours, at about seven-thirty, under the sheet, in her left thigh. No one saw me. They only discovered yesterday morning that she had died. Death must have occurred at about twelve-thirty in the morning, I was told when they called me up. That is, insofar as death hadn't occurred long ago. In the afternoon I was able to see her in the morgue. She reminded me of a fawn, she'd become so small."

"And she was cremated today? It's only Monday today. Isn't that very quick?"

"Of course that struck everyone. I called your lawyer, Giltay Veth, and he said that according to the Disposal of the Dead Act there was a minimum period of thirty-six hours. They kept to that exactly at the hospital. I think they were suspicious, just as Giltay Veth was for that matter. Perhaps they discovered the hole in her thigh at the postmortem and wanted to get rid of the evidence that anything untoward could have happened at their hospital as soon as possible. There was a short notice in today's newspaper saying that Mrs. Q. had died a natural death after seventeen years."

"Wait a moment . . . this is . . . this is just impossible . . . I have to write it down. So you gave her that injection on Saturday evening. It was seven-thirty. She died at twelve-thirty. In the morning she was taken to the morgue, where she lay yesterday. This morning she was put in a coffin and taken to the crematorium. And she was cremated there an hour ago."

"Yes. What's so important about those times?"

"What . . . how can . . . I . . ."

"Onno? Hello! Onno? Can you hear me? Are you still there?"

"There's something wrong with my head, Sophia, I can feel it . . . I can't write anymore ... the whole of my left side ... Eighteen months ago I had a ..."

"For heaven's sake, Onno! Where are you?"

"Hotel Raphael ..."

"Get them to call for a doctor at once. I'll take the next plane. I'm coming to get you both."

EPILOGUE

—*That's enough! You must know when to stop. Think of Goethe's words:* "Restriction shows the master's hand."

—But to be on the safe side he also said: "The fact that you cannot end is what makes you great."

—*Yes, those writers are like that. Always having the best of both worlds. You've accomplished your mission, and I've got six hundred and sixty-six questions about your machinations, but I won't ask them. The main thing is that we've got the testimony back just in time. Where's our man now?*

—Returned to the Light.

—*By now you might just as well say: to the Twilight. And what happened to the fragments of the two tablets?*

—Collected by the Jerusalem Sanitation Department. Taken to a rubbish dump with all the other rubble in the Dome of the Chain.

—*Well, for that matter, the testimony itself is a mess too. It looks like an upturned compositor's typecase.*

—If you must use terrestrial imagery, you'd better choose a more modern one: like erased *software.*

—*That is precisely the language of a world that we've no use for anymore. I suppose the sapphire tablets of the Law were the* hardware, *then?*

—As it were.

—*Yes, since Bacon the devil speaks English. It's becoming the world language. So let's keep to Latin:* consummatum est. *It has been accomplished. My strength is exhausted. We're done for. The world is done for. Humankind is done for. Everything is done for—except Lucifer. What we thought would never be possible has happened: time has gained a hold over us. Time—that was Lucifer's secret weapon. The only thing left to us after more than three thousand years was to take back those ten words. An impotent gesture, of course: like a jilted girl reclaiming her engagement ring. A poor consolation, a symbolic act, a melancholy farewell. But the Decalogue was the ultimate thing on earth: the Chief's contract with humankind, concluded with its deputy, the Jewish people, represented by its leader Moses in the role of notary. From now on Lucifer has a free hand. Let him carry off all those human things. I really don't care anymore.*

—Perhaps someone will appear on earth to put everything right.

—*The person would have to come from here, but nothing can come from here anymore. In Moscow an enlightened character assumed power a short while ago—the greatest human being in the human twentieth century in a positive sense, just as he whose name I shall not mention was in the negative sense. Within five years the Berlin Wall will be demolished, Russia will lose its colonies, the whole world will rejoice at the dawning of a new age . . . then in the liberated areas, the ultimate bloodthirsty backwardness will be in control again. Migrations of people will take place, shots will ring out again in Sarajevo, and as the third millennium approaches the disgusting twentieth century will be revived due to overwhelming popular success.*

—I can't believe that.

—*You'll learn to believe it. And it's all the same old thing—politics means nothing. The rise and fall of world empires has gone on forever. Politics are the rippling of the waves in a storm—makes no difference at all to the waves, because they come from somewhere completely different: they come from the moon. To the old global disasters are now added the ravaging tidal waves of the new: with their Baconian control of nature, people will finally consume themselves with nuclear power, burn themselves up through the hole they have made in the ozone layer, dissolve in acid rain, roast in the greenhouse effect, crush each other to death because of their numbers, hang themselves on the double helix of DNA, choke in their own Satan's shit, because that swine didn't conclude his pact out of love of humankind, only out of hatred for us. All hell will break loose on earth and human beings will one day remember the good old days, when they still listened to us—and probably they won't even do that anymore. It won't even be tragic anymore, just wretched. It's hopeless. Forget it.*

—And if they find out what we have done, won't that bring about a change of heart? I can see to that. At the moment there's one person on earth who knows about it.

—*You've suggested that before. Don't fool yourself. If they find out, not a soul will believe it. The news will be reported here and there; perhaps a few thousand righteous people, a few hundred theologians, and ten archaeologists will get very excited, but then it will be drowned out by the constant cataract of other news items, and a few months later it'll be forgotten. No, drop it, it's over.* Finis comoediae.

—We can at least try!

—*No, I'm not even prepared to give that knowledge to those treacherous off-spring of ours anymore.*

—Am I hearing you correctly? Is Onno Quist in danger if he tells anyone else?

—*That must be prevented. If that happens, just throw a stone at his head, like you did with Max Delius. Quiet a moment . . . I'm being called. I have to give a report on what you've told me.*

—Let's think of something else, then. We must fight to the last—we can still do it! Better to fail than to give up! Can't we do something about that pact that Lucifer concluded with Bacon? Give me another mission at once!

—*Those days are gone. You're retiring. Thanks for everything, on behalf of the Chief, too. Adieu.*

—Then I'll do it on my own initiative! Do you hear me? I'm not leaving it at that! How do they have the nerve! Who do they think they are, the up-starts! Answer me!

refresh yourself at penguin.co.uk

Visit penguin.co.uk for exclusive information and interviews with
bestselling authors, fantastic give-aways and the
inside track on all our books, from the Penguin Classics
to the latest bestsellers.

BE FIRST ▼

first chapters, first editions, first novels

EXCLUSIVES ▼

author chats, video interviews, biographies, special
features

EVERYONE'S A WINNER ▼

give-aways, competitions, quizzes, ecards

READERS GROUPS ▼

exciting features to support existing groups and
create new ones

NEWS ▼

author events, bestsellers, awards, what's new

EBOOKS ▼

books that click – download an ePenguin today

BROWSE AND BUY ▼

thousands of books to investigate – search, try
and buy the perfect gift online – or treat yourself!

ABOUT US ▼

job vacancies, advice for writers and company
history

Get Closer To Penguin . . . www.penguin.co.uk